THE BLACK MONK;

OR,

THE SECRET OF THE GREY TURRET.

A ROMANCE.

BY THE AUTHOR OF

"ADA, THE BETRAYED;" "JANE BRIGHTWELL;" "BLANCHE, OR THE MYSTERY OF THE DOOMED HOUSE;" "THE MILLER'S MAID;" ETC., ETC., ETC.

BY

Most featly do the minstrels sing
Of Brandon in its might,
Of song, of dance—of dame, of page,
And many a gallant knight;
For long as stone on stone remained
Of those embattled towers,
The light of love was beaming there,
And sweetly fled the hours.　　　OLD LEGEND.

LONDON:
E. LLOYD, 12, SALISBURY SQUARE, FLEET STREET.

1844.

PREFACE.

At the conclusion of the Legendary Romance of "The Black Monk; or, The Secret of the Grey Turret," the Author feels again devolving upon him the grateful task of saying a few words, if but to express his sense of the manner in which the Romance has been received, as well as to thank his numerous kind patrons for the favourable opinion they have been pleased to express concerning the work; an opinion expressed in the very best and conclusive manner—namely, by its great sale.

The Author of the "Black Monk" has always believed that much remained to be done with the manners, habits, customs, and incidents of the middle ages, which in many cases had been but feebly attempted, at the same time that he felt, human nature being the same some hundreds of years since as it is at present, that there was nothing to mar the domestic interest of a story, in the fact of its being thrown back for its time as far as the Crusades.

Of course, in such ages, the more violent feelings of human nature were likely to exhibit themselves with greater lawless ferocity, than in our own times, when people are more in the habit of succumbing to legal and social restraints. Neverthe-less there was a sense of honour and chivalrous feeling existing at that period which has to be completely made up now by merely legal enactments, so that as far as regards stirring incidents by flood and field, and remarkable contrasts of character, the middle ages may claim a supremacy over those that have succeeded them.

From the first number the Romance acquired a popularity which certainly greatly incited its Author to pursue the thread of his narrative in a manner which should prove satisfactory to his numerous readers, and consistent with the widely spread popularity of the publisher.

In announcing that the result, as to sale, more than equalled the warmest expectations of both, the Author respect-fully takes leave of his patrons, with a repetition of his thanks for an indulgence to his literary exertions, which has sunk deeply into his heart.

March, 1844.

THE BLACK MONK;

OR,

THE SECRET OF THE GREY TURRET.

BY THE AUTHOR OF ADA, &c.

CHAPTER I.

It was a night of horrors. E'en the pale moon did seem to shrink;—screams can
upon the howling blast;—cries wild and fearful smote the ear, and a voice cried from ear
to Heaven for help! help! help!—ANON.

> I saw it at the evening hour,
>   When all around was still,
> Save the gentle sighing of the wind,
>   As it swept adown the hill.
> My straining eyes no form could trace,
>   Yet—yet I knew 'twas there;
> For music of another world
>   Was floating in the air.
> I leant me 'gainst an aged tree,
>   I could but gasp the name;
> *   *   *   *   *
> Loud blew the wind, and the murky night
>   In double darkness came.—THE SPELL.

THE TEMPEST.—THE TURRET.—A NIGHT OF HORROR.—THE MONK

AND THE MYSTERY.

PEAL after peal of thunder rattled among the old battlements and gr
towers of Brandon Castle, the vivid lightning lit up the ancient and tim
worn fortress with fearful grandeur. Tower, moat, gate, battlement, a
donjon-keep would flash for a moment into existence like the aerial cre

No. 1

tions of the fancy, and then, ere one could say "behold," be lost again in a darkness so black and profound, that sky, earth, and water seemed alike covered by an awful canopy of gloom. A storm such as had not for many years visited the spot, was expending its utmost fury over the feudal residence which had been the mute witness of the changing manners of several centuries.

The Castle of Brandon and Weare, as it was called, from the names of two noble families, was of immense extent. Hardly one of its lordly possessors had dropped into the grave without adding something to it; so that, in the course of time, what had been originally but a small fort, flanked by four small towers, and surrounded by a stagnant moat, became an extensive castle of irregular design, yet grand in its proportions.

There were innumerable towers, court-yards, outer and inner fortifications, moats, bastions, turrets, and, in fact, every age had contributed something towards the defence and extent of the ancient castle, until, at the period when our tale commences, it frowned upon the surrounding country in all the dignity of feudal magnificence, a fit representative of that iron age when there was no intermediate dwelling between the castle and the cottage, and scarcely any society, except the ambitious and lawless nobles, and the tillers of the soil, who they consider as their slaves.

It was within one hour of midnight on the fourth of June, in the year twelve hundred and two, that Brandon Castle was visited by the frightful storm we have mentioned. But, oh! what was the storm that raged around the ancient battlements, compared to the hurricane of woe that at the same time swept over the heart of the lord of that stupendous edifice? .

The large hall of Brandon was hung from the ceiling to the floor with black hangings; massive silver candlesticks, in which were burning wax candles, lent a dreary magnificence to the vast apartment; and vast indeed it was, for six hundred knights, the flower of England's chivalry, had in the preceding reign, that of the ill-fated but chivalrous Richard of the Lion's Heart, held feast and revelry within it.

Time-worn banners floated from the carved ceiling, the floor was of polished oak, and the high gothic windows, filled with rare stained glass, imparted an air of cathedral-looking grandeur to the hall.

The lights were barely sufficient to render objects visible, and the intense lurid flashes of lightning completely overpowered their dim radiance, and lit up the apartment with an awful brilliancy,—a brilliancy the more awful and striking, on account of the objects it revealed.

In the centre of the hall was a bier, on which reposed a corpse, the face of which was uncovered. The bier was surmounted by a costly canopy, and the pall of velvet swept the ground. In fact, the sad remains of mortality were surrounded with every pomp which the rank of the departed, or the dear affection of those who remained, could suggest.

The fair and youthful face—fair and beautiful even in death,—that met the gazer's eyes upon that bier, would still, even in its sweet repose, have graced the festive bower. Death was indeed there, but it was not robed in its usual terrors. There was nothing repulsive in that fair pale face. A flower plucked from the stem that gave it life is still beautiful till time has robbed it of its blossom;—so it was with the fair and guileless being who there slept "the sleep that knows no waking." The flower was plucked, but it was a flower still. Death had taken away life, but had added nothing of its own as yet to mar the beauty of the shrine from whence the soul had escaped. The still form might have been sleeping in health and beauty but for the insignia of the fell destroyer that in the gleaming lightning met the gaze of the one person who watched those dear remains, and but that his heart was seared by the conviction that all he loved next to Heaven was lost for ever, he might have doubted for one happy moment that it was death he looked upon, and the feeling conveyed in the matchless lines of the poet might have crept across his bursting heart.

> He who hath bent him o'er the dead,
> Ere the first hour of life hath fled,—
> The first sad hour of nothingness,
> The last of sorrow and distress,—
> Ere yet decay's offensive fingers
> Have moved the lines where beauty lingers,
> And marked the mild angelic air,
> The rapture of repose that's there.—BYRON.

The one person who watched the corpse upon the bier was the lord of the castle and of all its proud domains. Sir Rupert Brandon was his name, and he was esteemed not only as a gallant soldier, but as a man of rare and high qualities and virtues. In short, he was one of the few who by their personal qualities have lent so great a lustre to the ages of feudal barbarism. He had fought by the side of King Richard in the Holy Land. Honours had been heaped upon him. King John, who was on the throne at the period of the commencement of our tale, had taken especial care to stand well with Sir Rupert Brandon, lord of vast possessions,—arbiter of life and death for miles around him, reigning in his ancient baronial castle like a despotic monarch, beloved by all who loved goodness and virtue, he ought to have been happy ; nay, he was happy, until fate deprived him of her who had been his dream of hope and joy from his boyhood. His Alicia, to whom he had been wedded but one short year, and who now lay upon the bier in his hall, watched in bitter anguish by him who had loved her with a love so intense and enduring that her loss seemed to have crushed his very heart for ever.

He was encased in armour from top to toe; a plume of black feathers waved from his casque, and no one had seen Sir Rupert's face, since the death of his wife, for he kept his visor closed, except when alone with the dead, which he had now watched for seven nights—seven weary nights of solitude and gloom.

His visor was now raised, and he stood with his arms folded across his breast by the head of the bier, gazing upon the face which in life had ever lighted up with smiles at his approach, but which in this world would never welcome him again.

Still the thunder pealed over the castle and awakened a thousand echoes among the towers and battlements ; the flashes of lightning succeeded each other with fearful rapidity ; but amid the strife of the elements—unchecked by the thunder or the lurid lightning, in that ancient hall might have been heard the deep agonizing sobs of the mail-clad warrior, as he stood there in all the bitterness of woe.

How terrible was the grief that wrung that noble heart! He who had never quailed before the foeman's lance—he who had seen death around him arrayed in all its terrors,—he whose gallantry and courage were bye-words,— he now loaded the air with such wild exclamations of grief, and wept so bitterly that a trembling fear came over his vassals, who from the corridor heard the deep sobs of anguish, and they crossed themselves with eager hands, muttering prayers for their bereaved master.

"Alicia! my Alicia!" he cried. "God of Heaven, can it be possible? —Art thou really gone from me ?—My Alicia !—my Alicia !—I who loved you so fondly,—I who—God forgive me,—loved you next to Heaven. My Alicia ! my Alicia ! Shall I never see thee smile again ?—Never hear the music of thy voice ?—Is it some horrible dream, or art thou indeed gone from me, my Alicia ——"

Sobs choked his utterance,—he clasped his hands, and bent over the cold face.

"Alicia! my Alicia!" he gasped. He kissed the cold lips, burning tears fell from his eyes upon the inanimate features. In a paroxysm of grief, he twined his arms around the lifeless form. "Alicia! my Alicia! my Alicia!" was all he could say.

His voice sounded through the hall, and amid the pauses of the tempest his vassals heard it, and with blanched cheeks again they prayed for him, for they thought his reason must have left him in that dreadful agony of feeling.

For a few moments now he only wept in silence as he hung over the bier with his arms twined round the dear form who never more could answer his embrace.

The fury of the storm seemed somewhat to have abated, for the thunder came at longer intervals, and a heavy splashing of rain sounded upon the windows of the hall. The wind was rising, and with a melancholy moan it swept over the castle, sighing around the tall turrets, and dashing the rain before it.

Still Sir Rupert wept. The tears were a relief to his wounded heart, and as the conflict of the elements of nature gradually subsided, the wild storm of passion which had rent his heart lost some of its violence, although none of its bitterness and anguish.

Suddenly there came upon the wind a dull booming sound, as of a heavy bell;—it was the castle clock. Twelve it struck, and each sound seemed to shake the heart of Sir Rupert. With a cry of anguish he stood erect.

"The time has come!" he said. "The time has come! Alicia! Alicia, we must part."

The doors of the hall were thrown open. Sir Rupert closed his visor with a clang, and stood still as a marble statue by the head of the bier on which reposed all that he had ever loved.

CHAPTER II.

" He was in truth an aged man
Of holy faith and deed,
Stood by that altar's sacred shrine
In sacerdotal weed."

A SOLDIER'S GRIEF.—THE DEATH WATCH.—A MYSTERY.—THE MIDNIGHT
VIGIL AND THE CLOSED VISOR.

A custom had subsisted for many years in the family of Sir Rupert Brandon, of interring their dead at the solemn hour of midnight, and everything had been prepared for the obsequies of the Lady Alicia, accordingly. She had died in child-birth, and the grief of Sir Rupert was probably more excessive on account of his severe loss occurring just as he was congratulating himself upon the probability of an heir to his name, his honours, and his estates.

A glare of light from many torches lit up the old hall as the doors were thrown open to admit the funeral retinue, and solemnly two by two, the retainers of the family, all clad in deep mourning, entered the chamber of death. In silence they ranked up on each side of the bier, and regarded Sir Rupert as he there stood *cap-a-pie* with feelings of respectful commiseration. From out the throng of servitors there now advanced two persons, a male and a female, who by the richness of their mourning attire, belonged evidently to the family of Sir Rupert.

They both bowed to him, and then silently took their stations behind him as mourners next in rank for the deceased.

Now there entered with slow and tottering steps an aged ecclesiastic, who made straight to Sir Rupert, who seemed much moved at his approach.

The old man laid his thin shrivelled hand upon the knight's arm as he said,—

"My son! my dear son! How is this? This garb ——"

"I will explain anon," replied Sir Rupert, sadly.

"Be comforted," said the aged priest. "Be comforted—she is with God."

Sir Rupert tried to speak, but his lips only gave forth a hollow sound within the cavity of the helmet, and he clasped his hands together in evident and deep emotion.

The bell of the castle chapel now selemnly tolled, and at its first stroke the priest made a sign to the attendants, who immediately prepared to lift the bier, and convey the corpse of their regretted mistress to its last resting-place.

The female mourner who had glided behind Sir Rupert, now whispered to her companion and pointed to the door of the hall from which at that moment, the shadow of some one glided quickly away.

"'Tis he!" she muttered; "'tis he."

"Hush—hush, Agatha," he replied in a tone of alarm. "Sir Rupert will overhear us, and then ——"

"What care I?" interrupted the female in a low stifled voice. "I will have revenge. Revenge, I say, I will have."

Again the bell tolled, and the bearers raised the bier with the body, and commenced slowly moving towards the hall-door.

Sir Rupert started as the corpse was carried onwards, and exclaimed,—

"No, no, no! Alicia! Alicia! God of Heaven!"

"My son! my son!" said the aged priest; "bear with resignation the decrees of Heaven. God has called her to Himself. If your voice would summon her from Him, would you raise it for the purpose?"

"Forgive me," said the knight, shuddering. "I—I knew not what I said—I'll follow you, holy father."

The priest crossed his hands upon his breast, and walked slowly after the bier, followed by Sir Rupert. The two persons we have mentioned came next, they were the brother and sister of the deceased Lady Brandon, whose maiden name had been Weare. Their names were Agatha Weare and Eldred Weare.

Agatha had always resided with her sister since her marriage to Sir Rupert, and Master Eldred Weare, as he was usually called, had been only summoned to Brandon Castle to take part in the expected festivities upon the birth of a son or a daughter to the noble owner, little imagining that a gloomy funeral would take the place of revelry and mirth. He held a lucrative appointment about the person of King John, and from his pleasant temper and sycophancy, was in high favour with that rather questionable monarch.

A crowd of vassals and men-at-arms, all retainers to Sir Rupert, filled up the rear, walking decorously two and two. In this order the procession reached the hall-door, where it was joined by several monks from the neighbouring monastery, who commenced chaunting prayers for the soul of the deceased.

The loquacity of Agatha Weare could not be subdued even by the solemn occasion upon which all were assembled, but with a voice of sneering inquiry, she said to her brother—

"Can you form no guess why Sir Rupert arrays himself in complete armour upon this occasion, Eldred?"

"No," replied Eldred; "in truth I cannot; 'tis very strange."

"Have you seen since sunset Morgatani?"

"Hush—hush. No—no."

"He is in the castle."

"In the castle? How could he ——"

"How could he dare, you mean? Brother, Morgatani has been a soldier. He dares anything."

"You quite alarm me, Agatha," said Eldred.

"Alarm you!" cried Agatha, in a voice above her habitual caution. "Weak fool! for whom am I plotting and scheming, but yourself? For whom ——"

"Hush! hush!" cried the timid Eldred. "Tell me another time ——"

With an expression of scorn upon her lips, Agatha relapsed into silence. The procession wound slowly along towards the chapel of the castle, in a vault underneath which the body of the fair baroness was to be deposited, according to the custom of the family, barefaced upon the bier which conveyed her thither.

The distance from the large banquetting hall in which the Lady Alicia had lain since her decease to the castle chapel was not great, and the mournful procession soon arrived at the entrance of the sacred edifice.

The chapel was brilliantly illuminated, and presented a gorgeous and imposing appearance. The solemn tolling of the great bell was now painfully distinct, and in the intervals, the rain which seemed to be descending in torrents beat wildly against the casements, and the wind howled dismally around the venerable pile.

The vault opened in the floor of the chapel, and the bearers of the bier sat down their burthen on the brink of the black yawning chasm. There was a dead silence for a few moments, a silence which was suddenly broken, to the dismay of all present, by a lengthened shriek, which seemed to come from the exterior of the chapel, and to proceed from no mortal lungs.

"There again!" cried Sir Rupert. "The wail of my house. The hand of fate still lies heavy upon me and my fortunes."

"What—what—is—this?" muttered Eldred Weare, turning as pale as death and glancing fearfully around him.

"It is known to many here present," said Sir Rupert Brandon, mournfully, "that such sounds as we have just heard, have ever preceded death or treachery to the house of Brandon."

Agatha was seen to start as the knight spoke, and she said, with a hesitating manner,—

"You—you do not suspect any one here of—of treachery?"

"As Heaven is my witness, I do not," said Sir Rupert. "Hark—there again."

The shriek once more filled the air, and many a manly heart beat with terror and undefined fear.

"That cry has haunted the castle," said an aged servitor, "ever since Sir Montague Brandon, who lived one hundred and thirty years ago, shut up the grey tower. I've heard my grandfather speak of it many a time."

"And it bodes ill to the house of my fathers," said the knight.

"It does, my honoured master. That sound never comes except there be death or treachery in these old walls."

"Death has been," said Sir Rupert, with a deep sigh.

"And treachery will ——"

"For shame, Sir Rupert," interrupted Agatha, pushing the ancient servitor unceremoniously on one side. "How can you at such a moment as this allow your judgment to be taken prisoner by superstitious fancies?"

"It is at such a time as this," said the old priest, shaking his head, "that the judgment gives the rein to fancy."

"We shall hear that cry once again," said the old retainer, whose name was Hugh Wingrove; "it always sounds three times."

"We will wait," said Sir Rupert, solemnly, waving his hand to the attendants, who were gathered round the bier.

The words had scarcely escaped his lips when the scream came again louder and clearer than before, blanching every cheek and causing an anxious flutter at every heart.

"Fate," said Sir Rupert, "cries to me in vain. The heaviest blow has fallen. Alicia, thou art gone from me, and now I may defy misfortune. I need no voice to tell me to be unhappy. I am desolate! The last of my race!"

The tone of heartfelt grief in which these words were uttered, went to the hearts of all who heard them, except one, that one was Agatha Weare. The only emotion she betrayed, was a slight quivering of the lips and an increased flush of the countenance, which might have betokened sympathy or conscious guilt of some kind, which it was, time will unravel.

Eldred Weare trembled excessively, and was forced to hold by the rails of the altar in order to preserve any degree of steadiness and composure.

The priest now made a sign to those who had borne the corpse to the chapel, and again it was lifted from the ground, and with great care carried down the broad marble steps which led to the vault.

"So soon? so soon?" cried Sir Rupert. "Must I never more look upon you, Alicia, even in death?"

"You will look upon her, my son," said the priest, "in imperishable immortality. Bid this clay adieu, and hope to meet the pure spirit that did but for a brief space inhabit it, in Heaven."

"I will, I will," said Sir Rupert. "But God who made one so beautiful and good will forgive me even clinging to the casket that contained the rare jewel."

"He will," said the priest. "He will, my son. The sins of our affections are surely most venial in the sight of Heaven."

The attendant monks now chaunted a solemn service for the dead, and Sir Rupert Brandon lifted his visor, and unmoved his helmet from his head for the first time since his Alicia's disease.

His grateful and attached followers were unexpectedly shocked at the change which six days and nights had made in his appearance. His eyes, which were wont to flash with fire and energy, were now hollow and lustreless. His cheeks were ghastly pale, and grief had planted more furrows on his ample brow in that short space of time than twenty years of active service on the battle field.

Sir Rupert would have descended into the vault, but the old priest gently restricted him, saying—

"Stay here, my son. Descend not into that dreary habitation. 'Twill conjure up in after years images of gloom and desolation. Take from here your last look on earth of her you loved, and then wait but for a brief space ere that you meet her never more to part."

Sir Rupert acquiesced in the judicious counsel that fell from the holy man, and he stood upon the brink of the abyss watching the countenance of his beloved Alicia till she was gone from his sight. Then a cry of anguish which he could not control, burst from his lips, and he dropped his plumed casque upon the chapel-floor, as he exclaimed—

"Farewell ! Light, joy, sunshine, all farewell. I may not, contrary to God's great ordinance, rush impetuously after you, Alicia, through the gates of death; but if kind Heaven will grant a boon to a desolate and broken, hearted man, it will take me from a life, the charm of which has departed for ever."

The bell now ceased to toll. The attendants ascended from the vault. All was over, and they crowded round Sir Rupert with words of sincere though rough condolence and proffers of good will and service.

"My friends," said the knight, with a faltering voice, "I will now tell you, wherefore I have kept myself encased in this warlike guise till now."

A respectful silence immediately ensued, and all bent eagerly forward to listen to their honoured master.

"As I kept watch by the sad remains——" Here his voice became broken, and he could scarcely proceed. "Pardon me, my gallant comrades," he then continued, "I am not used to woe, and hence it does affect me much. As I then kept watch the first fortnight in the hall, the first night of death there came some one with stealthy steps to disturb the sanctity of the dead or aim at the existence of the living."

An universal murmur of astonishment burst from the assembled throng.

"I saw," continued Sir Rupert, "a tall figure glide along the wall, but there must have been some secret outlet unknown to me, for when I would have grasped the intruder he fled, and I distinctly heard a door closed upon his flight."

"'Tis very strange, my lord," said Hugh Wingrove.

"It was, indeed," said Sir Rupert.

"My lord! my lord!" cried several voices.

Sir Rupert looked in the direction in which several of his vassals eagerly pointed, and he saw a dark figure crawling along the wall of the chapel, furthest from where he stood.

"'Tis the same," he cried, dashing forward. "Villain, whoe'er you be, you shall pay dearly for——ha! gone?"

By some means, the figure had eluded his grasp, and the attendants, who immediately dispersed themselves through the chapel with their torches, could discover no one.

CHAPTER III.

" Farewell—farewell, my ancient towers,
    A long farewell to thee ;
The home of joy, of hope, of love,
    Thou never more can be."

THE OBSEQUIES.— THE KNIGHT'S EXPLANATION.—THE DEPARTURE.— THE WARDER'S HORN.—THE DEEP, DEEP FOREST.

ELDRED WEARE trembled anxiously, and his sister Agatha regarded him with a look of deep meaning. She whispered in his ear,

"There is a time for all things, Morgatani will yet succeed."

"I—I—begin to fear," stammered the timid and irresolute Eldred.

"Fear?" echoed his more masculine sister. "Shame on your manhood. Were it not that I ——"

"Hush, hush," said Eldred. "Hugh Wingrove is watching us."

"Hugh Wingrove? That old babbler?"

"Yes. He regards us with an eye of suspicion."

"He shall die," whispered Agatha. "I will not have my purposes crossed by such as he. He shall die!"

"Why—why sister," said Eldred; "you would not kill him, surely?"

"No," replied his sister, "but you shall."

"I? Oh, lord—I—I ——"

"No words! I say you shall kill him. The how and the when I will tell you anon. Be still, Sir Rupert speaks."

"There is something," said the knight, "that I cannot divine, in all these mysterious appearances, and were it not that my mind is so full of grief, that there remains no vacancy for meaner thoughts than those that dwell upon the image of my—my lost—Alicia, I would fain ascertain who dares to play the eavesdropper in the ancient dwelling of my race. But now—now, my friends, what heeds it? Sir Rupert's heart is in the tomb. He is a man more desolate than the meanest of his vassals."

"Time," said Agatha, addressing the knight in fawning accents. "Time will assuage all our griefs, and you, Sir Rupert, in the duties of your station, as Lord of the Castle and its vast domains ——"

"Very rich domains," whispered Eldred.

"You will," continued Agatha, "find ample employment to wear away the fine edge of a grief which is as remarkable as it is rare."

"Agatha Weare," said Sir Rupert, "you know I am a man who will not dissemble. You know I have no cause to love you, but that is forgotten. The active pursuits of war can alone lend to my breast a small portion of that peace which erewhile went by the dearer name of happiness."

"Of war?" said Agatha. "Our country is now peaceful."

"Yes, thank God," said Eldred Weare. "One can go about now without the danger of a broken crown. There is no war."

"There is still," said Sir Rupert, "a small remnant left of the gallant
No. 2

band who fought for the redemption of the holy sepulchre. I have advices that they wage unequal and a desperate war with the infidels in the Holy Land."

"You—you will not leave Brandon?" cried Agatha.

"I shall leave it," answered the knight.

"Think better of this, my son," said the priest. "Remain here, and by the acts of peace and the social duties repairs the still bleeding wounds of our own country."

"No, no," cried Sir Rupert, "I cannot."

"As Lord of Brandon," continued the priest, "set an example to our lawless nobles, an example they much want."

"No no," again said the knight. "Urge me not, father, I cannot."

"For all our sakes," still remonstrated the aged priest.

"No, no," was the solemn reply.

"For the protection of those who love you."

"I cannot, I cannot," said Sir Rupert, in a trembling voice. "She who —who loved me best of all is gone. Why then should I stay?"

"I can say no more," cried the priest. "Bless you, my son ; bless you."

"You—you don't really mean to—to go?" said Eldred Weare.

"I have said it," replied the knight.

"You cannot seriously think of leaving Brandon Castle," said Agatha. "Would you exchange wealth and power here for peril and hardships in a foreign land ?"

"I would," answered Sir Rupert, "wealth I never coveted."

"It's a very good thing though, sister," whispered Eldred Weare.

"Power," continued Sir Rupert, "is only delicious to those who would tyrannise."

"But you will stay ?" said Agatha.

"No, no—I cannot," he cried. "I have already refused this holy man who merits my best esteem and respect. I cannot—may not stay."

Sir Rupert put on his helmet as he spoke, and he strode a pace or two towards the door of the chapel.

"My lord ! my lord ! Honoured master !" cried his numerous retainers and vassals. "Do not leave us. Stay with us ! Oh, stay."

Sir Rupert shook his head.

"Stay ! stay !" they cried.

"No, no !" said the knight, mournfully.

They dropped on their knees, and the foremost of them clung to his feet with tears in their eyes, for they were one and all enthusiastically attached to him.

"Master ! Sir Rupert ! Do not go. Stay with us ! stay !" was the universal cry.

The knight turned to them, and waving his hand, he said—

"Friends—dear friends, and many of you companions of the battle field, I thank you. But urge me not, I cannot stay."

There was a dead silence among his retainers. They felt that entreaties were in vain, and their hearts bled to lose so good and brave a master.

"I—I was wrong," said Sir Rupert, "when I said that I had lost all that loved me. I was wrong, my faithful friends."

They knelt around him, but they said no more.

"I leave Brandon Castle," said Sir Rupert, "to the joint care and superintendance of Master Eldred Weare, and you, my faithful 'squire, Hugh Wingrove ; and I charge you both always to take the advice of this holy man, who for his high virtues, I have made in virtue of authority vested in me, Abbot of Brandon Monastery."

"We shall see you again, my honoured master," said Hugh Wingrove.

"As Heaven is my judge, I hope so," said the knight.

A murmur of satisfaction came from the vassals at this earnest avowel from Sir Rupert.

The knight now closed his visor, and from behind its grating, he said,—

"Now friends, all, farewell. Years must roll over, ere that I can again look with calmness upon Brandon's ancient towers. Each spot would remind me of her. The moaning wind would repeat her name. If by the blessing of Heaven I am to recover serenity it must be in other climes, amid other scenes, in the tumult of war, where reflection may be drowned in the clangour of the trumpet, and the body's fatigue insure repose."

Again Sir Rupert strode a pace or two towards the door, and again he paused to say farewell.

Murmured adieus and blessings rose on every side.

"We shall hear of you ?" said Hugh Wingrove.

"Aye," cried Sir Rupert.

"By what token ?"

"This sable plume shall never leave my helmet till my head is laid in the grave," said the knight.

"You will not go alone, my son ?" said the priest.

"Yes, father, alone. I go alone."

He strode to the chapel-door. Then again he turned, and said—

"Farewell to all. Farewell ! farewell !"

His mailed foot echoed through the chapel, as, followed by his retainers, he gained the doorway and passed through it.

"My horse !" he cried.

Some kissed his hand and others vociferated prayers and blessings on his head.

Along the many winding passages the warrior took his way with a slow and stately step. He passed through his ancient halls without a moment's pause. Now he arrived at the court-yard which led to the outer gate, which was defended by a portcullis, beyond which was the wide moat, which with its black waters rippled with a melancholy sound round the stately battlements.

"My horse," again cried the knight.

His war steed, fully caparisoned, was in a few minutes led into the court-yard, and the noble animal recognised its master by rubbing its head upon his mail-clad breast as he laid his hand caressingly upon its arched neck.

The grey cold light of morning was beginning to steal over the scene. The wind was still high, but the rain had entirely ceased. Now the castle clock struck three, and Sir Rupert, with one bound, without touching the stirrup, vaulted upon his gallant steed, and waved his hand to his retainers.

Once more he cried,—

"Farewell ! Years may pass ere I again see Brandon Towers, but when I do return, may I be greeted by the same faces that I see around me now."

The warder at the gate now blew a loud blast from his trumpet, as was the custom when the Lord of the Castle was about to leave it either for a short or a long period of time, and Sir Rupert ordered the portcullis to be raised, and the great gate opened. The drawbridge, too, was promptly lowered, and amid the regrets of high and low, the noble but heart-stricken knight, pranced forth alone from the home of his fathers.

"Brandon, adieu !" he cried aloud. "My happiest and my most wretched hours have been spent within thy walls. Time may heal partially the wound my heart has received, and I may some day be able once again to look upon the walls that enclose the remains of my Alicia. Till then, my noble castle—ancient home of my race, farewell."

Again the clangour of the warder's trumpet rent the morning air. Sir

Rupert clapped his spurs to his charger, and in a few minutes was lost to the gaze of his faithful vassals, who strained their eyes to catch the last glimpse of his black plume and glittering helm.

In the immediate vicinity of the castle was a thick forest, and into that the knight plunged by a bridle path, leading far into the intricacies, so that he was very soon lost to the affectionate gaze of those who would have esteemed it a pleasure to watch his retreating form.

"He is gone," said Hugh Wingrove, "and a better soldier or a kinder master, never yet lived.   May the saints preserve him !"

"God bless him," cried the retainers.   "May the virgin have him in her holy keeping."

"Now, my friends," said Hugh, "we must be careful and cautious what we do, for we have those over us who are not so easily pleased as Sir Rupert.   Each man to his post, and ——"

Hugh was interrupted in his speech by an imperious voice, which cried in a tone of high command,

"Raise the drawbridge."

"The saints be good to us, it's Mistress Agatha," whispered a stout yeoman to a comrade near him.

The drawbridge was raised according to her orders, and the next command was to shut the gates, which was likewise obeyed.

"Now, ye idle hinds," cried Agatha Weare, "to your own quarters immediately.   I will have no roaming or lounging about the castle."

The vassals departed to a wing of the castle devoted to them, muttering as they went, something which did not sound like a blessing on the head of their new mistress.

"Don't you think, sister," whispered the timid Eldred, "that you had not just yet, you understand ——"

"What, coward?" cried Agatha, in a tone that made Eldred jump again.

"Why, I only meant," stammered Eldred, "that you might wait a little before you carried things with so high a hand, you know."

"Fool," cried his sister.   "These hounds must be taught obedience at once, and they will never forget the lesson."

"Well, you know best," muttered Eldred.

"I believe I do," replied his sister, as she walked with a stately air from the spot towards the private apartments of the castle.

CHAPTER IV.

> Some called him mad—while some
> Esteemed him as a wizard, who
> Could read men's birth and see
> Things coming ere their time.—OLD PLAY.

THE WIZARD OF THE RED CAVERN.—AN ADVENTURE AND ITS RESULTS —THE MYSTERIOUS COMMUNICATION.—REVENGE OF MORGATANI.

THE morning light was momentarily increasing as Sir Rupert plunged into the depths of the forest, his intention being to ride to the nearest sea port, and there take shipping for the east.

He galloped, however, out of the strengthening daylight, for the tall trees, among which he now picked his way, hid the light of Heaven, and converted even mid-day into a gloomy and uncertain twilight.

With a heavy heart the knight pursued his way as quickly as the nature of the ground over which he trod would enable him.   He sought to overcome reflection by rapidity of action, but the attempt was in vain. Deep sighs would burst from his breast, and the name of Alicia would rise in sobs to his lips in spite of his efforts to forget.

He raised his visor to enjoy the cool refreshing morning, but it had no cheering effect upon him, although it blew deliciously upon his fevered cheek.

Now he came to an open glade in the forest, and the blue sky looked down in beauty upon the spot which was covered with wild flowers. Sir Rupert allowed his steed to pause, and taste the fresh young herbage which grew in abundance, and throwing the reins upon the sagacious animal's neck, he looked around him with a deep sigh upon the sylvan beauty of the scene.

It was one of these rare sweet spots, which are sometimes to be found in English forests, where a combination of vegetable life, as if arranged artificially, to produce the most beautiful effects, meets the eye. As far as the vision could extend, was a diversified open glade, fringed by noble chesnuts, interspersed with oaks of the most majestic growth, among which, too, would rise the dark green of the fir tree and the graceful poplar, all uniting to form a pleasing variety, and enchant the eye with verdant beauty.

Sir Rupert was far from insensible to the sweetness of the scene, but the more he felt compelled to note its beauty, the more agonised his feelings became, for he could not help associating with all that was lovely, the thoughts of his lost Alicia, who had been torn from him in all her girlish beauty and youthful bloom.

"Alicia," he cried. "My Alicia! Why did I know you? Is thy image to be for ever brought before my imagination by everything beautiful; thy goodness and purity by everything virtuous? I look upon the various tints of these trees, their beauty extend into my soul, and I think then of thee, Alicia. I see the deer bounding in grace amid the gigantic denizens of the forest, and still I think of thee, Alicia; for thou wert beautiful as a dream of joy, graceful as a wreath of summer's cloud fresh blown from Heaven!"

The knight became silent from excess of emotion, but scarcely had the sound of his voice ceased, when some one who was hidden by the trees, exclaimed—

"Joy? who talks of joy? Ha! ha! ha! There is no summer, no joy, no beauty. Away, away! Fiends, away!"

Sir Rupert started, and looked narrowly around him, but he could see no one, although still wild laughter broke the silence of the verdant spot.

"It must be he," at length cried Sir Rupert. "It must be that strange being of whom I have frequently heard, but never yet seen, who goes among my vassals by the name of the Wizard of the Red Cavern."

"Away! away!" cried the voice again. "Mock me not. There is no joy, no summer; the birds and flowers are dead, and—and Nemoni is dead too—dead—dead—dead."

The most agonised sobs followed these words, and they were immediately succeeded by wild and unearthly laughter.

"How dreadful," thought the knight, "must be the state of this poor maniac, unless it may be, that Heaven in its mercy has deprived him of reason to drown the memory of some overwhelming misfortune, such as— as the death of one he fondly, dearly loved. I would fain see him."

"Lost, lost, lost!" cried the voice, "for ever lost! Ha! ha! ha!"

"What, ho!" cried Sir Rupert. "Come forth!"

A rattling among the branches of a majestic tree overhead induced Sir Rupert to look up, when to his surprise, he saw a strange being, attired in uncouth skins of beasts, rapidly descending, and in a few seconds, with a tremendous bound, and a shriek of wild laughter, the singular creature alighted, close by the side of the knight, and placed a large bony shrivelled hand upon his charger's neck.

The animal reared and seemed alarmed at the sudden and strange appearance, and it was with some difficulty that Sir Rupert could calm the frightened steed.

"What want you with me?" cried the strange being. "I, that am neither earth, fire, air, or water, neither good nor beautiful. Ha! ha! ha! Zenic was—Zenic was—but not now—not now! Away, away!"

"Who are you?" said Sir Rupert.

"Who am I?" said the wild creature. "Ha! ha! ha! An outcast of God and man—a pestilence—a loathing—a reader of the stars. The magi owns me as a brother. Sir Rupert Brandon, I feel nearly human towards you. Ha! ha! for—for you have suffered—you have still to suffer."

"You know me, then?" said the knight in a tone of surprise.

"Hush, hush—I know all—I know all!"

"Can you or will you name yourself?" inquired Sir Rupert.

"A name?" cried the being. "A name—I had a name. Men call me many names. Some call me madman—some, the wild man of the wood—others call me the Wizard of the Red Cavern!"

"Wherefore are you called that?" said Sir Rupert.

"Because I have passed through life once and come back again with secrets from the grave," replied the wizard, mournfully. "Because I know where evil lurks—because I can read men's hearts."

"Indeed!" said the knight.

"Even so—even so. But hark—hark. Hear you nothing?"

"I hear the light wind among the leaves of the forest trees," said Sir Rupert.

"Nothing more! nothing more?"

"The whistles of the hedge sparrow and the carol of the lark, I hear."

"Nothing more?"

"Nothing."

"Listen again—again."

"What do you hear?" said Sir Rupert, interested strangely by the manner of his companion.

"Hark! hark!" cried he, whom for want of a truer designation, we must call the wizard. "Hark, Sir Knight. Do you not hear them now?"

"Hear what?"

"The cracking of the blazing timbers."

"Blazing timbers?"

"It was—saved—saved. I come—I come."

With a wild shriek the unhappy creature rushed from the spot, bursting madly through the thick bushes, and bounding past the trees like a hunted deer, shouting,—"I come, I come. Saved! saved! saved!"

Sir Rupert sat for some minutes silent upon his charger in deep amazement at the sudden fury of the maniac, for such he considered him to be.

"What awful calamity," he said, "can have reduced this poor creature to such an extremity of wretchedness? His bearing and form are noble and imposing, and his speech is not rude or unlettered. Some direful mischance has taken his reason from him, and made him what he is. Heaven help him!"

Absorbed in these reflections, the knight gave the rein to his charger, and slowly pursued his way through the forest.

The sun was now high in the Heavens, and streaming down between the high tree tops—

"Dappling the sward with light and shade,"

and the birds were singing merrily from tree to tree. The many shadows agreeably tempered the heat, and it was with a sensation of calmness greater than he had ever felt since the death of his lady, that the gallant Knight of Brandon urged on his noble steed to a canter, and cleared the open glade of the forest.

He had not, however, proceeded far before his sagacious steed paused, and moved its ears in the attitude of listening. Sir Rupert, at the same moment, heard a low moaning sound, issuing apparently from some thick underwood to his right hand. In a moment he dismounted, for the voice of distress never sounded in vain in the ears of the Knight of Brandon, and leaving his steed under the shadow of a tree, where he well knew the gallant creature would faithfully await his return, he plunged at once among the thickets in the direction of the sounds.

He had not to walk far before he discovered lying upon the ground in a pool of blood, the unhappy being who had left him so suddenly a few minutes previously. The knight, who was of uncommon personal strength, lifted him immediately from the ground, and then perceived that he had a wound upon his forehead, from which the blood was oozing.

Sir Rupert conjectured immediately that the poor creature must have struck his head against some projection of a tree in his headlong flight. He removed the matted hair from his forehead, and satisfied himself that the wound, although large, was but superficial, then he laid him gently down upon a sloping bank, for he still moaned as if in great pain.

The knight was quite at a loss what to do, for he did not like to leave a poor maniac in such a state unattended, and he had no means at hand of rendering him any effectual assistance.

As he remained in doubt a moment, the wizard slowly opened his eyes, and looked with a dull glare upon the countenance of Sir Rupert.

"What now?" he said. "What now? More torments. Who said Nemoni was dead? Who said so? Tell me that, and I will be your slave. Tell me she is dead—dead ——"

"You have struck yourself badly," said the knight.

"And where is Morgatani?—where is he?" cried the wizard, starting to his feet with sudden energy.

"Morgatini," said Sir Rupert, his brow darkening.

"Where is he?" cried the wizard. "Let me tear him limb from limb. Let me feed upon his heart."

"Tell me," cried Sir Rupert, "what know you of Morgatani?"

"The villain!" cried the wizard.

"Yes," said the knight; "the black-hearted villain."

"Down with him," shrieked the maniac. "Down with him to the earth, tear him to pieces. See! see! his blood boils with unholy passions. There is a word that is shrieked in hell as a word of fear ——"

"What word?" said Sir Rupert.

"Morgatani!" cried the wizard. "Morgatani!"

"There is some fearful mystery here," thought Sir Rupert. "A mystery which, I fear, this poor creature feels the effects upon, while he cannot explain or unravel it."

"Your name is Rupert?" suddenly said the wizard.

"It is," answered the knight.

"You are the Lord of Brandon?"

"I am."

"Beware of Morgatani. Beware! beware!"

"Morgatani," said the knight, "dare not pass my threshold for his life."

"Beware! beware!" cried the Wizard.

"Man's enmity," said Sir Rupert, with a deep sigh, "is now to me as nothing."

"Beware, beware," cried the wizard. "I was powerful."

"I allude not to my power," said Sir Rupert, "I am desolate!"

"Desolate? Desolate, say you? 'Tis I that am desolate!"

"I am the last of my race," said the knight.

"Is the house of Brandon extinct with thee?"

"It is; I am the last."

The wizard pressed his hands for a few moments, and then said in a solemn tone :—

"No, no, not extinct. No, no."

"Quite extinct," said the knight; "I am the last."

"No, no," persisted his strange companion; "not so. Thy children ——"

"Children !"

"Aye. Thy children will be happy, although thou may not."

Sir Rupert shook his head. "You rave, you rave," he said. "I have no children."

"Beware of Morgatani! Beware, I am the Wizard of the Red Cavern, and I tell you to beware of Morgatani."

"I am leaving Brandon," said the knight.

"I know it," replied the wizard.

"For ever, I believe," continued Sir Rupert. "I shall never again see its towers and battlements."

"You will," cried the mysterious man. "You will; in peril and misfortune you will see Brandon again. You have spoken kindly to me. I will watch over your children."

"What a strange delusion," thought Sir Rupert. "I tell thee I am childless."

"Away! away!" shrieked the wizard. "The fiend is coming!—Nemoni—Nemoni! Art thou really dead? I will follow thee. Ha! Morgatani! villain! monster!—I'll have thee now. Ha! ha! ha!"

Again he darted from Sir Rupert with extreme speed, and was lost in the mazes of the forest.

CHAPTER V.

"Thrice the horn blew at the castle gate,
A blast of dread and fear;
And warriors stern, with blanched cheeks,
Did shake that sound to hear."

MIDNIGHT AT THE CASTLE.—AN ALARM.—THE SUMMONS.—THE MYSTERIOUS HORN,

SCARCELY had the midnight watch taken their stations upon the battlements of Brandon Castle, on the night succeeding the departure of Sir Rupert, when a horn sounded loudly from the further side of the moat.

The guards started, and looked at each other by the dim light for a few moments in amazement, for the sound was peculiar and familiar to their ears as that which Sir Rupert himself always blew from his bugle upon his return to the castle.

"By the holy rood," exclaimed one, "it must be our dear lord returned."

"It is his horn," exclaimed several with delighted eagerness.

"He has changed his resolution," said another. "Our own dear mas-

ter will come back, and take us out of the hands of the she-devil, Mistress ——ahem! you know who, comrades."

Again a blast came from the horn.

"I could swear to it now," exclaimed the first speaker. "And hark! my friends, the warder answers him."

As the man spoke, the warder's horn sounded clear and prolonged upon the night air, and the command was given by Hugh Wingrove to lower the drawbridge instantly.

A third time the horn sounded, as the drawbridge was let down quickly, and the great gates were thrown open with joyous precipitation.

A crowd of the vassals assembled hastily with lighted torches to welcome home their lord, who they expected to see immediately cross the drawbridge upon his well-known charger.

The light from the torches gleamed across the black waters of the moat for a considerable distance, but the radiance did not reach far enough through the darkness to enable them to distinguish who or what was upon the other side.

Again the warder blew a joyous blast upon his horn;—a shout of congratulation arose from the vassals, and all pressed eagerly forward, each being desirous of being the first to welcome back Sir Rupert.

The echo of the horn, however, as well as the shouts of the retainers, died away upon the night air, and still no step was heard upon the drawbridge; nor, in fact, could they hear any footsteps either of man or horse in advance or in retreat.

A dead silence now ensued of several minutes' duration, and then an undefinable fear crept over all those present, and they glanced at each other with looks of dismay and apprehension.

"He—he does not come," stammered one.

No. 3

Hugh Wingrove stretched a torch as far as his arm could reach over the murky flood that rolled lazily past the castle walls, but he could see nothing.

"Sir Rupert!" he cried; "Sir Rupert!"

The sound of his voice was echoed from tower and wall, but there was no reply, and with a blanched cheek the old man leant against the ponderous gate for a moment or two, lost in thought.

"It was his horn," he at length exclaimed. "Comrades, let us cross the moat; our dear master may be wounded, or in some sore strait, unable to do more than summon us to his aid by his well known bugle sound. Come, comrades, come."

The vassals were not backward in obeying the summons, and they all rushed forward to cross the drawbridge.

The voice of Agatha arrested them for a moment, as she exclaimed:—

"What means this tumult? What! the castle gates open at this unseemly hour! Speak, knaves, what mean you?"

She was attired in a loose black robe, and was of a death-like paleness, as she stood trembling with passion and apprehension within the gate.

Behind her was her brother Eldred, who presented the picture of cowardice and unmanly consternation.

"We heard Sir Rupert's bugle," said the blunt Hugh Wingrove, doggedly.

"Sir Rupert's bugle?" cried Agatha, starting back.

"The—the horn of Sir Rupert, eh?" stammered Eldred. "You—you don't mean that, do you?"

"It has sounded thrice from across the moat," cried a soldier. "Come, my brave comrades,—hurrah for our noble master!"

A loud hurrah rent the air, and the armed vassals resolutely crossed the drawbridge, headed by Hugh Wingrove, to seek their lord.

"Do you really, sister, think—that is, can he really have come back so soon?" said Eldred, in a voice of dismay.

"I hope so," said Agatha; "and yet, I fear the cause that could again bring him back to Brandon."

"The—the secret, sister, is surely safe?—I ——"

"Peace!" cried Agatha. "Whisper it not to the very stones of Brandon Castle. Peace, I say, peace!"

The eager retainers of Sir Rupert soon gained the opposite bank of the moat, and raising their torches high in the air, they looked inquiringly around them for their master, but to their surprise and alarm, neither horse nor man met their eager and straining eyes.

"By the mass," said Hugh Wingrove, "this is most strange. Let us disperse ourselves about the banks of the moat, and narrowly examine the place."

They did so, but no appearance of any one having been there recently rewarded their toils, and in deep wonderment they silently assembled at the end of the drawbridge.

"It is useless searching," said the soldier who had first drawn the attention of the guards on the battlements to the sound of the horn. "I feel quite positive that the bugle strain came from the very spot on which we now stand."

"And I feel equally positive," said another, "that it was Sir Rupert's horn that we heard. Well I know it."

"Let us ask Ambrose, the warder, what he made of the call," said Hugh Wingrove. "It is quite clear Sir Rupert is not here."

"He or his ghost has been here," said a soldier; "that I would swear to, for I have heard him blow that same call upon his silver bugle hundreds of times, and I know it as well as I do my own name."

"Let us return," said Wingrove.

Slowly they paced their way back to the castle over the drawbridge.

"What ho, Ambrose!" cried Hugh Wingrove to the warder who watched from his tower above the gates. "What made you out of yon bugle's sound?"

"It was Sir Rupert's," said the warder; "and yet I saw nothing."

"Nor I, nor any of us," muttered Wingrove. "Now Heaven help our honoured master, if he be not past Heaven's help."

The vassals and retainers crossed themselves devoutly as they thronged in at the great gates.

"Well," said Agatha, "what mummery is this?"

"Aye, aye," muttered Eldred, "what mummery is this?"

"'Tis no mummery," replied Hugh Wingrove. "We all heard Sir Rupert's bugle, and now we find he is not there."

"Indeed!" sneered Agatha.

"Yes," continued Hugh, "and I pray Heaven he may not have met with some foul play from those who love him not."

"What mean you, knave?" cried Agatha, furiously.

"Ah! what mean you, knave?" muttered Eldred behind her.

"I mean what I say, madam," replied Hugh Wingrove. "Heaven help my noble master, Sir Rupert Brandon."

"You are too free of speech, sir," said Agatha, as she retired, followed by Eldred, who muttered after her :—

"Yes, a great deal too free of speech ;—on my conscience too free."

Old Hugh shook his head, and walked with slow and mournful steps to the great hall, in which the castle guard kept themselves ready for active service the whole of the night.

Some fresh faggots were cast upon the ample hearth, for although it was the month of June, those large stone-paved halls were chilling and dreary after nightfall, without a cheerful fire to lend them comfort and animation.

"Good Master Hugh," said a rough soldier, throwing his heavy sword with a clash upon the large oaken table, which was graced with sundry flagons; "you promised some guard-night to tell myself and Peter Riches here why Sir Montague Brandon shut up the Grey Turret, and never would go into it in all his life afterwards."

"The tale is an old one," answered Hugh Wingrove; "but 'tis no secret, comrades, and I marvel that you have not heard it before."

"Well, let's hear it now, good Hugh," they cried with one accord.

"Listen, then," said the old faithful servitor.

Every one was immediately still, and each countenance betrayed intense curiosity.

"The Grey Turret, then," said Hugh Wingrove, "was shut up by Sir Montague Brandon a good many years ago. My grandfather has often told me the story. Sir Montague was very hospitable. His castle gates were always opened to the traveller, and no one, be his condition high or low, need then have passed Brandon Castle without food and shelter for as long as he chose to remain.

"The Grey Turret was fitted up as a handsome sleeping-chamber, and when any traveller—who from his appearance or manners seemed a gentleman,—came to the castle, he was always conducted by Sir Montague himself to the sleeping-chamber in the Grey Turret.

"Well, it happened that one night there came very late a summons for admission to the castle, and in answer to questions from the warder, it turned out to be a traveller, who solicited bed and board till the morning's light should enable him to pursue his journey, which, he further said, was of haste and importance. He was admitted, as a matter of course, and Sir Montague, who was just about retiring to rest, came from his chamber down to the hall, as was always his custom, to welcome the guest.

"After a collation, which Sir Montague, although he had supped, partook of from courtesy, the traveller rose and signified his intention of retiring for the night, as he wished to pursue his journey by sunrise on the following morning.

"Sir Montague then took a branch candlestick from the table, and preceded his guest to the Grey Turret, as was his custom."

"Well, Hugh, what then?" said a soldier, whose curiosity had been much aroused by the narrative.

"I am telling you, I believe," responded Hugh Wingrove, not in the best of humours at being interrupted in his story. "You want me to give it you, I suppose, like a blast from a bugle horn, all in one breath."

These words had scarcely left Hugh Wingrove's mouth, when they were all startled by a loud trumpet-call from the front of the castle,—a call in every respect similar to the one which had excited so much surprise and speculation, from its strong resemblance to Sir Rupert's summons.

The soldiers looked at each other aghast at the sound, and for some moments so breathless was the silence, that a pin might have been heard to drop.

"That is it again," cried Hugh Wingrove, starting from his seat.

"It's the same call," said one of the soldiers. "Sir Rupert's horn it must be."

"I should take my oath of it, myself," said Hugh Wingrove. "I taught him to blow it when he was a boy, and I think I ought to know the strain."

"Hark!" cried several.

Again the long peculiar blast from a bugle came upon their ears, and echoed around the ancient walls.

"To the gate once more!" cried Wingrove, snatching up his sword from the table upon which he had laid it. "To the gate, comrades, to the gate. Be it fiend or man, I'll ascertain who mocks us by that well-known call!"

Weapons were hastily snatched from various places where they had been deposited, and Hugh Wingrove at the head of the night-guard of the castle, hurried once more to the gate, in answer to the mysterious and inexplicable summons.

The distance was not great from the guard-room to the gates, and the party soon stood within them by the side of the sentinel whose duty it was to look to their security.

"What have you heard?" said Hugh to the man, who was standing in an attitude of fixed attention at his post.

"A horn!" was the reply.

"Did you know the sound?"

"I did."

"Whose—whose was it?"

"Sir Rupert's, I'll swear," answered the sentinel. "It was the same call that took us all over the drawbridge half an hour ago."

"It's very strange," muttered Hugh.

Even as he spoke a third blast, evidently from the other side of the moat, rang clear and loud upon the night air, and was prolonged by a thousand echoes among the battlements and towers.

CHAPTER VI.

The midnight hour had sounded
Throughout that dreary pile;
And a heavy footstep loudly rang
Along the chapel's aisle.—ANON.

MORGATANI, THE BLACK MONK.—THE CHAPEL.—THE TIME IS COME.—HESITA-
TION.—THE CASTLE CLOCK.

WHILE the retainers and servitors of the lord of Brandon were lost in astonishment and dismay at the singular trumpet calls in front of the castle, a
scene was being enacted within its ancient walls, which, had they witnessed,
it would have filled them with horror, and converted their surprise and astonishment into indignation and rage.

Hardly had the castle clock struck the midnight hour, when a figure might
have been seen slowly crossing the chapel.

The figure, by the flickering light of a lamp which it bore in its hand, appeared to be of gigantic proportions, and its shadow fell in grotesque and
strange shapes upon the walls and carved roof of the sacred and time-honoured
edifice.

The garb in which the form was clothed was that of a monk, and the flowing habit added greatly to the apparent height of the figure.

With a stately and slow step it advanced across the chapel until it reached
the altar, upon which it deposited the lamp in silence. The dim light then
fell clearly upon the features of the individual, as he stood still as a statue by
the side of the altar, with one hand resting upon it, and the cowl of his habit
thrown back from his head.

The face was that of a man who had passed the prime of life, but it would
seem as if time had not succeeded in dimming the fire of his eye, or in quench-
ing the passions which betrayed themselves in every feature of his face.

His complexion was remarkable as being of so swarthy a brown that he
might have been taken for a native of a warmer clime than is to be found in
Europe.

The features were large and bold, but well proportioned, and the mouth,
although almost colossal, might have been esteemed beautiful, were it not for
the habitual sneer which sat upon it, and which had been indulged in for so
many years, that it had become the natural expression of the face, and not a
fleeting passion.

His eyes were as black as jet, and few could stand their flashing scrutiny.
His neck and shoulders were of enormous strength, and he was evidently
considerably above the ordinary height of men. Altogether, his appearance,
as he stood by the altar, with his form just sufficiently illuminated by the
lamp to render its large outline visible, was one of singular grandeur, and
would have engendered in most breasts an involuntary awe of the man.

The hand that rested on the altar was immense, and seemed to be indicative
of enormous muscular power.

Silently he waited for some minutes by the altar, then a gesture of impatience betrayed that he waited for some one, and he muttered in low deep tones—

"Past the time—past the time. These puppets are too loose-minded to be
punctual. How I despise them."

Then folding his arms beneath his ample robe, he again stood fixed as a
statue.

A quarter of an hour had elapsed, and still no one came. Then, with a
very unpriestly execration from his lips, he took the lamp from the altar, and
striding towards a part of the wall of the chapel upon which was hung some
black drapery, he pushed the folds aside, and pressing a spring in the

panelling, a small concealed door sprang open, and presented beyond a narrow, low, arched passage.

The gigantic monk stood for a few moments at the entrance, listening attentively, then muttering an oath, he was about to plunge into it, when a faint light appeared at some distance off in its recesses.

He paused, and drew back, concealing his lamp under his garment.

The light approached from the narrow passage, and presently its bearer, who was no other than Agatha, the sister-in-law of the absent Sir Rupert, entered the chapel.

She paused a moment as she passed through the door-way, and shading the light she carried with her hand, she looked cautiously around her. The monk had returned back to the altar, and she could not see him at that distance from where she stood, for the rays emitted from the light she carried were feeble, and shed but a dim radiance for a few feet around the spot on which she stood.

She then turned again towards the narrow passage, and stepping just within it, she called, in a low voice—

" Eldred, Eldred !"

No one replied, but a confused shuffling of feet could be heard as of some one approaching with great reluctance.

" Eldred !" she again cried.

" Ye—ye—yes," said a trembling voice from the passage.

" Hasten," cried Agatha, in an earnest whisper. " Hasten, I say ! Why do you tarry behind thus ?"

" I—I—am coming," answered Eldred Weare, just making his appearance from the secret passage, very pale and frightened.

" Coward !" said his sister. " Dastard ! Why do you tremble ?"

" I—I—think it must be the—the—the cold, sister," replied the shivering Eldred Weare, whose teeth chattered fearfully.

" It is your courage that is cold," sneered his sister.

" N—n—no. Oh, no," stammered Eldred ; " I am as bold as a—a lion—a cold lion, I mean."

" Close the spring door and follow me," said his sister, imperiously. " We do not want so many lights ; extinguish yours."

" Y—yes," said Eldred, closing the door, which shut with a snap that made him give a great jump.

" What now ?" cried Agatha.

" I—I really don't know," said Eldred. " Something made me jump."

" Come on," said Agatha. " Assume a little courage if you can, and do not bring the contempt of *him* upon your head."

" Him, sister ?"

" Yes ! You know well who I mean. Be silent and follow me."

" Well—I'm coming," stammered Eldred, following his sister as closely as he possibly could.

Agatha advanced to the middle of the chapel, and then she said in a low voice, but still one sufficiently clear and distinct to reach any one's ears who might be in the place,

" Morgatani !"

" Here !" immediately replied a deep voice.

Eldred trembled violently, as he muttered to himself,—

" That's him, sure enough—*The Black Monk*."

" Hush," cried Agatha. " Beware, Eldred, how you offend Father Morgatani ; the name that you have uttered is not one that pleases him."

" I—I—only remarked," said Eldred, " that ——"

" Silence," interrupted Agatha. " Beware what you say, and offend not by an imprudent word your best friend."

"I only said ——"

"Hush, I say," cried Agatha. Then again raising her voice, she said,—— "Morgatani—I am here."

"And I am here!" said the monk, suddenly advancing.

"Ye—yes—yes," stuttered Eldred. "How—do you—you—do?"

"Daughter," said the monk to Agatha, "you are welcome. I have waited long for you."

"A circumstance occurred that delayed us," answered Agatha, "of which I will speak to you at a more fitting time."

"As you please," said Morgatani. "The night is wearing on ; we must to our work quickly."

"Perhaps," said Eldred, in a hesitating voice, "as we are all three here, you—you know—Father Morgatani, you don't mind, you see, being a little confidential or so—and—just telling me what's to be—done, eh?"

The Black Monk looked at Agatha for a moment with a peculiar expression, and then said, calmly :—

"Master Eldred Weare,—I thought you understood that I consented to aid you in becoming the master of Brandon Castle, and lord of its estates, on one condition, to which you agreed."

"Yes—yes," said Eldred ; "I—I—know. You are to be created Abbot of the Monastery instead of the present abbot."

"Yes," said the monk, with a sneer. "In order that I may extend my sphere of usefulness as a member of the Church."

"Oh, I know all that," said Eldred. "But—but ——"

"But what?" cried his sister, impatiently.

"Why I—I want to know why we come here to-night?"

"Description," said Morgatani, with a sardonic smile, "always falls so far short of reality, that I prefer shewing Master Eldred Weare the object of our meeting here to describing it to him."

"Certainly," said Agatha. "You are satisfied now, Eldred?"

"I—I—oh, dear,—I suppose so," stammered Eldred, with a vacant look.

"Precisely," said Morgatani.

He exchanged a look with Agatha as he spoke, which indicated the supreme contempt in which they both held the trembling Eldred, who, it was evident, was a mere instrument in their hands for working out their own wicked and ambitious ends.

The castle clock now struck one, and the belfry being immediately above the chapel, the sound came amid the stillness of the night with startling loudness to the ears of the parties assembled there.

"Time warns us," said Morgatani.

"Then let us at once proceed to the vault," cried Agatha. "You are fully prepared, Morgatani?"

"I am," replied the monk.

Eldred looked aghast from one to the other as they spoke.

"You—you don't say vault, do you?" he stammered.

"Yes," said Agatha, coldly, "I said vault."

"W—w—what vault?"

"The vault which was opened to deposit within it the deceased Lady Brandon," said Morgatani.

Eldred looked still more astounded at this announcement, and he glanced at Morgatani with his mouth wide open with amazement.

"We waste time," said Agatha, impatiently.

"We do," said Morgatani. "The slab that covers the entrance to the vault, is as yet, I presume, but merely laid in its place."

"Merely so," answered Agatha. "It is usually fastened down with strong cement, but that is not yet done, so it can be removed the more easily, and without exciting remark."

"But," said Eldred, "you—you don't mean to say both of you that—that you mean to—to go down to the vault?"

"Yes," answered Morgatani, in a tone that thrilled through the veins of the cowardly Eldred. "You, too, shall accompany us."

"I—I—oh, dear, no—I cannot ——"

"You must," said the Black Monk, in a hissing whisper in Eldred's ear, at the same time grasping his arm as if it were in a vice. "You must, I say. You have gone too far to retreat; you have consented to become Lord of Brandon, and you cannot—you dare not now shrink from the means which shall make you so!"

Eldred trembled, but made no further opposition, for his awe of Father Morgatani, the Black Monk, was excessive.

"To the vault, then!" said Agatha.

"Aye! To the vault!" cried Morgatani. "To the vault!"

Eldred moaned, and shook his head in extreme terror, but he said nothing, for he dreaded the vengeance both of his sister and the monk, and he was weak enough to believe their protestations that it was to confer upon him the castle and estate of Brandon that they thus met in secret at the solemn hour of midnight to desecrate the ancient tomb of the Brandons.

CHAPTER VII.

Of giant form, of giant mould,
He was for good or evil,
Terribly great.—GODWIN.

THE HERCULEAN STRENGTH OF THE MONK.—THE MARBLE SLAB.—THE PLOT.
—REVENGE.—THE VAULT.

THE monk took his lamp from the altar, and paced along the chapel till he came to the large block of black marble which closed the opening of the vault, where slept many of the race of Brandon, and last, although not least in loveliness and virtue, the lady of Sir Rupert, who was by that gallant knight so bitterly mourned and so sincerely regretted.

The monk stood by the side of the slab, and turning to Eldred, he said :—

"How many men did it take to lay down this marble block in its place? You know I am in bad odour with Sir Rupert, and could not shew myself at the obsequies of his lady."

"I—I should say five or six of the knaves," stammered Eldred, "laid down the stone, and a hard job they seemed to have of it."

"Humph," said the monk, "we shall see now what one can do."

He laid down his lamp, and bent his herculean form over the marble slab, in the face of which was inserted several large iron rings, by which it might be lifted from its place.

His huge form shook for a moment, and then, to the surprise of Eldred and Agatha, he lifted from its place the heavy piece of stone, and laid it upon one side of the yawning chasm which appeared beneath it.

The effort was evidently very great, and even the stalwart frame of the Black Monk shook as he rose, and he drew a long breath as he said :—

"'Tis done, and by the blessed virgin it's a weightier mass than I took it to be."

Below the stone appeared the staircase which led to the vaults, and Mor-

gatani, after a few moments' pause to recover the extraordinary exertion he had made, and which no man of ordinary strength could have accomplished had his life even hung upon the issue, again took up his lamp, and turning to Agatha, he said in his usual deep tone,—

"Let us now descend."

"We are ready," replied Agatha. "Brother, how heavy a debt of gratitude you owe the good Father Morgatani."

"Ye—yes," said Eldred. "He—he nearly broke his back, I think, but I don't yet see how I am to be made undisputed master of Brandon. You see now as it is, I have a sort of authority."

"But you have not the name nor the wealth," said his sister.

"N—no—no. That's very true," sighed Eldred. "I—I always was ambitious, you know, sister."

"And your ambition shall be gratified," said Morgatani, as he descended the staircase, adding to himself in an under tone, "most likely at the expense of your neck, while I reap the fruits and satisfy a desire for revenge that scorches my soul as if it were environed by a flame from the hottest region of hell."

"Come!" said Agatha, and seizing the trembling and reluctant Eldred Weare by the arm, she hurried him, whether he would or not, down the stone steps after the monk.

A few minutes brought the party into the vault, which extended throughout almost the whole space beneath the chapel floor.

"The roof, which of course was the flooring of the chapel, was composed of large blocks of stone, firmly cemented together, and supported by numerous massive pillars, which terminated in low groined arches, such as were commonly used in Gothic residences.

The air within the vault seemed to be very much vitiated and unfavourable

No. 4

to combustion, for the light which the Black Monk held high above his head, burned but dimly, and left the vault, except upon the spot where he stood, in great obscurity.

After a time, however, the pent up bad air appeared to escape into the chapel, and to be replaced by a purer atmosphere, for gradually the lamp burned brighter, and objects in that dreary home began to assume more distinct hues and shapes.

The dead lay upon biers, ranged side by side, each corpse being covered, with the exception of the face, by a rich pall of velvet, which had, however, in the majority of cases, yielded to the touch of time and crumbled into dust, exposing the ghastly remains beneath it of the form it was intended to cover.

Upon some of the biers there could be traced nothing but a mass of whitened bones. The progress of decay had dissipated all else belonging to frail humanity.

Others of more recent date were not so much decayed, and some portions of the embroidered pall would be still clinging to the ghastly tenant of the tomb. Then again there were others that still retained some of the lineaments of the face as it peered in hideous shrunkenness from the rich covering which reached but to the chin. Altogether, that vault of death—that apartment of the departed, presented to the eye a horrifying spectacle. It was the custom of the Brandons to leave their dead thus exposed, a custom which had taken its rise from some early family legend, which had perished in forgetfulness itself, while it left its foolish and revolting result behind.

The monk walked slowly, holding his lamp above his head, and casting an indifferent glance upon the ghostly occupants of each open bier as he passed it.

Agatha followed closely in his footsteps, but after gazing upon the first bier that met her eyes, she turned from the others, and resolutely abstained from looking at them. Even her iron nerves appeared to be shaken by the fearful spectacles which that vault presented.

Eldred Weare, whose imagination had never in its wildest flights, conjured up anything so horrible and terrifying as the vault of the Brandons, stood for a few moments as if stupified, gazing around with an expression of terror, which it would be in vain to attempt to describe.

"Let us go ! let us go !" he cried, wildly. "I give up all—all—only let me leave this place."

"Stir from this vault without my permission," said the monk, "and I will leave you here for ever."

Eldred was so terrified at this threat, that he said not a word more, although he was nearly bereft of reason by his fears. He clutched with nervous energy the dress of his sister, and followed her with many groans of anguish and mortal terror.

The priest walked on for some moments in silence, then his step became slower, and finally he paused, and turning to Agatha, he said, in a voice which was evidently struggling with some kind of emotion :—

"It is here, the one near at hand."

There was that in his tone which surprised Agatha, and she said to him in a suppressed whisper,

"What, Morgatani ! Can you feel ?"

"No," he answered in his usual tone, for whatever had occasioned the temporary weakness, he had now overcame it. "No, Agatha, I was only faint for an instant from the noisome vapour of this place."

"I'm glad it has passed," said Agatha, " for ——"

"Say no more, say no more," interrupted the Black Monk. "Here is the bier of—of ——"

"Lady Brandon," said Agatha.

"Aye," said the monk. "Even so."

They now stood by the mortal remains of the fair and faultless being, who had been so lately consigned to that last resting-place.

Even yet a shadow of beauty lingered upon the fair girlish face. The long flaxen hair hung still in grace upon the snowy neck—

> "She seemed more beautiful than death,
> Though all too sad to look upon."

The pall had shrunk down to the light agile figure that slept beneath its ample folds.

> "And as it settled to the still proportions,
> It betrayed the matchless symmetry,
> The grace of form, which but a little while
> Had charmed all eyes and seated them with beauty."

The Black Monk stood by the bier in silence, and that he lived could only be perceived by the troubled heaving of his breast.

"Morgatani!" said Agatha.

He stopped as if the sound of his own name had dissolved some spell, in which his senses had been wrapped.

"Who calls?" he cried wildly. "Who said Morgatani? I—oh, Agatha, forgive me. I was transported in thought far from here. I—I—to our work, Agatha; to our work."

"You betray unwonted emotion," said Agatha, inquiringly.

"'Tis past, 'tis past," said the Black Monk. "Heed it not, Agatha. But do you not think it many pities to—to ——"

"To what, Morgatini? This from you? I am amazed."

"She sleeps in beauty," said the monk.

"A beauty which has scared my heart," said Agatha.

"I know it," answered Morgatani. "Her beauty was a fatal light which lured to destruction."

"Good God," said Eldred. "How long are you going to stay here whispering? It's perfectly horrid."

"To our work!" cried the monk. "To our work. Come forward, Eldred Weare."

"Approach," cried his sister, imperiously.

The trembling Eldred approached the bier, and gazed upon the still features if his dead sister.

"Ah," he cried, "there she lies, poor thing. Well, who'd a thought it? So young and so very pretty, too; so uncommonly pretty."

"Silence!" cried his sister Agatha. "Attend to Father Morgatani."

"Eldred Weare," said the monk, in a hollow voice, which made the blood run cold in the veins of the trembling, yet ambitious and greedy coward. "Eldred Weare, listen."

"Ye—yes—yes," said Eldred; "I—I will."

"Wealth is your God?"

"I—I like money."

"Power you court, because you like its constant exercise?"

"Ye—yes—oh, dear, yes."

"You have a great mind, Eldred Weare," continued the monk, with a sneer that would have been detected by any one else but the weak man to whom he spoke.

"Why—yes," answered Eldred. "I—I think—I rather have in a manner of speaking a great mind—oh, yes; you're right."

"Of course you have," continued the Black Monk. "And you would be, if possible, Lord of Brandon and its rich possessions, which would ensure you both wealth and power?"

"Yes! oh, yes," said Eldred. "Besides, Sir Rupert hit me a thump on the back once, with a sheathed sword, and called me a coward, besides putting me in a perspiration."

"A gross insult," said the Black Monk.

"Oh, very," said Eldred. "I'll never forgive him."

"Then you work for money, power, and revenge."

"Yes! oh, yes!"

"I work for revenge, alone; wherefore it is no matter. But I will help you. Now, Sir Rupert's death would give you a fair chance for the possession of Brandon."

"Only a chance," said Eldred, shaking his head. "Some fellow would offer to fight me, to a dead certainty, as soon as I should mention it to the king, and there would be a pretty job."

"Very true," said Morgatani. "Sir Rupert's disgrace, and perchance his execution, would be better."

"Execution!" exclaimed Eldred.

"Aye," said the monk; "execution."

"F—f—for what?" stammered Eldred.

"Murder!" said the Black Monk, in a hissing whisper, that penetrated to the farthest corner of the vault, and echoed fearfully among the solemn arches.

CHAPTER VIII.

Murder most foul, as at the l est it is,
But this most foul and unnatural.—SHAKSPERE.

THE DEAD.—DECAY AND ITS PROGRESS.—THE SKELETON THRONG.—HORROR OF ELDRED.—THE DEED OF BLACKNESS.

ELDRED WEARE looked aghast at the monk, as he uttered the word murder, and then glanced fearfully around him, as if he expected some sudden occurrence to take place, in keeping with the words of Morgatani.

"Whose murder?" he at length said, in a tone of apprehension.

"The murder of Alicia, his wife," said the monk. "She who now lies dead before us in such—such ghastly beauty!"

"Of her?" cried Eldred.

"Yes," said Agatha; "it must appear so."

"And to make it appear so," said Morgatani, "we have come here to this dismal place this night."

"But, but,—" said Eldred.

"But what?" cried his sister, impatiently.

"Nobody will believe it," stammered Eldred; "because, you know, he was so fond of her, and all that sort of thing, you know."

"Hence," said Morgatani, "if the crime be proved beyond a doubt, the more damning will appear his guilt."

"Why, yes," said Eldred, "there is something in that."

"There is everything in it," said Agatha.

"But what an idea it is, to be sure," said Eldred. "Now, if you'll believe me, I never should have thought of such a thing as long as I lived. That I shouldn't."

"I can believe you," said the Black Monk.

"You are very good," answered Eldred. "But what do you mean to do? How can you make it out, I should like to know?"

"We monks," said Morgatani, with a bitter and contemptuous smile, "possess secrets unknown to the rest of the world. Secrets which awe the vulgar, and, in many cases, astonish the learned."

"So I have heard," said Eldred. "You can raise the—ahem !—I believe.

"The devil, I suppose you mean ?" said Morgatani.

"Why, yes," stammered Eldred.

"We can," said Morgatani. "We can raise a thousand devils ——"

"A thousand devils ?"

"Yes, the devils engendered by human passion. Those are our tools, the implements by which we work."

"How very odd," said Eldred, taking everything the monk said in the bitterness of his own black heart, in a literal sense.

"Look at this small phial," said Morgatani, drawing one from his vest, and holding it up between him and the light.

"What is it ?" said Agatha.

"If this corpse," said Morgatani, indicating the body of the Lady Alicia, "be sprinkled with the contents of this small phial, the progress of decay will be stayed. The hand of time will assault it in vain. Years hence it will present the same appearance as it does now. The remnant of beauty, that, like the last faint flush of day, is still glorious and Heavenly, will be as it is now, still a lingering guest upon that face."

"Can this be possible ?" said Agatha.

"It is as I say," answered Morgatani.

"What an astonishing thing," said Eldred. "But still, do you know, I don't see exactly see how that ——"

"Listen," said Morgatani, "and you will understand all."

"I attend," said Eldred. "It's quite wonderful."

"It may be years," said the monk, "before Sir Rupert Brandon returns to claim the government of his castle."

"That's very true," said Eldred.

"During his absence," continued the monk, "we can contrive among us three to share the power and the revenues of Brandon, but when he returns there will be an account to render."

"Dear me, yes," said Eldred. "That would be very unpleasant indeed. A most disagreeable thing ; and Sir Rupert such a violent man too, as he is."

"Exactly," said Morgatani. "Now, when Sir Rupert does return, he must be met by a charge against himself of so serious a nature as to destroy him at once, ere he has time to look around him."

"And that charge," said Agatha, "must be one of murder."

"Yes," said Morgatani, "a murder so well proved, so monstrous, so horrible, that to extricate himself from the accusation will be the next thing to impossible."

"Dear me," said Eldred, "how vehement you both are."

"When Sir Rupert is executed," continued Morgatani, "who is to step into Brandon Castle as its lord but yourself?"

"That's very true," said Eldred.

"Now, you see," continued the Black Monk, "there must be sufficient evidence upon the body of the Lady Alicia to indicate a violent death, and lest Sir Rupert should be long in returning, the body must be preserved from decay, in order to preserve those evidences of murder fresh and entire."

"Ye—ye—yes," said Eldred.

"You understand me now ?" said the monk, in that awful hissing whisper in which he was such an adept.

"Yes, yes," answered Eldred ; "oh, yes, I do."

"You see the whole plan ?" said Agatha to her brother.

"Oh, dear yes ; oh, yes," he replied.

"You may always rely upon my secresy," said Morgatani.

"Eh?" said Eldred.

"And mine," said his sister.

"I promise, on my holy character," said the monk, "that I will never breathe to mortal soul that you have yourself wounded the body of the Lady Alicia Brandon."

"Nor I," said Agatha. "You can do it in safety, Eldred. We are your fast and sure friends."

Eldred looked from one to the other in perfect amazement, for he could not possibly divine what they meant.

"Why—why," he said; "what do you both mean?"

"We mean that we will not betray you," said Agatha.

"And I will advise you, as a friend," said the Black Monk, "of the best mode of proceeding, so as to produce an appearance of foul play against the life of the Lady Alicia having been perpetrated."

"Yes," said Agatha, "Father Morgatani will instruct you how to proceed in this matter with safety and success."

"I!" cried Eldred; "I proceed?"

"Yes, you," said his sister.

"Who but you?" said the Black Monk, in his hissing awful whisper, in Eldred's ear.

"I—I cannot," he stammered.

"You must," said Agatha.

"You shall!" whispered the monk.

"Bless my heart and life, what can I do?" said Eldred, wringing his hands in an extremity of terror.

"Do you see this small poniard?" said the monk, drawing one from his breast.

"Ye—yes," said Eldred.

"It belonged to Sir Rupert, and was much valued by him. He bore it always about with him. You see by its size it is more ornamental than useful."

"Yes," said Eldred.

"We will try its temper," said the monk, and stooping to the ground, he thrust the poniard up to the hilt in the soft mould, and giving it a sudden jerk, he broke the blade short off by the handle.

"Now we have a fitting weapon," he said, as he ploughed up the earth with his heel, and picked the blade of the dagger from the ground.

"W—w—what's that for?" said Eldred.

"Take this blade," said the monk, "and do as I bid you."

Eldred took the blade in his hand.

"Now," continued Morgatani, "plunge it, by the assistance of the handle, or the hilt of your sword, into the heart of the body of the Lady Alicia."

"God bless me!" cried Eldred, "I couldn't if you would make me King of England."

"Then," said the Black Monk, "one or both of us shall never leave this vault alive. Prepare for mortal strife, Eldred!"

"Coward!" cried his sister. "Will you do nothing for Brandon?"

"Oh, dear, oh, dear," groaned Eldred. "I didn't expect this. Indeed, I didn't; I don't like it all."

"Do it," cried the monk, "or dread my vengeance!"

Eldred looked around him in despair; he saw there was no escape, and with fear and trembling he approached the body.

"Strike!" cried Morgatani.

"Remove the pall," said Agatha.

"Quick!" shrieked the monk.

Eldred removed with a trembling hand the pall from the breast of the corpse.

"Strike !" again cried Morgatani, stamping violently upon the floor.

Eldred, in his terror of the living, struck the blade of the dagger home to the heart of the dead.

"Is it done ?" cried the monk.

"Oh, dear,—yes, yes, yes," said Eldred.

"Replace the pall," said Agatha, in a low voice.

"Come—come. Away !—away !" cried Morgatani, as he rushed up the steps leading to the chapel. "Ha ! ha ! ha ! 'Tis done—'tis done ! Revenge ! Revenge !"

CHAPTER IX.

Beshrew that heart that makes my heart to groan,
For that deep wound it gives my friend and me;
Is't not enough to torture me alone?—SHAKSPERE.

THE SEARCH.—A STRANGE MESSENGER.—MORE MYSTERY.—THE ARROW IN THE CASTLE GATE.—THE PLOT THICKENS.

WHEN the retainers of the Lord Rupert, headed by Hugh Wingrove, rushed to the castle gate upon hearing the second summons from what they supposed to be the horn of their master, they were determined to lose no time in discovering who it was who could so closely imitate his peculiar bugle sound, if it were not himself, or something more than mortal that had thus mysteriously come to warn them of some coming misfortune, or perchance his death.

"Lower the drawbridge, instantly !" cried Hugh Wingrove. "Let us lose not a moment in crossing the moat."

The drawbridge fell with a clanging sound, and the soldiers rushed across it, bearing flambeaus in their hands.

They were upon the opposite side of the moat in a few seconds, and then with one accord they halted, and preserved a breathless silence as they held their torches high in the air, in order to shed as extensive a light as possible over the spot.

Their surprise was extreme to behold no indications of the presence of any one, nor could they detect the least sound of footsteps either of horse or man by the most vigilant attention.

Hugh Wingrove placed his ear upon the ground in order to endeavour to detect the least sound of departing feet, but he rose with deep disappointment, all was as still as the grave.

"Comrades," he said, " I fear there is something supernatural in this, for we have been so quick in our movements, that I feel confident no one could have removed many yards from this spot since we heard the last blast from the bugle horn which we supposed to belong to Sir Rupert."

The soldiers shook their heads, and muttered their acquiescence in what fell from Hugh Wingrove.

"I trust," said one, " no ill-fortune has befallen our noble master."

"I trust so too," said Wingrove ; "and yet I much suspect that such is the case, for, my friends, it is not unknown to you that Sir Rupert has enemies."

"Aye, aye," cried a soldier ; "the monk Morgatani was not scouted from the castle by Sir Rupert for nothing."

"And I," said another, " heard him mutter threats of revenge as he crossed the drawbridge, when Sir Rupert forbade him from ever again entering the castle."

"Time will tell all things," said Wingrove; "and let us hope that Heaven has protected our worthy lord."

After again casting some anxious and searching glances round the spot, the soldiers returned to the castle, much disappointed at the result of their inquiry, and filled with many superstitious fears upon their master's account.

Nothing further happened that night to cause any disturbance to the castle guard, and it was with feelings of grateful relief that they welcomed the grey light of morning, after passing a night of so much annoyance and anxiety.

Hugh Wingrove felt it to be his duty to repeat the circumstance of the repetition of the mysterious bugle sound to Agatha and Eldred Weare, considering that Sir Rupert had left them in some kind of authority over the castle during his absence from it and his faithful followers.

It was late in the day before Hugh Wingrove could obtain an interview with Agatha, and when he was admitted to her presence he could not but observe the air of extreme languor and fatigue which appeared to pervade her frame.

"I came," said Hugh, "to state that again the castle guard were disturbed by the bugle sound which so much resembled the summons of my noble master, Sir Rupert."

"Indeed!" said Agatha, turning a trifle paler, and she looked perplexed and much annoyed at the information.

"We once more," continued Hugh Wingrove, "crossed the drawbridge, but we could see no one."

"Heard you nothing?" said Agatha.

"Nothing," answered Wingrove.

"'Tis very strange. How often did you hear the sound?"

"The horn blew three times as before, and so quick were we, that I feel positive I stood with the castle guard upon the spot from whence the strain proceeded before its echoes had died away among the battlements."

"And even then you saw no one?"

"Not a soul."

"Nor heard nothing?—No retreating footsteps?"

"Nothing. Neither horse nor man could have left the spot so suddenly, and at the same time so quietly."

Agatha appeared for a few moments lost in thought; then she said:—

"Think you it will come again?"

"Truly I think it will," said Hugh, "for it doubtless comes to warn us of something."

"Of what could it warn you?"

"Alas!" said Hugh Wingrove; "I fear me something has happened to the noble Sir Rupert."

"Ha!" cried Agatha. "Think you so?"

"I fear——" said Hugh.

"That he is dead?" said Agatha.

"The saints forbid," ejaculated Hugh. "But the circumstance of his horn being blown outside the castle so mysteriously cannot portend any good to him."

"What could have happened to him?" suggested Agatha.

"He has enemies," said Hugh.

"Enemies?"

"Yes, lady; I fear he has at least one deadly enemy."

"Whom do you mean?"

"The Black Monk!"

Agatha started, and a flush of colour came across her pale cheek as she said:—

"Why do you think that?"

"Sir Rupert turned him out of the castle with contempt and ignominy some three months since," replied Hugh.

"Know you the cause?" said Agatha.

"No," replied Wingrove, "but I'm sure it was no trifle, for I never saw Sir Rupert so angry in my life, and he said, had it not been for his shaven crown he would have hunted him through the forest with his hounds."

"He dared not!" cried Agatha.

"If he had said he would, he would most certainly," said Hugh.

"Enough," said Agatha.

"I have only this much to say," grumbled Hugh Wingrove, as he left the room, "if Morgatani, or the Black Monk as he is called, has really used any foul play towards Sir Rupert, and I find it out, his shaven crown shall not stand in my way."

The midnight hour was now waited by every one within the castle with the most eager impatience, for the greatest anxiety prevailed to know whether the mysterious horn would sound from the furthest side of the moat.

Hugh Wingrove was particularly vigilant and kept himself ready to sally out upon the first blast.

The hours slowly winged their way, and now it wanted not many minutes to twelve. Expectation was at its height, and every ear was strained to catch the first sound of the clock, and the eyes of the sentinels upon the walls, were all fixed upon the further side of the moat, in order to detect any appearance which might present itself.

The hour at length struck, and it was counted with breathless eagerness by every one.

A dead silence ensued for several minutes, and had there been the slightest
No. 5

unusual sound either within or without the castle, it must have been heard by the anxious listeners.

No trumpet call, however, broke the stillness which reigned around, and the retainers of Sir Rupert began to look at each other with feelings of relief, that they were not again visited by the mysterious horn.

The silence was broken by Hugh Wingrove, who said,—

"All is still. There is no sound of a horn to-night, and the midnight hour being past there is now no likelihood of ——"

He was here interrupted by a loud shout of surprise from the sentinel at the castle-gate.

Without a moment's hesitation he rushed forward, and eagerly inquired what had happened.

"By my faith, good Master Hugh Wingrove," said the soldier, "I know not, but as I stood with my ear laid close to the gate to listen if any sound came upon the night air, there came such a blow exactly upon the other side of the gate that my head rings again."

"Indeed?" said Hugh Wingrove. "What can this mean?"

"I don't know what it may mean to other people," said the soldier, shaking his head, "but by the mass it didn't mean well to me."

"What did it sound like?" said a second one.

"Why, I should say, it sounded like something determined to come through the gate without having it opened," said the sentinel. "It seemed to me as if something was coming through the solid wood work, and I can tell you I snatched away my head as soon as I possibly could."

"Why, see here, Master Wingrove," said one. "Here is some blood on Bernard's ear."

"Eh?" said the sentinel, whose name was Bernard, putting his hand to his ear, and bringing it down again stained with blood. "By our lady it's true. There is blood on my ear."

"And here," said Hugh Wingrove, "is a small splinter knocked out by something from the back of the door."

"Then there's something sticking in the front of it," said Bernard, "and that was what gave my ear such a tingle."

"We will soon see that," said Hugh Wingrove. "Open the gates."

The great gates were immediately opened, and there sticking nearly up to the feathers, in the solid oak, was a singularly rude looking arrow or dart.

"Aye, there it is sure enough," said Bernard.

Hugh Wingrove made a desperate effort to draw the rude weapon from the gate, but it resisted all his efforts, and finally he broke it off short, leaving the point still sticking in the solid oak.

"This must have been sent with tremendous force," said Hugh, "it would have pierced a suit of mail."

"There is something wound round it," said Bernard.

"In sooth there is," exclaimed Hugh, as he unwound from the shaft a piece of paper on which were some written words.

"What is here?" said Hugh Wingrove. "Hold a torch nigh that I may see what is here written."

A soldier advanced with a light, and Hugh Wingrove read the following words, which were written in a large bold hand upon the scrap of paper:—

"To the friends of Sir Rupert Brandon.

"As often as the silver horn of the Lord of Brandon sounds by his castle gate, be assured he lives. If yesternight twelvemonths passes over and the horn sounds not, he is dead, and his son shall be proclaimed Lord of Brandon and Weare."

Hugh Wingrove looked astonished at the document.

"What can this mean?" he said. "Comrades, there is some mystery here. We can understand that possibly some good saint may blow Sir Rupert's horn to assure us that he lives, but this about proclaiming his son when we all know he has no son, is beyond my comprehension entirely."

The soldiers looked at each other very much puzzled, for it was quite well known that the Lord of Brandon had left his castle and his faithful followers principally on account of his deep disappointment at having no heir to his name, his honour and his large and beautiful estates.

"There may come a time," said Hugh Wingrove, "when we may better understand the meaning of all this."

"And till that time does come," said Bernard, "you may take your oaths, I shall not be in a hurry to place my ear against the gates of Brandon again. I like a race and a fight as well as any man, but I don't like such queer dealings as an arrow coming into a fellow's ear in cool blood."

"I must report this stange circumstance to the Lady Agatha," said Hugh Wingrove, "and see what she can make of it."

CHAPTER X.

Hor. What? has this thing appeared again to-night?
Ber. I have seen nothing.
Mar. Horatio says it is but fantasy.—HAMLET.

THE SOUTHERN GALLERY OF BRANDON CASTLE.—A STRANGE DISCOVERY.
—THE GREY TURRET.—THE HIDDEN CHAMBER AND THE MYSTERIOUS
LIGHT.

As early in the morning as he thought there was any chance of being admitted to an audience, Hugh Wingrove sent a message to Agatha Weare, that he wished to report to her the proceedings of the night.

He was directed immediately to attend her in an ancient oaken parlour, which had been a favourite apartment of the deceased Lady Alicia, who had been as much beloved by every one in the castle as Agatha Weare was disliked.

As Hugh Wingrove was proceeding in the direction of the apartment to which he had been summoned, not in the best humour at being kept so long from his morning's repose, he was met by the sentinel Bernard.

"Good Master Wingrove," said Bernard, "can you spare me a few moments of your time?"

"What for?" said Wingrove. "Have you had another arrow in your ear?"

"No," said Bernard, "it's my eyes are affected this time."

"Well, what is it?"

"Why, you must know, Master Wingrove, that since Sir Rupert left the castle things hav'n't been as they used to be."

"I know that well enough," growled Hugh.

"There has been nothing," continued Bernard, "but alarms and odd noises and all sorts of disagreeables."

"Well, well, man," cried Hugh, "to the point at once. What have you got to say, for I am half dead with sleep. You know I have kept watch two nights together in consequence of that horn sounding, that we can none of us make anything of."

"I know it," said Bernard. "I've been sound asleep myself for these six hours or more."

❦ " And now I suppose you want to keep me awake till you are sleepy again," said Hugh.

"No, no," whispered Bernard, coming close to Wingrove's ear. "You know when I was relieved from my post by the gate?"

"Yes, surely. You were gate sentinel till two o'clock in the morning."

"Very well," said Bernard, "then you must know when I was relieved I went straight to my quarters, for that deuced singing was still in my head you must know."

"Well, well, what then?"

"And to get to my quarters, you know, I had to pass through the great southern gallery."

"Yes, I know," said Hugh Wingrove, impatiently.

"Well, then," continued Bernard, "in the southern gallery is a window, that looks into the inner court."

"Yes, I know it. What then?"

"Why, I don't know how it was, but something induced me to go to the window, and take a glance into the court."

"You saw nothing?"

"Not in the court; but you know one can get a side glance of the Grey Turret from that window."

"True, but not at night, Bernard," said Hugh.

"No," replied Bernard, "unless there was a light."

"A light?"

"Yes, a light!"

"A light where? Not—in—in the Grey Turret?"

"Even so, Master Wingrove. As sure as my name is Simon Bernard, there was a light streaming from a loop-hole in the Grey Turret."

"Are you quite sure, Bernard?"

"Quite! I'd stake my life on it."

"You are sure that singing in your ears hadn't confused your faculties? Eh! Bernard?"

"Pho! pho!" cried Bernard, "one don't *hear* a light, good Master Hugh."

"That's true," said Wingrove.

"I tell you then, I saw it," persisted Bernard.

"In the Grey Turret?" pondered Wingrove.

"Aye, in the Grey Turret," repeated the soldier.

"Why it has not been opened for many, many years."

"So I have heard, and that was what made me stare at it so."

"No one," continued Wingrove, "not even the oldest retainer of Sir Rupert's, ever saw the inside of that turret."

"Well, there was somebody there last night," persisted Bernard. "I saw the light stream from the loop-hole and fall in a pale streak across the court-yard."

"You are sure it was no delusion?"

"Delusion!" cried Bernard. "Do I look like a man to be deluded?"

"Why you are big enough," said Hugh Wingrove, with a smile, as he glanced at the ample proportions of the man-at-arms.

"I hope so," said Bernard.

"Well, my friend," said Wingrove, after some moments consideration; "will you do me the favour to keep this matter secret between ourselves?"

"Certainly," said Bernard.

"I am going now to make the guard report to the Lady Agatha Weare, who I believe stands equally high in both our affections. Eh, my good Bernard?"

Bernard grimly smiled.

"I shall say nothing of it to her," resumed Wingrove.

Bernard nodded approbation.

" I believe firmly," continued Hugh, " that something is going on against our worthy master, and between you and I, Bernard, if there is any mischief brewing, Agatha Weare is at the bottom of it."

" How very singular !" exclaimed Bernard. " Those are my very ideas, Master Hugh."

" Caution then must be our watchword, Bernard."

" What, for to-night, do you mean ?" said the soldier, taking Wingrove's words in their literal sense.

" No, no," said Wingrove, " I mean we must be cautious."

" Oh, yes. Exactly. I understand you."

" Be secret then about this light in the Grey Turret."

" I will."

" Meet me an hour hence in the private guard-room, and we will concert measures how to arrive at the truth ; that is, whether any one is in the Grey Turret or not."

" Agreed," said Bernard, " you may depend upon me, Master Hugh Wingrove, I will be cautious."

" Do. Farewell for an hour."

Wingrove hastened to the oaken parlour to lay his report before Agatha Weare.

Bernard stood for several moments profoundly still after he was left by Hugh Wingrove. Then he tapped his nose a number of times in intimation of the extreme difficulty anybody would experience in wringing a secret of any kind whatever from him.

" Caution," he whispered. " Caution is the word."

Then, as if he had been walking upon eggs, or that the sound of his feet would betray his secret, he left the place upon tip-toes, and with so singular and cautious a manner, that had he met any one, they must have come to the conclusion that he was, or had been engaged in some very wrong and nefarious piece of business.

Hugh Wingrove found Agatha Weare sitting with her brother Eldred, who wore his usually alarmed and nervous look.

" It came not again ?" said Agatha, quickly, as Wingrove entered the old time-worn but still costly apartment.

" You mean the horn ?" said Wingrove.

" Yes," she replied.

" No ; it came not again."

" There was no alarm then during the night ?"

" No particular alarm," replied Wingrove. " This scroll was left at the castle gate about midnight."

" What ?" cried Agatha, starting from her seat as Hugh Wingrove placed the written paper before her.

" You—you don't mean that ?" stammered Eldred, turning very pale as he ran his eye over the words.

" Why did you not detain the messenger ?" cried Agatha.

" The messenger showed no inclination to leave the gate," replied Hugh.

" Then you have him ?"

" Yes," answered Wingrove, placing the broken arrow upon the table.

" This ?" said Agatha. " Came it on this ?"

" Yes, lady. And there is a good eight inches of it now sticking in the guard-gate, where it is likely to continue to stick."

" At midnight ?" said Agatha.

" Yes," replied Hugh.

" Dear me," suggested Eldred, " if any one had been in—in—the way just then—oh, dear me !"

"Peace—peace," said Agatha, contemptuously. "I would I knew who had sped this shaft on its message."

"A strong arm you may depend, lady," said Wingrove.

"I will consider," said Agatha, "what can be done in this matter. At present I cannot fathom it. At all events we are of course pleased to hear that no harm has happened to Sir Rupert."

"Y—ye—yes," said Eldred, "we—we are delighted—I—I don't think I can stay here long, there's so many odd things happening. What do you think, sister?"

"Coward," muttered Agatha. Then turning to Hugh—"Should anything of an uncommon character occur to-night, I beg you will let me know instantly."

"It is not my watch to-night," said Hugh Wingrove, "but I will not fail to communicate your orders."

"I shall go to-morrow," muttered Eldred to himself.

Hugh Wingrove now left the room, and Agatha turned to Eldred with an expression of scorn upon her features.

"Dastard!" she cried. "Disgrace to your name. Why will you let the vassals in this castle see your craven heart?"

"I—I really," said Eldred. "Now, sister, don't get in one of your horrid passions, you know."

"If it were not for my persuasions," continued Agatha, "Morgatani would desert your cause, and you would never be Lord of Brandon."

"Ye—yes," said Eldred; "I—I thought it was more on your account, ster, that the Black Monk —"

"Hush!" cried Agatha, colouring to the very temples. "Wretch! what mean you?"

"There you go now," said Eldred, "in one of your passions."

"Fool that I am," muttered Agatha, "to allow myself to be discomposed by what this craven-hearted idiot utters. He can mean nothing. He can surely know nothing!"

"Well now, I'll take a walk on the battlements," said Eldred, "to give me an appetite for my lunch."

"Away, away," said Agatha, "and remember you are surrounded by spies."

"Yes—yes, I know," said Eldred. "They won't get anything out of me, I can tell them."

"Thanks to the prudent foresight of Morgatani," muttered Agatha, as Eldred left the room, "he is unacquainted with the principal secret—a secret which I would not breathe in the lowest whisper to my own heart."

She sat musing for a few moments, then suddenly starting up, she exclaimed,—

"That mysterious and inexplicable paper! Whence can it come, and what can it portend? It mentions a son of Sir Rupert's too. No, no, that at least is false. The grave stops a succession well. I will seek Morgatani. His judgment shall decide."

CHAPTER XI.

Angels and Ministers of Grace defend us!
Be thou a spirit of health or goblin damned.—HAMLET.

OLD ALE AND ITS TEMPTATIONS AND CONSEQUENCES. — A SOLDIER OF THE MIDDLE AGES.—THE CASTLE CHAPEL.—THE PLEASURES OF BEING ON THE SICK LIST.

THE time at which Hugh Wingrove had promised to meet Berrard, the rough soldier, had nearly expired when he left the presence of the imperious

Agatha Weare and her trembling brother, and he at once repaired to the private guard-room, where he found Bernard solacing himself with a flagon of humming ale, which he procured from the cellarer on the strength of Hugh Wingrove's name.

" Well, Bernard," said Wingrove, " I believe I am before my time."

" Drink," was the soldier's response, as he pushed the ale flagon towards Wingrove, who was by no means averse to the process, and took a deep draught accordingly.

" Good!" said Bernard.

" Very good," responded Hugh.

" Here's my service to you, then," said Bernard, emptying the flagon a one pull. " Now for business."

" Why it's only this," said Wingrove, " you must not be well."

" Eh! What?" cried Bernard.

" You must be off duty to-night," continued Wingrove, " on the score of indisposition."

" The devil!" said Bernard.

" As you please," said Hugh; " but ill you must be."

" But I—I am as hearty as a flag-staff. I—really —" remonstrated the soldier.

" Pho, pho, man," said Wingrove; " I want you to-night on secret service. Do you understand now?"

" Oh, oh," said Bernard, " I begin to see."

" Do you?" laughed Wingrove.

"Yes, yes; it's to be a sham."

" You have made a wonderful guess," said Hugh. " I hereby excuse you from duty till further order, on the ground of illness; and now attend to me, Bernard."

" All attention, good Master Wingrove."

" You will meet me at eleven in the southern gallery."

" The southern gallery?" cried Bernard.

" Yes."

" At eleven?"

" Even so."

" But ain't you—that is, don't you think—I mean —"

"You mean something very much to the purpose, I dare say," said Hugh; " but, I am sleepy, and can't stay to hear it. Remember, eleven in the southern gallery."

So saying, Wingrove left the bewildered Bernard to his own meditations, which consisted of looking into the flagon, and upon perceiving it to be quite empty, making a resolution to try again the credulity of the old cellarer of the castle.

He who had charge of the liquors of the castle, was an old man who had been many years in the service of Sir Rupert, and his orders were to deliver no ale to the guard without the order of Hugh Wingrove, who was their head and chief.

Bernard stopped, *en route* to the cellarer, and debated with himself on the most likely means of overcoming his scruples, which he at length concluded would be done best by hurrying the old man, and putting him out of his way.

He accordingly made a rush into a sort of little pantry, in which sat the old steward, and pushing the earthen flagon in his face so as nearly to upset him, he roared :—

" A flagon of the best for Master Wingrove! He swears he has swallowed a mouthful of sand, and he is now in the little guard-room stamping like a mad bull!"

"Is he ?" said Hugh Wingrove himself, stepping from behind the chair of the old steward.

"The devil!" said Bernard.

"Ha! ha! Master Bernard," said Hugh; "you see I am an older soldier than you are."

"Well, I suppose it's no go," said Bernard, looking ruefully into the empty flagon.

"Now, you really don't deserve it," said Wingrove, "for your attempted imposition; but I was just telling Mathew to let you have one flagon more, seeing that I myself drank some of the first."

"That'll do," cried Bernard. "Never mind the reasons. The ale, good Mathew. The ale! the ale!"

Bernard soon had his flagon filled, and was about to leave the place with it, when Wingrove said to him in a whisper :—

"Be cautious, comrade. Sick people, you know, are not seen drinking ale by the quart."

"Oh, I know," said Bernard. "Trust me."

"Well, I only warn you," said Wingrove; "for, although I could of course excuse you from duty on no excuse but my own will, you know I will not excite jealousy by doing such a thing. Remember, you are very ill, Bernard."

"I know," said Bernard; "I am very bad. Trust me, Master Wingrove. Caution and ale for ever !"

So saying, Bernard departed triumphantly with his flagon.

Now Bernard was by no means unmindful of Wingrove's injunctions, and after solacing himself by a draught of the ale, by way of quickening his perceptions, he set about seriously thinking where he had better betake himself to for the secure drinking of the remainder thereof, without any kind of interruption, or danger of being overheard, even should he feel inclined to indulge in a merry stave, as was his custom over the flagon.

After some thought, Bernard gave his thigh a great thump, exclaiming :—

"I have it! The very thing. I'll creep into the chapel by one of the painted windows, and drink it there. The doors are locked, and it's out of sight, and out of hearing. Yes, it's the very place. I'll go there and be jolly for an hour or two, at least."

With this determination Bernard started off for the chapel, which was situated close to a wing of the castle, which by reasons of its extreme age was not inhabited.

The chapel doors were always kept locked, and they had not now been opened since the interment of the Lady Alicia, for, as the reader is aware, Morgatani and his associates found an entrance to the sacred edifice by a secret passage.

Bernard carefully examined the several windows, until he found one that was not fastened; he immediately opened it, and drew his bulky form through the aperture.

"This will do," he exclaimed; "it's nice and cool, and there's nobody to say nay, when one lifts the flagon too often; not but what I like a comrade to share in a cup of ale, but just now the circumstances are very peculiar indeed. I'm ill—very ill, and excused from duty, and it don't look well to see a sick soldier swilling away at strong ale. Oh, dear, no—not at all."

Uttering these sage and apposite sentiments, Bernard walked through the chapel, looking about him to endeavour to select the most comfortable spot in which to ensconce himself.

He at length fixed upon a seat near to a confessional, and placing his flagon by his side and his back against the wall, he made up his mind not to stir while there was one drop of ale left.

"And very likely," he said aloud, when he had come to that determination. "And very likely I sha'n't stir then, for I generally go to sleep after my second flagon, and this is the second, barring the hearty draught of Master Hugh Wingrove, at the first."

"It's cooler than I thought, here," said Bernard again, after a pause. "Ale warms us wonderfully, though, so here goes. Here's towards your very good health, Master Bernard, and may you enjoy a great many ——"

"Ha! ha!" cried a voice at this moment. "Hunted—hunted to the death. Through forest and stream—glade and brook—ha! ha! ha!"

Bernard paused aghast at this interruption, and he did what he was never known to do in his life, held within an inch of his lips the ale flagon for full three minutes without drinking.

"What the deuce was that?" he exclaimed. "What an uncommonly uncomfortable laugh."

Bernard then looked carefully around him, but he could see no one from whom the singular words and mocking laugh could have proceeded.

"Well," he said, "I'll be hanged if I'm quite clear where that voice came from; it sounded just at hand."

"A hand! a hand!" cried the same voice. "A red—a blood-red hand!"

"The devil!" cried Bernard, starting to his feet.

"Ha! ha! ha!" cried the voice, and directed by the sound, Bernard looked at the window at which he had himself entered the chapel, and saw a head rapidly drawn away.

"Oh!" he cried. "You are there, are you? Now, I'll be bound this is some trick to frighten me of some of the guard, who are jealous because I am not well and off duty."

Bernard having thus satisfied himself resolved that he would not be interrupted in his enjoyment, and he went back to his seat with a determined

No. 6

air, and took a deep draught from the flagon, after which he cast a look of defiance at the window, and nodded several times, adding in a tone of independence,—

"Here's towards your patience, whoever you are, for if you wait till I move again, you'll be tired I think."

Again Bernard lifted the flagon to his mouth, but in the midst of his draught and while the humming beverage was trickling down his throat in a copious stream, he happened to cast his eyes towards the window, and there was evidently a head peering in from it; but whose head it was, or even what sort of a head it was, Bernard could not by any means tell, for before he could take the flagon from his mouth it was gone again.

"Now, confound you," he cried, "whatever you be, for you nearly choked me in the middle of my drink."

Bernard then set about reflecting what he had best do, for he entertained no doubt but it was one of his comrades who was trying to play upon his fears.

"Let me consider," he said. "Who can it be? Ah, it's that good for nothing knave, Saunders, I'll be sworn. He is always up to some tricks or another. I'll be even with him. The best way to provoke him is to take no notice whatever. I'll pretend not to see nor hear."

Notwithstanding this determination Bernard still kept an eye upon the window, for sometimes a sudden doubt would spring up in his mind as to the truth of his surmise.

"By the mass," he said; "if it should not be Saunders! And yet it must be. Who else could it be, I should like to know?"

After propounding to himself this question, Bernard took another deep draught to clear his faculties, and there again as he glanced down the sides of the flagon was the window darkened by a head as before.

"Curse you!" cried Bernard. "You are there again, are you?"

"Ha! ha! ha!" cried a voice as the head disappeared. "Not yet, not yet. Blood! red blood! red blood!"

"The deuce," exclaimed Bernard. "What a disagreeable voice. Hang you, Saunders, but I'll serve you out for this. Let me think."

CHAPTER XII.

The chapel was old, the chapel was grey,
The small latticed windows scarce let in the day,
And the tombs of the dead e'en were rotting away.
                                        COLERIDGE.

SOLITARY SOCIALITY.—THE SOLDIER'S DEVICE.—ALE IS A COMRADE.—
THE SURPRISE.—AN UNWELCOME VISIT.

"IT's a very hard case, indeed," resumed Bernard, "that a man can't enjoy himself for a few hours without some fool grinning at him through a window. It's too far off, or else the next time I saw his ugly face at the window I'd throw the—no—not the flagon, there's some ale in it —but I'd throw something at him, at the chance of hitting him, I will too. I'll put him off his guard by singing a song, and then creep under the window, and fetch him such a dab in the mouth as will mark him, I'll warrant."

With this cunning resolve Bernard leaned back in his seat with an air of pretended indifference, and chaunted the following stave, which was popular at the period, among the lawless military :—

ALE IS A COMRADE! ALE IS A FRIEND!

"Ale is a comrade! ale is a friend!
Who would not tipple old ale?

"Ah! who, I should like to know, would refuse a flagon, because—

"Ale is a comrade! ale is a friend!
Such pleasure can never grow stale.
It makes a man smiling,
Fond woman beguiling,
Who would not tipple old ale?

"You've an old soldier to deal with, I can tell you. We'll see whether your head or the flagon is the toughest.

"Ale is a comrade! ale is a friend!
Without it the heart gets but pale.
It makes a man jolly!
It kicks melancholy!
Who would not tipple old ale?

"Just let me see your ugly head again, will you?"

The soldier still kept an eye upon the window, but nothing appeared at it, and with a knowing wink he emptied the flagon, and crept with it in his hand towards the window, still chaunting in a lower key to disguise his approach :

"Ale is a comrade! ale is a friend!"

Cautiously stooping so as to keep his bulky form out of sight, and chuckling at his own extreme cleverness, Bernard advanced until he was exactly under the window, where he resolved to wait patiently till the head should again appear, when he would at once, from his favourable position, dash the flagon at it without fail of hitting it.

For about five minutes he waited with exemplary patience, but then he began to find his position irksome, and in five minutes more he felt very much provoked that the head did not appear to receive the flagon against it.

"Hang him," whispered Bernard, to himself: "I hope he hasn't gone. How very provoking, to be sure. After all the trouble I have taken, too. It's really too bad."

Another five minutes of expectation fairly exhausted the small stock of patience with which Bernard was blessed, and with an oath upon his lips, he suddenly popped up from under the window to look out.

For a moment Bernard stood transfixed with surprise and fright to the spot, with his face within an inch of the window, from whence he had not power to move it.

At the same moment that he had risen from his concealment to look out at the window a face rose from the outside apparently to look in, and such a face Bernard had never in his life beheld.

It was wild looking and ferocious. The eyes glared like those of some wild beast, and the matted hair hung in disordered black masses about the countenance.

"The devil!" cried Bernard, when he recovered the power of speech and motion, and he rushed from the window at the same moment that the mysterious head from the outside disappeared with a wild and unearthly cry.

Bernard ran to the door of the chapel to endeavour to escape, forgetting that it was locked, and that if he wished to leave the place he must do so by the same means that he had entered—namely, by the window which he now dreaded to approach.

Bernard was as brave a soldier as need be against mortal foes, but he lived in an age of superstition, and he was at once persuaded in his own mind that what he had seen was not mortal, but some hideous being of another world.

The thought then occurred to him that he was so persecuted for desecrating the chapel of the castle, by making it the scene of his carousals and profane singing; and Bernard, like most people in our own day, even felt his religious feelings go hand in hand with his fears.

"How shall I get out?" he exclaimed. "At the window is the—the devil, and the door is locked. Oh, Bernard, Bernard—you have brought all this upon yourself by your own wilfulness. By all the saints, to whom I promise a wax candle each, I never will again drink ale in a chapel."

Bernard stood bewildered as he uttered these plaints. What to do he could not imagine. The window he dreaded even to look at, and well he knew the door was too strong to be forced.

"Dear me," he suddenly exclaimed; "where's my wits? There are other windows besides the one, where the dev——a hem! is keeping watch and ward. They are all fastened inside, to be sure; but then I'm inside, too, and can unfasten one, and scramble out, and so give the old gentleman with the long tail the go by."

Bernard was quite delighted with this thought, and was proceeding across the chapel to open a window quite away from the one where he doubted not waited the object of his alarm, when he heard a footstep in his immediate vicinity.

He paused, and a cold perspiration came over him as he glanced fearfully round and saw no one.

Still he heard the step of some one apparently approaching, and his first fears partially subsiding, he thought the step was not actually in the chapel, but seemed to come from one of its massive walls.

"Here's a mess to be in," muttered the soldier. "I can't get out any way, and some devil or saint is surely coming to kick up a row with me. I'll hide if I can't do anything better."

Bernard accordingly ran behind the altar, and dropping upon his knees, he began to mutter such reminiscences of prayers as had stuck by him since his childhood.

The mysterious footsteps grew louder and more distinct, and by some means the person from whom they proceeded, had evidently without difficulty entered the chapel.

"Six wax candles to Saint Barnabus," muttered Bernard.

The footsteps immediately ceased, and the soldier made sure that his offer to the saint had been the cause.

"Who spoke?" said a deep hollow voice.

"That's the old 'un," thought Bernard, "for a certainty."

"Methought there was a voice," said the same tone.

"You thought right," muttered Bernard.

A dead silence of several minutes duration now ensued, and then it was broken by the same deep hollow voice, saying :—

"'Twas busy fancy which ever peoples solitudes. There can be no one here, and yet I should approach more cautiously. Long impunity from danger makes us over bold."

The footsteps now again sounded in the ears of Bernard, but they were evidently retreating from the altar.

"He's going," thought Bernard. "Those six wax candles settled the business. I should like to have a peep at him."

Just as the soldier was about to raise his head, in order to catch a glance at the form of him who was evidently in the chapel, he was startled by a loud crash, as of broken glass, and something rushed through the air with a hissing sound.

"Ha!" cried a loud voice, and in another moment Bernard heard the loud shutting of a door.

"Lost—lost!" shrieked a voice from the window at which the soldier had seen the strange, unearthly face.

All was then still—still as the grave.

Bernard was thoroughly bewildered at the rapid succession of noises, and he sat down behind the altar in a perfect agony of apprehension, for he believed himself completely surrounded by the agents of another world.

For a full half hour did Bernard sit in mental tribulation behind the altar in the chapel, and then at last, upon finding that all continued still, he began to think that his trials for that time were over.

"Perhaps if I move, though," he thought, "they will all begin again."

This thought kept him quiet for some time longer, and then he ventured, after much hesitation, upon an experiment, to ascertain if any noise upon his part would provoke a renewal of supernatural hostilities; so he cried, in a low, trembling voice,—

"Hem!"

There was no reply of any kind, and he felt much emboldened, so much so, indeed, that his next effort consisted of,—

"A-hem! Who's there—eh? Hem!"

All this produced nothing, and Bernard now gathered himself up, and carefully looked around him. He saw nothing but the ancient walls, and gloomy aisles of the chapel.

"They are gone," he said, "and the sooner I go the better."

He strode towards one of the windows, and undoing the fastenings in an instant, he was about to spring out, when he observed something projecting from the wall close to his head.

"What's this?" he exclaimed, as he tried to possess himself of it; but it was too far imbedded in the wall.

"It's an arrow, as I live," he cried, "and the brother shaft to the one that was sent so deep into the castle gate. That was what I heard hissing through the air, then. By Heavens, there's something very strange in all this: I'll e'en break off the shaft, and show it to master Hugh Wingrove. If the devil shot this, he has a good bòw, and a strong arm, I can tell, for it's up to the feathers nearly."

As he spoke, he broke off the end of the shaft, and with great precipitancy, and a feeling of relief, sprung through the window, and got clear of the chapel and its mysteries.

CHAPTER XIII.

"Revenge! 'tis a wild passion,
And o'ermasters reason. Nourish it not,—
'Tis a barbed arrow in the heart."

AGATHA WEARE.—HER WILD PASSIONS.—THE SECRET OF HER ENMITY TO THE KNIGHT.—REVENGE.—THE COMMUNICATION.

AGATHA was sitting alone in the oaken parlour we have previously mentioned, when a low knocking sounded upon the wainscoted-wall at a part where there was no appearance whatever of a door.

She immediately rose, and locked carefully the ordinary entrance to the apartment, and then approaching the part of the old wainscoting from whence the knocking proceeded, she, by means of some secret spring, opened a panel, and Morgatani, the Black Monk, entered the apartment, with a gloomy brow.

"Welcome," cried Agatha, "most welcome, Morgatani. I have long waited for you."

"There is one within the castle," said the monk, "who would fain have made you wait for ever."

"What mean you?" cried Agatha, in a tone of surprise.

"On my progress hither," replied Morgatani, bitterly, "an attempt has been made against my life."

"Your life, Morgatani?"

"Aye, Agatha, my life."

"Is it possible?"

"'Tis more than possible: tis true. The shaft was well aimed, but the hand that sped it knew not that I bear a charmed life. There lives not the hand that can lay me low."

"Tell me how this happened," said Agatha. "Surely no one suspects your presence here?"

"Of that," answered the monk, "I cannot be certain; but as I was passing through the chapel, on my secret route hither, I thought I heard some one within its walls; and, before I could well resolve upon what to do, there came an arrow, sent by no stripling hand, within a hair's breadth of my heart."

"An arrow?" said Agatha.

"More strange than welcome," answered Morgatani.

"Do you suspect any one?"

"I suspect all. There is not a knave in the castle who would not have done the deed, to boast of it to Sir Rupert."

"Believe me," said Agatha, "your danger touches me nearly."

"I do believe it," said the monk, in a lowered tone. "Feelings and passions in common have bound us together. From hating the same people, we have come to love each other."

"Hush!" said Agatha, "speak not thus; the very air is dangerous in this castle to us."

"It is," cried Mortagani; "but there may come a time when it may prove a more dangerous atmosphere to others who now sleep in fancied security."

"There are other matters for our consideration," said Agatha.

"Say on," said the Black Monk; "I attend."

"Listen, then," said Agatha, and she then related to him the circumstance of the arrow being found imbedded in the castle gate, and laid before him the written scroll which it had evidently been its object to convey.

The dark complexion of the monk assumed a sallower hue as he heard the relation, and read the paper, and for several minutes he seemed absorbed in deep thought.

"There is more in all this," he at length said, "than I can at present discover."

"You think there is danger?" said Agatha.

"I do," replied the monk.

"From whom?"

"That I must make it my business to discover as quickly as may be," said Morgatani.

"Can you, do you think?" said Agatha.

"I am a Jesuit," answered Morgatani.

"I know you have wonderful power," said Agatha.

"I have," answered the monk. "Trust all to me; all shall be as we wish. What I have undertaken that will I perform."

"And that is —"

"The destruction of Sir Rupert Brandon."

"Then I shall be avenged," said Agatha.

"You shall," answered Morgatani; "he has injured you in that way that no woman ever forgives."

"He has," said Agatha, trembling with passion; "he scorned my love, I—I offered him my affection, and he turned from me with courtly phrases and preferred her who now lies in the tomb."

"I know it all," said the monk; "he shall fall. Alicia, even the dead Alicia shall destroy him."

"Enough," said Agatha. "Aid me, Morgatani, and soul and body I am yours."

"For the present, farewell!" said the Black Monk; "I too pant for revenge against Sir Rupert. I go to fathom this mystery of the arrow. I will see you anon."

"Farewell, Morgatani," said Agatha; "be speedy for revenge."

"Revenge!" cried the Black Monk, as he darted through the secret panel, and disappeared in the black gloom of a narrow passage which led from it.

"Yes," said Agatha, clasping her hands. "If any one can give me revenge it is Morgatani: his power seems more than human. Tremble, Sir Rupert Brandon! Tremble! for your destruction is sworn, and Heaven or hell shall not save thee."

Bernard was very much disappointed to find that Hugh Wingrove had retired to snatch some repose before the evening, leaving strict and particular injunctions that he should not be disturbed unless something of moment requiring his presence should occur.

Under these circumstances Bernard was reluctantly compelled to bottle up his story for some hours, and as his plea of indisposition did not permit him to mingle with his comrades in the guard-room, he was altogether about as unhappy as a man-at-arms could possibly be.

Time, however, proceeds onward, alike to those who are sighing to retard his march, and those who with fretful impatience chide him for delay, and to the great joy of Bernard, ten o'clock at last boomed from the old castle clock.

He started at the sound, and thought he might as well go at once to the southern gallery and there wait for Hugh Wingrove, as remain where he was; but then again the thought came across him of how very liable he should be to all sorts of supernatural visitations, all alone in that dismal gallery for a whole hour, and he determined to wait some time longer before venturing upon his disagreeable duty of keeping an uncomfortable appointment.

Half an hour more at length passed away, and Bernard felt that it was then time for him to think of going.

Girding on his sword, and placing on his head the steel head piece which was then universally worn by the common soldiery, he sallied from his dormitory, where he had been sitting so long with no companion but his own reflections, towards the great gallery of the castle, which was called the southern gallery.

This gallery or long corridor was of great extent, spreading almost the entire length of the southern side of the castle, and into it looked many windows, and opened many doors, while it was a common landing, for several flights of stone stairs, that by many turnings and windings led to different parts of the extensive and time-worn edifice.

The moon had risen by the time Bernard reached the place of his appointment, and bright streaks of light from various windows were reposing in wild beauty upon the oaken floor.

"I'll never be ill again and off duty, if I know it," muttered Bernard, as he reached the gallery. "Here I've been unhappy and wretched all day, all through shamming ill at Master Hugh Wingrove's request, so that he might come and see a light in the Grey Turret! If I see a light anywhere else I'll keep it to myself, and then I shall have no trouble about it."

As Bernard uttered these complaints he reached the gallery, and being rather stout than otherwise, he paused a moment to recover his full modicum of breath, after ascending the stone staircase which led from the basement story.

"Moonlight," he muttered, "some folks like the moonlight, but I don't, it always makes such ugly shadows and throws such queer lights upon things, that it makes me jump sometimes, and fancy I see what I don't see at all."

Eleven now sounded from the clock tower, and the echoes reverberated throughout the long gallery in which Bernard was stationed, in prolonged and mournful sighs.

"That's unpleasant, too," said the soldier. "It's pleasant too in one way, because Hugh Wingrove will soon be here. In fact, he ought to be here now, and it's very wrong to keep a fellow waiting in a disagreeable cold —— Hilloa! what's that?"

Bernard gave a great spring forward, as he felt a heavy hand laid upon his shoulder.

"Why, who should it be?" said the familiar voice of Hugh Wingrove.

"Oh, it's you, is it," said Bernard. "Why—why didn't you speak first, eh, Master Wingrove?"

"A soldier should never be surprised," said Wingrove.

"I wasn't on duty," muttered Bernard.

"Well, well," said Wingrove, "is the mysterious light again visible in the Grey Turret?"

"I don't know," answered Bernard, "I've never moved from here since I came."

"Which was the window you saw it from?" asked Hugh Wingrove, in a low voice.

"The second from yon pillar," said Bernard, "there, where the streak of moonlight falls so bright and clear."

"Let us go there then," said Wingrove.

They both proceeded to the window indicated by Bernard as that which commanded a view of the Grey Turret.

The moon shone from behind the ancient tower, which went by the name of the Grey Turret, and it rose clear and black in the sky, its very outline being minutely defined.

"All is dark," said Wingrove.

"True enough," answered Bernard, "but I'll take my oath there was a light last night, although the devil may not think proper to show one to us now that we are on the watch."

"Ah! Bernard," said Wingrove, shaking his head, "your lively imagination must have deceived you. How could there be a light in the Grey Turret, Bernard?"

"Why, in consequence of a candle, I suppose;" said Bernard. "That's easily answered, I'm sure."

"Well, but I mean how could the light, or the candle get there"? said Hugh Wingrove, "you know it has been shut up for many years."

"That's all very true," replied Bernard; "but you know the devil, Master Wingrove, can ——"

"Pshaw!" cried Wingrove.

"You won't say pshaw! when I tell you what happened in the castle chapel, to-day."

"What was that, Bernard?"

Bernard suddenly grasped Wingrove by the arm, exclaiming,—

"See! the light in the turret!"

Wingrove looked, and there sure enough was a pale stream of light issuing from a loop-hole in the Grey Turret, and clearly distinguishable from the surrounding moonlight.

CHAPTER XIV.

Beshrew me but I do suspect this man.
His age sits not easily upon him,
But, like a borrowed garment,
Doth deface its wearer.—BEAUMONT.

THE MIDNIGHT MEETING.—THE LIGHT IN THE GREY TURRET. — AN ARRIVAL. — SUSPICION. — THE AGED PILGRIM. — A SPY AND HIS CONDUCT.

THE light came evidently from a loop-hole in the Grey Turret. Of that there could be no doubt whatever, and it was so very different in colour from the pale refulgence of the moon, that it precluded the idea of it proceeding from that luminary shining through the opposite loop-holes in the long deserted turret.

No. 7

"Bernard," said Wingrove, "this passes my comprehension completely. There is more in this than meets the eye."

"Well, I'm glad it's there," said Bernard, in a suppressed voice, "because you see it ain't pleasant to be accused of having an imagination. Now I assure you, Master Wingrove, I have no imagination. My father had no imagination—my grandfather had no imagination, and —— "

"Hush! hush! Bernard," cried Wingrove, "cease this idle talk and let us really consider what had best be done."

"But what can be done?" said Bernard.

"What I propose is this," answered Wingrove, "that you and I should now proceed to the Grey Turret, and endeavour to come to some opinion about this mysterious light."

"Go to the Grey Turret?" said Bernard.

"Yes, of course," said Wingrove.

"The devil!"

"Why, what objections have you?"

"You—you don't mean to say you would go into the Grey Turret, do you, Master Wingrove?"

"I don't suppose we could get in conveniently," said Wingrove; "but we can see if the door is fast."

"I don't half like the job," muttered Bernard.

"Will you come?" said Wingrove.

"Why, yes, of course—I—I —— "

"Well then, no more words about it. Come along.—Ha! the light is gone."

"So it has," said Bernard, "and the turret looks as black as—as— I don't know what."

"It's not much use going now," said Wingrove.

"I should think not," answered Bernard.

"I tell you what we will do," whispered Wingrove, after a pause of thought. "We will remain here some time, and if the light appears again we will at once proceed to the turret."

"Very well," growled Bernard.

"And if it comes no more to-night," continued Wingrove, "we will to-morrow watch its first appearance, and then hasten to the spot."

"How long do you mean to stay here?" asked Bernard, "it's not very comfortable."

"Not long," answered Wingrove. "Half an hour at the utmost. Hark! the castle clock strikes twelve."

"What noise was that?" cried Bernard, suddenly.

"Noise?" said Wingrove.

"Ay; I heard a sound as of a challenge to the warder for admission to the castle."

"Hark!" cried Wingrove; "I hear it now. They are lowering the drawbridge for some one."

"Who can it be?" cried Bernard.

"At all events, it puts an end to our watch for to-night," remarked Hugh; "for I must see who has arrived."

Bernard heard this with great satisfaction, and he said :—

"Well, Master Wingrove, I have something for your special hearing as soon as you are at leisure."

"Meet me, then, in the small guard-room as soon as you see I am disengaged."

"I will," cried Bernard

"Now then, to the castle gate," said Wingrove. "Visiters are rare, and particularly at this hour."

Wingrove and his companion soon arrived at the castle gate, where the former was told in answer to his inquiries, that a palmer from the Holy Land had claimed hospitality and shelter for the night in the castle.

"Admit him instantly," said Wingrove. "He may tell us some news of Sir Rupert. He may have met him, or heard of him."

"The drawbridge is lowered," said the warder. "He will be here anon, for a guard has gone across to conduct him."

"How know you he is a pilgrim?" said Wingrove.

"His habit showed clearly in the moonlight," replied the warder, "and in answer to my challenge, he said he came from Palestine, and was faint and weary."

"He is welcome," said Hugh Wingrove, "and I would that Sir Rupert were here to entertain him."

As he spoke a soldier appeared at the gate, upon whose arm was leaning an apparently aged man.

His hair was of a silvery whiteness, and his trembling limbs seemed hardly capable of supporting his bent and aged form.

"Blessings on all here," he said, feebly, and in broken accents, as he passed the gates.

"Welcome, father," said Wingrove.

"Bless thee, my son, bless thee;" said the aged pilgrim, as he leaned heavily upon his staff, and looked tremblingly around him upon the rough forms of the soldiers.

"If he were upright and strong," whispered Bernard to one of his comrades, "this pilgrim would be a marvellous big fellow."

"I think so, too," answered the soldier. "See, even as he stoops, what a frame he has. In his time he has been a taller man than any in Brandon Castle."

"There is a fire in the painted hall," said Wingrove. "Conduct the holy man there."

"Nay, nay, my son," said the pilgrim, in weak tremulous accents; "in —in my youth, I—I was a soldier."

"Indeed," cried Wingrove.

"And a stalwart one, I'll be bound," said Bernard.

"'Twas many—many years ago," answered the old man, with a deep sigh; "when—when good King Richard led the cross in—in holy Gallilee, and—and—"

Here a fit of coughing interrupted the old man's speech, and Wingrove said kindly,—

"Well, father, would you prefer to sit with us in the guard-room for a time, before you retire to rest?"

"Aye, my son, aye," said the pilgrim, "I would. The sight of—of arms—and soldiers, warms my old blood."

"A thumper, in his time, I'll warrant," muttered Bernard, whose estimate of people was always solely with reference to their real or supposed bodily powers. "Why, even now he has a hand that could take a good grip of a battle-axe."

"Follow me then, father," said Wingrove. "You shall tell us something of brave King Richard of the Lion Heart, and his doings in the Holy Land."

"That will I—that will I," said the pilgrim, as with tottering and uncertain steps he followed Wingrove to the room in which the night-guard remained, waiting their turns of duty.

"What a man!" cried Bernard. "Why, if he were to stand upright, there is not a suit of mail in the castle would fit him. A fine fellow—a most admirable fellow! A most worthy fellow! A most uncommonly big fellow."

"Well, how are you by this time, Bernard?" said one of his comrades.

"How am I!" said Bernard. "What do you mean?"

"Why, we all thought you were very bad."

"Oh, aye—true," said Bernard. "I'm better—a good deal better; but I have been very bad, indeed. Plague take being ill," he said, in an under tone; "I shall never hear the last of it. A man ought never to be ill but once, and then he ought to die; and a soldier ought never to be ill at all, for he ought to be knocked on the head some day in some most glorious fight."

Wingrove conducted the pilgrim to the guard-room, and ordered refreshments to be placed before him, of which he sparingly partook, after very piously blessing the meal.

"Have you been long from the east?" said Wingrove.

"No," answered the pilgrim, "but a short space, my son. I—I am on my road to London."

"I trust you will remain here, if you be weary and travel-worn, until you are quite recruited," said Hugh, kindly.

"I—I thank thee, I thank thee," said the old man. "Your lord, I know well, is good to—to the aged, the poor, and—and the wearied and soiled wayfarer."

"I regret his absence," said Wingrove; "but whatever I can do to render you comfortable shall be done."

"Is he absent?" asked the pilgrim.

"He is," answered Wingrove.

"Alas! I would have rejoiced to see him. I knew him when he was a boy; and when I came in sight of this place, I halted and cried to myself with joy, 'There is Brandon, and I shall once more, ere I die, see the good Sir Rupert.'"

"He has been gone some days," said Wingrove.

"And who—who," said the pilgrim, "enjoys authority here in his absence?"

"The Lady Weare, myself, and Master Eldred Weare."

"Um!" said the pilgrim; "I have heard of them. Those Weares."

"Have you?" said Wingrove.

"And—and," continued the pilgrim, inclining his mouth to Wingrove's ear, "I—I like them not."

There was an earnestness in the tone of the pilgrim that carried conviction with it, and Wingrove said,

"What ill know you of them?"

"Eldred Weare, I have heard, is a dastard," answered the pilgrim, "and Agatha Weare wants that charm of woman—softness."

"Why, truly, she is rather a rough specimen of the fair sex, Master Pilgrim; but you seem to know them well?"

"I do, I—I do," said the pilgrim; "eugh! eugh! I—I have a troublesome cough, my son. The old are—eugh! eugh! sorely afflicted."

"Do you come to England on any special errand?" said Wingrove.

"Yes, yes," said the old man, shaking his head sadly.

"I hope it is not one of pain?"

"Pain—pain!" said the pilgrim; "much pain. I—I come to seek a bad man; a—a villain!"

"A villain, father?"

"Aye, my son. One who has done me wrong."

"Shame to him then," said Wingrove. "Your years should have protected you from injury."

"Yes, yes," faltered the pilgrim; "but Morgatani ——"

"Morgatani!" cried Wingrove.

"Yes, Morgatani!" said the pilgrim, laying his hand heavily upon the arm of Hugh Wingrove.

CHAPTER XV.

There was a time when with my biting falchion !
I'd have made them skip again.—LEAR.

THE CONVERSATION.—INSINUATIONS.—THE CHAMBER AND THE SUIT OF MAIL.—THE MAN-AT-ARMS.—A SUDDEN DISAPPEARANCE.

A SILENCE of some moments ensued between Hugh Wingrove and the aged pilgrim, for the soldier did not know exactly how to receive such a communication from one who was an utter stranger to him, although he came in a sacred and a saintly garb.

The pilgrim seemed determined that the silence should be broken by Hugh Wingrove, for he stirred not, neither did he speak.

"The person you mention," said Wingrove, at length, "is not altogether unknown in Brandon Castle."

"Ah! Say you so, my son?" said the pilgrim. "Is he here?"

"No," answered Wingrove; "it is no secret here that some time since Sir Rupert Brandon forbade him the castle."

"Indeed?"

"Yes; his offence must have been great, for Sir Rupert is not a passionate man upon trifles, and I never saw him so enraged."

"Had you no suspicion of the cause?" said the pilgrim.

"None whatever," answered Wingrove.

"And since then Morgatani has not, I suppose, been to Brandon?"

"Never since then. He would not be admitted."

"He is artful and bold," said the pilgrim.

"He would need to be," answered Hugh, "to induce us to let him within the gates of Brandon, against the express orders of Sir Rupert."

"Yes, yes—true, my son, true. You have no suspicion that he has ever been within the castle lately?"

"'Tis impossible."

"You are sure?"

"Quite. Why do you ask?"

"Because if I were you, and found him here, whether it was in hall or chamber, closet or corridor, turret or chapel ——"

"Well, father ——"

"Humph!" said the pilgrim, who had been looking keenly in Wingrove's face; "I'd detain him."

"Well, then, I wouldn't," said Wingrove.

"What—what would you do?"

"I'd give him a swim across the moat."

"A good plan; a—a very good plan," said the pilgrim, "if—if it could be done."

"We would try, however," said Wingrove.

"I—I," said the pilgrim, "should be tempted to send a cloth yard shaft through his heart."

"It would serve him right," said Wingrove.

" Particularly if it took him unawares," added the old pilgrim.

" Now, shame on you if you be an old soldier," said Wingrove, " to think of taking your worst foe at an undue advantage."

" Young blood, young blood," said the pilgrim, " I—I did but try you, my son. Forgive me : it is my custom."

" Not such young blood either," said Wingrove.

"I am now weary," said the pilgrim.

" A soldier shall conduct you to your quarters, holy sir," said Wingrove, " and Heaven send you good repose."

" Thanks, my son, thanks. I will see you again in the morning."

" Good night," said Hugh.

" Yet, ere we part," whispered the pilgrim, " I would say a word or two."

" I attend," said Wingrove.

" You love not Morgatani ?"

" Well."

" Let us, then, concert some measure for his destruction."

" No," answered Wingrove, " I will have nothing to do with him."

" As you please," said the pilgrim.

He tottered to the door, preceded by a soldier bearing a flambeau.

" Bless you, my son ; good-night," he said, as he paused a moment upon the threshold, and then disappeared with the soldier.

" Curse you !" cried Wingrove, " for an impudent knave, whom I suspect to be about as much a pilgrim from the Holy Land as I am. We shall see —we shall see. What, ho ! Bernard, Bernard ; and you, Evans, come hither, both of you."

The two soldiers immediately appeared from the outer guard-room, at the call of their chief.

" What now ?" said Bernard.

" Attend to me," said Wingrove. " You both saw the pilgrim ?"

" We did."

" What do you think of him ?"

" An' I were to be hanged," said Joyce Evans, " I don't know what to think ; but I can tell you this much, Master Wingrove, that I saw the handle of a weapon—I think it was a curtal axe—beneath his garment as the wind from the gate flapped it on one side."

" Indeed ?" said Wingrove.

" I think he's a stunner," said Bernard.

" A what ?"

" A stunner : I mean one who can give a knock-down blow. His hand didn't belong to an old man ; it was like a haunch of venison."

" Who he is," said Wingrove, " I don't know ; but I feel pretty sure he is no old pilgrim. He has an eye like a coal, and once or twice he forgot his disguise, and his voice was as deep as a muffled bell. No; he is no pilgrim."

" Then what is he ?" said Joyce Evans.

" I know not," answered Wingrove ; " some cursed design is on foot that I fear is not for the advantage of Sir Rupert."

" Did you say he had a deep voice ?" said Bernard.

" I did," answered Wingrove.

" A heavy tread ?"

" Yes."

" Then I know who it is."

" Who, Bernard ?"

" The —"

" What ?"

" Devil."

" Pho—pho !"

" Ah ! you may pho—pho, as much as you please, Master Wingrove ; but I tell you, he came to me in the chapel to-day."

" You took a flagon of ale to the chapel, I dare say," said Hugh.

" Why, yes, I did take the ale ; but you know ——"

" Ah, yes ; we know a flagon of ale accounts for a great many things, Bernard ; so, if you please, we'll not exactly believe about your strange visiter."

" Well, now," exclaimed Bernard, " may I be smothered in a ditch ; but I tell you, he came to me, and ——"

" That'll do," said Wingrove, " another time—another time."

" Oh—oh," whispered Joyce Evans, " that was when you were ill and off duty, eh, Bernard ?"

" D—n that illness !" cried Bernard.

" What I propose is this," said Wingrove, " that when Anstey, who is lighting the pilgrim to a chamber, cames back, we all go and discover to a certainty whether he is really the old man he represents himself to be, for it may be dangerous to allow him to remain a night in the castle, to prosecute any villany he may think proper."

" Agreed," cried Bernard.

" And here comes Anstey," said Joyce Evans.

" Well," said Wingrove, " what do you think of the pilgrim ?"

" He's an odd one," said Anstey.

" How so ?"

" Why I took Lim into the small chamber by the armoury, and you know there hangs by the door a suit of mail that belonged to Count Baldwin years ago."

" Yes," said Wingrove, " 'tis an old-fashioned suit, and so heavy no one would wear it now that quality of metal renders thickness not so necessary as it formerly was."

" It is heavy," said Anstey, " and by some means it had fallen down, and quite obstructed the door-way, so I said, ' ellow, we must get assistance to move this lumber. It's beyond one man's strength, and I suppose your help wouldn't be great ?' said I, with a sort of laugh, you know, Master Wingrove."

" Well—what ?" said he.

" Why he stooped down, and, with an oath that beat all the swearing ever I heard all to nothing, he caught hold of the mail by one hand, and flung it a score of yards or so from the door, as any of us would a bundle of straw."

" What, then ?" said Wingrove.

" Why then he says something about the blessing of Heaven, and bids me good-night, as if he hadn't a minute to live."

" He is an impostor," said Wingrove, snatching a light from the table. "Come, my friends, we will see to the bottom of this business. Disguise always conceals villany of some kind or other. We will give this mock pilgrim a different lodging to-night."

Without another word Hugh Wingrove rushed from the guard-room, followed closely by the three soldiers, and took his way direct to the chamber of the pretended pilgrim.

They soon arrived to where the armour lay in a disordered heap, and a few paces more brought them to the door of the small chamber into which the mysterious guest had been shown.

Wingrove placed his finger on his lips, to indicate silence to his three companions, and then he knocked gently at the door of the pilgrim's chamber with the hilt of his sword.

No answer was returned, and, after waiting a few seconds, he knocked again, louder than before.

Still there was no notice taken from within, and Wingrove, placing his ear to the door, listened if he could hear any voice; but all was still as the very grave.

"Sir," he cried, "holy sir; I would a word with you."

Still no answer came.

"Call out fire," suggested Evans.

"No; I will enter at once," said Wingrove. "You take the light, Bernard, and hold it as high as you can, so that if the knave strikes at me, I may see to return the compliment."

Bernard took the light, and held it above his head, with great indifference, while Wingrove, laying his hand upon the lock, suddenly flung the door wide open, and stood upon his guard at the entrance.

"Where is he?" said Bernard.

They all immediately rushed into the apartment, but to their surprise and consternation it was empty, and the light alone remained which the soldier Anstey had lit for his guest.

~~~~~~~~~~~~~~~~~~~~~

CHAPTER XVI.

What devil was it
That thus hath cozened you?—HAMLET.

THE CONCLUSION OF THE LEGEND OF THE GREY TURRET.—A SUDDEN AND MUCH UNEXPECTED VISIT.—THE CLUTCH.—BERNARD'S GREAT DISCOMFITURE.—THE DEPARTURE OF THE SPY.

THE astonishment of Hugh Wingrove and his companions was very great at the sudden and mysterious disappearance of their guest, a disappearance which while it puzzled them to account for, at once confirmed all their suspicions of his being far other than he represented himself.

"All we can do now," said Wingrove, "is to take care that no one leaves the castle, and, at the first dawn of day institute an active search for our singular and I fear rascally visiter."

"He cannot leave the castle if he be human," said one of the soldiers, "for the moat is wide and deep—the drawbridge is up, and a leap from the battlements would, I think, make the boldest hesitate."

"Besides he would have to jump into the moat," said Bernard, "and I'll be bound there's mud enough at the bottom to hold anybody tight that once got plunged among it."

"See even now the morning is coming," cried Wingrove. "The knave must be in the castle, and the light will be strong enough in another hour to ferret him out."

"Good Master Wingrove," said one. "Perhaps you won't mind telling us the rest of the story of why the Grey Turret was shut up?"

"Come to the guard-room then," said Wingrove, "and while we wait an hour for a little light, I will finish my tale."

"I hope it's something dreadful," said Bernard, "for I must own I like a little of the horrible."

"Why, nobody knows exactly," said Wingrove. "The most of it is left to the imagination."

"Perhaps," said Joyce Evans, with a malicious smile, "Bernard had better go to bed as he has been so very unwell as to be off duty. The night might injure his delicate frame."

"Curse you," muttered Bernard. "Am I never to hear the last of that confounded illness?"

They were soon in the guard-room gathered round the cheerful wood-fire which was always kept burning on its ample hearth, for even at the sunniest period of the year, the old castles were cold and dreary, being composed mostly of stone and surrounded by water.

"Where did I leave off?" said Wingrove.

"Why," replied Anstey, "Sir Montague Brandon had just taken a light to show the stranger to his sleeping room, and everybody was waiting for him to come back."

"True," said Wingrove, "so I was. Well, you must know then, that many minutes elapsed before he did come back."

"Yes," said Bernard.

"Now don't be saying ' yes' every minute," cried Wingrove, "you put me out with your ' yes' and ' indeed.' "

"If he says ' yes' again," said Joyce Evans, " I'll let my halbert fall upon his ugly head."

"I'll hold you over the candle with my finger and thumb and singe you," said Bernard, " if you say another word."

"Silence, silence!" cried Anstey.

"Well," continued Wingrove, " if there's any more interruptions I won't tell it at all, so be quiet all of you.

"At length a heavy footstep was heard approaching," said Wingrove, continuing his narration, " and it was so different from the usual quick tread of Sir Montague Brandon, that nobody would believe it was him till he
No. 8

came into the room, and then they could all see that he looked vexed and annoyed.

" ' Some water,' he cried.

" Well, a basin of water was brought to him, and for the first time they then saw that he had a serious wound upon the palm of his hand, for he began washing it and fuming and fretting all the while, for he was evidently very much put out about something.

" No one liked to ask him a question, and he washed the blood from his hand and bound his handkerchief round the wound which I'm told was as ugly a cut as one would wish to see.

" Well, when he had finished dressing his wound, he turned to his friends and retainers and said, in a sorrowful voice,—

" ' My friends, it's a sad thing when a man betrays his guest to whom he is bound by the laws of hospitality ; but I think it's still worse for a man to come to another's house, receive a kind welcome and every attention, and then make a dastardly attempt upon the life of his kind and hospitable entertainer.'

" At this you may be sure they all looked astonished and crowded round Sir Montague Brandon to learn the particulars.

" ' I had scarcely,' he continued, ' lighted the stranger to his chamber, and had the words ' Good night' upon my lips, when he made a rush at me with a dagger and endeavoured to plunge it in my heart.'

" An universal cry of indignation arose from the vassals at this information, for Sir Montague was much beloved, and several snatched up their weapons and were hurrying from the room to take instant vengeance on the stranger when Sir Montague cried,—

" ' Hold! my friends and comrades.   Hear me out.'

" There was immediately a respectful silence, and he continued thus :—

" ' I heard his movement and turned just in time to see the uplifted dagger.   I clutched its blade in my hand upon the impulse of the moment and gave myself the wound you have seen.'

" ' The villain !' muttered the vassals.

" ' I kept my hold,' continued Sir Montague, ' and wrested the weapon from his grasp, for he seemed dreadfully terrified that he failed in taking me by surprise.'

" ' Death to him !' cried the vassals and retainers.   ' Death to the assassin !   Death to the villain !'

" ' He is dead,' said Sir Montague.   ' In the vexation of the moment, I killed him, which I regret, for such a scoundrel should have suffered a more ignoble death than by my hand.' "

" Is that all, Master Wingrove ?" said Bernard.

" Not quite," answered Wingrove, " for Sir Montague Brandon went on to say that he detested ingratitude so much, and was so grieved that his kindness and hospitality to a stranger should have been thus requited, that he would never go into the Grey Turret again as long as he lived in Brandon Castle, nor suffer any one else to sleep in it."

" And so it was shut up ?" said Joyce Evans.

" Yes," said Wingrove.   " I'm told that Sir Montague would not even have the body touched, and, in fact, he went himself and within the hour saw the door fastened up."

" Why you don't mean to say he left the dead man in the turret ?" said Bernard, in a tone of surprise.

" Yes, I do," resumed Wingrove.   " So the tale has been told to me. The turret was locked and nailed up from that hour, and no one even had a peep into it, at all."

" That's very odd," said Bernard.

" Yes, and so it has remained till the present day.   No Lord of Brandon ever would have it opened."

" And the dead fellow is there still!" said Joyce Evans.

" His skeleton, doubtless," said Wingrove, " for you must recollect all this took place many years ago."

" Well," said Bernard, " that's a most uncommon story."

" There's the first glimpse of the sun," cried Wingrove.   " Let us to our search, my friends.   We will unkennel this pilgrim, unless he be something more than a mortal rogue."

" Ha!" said Bernard, " there's the question you see.   Now I think he's the old gentleman himself."

" He's a strong old gentleman, however," said Anstey.

" And I've no doubt a bad one," said Wingrove.   " But come, friends, let us take a run over the castle, and endeavour to find him out, if he be hiding anywhere."

Wingrove rose as he spoke and walked to the door of the guard-room, but before he could reach it, it opened and to the surprise and consternation of them all, there stood upon the threshold, leaning upon his staff and trembling with apparent weakness—the pilgrim !

" Bless—you—my—my children," he said, in faltering tones, " a fair morning to you all, and—and a happy day—a happy day—Eugh! eugh! eugh! my cough racks me—eugh!"

" The devil !" said Bernard.

" Well, I'm bothered !" muttered Anstey.

Wingrove looked astonished, and for some minutes was at a loss what to say or do.

" Good morning," he at length said.   " Perhaps you will be so kind as to tell where you slept last night ?"

" In—eugh !—eugh !—Brandon—Brandon Castle," said the pilgrim.

" I know that," cried Wingrove, " but I want to know in what room ?"

" In—in that—eugh ! your great kindness placed me."

" Permit me to doubt," said Wingrove.

" Eugh ! eugh !" coughed the pilgrim.   " Fools are always tormented with doubts—eugh !—my cough is very troublesome."

Wingrove eyed him suspiciously as he shook his head, and said,—

" I expect, before we part, we must come to some explanation together, most holy and sanctified palmer."

" Eugh ; eugh ! very likely," said the pilgrim.

" Don't you find a heavy battle axe inconvenient to carry under your pilgrim's gown, eh ?" said Joyce Evans.

" Not—in—in the least, my dear son," said the pilgrim.   " Sometimes— eugh ! eugh !   I encounter a—a thick-pated knave—eugh ! eugh ! who asks impertinent and silly questions—then you know—it's—it's very useful —eugh !"

" Curse his assurance," muttered the soldier.

" I hope," said Anstey; " your old bones didn't ache through moving that coat of mail last night ?"

" No, no," said the pilgrim; " you—you are very kind, my son—but— but—eugh ! I am pretty well—if—if—eugh !—eugh ! it wasn't the cough that troubles me."

" You have a stong hand, father," said Bernard.

" I—I had once, my son,"

" What do you think of this one ?" continued Bernard, presenting his own muscular right hand to the pilgrim.

" Ah," said the old man—"there was a time, eugh !—when—when I could have grasped and made you—you wince again."

"Say you so?" cried Bernard, winking at his comrades, and adding to himself in an under tone, "You cursed hypocrite, I'll make you wince, for you are no more an old pilgrim than I am."

"Yes," said the pilgrim, "there was a time."

"Let's have a clutch now, then," said Bernard. "We can come to some judgment, even now, you know."

"I—I—eugh!" said the pilgrim. "I—have no objection my—son—but you know—eugh! I—am old—now."

"I'll make you raise your voice a little," thought Bernard, as he grasped the extended hand of the pilgrim.

In a moment Bernard felt as if his hand was in an iron vice—the bones of his fingers crackled again, so tremendous was the grip of the pretended old pilgrim.

"D——n," cried Bernard, as he looked at his benumbed and injured hand, when the pilgrim released it.

"Eugh!—eugh!" he said. "There—there was a time—eugh! eugh!"

"We will have an end of this mummery," said Wingrove, advancing towards the pilgrim.

The pilgrim stepped aside, and the lady Agatha stood in the door way.

"Lady, this man," began Wingrove.

"Must leave the castle unmolested," interrupted Agatha.

"Indeed?" said Wingrove.

"Lower the drawbridge," cried Agatha.

"Eugh! eugh!" coughed the pilgrim.

He passed with a tottering step through the gate and over the drawbridge, and was soon lost to view.

"That's either the devil or one of his imps," whispered Bernard to Wingrove.

"I know him now," said Wingrove, in whispered reply.

"Who is it?"

"Morgatani!"

"Morgatani? The—the Black Monk?"

"Even so. I'd lay my life on it."

CHAPTER XVI.

Arm'd say you?
Armed, my lord.
From top to toe!—HAMLET.

THE MEETING TO SOLVE THE MYSTERY.—THE OLD COURT.—THE STAIR-CASE AND THE FATAL DOOR.—THE APPARITION.

THAT evening Wingrove and Bernard met according to appointment in the southern gallery, in order to watch for the re-appearance of the mysterious light which they had seen the night before in the Grey Turret.

The night was windy and boisterous, and although the silver moon was high in the blue vault of Heaven, the clouds which flew rapidly across its radiant disc, for the most part obscured its beauty and dimmed its radiance. It was only therefore occasionally that its soft pale light fell upon tower and battlement, and even lit up the sleepy-looking waters of the moat with a temporary beauty.

"It is not the time, yet," answered Wingrove. "If you recollect, it was near upon the stroke of twelve last night when the thin stream of light glanced from the loop-hole."

"It was," said Bernard; "and now eleven has but just pealed from the clock tower."

"Let us be patient," replied Wingrove, "and I doubt not we shall again see it, and be able to come to some opinion about it."

"And do you really think yon pilgrim, with the hard hand," said Bernard, "was the Monk Morgatani?"

"I suspected it from the moment that I suspected he was no pilgrim," answered Wingrove. "If you recollect Morgatani at all, Bernard, you must recollect his great height."

"I do; he was above the tallest."

"So was the pretended pilgrim. Had he stood upright he would have matched the Black Monk to a miracle."

"It must have been him," said Bernard. "By the mass, he has a grip like a vice. I sha'n't forget his grasp for one while."

"It was a stalwart knave," remarked Wingrove. "But what convinced me most of all that it was Morgatani in disguise, was the conduct of the Lady Agatha."

"Ha," said Bernard; "I have heard something whispered on that head among the men-at-arms before to-day."

"Yes," continued Wingrove; "some do not scruple to say that Morgatani was the favoured lover of Agatha Weare as well as her confessor."

"So I have heard," said Bernard. "Ah, the rogue! by the mass, these monks sometimes hide a wolf's heart beneath their priestly garments, Master Wingrove."

"Yes," said Wingrove; "and of all the scoundrels that the world can produce, the most rascally and despicable variety are those who make religion a mask wherewith to hide their sensuality and baseness."

"They ought to be flayed alive," said Bernard.

"Some say," continued Wingrove, "that the reason why Sir Rupert turned the Monk Morgatani from the castle with such anger and contempt was the discovery of an intrigue between him and Mistress Agatha Weare."

"Very likely," responded Bernard.

"Then I differ with you," said Wingrove. "I think such was not the reason at all, merely from one circumstance."

"And what's that?" said Bernard.

"Why this—I am quite sure if such had been the case, Sir Rupert would have sent Agatha Weare across the drawbridge of Brandon Castle as quickly as he did the Monk Morgatani."

"Humph!" said Bernard. "There's something in that. So he would, Wingrove, so he would."

"It was a saying of Sir Rupert's," continued Wingrove, "that when a woman forgot her sex he forgot it too; so you see, he would in such a case have packed her off in a moment."

"And serve her right," cried Bernard. "D—n her, I hate her, and if I come across Morgatani again, trust me, but I'll square accounts with him, big as he is."

"The light—the light!" suddenly cried Wingrove.

"What?—From the turret?"

"Aye—see, it streams clear and bright from the same loop-hole that we saw it come from yesternight."

"By Heaven it does!" cried Bernard. "Now what do you mean to do Master Wingrove?"

"You are armed?"

"I am."

"And fear not?"

"Certainly not."

" Then come with me to the turret-door, and let us there keep watch if needs be till morning's light, and see who comes forth."

" Agreed," cried Bernard. " Be it ghost or devil, Wingrove, I'll stand by you, and face it."

" Come on then," said Wingrove. " Follow me, I know the nearest route to the place."

" Shall we have no light ?" said Bernard.

" No—the very thing we should not have is a light ; it would betray us—I wish our watch to be a secret one."

" As you please," answered Bernard. " Lead on, I'll follow you."

Wingrove immediately left the gallery, followed closely by Bernard, and as quickly as he could made his way to the uninhabited part of the castle of which the mysterious Grey Turret formed a most conspicuous portion.

They passed through many gloomy chambers, and corridors of vast extent, upon whose crumbling walls hung the damp of centuries. There were in some the remains of faded furniture and hangings, which at one time had excited envy and admiration, but now like the mortal remains of those who had sat beneath the shadow of their beauty, they were crumbling into dust, and like the baseless fabric of a vision, would soon—

" Leave not a wrack behind."

Having traversed more than half round the entire building, Wingrove suddenly paused at a small door, which yielded to his touch, and turning to Bernard, he said,—

" This door leads into the court-yard, from whence we can ascend a flight of stone steps to the very door of the Grey Turret."

" Are we so near ?" said Bernard.

" We are. Be cautious or we shall give the alarm if it be a mortal man like ourselves, who is in that long deserted chamber, and that it is I firmly believe, for you know, Bernard, I am no believer in spirits and devils."

" As you please as to believing or not believing, Master Wingrove," replied Bernard ; " but if you had been in the chapel with me when you know I had ——"

" The second flagon of ale," interrupted Wingrove, " all to yourself, and fell asleep."

" No—no," said Bernard, " the bit of arrow ought to have convinced you, Master Wingrove, that I did not dream it all."

" I own that staggered me," said Wingrove, " but we have now no time to spare. Do not speak a word, Bernard, when we are through this door-way, and tread as lightly as you can."

" I am used to secret watching," said Bernard, " when I was with the Elector of Bavaria, in ——"

" Pho ! pho !" cried Wingrove, " another time will do for that. Come—not a word more."

He gently pushed open the little door, and treading with extreme caution, he entered the small court-yard, followed closely by Bernard.

The small paved court in which they now found themselves had evidently been deserted for a long time. Rank grass was growing up between the large flag stones, with which it was paved, and under the walls weeds of various growths were waving in the night air. Altogether there was an air of mournful desolation in the place, which was greatly aided by the occasional glimpses of pale moonlight that struggled through the drifting clouds and fell clear and cold on the old grey stones.

And there rose high and black in the sky the old Grey Turret, within which was supposed to be still the body of the traitorous guest, who had attempted the life of the brave and hospitable Sir Montague Brandon, and paid so dearly for his treachery.

The streak of light still came streaming from the loop-hole, and Wingrove stood full in its path, to be assured that it was no delusion of the active imagination.

The light was immoveable, and after a time Wingrove beckoned to Bernard and advanced to the turret.

Leading direct from the court-yard was a winding stone staircase, which terminated at the actual door of the turret chamber, which had so very questionable a character in Brandon castle.

"There was a door here once," whispered Wingrove to Bernard, "but see! It has been forced from its hinges, and now lies against the wall. Some mortal arm must have done that."

"It has just struck me," answered Bernard, in a low suspicious tone, "that perhaps the ghost of the rascal that tried to assassinate Sir Montague Brandon, can't rest in peace, and so sits in the turret wanting some Christian to come and bury his remains."

"But a ghost wouldn't want a light," said Wingrove, incredulously.

"Who knows?" answered Bernard, shaking his head. "I've heard of such things often."

"Well, we will see if it be so," said Wingrove. "So come, Bernard, let us ascend the stone staircase that you see stands so invitingly before us. Come —you do not hesitate?"

"No, not I," said Bernard. "Ghost or no ghost, I am your man, Master Wingrove."

"Your teeth chatter with fear," said Wingrove.

"It's with cold," answered Bernard.

Wingrove now slowly ascended the stone staircase.

Notwithstanding his disbelief in supernatural agency, and his conviction that it must be some mortal man like himself who was in the Grey Turret, for some object, he could not prevent an undefinable fear from creeping over his heart as he slowly ascended the stairs leading to that chamber, where lay, to the best of his belief, so ghastly a spectacle as the unburied body of the assassin, who had been killed by Sir Montague, must present.

He breathed short and thick as he reached the top of the staircase, and knew that a few steps forward would lead him to the door of the chamber of blood.

Bernard, in spite of his fears, which were rapidly increasing, followed Wingrove closely, and they both stood silent and motionless as two statues for some minutes at the head of the staircase.

"Bernard," he said in a whisper, scarcely above his breath.

"Here," answered Bernard, in the same tone.

"We will stay here. Nothing can pass us."

"Hark!" said Bernard.

A deep groan came from the turret chamber.

Wingrove felt an icy coldness gathering round his heart, and Bernard could not refrain from a responsive groan himself.

"Sh—sh—shall we go, Wingrove?" he stammered.

"No—no," gasped Wingrove, "we are innocent of purpose, and—and we will stay."

A shriek now burst from the turret chamber,—a shriek so wild and awful that it took away very nearly the breath of Wingrove to hear it. Before they could recover from their alarm and horror, the whole landing place on which they were standing was lighted up by a sickly green light, and a figure passed them, over the whole surface of which played a flame of the same hue.

It walked slowly between them, and descended the stairs uttering deep and agonising groans till it was lost in the distance.

CHAPTER XVII.

" 'Tis said that when foul murder has ta'en place
The house is then accursed, and unclean spirits
Stalk in pale horror through it's chambers."

SWOON.—SPECULATION.—THE INTERVIEW WITH AGATHA.—THE BEGINNING OF THE END.—THE FIRST LINK IN THE CHAIN OF GUILT WOVEN FOR THE INNOCENT.

WINGROVE could not tell exactly how long it was before he recovered from the shock his mind had sustained by the strange visitation he had been subjected to ; but when he did recover sufficiently to speak, he was in utter darkness, and his throat felt parched and dry.

"Bernard," he cried, "Bernard."

No voice replied, and Wingrove began to be seriously alarmed with regard to the fate of his companion.

"Bernard !" he again cried ; but no answer being returned, he began slowly and cautiously to descend the staircase.

He had not passed over many steps, when he trod upon something soft, and he heard a groan, which he thought was in Bernard's tone.

"Bernard," he cried, "are you here ?"

"Good and gracious devil," said Bernard.

" 'Tis I," cried Wingrove ; "get up, and let us leave this place."

"Where would you take me ?" groaned Bernard. "I'm a poor man-at-arms, master ghost, devil, or whatever you are."

" 'Tis I," said Wingrove, "I, Hugh Wingrove."

"Eh ?" said Bernard.

"Come, get up ; we have had enough of horror for one night. I am sick at heart, Bernard : let us leave this fearful place."

"Is it really you ?" said Bernard, rising.

"Yes, yes ; come on, come on."

"Oh, Wingrove ; wasn't it awful ?"

"Hush—hush !" said Wingrove. "Speak not of it here. Our cooler judgments must decide upon what we have seen and heard."

So saying he hastened through the court-yard, and Bernard, through fear of being left behind, kept closely upon his companion's heels, nor ever once looked behind him.

They soon found their way to the inhabited part of the castle, and Wingrove led Bernard to the small private guard-room, after ordering a soldier to bring him immediately some refreshment, for he felt faint and weary, both in mind and body, from the excitement he had gone through.

He took a deep draught from a flagon of ale which was brought him, and then tendered it to Bernard, who, with a preliminary nod, finished the remainder without taking it from his lips.

"How do you feel now, Master Wingrove ?" said Bernard.

"Better, certainly," answered Hugh, "for I was choking with thirst."

"Don't you think ?" suggested Bernard, looking into the empty flagon.

"Think what ?"

"Why, that we had better—eh ?"

"Have that filled again ?"

"Yes."

"I do, Bernard, for I an chilled and miserable."

The flagon was again set before them, filled to the brim with that rare old ale, for which "merrie England in the olden time" was so greatly famous.

"Bernard," said Wingrove, "did you see the— the —"

"The ghost?"

"I can't say what it was; but did you see what came out of the Grey Turret so suddenly?"

"I did."

"What did it appear like to you?"

"The figure was in half armour, and an arm was in the sleeve of a jerkin, which was hanging nearly to the ground."

"I noticed that," said Wingrove. "The figure appeared either to have been putting on or pulling off an upper garment, which covered a half suit of mail. Did you mark anything else?"

"Nothing, master Wingrove," said Bernard; "and I can only tell you this much, that I never will again set my foot upon those turret stairs while I know it."

"I do not wonder at your determination," said Wingrove. "The appearance of that strange figure was sufficiently startling and alarming to warrant you in such a resolve."

"Oh, Master Wingrove," said Bernard, "you always doubted about ghosts and such like things, and you see now what it has come to."

"I cannot dispute," answered Wingrove, "that we saw a strange being, but who or what he may be, I cannot yet determine. I would I had had presence of mind to follow it."

"Follow it?" cried Bernard.

"Yes. I only regret now that I did not do so."

"I wouldn't have followed it," said Bernard earnestly, "for the castle and domains of Brandon!"

"Now, what may be your opinion," said Wingrove, after a pause of some moments, "as to what this appearance was?"

No. 9

"Why," said Bernard, "it was, of course, the spectre of the man whose body lies there, who was killed by Sir Montague Brandon."

"Think you so?"

"On my soul, I do, Wingrove. The dress was ancient, and the half armour such as is not worn now-a-days."

"I cannot say it is not so," answered Wingrove.

"Because of course it was he," said Bernard, whose mind seemed to be quite made up upon the subject.

"I would Sir Rupert was back," said Wingrove.

"Aye," said Bernard. "He'd soon set this all to rights, I'll warrant you, Master Wingrove. He fears neither man nor devil, and is pious as well as brave, God bless him!"

"Amen!" said Wingrove. "We've had nothing but trouble since he has been gone, and we shall have nothing but trouble till he comes back, you may depend."

"Here's to his health and speedy return," said Bernard, emptying the second flagon with one long pull.

"I will report all that has occurred to Agatha Weare," said Wingrove. "I am yet undecided as to the character of the mysterious inhabitant of the Grey Turret, and as I tell the circumstance to Agatha, I will watch her countenance narrowly, in order to detect if she is in any way concerned in getting up the thing to favour some scheme of her own, for as I live I suspect that woman to be in league with Morgatani, the Black Monk, for some purpose contrary to the interests of Sir Rupert."

"Oh, she's a bad one, you may depend," said Bernard, nodding his head, "I never met with such a woman. I only wonder why Sir Rupert allowed her to remain here in his absence"

"Why, Sir Rupert feels now that he is alone in the world," said Wingrove. "He is the last of his noble race. He leaves behind him in this castle no one to whom she can do any mischief, so you may depend he didn't care to trouble himself to order her out."

"Ah, that's it, I dare say," said Bernard.

"Now then, Bernard," said Wingrove, rising, "I will endeavour to snatch an hour or two's repose before I see Mistress Agatha upon this subject, which I am resolved to do."

The comrades in arms then separated, and the sun was shining serenely and warmly upon the old castle walls, ere the exhausted Hugh Wingrove, who had now passed several nights of anxious watching, rose from his couch, and hurriedly attiring himself, sought the presence of Agatha Weare in order to converse with her on the events of the night.

Agatha received him with unusual celerity, and affected a degree of graciousness in her air and manner, which sat but poorly upon her haughty countenance.

Wingrove looked earnestly at her, at the same time cautiously, and he fancied that he observed a slight heightening of her colour as he said—

"Lady, an extraordinary circumstance occurred last night, which I think it is fitting you should be made acquainted with."

"Indeed !" she replied. "Another trumpet summons was it ?"

"No," said Wingrove. "What I allude to has happened within the castle walls."

"Say you so?" cried Agatha, "I trust we have none other than friends within the walls of Brandon."

"I hope so, too," answered Wingrove; "but I suspect that some one even makes Brandon Castle his home, who would not dare to cross its threshold were its lord at home."

"'Tis false," said Agatha, suddenly rising. "'Tis false, I say."

" Lady !"

" False, I repeat.   He—he is not here."

" Who, lady ?"

" Who ?—you—you said that—You mentioned a name ?"

" I did not.   I mentioned no name," said Wingrove.   " I gave no voice of my suspicions."

Agatha dropped into a chair, and for a few moments leant her head upon her hand.

" Fool !   Fool that I am," she muttered, " to allow passion thus to play upon my brain.   I—I thought you named some one ?"

" No," said Wingrove.   " I merely said that there was some one in the castle who might be an unwelcome guest."

" Whom mean you ?"

" He whom I saw last night."

" Last night ?"

" Even so, lady."

" His name ?"

" That know I not.   I came to tell you of a circumstance that was strange and appalling, that even now, I tremble at its recollection."

" Say on," cried Agatha.

" You know the Grey Turret ?"

" I do."

" And the cause of its being closed so long from mortal eyes ?"

" Yes.   The body of an assassin lies there."

" Even so," said Wingrove.   " Well, lady, for two nights I have observe a pale light issuing from the loop-hole of that deserted place."

" Can that be possible ?" said Agatha.

" I doubted it myself," continued Wingrove, " until I actually stood in its rays.   Lady, there was a light last night in the Grey Turret."

" What more ?" said Agatha.

" With a brave and faithful comrade," said Wingrove, " I sought the spot. We ascended the staircase leading to that long closed turret chamber."

" What saw you ?"

" Scarcely had we decided how to act, when deep groans burst upon our ears."

" Groans ! that speaks of murder," said Agatha.

" Then," continued Wingrove, " came a shriek more horrible than tongue can tell.   Even now its echoes ring through my brain."

" Your tale is strange.   Go on, I pray you."

" So close upon that scream that the air was still filled with the sound, there came, apparently from the turret-chamber, a form of wild and singular appearance."

" Was it human ?"

" I know not.   Solemnly it passed and a lurid light played around it, as with groans, such as I never before heard, and hope never to hear again, it disappeared down the stone staircase, by the way we had ourselves came."

" Did not this congeal your blood with horror ?"

" I own," said Wingrove, " I knew not what to think."

" 'Tis very horrible !" cried Agatha.   " Some crime must have been committed in this castle, or such a spirit would not with such hideous sounds visit it in the silence of the night."

" Crime !" said Wingrove.

" Yes.   Nothing but murder could bring such a visitation upon Brandon Castle.   There has been some foul deed committed."

" Impossible !" said Wingrove, " there has been no opportunity."

" Some murder I say," repeated Agatha.

" Murder !"

" Aye, murder. How suddenly —"

" Suddenly what, lady ?" said Wingrove, observing that Agatha paused.

" How suddenly my poor sister died."

" Suddenly, lady ?"

" Aye, did she not ?"

" True, but we all know that all that human skill could do was done by Sir Rupert to save the Lady Alicia's life. She whom he loved so tenderly that he has even left his ancient castle now that she is no more here to make it to him a happy home."

" Enough—enough !" cried Agatha. " I must—I will not say more—I will consider further of this matter connected with the Grey Turret, and let you know my resolve."

" An' it please you," said Wingrove, " I will send to the Monastery for the Holy Father Abbot, who was so much attached to Sir Rupert, and take his advice upon it."

" No," said Agatha, coldly, " I have reasons for not wishing his presence."

" But," persisted Wingrove, " Sir Rupert left a special charge that he should be consulted upon any matter of moment."

" There are reasons, my friend, for not requiring his presence, which I will at a more fitting moment explain to you," said Agatha.

Thus the interview terminated, and Wingrove left the room completely puzzled by Agatha's behaviour, and the obscure and dreadful hints she had thrown out.

CHAPTER XVIII.

" Woman in her purity and loveliness most like an angel is ;
  But yet how fierce a devil is she when the charm
      Of grace and virtue is forgotten."

AGATHA ALONE. — A MIND DISEASED. — FRENZY. — THE BLACK MONK. — THE JESUIT.—WINGROVE'S RESOLVE.

SCARCELY had Wingrove left the room in which he had held the interview we have just recorded with Agatha Weare, when she rose, and, clasping her hands with vehemence, she exclaimed,—

" It is begun : the plot has commenced. Tremble, Sir Rupert Brandon, tremble ! You shall see what a woman's revenge is capable of—a slighted woman !"

These last words were uttered with a shriek of passion, and for a few moments her countenance assumed an expression perfectly demoniac, and fearful to behold.

" I shall have revenge !" she cried ; " revenge, for which I have given all —all—to—to him—to him—to Morgatani."

She sat down, and leaned her face in her hands for some minutes ; then, suddenly rising, she cried,—

" I loved him—I—I—the proud and scornful, because I felt myself, in all the attributes of mind, above my sex. My heart, which had resisted all fond sensations, was at length prostrated. I—I loved— loved—I adored—I worshipped him ! Sir Rupert Brandon, oh, God !—oh, God ! My love was like a mountain torrent— an avalanche—it overwhelmed reason, faith, religion, duty—all."

She paced the room with her hands pressed convulsively to her brain, and deep groans burst from her labouring breast.

" And—and," she muttered ; " he—he, the bold, the beautiful, could not love me. He had a lion's heart, and so had I. He was scornful and proud, and so was I.   Fool, fool that I was not to know that such natures are always attracted by their opposites.   He—Sir Rupert Brandon, passed me by, and knelt at the feet of my sister, Alicia, the trembling, soft-spoken girl, whose passion, like the dead sea we read of, no storm could ruffle; whose skill was in her gentle lute ; whose tears were ready as her smiles.   Then—then I swore revenge—revenge !   She is gone—gone by the decree of Heaven.   But he—he shall perish for his scorn.   I stooped to sue, and he turned from me. The next time I stoop to Sir Rupert Brandon, it shall be to whisper—to shriek despair into his dying ear.   Ha !—ha !—yes—yes.   I—I shall have dear revenge ; revenge—I—oh, Morgatani !"

The Black Monk stood before her.

" What means this storm of passion ?" he cried, in his customary deep, sepulchral tones.

" Sometimes," gasped Agatha, sinking into a chair ; " sometimes thought will oe'rmaster reason.   I—I think I am for a brief space at certain periods mad ; aye, mad, Morgatani."

" You do not shrink ?" said the monk.

" Shrink !" she exclaimed ; " shrink from revenge ?"

" Aye."

" No—no ; were hell to open at my feet, I would not shrink while that word revenge is written in characters of living flame upon my brain.   Morgatani, you know me not."

" Well I know your indomitable resolution," said the Black Monk. " Agatha, I doubt you no more than I do myself."

" And your heart, Morgatani ?"

" Ha ! ha !—my heart—my heart is marble."

" And mine, and mine," cried Agatha.

" Whence arises," said the monk, " this unusual agitation ?"

" Listen !" said Agatha.

" I do."

" I have commenced."

" Ah ! say you so ?   Speak on, and let me drink in the sweet words of promise, Agatha."

" The first drops of the subtle poison, suspicion, I have distilled into the ear of him whose blunt honesty, and dogged integrity, we have most to fear from."

" Hugh Wingrove you mean ?" said Morgatani.

" The same," answered Agatha.   " I saw him tremble as I spoke."

" 'Tis well," responded the monk.

" The subtlest poison," cried Agatha, " that the art of man has ever succeeded in extracting from nature shall not work so deadly an effect as the words of suspicion which now, from time to time, I shall utter to poison the fair fame of him upon whose head I would have fell destruction fall."

" You are right, you are right," cried the monk ; " slander is a poison of most deadly venom."

" We shall, we must succeed," remarked Agatha, vehemently.

" The plot is well laid," said Morgatani, calmly ; " recollect who I am."

" I know—a Jesuit ?"

" Yes ; and I and my order know secrets unknown to meaner men.   The secrets of science are revealed to us.   We know arts by which even the dead may seem to rise."

" The dead ?" said Agatha.

" Aye, the dead," said the monk.   " But I said seem to rise, only.   Real miracles we despise."

" I believe you have little faith," said Agatha.

" Priests generally have but little," sneered Morgatani.

"Think you I was premature," said Agatha, "in hinting the commencement of our plan?"

"No," answered the monk, "opportunity was everything, and I know none so fitting as yourself to judge when that presented itself. Tell me what passed."

Agatha then related to him the conversation she had had with Hugh Wingrove.

"Humph!" said the Black Monk. "The knave seems to suspect my presence here."

"He does," said Agatha. "And yet knowing not the secret means you have of approaching and leaving this castle at pleasure, his mind is involved in much doubt upon the subject."

"Superstition," said Morgatani, "will exert its giant influence upon his mind in due time. He will then be ours."

"There is no one else in the castle," remarked Agatha, "who may not be made as mere puppets in our hands."

The conference between the Black Monk and Agatha Weare continued for a long time, and we must leave them to discuss and mature their villanous projects in order to revert to the proceedings of other personages connected with our tale.

Wingrove was not at all satisfied by what had passed in his conversation with Agatha Weare, and her opinion that the appearance he had seen was some apparition, which haunted the castle on account of some deed of blood —some unjustifiable death having taken place within its walls, was by no means satisfactory to his mind.

"Nothing of the kind," he reasoned with himself, "could have taken place, for I have been here now many years, and never such a thing as a light was seen in the Grey Turret, or an apparition reported to be in the castle. Besides," he said, "as he thought the matter over in every possible light, no one has been to the castle who has not left it as hearty as he came. In fact, the death of the Lady Alicia was the only death that has taken place within the walls for many years, for Sir Rupert's brother was killed in the battle field."

Then Wingrove began to try to recollect exactly what Agatha Weare had said about the Lady Alicia, which had left a disagreeable impression upon his mind, he knew not why.

"What was it?" he said to himself. "Gracious Heaven, was it a hint of any foul play, with regard to the death of the Lady Alicia? It must have been that she meant. Can there be any grounds for such a supposition? The very thought is distressing. I must speak to Mistress Agatha Weare again upon this subject."

How soon does a hinted suspicion fix upon the mind and grow into a monstrous evil to the excited imagination.

The few hinted words of Agatha Weare, had, as she intended they should, made a strong impression upon the mind of Hugh Wingrove, excited and prepared as it was to receive any new and extraordinary impression by the sight he had witnessed on the steps leading to the Grey Turret the preceding eventful evening.

After an hour or more spent in reflection, he made a resolution, that now in broad daylight he would go to the Grey Turret, and personally examine the door, to see if the fastenings had been tampered with, or if it still remained close locked and nailed up according to tradition.

More for the sake of having a witness to any discovery that he should make than from any dread to go alone, Wingrove summoned Bernard, and proposed the expedition to him.

Bernard did not seem at all pleased at the prospect of again risking an encounter with any of the horrors connected with the mysterious Grey Turret, and he looked rather ruefully at Wingrove, when the proposition was made to him to go.

"It's broad and sunny daylight, now," urged Wingrove ; "and I would rather take you than another because you are already acquainted with the whole of the circumstances, which under such an examination is almost absolutely necessary."

"Why, Master Wingrove," said Bernard, "of course I'll go ——"

"I knew you would," answered Wingrove. "When were you ever found lagging even when danger was at its hottest ?"

"I don't mind danger," said Bernard, "and to tell the truth I rather like a fight than otherwise, but ——"

"But what, Bernard ?".

"Why, in a manner of speaking, you see, Master Wingrove, I—I—"

"You what ?" said Wingrove, impatiently.

"Why, I really shouldn't like to meet that odd-looking fellow again that we saw last night on the turret stairs, and that's the honest truth, Master Hugh Wingrove."

"Nor to tell the honest truth," replied Wingrove, "should I. But what I want to make sure about is, that we are not taken in."

"Taken in ?"

"Aye—that we are not the victims of some trick, some delusion in which that confounded Monk Morgatani ——"

"And Agatha Weare," put in Bernard.

"Aye, and Agatha Weare have got up between them."

"Well, curse me if I should like to be imposed upon in that way," said Bernard. "I'd rather it was a real ghost a hundred times."

"That's what I want to find out," said Wingrove.

"Then I'm your man," cried Bernard, "and all I've got to say is, it had better not turn out to be a sham ghost, that's all."

"Well, it strikes me," said Hugh Wingrove, "that we are quite clear upon one point."

"And what's that ?"

"Why, that the appearance, whatever it was, came out of the turret chamber, and was not upon the staircase when we arrived there."

"Oh, there's no doubt about that," answered Bernard.

"Well then, if what we saw was supernatural, it could have came out perhaps without moving the fastenings, and at all events, be that as it may, we know if it were human like ourselves it could not."

"That's very true," said Bernard. "You've got a head, Master Wingrove."

"Thank you," said Wingrove. "I always considered I had. Will you accompany me now ?"

"You don't think of going into the turret ?"

"No—by no means, unless ——"

"Unless what ?"

"Unless it's open. Then even you can have no objection. I'm told it was nailed and screwed up with great care."

"Well, well," said Bernard, "if it's open you know we are not the first that have been in, that's clear."

"Certainly not," said Wingrove, "and I promise you, I will not attempt to interfere with the fastenings if they be still there, which I strongly and conscientiously doubt."

"Besides, you know," said Bernard, "to do so would be against Sir Rupert's express order."

"I know it," answered Wingrove, "and without his word would not attempt it, so come on."

CHAPTER XIX.

" 'Tis only at the midnight hour that spirits
Can gibber to the sky, because the eye of
Heaven is then unopened, and they are
Stricken not by its pure light."

THE NOON-DAY ADVENTURE.—THE GREY TURRET DOOR.—A FEARFUL SIGHT.—
HORROR!—HORROR!

BEING daylight, Hugh Wingrove and Bernard found their way much quicker to the uninhabited wing of the castle, adjoining to which was the Grey Turret, that was the object of their surmises and their destination.

Carefully avoiding meeting any one, and walking with cautious footsteps until they were so far from the rooms which were in daily use, they rapidly passed on their way until they came to the small door which has been already mentioned, as leading into the court-yard, from whence the winding flight of stone stairs arose, that conducted to the door of the mysterious chamber.

" How different things look in daylight," said Bernard.

" They do indeed," said Wingrove. " Night adds many artificial terrors to a place."

" I don't seem now," said Bernard, " to care much about the Grey Turret. If I am to see ghosts, I should like always to see them at broad daylight."

" Aye, but they won't come then, Bernard. They don't like the morning air."

" Well, it's very wrong of them," said Bernard, " they ought to know better than to come frightening a fellow at night."

" They might show better taste," said Wingrove. " I wonder if it was a ghost that pulled down this door that shut up the staircase from the court-yard, Bernard?"

" Ah! you may joke," said Bernard; " but I'll wager anything you like now, Master Wingrove, you will find that secret door as fast shut as it was in the days of Sir Montague Brandon."

" What makes you think so?"

" Because I'm sure it was a ghost we saw last night."

" Well," said Wingrove, placing his foot upon the first of the stone steps, that conducted to the Grey Turret, " we shall now see, but for my own part, I have every expectation of finding that the door is open, or that it has been opened recently."

" A quart of canary on it," cried Bernard.

" Agreed," said Wingrove, " and should you win I shall not grudge the price, for you have had some extra duty."

" Come on, then, cried Bernard.

They quickly ascended the stone staircase: sufficient light streamed in upon the stone steps from various loop-holes, as well as from the door-way below, to render them quite light, and in a few moments Wingrove and his companion stood upon the landing-place, exactly opposite the actual door of the mysterious turret chamber.

The recollection of the preceding night's adventure induced a degree of nervous excitement in Wingrove's breast as he again stood upon the precise spot which had presented to him so inexplicable an appearance.

For several moments they both paused as if struck by the same feeling, when they arrived at the top of the stairs, and they simultaneously cast a hurried and anxious glance around them as they expected to see some indica-

tions of what had been there on the night before, when they kept their dreadful watch.

All was, however, profoundly still, and nothing met their gaze but the cold grey walls, and immediately opposite to them was the door—an examination of which was, in some measure, to realise their doubts upon the natural or supernatural origin of the apparition which had crossed them so strangely.

The door seemed to be of great strength. It was panelled into four distinct compartments, each of which were sunk deep in the solid mass of the wood work, and adorned with rich gothic mouldings, standing out in bold relief.

A broad streak of light fell full upon it, and there was in consequence every facility for a full and ample examination of the entrance to the long deserted chamber.

"Now, Bernard," said Wingrove, drawing a long breath. "We are here with plenty of light and leisure. Let our examination be complete."

"The place is as still as the grave;" said Bernard, in a low voice. "That door don't look as if it had been moved for centuries."

They both advanced close to the ancient entrance, and Wingrove ran his eye carefully over the door.

"This door opens outwards," said Wingrove; "for see, Bernard, it is fastened by pieces of solid oak being laid across and screwed both to the door and these massive wooden side-pieces to which it is hung."

"And I'd swear," said Bernard, looking closely, "that not one of those screw heads have been touched for many a year."

"I believe so too;" said Wingrove, in a suppressed voice. "See, there are even spiders webs over the very opening of the door."

"There are," said Bernard, "and the lock is covered with cobwebs. See the black dust upon the handle."

No. 10

He touched the handle with his finger, as he spoke, and showed that the accumulated dust was as thick as moss.

"The door has not been opened," said Wingrove. "By Heavens, Bernard, I know not what to think."

"Why, I told you before you came," said Bernard. "I hope you are quite satisfied that I have won my canary!"

"Quite, quite," said Wingrove, anxiously. "I own I was unprepared for this. The door cannot have been opened for many years, I am perfectly convinced, Bernard."

"Of course not," answered Bernard. "Why, there are a couple of dozen large screws. It would take a good workman some time to get in here, Master Wingrove."

"Is it locked, I wonder?" said Wingrove.

"Locked? Of course it is."

"Shall we try the handle?"

"The devil!" cried Bernard. "By no means!"

"Now that we are here," said Wingrove, "it would be a pity not to ascertain the precise condition of the door."

"But—but," interposed Bernard, "who knows, if we try the handle, what may happen?"

"There can be no harm," said Wingrove. "Stand aside, Bernard, and let me try it."

"Well, it's all your own doing, you know," cried Bernard, retreating down three of the stairs. "If anything pops out, I have nothing to do with —— I, Bernard, don't mean to try the lock, ahem!"

These last words were repeated in a higher tone, as a sort of warning to all ghosts and apparitions to hold him harmless in the matter of tampering with the lock of the door of the Grey Turret.

"Pho! pho!" cried Wingrove; "your fears are groundless. See, now, I have tried the handle, and find the door to be as I supposed, locked."

"Of course it's locked," said Bernard. "Now come away."

Wingrove still seemed loath to depart, and lingered by the door.

"The very key-hole," he said, "is blocked up with black dust and spiders' webs, Bernard."

"It's cold and uncomfortable here," replied Bernard. "Won't you come away now, Master Wingrove?"

"Presently, Bernard, presently. While we are here let us leave nothing undone, to assure us of the character of the appearance we saw last evening."

"Well, ain't you assured?" cried Bernard.

"Yes ; but don't you think we could clear the key-hole with the point of your poniard?"

"What?" cried Bernard, precipitately rushing down three more of the stone steps. "The key-hole did you say?"

"Yes," answered Wingrove. "We might, you know, even get a peep into the turret."

"A peep at the devil!" cried Bernard. "Are you mad, Master Wingrove?"

"Well, Bernard," said Wingrove, "I do not enforce your presence. You can go, you know."

"I—I don't say I want to go," growled Bernard.

"Well, then, hand me your poniard, and let me try if I can get a peep into the much-talked-of turret chamber."

Bernard sullenly complied, and Wingrove with the point of the dagger cleared the cobwebs and dust from the key-hole.

"Come, now, Bernard," he said, "will you have the first look?"

"I ?" cried Bernard. " You won't catch me putting my eye to the key-hole of this door, I can tell you."

" Well, I have no fears," said Wingrove.

He stooped as he spoke, and placed his eye to the key-hole, but in an instant he started back, exclaiming :—

" God of Heaven !"

Bernard heard the exclamation, and in one moment cleared the steps, and rushed into the court-yard.

" I told him so," he cried. " Now it's coming again, no doubt."

In a moment or two Wingrove came down the stairs looking pale and alarmed.

" That place is full of horror and mystery, Bernard," he said. " Let us leave this spot. I will come here no more."

" It serves you right," grumbled Bernard. " You would look, you know But what did you see, Wingrove ?"

" Come away," said Wingrove ; " I will tell you presently."

They hurried from the spot, and rapidly traversing the various apartments they had of necessity to pass through, they at length arrived at the little guard-room.

" Well, now," cried Bernard, "I am dying with curiosity, Master Wingrove. What did you see ?"

" I am more puzzled and bewildered than ever," said Wingrove.

" You saw the dead man ?"

" No."

" The ghost ?"

" I don't know."

" But you saw into the turret ?"

" No."

" Then what the devil did you see ?"

" An eye !"

" A what ?"

" The moment I placed my eye to the key-hole, it was confronted on the inner side by a glaring horrible-looking eye !"

Bernard opened his mouth aghast.

" You may well look surprised," continued Wingrove. " I was so startled and astonished myself, that it was only by a powerful effort I could withdraw my eye from the key-hole, so horrible and fascinating was the glare that met me."

" Well," cried Bernard, drawing a long breath ; " I never in my life heard anything equal to that."

" I am now done with the Grey Turret," said Wingrove. " I will go there no more."

" Then you did not see into the chamber at all ?"

" No ; the eye was within a quarter of an inch of the other side of the key-hole, and I could see nothing but it glaring upon me."

" You may depend," cried Bernard, " it had been looking at us all the time we were there."

" No doubt," said Wingrove.

" If I had known that !" cried Bernard, with a shudder, and holding up his hands. " Master Wingrove, you won't catch me there again, I can tell you."

" Nor will I tempt my fate any more," said Wingrove. " I would that Sir Rupert were here. Till he returns this inexplicable matter must now rest."

" And now for the canary !" said Bernard, smacking his lips in anticipation ; " for I declare you have made me quite thirsty with your description of that horrible eye."

CHAPTER XX.

" They met at the silent midnight hour,
  The moon was sailing high ;
There was scarce a breath of balmy air,
  To stir the chequered sky."

THE MONK AND AGATHA.—THE DREAM OF A DISTURBED CONSCIENCE.—THE
CONSULTATION.—WICKEDNESS ITS OWN PUNISHMENT.

THAT night, as the castle clock of Brandon struck twelve, Agatha Weare
stole from her own apartment in the western wing of the edifice, and after
glancing cautiously around her, and listening attentively for some anxious
moments, she, with a taper in her hand, which shed a faint and sickly lustre
on her path, betook herself towards a long gallery in the castle, from whence
many chambers opened.

Her face was ghastly pale, and her whole aspect and demeanour betrayed
an agitation of mind strangely at variance with her usual manner—so cold, and
firm, and sneering.

In her hand she carried a massive key, which opened most of the doors in the
castle, and was, in fact, a master key, which Sir Rupert had had made for
himself some months before the death of his much-loved, and bitterly-regretted
Alicia.

After proceeding some distance along the gallery, she, with trembling
hands, unlocked a door that conducted her into a suite of apartments long
disused by the small family that for the last fifty years had occupied the old
baronial residence. These antiquated and time-worn chambers were, however, far from being new to Agatha now, and she walked through them without
hesitation, or wasting one glance upon the faded grandeur and remains of
former richness and beauty they at every step exhibited.

It was at the fourth one of these chambers that she paused, and, drawing
aside a magnificent piece of arras, which time and the moths were rapidly destroying, she pressed upon a small brass nob in the wall, when immediately a door, turning upon a centre, was discovered, and presenting beyond
it a narrow, dark, winding passage. After a moment's hesitation she entered
the passage, and, closing the door behind her, she pursued her way, with a
strange mingled expression upon her countenance, of doubt and resolution.

The flooring of the secret passage rapidly ascended—and, by the time
Agatha had reached its extremity, she was many feet above the level of the
gallery, from whence it had taken its rise.

Another door now presented itself, which, although artfully concealed from
observation on its outer side, was rough and unhewn on the side next to the
passage, and presented clearly the spring by which it might be easily opened.

Agatha was evidently quite familiar with the place in which she now was,
and pressing the spring she stepped from the secret passage on to a staircase to
which the door immediately opened. Some winding steps brought her to a
door, through the half opening of which the cold air came with a moaning
sound. Agatha passed through the door-way, and allowing the wind to catch
her long hair, she stood upon the battlements of Brandon Castle.

She had taken the precaution to place her taper on the staircase, so that it
was protected from the wind which always blew freely on the ramparts, they
being at a considerable elevation from the general level of the surrounding
country.

Agatha looked scrutinisingly about her, and then being satisfied she was
alone, she sat down on a rude stone bench, and with a shudder she muttered,

"Dreams! What are they? Why am I thus tormented by fearful visions? I cannot sleep, my couch is like a bed of fire on which I lie in torture. Oh, that dream—that awful dream! Can I—dare I ever sleep again with the terrible chance of such another vision sweeping across my terror-stricken soul, and nearly driving me to madness?"

"Agatha!" said a deep-toned voice near her. She started from the stone-seat, and casting her eyes in the direction of the sound she saw the tall figure of Morgatani standing clearly defined against the sky.

"Morgatani," she replied.

"Aye, you are early at our place of meeting."

"I am, but ——"

"But what? Do *you* tremble? You who have in a woman's frame the heart and soul of a brave man!"

"'Tis but a passing weakness, Morgatani. I have had a dream."

The monk started slightly as he replied,—

"A dream? Why, so have I—and yet my blood flows calmly through my veins—my tongue falters not, and my brain thinks as actively as before the vision."

"But my dream, Morgatani, was full of horror. A dream to blanch the cheek, to take the reason prisoner while wild imagination should assume the throne."

There was a scarcely perceptible sneer in the monk's tone as he said,—

"And has this dream brought you half an hour earlier than the hour of appointment here?"

"It has. The air within my chamber was oppressive, and I sought this spot to cool my fevered brow."

"Think you he will come?"

"Eldred?"

"Aye!"

"He dare not break his faith with me, much less with you, Morgatani. He will surely come, but he will shrink from what you wish him to do."

"And yet he must find a man to do it, or we shall incur much danger. There is now so much prying on the parts of these vassals about the castle, that a body will be found at some disagreeable moment in the Eastern Turret."

"The dead body of Beatrice?"

"The same. You recollect when she returned from performing us a service as rare as it was useful, she died."

"She did die, Morgatani."

"Eldred Weare struck the blow," said the monk, in a tone of triumph, "and he must dispose of his own handy work. The finding of that body would be enough to bring a hornet's nest about your ears, and would last the knaves in the castle for ever as a prolific source of conjecture, surmise, and never-ending suspicion."

"It would."

"Then, Eldred, as I may not be seen, must remove the body to some place of more ample security."

"Would it be likely to be discovered," said Agatha, "where it is?"

"It would. Dogs scent carrion a long way. The body or rather the remains of it, lend no agreeable perfume to the turret."

"Hush! hush! 'tis the step of Eldred. He comes."

The timid, shrinking Eldred, now, with a sidelong shuffling gait, approached his sister and the monk.

"I—I believe I'm in time," he muttered. "Hark! there goes the half hour. It was to be half-past, you know."

"It was," said the monk. "Listen to me, Eldred Weare. You committed a murder some time since."

"I—I—I. Oh, dear."

"You did," hissed the monk. "You recollect the eastern turret?"

Eldred trembled and faltered out,

"You, you know you made me mix the—the arsenic."

"But you did mix."

"Oh, I ; that is, yes."

"And you gave it to your victim."

"My victim. Well, I—like that. It's very good, indeed. You know, you said —"

"Peace, driveller, peace. Receive your instructions from me, or I leave you to your fate. You must find some means of removing the dead body which lies in the eastern turret. Should it be found it will give rise to too much useless conjecture, and probably be the means of urging on an inquiry that might terminate in your death at the hands of the common hangman."

"My—death—you surely don't mean to say there's the—the remotest chance? Bless me, I'm all in a perspiration."

"You must remove that body, or some day Brandon may tumble about your ears, while she who now sleeps the sleep of death in the vault of the Brandons, may drag you shrinking through the crumbling mass, and while —"

"Hold, hold," said Agatha; "tell me, in mercy, did you dream that?"

"I did."

"Then, then it was the same dark vision that disturbed my slumbers. I dreamt that Brandon was crumbling to decay, that stone by stone it was falling, while hideous noises, more terrible than thunder, accompanied the loosing of the deep foundations. Then through the ruins stalked one, who I will not name; and she was dragging him, Eldred, with her. He shrieked for mercy, but the long bony fingers of the corpse were clasped around his heart, and—and—I knew that my time would come. I—I— Morgatani, Morgatani, save me!"

She clutched convulsively the robe of the monk, and pointed along the battlements, while her lips moved, but it seemed as if terror had deprived her of the power of utterance, for no sound came.

Gliding slowly along the battlements was a dim spectral figure. It approached the extreme verge and then melted away into the air or down the deep abyss.

The monk spoke not nor moved, but he kept his eyes fixed upon the figure until it disappeared from his sight. Then, as if some spell had been taken off his faculties, he rushed forward, but Agatha clung to him, crying,

"For mercy's sake, do not go. Morgatani, do not leave me now."

He paused, and in a deep sepulchral voice said,

"It is gone. Could it have been real, or some exhalation of the night?"

Eldred, when he saw the figure, had got as far back as the stone bench would permit him, and had slid down to the ground where he now sat with his mouth and eyes wide open, looking the very picture of fright.

CHAPTER XXI.

——— Can such things be,
And overcome us like a summer's cloud
Without exciting our especial wonder?—SHAKSPERE.

THE SECOND PLOT FOR THE DESTRUCTION OF SIR RUPERT.—A GUILTY CONSCIENCE.

FOR some few minutes neither of the three persons so associated to-gether by the terrible links of a chain of crime which they could not snap asunder, spoke, and then the monk, recovering from the effect which the strange appearance had had even upon his haughty mind, turned to Eldred and said firmly,—

"Were all hell to be let loose you must do my bidding. We may have a harder struggle for Brandon yet than we conjecture, and there must be nothing to provoke other inquiry than that we choose to set on foot. The body I have mentioned must be removed."

"I—I'm sure it was a ghost," said Eldred. "If I'd been by myself I should have been half dead with fright."

"Listen to me," cried the monk, "and do not occupy valuable time by prating of your silly fears."

"Silly fears? Why, you saw it as well as I did. Silly fears, indeed!"

"Peace! You must take that corpse and place it where I shall direct you."

"W—w—where?"

"You know the small chamber which was usually occupied by Sir Rupert?"

"Yes, yes; he locked it up when he went away, and threw the key in the moat."

"That chamber contains various mementos of her who is dead."

"Alicia?"

"Yes. Sir Rupert does not wish it opened by any one but himself, and those hinds who have made themselves so troublesome to us will on that account abstain from making any attempt to enter it. I, however, have a key."

"Have you really?"

"I have."

"And have you been in? What is there in the room? Really I like curious things."

"You shall go in."

"I wonder now if Alicia's diamonds are there."

"They are. At least I have taken care of them myself."

"Oh!"

"In that room you shall place the mouldering remains of Beatrice, the handmaiden of the late Alicia."

"It always puzzled me," said Eldred, "why you killed her."

"I kill her? You took her life yourself, because you remarked, and certainly with truth, that common people were always better out of the way after being useful in some affair of magnitude."

Eldred stared at Morgatani as he said this, with eyes of wonder and amazement.

"Well," he said, "if I couldn't have sworn it was you that said those words and not me."

"Beware!" said the monk.

"Oh, no offence. Only—I—thought—"

"Beware!" again said Morgatani, and Eldred shrunk back without daring further to contend the matter.

"You will gather together the remains of the body," continued the monk, "and place them in Sir Rupert's room. There is a cabinet there, into which you can thrust your victim."

"My victim? There you go again. What do you call her my victim for?"

"She was the victim of your deep policy, Eldred Weare."

"Oh, my deep policy—was she?"

"Yes; one of the steps as it were by which you were to climb to the summit of your high ambition."

"Ah, yes—I dare say—oh, yes—I am ambitious, I like to order people about and say do this and do that, and do the other thing, and make 'em do it. Then what a delightful thing lots of money is. You can chess as bravely as you like—keep out of all danger, and make much of yourself."

" All that by following my counsels you will be able to do. Come now. To your work."

" What ? to-night?"

" Yes—this hour. A more favourable opportunity you would look for in vain. To the eastern turret. Come."

Eldred trembled in every limb, and his sister cast a glance of scorn and indignation at him, for she had recovered from her nervousness at the sight of the apparition.

" Follow us," she said. " Lag back at your peril, coward."

" Ah, it's all very well," muttered Eldred, " but they give me all the disagreeable jobs to do always. Upon my word I don't like it—messing about among dead people."

" Quick," cried Agatha, looking around, and her voice had much the same effect upon her cowardly brother, as a whip upon a jaded horse, for he started forward a step or two, and then crept on as before, muttering to himself.

" Morgatani," whispered Agatha, as she walked by his side, " what think you of the figure we saw upon the battlements ?"

" It was but a misty exhalation from the moat, or a passing cloud," replied the monk, " but I defy it, be it what it may. Are you well acquainted with Sir Rupert's writing ?"

" His peculiar character mean you ?"

" Yes."

" I have seen many of his letters to my sister."

The monk by some chemical means procured a light, and holding an open letter before Agatha, he said,

" Whose writing is that ?"

" Sir Rupert's."

" No, 'tis mine. I am glad the imitation is so successful."

" What is the purport of that letter?"

" Simply this, that if all other evidence should fail, it forms a damning link in the chain of evidence against Sir Rupert, for the murder of his wife."

" But this woman—this Beatrice acted with us."

" She did—and so came by her death when we wanted her no more. Her body must be found in Sir Rupert's private room—the room he has so carefully locked up—and among the festering remains the letter will be found, purporting to be from him to her, urging her to assist him in the murder."

" I understand."

" It will appear then that she refusing, or having become dangerous, after-wards met her death from him. Hence, will he have a double murder to answer for, and each corroborating the other."

" That cannot fail."

" No. It cannot. Lord of Brandon, I have you in a snare from which you never can—never shall escape. You will learn my power which you braved once, and with the experience you shall ascend the scaffold. Re-venge ! revenge !—I will have revenge."

The monk shook his clenched hand in the air as he spoke, and even Agatha shrunk from the violence of his passion.

They had now traversed nearly the whole of one side of the castle along the battlements, and the monk paused at the bottom of a small flight of stairs leading to the eastern turret.

In a few moments Eldred reached the same spot, and Morgatani, turning to him said,

"Ascend.   You will find her whom you seek lying in an old chest at one corner of the small chamber at the top of these steps."

"But—you—you don't mean to say that I can lug down a chest with a dead thingummy in it?" stammered Eldred.

The monk stamped impatiently as he said, "Is not your strength sufficient for so small an object?"

"I should think not."

"I will go with you and help you."

Morgatani pushed Eldred before him, and the two ascended the narrow staircase.

The door of the turret readily opened to a key which the monk produced, and they entered a small octangular chamber, in which was a most horrible and noisome odour.

The monk then lit a taper, and holding it high above his head, he said,

"Yonder is the chest, and in it is the body of Beatrice."

"It seems very heavy," said Eldred, his teeth chattering with fear.

"Pshaw!" cried Morgatani.   "Do you hold the light, and I will carry it down the staircase for you.   You must then carry it yourself, because, should you meet any one on your route to the room in which it is to be left, no questions can be asked of you, while I would be open to all kinds of suspicion."

"Dear me." ejaculated Eldred ; "it's a shocking thing that I'm obliged to do all the dirty and disagreeable work."

The monk took him by the collar and shook him as if he had been an infant.

No. 11

" Do you dare," he said, " to dispute my commands? Coward, one word of mine would hang you on a gibbet as high as Haman."

" Oh, oh—you're a choking me—oh—oh. I really—sister, do tell him not to be so violent. Oh, dear me. It's a thousand mercies I preserve my life among you."

" Once for all, Eldred Weare," said the monk, sternly, " listen to me. To accomplish the desires nearest to your heart, you have sought my assistance—I gave it on one condition—namely, implicit obedience."

" Yes, yes—oh, dear me. You know quite well I always do—do whatever you and Agatha say I must do, although between you I certainly might as well, in a manner of speaking, be —"

" Peace, peace," said the monk. " To our work—to our work."

" Well, if it must be, why then I suppose —"

" Another word and I will hurl you from the battlements. This prating may alarm some of the idle knaves who keep watch and ward, and consume the revenues of Brandon—revenues which ought and which shall be yours, Eldred Weare, if you do but trust in me."

" Of course I'll trust in you."

" 'Tis well, now for the chest."

As the monk spoke there was a heavy splash heard in the castle moat, and then followed a strange dashing sound of waters, after which all was still as if some one had been cast into the stagnant water and struggled for a brief moment for existence ere he sunk to rise no more.

Agatha involuntary grasped the arm of the monk, as she said,—

" What sounds are those, Morgatani?" and Eldred stood trembling with fear.

The monk stalked to the edge of the battlements, and strove in vain to pierce with his eye the dim obscurity between him and the moat ; but although he could see nothing, he could distinctly hear that the guard was disturbed, for the voice of a soldier rose in clear accents upon the night air, crying,—

" Who goes there ?"

No reply came to his challenge, and then he cried, " Guard—guard !" and a bustle at the portal speedily announced that his summons of the castle guard had been obeyed.

Morgatani rose from his crouching posture, and stamped violently upon the earthen flooring of the rampart, as he cried,—

" Ever thus—ever thus. These knaves, now that they have grown alarmed and suspicious, are ready upon the slightest noise of an unusual character to rush forth and place us all who are working for our own ends in great danger."

" Danger ?" echoed Eldred, " bless me, you don't think there's danger, do you ?"

The monk turned from him with a look of contempt, and addressing himself to Agatha, he said,—

" Some means must be discovered of either calming the fears of the dwellers within the castle, so that they may hear an idle noise without rushing forth with sword and buckler, or of increasing their fears to such an extent that they will be afraid so to do."

" I do not think," replied Agatha, " from what I have seen of the soldiers Sir Rupert has left behind him, they would easily be frightened."

" Doubtless not ; I would try the experiment though at some moment of revelry when they were in their cups, and least likely of all to adopt any sudden course of action. It may be possible to prey upon their superstitious fears sufficiently to make them not so ready in action and in search about the castle."

" Hugh Wingrove is your greatest enemy."

" He shall die."

" 'Twere well he were disposed of, for he is looked up to by the men-at-arms as an oracle of soldierly wisdom, and once deprive them of him as a leader, they will —"

A cry of terror from Eldred Weare, as he rushed to the side of Morgatani, and laid hold of his sleeve, abruptly terminated the conference, and upon the monk and Agatha hastily glancing around them, they saw, at some distance from where they stood, a tall dark figure standing between them and the sky, upon the very extreme verge of the parapet.

CHAPTER XXII.

THE MONK AND THE APPARITION ON THE PARAPET.—THE MIDNIGHT PATROLE.—AN ALARM.

THE iron nerves of the monk seemed for a moment shaken, as he saw the strange supernatural-looking figure between him and the sky, and he hesitated just long enough to destroy all possibility of discovering who and what the appearance was, for before he could recover from his astonishment, the mysterious apparition sprung from the giddy height on to the rampart, and disappeared in the gloom and long shadows cast by the turrets.

" What can that be ?" exclaimed Agatha.

" Nay, I know not," replied the monk, in a voice of doubt and hesitation. " If this castle be haunted by evil spirits, I care not. They shall not turn me from my purpose. The darkest fiend in hell shall not stay me in what I have undertaken. I have sworn the destruction of the Lord of Brandon, and I will keep my oath."

" You—you think then it was a ghost ?" stammered Eldred.

" I care not—angel or devil, 'tis the same to me. I defy them both, and take the even tenor of my way. To our work once more. Ah ! who comes here ?"

A solitary figure with a strange bounding step came from the further end of the rampart, and stood looking into the moat. Then it stretched forth its hands, and raised a wild unearthly cry, and with a bound retired again from whence it came.

" Follow me," said Morgatani, as he drew a short two-edged sword from beneath his friar's gown. " This must be seen to."

As he spoke, he hurried from the turret on to the parapet, followed closely by Agatha, to whose dress Eldred clung in great fear, not that he wished to follow the monk, but that he feared to be left alone.

Morgatani in a moment crossed the spot on which the figure had stood, and darted in the direction it had taken, but he found himself only at the base of another of the turrets that flanked the battlements, and the low door which led to its chambers was so securely fastened by bolts on the outer side, that there was no remote possibility of the figure having escaped that way, unless it had had an accomplice to bolt the turret door.

The monk paused irresolute for a moment, and then he muttered to himself,

" It matters not—it matters not. Let them do their utmost, be they mortal or immortal beings, that prowl about this ancient pile. They shall find a Jesuit their equal in craft, and more than their equal in unscrupulousness."

"Hide, hide!" cried Agatha. "The guard is coming this way. The troublesome Wingrove is leading a search through the castle."

The monk turned sharply, and listened to the heavy tramp of the small party of men-at-arms, who were led by Wingrove in the nightly patrole round the battlements.

"Curses on the meddling fool!" he muttered. "Some means must be adopted of ridding us of him. Adieu, we shall meet soon again."

So saying, Morgatani walked stealthily along the rampart, until he came to a part which overlooked a lower fortification. A flight of steps for the purpose of descending from the upper to the lower rampart, was a short distance in advance, but he jumped from where he stood, although the height was very considerable, and when he alighted, he walked forward for a few paces, to what appeared to be a dead wall, with a massive iron ring fixed in one of the stones. This ring he laid hold of, and pushed towards the wall, when the stone turned upon a centre, leaving an open space of about three feet square. Through this the monk crawled, and closed the stone from the inner side, when all appeared as undisturbed as before.

Meanwhile the castle-guard with Wingrove at their head, had come up to the spot on which stood Agatha and Eldred Weare. Agatha stepped forward, and in a sneering voice said,

"Methinks in time of peace, this foolish patrole around the ramparts may be dispensed with."

"We have dispensed with it," replied Wingrove, "but there has been an alarm to-night. Some one crossed the moat I am certain, but whether to or from the castle, I cannot say."

"Pshaw—it must be your own fancy that peoples this castle with spectres, and makes every incidental noise an alarm."

"I'm sure it ain't my fancy," grumbled Bernard, "for I ain't fanciful— never was—never shall be, and I'll wager my head to a flagon of ale, some one jumped into the moat."

"Peace," cried Agatha. "Your head and a flagon of ale are too often in juxtaposition."

"Hilloa!" whispered Anstey, "she had you there, Bernard."

"Too often did she say? I'm sure she's wrong there. Why, I haven't had but five."

"Dismiss the guard," cried Agatha imperiously. "Let us have no more of this idle parading up and down the battlements by night."

"We have completed our rounds," said Wingrove, in a surly tone; "Sir Rupert likes military usages kept up."

"What!" cried Agatha. "Durst parley words with me! Eldred, you are a man, and stand by to see me insulted."

"Ye—ye—yes," stammered Eldred; "how dare you? Eh! I've half a mind really to—to—give you quite a push."

Bernard burst into a horse laugh at this speech of Eldred's; and Agatha, foaming with rage, turned so sharply upon her brother that he nearly fell down with fright.

"Coward, dastard, wretch!" she said in a suppressed voice. "Follow me at once, and remain not to earn the contempt of every paltry man-at-arms."

"Oh, I can tell them they had better not treat me with contempt," said Eldred, trying to muster up some courage. "I've a good mind to knock some one down."

Bernard was so tickled at Eldred's mock valour, that to prevent himself from laughing aloud, he turned round, and stamped so violently upon the ground, and made his face so red, that one of his comrades thought it necessary to pat his back, which he accomplished by giving him such a swinging blow with his halbert, that a weaker man than Bernard must have been felled to the ground.

Without saying another word, Agatha abruptly left the spot, followed by her brother, who considered in his own mind that he had acted with very great courage indeed.

When they had reached the commencement of the suite of rooms which were occupied as chambers, Agatha turned to Eldred, and with a bitterness of voice and manner that quite alarmed him, she said,

"Fool, idiot! Cannot you even here, where none dare raise a hand against you, assume a courageous air and manner, although your craven heart may be a stranger to the feeling? Dastard! you are a disgrace to your race. I hate you!"

"Bless me," said Eldred, "how violent you are all of a sudden. Haven't I done all sorts of disagreeable things, and now you want me to set about fighting a parcel of lazy men-at-arms, who have nothing in the world to do but eat and drink, and give hard knocks upon people's heads. The very idea gives me quite a pain, I declare."

"Idea," sneered Agatha. "You never had one."

She then passed through a doorway, and when Eldred would have followed her she slammed it in his face with a vehemence that startled every nerve in his composition.

When Agatha reached her chamber she stood for some few minutes as still as a marble statue. Then she threw herself into a chair, and a deep groan burst from her labouring heart. She started at the echo of the mournful sound, and could scarcely believe that it proceeded from her own overburthened conscience.

"What feeling is this," she whispered, "that comes over me occasionally now when I am alone—an awful feeling of horror and fear. The very air seems peopled with strange unearthly shapes that gibe and mock at me, and sometimes a voice appears to whisper in my ear, 'Agatha Weare, Agatha Weare! what have you gained by the awful crimes you have committed?' No, no, I have committed none—only instigated them, and—and consented to their commission. But does Heaven draw such nice distinctions? Why do I tremble—why does my heart beat within my bosom like a bird striving to burst its prison-house?"

She rose from her chair, and walked hurriedly to and fro in her room, while a host of mournful feelings like a legion of fiends kept gnawing at her heart.

"Agatha, Agatha!" she cried, "shake off these terrors of the imagination. Be yourself again. Where is now the spirit that never quailed before aught human? What have I gained?—What have I gained?—only a prospect of revenge. Such deep revenge as a woman pants for against the man she has loved once, and then taught herself to hate. Yes. If there be one feeling which in its wild intensity exceeds the love of woman it is her hate. Beware, Sir Rupert Brandon, you have made a foe who will cling to you until her death. Yes, till death, and when I have had my revenge, I shall be happy—happy! Yes, yes, I must then be happy.— Who says no?"

Her over excited fancy had made her convert the suggestions of her own mind into a voice addressing her, and she sunk trembling into a seat as she whispered,

"I—am sure I heard a voice say no. These chambers are very desolate. I cannot sleep, and 'tis better I should not now, for dreams might come with what would else be a blessed repose for the o'erwrought mind, converting the deep slumber which should recruit nature into a period of horror and mental exhaustion. No, I cannot sleep; the very air here feels suffocating to me. What sound is that?"

The solemn tones of a bell reached her ear amid the stillness of the night.

"The monks of the neighbouring monastery are going to their prayers," she muttered. "I never pray, and yet there was a time when I used to bend the knee to Heaven and lift up my voice to—but I must not think of such things now. I have staked my soul upon a cast and I must stand the hazard of the dye. Oh, Heavens! if I could but even now recal from the grave—no, no, that way lies madness. Let me be calm. Agatha, Agatha, where—where now is your vaunted spirit, where your ambition, where your master spirit? Revenge! revenge!"

With her arms stretched across the table at which she sat she remained for some minutes silent; then in a mournful voice she said,—

"Hours must yet elapse ere daybreak. What shall I do to take me from myself? What shall I do to drive my thoughts into another channel? No sleep—no sleep. I dare not sleep to-night. I will read—yes, reading. The page may charm, by its fiction, the pangs of reality. I will read."

She took from among the few books that were in her chamber, a volume containing some of the choicest of the chivalrous romances of the period, and read as follows :—

"The clock of the Castle of Wernsberg had tolled the hour of midnight, when the form of the *petite* Laura might be seen issuing with a lamp in her hand from the door of her chamber. Cautiously she looked around, and with hurried and agitated steps paced the gloomy passages of the dismal place.

"On a sudden her steps were arrested by the creaking of a distant door, and fearful of being seen, she secreted the lamp beneath her mantle until the individual who had startled her should have passed away. It was her father retiring from his study to his chamber, and Laura, with emotion, beheld his pale and care-worn features.

"For a moment she hesitated whether she should not return to her chamber; on the morrow to again fulfil the domestic duties which devolved upon her, and with filial tenderness attend to the wants of her aged father; but love, all-powerful love, impelled her forward. She felt assured her beloved Henri would tarry for her, and she could not forego the interview; besides, to be for ever shut within the gloomy walls of Wernsberg Castle chilled her youthful heart; she, therefore, listened to its voice, and when her parent had closed his door again she proceeded forward.

"When she reached the hall the wind blew in gusts from the various passages, causing her to shiver and draw her mantle round her; and as she placed her hand upon the massive key of the door, she again stopped to consider the step she was about to take.

"She had not undertaken the thing rashly; she had well considered all the most material points, and the result was, that poverty with the man she loved was preferable to being secluded in a gloomy abode, although surrounded by pomp and riches.

"As yet she was perfectly unacquainted with the pursuits of Henri. She knew him by name only. He might be surrounded by poverty, although his appearance betokened rank; but even were he poor, her soul was too noble to despise him for it, as long as he continued the same generous being she had known him.

"But her father, would not his soul be tortured when he discovered she had left her home? How could she bring his grey hairs with sorrow to the grave? Would not her conscience-stricken mind at some future day repent the fatal step she was now about to take? But all might yet be well. Henri might be possessed of wealth and honours, and she doubted not that his forgiveness might be obtained.

"Then she reflected on the noble bearing of her lover, his manly form embodied all that she had ever pictured to her imagination of masculine perfection ; his noble and lofty brow, which seemed the abode of refined and elevated thought, appeared to shadow forth the happiness she should enjoy as his future wife ; his dark intellectual eye, which seemed to comprehend all subjects at a glance, filled her with delight, and when it beamed on her, how could she resist the feeling of love it conveyed? and when that feeling was expressed by the deep impassioned tones of his voice, so full of pathos, what maiden would not feel the power ?

"While her hand yet lingered on the lock, a single note breathed from a flute announced the impatience of her lover. Her reverie for the time was dispelled, and she opened the creaking door. The wind immediately put out her lamp, and blew her tresses in wild disorder. She then closed the door, drew her hood over her head, her mantle more closely round her, and descended the precipitous pathway that led to the river, which ran round three-fourths of the rocks upon which her father's castle was situated.

"The night was clear and cold, the wind blew keenly over the rocky eminence, and the moon gleamed with a piercing and frosty brightness, casting the reverse of every object into a deep and pitchy gloom, of which Laura availed herself as she hastened forward.

"Once, and only once, did she venture to look back upon her childhood's home, and as a straggling ray from the lamp of some retiring domestic shone through the casement she felt half tempted to retrace her steps.

While the thought was yet passing through her mind, Henri started from beneath the deep shadow of a rock that overhung the pathway, and once more clasped her to his breast. She trembled from head to foot, an involuntary scream was about to escape her lips, till perceiving she was enfolded in her lover's arms her fears relaxed.

"'Hush—hush! my life,' said he ; 'for Heaven's sake do not utter a single sound ; there are those near that seek my life.'

"At this Laura clung tremblingly to the arm of her lover as they hurried forward.

"'Quick,' said he again ; 'keep close : do you not hear a sound ?'

"'Laura listened attentively and discovered the sound of footsteps among the rocks. 'What means this caution ?' whispered Laura.

"'This way,' replied Henry hastily, and immediately drew her into the deepest recess he could find at hand, and directly after two men with carbines were seen approaching.

"'They say he woos old Wernsberg's daughter,' said one, as they approached.

"'There's little doubt of the matter,' replied the other ; 'the boat at the bottom of the path tells he is somewhere hereabout.'

"'Certainly,' returned his companion.

"'And if I could only get my piece within range of him, I'd ——'

"'There, what's that ?' interrupted the other.

"'Yonder goat.'

"'Just push your carbine into the shadow there, will you.'

"'Nonsense ; you don't think he'd be such a fool as to remain just under our very noses.'

"'I don't know that.'

"'Well, then, to satisfy you,' replied his companions, 'I'll do it : there then,' as he said this he thrust the bayonet into the very spot where Henri and Laura were concealed ; but by good fortune it passed between the arm and body of the former and touched the rock behind them.

" Laura nearly fainted with alarm ; and as soon as those in quest of him had gone further up the ascent Henri took the agitated girl beneath his arm, and covered by the shadow of the overhanging rocks regained the boat, near which was moored another belonging to his pursuers.

" With the greatest caution Henri placed Laura upon the cushioned seat of the fragile vessel ; he then removed the oars from the second boat into his own, and pushing from the shore was carried silently down the stream.

" After pursuing their course for some distance Henri pulled the boat beneath a rock, where the stream was widest, and lifting Laura from her seat placed her on shore, and they continued their way for some distance in total darkness ; at length they emerged from beneath the arch of a small ruin, and Laura perceived they were in a thickly shaded wood, as the brightness of the moon could scarcely penetrate the overhanging foliage.

" The agitation she had undergone and the command of silence imposed by her lover (who seemed less disposed to converse) had hitherto restrained her speech ; but now she breathed more freely, and in gentle accents, soft as a whispering breeze, she inquired, ' where go we, Henri ?'

" ' To where we can ever love without the fear of interruption.'

" ' And where is that ?' asked Laura.

" ' The name it imports little,' said her lover ; ' your affection is as dear to me in a cot as in a palace, and I trust mine to you is the same.'

" ' Yes, dear Henri,' she replied, ' the die is now cast ; and come weal or woe I'll share it with you.'

" ' Sweet love,' returned Henri ; ' but should the woe bear the predominance, have you courage to sustain it ?'

" ' Why do you ask me ?'

" ' To know the tenor of your mind, that ere it be too late and repentance smite your breast you may return.'

" ' I told you once, dear Henri, that I confided in you ; but wherefore do they seek your life : what have you done that you should be pursued ?'

" ' Why, sweet love, should I distress your mind by the narration of deeds that you might not approve of ?'

" ' Can it be possible that you have acted thus ?'

" ' I have, dear Laura ; long have I strayed from the path of honor and virtue, and it is only near you that I find peace or happiness.'

" ' For Heaven's sake, dear Henri, confide to me your cares and sorrows, and it shall be my constant pleasure to dispel them from your mind.'

" ' I would, dear Laura ; but the recital would fill your gentle breast with pain ; hitherto you have known me but as Henri, your adoring lover, and to dispel the illusion I am loth.'

" ' And are you not so still ?' asked Laura eagerly.

" ' Yes, dear Laura, I ever shall adore you, and to you will be the same ; but to others my name is ———'

" ' What ?' eagerly inquired Laura, as she pressed her lover by the arm.

" Henri was about to reply, but the notes of a horn arrested their attention, and in a few minutes a troop of horsemen drew near, and having dismounted led their horses down a steep ascent, the mouth of which was covered with a massive piece of rock, and seemed as if raised by some powerful machinery.

" On a sudden Henri stopped and taking Laura by the arm, to her surprise led her down the same declivity. At a loss to conjecture the intentions of her lover she clung still closer to his arm, while a whirl of strange imaginings ran through her mind.

" " After pursuing the descent for some time a red glare of light suddenly met her view, which was soon discovered to proceed from torches placed against the wall, while the coarse voices of the horsemen before struck her with the most dreadful astonishment.

" After proceeding through two or three low vaulted chambers strewed with merchandise he led her to one of a similar size, but better furnished : here were couches of the finest manufactures ; rich tapestries, but ill concealed the rough and rugged walls which were hewn out of the solid rock ; here and there were sconces of the most valuable metal in which were tapers of more than ordinary size, and appeared as if they had once done duty before the altar of some temple ; from the centre hung a massive silver lamp, while around were various articles of elegance, materials for drawing, music, books, &c.

" Laura gazed upon the scene before her with looks of deep astonishment ; her faculties were perfectly paralysed, so different was everything from what she had expected.

" ' This, my love,' said Henri, addressing her, ' is your own apartment ; nought here can interfere with the current of our happiness ! name but your wishes and they shall be instantly gratified !'

" ' Dear Henri !' returned Laura, ' surely there must be some mistake ; you do not mean to doom me to solitude in this chamber ?'

" ' No, my sweet girl, here I shall enjoy your blest society and revel in the delights of mutual love.'

" ' But I have some dread forebodings.'

" ' Then banish them from your mind.'

" ' Indeed I cannot.   Tell me ——'

" ' That you repent your choice ?'

" ' No, dear Henri, I dearly love you ; but I could be happy anywhere else but here.'

No. 12

" ' And why not here ? did you not agree to share my fortune good or bad ?'

" ' I did.'

" ' Then why repent your choice ?'

" ' A fearful undefined dread of horror rushes through my mind.'

" ' A mere phantom of the brain.'

" ' No, dear Henri, although you are dear to me, I can never abide in this dark and gloomy place, where the light of the sun never enters.'

" ' Habit, my dear girl, the force of habit ; because you have always been perched upon a rock in yonder old castle, you imagine no other place is fit to live in.'

" ' No, dear Henri, I do not imagine that.'

" ' Then why complain, my love ; have you not here all the elegancies and conveniencies of life ?'

" ' Yes, but ——'

" ' Let me entreat you to be happy and content ; do not make yourself unhappy without knowing why ; for the present I must leave you.'

" As Henri said this he left the place, and Laura, reclining upon a couch of purple and gold, gave way to a train of reflections no ways calculated to relieve her mind.

" ' Can he be connected with those fearful men I saw enter this cavern before me ?' said she mentally ; ' if so, what can be the nature of his employment ? Why should he dwell beneath the ground ? Why should the men I saw near my father's house seek his life ? There must be some deep and mysterious cause for this.'

" As this mental soliloquy passed across her mind, she shuddered with apprehension, and the oppression of the atmosphere caused her to fall into a restless slumber.

" She had not lain long before a horrid dream disturbed her ; she saw her lover standing near a low and miserable bed, upon which was an aged man, who entreated him to spare his life ; the pionard, yet reeking with human gore, was already about to be plunged into the aged victim's heart ; the arm was raised on high for the fatal blow ; it then descended, and—she uttered a faint scream and awoke trembling and exhausted.

" How long she had lain she know not ; the lamp from the ceiling cast a dull and flickering light ; not a sound met her ear ; all seemed as still as death.

" Thus situated she knew not how to act ; curiosity at length prevailed, and she determined to explore the place in which her fate had placed her.

" With a faltering step excited by her late dream, and by the uncertain light of the lamp, she reached the entrance of her apartment ; it led into a labyrinth of dark and subterraneous passages. She was uncertain which to take ; but when her eyes became accustomed to the gloom in the distance, she perceived the lurid red of one of the torches she had noticed at her entrance, reflected against an angle of the passage ; she, therefore, chose it to direct her course.

" After pursuing the winding of the passage for some distance, the sound of footsteps behind her made her hurry forward : the footsteps still drew near her, and fear taking possession of her mind, she insensibly stood still ; her pursuer was now within a few paces of her ; no time was to be lost ; and in the excess of her trepidation she fell against the side of the passage, and in another instant Henri passed her.

" She was about to pronounce his name, but prudence compressed her lips ; her fears for the instant were removed, and she resolved to follow him whatever might be the consequence ; any state was preferable to the loneliness of the cavern she had quitted.

" As she hurried after his retiring footsteps the sounds of mirth for the first time met her ear, and she heard her Henri (as he entered the vault from whence the voices came,) saluted with,—

" ' Hail, captain ! we are glad to see you safe returned.'

" ' Yes, thanks to the saints, I'm sound wind and limb,' returned the voice of Henri.

" At this moment Laura reached the entrance of the vault, and then saw her lover take possession of a seat at one end of a rude and coarse table, around which were seated men to match, while swords, pistols, daggers, drinking-cups, and bottles formed the chief furniture of the place.

" The cavern was well lighted from a large and massive candelabra, which from its make appeared to be of silver, although much corroded, and Laura stepped into the dark shadow of the entrance, that she might not be discovered by its light, and at the same time remark all that passed within.

" ' And now, captain,' said one of this goodly company, who appeared to have some command, ' I suppose you never intend to roam again in search of bright eyes and pretty ankles ?'

" ' Not at least for some time, until the air of this infernal den tarnishes the colour of her skin.'

" ' Of course not,' returned the lieutenant.

" ' You know, Leonardo, that beauty is only skin deep, and will not last for ever.'

" ' Just so ; it's worse than the silver of yonder candlestick, that will rub up a bit when we want to make it smart ; but the more you rub up a beauty the worse you make her.'

" ' Ha ! ha !' joined in another of the band : ' if you had said like plated ware, 'twould have been more like, which by polishing leaves the copper underneath.'

" ' Ha, ha, ha !' laughed all in chorus, while the others knocked their cups in approbation of the sentiment.

" As Laura listened to these rude and brutal jests her heart died within her, for it left no doubt of her lover ; Henri, he was, then, the captain of a band of lawless bandits.

" ' Is it to-morrow night we take a peep into Wernsberg castle ?' asked the lieutenant.

" ' Yes !' replied the captain.

" ' Do you think it worth the risk ?'

" ' I do !'

" ' And how shall we get information of the spot where the old man's wealth is kept ?'

" ' I'll pump it out of Laura !' was the reply.

" ' If we once get our noses within its crazy walls, I'll warrant we find that out,' said another of the party.

" ' By clapping a pistol to the old man's head,' rejoined the lieutenant.

" ' Exactly so.'

" ' It's as good a method as the rack of the inquisition,' said the captain ; ' it never fails to elicit the proper answer.'

" ' Never,' said several.

" ' And at what time shall we be ready, captain ?'

" ' At midnight.'

" ' Good, good !' said the lieutenant.

" ' And keep a good look out, for we are tracked,' said the captain.

" ' How so ?'

" ' While I waited for my pretty Laura, I heard the sound of oars and voices, and soon after two of the government officers left their boat near mine, and searched amongst the rocks ; how they got the information I know not.'

" ' And how did you manage to escape them ?'

" ' By a miracle ; one of their bayonets passed within an inch of me, and I was afraid the timid Laura would scream, but fear kept her silent. When they passed I left in safety.'

" ' A narrow escape,' murmured several.

" ' But now for a song, boys,' said the captain.

" ' Aye, aye ! a song !' echoed the lieutenant.

" ' Come, Paulo, strike up,' said the captain, addressing one of the band.

" ' Varroni can do it better,' said the man spoken to.

" ' Well, it makes no difference so as we get it,' replied the lieutenant.

" ' All right,' said Varroni, and after clearing his throat, in a hoarse voice, sung,—

> " ' Over mountain, over dale,
>   - We roam both gay and free ;
>   The morning breeze we fresh inhale,
>   Who then so blithe as we ?
>
> " ' Nor do we pine with care,
>   Or grief consume our years ;
>   We drink our wine so red and fair,
>   Free from both frowns and tears.
>
> " ' 'Tis true no scolding wives annoy
>   Our ears with ceaseless tongue,
>   Yet still the song of heartfelt joy
>   By youth for us is sung.'

"When the last lines of this had been repeated in chorus by twenty different voices, it was acknowledged by the accustomed clattering of the wine cups upon the board, and soon after all commenced to drink deeply, the lover of Laura not excepted.

" They soon fell asleep, and while in this state, Laura took one of the torches to trace the passages of this subterranean abode.

"After wandering for some time, and passing through many dreary vaults and passages, she came to a spot where the water oozed through the rock, and beyond which a gleam of daylight broke upon her sight.

" With anxious steps she hastened forward, and with joy found herself in the cave where the boat had been moored. The water was now low, and she walked to the margin of the river, upon reaching which she fell upon her knees, and returned thanks to Heaven for her deliverance.

" She now hastened homeward by pursuing the stream in an opposite direction to the current, and after walking many miles faint and weary, she discovered the towers of her father's lofty castle towering against the clear cold sky.

When she reached that part of the river opposite the steep ascent she found a boat, and getting into it rowed herself across, and with a palpitating heart, once more ascended the steep ascent and gained the castle entrance.

Upon loudly knocking at the door, it was soon opened by the seneschal, and without waiting to answer his interrogatories, Laura rushed wildly by him, and sought her father's chamber.

" In a few minutes she waited at the door to collect her mind before entering into her father's presence, when a gentle murmur met her ear ; for an instant she listened, and plainly discovered it was the voice of her aged parent, offering up a prayer to Heaven for her protection. She knocked gently.

" ' Come in,' said the baron.

" Laura opened the door, and saw him rising from before a small altar-piece.

" ' Merciful Heaven !' said he, ' do I once more behold my child !'

" ' Yes, dear father,' said Laura, casting herself at his feet ; ' forgive me, forgive me !'

" ' Thou hast caused me much unhappiness!' said the aged baron, 'and with tears I have deplored thy absence.'

" ' Dear father,' said Laura, ' I have offended Heaven by my disobedience, and dearly I have paid the price : in mercy do not upbraid me more.'

" ' I need not say more to thee than thy own heart speaks, Laura ; but never, I entreat you, cause your father such pain again.'

" ' Never, dear father, will I cause you the slightest pain. Oh, Heaven, forgive me for my wickedness!'

" Laura here burst into a flood of tears, overcome by her emotion : her parent endeavoured, by every endearing term, to recal her to herself, but she swooned away, and in this state was carried to her chamber, where, after a short time, she recovered, and then fell into a gentle sleep.

" The brigands, on the other hand, slept long and soundly : their chieftain felt secure of the love of Laura, and conceived he could visit her at his idle hours ; he, therefore, for the present, did not think it worth his while ; but, after having charged one of the troop to attend to her wants, he, with the rest of the band, set out in quest of the castle, unconscious that Laura was there before him.

" When they arrived near the spot opposite the castle, they, with their horses, forded the stream, and began to ascend to the lofty portal of the castle, and by the help of ladders reached the outward rampart, the warder of which was fast asleep ; and, lest he should raise an alarm, a poniard was planted in his bosom, and the keys taken from his possession.

" There was now no difficulty—every door yielded at their approach, and with cautious steps they proceeded through different apartments of the castle, placing every valuable they could find in readiness to be carried off.

" ' But where are the old man's riches?' asked the lieutenant.

" ' His coffers are, no doubt, in the vaults of the castle,' returned the captain.

" ' If we but knew his chamber, we could force him to give the keys.'

" ' Certainly ; let us discover it once.'

" ' We must be cautious not to alarm the domestics, and, above all, the women ; they always make such a clatter,' returned the lieutenant.

" ' Keep a sharp look out,' said the captain, ' and I doubt not I shall soon find the old miser.'

" As this was said the captain went in search of the baron's room, which at last he found.

" ' Who's at the door?' demanded the baron from within.

" ' Your servant Pierre,' replied the bandit chief, in an assumed voice.

" ' And what's your business at this hour?' demanded the baron.

" ' I have particular intelligence to communicate concerning the Lady Laura,' returned the bandit.

" At this intelligence the baron leaped from his bed, anxious concerning the fate of his child, and upon opening the door, the robber rushed in, and seizing him by the throat, exclaimed,—' Silence!'

" With a wild and bewildered gaze the aged man fixed his eyes upon the robber, and then, in choking accents said,—

" ' What is your business here?'

" ' Money,' returned the robber.

" ' Alas! I have none to give,' rejoined the baron.

" ' Liar!' growled the bandit. ' This instant lead me to your coffers, or death shall be your portion.'

" ' If that will give you satisfaction, you are welcome to a life that I am weary of.'

" ' Come, come, do not think to evade my question by such a subterfuge as that. Where are your plate and jewels?'

"'Once more, I tell thee, I have none: thou canst not take what I have not.'

"'Avaricious miser!' cried the bandit; 'this instant produce the key, or another moment shall see you in eternity!' Saying this, he placed a poniard to the old man's breast.

"'Nay, spare my life, but for my daughter's sake!' supplicated the aged man, 'to me all else is worthless.'

"'Your daughter?—ha! ha!' returned the bandit; 'she is many miles from here.'

"'Oh, my child—my Laura! Return her but to her aged father, and name what sum you will for her release.'

"'We'll consider that presently,' cried the bandit; 'the key to your wealth, I say, or another moment shall not be your's.'

"'Never,' cried the baron.

"'You then refuse?'

"'Never shall it be said that the Baron Wernsberg yielded to the threats of an outlawed ruffian!'

"'Then receive your doom!' said the robber-chief.

"The poniard was again raised and descended with the lightning's speed; but, instead of entering the breast of the aged baron, it pierced his own, and he fell dead upon the spot, for Laura had guided his arm. She had awoke; and, hearing the sound of voices within the castle, fear took possession of her frame, and for protection she sought her father's chamber; but what was her horror upon perceiving her once-loved Henri standing over the prostrate form of her parent.

"The love which once had animated her breast, had turned to the most deadly hatred in consequence of the deception he had practised, and now she viewed him in no other light than an assassin about to take the life of her fond and aged father. Stealthily she crept behind him, and, when the fatal weapon was about to pierce his heart, by the aid of Heaven the murderer had received the desert he merited.

"The tumult within the castle had now become general; the servants and men-at-arms, hastened from every part to defend their lord; the sound and clash of arms was heard in every room and passage; blood flowed in streams down the marble stairs, while at intervals the bodies of the disputants choked up the way.

"The castle had been fired in many places by the robbers, to favour their escape, and it required all the activity of the inhabitants to quench the flames, and, at the same time, to defend themselves from their foes.

"But now a shout was heard: a band of soldiers had arrived; the clash of swords reverberated again through the lofty halls, and finally subsided; but the bandit gang was vanquished; they had lost themselves in the intricacies of the castle, and each man, separated from his fellow, had fought with desperation, nor gave up the contest with his life.   *   *   *

"The beautiful Laura never ceased to reproach herself as the cause of all this bloodshed; a deep melancholy settled on her once laughing face, and never more was she seen to smile. Upon the death of the baron (which happened a short time after these events, in consequence of the fear he had endured), Laura, being the heiress of Wernsberg, made over the castle and estates to a neighbouring convent, and devoted the remainder of her days to Heaven."

*   *   *   *   *

"The remainder of her days to Heaven!" muttered Agatha; "poor fool; not so would I have done. But the morning is breaking—hail to daylight, for there is uncertainty and dread in the shadows of the night—hail to daylight, for then I am myself again."

CHAPTER XXIII.

Ere you could say behold ! 'twas gone.—BYRON.

THE VISION IN THE GUARD ROOM.

WHILE Agatha was suffering the pangs of a conscience ill at ease, Hugh Wingrove and the retainers of Sir Rupert, who had been disturbed by the alarm given by the sentinel when the strange noise and the plunge of some heavy body in the castle moat were heard, determined upon sitting up for the remainder of the night, it being, as Bernard remarked, quite an insult to one's bed to go back to it again after once getting up, more especially as ale might be had in the guard-room, and none in the dormitory.

This last argument was quite conclusive, as regarded even the most sleepy, and Hugh Wingrove, after repeatedly shaking his head, and declaring he would give no orders for ale, concluded by sending Bernard and Anstey for two flagons.

Who thought of sleep then, when the foaming humming ale was placed on the oaken table, worn quite black by time, which was in the centre of the guard-room? No one, and by the time each man had taken a hearty draught of the liquor, and drawn breath afterwards, which in Bernard's case took nearly half a minute thoroughly to effect, there was not a drowsy eye among them all.

"Bless me," suddenly exclaimed Bernard, seizing the flagon next him; "I forgot."

"Forego what?" said Wingrove, arresting the ale, on its rapid transit to Bernard's mouth.

"Why, to drink health, long life, and happiness, to Sir Rupert, to be sure."

"Then mind you don't remember to forget another time," said Wingrove. "It aint your turn at the flagon, yet."

"Eh? Remember to forget, eh? Hang me if I understand you."

"I'm not obliged to find you brains, Bernard, nor do I think you would be a better soldier if your skull was thinner, so make yourself easy. Your turn for the ale will come round in due time, depend upon it."

"Oh, just as you like," said Bernard; "but I can tell you something, Master Wingrove, and comrades all, that will astonish you."

"What is it?"

"Why, it's this, as we rounded the barbican tower, and were coming up theli ttle steps, mind you, opposite the green hall, you know, next to the painted gallery that leads to the ——"

"Now, hang you for a prolix knave," cried Wingrove, "what has all that to do with astonishing us?"

"You shall hear; as I was a coming round the barbican tower and up the little ——"

"Take that," said Anstey, who had just emptied one of the flagons, and gave the vessel a heavy blow against the side of Bernard's head.

"There's nothing in it," exclaimed Bernard.

"I know there aint," said Wingrove.

"I mean the flagon," roared Bernard, amid the general laugh that arose at his expense. "Well, I tell you, I saw three people on the battlements to-night."

"Three?"

"Yes! There was some one else, besides Mistress Agatha, and that terrible nervous Eldred Weare."

"Are you sure?"

"Have I got two eyes ?"

"I believe so."

"Then I saw these people, and one of them, a tall fellow, by the mass, shrunk away before the guard reached the spot, and must have jumped into the moat."

"Impossible," said Wingrove, "and yet if we are, as I much fear, haunted in the castle by spirits, one of them might do such a thing—who knows ?"

"Ah ! who knows ?" cried Bernard. "That's the question. Now, all I've got to say, is that if there be anything strange and out of the way to see or hear in Brandon Castle, I'm the man to see or hear it."

"Are you ?" said Anstey, "then all I've got to say is—the devil !"

He started from his seat as he spoke, and glanced in the direction of the door which lay in the gloom at the further end of the large apartment.

All eyes were immediately turned in the same direction, when they beheld a tall figure, attired in the garb of an ecclesiastic, standing on the very threshold of the door.

"The Black Monk !" cried Wingrove.

"The Black Monk !" echoed the guard, and a general rush was made to the door, which was on the instant slammed shut.

For the space of one moment, and no longer, did the door remain closed, and then Hugh Wingrove, with his drawn sword in his hand, rushed into the passage which led to the gate. Before him, at about the distance of half a dozen yards, he saw the same figure, or what he supposed to be the same, standing perfectly motionless. By the dim light that came from the lamp which hung in the guard-room, he, at once, recognised the garb of the monk.

"Villain ! I have you now," he cried, and rushing forward, he made a cut with his sword at the figure which, on the moment, appeared to sink into the earth at his feet.

"Lights ! lights!" cried Wingrove.

A soldier rushed from the guard-room with a blazing piece of wood he had snatched from the fire, and as it crackled and roared in the cool air of the passage, the flame arising from it made every object clearly visible. No monk was to be seen, nor was there upon the sword of Wingrove the least trace of blood, the only mark of the blow he had struck appeared in a splintered cut on the wainscoted wall. For about a moment no one spoke, but Wingrove took the light and looked carefully down upon the spot where he could have sworn the monk had stood, and through which he seemed to have disappeared. Nothing, however, in the appearance of the flag stones could for a moment countenance such a supposition, and Wingrove, as he wiped the perspiration from his forehead, looked much perplexed and very pale.

"Now, by my faith, comrades," he said, "there is more in this than I can make out. I could take a solemn oath I saw Morgatani, the Black Monk, in the same habit he wore when Sir Rupert turned him out of Brandon, standing here on this very spot, and made a slash at him with my sword, which would have cracked his shaven crown had he not been an imp of the devil's, and disappeared even at my feet."

The men-at-arms looked at each other in dismay, for superstition had a strong hold of their minds, and they very soon believed that that which they had seen was supernatural.

"I saw him too," said Bernard, "and there's one thing I must tell you, Wingrove, that sword will never be of any further use to you as long as you live."

"Indeed, and why ?"

"I've heard my grandfather say, that a sword which had been used against anything not human was sure to play its owner some trick in the hour of

need, most probably breaking, when there was most occasion for it holding together to do good service."

Hugh Wingrove glanced at his sword-blade, and was half inclined to lay it down, but he was ashamed of his temporary weakness, and replacing it in its scabbard, he cried,

"Monk or devil, it has no business here, and I will cut and slash at it whenever it crosses my path. Comrades, my idea is, certainly, that this monk is haunting about the castle ; we know that such fellows are up to as many tricks as a cat has hairs on her back."

"I believe you," remarked Bernard. "I've been served out in one way and another, I can tell you. I've had a singing in my ears ever since that cursed business."

"Well, never mind that, now," cried Wingrove. "The morning is breaking, and we shall have, I fear, many more days and nights of trouble before our noble master, Sir Rupert crosses the drawbridge of Brandon Castle."

"You may say that," sighed Bernard, "and what do you think the cellarer told me, quite in strict confidence, comrades ?"

"What ? what ?" cried several.

"Why, that he was going to-morrow to tap the last ale barrel."

"Oh, is that all ?"

"Not quite. He added, that he very much feared Mistress Agatha would not order in any more, but make us all drink water from the well in the court yard."

"Water ? water ?"

"Ah, water, instead of ale too. I mean to say, comrades, that when water comes to be drank in Brandon Castle instead of ale, it's enough to make the old walls topple down, it is."

No. 13

CHAPTER XXIV.

"Dark passion filled her breast with fire,
A thing she was of dread.
No peace nor calmness could she know
Till numbered with the dead."

AGATHA AND THE MONK.—A STRANGE MEETING.

THE sun was glowing on the battlements of the castle, and the blithe birds were gaily singing as they perched upon the tower-wall and turret grey, when Agatha Weare rose from a restless couch, on which she had thrown herself not an hour before, and opening the secret outlet from her chamber, she passed into an exceedingly narrow passage, which, by many tortuous windings led into the southern gallery, from whence Bernard and Wingrove had watched the mysterious light in the grey turret.

Want of rest and her agony of mind made her look ghastly pale, and her steps tottered as she took her solitary way. It was the least likely hour to meet any one stirring within the castle walls, for the night-watch was considered over by the first streak of sunshine, and the tired guard retired to snatch a few hours rest before breakfast time made the old hall as merry as a fair.

Agatha's hands were clasped and her lips were compressed as if she were making an effort almost beyond her strength to preserve her apparent calmness of demeanour. Her footsteps faintly echoed through the long gallery, and now and then she would shudder and pause a moment to listen if any sounds disturbed the silence that reigned throughout the ancient building; all was as still as the grave, and the unhappy woman proceeded on her way until she came to the same window from whence Wingrove and Bernard had watched the light.

Agatha then paused, and taking from her bosom a small piece of crimson silk, she fixed it in the window in such a manner that it fluttered outside in the morning air. She then retired as she had came and in five minutes more was seated in her room.

Her former gloomy train of thoughts began now to oppress her, and she was leaning her head upon her hands, when a low knocking sounded on the secret panel. She sprang to her feet, and in an instant admitted Morgatani to the chamber.

"Never more welcome," said Agatha; "you saw the signal?"

"It is here," said the monk, as he laid the piece of silk before Agatha, "but you look jaded and worn. What has happened to distress you?"

"Nothing—nothing," replied Agatha. "But solitude begins to have terrors for me."

"Solitude? chase such fancies from your brain. You, a woman with a mind far above the ordinary weaknesses of your sex, should rise superior to these feelings which make fools tremble and the wise smile."

"Nature will be nature still," said Agatha, in a faint voice. "I have passed a night of terror; my very chamber has seemed peopled with frightful fancies and hideous shapes. The faces of grinning fiends have come close to me and almost choked me with their pestiferous breath. Oh, I have, indeed, passed a night of horrors."

"You surprise me," said the monk. "The mind that could conceive that which we have executed in this castle should augur an imagination more under strict control."

"But when we sleep?"

"Well? when we sleep?"

"Then the judgment cannot control the wayward fancies of the brain, and terror runs riot through the chambers of the soul."

"You have had a dream."

"I have. A dream which, if it prove prophetic, will work us much woe."

"Indeed!"

"You shall hear. Methought I was in the mazes of a forest, from which I could not extricate myself, and that a young boy came up to me, saying, 'aunt, prayer only can relieve you.' I started to hear myself called by such a name, and then he added, 'I am Sir Rupert Brandon's son and heir.' Then there came from every tree, from every shrub, from every brake and covert of the wood, such gibing laughs as made my blood curdle in my veins and my brain to throb with such intensity of agony that mere pain awakened me from my vision."

"Aye," said the monk, "you have rightly named it a vision. Sir Rupert might yet marry and yet have children, but that he had made so powerful a vow that since Heaven had seen fit to take from him Alicia, whom he nearly worshipped, never again should female form delight his eye."

"I heard the vow."

"You did, and as you heard it, your own faint hopes were buried a thousand fathoms deep in the grave."

Agatha shuddered. "I had no hopes," she said in a faltering tone.

"It matters not. I, Morgatani admire and love you, can and will help you to your revenge. You should be happy. All is prosperous; Sir Rupert may die in the wars, and if so all trouble is at once spared, for I can produce his will, leaving Brandon and all its rich possessions between you and your brother."

"And yourself."

"My monastic vows prevent me from personally possessing property, but for my wants I shall trust to you."

"You may and safely. He who has helped me to wealth and revenge, shall merit my eternal gratitude."

"But," whispered the monk, "should he return, as something seems to tell me he will, we must play the bold game of which we have laid the groundwork, and when Sir Rupert is executed, the castle and estates will descend in succession entirely to your brother Eldred."

"I know so much," said Agatha, "but he is most unworthy."

"True, but you and I can assist him. He dares not for his life, even now, gainsay us in a single wish; but then how much deeper will he be committed as our slave, when he has added perjury to ———"

"Hush! hush!"

"Murder," added the monk. "Why do you fear a word like that? It brings no terrors to me. Agatha Weare, I thought you had a spirit high-reaching and ambitious."

"I have, but I will confess my soul was shaken by yon strange figure we saw upon the battlements. Say, Morgatani, what think you that figure was?"

"I know not, and I care not," said the monk. "I fear nothing—believe nothing."

"Believe nothing?"

"No. By my own scientific lore, such as is only known to the brotherhood I belong to, I can make most magical appearances. Even the night that has now passed away has witnessed a scene that will furnish food for gossip and a winter's tale to many an idle head."

"This night?"

"Yes. A spectre has appeared to the night-guard."

"A spectre?"

"Aye of my contriving. I have means, gathered from a knowledge of nature, of producing strange effects, but it matters not now how I made a form, which was but a shadow, appear before the eyes of the night-guard. What I now wish is for you, when Wingrove makes his report, to tell him you have received certain news of my death through a dream, and that a vision told you I had died at half-past two this morning. Such a tale from you, coupled with what they saw themselves at such an hour, will convince them that in a super-natural form, I haunt the castle, and hence I can come and go more freely to and from your chamber; for who will stop a spirit on his nightly walk?"

"The plan is good," said Agatha, who from the presence and conversation of the monk, had recovered, in a great measure, from her state of mental depres-sion. "I will second it, you may depend, with every circumstance that can seize upon the imaginations of the soldiery."

"Do so, for until Sir Rupert returns, or is dead, I may not show myself bodily without danger here."

"Morgatani," said Agatha, " you never yet told me why Sir Rupert con-ceived so great an indignation at you."

"'Twas nothing ; a mere dispute about the neighbouring monastery, which you know is in his gift ; a mere trifle."

Agatha said nothing, but she too well guessed in her own mind, from stray expressions of the monk, that the real cause was some insult to the Lady Alicia while she was yet in life, for nothing else would have so stirred the brave, gallant, and temperate Sir Rupert.

"Should we hear nothing of the Lord of Brandon within a few months, I will adopt some means of ascertaining his fate in the Holy Land," said the monk ; " and it may be I shall find some one of my own order to set at rest with a dagger all question of his life or death, provided I am assured he has no intention of returning."

"You did not think to adopt such an expedient ere he went."

"Not think, not think? I thought, but my brain seethed, and the blood rushed through my veins like scalding lava. Hear me, Agatha Weare ; there are injuries that death cannot satisfy. Mine is one of those. The simple death of Sir Rupert would give me no revenge. He—I—you—all of us must die ; and by the means I might be compelled to adopt, I might be sparing him pain, not inflicting it, and where then would be my revenge? Out upon a mere assassination as an act of vengeance—I despise it! As he watched by the bier of Alice I could have sent a shaft to his very heart! I could have stolen behind him and cleft him down with an axe! But what was that to me? Would that have given me revenge? Never! The mind—the feelings—the affections must suffer! Death—a death of ignominy and shame shall follow months of mental torture, and then—then part of my deep revenge may be gratified!"

As he spoke his eyes seemed to flash with fire, and his gigantic form to di-late with the excess of his passion.

Agatha trembled before him as she said :—

"Then you wish for the return of Sir Rupert to his ancient home?"

"I do," said the monk with startling energy, "and I will take some means to force him home, if possible, but not at present. His feelings are too fresh for the loss of his beloved ; and then should he resist all attempts to bring him to England, he shall die in the East as lingering a death as I can have inflicted."

"Can a slight injury, as you say yours was," said Agatha craftily, "stir you to so much passion?"

"I said not my injury was slight," replied the monk. "The provocation was slight, but the injury to me immense. Was I not chased like a stranger cur from the castle? was I not struck?"

"Nay, I knew not he had struck you."

"He did; curses on him; but enough—enough of this. I will have my revenge, and in having my revenge, you can be gratified, for you can fancy it yours Agatha, and the insult he gave to you will be effaced in the agony you shall see him suffer."

"'Tis dangerous," said Agatha, "I have heard, to scorn the humblest, poorest heart that ever beat; but when such as mine meets not with the devotion it exacts, the vengeance it pants for must be great. Morgatani, I have surrendered my very soul to you. The price is, revenge on Sir Rupert Brandon!"

"It shall be paid," said the monk. "Be assured it shall be paid."

CHAPTER XXV.

The heart that ne'er in battle shrunk,
Nor cared to think of life,
May well beat high and shrink before
The assassin's deadly knife.—ANON.

ELDRED WEARE'S EFFORT OF COURAGE.—THE PROJECTED ASSASSINATION.

WHILE the monk and Agatha were conversing in the impassioned manner that usually characterised their discourse, Eldred Weare sat in his own room revolving in his mind, what for him was quite a mighty project, and one which, even to think of, required him to muster into one spot in his brain every latent spark of manhood, if such there were in his composition.

"They are always twitting me with being a coward," he muttered. "Upon my word I must do something really to show them that when I like, that is when I'm quite aggravated, I can do something. Plague on that knave Wingrove, to laugh in my face; a pretty thing indeed. And I, although I'm in authority here, can't turn him out of the castle, because old black muzzle, the monk, says he'll be off to Sir Rupert, if I was to do so, and like nothing better."

Eldred rubbed his hands together and shook his head in great indignation.

"Now I could find in my heart, I'm in such a rage," he muttered, "to cuff anybody soundly. If there was but some boy now in the castle, I'd go to him and deal him such a whack on the head, I would, as should make him dance again—ah, I would. But hang these men-at-arms, with their great broad shoulders and their fists like legs of mutton, the vagabonds to laugh at me. I really must do something just to show sister Agatha that I ain't going to be put upon by everybody for nothing; oh dear, no. Now if I could come behind that Wingrove slily some time and give him a progue with a pike, how satisfactory that would be. Yes, I—I must really do something—I must."

Convinced as was Eldred of the necessity of doing something, he felt like a great many persons with the same impression, in a very great perplexity to know what that something should be.

He resolved in his mind various schemes of aggression secretly against Wingrove, but none of them seemed to him at all feasible, that is to say, he could think of nothing that was not attended with some small personal risk, which was something to which Eldred Weare had certainly the greatest possible objection.

"Now, if I could but manage to do him some very grievous harm from a long way off," he muttered. "By heavens I have it—I have it now—a most bright idea—a most brilliant idea ; there never was such an idea surely. I'll get a cross-bow and wait behind some door while Wingrove passes, and have a pop at him with an arrow. If it hits him, down he goes—if it don't, away I run—a capital idea. Then if I should kill him, I can tell Agatha what kind of story I like, while the men-at-arms need never know from whose hands he came by his death. There never will be such another idea as that. I rather believe I have some brains, though Morgatani pretends I haven't; and there's that little waiting-maid Anna, of my sister's, I overheard her telling that great oaf Bernard, that I was a fool. A fool, indeed. I'll—I'll frighten her some day, when she's going along in the dark. I'll bounce out of some door-way, and cry bo ! I will. Yet she is a remarkably nice little creature, and if I was a serving man instead of a gentleman, I would certainly cut out that great two yards of bad stuff Bernard, and marry her myself. She's quite a dear with her black eyes. What a bore it is to be a gentleman, and to be bothered as I am about one's courage, and to be expected to knock down this one—fight that one, and bully t'other one, when I would much rather be in the kitchen enjoying myself."

Buried in these reflections, Eldred Weare left his chamber, and proceeded to the armoury of the castle, in order to select a cross-bow which should serve him to wreak his vengeance upon Wingrove with.

The armoury of Brandon Castle was of great extent, and rich in all kinds of weapons from the very earliest and rudest ages to the more polished and skilful, if not the more really civilized. Many magnificent suits of chain, scale, and plate armour hung upon the walls, and some of the more costly mail was richly inlaid with threads of gold curiously wrought in all manner of rich and varied devices.

Every succeeding warlike possessor of Brandon Castle had added to the stock of defensive and offensive weapons, by placing upon the walls some of the choicest specimens of the age in which he lived. The collection, therefore, was not only of great extent, but very costly.

Eldred Weare glanced around him upon the various weapons, until he came to where a number of cross-bows hung in fanciful grouping between two of the deeply set windows.

" Oh, these are the kind of things for me," he said ; "they are so very safe. All you have to do is to get behind something, and take care not to catch your finger in the cord, and you are all right—all safe, I mean, which is just the same thing."

He took down one of the bows, but it was too powerful in its spring for him, and when he did succeed in bending it, he was half afraid of the jerk it would give him when he pulled the catch.

" I won't have you," he muttered. " Some milder one will do just as well. I don't want it to go off with such a vengeance as almost to knock one backwards."

Bow after bow he tried till he found one that was fitting for his purpose, because it was easily worked, and yet seemed to possess a considerable power of projection. He next selected three sharp, straight arrows, and fixing one of them in the bow, he took aim at a suit of mail which hung at the further end of the armoury, in order to make trial of his skill.

" I'm sure Wingrove is quite as broad as yon suit of plate armour," he said, " and if I can hit that, why I dare say I can hit him."

After winking a great many times, and taking a very long and elaborate aim, Eldred let the arrow go, when it struck the suit of mail so sharply on the side that it swung off the ponderous hook on which it was suspended, and fell to the floor with a crash that echoed again throughout that whole wing of the castle, and so alarmed Eldred that he rushed to his own room with the crossbow in his hand, and his hair nearly on end with fright.

"What's that noise?" said Bernard to Anstey, as the distant rumble of the falling armour came to their ears.

"I don't know," replied Anstey, filling his mouth with a huge cut of a venison pasty. There is nothing but odd noises and uncommon sights now in the castle, and the best way is to take no notice of them. My opinion is ——"

"Is it," said Bernard, snatching the ale flagon from Anstey. "Mine is that you had the last pull at the flagon, and it's my turn now, comrade. My service to you."

Bernard immersed his face in the huge pewter flagon, which, when full, required two hands to lift, and while he was so engaged, Anstey passed the edge of his knife sharply against the bottom of the vessel, producing a curious shrieking noise, that sounded to Bernard, as it vibrated through the interior, like something most awful and unearthly.

"The saints preserve us! What's that?" he cried, bringing down the flagon with a dab upon the oaken table.

"What's what?"

"A most singular noise."

"I heard nothing."

"You heard nothing? Why it was like the very devil himself having a tooth pulled out, with fangs reaching from his jaw to his great toe—his great hoof I mean."

"That's all your imagination, Bernard."

"It ain't, I tell you, I have no imagination—I never had any—don't like it—and never mean to have any. D—n it, for this day or two everybody has been accusing me of imagination, and all that sort of nonsense. 'That's your fancy, Bernard,' says one. 'All your imagination, Bernard,' says another; d—n it I say I haven't any fancy at all, nor imagination either, and I'll punch any one's head who says I have."

"Well, well, you needn't be in such a rage."

"But I am in a rage."

"Ah, that's all fancy."

"What?"

"Imagination."

Bernard reached across the table to give Anstey a blow on the head, but the latter with a laugh, stepped from his seat, and Bernard's weight upset the pasty and the remainder of the ale, which mingled together in delightful confusion.

"Peace, peace," said Wingrove. "Quarrelling over your meals?"

"No," said Anstey, as he left the guard-room, "it's only Bernard's imagination."

"Wait till I catch you," cried Bernard, "and you shall have as real and unfanciful a punch in the head as can be. My fancy and imagination indeed! What next, I wonder? They'll be pretending I'm such a milksop as to read and write, next."

"Nobody ever thought of accusing you of such great enormities," laughed Wingrove; "but I must now go and make my report, I suppose, to Mistress Agatha Weare, and be hanged to her."

"Amen! say I to that, Master Wingrove. She don't look upon me with any great favour. The idea of asking that Eldred to knock me down. Oh —oh—oh; ha—ha—ha!"

"Don't make that dreadful noise. You'll alarm the whole house, you will. It's as bad as an earthquake when you laugh."

So saying, Wingrove left the guard-room to report to Agatha the proceedings of the night, among which he was sure not to forget the mysterious appearance of the spectre monk at the door of the guard-room.

"She won't fancy much my hacking at him with my sword," thought the honest soldier; "but I don't care what she minds, and what she don't. If I see an enemy, be he priest or layman, it matters not to me, I will have a slash at him; so I'll just tell her the truth, and she may come and see the wall, if she likes, where there's a notch that I wish had been on the shaven crown of the Black Monk instead."

Eldred, when he reached his chamber with the cross-bow and the two arrows, immediately locked the door, and in his extreme fright tumbled into bed and drew the clothes up to his very nose.

There he remained for some minutes, expecting to hear an universal alarm all over the castle, when he made up his mind to pretend not to have yet risen; but after a time, upon finding all as silent and quiet as before, he began to have some confidence and slowly crept out of bed.

"Was there ever such a clatter as that confounded armour made," he said to himself. "It was enough to frighten the very devil. Well, however, I hit it; that was quite clear, and shows what a great warrior I should have been had I been brought up to carry arms and command armies. But it's just as well I wasn't, for I don't like danger at all: oh, dear no, and as for getting hurt it's positively dreadful. Now, there was father, as great a fighter as needs be, what good did he ever get by it?—a cracked crown! that's all; and so with all his glory he was popped into the family vault. Ah! the cross-bow for me, behind a door, where there is no danger."

Eldred then cautiously unlocked the room door and peeped out.

"There's nobody there," he whispered. "I think I may venture now, all's safe. Oh, dear, if I should meet anybody now with this cross-bow in my hand, what would they think? Well, one must run some risks; so here goes. Let me see: he comes to make his report about now, so as he passes through the rooms to the left here, which he must, I can have a pop at him. Good gracious, there he is!"

Eldred precipitately retreated into the first room that presented itself, as he saw Wingrove leisurely advancing from the farther end of the long corridor.

Eldred galloped through the room as if he had been chased, and bolting through a door-way which led into a second chamber of the suite, he there paused to take breath.

"He didn't see me," he muttered. "I'm sure he didn't see me. Here's the key too in this door; and let me consider, these rooms lead on to the east wing of the castle, so now if he would but have the extreme kindness. Good gracious!"

CHAPTER XXVI.

———— Now take aim,
His heart shall soon receive the barbed wound.—Old Play.

THE CROSS-BOW.—WINGROVE'S DANGER.—THE MONK AND ELDRED WEARE.

Eldred's exclamation arose from seeing Wingrove at that moment enter the room and fling himself into a seat.

Eldred was afraid to move, and the door being open several inches gave him a good view of Wingrove as he sat.

"So," said Wingrove, "she's busy, is she, and can't receive the report yet. Well, I can wait, I've nothing very particular to do, but to go to bed; I'm very drowsy. In ten minutes she can see me, I think she said. Well, well, I'll give her a quarter of an hour and then go to her again."

"Here's a chance," thought Eldred. "He's going to sit there a quarter of an hour. I can be ten minutes, if I like, taking aim. What an opportunity! I think I have you now, Master Wingrove; you won't laugh at me any more, I'll be bound. If I can hit a great suit of plate-mail and knock it off its hook, I'm sure I can hit you, you great old vagabond. Oh, I hate you. You laughed at me, did you? I'll make you laugh on the other side of your mouth."

"I cannot account for that strange appearance," said Wingrove, in a low tone of voice. "If ever there was anything supernatural revealed to mortal eyes, surely that appearance was."

"Whatever is he talking about," thought Eldred, as he took one of his arrows from his vest.

"'Tis strange, very change," continued Wingrove.

"So it is," muttered Eldred.

"Since Sir Rupert's departure, there has been nothing but alarm."

"I'll alarm you in a few minutes," said Eldred.

"Supernatural sights and sounds—night ones, and that strange eye that glared upon Bernard and myself from the Grey Turret."

"What does he say?" muttered Eldred. "An eye in the Grey Turret?"

"'Twas horrible."

"Gracious, I'm getting frightened. I—I must make short work of it. Lord, if some one was to come behind me now and catch hold of me; what a horrid idea. Suppose a skeleton was to catch me by the leg. Goodness gracious! I should faint clean away."

No. 14

"Conjecture is idle and useless," remarked Hugh Wingrove, as he changed his position. "I have but to do my duty, in spite of the pusillanimity of the cowardly fool Eldred, the unruly passions of his sister, and all the strange sights and sounds which now begin to be familiar things in the castle."

"Oh," thought Eldred; "that's a new name for me. I'm a pusillanimous, cowardly fool, am I? We shall see, we shall see, Master Wingrove, how much good you have done yourself by that remark."

Eldred now commenced adjusting the cross bow, for the last remarks of Hugh Wingrove had aroused all the animosity of his despicable nature, and it would have given him infinite pleasure to see his victim writhing in pain.

His own hands trembled, however, so excessively with fear while he was adjusting the arrow, that he could scarcely do so; but when he at last succeeded in placing it well in its groove, he smiled to himself, and projecting the head of the weapon just a hair's breadth or so beyond the crevice of the door, he commenced taking the cool and deliberate aim which he wished should cause the arrow to reach the heart of Wingrove, who sat all unconscious of his imminent danger.

Another moment, and the shaft would have winged it way to the bosom of the soldier; but just as Eldred was about to release the string, a heavy hand was laid upon his shoulder, and the voice of the monk said in his ear,

"Forbear!"

Eldred uttered a cry of terror, and Hugh Wingrove sprang from his seat.

In an instant Morgatani had closed and locked the door. Then seizing Eldred by the collar, he without a word dragged him through several apartments, until they reached one of very small dimensions, the door of which the monk locked carefully, and then turning to his trembling companion, he said,

"Eldred Weare, what fiend tempted you to take up arms?"

"I—l—oh, dear me."

"Speak. Tell me what you wished to accomplish with your crossbow?"

"Bless me, you nearly take my breath away."

"Speak, I say!"

"Well, I am speaking as fast as I can, only you are so dreadfully impatient that you put me out ever so many times, you do."

"Tell your story then in your own style."

"Well, I mean to do so. What made you come and lay hold of me in such a manner? Upon my word, you quite alarmed me."

"Eldred Weare, am I a man to be trifled with?"

"I should say decidedly—a-hem!—not."

"Then tell me at once what purpose you had with that cross-bow?"

"Oh, the—bow—bow?"

"Yes."

"The cross-bow, you mean, I suppose, eh?"

"Prevaricating fool! Think you to escape my questions by such common trickery? Answer me at once, or I abandon you for ever."

"Well, I—I don't mind. It was to shoot somebody."

"Who?"

"Why, that vagabond, Hugh Wingrove, to be sure."

"And what put so unusual a thought into your head?"

"He's always laughing at me."

"Pshaw!"

"Ah, you may pshaw! but he call me a pusillanimous, cowardly fool, he does, I assure you."

"I have no doubt whatever. But now let me tell you, if you venture upon any such proceedings without my sanction and previous orders, I will give up having anything further to do with you. You know not what danger you may bring upon all of us by one such a silly act."

"Danger!"

"Positive danger."

"There couldn't be much, because you see I meant to run away the moment I had done it."

"Of that I have no doubt; but let me now inform you, Eldred Weare, that the same stroke of master policy that destroys Sir Rupert Brandon will likewise drag to the scaffold this meddling Hugh Wingrove, for I intend to accuse him as an accomplice."

"Do you, indeed?"

"I do. Therefore, leave him alone. Run no useless and foolish risks; he is quite harmless at present. Nay, I mean to make him useful as evidence of things which must militate against his master, Sir Rupert Brandon."

"Good gracious! what a head-piece you have got to be sure."

"I have need of one," muttered the monk, "when I have such tools to work with."

"Eh, what did you say?"

"Nothing; but remember my advice."

"Oh, dear, yes. I won't trouble my head about him any more. It's given me a great fright as it is, I can tell you. I'm sure he may just say what he likes; not that it's pleasant to be called a pusillanimous, cowardly fool, you know."

"Certainly not."

"But I hope you see I have courage, and can resent an insult, If you hadn't popped upon me unawares I should have settled the business of that Wingrove, and he's a big fellow."

"Certainly, you have shown the most extraordinary courage," said the monk, with a sneer.

"I believe I have."

"It is only to be equalled by your discretion in keeping the door between you and Wingrove."

"Yes, exactly. There was generalship for you. It isn't many would have thought of that."

"Very few."

"Well, I'm glad to find that you appreciate my spirit."

"I do most certainly."

"Now that's a comfort."

"Rest content, Eldred. Your courage and wisdom are fully appreciated by, I believe, every one in the castle, and by none more than by myself. For the future, when there shall arise any particularly dangerous piece of work, you shall do it."

"Oh, thank you. Never mind, I ain't presuming."

"True merit never is."

"Certainly not. So—so—so —"

"So what?"

"You may do all these pieces of dangerous work yourself, and I sha'n't feel offended in the least."

"What rare modesty."

"Yes, I believe you."

"Well, well, I am busy now. We will talk more of this another time. Farewell."

"Oh, are you going?"

"No; but you are."

" I ?"

" Yes, I remain here. I have a means of leaving this room known only to myself, I believe, now that Sir Rupert's away."

" Bless me, I like secrets. Show me."

The monk shook his head.

" You won't ?"

" I will not."

" Oh, very well. Never mind. I ain't at all anxious, you know. Very far from it. I'll go if you wish it."

" I do wish it."

" Good morning, then. I dare say Wingrove didn't at all suspect it was me."

" Good morning," said the monk.

" Well, good morning—I——"

Morgatani took him by the arm, and pushing him out at the door without any further ceremony, locked himself in again.

" Well, that's cool," said Eldred, " uncommonly cool, but I don't mind a bit. He has an opinion of my courage now. He sees I am a person of some courage, ha! he feels now that I am somebody, ha! that I can use a cross thingemmy, ha! and that I am a dangerous man to my enemies, ha! I should like to see anybody laugh at me now, I should."

Full of self complacency, Eldred strutted along the corridor, and nearly run his nose against his own chamber door, so jerked up was his head on the strength of what he considered his late great achievement.

~~~~~~~~~~~~

CHAPTER XXVII.

—— I had a dream—
A strange unearthly vision crossed my soul
And spoke of death.—Anon.

THE DREAM OF AGATHA.—WINGROVE'S SURPRISE.—MORE MYSTERIES.—
THE CROSS-BOW.

HUGH WINGROVE, when he heard the sudden cry of Eldred, recognised his voice in a moment: but the sudden closing of the door by the monk, prevented him from ascertaining its cause, and he stood for a moment or two irresolute what to do.

His next impulse then was to try the door, which finding quite fast, stopped his proceeding in that quarter, and then he paused again, saying,

" Pshaw, 'tis not worth the looking after, and discovering what has frightened that booby, Eldred Weare, for it was his voice I am certain. In all probability it was merely the sight of me here, when he did not expect it, that caused his exclamation and precipitate retreat, so it's not worth while to take any trouble about him."

Wingrove then left the room, and for the second time that morning, proceeded to the apartment in which Agatha Weare sat, namely, the oaken parlour, which we have before mentioned to the reader.

She was now ready to see him, and when he entered the room, she held her hand to her head, as if racked by some dreadful pain.

" You do not seem well this morning, madam," said Wingrove. " The report will keep till to-morrow."

" No, no," said Agatha, " I would rather hear it now. I am well, with the exception of a head-ache, which is either the cause or the effect of a singular dream."

" A dream, madam ?"

" Yes—I thought a voice came upon my ears in the dead of the night, saying, ' At half-past two, died Morgatani, but his shadow will haunt the Castle of Brandon.' "

Wingrove was certainly a little staggered by this seeming coincidence of Agatha's dream, with the appearance of the monk in the guard-room, and he said,

" Part of the report I have to make to you, relates to Morgatani, the Black Monk."

" Indeed !   To him ?"

" Yes—at about the hour you heard the noise you mention, there came a figure to the guard, bearing an exact resemblance to the monk. I followed it, and after cutting at it with my sword, it disappeared most strangely."

" Your sword was well employed," sneered Agatha, " in cutting at a defenceless man, and a minister of Heaven."

" With all deference to you, madam," rejoined Wingrove, " I doubt very much if Morgatani is the man to go unarmed ; and as for being a minister of Heaven, I should much sooner take him to be minister of the other place."

" Peace, peace," cried Agatha, " nor speak thus irreverently of the dead. I feel a conviction that the words I heard in my dream were true."

" Then Sir Rupert Brandon has an enemy the less," said Wingrove, " and as for the ghost of the Black Monk, it's quite welcome to glide about the castle if that be its taste, to all eternity, for all I care about it."

" But," said Agatha, " the knowledge that the strange being you have observed, or fancied you have observed, belongs not to mortal existence, should induce you to shun contact with it, and not lift mortal weapons against the spirit, which, for some purposes of Heaven, is permitted to revisit the earth in the shape it wore when it belonged to humanity."

" There is something in that argument," said Wingrove, seriously ; " I wish not to war with Heaven, or its wise purposes and decrees."

" Then leave this perturbed spirit of Morgatani to take its own course through Brandon, without interruption—it is tempting Providence to raise an arm of flesh and blood against the emanations of spirit merely."

" If I was quite sure," said Wingrove, " that it was the spirit of the Black Monk."

" Can you doubt ?"

" Yes—he is, or was a Jesuit, I have been told, and they are as crafty, if not more so, than the devil himself."

" You speak of that you do not comprehend," said Agatha ; " but enough of this subject. It appears that Brandon Castle last night was visited by some one, as well as by the spectre of the monk."

" That I cannot take upon myself to say, but certain it is, there was a great splash in the moat, as if a heavy body had plunged into it, but whether from the open country, or the ramparts, neither I nor any of the guard can tell."

" Saw you nothing ?"

" I saw nothing, but Bernard declares, that before the guard reached you and Master Eldred Weare, upon the battlements, he saw a third figure apparently in conversation with you."

Agatha slightly changed colour, as she said,

" Impossible !"

" He is ready to swear it."

" He is mistaken. There was no one but ourselves. My word is surely good against that of a drunken man-at-arms."

"Bernard was sober, madam; but he may have been mistaken."

"What figure does he say he saw?"

"One closely resembling Morgatani."

"Ah, then it may have been, for sometimes I have heard that these dis-embodied spirits only appear to certain people at certain times. The spectre of the monk may have stood by me and I not know it. There are philosophers who scruple not to assert that we are never alone; but even in what we imagine our greatest privacy, we are closely hemmed in and surrounded by the spirits of the dead."

"That's a very uncomfortable philosophy."

"And yet it may be true. Their subtle natures may defy the observation of our mortal senses, but still they may be present. Even now Morgatani may be listening to our words."

A deep groan at this moment sounded in the room, and both Agatha and Wingrove started in alarm, although a moment's thought told the former that the sound proceeded from the lips of Morgatani, who was listening to their conference behind a secret panel.

"I could have sworn I heard a hollow groan," said Wingrove.

"And so did I," remarked Agatha. "It is as I suppose. We are surrounded by the dead. Let us talk no further upon such a subject, lest we tempt them to make themselves more visible to our mortal senses, and drive us mad by the assumption of some shape too terrible for human eyes to gaze on."

"Madam," said Hugh Wingrove, shaking off the feelings of superstition which Agatha was so artfully awakening in his breast, and which, despite his better reason, he at moments almost gave way to—"madam, I fear nothing living, and I will fear nothing dead. Heaven never will, how-ever, permit one class of its creatures to make an amusement of the nerves of another."

"Feel as you please—boast as you please," said Agatha, "I will not defy the powers of another world, lest some terrible sight blast my eyes, and convince me of the existence of spirits, at the same time that it implants eternal terror in my heart. Now leave me, and should aught occur this night, be sure to let me know by an early hour in the morning."

Wingrove left the room, and as he did so, he saw Eldred sneaking along at the further end of the corridor.

"I will just ask him," said Wingrove, "why he screamed out and locked the door when he saw me sitting down a few minutes since."

The hardy veteran then quickened his pace to come up with Eldred, who no sooner perceived that such was the case, than a sudden fright seized him that by some means his designs against Wingrove's life had been divined, and he accordingly took to his heels, and scampering along the corridor, ran down a flight of stairs with a speed and precipitancy that astonished Wingrove to account for.

"Upon my faith," he said, "this castle is as full of mysteries as it can very well be. Surely there must be something very odd-looking about me this morning that Eldred Weare screams out when he sees me, and runs away as if a cloth-yard shaft was singing after him. There's more in all this than I understand just at present. Well, no matter. I won't perplex myself about all these things, for I've got my duty to do, and if I once get into a maze of conjectures about ghosts and all sorts of noises, 1 sha'n't be able to do it, that's quite clear. Oh, that Sir Rupert would return. Then all this plague and torment would soon cease, I'll be bound. Patience—patience, Hugh Wingrove. The day may come at last when I shall see my beloved master again in his ancient halls, and till then, why I must rub on the best way I can."

With these reflections, Hugh Wingrove repaired to his chamber, and soon slept the calm, sound sleep of a healthful frame and an unburthened conscience.

CHAPTER XXVIII.

Anon with passion wild,
He'd shout his wrongs from earth to Heaven;
Then breaking to a gentler humour,
He would weep awhile.—BEAUMONT.

THE WIZARD'S HUT.—THE MYSTERY OF THE TWO CHILDREN.—A MIND
IN RUINS.

THE morning sun was shining brightly among the trees of the forest in the immediate vicinity of Brandon Castle; the birds, with their sweet, dulcet notes, were calling to each other from bough to bough; the wild flowers that grew unloved and unknown in that solitude, were spreading their bosoms to the genial air, and all animate and inanimate nature seemed happy in the sole delight of existence. No human voice disturbed the feathered tribe, no human foot for some time had startled the timid hare from her covert, or raised the hunter's cheer to the affrighted deer; for he who, hermit-like, made the forest his home—he, the strange wayward creature who had been met by Sir Rupert when he left his castle, looked upon the dumb creatures of the woods with eyes of kindness, and he would creep softly through the mazes of the luxuriant vegetation, and murmur his strange thoughts in low tones when he was in his usual state, and not excited out of his ordinary routine of existence. When, however, it did happen that a wilder spirit took possession of his faculties, the storm of feeling that raged within his breast overcame every other consideration, and apparently stung to madness by some real or supposed injuries, he would rush through the forest shrieking and yelling in his rage. It was not often that such a mental tempest occurred, and when it did, its termination was generally in some accident, such as the Lord of Brandon had witnessed when he held the singular conversation he did with the wild son of nature.

Fits of deep despondency too would occasionally cast their shadow upon the soul of the brain-stricken man, and he would sit for many hours with his head buried in his hands weeping in the bitterness of his grief and despair with an intensity that would, had any mortal been near, have filled his breast with terror. Then slowly the mind would recover, and although the reason was gone, or at all events, so far blighted as to make strange confusion in the imagination, he would stroll quietly through the old forest glade musing upon the ancient trees, and gathering from every blade of grass, every wild flower and weed, matter for contemplation. By much labour he had formed himself a hoard, in which he kept a store of wild fruits, and such game as he killed in the wood for his subsistence. The hut was more like a cavern when viewed from the interior than what it really was, for he had plastered the interlaced branches of the trees of which he had formed his rude house, with clay and earth, which drying and burning hard, assumed the appearance of the roof of an excavation.

There was one occupation which the poor being spent always some part of each day in—that was in sharpening and polishing a long double-edged sword, which he seemed ever to regard with a degree of veneration and care. He would lay it on his knees as he sat upon the trunk of some fallen tree, and talk to it as if it were a living thing.

" Be firm and fleet," he would cry. " Reach his heart when the time
shall come, as it will—as it will. Sword of my destiny, thrice blessed blade,
you must give me joy by giving me justice. I seek not revenge, but I will
have justice meted out to the oppressor."

Then he would hide the blade within the hollowed trunk of an ancient
oak that grew near to his hovel, and from whence he could draw it in a
moment, but where it was completely hidden from the observation of any
chance wanderer in the forest.

The wizard, as he was called, was well known to the whole country side,
and sometimes he would wander to the cottages of the peasantry, and they,
with a dread of his violence if refused, would give him many little comforts
to carry to his forest home.

The village of Brandon was within half a mile of the castle, and its inhabitants were all dependant upon the lord of the feudal residence, the only
other person in any kind of authority being the superior of the monastic
institution, which was at a very short distance from the castle, lying mid-
way between it and the village.

About the time that the wizard made his first appearance in the neighbourhood, there came a travel-worn and weary woman, and claimed the
hospitality of the villagers. She said she had come from another land,
although she spoke the English language purely and fluently, and that she
and another had been the objects of great oppression. With tears and sobs
she begged to be allowed to remain in the village, and Sir Rupert, upon
being applied to, had given her a vacant cottage. Then the rumour arose
that the forest was haunted by the strange man who called himself Nemoni,
and who soon acquired the reputation of being a wizard, and one who possessed many rare spells and charms. By the command of Sir Rupert, he
was not molested, and he built himself then the strange cavernous-looking
hut in which he lived.

On the morning to which we have alluded, Nemoni had but just recovered from one of his fits of melancholy, and he was leaning against the
trunk of a tree with the traces of recent tears upon his cheek, when a
rustling among the boughs of a neighbouring tree, the long branches of
which touched the ground, caused him to start from his posture and glance
in the direction of the sound.

" Who comes ? who comes ?" he cried. " Where is my brave sword ?
who comes for poor Nemoni ? Want you a charm to scare the night-mare
from your couch—a cure for an unthankful heart, or a potion of love ?
Come forth—come forth—I am here. The wizard is here."

The figure that appeared from among the roots and branches of the tree,
was a female one. Her steps were slow and solemn, and although she
could not have numbered thirty summers, there was such an expression of
long suffering depicted on her face, that it seemed as if she had lived a
century of woe. She approached Nemoni, and he, as his eye caught her
face, muttered to himself,—

" 'Tis she—'tis she. From the tomb she has come again. Welcome—
welcome."

There was an earnest tone of feeling in the voice of the female as she
accosted Nemoni, that betrayed an interest in his fate beyond that of mere
compassion.

" Brother—brother," she said, " I have come to see you, as you said I
might. Will you speak to me ?"

" Aye," said Nemoni, his eye lighting up with the strange fire of insanity. " God of Heaven, why should I not speak to thee, my sister's
spirit ? Ah ! 'tis merciful and great of Heaven to give you leave to live
again."

"Oh, brother, brother," she cried, as she leant upon his arm. "Even as you live so live I."

"No, no," he cried; "I saw it—I saw it. They built you up in a living tomb—'twas done in Italy, the land of sunshine and song. Yes, they killed you; the foul fiend tear his eyes from his head; the imps rack him. Morgatani—when will the day of vengeance come? Is poor Nemoni to wait for ever?"

"Leave vengeance to Heaven," said the sister, who was the female who had claimed the shelter of a home on the Brandon estates. "It is not for us to take it. Oh, come away from this place—tarry not here, my brother, your danger is excessive."

"Yes—yes; I see it now—I see it now," cried Nemoni; "there, through the branches of yon elm—the pale face is distorted by pain, the beautiful brow has spots of blood upon it. Now—now they turn the rack, and I am held by bands of iron, and forced to see the sight that curds my heart, turns each artery of my body into a channel for liquid fire, dries up my brain, and fills the hollow of my skull—the void where once was glorious reason—with despair, and fiends that mock me. See, see—the face of my bride—she who loved me. They will not moisten her parched lips; they heed not her groans. Oh, save me, Heaven."

With a wild convulsive shriek he dropped on his knees, with his hands out-stretched in the direction of the tree, between the branches of which his fancy had conjured up the vision which so much disturbed his soul.

"Allan, Allan!" cried the sister, wringing her hands in grief. "For the love of Heaven look up."

He slowly struggled to his feet, and an expression of terror came across his face.

"Hush! hush!" he said. "Hush! call me Nemoni; some busy fiend else will carry your words to the Black Monk—he who has made me what I

No. 15

am—then he will place me on the rack ; yes, he will torture me, and then I cannot kill him.   Hush! hush! hush!"

"Alas! alas!" sobbed the sister.   "This mental malady will last till the grave closes over him.   My poor, persecuted, suffering brother."

"Ah, you weep," he said.   "Do angels ever weep?   No, no—there are no tears in Heaven.   Let me think!   What dream is that which ever comes so freshly to me when you are here?"

"The children?"

"Ah, the children.   Can that be true?"

"It is true.   Come this way—this way, brother."

"Whither would you lead me?   Is my grave dug?"

"No, no.   Speak not thus.   Come hither, I have a spectacle to shew you, which should make you smile—come, come."

He suffered himself to be led towards the large tree, from among the branches of which his sister had come.   On a small green spot shaded from the sun's too fervent rays, immediately on the other side of the tree, were two very young children.   They were smiling at each other, and one was with childish earnestness holding by its slender stem a wild flower, so that the reflection of its bright colours came upon the other's cheek.

Nemoni passed his hand across his brow, as if he were endeavouring to recollect something or arrange his ideas in a connected form.   Then he said,

"Bless them—bless them.   The day will come."

"Will you not trust me with the mystery concerning these children?" said his sister.

"No, no, you might breathe it in your sleep.   They were benighted in the forest ; let that suffice I found them."

"The villagers are annoyed at the mysterious manner in which they came among them.   Will you not tell me all?"

"The foul fiend wears a cowl," muttered Nemoni, abstractedly.   "The time will come though, when his shaven head will lie low, and then, aye, then you shall know all.   Heaven help poor Nemoni.   There—there again.   On his red horse—blood—blood from head to heel ; he comes.   The Black Monk. No—you shall not.   I have wedded her.   You say she is a nun.   Heaven recognises such vows ; I love her.   Before God's throne we became man and wife.   You shall not kill her. Help! help! a sword to slay the Black Monk."

He darted off with tremendous speed and was soon lost to sight, amid the mazes of the forest.

The sorrowing woman then took the children in her arms and slowly walked towards the cottage, which was but a very short distance from the road. "There is no hope.   There is no hope," she sighed, " no hope but in the grave."

CHAPTER XXIX.

"A warrior grim was he—
He had been bred in camps and knew not
All the smirking courtesies of life."

THE MESSENGER.—THE MONK'S SUSPICIONS.

THE state of feeling which Morgatani had wished to produce among the men-at-arms in the castle was rapidly working its way in their superstitious minds, and several of them who would have looked unmoved upon the stoutest mortal opponent, were becoming timid at the slightest noise, and fully believed the castle of Brandon to be the haunt of a legion of evil spirits.

Wingrove struggled hard against a belief in such things; but what other resting place for thought had he, than in ascribing to supernatural agency the various sights and sounds which were rapidly converting the castle into a very disagreeable abode. Everything seemed to prosper the designs of the monk and Agatha Weare. They had but one great source of anxiety, and that was to ascertain if Sir Rupert Brandon were dead or alive; and in the then troubled state of the Holy Land, whither he had betaken himself, it was next thing to an impossibility to procure authentic information concerning any of the various champions of the Cross who fought for the Holy Sepulchre.

The gallant exploits of Richard Cœur-de-Lion were filling Europe with wonder, and it was supposed that the Knight of Brandon was following his fortunes instead of being among the English knights ranked under the banners of Count Baldwin; but this was all conjecture, and as day after day had passed on without bringing any intelligence of him, Morgatani began to fear that he was dead—to fear it we say, because the death of the knight would have baulked him of the vengeance he wished to wreak upon him, for turning him out of the castle with such marked ignominy.

Nothing but Sir Rupert's death upon a public scaffold could have satisfied the dark malignant spirit of such a man as Morgatani, and now that he had completed all his arrangements, no one panted more for the return of Sir Rupert to his ancient home, than did he. However, the life he was leading within the castle was an irksome one, and he longed to exercise openly the power which he grasped at. The possession of so much consequence as the virtual receipt of the immense revenue of the Brandon estates would have given him, he flattered himself might induce the Pope to grant him a cardinal's hat, when to his ambitious soul a career of ambition would be opened to him that he considered worthy of his energies.

With his usual glowing language and plausible manner he explained those thoughts and projects to Agatha Weare, even at the same time flattering her that she should secretly share his wealth and his power in addition to gratifying her hatred against Sir Rupert.

"The capital will then," said Morgatani, "be the place in which we can best enjoy the smiles of fortune. Then wealth and power will make our days pass pleasantly, and I shall be able to raise you to a height above even your ambition. We will leave Brandon and its gloomy associations, seeing nothing of it but the bright gold which it produces to us."

"The place is hateful to me," said Agatha, "but think you, Eldred will be satisfied?"

"He shall be satisfied," cried the monk; "he dare not complain, and should he prove troublesome beyond expectation, some means must be taken to silence him."

Agatha shuddered as she said,

"You cannot mean his death?"

"No, that would be impolitic. But I will so work upon his fears, that far from disputing with us the possession of the estates of Brandon, he shall think it a gracious boon to be permitted to live."

"Be it so—but cannot you, with all your ingenuity, bethink you of some means of bringing home again Sir Rupert Brandon?"

"He is a favourite with King Richard," said the monk; "should that monarch be slain or captured we should then have a far better chance of proving the death of Sir Rupert, and that he will be slain or captured soon, I have means of knowing."

"How is that, Morgatani?"

"His brother John is ambitious—that is the answer. Ha! what sound is that?"

The monk started from the chair on which he sat, as a trumpet sounded from the exterior of the castle.

"Begone," cried Agatha, "secret yourself—there will be some one here."

A knock came at the room door as Agatha spoke, and the voice of Eldred, said,—

"Sister, here's some one demands admittance to the castle. He says he has news of Sir Rupert, and the moment the knaves in the guard-room heard so much they down with the draw-bridge with a crash that made me jump again."

"Come in," said Agatha, unlocking the door when the monk had passed from the room by the secret door-way, of which Eldred was ignorant. "Do not be prating there, but tell me at once who this is who comes with such tidings."

"Why, that I really don't know."

"Then go at once, and bring me information. Quick, Eldred, it is necessary I should know the rank of the visiter ere I see him."

"Hilloa !" cried Wingrove, as Eldred ran full against him in the doorway.

"Murder !—fire !—oh, it's you, is it ?" said Eldred, who had struck his head a hard blow against the half mail that Wingrove always wore when on active duty, and which he had snatched from the wall of the guard-room, and hastily put on upon seeing that the visiter was a Knight Templar.

"There is some one at the gate ?" said Agatha.

"He is in the painted chamber now, lady," said Hugh Wingrove. "'Tis a gallant knight, one Sir Kenneth Hay. He brings news of Sir Rupert."

"And—and the import of his tidings ?"

"Good, for Sir Rupert is well."

"I will see him. In the painted chamber ?"

"Yes ; we have done him all honour—we turned out the guard, and have offered him the best the castle affords."

"Well, well, I will see him," said Agatha ; "Eldred, attend us."

"Who ?—I, sister ? I really had better stay here, you know. These knights and I never could get on well. They think of nothing but fighting, and ——"

"Peace !—follow me directly."

Agatha, with a hasty step, proceeded to the room of state, into which the knight had been shown—there she found a tall, chivalric-looking man, whose face was bronzed by exposure to the sun of a warm climate, and whose iron frame appeared well fitted to cope with every kind of adventure which the lives of the crusaders abounded in.

He made a rough bow to Agatha as she entered the room, and without any preface he said, "are you the Lady Agatha Weare ?"

"I am, sir."

"Then I am Sir Kenneth Hay : you see, lady, I am a Templar by my habit. The last time I saw Sir Rupert Brandon he was alive and well, and gave me this scroll for your reading and that of Master Eldred Weare."

As he spoke, he handed a small folded note to Agatha, who read upon it the following words :—

" ' From my means within my castle of Brandon let Sir Kenneth Hay have three hundred pieces of gold.   " ' RUPERT BRANDON.' "

" 'Tis a large sum," said Agatha. " Is Sir Rupert a prisoner ?—and is this for ransom ?"

"No, lady, but another is a prisoner—one much loved by Sir Rupert."

"I know not if so much be within the cabinet of which Sir Rupert gave the abbot of the neighbouring monastery one key, and me another."

"Will it please you look, lady," said the knight, "for I must sleep but one night here, and then hasten to the coast again to leave England for Germany."

"Germany? I thought you came from Palestine."

"So did I; but I am to meet Sir Rupert in Germany—the crusaders are all dispersed."

"Then may we expect Sir Rupert home again?"

"By the mass, yes, if he live so long. But an' it should turn out you have not the money, I must e'en borrow it among the friends of Sir Rupert, for it must be had."

"I will not trespass long on your patience, sir," said Agatha, as she left the room.

"Humph!" said Sir Kenneth, "mind you don't. I should never like that woman. Now, let me once more look at the instructions given me by my esteemed comrade, Sir Rupert."

He took a slip of parchment from his vest, and read :—

"Firstly, to find out that all the tenantry are comfortable and undisturbed. Secondly, if Hugh Wingrove be agreeably supported in his duties by Agatha Weare. Thirdly, if any rumour or suspicion exists that Morgatani, a monk, has visited the castle; for the satisfaction of all which, consult Hugh Wingrove, and pleasure much your loving friend."

"He don't say what I'm to do though, if it be not all right. Well, that's left to my discretion, I suppose ; somebody may want a knock on the head, and I'm not the man to grudge it, should it be necessary."

While the knight was thus reflecting Agatha had made speed to her own room, and immediately proceeding to the secret door through which the monk had passed, she knocked in a peculiar manner at it, when it opened, and Morgatani appeared.

"A messenger has come with a demand for three hundred gold pieces in the name of Sir Rupert," she said.

"Ah!" cried the monk; "then he is a prisoner. Such a sum could not be required but for such a purpose."

"It struck me too that such was the fact," said Agatha; "but this messenger denies it."

"And yet it may be true. Agatha, let him have the money, and leave the rest to me. Does he purpose leaving the the castle immediately?"

"No : he talks of staying the night."

"'Tis well. Give him the gold ; I will bring it back again to-morrow ere it be clear of the forest."

"Beware how you run into danger, Morgatani."

"Danger!" sneered the monk. "What fear I? Nor man nor devil can raise a flutter in my breast! I fear nothing. What is the quality of this messenger?"

"A knight ; by name Sir Kenneth Hay."

"Indeed! A stout and well tried soldier—I have heard of him. Were Sir Rupert in my opinion at liberty in Palestine, I would do something that should ensure this knight making such a report to him as might induce his return ; but believing him a captive, he shall remain one. That is punishment for such a man, and a good prelude to death here."

"Yet, such may not be the case," said Agatha.

"There can be scarce a doubt," replied Morgatani. "Get from this knight what particulars you can of Sir Rupert's acts since he left here. A trifle may impart us much."

"Yes—yes," stammered Eldred, who had entered the room unperceived, in consequence of Agatha, in her excitement, forgetting to lock the door.

"You here?" she cried.

"Yes, I. You know there may be danger, and as I'm plucking up a spirit, I ought to be here, there, and everywhere, sister. I'm not going to be snubbed, I can tell you."

"Peace, peace," said the monk. "Eldred Weare, since you say you have become courageous, I will seek out some dangerous work for you to do, something that would appal the stoutest warrior, and by achieving it you shall approve your courage."

"No, no, no," cried Eldred, in alarm. "True courage, you know, never courts danger, but always faces it—behind. I wouldn't mind fighting anybody now—he to shoot arrows through one hole in a door, and I through another."

"Why did you not follow me to the painted chamber?" said Agatha.

"Why, I did as far as the door ; but, you see, sister, that Sir Kenneth has such a brown look about him, and is so big, that I didn't much like to go in."

"Your courage!" sneered Agatha. "Talk no more of it. You are beneath contempt."

"Ah, you always were violent," replied Eldred. "Now, you see, I —"

At this moment another trumpet call from the outer side of the castle moat awakened the echoes of the ancient fortress, and filled Agatha and the monk with astonishment, while Eldred trembled through fear.

"More visiters to Brandon," cried Morgatani, "What can be the meaning of all this?"

"Eldred, I command you," cried Agatha, "to go at once and see who is this new comer."

"I—I don't like," stammered Eldred. "You had better go yourself, because if—if there should be a row, you know, they wouldn't hurt a woman ; and I might get such a rap on the head as I should never forget."

"Keep the door locked," said Agatha to Morgatani. "I will return quickly."

She then hurried from the apartment, just as another blast from the horn rung again upon the morning air.

<center>~~~~~~~~~~~~~</center>

CHAPTER XXX.

With sound of horn they came,
Two gallant knights I ween :
The sun gleamed on their glowing casques,
In bright and golden sheen.— Scott.

THE ARRIVALS.—A PROCLAMATION.—THE TRIAL BY COMBAT.

WHEN Morgatani was alone, for, Eldred, always dreading to be with the monk, had made an affection of going after his sister, he knit his brows for a few moments, and folding his hands in his monastic garb, he paced the apartment with a troubled air.

"What mean these sudden arrivals to Brandon Castle?" he muttered. "Can it be that Sir Rupert has any suspicion of my presence here, and is adopting a means of discovering it by these precursors of his own presence? or are these visiters just what they avow themselves, and without hidden purpose? I must be cautious, bold, resolute, and cunning as a fiend. Let him come ; aye, let him come, I am fully prepared for him. He shall learn that a Jesuit, although he may appear to suffer insult and ignominy in silence, is only like the deceitful calm upon the ocean's breast lulling the mariner to fancied security, in order that the tempest, when it comes, may hurl him to destruction. Let Sir Rupert Brandon beware. I loved his wife with a fierce passion, that knew no bounds. 'Tis said we most admire our opposites, and she was gentle and soft of speech, while I am stern and rough. I loved her. God—how I loved her! His love for her, that love of which he made such boast was, compared to mine, as a soft murmuring streamlet to a mountain torrent, wild and fierce. Well, well, she is gone—gone. I have had my revenge, although I have seared my own heart. Revenge is nearly as sweet as love ; at least, it is the only recompense for the heart's bitter disappointment. I have had revenge on her, and I shall have it upon him."

When Agatha, with agitated steps, reached the castle-hall, she found the guard, with Hugh Wingrove at their head, all under arms, and standing just within the gates, was a herald in his gaudily emblazoned coat, and a knight equipped in half armour.

"What is this?" said Agatha ; "whence came you?"

The knight advanced, and turning to Agatha, he said,—

" Lady, it is my mission to make a tour with the herald from castle to castle of the noblest barons, to proclaim King John."

"King John?" cried Wingrove ; "God's mercy! Has the gallant Richard fallen?"

"King Richard is no more," said the knight, "and John is on the throne of England."

The herald raised his trumpet to his lips, and blew a short enlivening blast. He then cried,—

" God save King John !" and the knight, moving his hand, pointed through the open gate, and across the draw-bridge to his horse, which was then held by a page richly caparisoned.

"I will take a cup of wine to the king's health," he cried, " and then begone."

" Then, Fitzhugh," cried Sir Kenneth Hay, suddenly striding forward, " it shall be to King Richard you drain the cup."

The knight seemed perfectly paralysed at the sudden appearance of Sir Kenneth Hay, and he reeled back a few paces, as if he had been a spectre. A grim smile came across the face of Sir Kenneth, as he said,—

" By my knighthood you don't seem glad to see me."

" I—I thought," said Fitzhugh, " you were in Palestine."

" Pho—pho !" laughed Sir Kenneth, " a man can't be in two places at once. You see I am here. So you come to proclaim King John."

" I do."

" You do? Then ere we part, I shall trouble you to alter the names."

The knight then raised his voice till it rang like a trumpet all through the castle.

" Friends of Richard of the Lion Heart," he cried, " you who love God, your country, and your king, hear me. King Richard lives. Lives to confound his enemies, and once more reign in merry England—hurrah ! hurrah ! for King Richard, the champion of the Cross."

The men-at-arms, with Wingrove at their head, echoed the shout of Sir Kenneth, and Fitzhugh looked pale and irresolute, while the herald half-raised his horn to his lips and seemed doubtful what to do.

" The wine-cup—the wine-cup," cried Sir Kenneth, " Fitzhugh, although you have scarcely won your spurs you shall drink a health to King Richard. Ho ! there, the wine ! Sir Rupert Brandon is my most excellent friend, and I may make a little free in his ancient halls."

" King John," interposed Fitzhugh, " has received certain intelligence of of Richard's death."

" Who says so, lies," cried Sir Kenneth, " and who repeats the saying is a traitor. Fitzhugh, I know you well, you were ever a courtly smooth-spoken man, one who would serve the devil for a consideration ; I am plain of speech, and tell you what I know. If you refuse to drink the health of King Richard, I will kick your spurs from your heels."

The face of Fitzhugh turned sallow with rage, as he said,—

" Sir Kenneth Hay, you are trying to fix a quarrel on me, but King John is my master, and I will acknowledge none other."

" Then I proclaim you a traitor," cried Sir Kenneth.

" Traitor in thy teeth," said Fitzhugh, goaded nearly to madness by the evident relish with which Sir Kenneth's words were received by all the men-at-arms.

" Ha ! say you so," cried Sir Kenneth Hay, " have you so much courage ? Will you maintain your words ?"

" I will.   The wine—the wine—pledge me King John ! Long live the king."

" Hold," cried Sir Kenneth, as one of the guard advanced with a massive silver goblet filled with wine.   " Myself and this new-made knight Fitzhugh, a man whom I left a humble 'squire of the king's brother, have an affair now to settle ere any healths be drunk by name.   Since he comes here in sem-blance of a knight, I will put his manhood to the proof—and here I challenge him to combat in the castle-yard of Brandon, which well I know has witnessed many an encounter."

" Hold, sir knight," cried Agatha.   " As one left by Sir Rupert Brandon in care of his castle, I cannot permit bloodshed within its walls.   If it be that King Richard is known to be no more, why then, is John our monarch, and this gentleman newly come from court must know."

" Indeed, lady, you are wrong," said Sir Kenneth.   " This gentleman as well as his master only speak their wishes, not their knowledge.   King Richard lives, and as for a combat between knight and knight within the walls of Brandon being contrary to Sir Rupert's will, I know him better—what say you, soldiers ?"

A cheer burst from the castle-guard, and Wingrove cried,—

" Long live Sir Kenneth Hay."

" Lady, you hear," added Sir Kenneth, " you shall return to your distaff, and you embroidery.   Mayhap you will work some scarf in rare devices to grace the victor with."

There was a tone of irony in the voice of Sir Kenneth Hay that vexed Agatha beyond expression, but summoning up all her resolution, she said :—

" I forbid this combat ; it shall not take place within the walls of Brandon."

" Why, then, if not within the walls it shall take place without ; for Fitz-hugh must fight me somewhere."

" Now I bethink me," said Fitzhugh, " I am not free to accept your chal-lenge, for I am on a mission for my sovereign."

" Then carry your soiled knighthood back to him who gave it you," cried Sir Kenneth, " for I here proclaim you a dastard and coward."

As the knight spoke he took one of the heavy gloves he wore and threw it in the face of Fitzhugh, who with an inward groan felt that he had no alterna-tive but to accept the combat.

" Let it be so," he said.   " There is my guage," throwing down his glove.

" It shall not be," cried Agatha.   " Take back the wine. Sir Kenneth Hay, if that be your name, why should you come hither to make disunion in Bran-don Castle ?   That which you came for you shall have, but begone ; nor by your longer stay offend our peaceful home."

" Lady, I would you were a man," said Sir Kenneth, with a smile.   " But did the gallant Sir Rupert leave you alone with full power in Brandon ?"

" No," cried Wingrove.   " Master Eldred Weare and myself were to be consulted as well as the abbot of the neighbouring monastery in all matters of moment."

" Then you give me free leave to fight here ?" said Sir Kenneth, with a laugh.

" Leave ?" cried Wingrove.   " Aye, for a month, if you like ; and there is Master Eldred."

Sir Kenneth glanced in the direction in which Wingrove pointed, and seeing the half silly-looking Eldred Weare, he in three strides stood close to him, and in a voice of thunder, said,—

"May I fight here?"

"Ye—ye—yes. Oh, dear—bless me, yes. Just do w—w—whatever you like—oh, certainly—I—I don't feel very well."

"Thank you," cried Sir Kenneth, in a voice that made Eldred jump again; and then scarcely able to control his laughter, the knight turned to where Agatha had stood, but she was gone.

"Well, well," he cried; "since a fair dame will not grace me with her presence, I must e'en do the best I can without. Ho, there; the wine cup. Now, Fitzhugh, it ill becomes us as men who are to meet in strife, to make more words; so here, I drink to the King of England, without mentioning his name. My friends, I shall sleep here to-night, and to-morrow early we will have this little affair over, when Heaven protect the right."

"Let my horse be seen to," said Fitzhugh. "I am weary with riding, and will go no further this day. My horse!"

The page walked his horse over the drawbridge, and with a gloomy countenance, Fitzhugh, who dreaded the combat, yet felt it to be inevitable, took off his casque, and wiped the moisture from his brow as he slowly walked into the recess of a deep oriel window.

In a few moments a serving man appeared, and whispered to Fitzhugh,—

"An it please you, sir, the Lady Agatha Weare would speak with you. If you will follow me I will conduct you to her."

"I attend her with much pleasure," said Fitzhugh, as he walked after the attendant, a sanguine hope springing up in his breast, that after all Agatha might find some means of enabling him to get off the combat altogether, a consummation he devoutly wished.

No. 16

CHAPTER XXXI.

Saw you the disembodied spirit?
Aye, sir, we did.
Was it an angel, or a devil?—FLETCHER.

THE SKELETON ARM FROM THE GREY TURRET.—THE MIDNIGHT ASSIGNATION.

SIR KENNETH HAY turned to Wingrove, and said to him, in a low voice,—

"My friend, I wish some private converse with you, upon matters entrusted to me by Sir Rupert."

"Will it please you, sir, to walk with me upon the battlements," said Hugh Wingrove, "and I shall be proud to hear from you any message from my dear master."

The knight and Wingrove accordingly walked together up the broad flights of stone steps that conducted to the castle ramparts, and from where a magnificent view of the surrounding country could be obtained.

When they had arrived and were perfectly free from observation, Sir Kenneth said,

"I was told by Sir Rupert, that I might confide in you, for you were a brave soldier, and a faithful retainer of his house."

Wingrove's eyes sparkled with pleasurable emotion, as he replied,

"Heaven bless my noble master for speaking so of me. I were, indeed, a disgrace to mankind were I otherwise than faithful to so gallant a knight, and so brave and good and noble a master."

"Then I must tell you," continued Sir Kenneth Hay, "that Sir Rupert, upon his arrival in the Holy Land, was made one of a body of six knights, who attended the king in all his personal excursions to reconnoitre the enemy, and many a brave exploit has your gallant master been foremost in on these occasions. Shortly, however, after he had arrived, there arose serious jealousies and disputes among the ranks of the crusaders, and to such an extent did they go that all thoughts of the enemy were forgotten in their private quarrels. The armies became disorganised and broken up, and notwithstanding all King Richard could do, disorder and tumult took the place of regular and systematic warfare."

"I grieve to hear these tidings, sir," said Wingrove, "but what became of my gallant master?"

"He, and I only, along with the king, determined to ride across a large district of Hungary, in order to urge Phillip, the warlike Elector, to send a large force to coalesce with the English army, and prevent the war. We urged our steeds forward as quickly as consistent with their strength, until we had accomplished one half of our journey, when travelling through a forest we were attacked by overpowering numbers and taken prisoners."

"By the enemies of our religion?"

"No, we were in a Christian land. Treachery and guilt had been at work, and the owner of a small obscure principality had been bribed by John, whom you heard yon craven knight proclaim king, to stay the gallant Richard as he passed."

"Then he is no more?"

"You are wrong. He lives, and safely too. His life is looked upon by his captor as a never-ending mine of wealth. He is kept with the most zealous care in a dungeon, and his keeper hugs himself with the hope of continually extracting large sums from John, for keeping up the report of Richard's death, and never allowing him his freedom. By the connivance of our gaoler, who we bribed with valuable jewels we had about us, Sir Rupert and I escaped from our prison, but we could not move in the release of the king, because our means were exhausted. Sir Rupert, then, in the disguise of a peasant, remains in the vicinity of the gloomy abode of his sovereign, while my mission to England is to procure gold to attempt his release, failing in which we must resort to force."

"Would not force, in the first instance, have been the better plan, Sir Knight?"

"No," said Sir Kenneth, sadly. "It grieved us much to come to the contrary conclusion, but we were assured that any attempt to rescue the king by force of arms, would be looked upon with such terror by his gaoler, that he would at once put him to death. Hence is it that we are compelled to use stratagem; I forgot to mention to you, that Blondel, his faithful minstrel, is with Sir Rupert, and together they await with much anxiety my return."

"These are sad tidings."

"They are, but King Richard lives, and in that there is great hope. To-morrow morning, I will punish this new-made knight, Fitzhugh, who I know well to be a mere creature of John's, and then I shall make what haste I may back to my royal master."

"And has Sir Rupert," asked Hugh Wingrove, "overcome his grief for the death of his beloved wife?"

"In part, but not wholly, he has. Sometimes he will grieve sadly, but the active life he has led in the Holy Land has done much to temper his grief, and make it wear more the semblance of resignation."

"Then he will return once more to his ancient halls?"

"He will. His heart is here; although, to soothe his grief, he tore himself away. And now let me ask you, in accordance with his wishes, if anything has gone amiss during his absence?"

"Nothing has gone right," said Wingrove; "we have had all sorts of alarms, and the castle seems haunted by a legion of devils."

"You amaze me."

"It is but too true. One day we have one kind of alarm and the next another. The guard have scarcely a quiet night now, and what with strange noises and strange appearances, we sometimes scarcely know if we are upon our head or our heels. For my part, I sometimes think some of us must be bewitched, or that the castle, now that Sir Rupert is absent, is given up to the evil one as a place of amusement."

"That is strange news. Sir Rupert wished to know if one Morgatani, an Italian monk, had given you any trouble?"

"Ah, there it is," cried Hugh Wingrove. "May I be brained by a boy, but I believe that devilish monk to be at the bottom of it all. He is either living and leagued with fiends, or he has died and left us his curse."

"Have you seen him?"

"Why, I may say I have and I have not. He has been here and he has not."

"What mean you? You speak in riddles."

"I made a slash at him with my sword and yet cut him not; I saw him and yet he was not there; an he be not the devil himself, he is some very great acquaintance of his. Then, there's scarce a man-at-arms now will venture out of the guard-room after sunset, for with what they have seen, and what they imagine they see, they are scared to death nearly."

"In sooth you seem in a strange state altogether here."

"We are; but the worst of all is the mystery of the Grey Turret."

"What mystery is that?"

"Simply, that old Nick has himself taken up his abode in it, or at least one of his imps. We have seen strange sights that are enough to curdle one's blood,—heard strange sounds that stick by the ears for days afterwards in terror."

" The Grey Turret !　I have heard something of it, now I recollect." ｔ

" You may see it, if you will step a little this way," said Wingrove. " There, yonder is the Grey Turret, and a great curse to the Brandons is it."

The knight gazed upon the time-worn turret with interest, and then turning to Wingrove, he said,

" Does not a legend say there lies the body of an assassin in that turret ?"

" It does, Sir Knight, and it says the truth, for a scoundrel who attempted the life of a former lord of Brandon, lies there dead.　The door has been nailed up ever since, and not a soul in the castle chooses to undo it."

" Then that will I, ere I leave Brandon," said Sir Kenneth, " for I would fain convince you all that there can be no danger from a dead man.　I am no believer in the dark superstition that peoples every solitude with loathsome spectres."

" Nor I," said Wingrove; " but seeing is believing, and I've seen enough in Brandon castle to puzzle me, Sir Knight."

" Good Heaven !　what is that?" cried Sir Kenneth.

He pointed to the turret as he spoke, and from one of the loop-holes there dangled the hand and fore-arm of a skeleton.　The long ghastly fingers seemed clutching at the outer stone-work of the turret, and the impression conveyed was that of a skeleton trying to get out of the turret.　In a moment the arm was hastily withdrawn, and all was as before.

The knight looked at Wingrove in intense surprise, while the latter shrugged his shoulders, and remarked,

" We are getting used to those things, Sir Kenneth, and what would have furnished gossip for the guard-room for twelve months or more, now passes by us with no more than a passing shudder."

" By Heavens !" said Sir Kenneth, " I am astonished.　I was going to propose a visit to yon turret."

" I should be loth to say nay to you, sir," said Wingrove, " and yet I should be loth to go."

" But will you go with me this moment ?"

" Nay, sir, if it be, that after all our senses are only deceived by the devilish cunning of the monk Morgatani, who I cannot help believing, haunts somewhere about the castle, we had better go at some time when we may not be seen, or at all expected."

" True—let it be night, Wingrove.　I would fain, when I relate to Sir Rupert Brandon the mysterious sight I have seen, be able to add, that I made an effort to discover what it really was."

" I will meet you, sir," said Wingrove, " but let me beg of you to say nothing to the Lady Agatha of your intention, for on my conscience, I believe her no friend to Sir Rupert."

" Indeed.　Then she shall meet no friend in me.　There is a devil in her eye that I like not.　She would fain have spoilt my combat with Fitzhugh."

" She would, Sir Knight, and I take it that would have been grievous to us all."

" And worst of all to me, good Wingrove.　When and where shall we meet ?"

" I will ascertain where mistress Agatha orders you to be lodged for the night, and then take some means of communicating with you."

" Thanks, good friend ; your kind reception and frank behaviour, shall reach the ears of Sir Rupert, before I have been an hour in his good company. I pledge you so much on my knightly word, and if in the space of one night the mysteries of Brandon Castle may be fathomed, they shall be to-night."

" Heaven grant you success, Sir Knight. We are all here weary and sick at heart for our noble master's return, and my mind strangely misgives me that there is something brewing to his prejudice."

" There can be no prejudice done to the gallant Sir Rupert Brandon, that he cannot put right with his own sword."

" I rejoice to hear you say so, but there is another matter as mysterious and strange as any I have hitherto recounted to you."

" Upon my faith, Master Wingrove, you abound in marvels here. Pray tell it to me."

Wingrove then recounted the story concerning the mysterious horn sounding so like Sir Rupert's own trumpet-call, and the arrow with the written scroll, which had been shot into the oaken gate, when Bernard had his ear to it.

" That must be the act of some madman," said Sir Kenneth, " for the great grief that lies so heavy at the heart of the gallant Sir Rupert is, that he is childless. Oh, if he had but a child upon whose head he could lavish all the deep love and tenderness of his nature, he would be happy even yet."

" He would—he would," said Wingrove. " I never shall forget the night when Sir Rupert was pacing his own room, expecting each moment the welcome intelligence that a child was born to him. My lady had an attendant well skilled in such sickness, called Beatrice, and from her lips Sir Rupert expected the welcome news. Minute after minute, however, passed away, and she came not. Then Sir Rupert said to me,—

" ' Wingrove,' he said, ' hie thee to the apartment of your lady, and from the corridor ask for me what news there is—I am myself too agitated to go.' I went, sir, and as I neared the chamber, I thought I heard the cry of an infant. Then Beatrice came from another room, and upon seeing me, she staggered, and nearly fell to the floor from sudden fright.

" ' What news,' said I, ' for my noble master ?'

" ' I am going to him now,' said she; ' away with you. This is no place for a soldier.'

" I went to the guard-room, and soon after that, we all heard that the Lady Alicia was dead, having given birth to a dead child, over which the noble Sir Rupert wept bitterly, and then could never look upon it again."

" 'Twas a sad mischance."

" It was. Then my gallant master took such grief upon him that he placed a helmet on his head, and closed the visor, that none should see how great was his anguish from his countenance. The Lady Alicia was buried. You know the rest, doubtless, from my master's own lips."

" He told me the castle had grown distasteful to him since every object reminded him of her he had lost."

" Such was his feeling; but I and all here who love him have had but one hope since his departure, and that has been that, overcoming his grief, he will come once again to the home of his fathers, and live among his vassals and companions in many a well-fought field."

" That will be, good Wingrove. But who comes here ?"

" It is a messenger from the Lady Agatha."

The same attendant who had summoned the knight who came to proclaim King John now approached Sir Kenneth with great apparent deference, and said,—

" My lady begs the favour of your presence at a poor banquet she has on short notice prepared, to do you honour as the representative of her noble kinsman Sir Rupert."

"By the mass !" cried the knight, "your lady is most courteous, and for the banquet, it is right welcome, for we who have fought and bled in Palestine have almost forgot what a banquet is."

"This way, an it please you, sir."

"You will not forget our assignation?" whispered the knight to Wingrove.

"I will not; you shall hear of me ere the time of rest."

Sir Kenneth Hay then followed the attendant towards the inhabited part of the castle, and as the man went some dozen paces before him, the knight was surprised to see an arm thrust out from a doorway and a slip of paper in the hand.

He took the paper, and in a moment the arm was withdrawn, and the knight passed on in great surprise, scarcely believing he was really awake.

CHAPTER XXXII.

With passion wild she answered him,
Her words were of despair.—ANON.

THE INTERVIEW.—THE POISON DRAUGHT.

WHEN Agatha had so suddenly left the two knights by the castle gate, she had hurried to her chamber, in order to take counsel of Morgatani what should be done. She found the monk anxiously expecting her, and when she had informed him of the wrangling between the knights, a smile came across his features, and he said,—

"I now better understand this matter. By the machinations of John, King Richard is in some sore strait, and it may be that for him after all this money is wanted. Now it suits both the interests of the church to which I belong and my own revenge, that John should be king, and not Richard. Do you not perceive, Agatha, how much easier it would be for us in the event of any accident to substantiate a charge against Sir Rupert to King John, instead of King Richard? The latter thinks highly of him, has fought by his side, and it would take such evidence as perhaps no mortal could bring to convince Cœur de Lion of anything to the prejudice of Sir Rupert Brandon. With John the case is different. He will eagerly embrace any opportunity of crushing the personal friends of Richard."

"You reason justly," said Agatha; "and yet upon only assumed facts you know not that this mission of Sir Kenneth Hay's has reference to Richard the king."

"Jesuits know much," said Morgatani. "I had secret intimation from one of my order that a plan was on foot to sow dissension among the crusaders, and then destroy Richard, in order to place John, who has promised immense concessions to the church, upon the throne of England."

"Then what do you propose doing?"

"I purpose that the combat between Sir Kenneth Hay and this Fitzhugh shall proceed; and further, I purpose that Sir Kenneth Hay shall be conquered."

"Can you accomplish so much as that and be human?"

"I can, and easily. Hearken to me. From the effects of a subtle drug which I will mix with a cup of wine for Sir Kenneth Hay, he shall rise wearisome, confused, dizzy, and enervated. He shall not be in strength equal to a child of ten years old ; so shall Fitzhugh, whom I have heard of and whom I know to be the veriest coward that ever breathed, achieve an easy victory over the man who, otherwise, would in five minutes trample over him in the lists."

" Mean you then he should slay Sir Kenneth ?"

" No; I will have him live, and the only price of his life, shall be a full disclosure to me of where King Richard is, and under what circumstances he left him."

" Wonderful man," said Agatha, " what can you not achieve when you bend your mind to its accomplishment !"

" If," said the monk, while a fierce glance shot from his eyes, " if I cannot have my wish, I at least will contrive to have a full and deadly revenge on him who thwarts it."

" I know to what you allude," said Agatha. " Each day, Morgatani, I can perceive how much you loved my sister."

" Hush—hush," said the monk. " Do you want to drive me mad? Mutual hatred of the same person has brought us together. Such love as I can feel for woman, Agatha, I now feel for you, for you have a mind in unison with my own. Speak not of the past—let that which is to come alone be written in your brain, and let the characters be traced with blood. Revenge—revenge shall be our only cry."

" 'Tis a dreadful life into which we have plunged," shuddered Agatha.

" Dreadful !" cried the monk, as he clasped her wrist with violence. " Do you forget? Can your woman's heart forget him to whom you said —"

" Peace, peace," said Agatha.

" Him," continued Morgatani, " to whom you, forgetting the modesty of woman, avowed a passion."

" Hold ! Morgatani, I —"

" Him to whom you knelt in your despair."

" Not even from you," cried Agatha, rising from the chair into which she had sunk, " not even from you, Morgatani, will I hear this any more. Taunt me thus, and I will bury a dagger in your heart. My brain is fire itself while you use such words. My blood boils and I—I—would tear his heart—his living panting heart from his breast. I could revel in his gore— I—I—will have revenge—air—air—the window—let me have some air !"

" So," said Morgatani, as he threw the casement wide open. " So you can yet feel the memory of your injury. It still rankles in your heart, Agatha Weare. Methought you were turning cold upon your revenge, and that it was necessary to use the goad of recollection to urge you on to your blunted purpose."

Agatha said nothing for some moments, but she leant towards the window and allowed the cool air to play upon her fevered brow. Then in a low voice, she said,—

" Morgatani, never again tempt me so far. You know the depth of slumbering passion that lies hidden in a slighted woman's heart. It needs no goading to revenge. Be satisfied I will not pause in what I have undertaken, and do you let any passing remark that may be wrung from the weakness of human nature go unheeded. My purpose is as fixed as the decrees of that fate which we must all obey. I will have revenge even unto death upon Sir Rupert Brandon."

" Well said," cried the monk. " Of a verity I was wrong to say so much. We understand each other better from this moment, Agatha Weare ; and now it is necessary you should summon this Fitzhugh, and assure him of his safety in the coming combat, or else he will by some means yet escape it."

" Can he be so assured with safety ?"

" He can. You need tell him no more than that you are a friend to King John, and will mingle something in Sir Kenneth's drink that will take the manly strength from his sinews and enfeeble even his mind. He, Fitzhugh, will most eagerly second you, and moreover we shall be making a friend at court."

" I will send for him now."

" And be sure you trust him not too far. Say nothing of me, for the true policy of having a confederate, is never to let him know more than may make him useful. I will now leave you, but meet me before nightfall on the staircase of the Grey Turret, when I will give you the poison draught that shall not kill, but yet shall reduce to second childhood the flower of English chivalry, Sir Kenneth Hay ; he shall to-morrow appear in the lists like one stricken by the hand of Heaven to his destruction."

" Let it be so," muttered Agatha. " 'Tis well, Morgatani, your policy is deep and terrible."

" Success will insure it, Agatha Weare. Let us now part ; and do you entertain both these knights with seeming equal courtesy, that no suspicions may be awakened. When you reach the turret staircase, make the accustomed signal, and I will have the subtle fluid, which will work such woe to Sir Kenneth Hay, prepared. Farewell for a time."

The monk turned from Agatha and disappeared through the secret doorway leading from Agatha's chamber.

At the same moment a small figure glided from the corridor immediately outside the ordinary entrance to the apartment. It was the page that Fitzhugh had brought with him. He glided into a window seat and remained a moment or two in deep thought. A convulsive sob then shook his frame, and he started at the sound he had made.

" Hush, hush," he whispered. " O, God, that we could dictate to our affections ; but we cannot—we cannot. I must save this gallant knight from the treachery that is around ; and oh, that I may perish in the attempt."

The page then glided from the window seat, and wrote some words on a scrap of paper, which he handed to Sir Kenneth Hay in the mysterious manner we are already aware of.

The monk left Agatha in a fearful state of mind. The awful nights she sometimes passed, crowded with fearful dreams, had shaken much of the resolution with which she had commenced her career of crime ; and there were times when remorse would bring such pangs to her heart that she could have shrieked aloud in her mental agony. The monk had well noted this occasional wavering spirit in Agatha, and he had resolved occasionally, let her anger be what it might, to remind her of the insult she had received from the rejection of her proffered love by Sir Rupert Brandon.

By this course, Morgatani judged rightly that he should succeed in keeping alive the wild fire of her feelings and stimulating her to take part in crimes she, otherwise, would have shrunk from aghast.

" It shall be done," she muttered ; " he shall have the poison. I feel as one who has commenced the deep descent of some slippery path,—I must go on, for to return were instant destruction : he shall have the poison. And should there ever come a day when life to me is too terrible, I can die ; surely I can die ; and let doating churchmen say what they will there is— there must be—peace for ever in the grave !"

Eldred now made his appearance at the door, and in a whining voice, said, " Sister, now don't be in a passion ; you know that I could not help it ; yon Sir Kenneth is such a big fellow, and he came up to me with such a bounce that I thought he was going to snap my head off."

" Disgrace to your name !" cried Agatha. " Disgrace to your sex. I

have scarce patience to answer you. Eldred, Eldred, when will you show one spark of that courage which so well becomes a man ?"

"Courage ! Oh, I,—if I must say it,—I think one of the greatest possessions of life is a whole skin. I don't like fighting ; you know I never did. Don't you remember, Agatha, you used to knock me about, and always got the better of me when we were quite children ?"

" Peace, peace."

" Well, that's just what I say, especially when there's any likelihood of a row. Peace, I say ; peace always."

" Go you to the servants' hall and order a banquet, consisting of the best viands the castle can afford, to be served up with what expedition it may, in the painted chamber. These knights must be entertained."

"A banquet ?" cried Eldred. " Oh, certainly. Now, that's what I do like, I like the sauces. They are so nice and rich. By the bye, I ain't a bad hand at making a sauce or two, so as I dare say I shall not be wanted here or anywhere where these fighting fellows are, I'll just amuse myself in the kitchen helping to make the sauces—it's well to be useful."

" Can this be a brother of mine ?" muttered Agatha, as she left the room, Eldred having made off without waiting for her answer. " Can it be that kindred blood to his flows in my veins ?"

CHAPTER XXXIII.

A dastard wight I ween was he,—he loved not noble deeds;
But far preferred to deck himself in lowly menial weeds.—ANON.

ELDRED'S COOKERY.——THE PAGE AND HIS SONG.—TREACHERY.

WHEN Sir Kenneth unfolded the written paper which had been handed to him in so mysterious a manner by the page of Fitzhugh, he found it to contain these words,—

No. 17

"Beware of poison!"

The knight started as he read them. "What can this mean?" he thought. "Beware of poison? Can it be possible that there is any such danger here, or is this some deep device to scare me from the banquet? I have heard often of such warnings as these, having no other foundation than the fancy of their writers—I will heed it not. Besides, 'tis too indefinite, for how am I to beware of poison, unless I refuse to let anything pass my lips within this place, and that would be a hard penance. Stay, the person who handed me this note may still be lurking in the same spot."

The knight turned, and hastily striding back, he pushed the door, from a small opening from which the page had given him the note. It opened on to a flight of stone steps leading to a platform below the ramparts. He could see no one, and just as the attendant hurried up to him with the words—

"Noble sir, you have mistaken the way," he had closed the door again."

"I will follow you, friend," said Sir Kenneth. "This castle seems full of mysteries. How long have you lived here without being frightened out of your wits?"

"By the mass, sir, not long. Brandon Castle is enough to make a serving man's hair stand an end from morning till night. We don't see or hear much in the east wing, but Bernard, and Anstey, and Joyce Evans tell us sometimes such things that the cook is fain almost to get up the chimney, and we are all afraid to go to bed for days afterwards."

"Why, you don't go to bed in the day time, do you?"

"Yes! Since the ghosts and lights in the Grey Turret we have taken it by turns to go to bed in the day time, and we sit up at night; because you know, noble sir, that spirits are not known to walk in broad daylight."

"Upon my word," said Sir Kenneth, "my friend Sir Rupert has a pleasant property of this Brandon Castle."

"Oh, sir; it wasn't near so bad when our master was here. We certainly did now and then have a scream from some of the maids at their own shadows belike on a wall, or somebody would fancy they thought they imagined they saw something; but now—oh, it's dreadful."

"Then the sooner Sir Rupert returns the better," said the knight, "and so I shall tell him."

"Bless you, sir, do. We shall have no peace till he does come home."

"I don't know that. Some one else may do a little good. Now can you tell me if ever you saw one Morgatani, a monk?"

"Gracious, sir, don't mention him."

"And why not?"

"It's thought, sir, that he has dealings with the thingummy."

"The devil?"

"Yes, sir."

"Pho, pho! All monks do. Has he been in the castle since Sir Rupert kicked him out?"

"Why, noble sir," said the attendant, glaring around him timidly, "I won't say he has; but I can't say he hasn't, for some say as they have seen him."

"Then you may depend he is at the bottom of all this devilry in Brandon."

The servant now approached the knight very carefully, and standing on tip-toes, he placed his mouth close to his ear, and whispered—

"I—think—so—too."

Sir Kenneth mysteriously beckoned to the attendant, and when he came close to him, he said in the same tone—

"Do—you?"

"Oh," said the attendant, evidently disappointed at not hearing something very dreadful, which he might have had the pleasure of retailing again in the hall.

" Now pray go on towards this banquet," said the laughing Sir Kenneth, " for my stomach groans for food more than does my imagination for the marvels of Brandon Castle."

The attendant led the way, and the knight was conducted to the same painted chamber into which he had been shown on his first arrival. There were several attendants present laying upon a large oaken table an ample repast, the main dish of which consisted of a magnificent venison pasty, sufficiently large to have amply dined twenty hungry troopers.

" Ha !" cried Sir Kenneth, " that looks well ; yon pasty is food for the eyes as well as the stomach. Truly I am thankful for such good cheer. Where is your lady ?"

" She will be here anon, sir," said a serving man.

In a few moments Agatha made her appearance, and so well had she schooled her features, that no traces of the dark passions that had been so very recently struggling at her heart were visible in her face. She bowed courteously to the knight, who returned her salutation with the practised ease of the man of the world.

" I will take her civility," he thought, " as it comes, without testing too curiously its sincerity."

" It is," said Agatha, " my duty as well my pleasure to make welcome a friend of Sir Rupert Brandon's ; and if I too strenuously opposed the combat you wished to have with the knight from court, it was more that I should avoid a reproach from Sir Rupert upon his return for permitting brawling in his ancient home, than from a wish to favour one knight before another."

" Oh, lady," replied Sir Kenneth, with a smile ; " Sir Rupert would scarcely consider a lance broken in good King Richard's name as a brawl. Nay, I am sure he would be the first to blame me for not defying yon messenger from court. Nevertheless, as he, Fitzhugh, has accepted my challenge, I shall now treat him with as much courtesy as befits one knight to another, although I have a contempt for him and his knighthood, which I am convinced he has won not fairly."

" Let peace and apparent concord, at all events, reign at the festive board," said Agatha.

" It shall, as far as I am concerned."

" Sir knight, I thank you, Will it please you to be seated. I will be with you soon, and in the meantime, perchance you may be amused by the strains of a young page belonging to Fitzhugh, who even now has asked my leave to sing to you after the banquet."

" Let him come," said Sir Kenneth ; " I delight in minstrelsy much. The strains of Blondel, King Richard's rare minstrel, have soothed many a pang of his heart, and reflected joy upon mine. Let the boy come, lady."

" He shall," said Agatha ; " and by the time the tables are spread I will be with you."

Agatha then left the painted chamber, in order to have a few words conversation with Fitzhugh. She found him, according to the orders she had given, in the small oaken parlour in which she usually spent her mornings, and when she entered the room, he rose, and bowing low, said :—

" Lady, I am here in obedience to your commands. May I presume to hope I have found so much favour in your eyes, that you will permit me to ask a boon ?"

" I will first, sir, inform you why I seek this private interview," said Agatha. " Firstly, it is to tell you that myself and my brother are great favourers of King John in preference to Richard."

" Lady, that were good news if Sir Rupert Brandon were dead."

" There is a time for all things," said Agatha ; " but secondly, I came to talk to you of your intended combat with Sir Kenneth Hay."

"And it is upon that subject that I humbly wish to consult you, lady," said Fitzhugh ; "I am awkwardly situated, for, as a special messenger of King John's, I am not free to take up this quarrel. King John cannot just now afford to have his friends picked off by hot crusaders, who have been in practice of fighting for months—nay, years. It might be, then, that this Sir Kenneth Hay, who bears with him a reputation, would conquer me."

"'Tis more than probable," said Agatha.

"Perhaps kill me."

"I think he would."

Fitzhugh changed colour as he said,—

"Then, lady, my boon to you, is that some time after midnight you allow me to leave Brandon and proceed on my mission without encountering this turbulent man. Not that I fear him, but I think my duty stands full in the way of my combat of to-morrow."

"I quite understand you, sir," said Agatha, with a scarcely suppressed sneer ; "but should you be assured of conquering Sir Kenneth Hay, your duty probably would not stand in the way of the contest."

Fitzhugh shook his head as he said,

"The issue of a combat can be only surmised. I fear me he is the stronger."

"So that you do conquer him, you care you for the means ?" said Agatha.

"The means ? Certainly not. I have no such troublesome scruples."

"Good ; then you shall be the victor to-morrow. I have a potion which I will administer to Sir Kenneth in his wine, and which by to-morrow's dawn will have bred such havoc in his frame, that his strength will be as nought, and you can easily overcome him."

"Indeed ! Can this be done ?" said Fitzhugh, with exultation. "The renown I shall acquire in conquering such a knight as Sir Kenneth Hay will rescue my name from every evil speaker ; I shall be a made man. If you can and will, lady, accomplish so much for me, my unbounded gratitude shall be yours while I have life."

"All I require is, that you commend me to the king your master, and tell him that although he has a dangerous enemy in Sir Rupert Brandon, he has a warm friend in Agatha Weare, who, if needs be, would even maintain the castle against Sir Rupert, or give him up as a traitor."

"Your devotion to the king shall not go unreported," said Fitzhugh. "Now, indeed, I long for to-morrow as a day of triumph. You are quite sure the poison draught will be effective ?"

"Quite. It is prepared by a Jesuit."

"Then there can be very little doubt, for I do believe the Jesuits can raise the devil himself to aid them if they have a fancy so to do."

"Come now to the banquet—be courteous to Sir Kenneth, as he has promised to be to you, and wait the morning with confidence, for as sure as that you are now alive you shall win the fight."

"A thousand thanks, lady. The devotion of my heart will be ever yours. To have inspired in the heart of one so fair—a feeling ——"

"What, sir ?" cried Agatha, turning upon him, and her eyes flashing with rage.

"I merely ventured to hope," said the unabashed Fitzhugh, "that you had deigned to regard your humble servant with an eye of favour."

"You ?"

"Aye, lady ; among men, I flatter myself I am passing well-looking."

"Wretch—coward," cried Agatha, stepping towards him, "how dare you presume so far ?"

"Nay, lady, the great care you have had of my life gave me hopes ——"

"Hopes, sir. Beware what you say, or you may raise a spirit you fain would quell again—I look upon such as thou with favour !"

"Your words are harsh, but wherefore do you take such kindly interest in me, an it be not for myself? Smooth your brows, lady, and give a smile to one who is smitten with your charms,—one who owes you so much."

"Are you a fool as well as a coward?" said Agatha, endeavouring to smother her rage.

"Now you are unkind," murmured Fitzhugh. "If love has not prompted, what other passion could make you so solicitous for my safety?"

"Revenge!" cried Agatha, as she left the room, leaving Fitzhugh quite bewildered at the scene he had gone through.

CHAPTER XXXIV.

"Shun the cup with treacherous wine.
Let the lips—let the lips
Of the goblet ne'er touch thine."

THE WARNING.—SIR KENNETH'S CARELESSNESS.—THE BANQUET.

THE day was now rapidly drawing to its close, and huge wax tapers were lighted in the painted chamber, to do honour to the guests. The room was of considerable extent, and the roof, from which it took its name, was splendidly emblazoned over its whole extent with the arms of the Brandon family. The walls were hung with damask, and the highly-polished oaken floor was lightly strewn with fine rushes.

Sir Kenneth was seated in a high-backed chair, which was richly carved, and covered with Genoa velvet. When the page entered the room, there was a look about the boy of timid bashfulness, extremely different from that usually to be noted upon the countenances of the dissolute and impertinent youths who at that period followed knights and ladies in the idle capacity of a page.

"Come hither, boy," cried Sir Kenneth. "They say you desired to sing to me. In truth you look by far too bashful to sing if you were asked so to do. Did you really desire to give me an old ballad?"

"I did, Sir Knight," said the page, timidly, as he glanced around him on the serving men who were dressing the table.

"Then let me hear it, boy. Let it be of war, and, if possible, of Richard Cœur de Lion."

"Nay, sir, I know but few songs of war; but I can sing you a ditty of a knight who was put to death by poison."

"Poison?" said Sir Kenneth, his mind instantly reverting to the note he had received.

The page glanced at the attendants, and then, hanging down his head, he said,—

"Shall I sing the strain, sir?"

"Aye, do," said Sir Kenneth, who began to suspect the page to be the author of the note of warning which had been put into his hands. "Let me hear it, boy. If you have a good voice, and the song please me not, I still shall listen with pleasure."

The page commenced in a low, but exceedingly sweet voice, the following song :—

"Gallant knight, gallant knight,
Shun the cup with treacherous wine;
Let the lips, let the lips
Of the goblet ne'er touch thine.

> Poison lurks in many a flower,
>   With colours rich and fine;
> Why may it not be found for thee
>   In the juice of the blushing wine?
> Gallant knight, gallant knight,
>   Shun the cup with treacherous wine;
> Let the lips, let the lips
>   Of the goblet ne'er touch thine."

The page ceased, and Sir Kenneth Hay, bending forward, said,—

"Boy, has your song a meaning?"

"Hush!" said the page, as Eldred Weare at the moment came into the room.

He was attired most singularly, having on his head a white night-cap, and a napkin being tucked under his chin, in order to save his clothes from grease in his culinary operations.

"Now, knaves—now, knaves," he cried; "come one of you to the kitchen. The sauce I am making wants to be perpetually stirred, and ——"

He now saw Sir Kenneth, whom he did not suppose was yet in the room, and he paused suddenly in his cooking explanations.

"Well, Master Weare," laughed Sir Kenneth; "you are taking much trouble on my account,—or, do you usually assist the cook?"

"I—oh, I? You mean me?" stammered Eldred, as he snatched off the night-cap; "it's only a joke—ha! ha! ha!—I just wanted to amuse myself a little—you understand?—ha! ha!"

"Upon my word I never heard a more unmeaning laugh in my life," said the knight. "Is that your sister, Mistress Agatha, I see coming?"

"My sister?" cried Eldred, in a great fright. "Bless me! she won't see the joke—she never does see a joke. What a rage she will be in to be sure. I shall never hear the last of it. Here, you Master Page, take this night-cap and napkin to the kitchen. On the fire you will see a small stew-pan, and a large woman stirring what's in it. The small stew-pan contains the most delicious sauce ever you tasted; but don't taste it, for there can't be much of it. The large woman is the cook; and, as I dare say she is tired of stirring it by this time, do you take her place."

"I am a knight's page," said the boy, haughtily; "not lacquey to a cook's assistant."

"Well, I never!" exclaimed Eldred. "Did you ever hear the like of that? Do you mean me by the—the cook's assistant?"

"Yes."

"Oh, you—you. I've a good mind to thrash you soundly, and I will too—yet—dear me, what's to-day?"

"Thursday, Master Eldred," said a servant.

"Oh, Thursday. Well, my lad, Mr. Knight's page, it's an amazing lucky thing for you it does happen to be this day."

"Indeed?"

"Yes, indeed; I never fight on a Thursday, or else I would have beat you dreadfully!"

"I shall be here to-morrow," said the page.

"Ah! but I don't bear malice. If I don't beat my man at once, I never touch him at all. You have escaped, young fellow, for once, with a whole skin. Learn discretion and respect for your superiors, or you may not always be so lucky, you know."

Sir Kenneth Hay could no longer command his countenance, but laughed aloud as he cried,—

"Why, Master Eldred, the boy will brain you if you say too much. That sauce you were making must have got into your head."

"Ah! it's all very fine," said Eldred. "When I'm roused, I'm tremendous—awful in my rage—I—".

As Eldred attempted to throw himself into a heroic attitude, he ran against a man who was bringing in some hot soup, and upset himself, soup, and man, with a great crash.

Sir Kenneth Hay forgot all about the mysterious hints of the page in his great enjoyment of the scene, and he laughed till the tears ran down his face.

"Whence arises all this tumult?" said Agatha, as she appeared at the door of the room.

Eldred immediately scrambled to his feet and ran off, leaving who liked to explain the affair.

"Lady," said Sir Kenneth, with difficulty moderating his laughter, "your valiant brother ran against a serving man."

Agatha bit her lips with vexation, as she said,

"My brother fatigues his brain too much with study, to know what he says or does one half of his time."

"Oh!" said the knight, "study always makes me ill; I like fighting a vast deal better."

Fitzhugh now entered the room, and bowed very low to Sir Kenneth Hay, who returned the salutation by slightly bending his head. Then he said,

"Fitzhugh, we are now guests of this honourable lady, and while we are so, we will lay aside private quarrels, as in duty bound."

"Your sentiment, Sir Kenneth, finds an echo in my own heart," said Fitzhugh, blandly. "Will it please you to drink with me?"

He poured out a goblet of wine as he spoke and handed it to the knight.

"Or shall I sing you the ballad of 'Shun the wine cup?'" interposed the page.

Fitzhugh turned hastily, and looked surprised at the interruption.

"Away, sir," he cried, "by the mass, the boy has lost his wits; I never knew you so forward before."

The page shrunk away to the further end of the apartment, and Sir Kenneth looked grave for a moment, when he said,—

"Fill for yourself, Fitzhugh."

Fitzhugh filled himself a bumper from the same flagon, and drank first, which perfectly reassured the knight, and he drained his own glass on the instant without suspicion.

The banquet now proceeded merrily, and each moment Sir Kenneth Hay thought more and more that the page must be wrong in his suspicions, for Fitzhugh and Agatha both drank freely from the same flagon of wine from which his glass was filled. The hours flew quickly and pleasantly by, until Agatha rose from the table and said,—

"I will leave you now. Pray make good cheer. There is in the castle some rare wine which Sir Rupert has ever kept for his own use. It has been blessed by a saint, and one cup of it is bestowed upon every guest we wish to honour. I will see that it be sent to you. The saints guard you, farewell!"

The knights rose and bowed to Agatha as she left the room, and Sir Kenneth Hay, who had drank rather deeply of the generous wine, cried,—

"Aye, lady, send us the rare liquor. I will report its flavour to Sir Rupert, when I see him."

The page now, in a careless tone, as if singing merely for his own amusement said,—

"Shun the cup with treacherous wine,
Let the lips—let the lips,
Of the goblet ne'er touch thine."

"What do you mutter there, boy?" cried Fitzhugh, with sudden anger.

" Merely a fragment of an old ditty, sir," said the page. " It tells how a noble knight was poisoned by drugged wine, and how after that he ——"

" Peace," roared Fitzhugh, " leave the room or I will chastise this forward insolence. Tempt me to strike you, boy, and you will repent it bitterly. My hand falls heavy in anger."

" Nay, moderate your wrath, Fitzhugh," said Sir Kenneth, " those lads who can sing are proud of their art, and no doubt the youngster thought to lure us to ask him for a song."

" He is too forward," said Fitzhugh, " begone, I say—begone."

The page with a reluctant step left the room.

" I know not what has come over the boy," muttered the alarmed Fitzhugh, " I used to find him ever obedient and gentle, and never knew him speak till called upon to do so."

" Have you had him in your service long ?" said Sir Kenneth.

" Not above a few months. He came and solicited service of me, commending himself much for discretion beyond his years ; upon which I entertained him, and have found him faithful."

" He seems a delicate youth, and has a sweet voice ; he sang me a song even now."

" 'Tis strange ; I can scarcely myself ever induce him to sing."

" It is strange," said Sir Kenneth. " Drink—the wine stands with you."

" I thank you," said Fitzhugh, " but as I have in the morning to encounter so renowned a warrior as Sir Kenneth Hay, I think it wise to retire early to repose."

" As you please," said Sir Kenneth. " What now ?"

A servant entered the room with a small slip of paper in his hand, which he handed to Sir Kenneth Hay. On it were these words,—

" The guard of Brandon Castle request the favour of Sir Kenneth Hay inspecting their arms and accoutrements, ere he retires for the night, in order that when he shall next see their noble master he may report to him concerning such matters."

" Good," cried Sir Kenneth, who took this as it really was, merely a hint from Wingrove to meet him in the guard-room. " I will come directly."

He then threw the slip of paper upon the table in order that Fitzhugh might read it if he chose, and not have any suspicions awakened concerning his, Sir Kenneth's, intentions of exploring the castle, and rising, said,—

" A pleasant night's repose to you. We meet early to-morrow ?"

" As early as you please," said Fitzhugh, " I consider myself much honoured in the chance of breaking a lance with so renowned a knight as Sir Kenneth Hay."

" Oh, sir, you have lived in court and learnt to flatter," said Sir Kenneth, as he left the room, preceded by the attendant, who volunteered to guide him to the guard-room.

" Do I flatter?" muttered Fitzhugh, when he was alone. " In truth, I do ; for if this revengeful lady keeps her word, your laurels will be transferred to my brows, Sir Kenneth Hay. But then if she should not, or if the potion should fail in its effect, or he refuse to drink it from some cause. Where am I then ?"

A cold perspiration of intense fear broke out upon the forehead of Fitzhugh as he began to repent of having placed reliance upon Agatha.

" Even now if I could find a means, I would leave Brandon," he muttered ; " but that is quite impossible. I must abide the issue of to-morrow, now."

CHAPTER XXXV.

Take thou this potion—it bears great
Animosity to life,—
I will use it on mine enemy.—OLD PLAY.

THE APPARITION IN THE SOUTHERN GALLERY.—AGATHA'S TERRORS.—THE POISON.

AGATHA, when she left the two knights carousing in the painted chamber, took from her pocket an ancient key, with which she opened a door leading into a suite of apartments that had long fallen into disuse, but which led by a near cut to the southern gallery, and from thence to the Grey Turret. She carried in one hand a lamp, which shed an uncertain and a flickering light around her as she entered the gloomy precincts of the long deserted rooms.

"Oh, how I hate this abode and all connected with it," she muttered. "It ever reminds me of the bitter—the awful feelings that crossed my heart when, with cold courtesy, Sir Rupert rejected the wild love I offered him. I could never be happy here—happy—shall I ever again be happy?—but I must not think that way now. To-night I have to act, not to reflect. This knight must have the subtle poison Morgatani is even now preparing for him; so will King John, by such a trifling circumstance, perchance succeed in wresting England's crown from Richard. Then too, an accusation against Sir Rupert Brandon will gain ready credence. The monk reasons well,—Morgatani is right."

Agatha passed through room after room, each more or less presenting to the eye the remains of former magnificence. Here were faded hangings, half dropping from the walls—there rich, carved furniture, covered with the dust of years. Antique cabinets—rare oak tables, and carved chairs, all destined

No. 18

in another age to be admired by the vertuosi, and to form the ornaments of a more polished race.

The dim rays of the lamp glanced upon the gilding, that still retained some of its pristine lustre, on the roofs and cornices, giving an air of gloomy yet grand magnificence to the stately rooms.

Agatha's mind was, however, too much occupied with its own dark and terrible thoughts to heed the interesting records of a former magnificence, which greeted her on every side. Her whole soul was absorbed by her own passions as hatred, revenge, despair, and remorse struggled for mastery at her heart.

" Let who will suffer, I care not," she muttered, " so that the suffering ministers to my revenge."

Her last word echoed through a large apartment she was in ; the word revenge appeared to fall back upon her ear as if uttered by some awful voice from the tomb.

Agatha turned ghastly pale, and with a shudder she quickened her steps, in order to get through the long suite of gloomy apartments. She was now in the last one, and with a feeling of great relief she opened the door, passed out into the southern gallery from whence Bernard and Wingrove had watched the mysterious light in the loop-holes of the Grey Turret.

" He is surely ready," she thought. " This wing of Brandon is most dismal, and, unbeliever as I am in all the supernatural world, busy fancy will ofttimes people solitudes like this with strange forms. Gracious powers !"

Agatha dropped the lamp and started back in terror, as a ray of light came through a window, and falling upon the opposite wall of the gallery, continued to increase in size, until it assumed the appearance of a skeleton head—the ghastly moisture of the tomb seemed clinging to it, and from the rotting gums the teeth seemed as if in the act of dropping one by one.

It was but for one fleeting moment that Agatha saw the fearful sight, and then it was gone, leaving the gallery in impenetrable darkness.

For a few moments then she stirred not, for terror had nearly frozen up her faculties. When she did move it was with trembling steps, and she gasped in choking accents,—

" What awful messenger from another world was that? Did it come at the moment of my expression of unbelief to scare me into faith, in all which I would fain disbelieve or go mad in the believing? Hence—hence horrible shadows ! I will speed to Morgatani—he shall assure me that that was some phantom of the overwrought brain. I will not be scared from my revenge by such images. No, no—though all hell should open at my feet, I will have my revenge !"

She advanced to the door which opened from the gallery, and, conducted by the narrow winding staircase, came to the small paved court, from whence the Grey Turret rose in all its gloom and decay. Shading then the lamp with her hand, as she came into the open air, she moved with a noiseless step across the old flag-stones, between which the rank grass was growing, until she reached the door at the foot of the staircase leading to the turret. It yielded to her touch, and in another moment she had passed from the open air, and with a shudder stood within the precincts of the unhallowed spot, which by common belief was peopled with horrible shapes—a belief which even Agatha, scorning, as she did, most vulgar superstitions, could not at that moment rid herself of, so powerful had been the impression made upon her by the sight she had witnessed in the gallery, and so highly wrought up were her nerves to the deed of iniquity she had come to that place to find the means of perpetrating.

Never had Agatha ventured to intrude upon the privacy of Morgatani in that lonely turret; and now she stood upon the staircase, holding the lamp above her head, so as to cast its rays as far as possible up the gloomy ascent, in momentary expectation of being joined by the monk, who she doubted not was in the turret.

Not long had Agatha to endure the suspense she was in, for scarcely had she began to breathe freely after the terror she had experienced in her passage to to the turret, than the deep-toned voice of the monk pronounced her name.

"I am here, Morgatani," she replied.

"Ascend," said the monk.

Agatha obeyed the mandate, and slowly ascended the time-worn staircase, until she reached the landing immediately outside the turret-door, where stood the monk, his tall form thrown into bold relief by a lamp which burned at his feet and cast his gigantic shadow upon the turret door and the blackened walls.

"You are punctual, Agatha," he said ; " saw you nothing as you passed through the southern gallery ?"

"I saw that which, had I been weaker than I am, would have curdled my blood with horror."

"'Tis well and ill," said Morgatani. "When that sight met your gaze I knew not that 'twas you in the gallery, or you should have been spared it. Agatha, heed not what sounds you hear or what sights you see in Brandon Castle—superstition is the weapon we wield to subject human nature to our sway."

"Then by your art you produced that frightful object which met my gaze ?"

"I did ; know, Agatha, that the secrets of nature are much revealed to my order, and we can do things which may well appal the bravest."

"Then whatever sight of terror meets my eye, may I indeed believe that it is produced by your science ?"

"You may—so rest in peace. We have a deep and dangerous game to play, and I would fain relieve your mind from all fears but one."

"And that ?"

"The fear of failure, which may itself be made to dwindle even into nothing by our own perseverance. We have but to keep the one great object in view —the utter destruction of Sir Rupert Brandon, and we must succeed. Even this circumstance of Sir Kenneth Hay arriving here will eventually aid us in our purpose : for by the means we shall adopt to spoil his mission from the Holy Land we shall acquire great favour with King John, who will then be possessed with two reasons for listening greedily to an accusation against Sir Rupert Brandon—namely, favour to us, the accusers, and disfavour to him, the accused."

"I understand you," said Agatha. "Have you ready the potion which is to seize upon the faculties of this Sir Kenneth Hay, and give the fortune of the fight to his opponent ?"

"I have, Agatha ; 'tis here. Three drops of this subtle fluid will suffice to make him weak as an infant by to-morrow's morn—then shall the craven-hearted Fitzhugh—who, but that he is useful at the present juncture, I could myself brain for his cowardice—overcome easily one of the most renowned knights in Christendom."

"Will the effects of the poison continue on the frame of Sir Kenneth ?" asked Agatha.

"No," replied Morgatani ; " on the third morning from to-morrow he will be well again, but before then he will have found a home in one of the dungeons of Brandon Castle ; there he shall pine away his life a prisoner, until I shall think fit to release him by death."

"Why preserve his life now ?" said Agatha.

"Because I hope to make him useful yet. I have a plan for making even this Sir Kenneth an evidence against our common enemy, Sir Rupert Brandon. The mind, weakened by bodily suffering, will receive impressions, which in happier circumstances it would scorn and stand aloof from. Take you now the poison, and be sure it be administered by some means to Sir Kenneth Hay, at least six hours before the combat, and should no opportunity present itself until the matin meal you must use some pretext to put off the fight until near mid-day, when all will be as we desire."

Agatha took a small phial containing the poison which the monk had prepared, and then preparing to descend the turret stairs, she said,—

"Adieu, Morgatani—would this liquid ensure me a forgetfulness of the past, how gladly would I drain it to the dregs."

"Remember your revenge," whispered the monk.

"Hush, hush! No more of that—I need no tempting to pursue the path of vengeance I have chosen; but oh, Morgatani, if you could convince me there is no hereafter, methinks my heart would grow light within my breast."

"'Tis superstition merely weighs it down," whispered the monk. "We are the creatures of destiny; we each have our part to play until the grim hand of death lays us low in the grave, there to rot again into the humid earth from whence we sprung."

"You believe in nothing?"

"Nothing," echoed the monk, as he turned from Agatha to enter the turret.

Agatha tremblingly descended the narrow stairs, and with a sickness at her heart which made her brain dizzy and her steps uncertain, she took her way to her own chamber. Her movements were more mechanical than the result of present reflection, for she had before arranged all she meant to do, and she now went through it like a performer playing a part. She took from a cabinet in the room a richly-chased drinking cup of silver, and filling it with wine she dropped into it three drops of the poison.

"To Sir Kenneth's chamber," she muttered. "To Sir Kenneth's chamber —he cannot well refuse to pledge me in this goblet. I will tell him it is Sir Rupert's own wine-cup, and that it is the custom at Brandon to offer it to the most honoured guest. He will drink it—he will drink it."

CHAPTER XXXVI.

He was a gallant knight,
　　A knight beyond compare;
No danger e'er affrighted him,
　　His courage was so rare.—HERRICK.

THE GUARD-ROOM.—SIR KENNETH AND THE VOICE.—ELDRED'S FEAR.

WHEN Sir Kenneth Hay retired to his apartment, his first care was to take the light which had been given him, and examine all parts of it, for his own observation of Agatha, as well as the hints of the page of Fitzhugh, had began to work upon his mind, and induce him, however reluctantly, to consider that there might be danger even in the home of his best friend, Sir Rupert Brandon.

"Surely," he thought, "yon page must be aware of something evil intended me, or he wouldn't have taken so much trouble to warn me against exceeding a moderate dose of wine, for to such an end his warnings must have alluded. He feared my faculties might become steeped in the fumes of Sir Rupert's rare Burgundy, and then that I should fall a prey to the machinations of those who would do me injury. Well, I have been careful, and it will go hard with Sir Kenneth Hay, if, sooner or later, he finds no opportunity of returning a good turn."

While thus communing with himself, the knight carefully examined each nook and corner in the ancient chamber allotted to him, without, however, discovering anything of a suspicious character, and then, ever more prone to generous feelings than suspicious ones, he said :—

"Well, after all, the youngster may be wrong, and fain would I believe he is, though there is always something extremely suspicious about sudden kindness such as I have experienced from this Agatha Weare, when it follows so close upon contrary conduct. But now for my appointment with Hugh Wingrove, and much pleasure will it give me, while thus a solitary sojourner, as it were, within the ancient Castle of Brandon, to set at rest the superstitious feelings which seem to beset every one in it. I will see the inside of this much-dreaded Grey Turret, though all the evil spirits in Brandon were to say me nay."

Twelve o'clock had solemnly been given forth by the castle clock some time before, and now, taking in his hand his night lamp, the gallant Sir Kenneth sallied forth to keep his appointment with the faithful Wingrove, who with much pleasure had prepared the castle guard for the visit of the knight, whose fame had been the ready theme of every palmer or minstrel who had wandered homewards from the Holy Land.

Sir Kenneth was met a few paces from his door by Wingrove, who said in an under tone :—

"This way, Sir Kenneth. On my faith, it would seem as if those in the Grey Turret knew of the coming of a Christian, and were disturbed at the thought, for there have been strange sounds and gleaming lights coming from it for more than an hour past now."

"Indeed, Wingrove. Then it is time we went to it, and in the name of Heaven and a right cause, will I draw my sword against every evil thing that may bar my progress, and will not have to tell Sir Rupert that I found his castle disturbed by fears which I made no attempt to dissipate. Lead on, Wingrove ; I am ready."

"Will it not please you, first, Sir Kenneth, to bestow a few moments of your company upon my companions in arms in the guard-room. Many of them are old soldiers who have fought and bled with Sir Rupert."

"In good sooth, yes," cried Sir Kenneth. "Lead me to them, good Wingrove, and such kind phrases as I can now remember Sir Rupert has so often used when speaking of them beneath the beautiful night sky of the east, when we have lain down together to snatch a few hours' brief repose ere the morning's light should summon us to meet the foe, I will repeat to them."

Wingrove's eyes glistened with pleasure as he heard Sir Kenneth Hay speak, and with a voice of emotion he said :—

"I cannot find words to tell you how welcome you will be. If you will follow me, Sir Kenneth, I will conduct you to them."

A low whining noise now attracted their attention, and in a moment a large hound came up to the knight, and by every means in its power testified affection for him.

A tear started to Wingrove's eye as he stooped and patted the creature, saying :—

"This was a great favourite of Sir Rupert's. The faithful creature would follow him and my deceased lady in their walks through the forest, gamboling with them, sometimes carrying a glove for the Lady Alicia, and ever ready to do all kinds of loving service. Since Sir Rupert went away the creature has moped sadly, and you are the first person it has taken any notice of."

The knight patted and spoke to the animal which could scarcely testify enough its delight.

"This creature shall go with us," said Sir Kenneth, "on our enterprise to-night if you think it will be obedient, and not be too active when not required. What is its name, Wingrove ?"

"Its name is York," said Wingrove; "Sir Rupert called it so, because, when quite a pup, it followed his charger through the streets of the city of York, and would not leave him for many weeks until he brought it home with him.   It would lie down when Sir Rupert told it."

"Lie down, York," said the knight, and the dog immediately lay at his feet, perfectly passive.

"He never would be so obedient to any one before, but his master," remarked Wingrove.   "I pray you take him with us, Sir Kenneth."

"He shall go ; ho ! York. Come on—come on."

Sir Kenneth followed Wingrove closely, and the dog kept by his side, testifying in every possible manner his pleasure at being with him.

The guard-room was soon reached, and Sir Kenneth was, on the moment, surrounded by the men-at-arms.

"My friends," he said, " I have the satisfaction to tell you that your noble master, Sir Rupert, never once forgot you, but always when he spoke of England and home, mentioned his soldiers—his dear companions in arms, with much kindly emotion, and hoped the day would come when, with a lightened spirit, he could once more be among you to share your pleasures and your toils."

The guard would have raised a shout of pleasure, but Wingrove interposed, saying ;—

"Hush, hush, remember Sir Rupert is not here, and this noble knight who has honoured us with a visit is on a secret enterprise."

"Perhaps," said Bernard, advancing, " Sir Kenneth now he's here, wouldn't mind, in a manner of speaking, you see, Master Wingrove, and comrades —"

"Well, what ?" said Wingrove.

"Why, I'm rather diffident. It's my weakness, but I only just thought—"

"Hang your diffidence," said Wingrove, " I'll let fall my halbert on your thick skull if you don't speak out at once what you mean."

"Well then," said Bernard, with a desperate air, " all I have to say is —ale !"

There was a general laugh as Bernard spoke, and then turning indignantly to his comrades, he said,

"Well, now, you'll all be ready enough to drink it, I'll warrant, when it comes.   Mind, Master Wingrove, all those that laugh, don't want any of the ale."

His remark immediately produced a degree of serious gravity that much amused Sir Kenneth, who, turning to Wingrove, said,

" For my sake let them have a few extra flagons."

"They shall have it, Sir Kenneth, but I expect you will come with us, Bernard."

"Me—oh.   What to the—the—"

"The Grey Turret."

"You surely don't mean that, and just as the ale's coming too.   Now you are so full of jokes, Wingrove."

"That is no joke," said Wingrove.   "You must come."

"Nay," said Sir Kenneth, " let us leave him to the enjoyment of his ale. We can manage by ourselves, I dare say."

A flush of colour came over the face of Bernard, as he drew his tall form up to its full height, and said,—

"Sir Kenneth Hay, I am fond of a good flagon of ale.   No man more so, but I am fonder of my honour and my duty. I will go with you, if as a consequence, not another cup of ale shall ever pass my lips. You know, Wingrove, for you have seen me fight, that I am no coward."

" A better soldier never fought," said Wingrove, "but the truth is, we do not want you, Bernard. There will be no fighting. If there were we should not go, where we are now going, without you."

"That's satisfactory," said Bernard. "Come along with me, Anstey, and fetch the ale."

"We will now proceed, if you please, on our enterprise," said Wingrove to Sir Kenneth.

"I am at your service," said the knight, taking from the wall where it hung, as he spoke, a heavy mace of much too great a length for the use of any ordinary man.

"This will be handy," he said, "if a door should obstinately stand in one's way."

He threw the massive piece of iron high up to the roof and caught it again as it descended, to the great admiration of the men-at-arms, who considered personal strength as one of the greatest of human attributes.

Wingrove thus led the way, and Sir Kenneth following him, they left the guard-room, accompanied by the hound, on this mission to explore the secrets of the Grey Turret.

"I have a lamp here," remarked Wingrove, "with a shade to it, by which we can remain enveloped in darkness, for as long a period as we please, or at once illumine any spot we may happen to wish to examine. The castle and all its various intricacies are so familiar to me, that by night or by day I could have gone almost blindfolded to any part of it, so, if you will let us now proceed in darkness and trust to my guidance, I think it will afford us a better chance of success in our undertaking."

"I will be guided by you," said Sir Kenneth, "as long as you will permit me to advance."

Wingrove then led the knight by the most unfrequented part of the castle towards the gallery which was so near to the Grey Turret; for, although he had seen sufficient in his own and Bernard's visits to the turret to warrant almost any superstitious construction he might choose to put upon the strange sights and sounds that had attacked his senses, he was yet not without a lingering belief that it would turn out that Morgatani was at the bottom of all the mischief, and that it would be a good thing to take him unawares, if possible.

They proceeded in silence for some time, and passed through many gloomy rooms, which, by the very dim light of the midnight sky, seemed covered with dust, and to have been much neglected, although of superb dimensions. Finally, they reached the southern gallery, and, in consequence of the number of windows in it, there came more light into it than into almost any other part of the building, and its long extent, except in the dull depth of the winter season, was perceptible at almost any hour of the night.

"We are now near the turret," whispered Wingrove. "From one of these windows we can command a clear view of the loophole from whence I have now several times seen issue the mysterious stream of light."

"Then Heaven send it may issue to-night," said Sir Kenneth Hay.

Scarcely had he spoken, when Wingrove laid his hand upon the knight's arm, saying, in an anxious whisper,—

"Gracious Heavens! some one is coming from the turret."

The knight placed his eye close to the window he was at, and saw a figure flit across the court-yard at the base of the turret, apparently coming from it towards the gallery. Neither of them spoke for several moments, and then the door conducting to the court-yard opened, and Agatha Weare, bearing a light, entered, on her route back from her last visit to the monk.

The slightest whisper from either Sir Kenneth Hay or Wingrove must have discovered them to Agatha, for she passed so close to them as almost to brush them with her garments. Above her head she held the lamp, and as its feeble rays fell upon her face, it presented to the eyes of those who saw her, a countenance so ghastly pale and so distorted by evil passions that it was dreadful to look upon : see to what a sad pass human passions could bring the features which God had stamped with intelligence, and which, under happier culture, might have shone resplendent with humanity and happiness.

Oh, let those who feel angered at evil doers banish the feelings from their breast. Let them not be anxious to punish the guilty; for as surely as there is a sun in the Heavens, will pangs far greater than human tortures could inflict, rend the hearts of those conscious of crime, and there will come a day, as it had come to Agatha Weare, when the hell within their own breasts will far exceed, in the exquisite agony of its torments, any that the fabled flames of the mansion of the evil one could inflict upon a disembodied spirit. Agatha passed on, more like a sceptre than a living, breathing being; not one particle of colour was visible in her cheeks or on her lips. Yes, she, even she, wicked as she was, and steeped in crime, might well be pitied even by her victims, for she could not make them endure one tithe of her own sufferings.

When she had passed on for some little distance, she suddenly paused and shaded her light with her hand. Then a loud cry came from a distant part of the gallery, and Eldred shouting,—

"Murder! fire! murder!" rushed towards her.

The sound of his voice seemed to convert in a moment the dull, torpid look of despair which had been upon Agatha's face into an expression of rage, and she in a moment placed herself in Eldred's way and grasped him by the arm, saying,—

"Wretch! how dare you make this alarm?"

"Oh! murder! fire! mercy!" cried Eldred. "Good Mr. Ghost, pray excuse me, I never did anything to anybody. Oh! pray let me go."

"Fool!" cried Agatha, "'tis I."

"Oh! oh! oh!" continued Eldred, lying on his back and hammering with his heels against the oaken floor. "Oh! oh! go to my sister Agatha, she don't mind a ghost or two, but I do."

"Coward!" cried Agatha.

"Yes, yes," said Eldred, "I know I am. Anything you like, but don't do me any harm. I'm very delicate, I always was, dear Mr. Ghost. Let me go pray. Oh, dear! oh, dear!"

Eldred was evidently too terrified to recognize his sister, and continued supplicating the mercy of the supposed ghost with all his might, until Agatha, stooping down to him, flashed the light in his eyes, crying,—

"Eldred Weare, look up, I am Agatha. Whence arises this consternation? Speak, I say—I am Agatha!"

CHAPTER XXXVII.

"Hark! hark! what awful sounds—
What dreadful form is here?
The stoutest heart grows cold,
The bravest well may fear."

THE APPARITION ON THE TURRET STAIRS.—THE SKELETON.

ELDRED now began to have some glimmering consciousness that it was his sister who was addressing him, and he gathered courage to open his eyes and assure himself of the fact by ocular demonstration.

"Is it really you?" he said. "Well, bless me, I thought to be sure it was another ghost. I never can stay here. It's no use your raving at me and telling me I must, and all that kind of thing—I can't. I shall be frightened out of my wits, and there's an end of it. Oh, dear me, it makes me shudder to think of it."

"To think of what, coward?" said Agatha.

"Why, I've seen a ghost, to be sure."

"Pshaw! Your own fancy has peopled vacancy with some form which you have mistaken for a supernatural visiter."

"No—no," said Eldred; "I never had any fancy for ghosts, nor ever shall. My fancy, indeed. I never was accused of having a fancy before. I tell you, sister, I saw it—all in white."

"Where?"

"Just by the great staircase. You must know that the old cellarer and I have got rather thick."

"How dare you demean the name you bear by herding with menials?" said Agatha.

"Oh, bother the name, sister. Besides, one must have some company. Now there's the cellarer is a most agreeable companion, for when we get dry, he says says he, 'Well, Master Eldred, bless us, let's have a cup of Burgundy.' "

"But what of this apparition you say you saw?"

"Well, as I was telling you, I was coming round by the great staircase, and I'm sure I wasn't giving offence to any ghost in the world, I was coming so slow and softly, when just as I turned by the suit of chain armour and the bucks' horns that hang there, something all in white came up to me and nearly frightened me to death."

No. 19

"Away with you to your chamber," said Agatha.   "You should not be prowling about the castle at this time of the night."

"Well, sister, no more should you, if you come to that."

"Dare you call in question my actions?" said Agatha, with sudden passion.

"Well—well, don't be in a rage. I'm going to bed in a minute; and as for prowling about the castle, I think I see me. Why, I wouldn't slink about it as you do of a night if after a week somebody was to say, 'Well, Eldred, now it's your own.' I didn't know I was here. I only run as fast as I could from the ghost and came here I don't know how."

"Away—away" said Agatha, and she immediately walked hastily down the long gallery towards the habitable part of the castle.

"Hilloa! hilloa!—sister, sister," cried Eldred, scampering after her. "For God's sake don't leave me here in the dark. Just show me the way to my room. Lord bless me, if that ghost should come again."

Sir Kenneth Hay, who much enjoyed the terror of Eldred, uttered a loud groan just as he commenced pursuing his sister, and the sound had such an effect upon the terrified Eldred, that he sprung forward like a hunted hare, crying.—

"Goodness gracious! it's coming again. Sister, sister—stop—murder—fire! It's coming again."

His voice died away in the distance, and the knight was alone with Wingrove.

"Let us now proceed at once," said Sir Kenneth, "or we shall run a chance of being surprised by the morning light."

"This way," said Wingrove, as he led Sir Kenneth towards the same door by which Agatha had entered the gallery. I much rejoice that we have seen Agatha Weare coming from the turret, for it assures me more and more that we have really nothing but mortal foes to contend against."

"I will not deny," said the knight, "but that Providence may think proper at times to accomplish its ends by the agency of supernatural beings; but I am strongly inclined to think that in this case we have to contend against some evil spirits still clothed in flesh, rather than those disembodied and belonging to another world."

A cold air was blowing in the court-yard, from which clear and black against the sky rose the turret. The open space was but of trifling extent, and in a few moments it was crossed, and Wingrove pushing open the door which was at the foot of the staircase, whispered to the knight,

"We are now on the turret stairs. This winding flight conducts to the apartment which has been so long nailed up, and in which repose the ashes of the unburied dead."

"Beware!" said a voice in deep hollow accents, and Sir Kenneth Hay started, as turning to Wingrove, he said,

"Did you speak?"

"No; but I heard a voice say, 'Beware!'"

"Beware!" again said the voice, and this time it seemed to sound close to the elbow of Sir Kenneth, who instantly made a sweeping blow round him with the trusty mace, in hopes of catching some intruder, but a mocking laugh was the only reply.

"I defy you," cried the knight; "be ye of earth or air, I defy you. If you be spirits of good you should know that my purpose here is good; and if that you be spirits of evil I defy you on my knighthood and my faith."

A deep silence followed this speech of the knight's, and then turning to Wingrove, he said,

"Come on. We will ascend the stairs, and he will be a bold man who stops my way."

A cry, something between a shriek and a howl, at this moment smote their ears, and Wingrove's heart grew cold despite his courage and faith in the might of Sir Kenneth Hay. The fearful cry echoed up and down the winding stairs, multiplying itself almost endlessly, until it died away in a low, melancholy wail, which seemed like a sigh from the grave.

"On, on," cried Sir Kenneth, as he strode up the staircase, swinging his heavy mace in his hand, and fully prepared to encounter any foe that might present himself. " On, Wingrove, on; we will this night penetrate the mystery of this much-dreaded turret."

Before he could proceed another step such a dazzling ray of light flashed into his eyes that he involuntarily put his hand up to them, with an exclamation of pain, while the same voice that had before spoken, said in deep hollow accents,

" What seek you here ?—Beware, beware.—Wake not the dead !"

The bright flash of light had disappeared as suddenly as it had shown itself, but it had had the effect of making the darkness more confusing than before, and so much injuring the distinctness of the knight's vision, that it was only by grasping the heavy balustrades of the staircase that he could tell which way to go.

" Your light, Wingrove, your light," he said, and Wingrove produced the small lantern he had with him, which, however, cast but a feeble illumination over the staircase.

They had, however, ascended so far now as to command a view of the door of the Grey Turret, and were on a wide portion of the stairs which led to a small room scarcely sufficient for two people to stand in, but which was used in time of war as a post for archers to annoy any foe, by shooting at them through loop-holes, who might have good a lodgment within the castle.

Here Wingrove paused, and said to Sir Kenneth,

" By leaving our light here we shall catch sufficient of its rays to enable us to undertake what operations we please against the door of the turret. Heaven direct us in our undertaking, and save us from the machinations of evil spirits."

" Amen !" said Sir Kenneth; " but I have no fear, Wingrove, for nothing but some undoubted warning from Heaven not to proceed, would weaken my resolution."

" Hush, hush. Heaven preserve us, what is that ?" cried Wingrove.

At this moment a light proceeded as if from some small orifice in the door of the Grey Turret, falling upon the wall exactly opposite to where they were standing. At first it seemed but about the size of a full moon as we see it sailing in the heavens ; but as Wingrove and the knight continued gazing at it, it gradually expanded, until nearly the whole of the wall was covered, as it were, with a thin sheet of white light. Then a confused mass of images appeared upon it,—myriads of colours danced before their eyes for some moments, until arranging themselves, they begun to take the outline of a human form, and before Wingrove and Sir Kenneth could utter the slightest exclamation of surprise, they saw before them the tall figure of a knight clad in half armour, and with a grave and serious expression of countenance. The eyes were fixed upon them with a sorrowful gaze, and then a low voice, with a great deal of sweetness in its tones, said,

" Sir Kenneth Hay, it is forbidden by Heaven to disturb the sanctity of the Grey Turret. There was a curse upon it, but 'tis now the haunt of chosen spirits, who watch over Brandon. Depart in peace—oh, depart in peace."

" Gentle spirit," said the knight, while he drew his breath short and thick, as believing himself conversing with one of another world.   " Gentle spirit, tell me who you were in life ?   Your arms bespeak you a warrior."

" My arms and armour," said the same voice, " are but coloured vapours lent by Heaven, to make the form I bear, more palpable to human eyes.   I am the spirit of Sir Rupert Brandon's ancestor, whose life was attempted by a treacherous guest in yon old Grey Turret."

" 'Tis truth—'tis truth," gasped Wingrove ; " there is a portrait in the castle, which represents him even as we see him now, Sir Kenneth."

A mist now seemed to envelop the figure, and it was fading gradually away, when Sir Kenneth recovering a little from his first surprise, said,

" Vision, I conjure thee to allow the Grey Turret to be explored, and the skeleton form of the assassin which is believed to be there, to be removed.   While that remains, terror will ever haunt the breasts of the inmates of Brandon.   Let this be done, in the name of Heaven."

A loud report like a clap of thunder, immediately followed the knight's words, and both he and Wingrove involuntarily stepped into the archer's room.

" We are lost, we are lost," cried Wingrove, as he closed the door that shut the room from the staircase.   " Oh, Sir Kenneth, you see the powers of Heaven are against our enterprise.   Let us go back.   Surely we have done enough now.   For Heaven's sake, let us return."

" I am resolved to see if the body of the assassin is really in the turret," said Sir Kenneth.   " Open the door, Wingrove, instantly."

Reluctantly Wingrove opened the door, and when he did so, he found that the whole staircase was lit up by rays of light, which principally, however, fell outside the door.

" What is that?" cried Sir Kenneth.

Wingrove cast his eyes down, and lying just before him on the wide stair, which led to the archer's room, he saw lying a hideous form, half skeleton, and half clothed with masses of flesh, which seemed to be rotting from the bones.   The ghastly form was lying on its back, with its head towards the archer's room, and the pieces of flesh that still hung to the grinning jaws, gave an awful appearance to the countenance, while a fetid odour arose from the yellow moist joints, which were relapsing into slimy corruption.   There were crawling things too, about the body—insects engendered by the process of decomposition, that seemed to riot in the rank corruption of the festering flesh, and to grow sleek and slimy in the moisture which arose from the mass of rottenness in which they lived.

It was a spectacle for humanity to shudder and grow sick at—an awful lesson to those proud of beauty—a terrible voice as it were from the grave, to living breathing men, saying, " Even as I am, so shalt thou be."

" This is enough," said Sir Kenneth, with a sigh ; " I am more than satisfied, and will now go in peace."

Wingrove shuddered, as he said,

" This must be the body of the assassin.   In compliance with your wish, it has been cast out of the turret to you.   It is a dreadful sight."

" So dreadful," said the knight, " that I wish not to look upon its like again."

Even as he spoke, the light which had so brilliantly illuminated the staircase, disappeared, leaving them in darkness, for after the vivid glare which their eyes had been accustomed to for the last few moments, the feeble light from Wingrove's lantern, was scarcely at all perceptible.

" Let us go," said Sir Kenneth.   " I am satisfied."

As he spoke, he unintentionally trod upon the lantern, and then all was total darkness.

" Wingrove," he said, " give me your hand.   I am a stranger here, which you are not, and must trust to your guidance back to my chamber."

"This way," said Wingrove.

The knight followed the voice, but to his horror, he found by the crushing sound under his feet, that he was treading upon the ghastly body that occupied the stair. A deadly sickness came over his heart, and for the first time in his life, Sir Kenneth Hay felt fear. It was not, however, the fear of mortal man, but the intense horror he felt of treading among that horrible mass of corruption that made an anxious flutter at his heart, and his cheeks grew pale.

Two more steps freed him from contact with the dead, and he followed Wingrove hastily down the steps of the Grey Turret. The cool fresh air from the court-yard, fell like balm upon his heart. Oh, how delicious it was, after what he had seen and heard, to stand once more beneath the canopy of Heaven, and breathe the keen free air as it blew along the battlements of the ancient castle.

CHAPTER XXXVIII.

The morning broke in beauty,
  Radiant was the sky,
And gallant warriors rose,
  To conquer or to die.—THE JOURNEY.

THE COMBAT.—THE EFFECTS OF THE POISON DRAUGHT.

SIR KENNETH HAY felt faint and weary when he reached his room, and it was a great relief to him to drop into a seat and take off some of the half armour he had worn on his visit to the Grey Turret. He remained for some time after Wingrove had left him, in deep thought concerning the very mysterious occurrences of the night, and his faith in the reality of the vision that he had seen was not at all shaken by calmer reflection.

"We could not both have been deceived," he said. "Had I alone seen the appearance I might have thought my brain had conjured it up to cheat my eyes, but two persons can scarcely at one and the same moment be the victims of the same mental delusion. It must have been real, and as terrible as it was real. Ha! who knocks?"

He started to his feet as a timid tap at his chamber door came upon his ears. Then striding towards it he flung it wide open, and beheld Eldred Weare standing on the threshold, bearing a large silver salver on which was a goblet of the same material.

There was an appearance of fright upon the face of Eldred, as he muttered,—

"It's—it's—an ancient custom, my sister says, a very ancient custom— dear me, and such a time of night too —"

"What do you mean?" said Sir Kenneth.

"Oh, I don't know really. Don't get in a passion."

"Explain yourself."

"Why you see, my sister says, as it's an ancient custom to—to—bring it—you see."

"Bring what?"

"This cup of wine. It's Sir Rupert's own cup, and it's always brought to the chamber of any much honoured guest, filled with choice wine; so says my sister, and she's a very violent woman you know, and won't be gainsaid in anything."

"Let the custom be ancient or modern," exclaimed Sir Kenneth, as he took the wine cup, " it is welcome, for I don't know anything that I should be more glad of at the present moment than a cup of rare wine."

" You are uncommonly welcome," said Eldred. " Bless me there's three o'clock striking. Much sleep I shall get to-night, with one thing and another."

As he spoke he shuffled off with the salver to acquaint his sister with the success of his mission.

Sir Kenneth Hay closed his door, and then without the slightest pause he quaffed off the wine.

" Generous rare wine, do they call this," he muttered. " It has a strange flavour—I like it not. Women are no judges of wine. I warrant Sir Rupert would not have offered me wine from the vat this was drawn from. 'Tis strangely bitter—sickening. Well, it cannot do much harm, surely. I feel drowsy, very drowsy. But no wonder, the night is far advanced, and I have travelled far to-day, very far. What a strange sight was that on the turret stairs—most strange. I will sleep now till the morning summons me to punish this Fitzhugh, traitor as he is, for daring to wear the spurs of a knight. Yes, the combat in the morning—the combat—the combat—the —"

He sunk dressed as he was upon his bed, and fell into a deep sleep. The drugged wine was already beginning to affect his system, and the brave gallant knight was rapidly relapsing into the state which the monk had prophesied he would, provided he drank of the poisoned goblet. Deep repose was now over the castle of Brandon, and all but the guilty slept in peace. Slumber would not, however, visit the eyes of Agatha. She sat the whole of that night in her chamber with her hands clasped, and her face of an ashy paleness, a prey to the most agonising thoughts—thoughts sufficient to goad the brain to madness, and convert the sweet oblivion of repose, could she have commanded it, into a curse instead of a blessing.

The grey light of early dawn was shining coldly on tower and battlement, when Wingrove aroused the slumbering guard, and bade preparation be made in the court-yard for the coming combat. The men-at-arms, to whom such a thing was the richest treat that could be presented to them, were soon all life and commotion. Ponderous beams of wood were placed in the ground for the purpose of forming temporary lists. The ancient banner of the Brandons was unfurled in honour of the occasion, and gaily fluttered in the fresh breeze of morning. Such an air of animation had not reigned through Brandon for many a day.

While all this was going on in the court-yard, a strange scene was taking place in the armoury of the castle, whither Fitzhugh had repaired early in the morning, to pick out from among the ample warlike stores there collected, such defensive pieces of mail as he thought would best protect him from any random stroke of Sir Kenneth's; for, notwithstanding the assurance of Agatha that the knight would be rendered harmless, he could not divest himself of a tremulous feeling as the hour for the combat rapidly approached.

Not many minutes had he been in the armoury when his page, who had taken so deep an interest in the fate of Sir Kenneth, joined him.

" How now," cried Fitzhugh. " Why were you not here earlier : here, take this casque; methinks it would be a hard dint to get through that."

The page took the helmet, and then regarding his master with a melancholy air, he said,

" Oh, sir, spare the noble knight, Sir Kenneth Hay. Let me implore you not to stain your new honours by taking the life of one unable to resist you."

Fitzhugh's eyes flashed with passion as he cried,

" Boy, what do you mean ? what dare you insinuate ?"

" Kill me, sir, if you like," said the page. " I will make no resistance ; but I will first confess that I am acquainted with the plot for the destruction of Sir Kenneth. Let it suffice for you to vanquish him, but spare his life : so will you accomplish all you ought to desire, and save yourself a great sin."

" Now of all the unparalleled pieces of assurance," said Fitzhugh, " that ever I heard of, this beats them. Boy, I could brain you, even now."

" Do, do," said the page, " and may you find a more faithful follower."

Fitzhugh answered in a lower tone,

" I will not deny, that for some reason, you have shown yourself much devoted to me ; but wherefore this strange solicitude for the life of Sir Kenneth Hay ?"

" Oh, sir," said the page, " I want the pleasure of looking back with satisfaction upon your actions. Spare the knight, I implore you, and you will have at least the credit in your own mind of stopping short in your revenge when you had the means of going farther. Say you will not take his life !"

" I care not," said Fitzhugh, " whether he live or die, provided I get the better of him in the approaching conflict. But tell me how came you acquainted with the circumstance you mention ?"

" I overheard Agatha Weare talk of drugging his wine ; and now, sir, I say to you, beware of her, for she is subtle, deep, and dangerous ; and the woman who would place poison in the wine cup of one guest is scarcely to be trusted by another."

" By Heaven there is sound reason in what you say, boy," cried Fitzhugh, " and I will not linger here beyond to-day : but, hush, here comes Wingrove."

Hugh Wingrove entered the armoury at this moment, and glancing around him, said,

" Has Sir Kenneth Hay not been here ? I came to help him to put his armour on."

" No," said Fitzhugh, " I have seen nothing of him. It may be that he has no stomach for the fight."

An angry answer was upon Wingrove's lips, but he repressed it ; as he thought how soon the braggadocia spirit would be taken out of Fitzhugh, when he really came hand to hand in conflict with Sir Kenneth. He remained, however, for some moments gazing round, and the expression of his face was one of surprise as he said,

" 'Tis very strange, but a suit of black mail armour is missing from here.'"

" Indeed," said Fitzhugh ; " a whole suit ?"

" Aye ; it hung here, and was of great size. By Heavens it has disappeared since yesterday."

Fitzhugh turned a little pale, as he thought the mysterious abstraction of the armour might possibly betoken some danger to him, and he said,

" Who could have taken it : there is no one here to wear armour but myself and Sir Kenneth Hay."

" None, to my knowledge ; but hark, they have finished the lists."

As Wingrove spoke, a cheer burst from the men-at-arms as they completed the formation of the temporary lists ; and he hurried from the armoury to the chamber of Sir Kenneth.

When Wingrove reached the dormitory of the knight he knocked loudly at the door twice or thrice, and receiving no answer he turned the handle of the lock, and entered the room.

"Sir Kenneth, Sir Kenneth," he cried; but the knight made him no answer, save by his heavy breathing, as he lay on the bed, suffering from the baneful effects of the potion which had been administered to him in the wine.

"Good Heavens!" cried Wingrove; "what unnatural and long sleep is this? Sir Kenneth; awake, awake!"

Slowly the knight opened his eyes and gazed upon the face of Wingrove, saying in an almost inarticulate voice,

"Is it time—is it time? the combat."

"It is time; you should arm," said Wingrove. "For the sake of your honour and of good King Richard, shake off the drowsiness that seems so strangely to cling to you. Rise, Sir Kenneth, and prepare yourself for the combat."

"Yes, yes," said the confused knight, making an effort to rise. "My armour, my armour—1 am strangely sleepy, and a numbness seizes all my limbs—my armour, quick; the combat, aye, the combat."

It was evidently with the greatest difficulty that he could stand upon his feet, after he had risen from his bed, and he staggered to and fro like a drunken man.

"What can be meaning of this?" cried Wingrove. "Sir Kenneth was quite well when I left him. Gracious powers; can he have taken poison? what a dreadful supposition! Sir Kenneth, speak; for Heaven's sake say what you have taken."

"The fight—the fight—my armour," was the only reply Wingrove could get from him.

"He is lost," ejaculated the honest old soldier, wringing his hands and sinking into a seat.

Some slight feeling of strength for a moment now seemed to animate Sir Kenneth's frame, and he drew himself proudly up, saying,

"Who says I am lost? Quick, my sword and charger, I must to the fight."

With a hope then that he was shaking off the strange feelings that oppressed him, Wingrove said,

"I will bring you your arms, Sir Kenneth, and send Bernard to assist you. My presence is wanted at the lists. Rouse yourself, for Heaven's sake, and show this craven knight Fitzhugh what a warrior really is."

"I will—I will," said Sir Kenneth; but when Wingrove left him, his head sunk upon his breast, and he had the greatest difficulty to keep himself from again falling into the uneasy, troubled slumber from which he had been awakened.

Wingrove now hastened to the court-yard, and beckoning to Bernard he said,

"For Heaven's sake, Bernard, go and assist Sir Kenneth to arm, or all our honours are at stake. Fly, you will find him in his chamber. Bring him hither as quickly as possible, while I on one pretence and another put off the fight beyond the appointed hour."

As Wingrove accompanied these words with a push, Bernard had no opportunity of seeking for any explanation, but started off in great wonderment towards Sir Kenneth Hay's bed-chamber.

At this moment, from a side door opening into the court-yard, the two horses belonging to the respective knights were brought forward, fully caparisoned for a tilt, and pawing the ground with pride and emulation. Then a trumpet blast was blown by the warder of the castle, and Agatha Weare, accompanied by Eldred, entered the arena.

"The hour is past," she cried. "Where are these two gallants who must

needs bring strife into Brandon Castle? If this fight must be, let it be quickly over, that we may take our morning meal without the sounds of strife ringing in our ears."

"Ah," said Eldred, "let it be soon over as you say, sister. I hate fighting as I hate ——"

"Silence!" cried Agatha, darting an angry glance at Eldred, which at once silenced him, and made him shrink back several paces. Then turning to Wingrove, she said,—"Summon the combatants. We will see this combat at once, and Heaven prosper the right."

Wingrove looked anxiously in the direction he knew Sir Kenneth Hay would come, but no knight was to be seen. Fitzhugh, however, had not arrived, and the afflicted soldier, turning to Agatha, said,—

"As neither of the champions are here, it may be rather premature to sound to arms."

"Indeed!" sneered Agatha. "You are most scrupulous, Master Wingrove, suddenly. But see, one of the champions even now approaches."

As she spoke, Fitzhugh presented himself, attended by his page, and fully armed for the contest.

"The trumpet—sound the trumpet," cried Agatha.

Wingrove was compelled to obey, and thrice the warder blew a shrill blast upon a trumpet, after which he cried aloud,—

"Sir Kenneth Hay, a knight of the Holy Sepulchre, here challenges to single combat Sir Giles Fitzhugh, knight, in defence of King Richard, his name and sovereignty."

"I am here," cried Fitzhugh, throwing down his gauntlet—"I am here, and Heaven preserve the right."

No. 20

CHAPTER XXXIX.

" They met in mad career,
    One was a gallant knight;
But treachery had marred his fame;
He lost—he lost the fight."

THE COMBAT LOST.—THE EFFECTS OF THE POISON.

There was now an anxious pause of some moments' duration, during which Wingrove glanced repeatedly towards the entrance to the court-yard, in expectation of the appearance of Sir Kenneth Hay, and an expression of ill-concealed triumph came across the face of Fitzhugh as he affected to be busy in arranging some of the trappings of his horse.

" Where," cried Agatha, " is the laggard ? Methinks the challenger should not be the last on the field."

" He will come, lady," said Wingrove. " Bernard is even now helping him to arm."

" Isn't he well ?" said Eldred.

Agatha turned and darted a glance at him that had so much ferocity in it, that he ran behind Fitzhugh's charger in a great fright, muttering,—

" Well, now, I thought that was a rather clever remark than otherwise, but certainly Agatha grows more violent every day, that she does."

" Let the trumpet sound again," said Fitzhugh, " and if Sir Kenneth comes not to meet me, I claim the victory."

Again the warder blew a shrill blast, and before the echo of the sound had ceased, a door was flung wide open, and the tall form of Sir Kenneth Hay appeared fully equiped for the fight.

More than one anxious glance was cast at the knight, as he made his appearance. Wingrove, with a beating heart, kept his eyes fixed on him to endeavour to assure himself that the strange lassitude that had affected him had passed away, while Agatha and Fitzhugh watched his every movement with the hope of discovering the weakness of his frame, induced by the poison.

Bernard crossed the court-yard to where Wingrove stood, and whispered in his ear,—

" On my faith, I don't know what to make of Sir Kenneth, he is either mad or drunk."

" Hush! hush!" said Wingrove. " Heaven help him—Heaven help him."

All eyes were now fixed on the knight, who with a wandering and unsteady step crossed the court-yard towards where his charger was standing. It was evident to every one that he moved with difficulty, and when he reached his steed which with a whine acknowledged the presence of its master, he leaned heavily against it, and lifting up his visor he exhibited a face so ghastly pale that it would seem as if he had risen from a bed of sickness to attire himself in the trappings of war.

Several of the men-at-arms, including Wingrove and Bernard, made a movement forward to assist him, but he languidly waved his arm and drawing two or three long breaths, like one sadly oppressed with indisposition, he shut the visor of his helmet with a clang and prepared to mount his steed.

" He is very ill," whispered Fitzhugh to Agatha.

" He is," she replied. " You will have an easy conquest. He has not the strength of a child. See, he cannot even mount his horse."

Sir Kenneth was making sundry abortive efforts to mount his steed, but he had not strength, encumbered as he was by his armour, to do so, and finally he fell on the pavement of the court-yard with a deep groan.   In an instant, Wingrove and Bernard raised him to his feet, and the former whispered to him,—

"For God's sake, Sir Kenneth, say you are very ill, and decline the combat."

"No! no! no!" gasped the knight.   "My horse.   Help me on my horse."

"He will not fight," cried Fitzhugh.

"He will!" shouted Wingrove; "though suffering from severe indisposition he will fight, and may Heaven protect him and give him strength."

A cheer burst from the men-at-arms, and the sound for a moment appeared to raise Sir Kenneth Hay from his lethargy.   Wingrove and Bernard helped him on to his horse, which to the dismay of Fitzhugh, he managed far better than could have been expected from the evidently feeble state he was in.

"I think he's getting better," remarked Eldred, as Fitzhugh with nervous haste sprung into his saddle.

The lists were now cleared, but it was evident to all, that Sir Kenneth could have no chance, for he was bending from side to side in the saddle, although with his bridle hand he contrived to manage well the paces of his steed.

The combatants were now placed opposite to each other at the greatest distance which the court-yard afforded, and it was doubtful even then, whether Fitzhugh's fear did not make him almost as incapable of conducting the combat successfully, as Sir Kenneth's feeble state did him.   When the lances, however, were handed to them, it was quite clear that Sir Kenneth's strength was insufficient to make him tilt at all, for the long heavy lance shook in his grasp, and the point instead of being directed against his opponent, was nearly trailing on the ground.

"This must not be," exclaimed Wingrove.   "A sickness has come over the gallant Sir Kenneth Hay, and who can wrestle with the decrees of of Providence?   The combat must be stayed."

"No," cried Agatha.   "He is the challenger.   Let him take his chance."

Sir Kenneth heard her, and waving his hand which held the bridle, to Wingrove, he contrived for a moment to raise the point of his lance.

Agatha then motioned to the trumpeter to blow the signal of assault, and in another moment the horses were dashing forward to the rencontre.

As Fitzhugh had marked the weakness of his adversary, he had himself gained courage, and never doubting of an easy conquest over Sir Kenneth, he aimed his lance full at his breast.

Sir Kenneth's lance took no particular direction as regarded his opponent, and it was clear that he charged without the least motive.   The point of Fitzhugh's weapon would have struck him full in the heart, had not the lances crossed, which had the effect of slanting it upwards, so that it only glanced harmless over the helmet, carrying away one of the feathers that waved in it.

Weakened and exhausted, however, as was Sir Kenneth Hay, the shock of the rencontre was too much for him, and his lance dropping from his nerveless grasp, he was on the point of falling from his saddle, when he was caught by Bernard, who dragged him from his alarmed steed, and placed him in safety upon his feet.

"Air, air," gasped Sir Kenneth.

Bernard raised his visor, and the cool air that blew upon his face, seemed to revive him for a moment, and he said in a faint voice,—

" What has happened—where am I ?"

" You have been tilting with Fitzhugh," cried Wingrove, who had approached him, " and have lost the fortune of the day, in consequence of your illness."

" Fitzhugh—lost "—said Sir Kenneth—" my sword—my sword !"

He drew his sword as he spoke, and assuming an attitude of defence, turned his pale face to Fitzhugh, crying,

" Dastard, come on ! Pain and sickness have not yet conquered me. Come on. For good King Richard ! Dismount, coward, dismount."

With a face nearly as pale as Sir Kenneth's, Fitzhugh dismounted from his steed, and drew his sword, for he was compelled to renew the combat upon foot, if Sir Kenneth wished.

" Can he be recovering," he thought, as a cold perspiration, induced by fear, came upon his brow.

The men-at-arms appeared now to be in the greatest state of excitement, and they crowded as closely round the knights as they could without impeding them, while even Wingrove began to entertain some sanguine hopes as he saw the fine attitude Sir Kenneth had assumed as he stood upon the defensive.

Again the trumpet sounded to the assault, and Sir Kenneth advanced amid a cheer from the men-at-arms, while Fitzhugh retreated step by step. Another attack of the deadly sickness, arising from the poison, was then evidently coming across Sir Kenneth, and his arm was seen to shake like an aspen leaf. Fitzhugh took advantage of the moment, and suddenly assumed the offensive, dealing the unhappy knight a heavy blow upon the shoulder. For a moment Sir Kenneth staggered, and then throwing into one effort all the strength he could muster, he gave Fitzhugh so stunning a blow upon the head in spite of his guard, that he, Fitzhugh, dropped upon his knees, and was perfectly bewildered for a moment.

This was, however, the last expiring effort of Sir Kenneth's consciousness, for he immediately afterwards fell backwards with a crash upon the ground, and lay perfectly insensible.

A rush was made towards the fallen knight, and when he was raised and his helmet taken off, it was found that he had fainted.

" Sir Kenneth is vanquished," said Agatha.

" Yes, yes," said Fitzhugh, shaking his head, and looking wildly about him, for the blow he had had quite confused his perceptions.

" No," cried Wingrove, in a voice that rung through the court-yard.

" Who dares say so ?" cried Agatha.

" I do," replied Bernard ; then placing his hand to his mouth he shouted " No," till the air rung again.

" Sickness," added Wingrove, " and not the sword of Fitzhugh, has conquered Sir Kenneth Hay ;—the hand of Heaven is heavy upon him. Had there been poison put in his wine he could not be worse."

" Poison ?" cried Agatha, turning first red and then as pale as ashes.

" Aye, poison, lady."

Eldred groaned and began slinking away as he thought the truth was coming out, and somebody might knock him on the head for his share in the odious transaction.

Before, however, another remark could be made by any one, an universal cry of astonishment burst from the men-at-arms, as a figure suddenly appeared from the same door-way at which Sir Kenneth Hay had come to the court-yard, attired in complete armour and wearing the visor down, so that not the smallest vestige of the face could be seen.

There was, after the first cry of surprise, a silence equal to that of the grave as each man looked at his fellow, and then at the mysterious visiter in speechless astonishment. Agatha was the first to speak, and it was with tremulous accents that she said,—

"What trick is this. Who dares come here in such a garb unknown and unsolicited?"

"I dare," said the stranger knight, in a deep hollow voice, "as the champion of Sir Kenneth Hay, on whom the hand of sickness sorely presses; I come in his name, and in his place to proclaim Fitzhugh a coward, a dastard, and a traitor."

The commotion that followed this speech, it is impossible to describe. It seemed as if Babel had broke loose, for every one had something to say on the occasion. There were shouts—cheers—hurrahs—questions—defiances, and expostulations in abundance, and it was not until a partial lull took place in the tempest of sound, that Agatha could make herself heard, as she said,

"Seize this stranger, soldiers. He is some robber in disguise. Seize him, I say."

"I do not see why he should be seized," said Wingrove. "Let Fitzhugh do battle with him."

"Hurrah," cried the castle guard. "Hurrah.

"I will not fight with a stranger," said Fitzhugh. "He may be no knight at all for aught I know. Let him declare who he is."

"I am a knight," said the stranger. "Who doubts my word let him prove it on my person."

"The combat has been lost and won," said Agatha. "Sir Kenneth Hay has been vanquished."

"True—true," cried Fitzhugh, "I am not to fight every brawling braggart, who by fraud or violence has forced his way into Brandon Castle."

"Then I proclaim you coward and recreant," said the unknown knight, "and if you will not fight me, I will hack your spurs from your heels with my sword, and let who will venture to hinder me from doing so."

"I will hinder you," said Agatha.

"Ah, lady," said the unknown knight, in a tone of irony. "How delightful would be your dear society in some fair summer bower, while your sweet voice mocked the tuneful birds, making still richer melody."

A roar of laughter burst from the men-at-arms as the knight spoke, for a gentle voice was certainly not one of Agatha Weare's blandishments, and her rage knew no bounds as she glanced round her, and felt that there was no one who had the courage to avenge her upon the unknown.

"Villain!" she shrieked.

"Sweet creature!" said the knight.

Agatha stamped with passion, and turning to the men-at-arms, she said,—

"Is there no one among all here who will avenge me upon this insolent stranger?"

"Aye," said the knight. "Is there no one? Perhaps, Fitzhugh, you will step forward—come. Be persuaded."

"He shall fight," said Bernard, "or he shall leave his spurs behind him."

"The fight! the fight!" cried several.

"Here," said Wingrove, "a couple of you convey Sir Kenneth Hay to his chamber and take off his armour. We will now see whether Fitzhugh can hold his way against a knight not borne down by sickness."

Fitzhugh saw there was no escape for him, and with inward curses accompanied with groans and fear, he slowly took his way towards his steed, while the stranger knight approaching Sir Kenneth's horse, placed his hand upon the saddle, and then with one spring safely alighted in it,—no trifling feat to perform in a suit of heavy mail armour.

He then made the horse gallop round the court-yard, and by a variety of manœuvres showed his perfect management of the steed, after which beckoning to one of the soldiers to hand him Sir Kenneth's lance, he threw it up in the air to a great height and catching it then as it fell, he curvetted round the court whirling the lance round his head as if it were a straw.

The admiration with which Wingrove, Bernard, and the rest of the castle-guard looked upon these proceedings of the knight was unbounded, and as for Eldred, he stood with his mouth open, quite transfixed with intense wonder and amazement.

Fitzhugh felt that his fate was sealed, and his only chance of safety he considered was to slip from his horse the moment he and the stranger knight met in full career and give up the contest, a manœuvre which he determined to put in practice as speedily as possible.

CHAPTER XL.

A being of strange mystery is he,
A knight of stalwart fame,
Encased in warrior's panoply—
A chief without a name.

ANON.

AGATHA'S FEAR OF THE STRANGER KNIGHT.—THE MONK'S COUNSEL.]

THE feelings of every one who witnessed the new conflict were widely different from those that affected them on the former occasion, when all were painfully alive to the fact of Sir Kenneth Hay's serious indisposition. Only Agatha and Fitzhugh were now in dread and consternation, not that the former cared one straw for Fitzhugh, or any danger he might run ; but her breast was full of consternation at the sudden and mysterious appearance of the stranger knight, an appearance to her so inexplicable, that she could not but imagine, with a shudder of anticipatory apprehension, that it boded her and Morgatani some serious evil.

Not a long time, however, had she or any one else to indulge in any thoughts or conjectures, for the approaching contest absorbed the faculties of all.

The knights were duly placed in their respective positions, and there was a pause of intense anxiety until the warder, in obedience to a signal from Wingrove, blew his horn. Fitzhugh's horse then dashed forward, being used to the lists, with more speed than its rider wished, while the unknown knight came sweeping on like the wind, with his lance placed freely and carelessly in its rest, and apparently taking the whole affair in the easiest manner imaginable. Then, before Fitzhugh could put in practice his intention of slipping from his horse, the stranger knight steadied the point of his lance, and hitting him full upon the chest, he sent him from the saddle with such terrible vehemence that the stirrup-leathers snapped like threads, and Fitzhugh, when he did reach the ground, rolled over and over as if he had been discharged from some piece of ordnance.

A shout arose from the men-at-arms, and the stranger knight, in an instant, waving his lance, quickly trotted his horse back to the further end of the lists.

When Fitzhugh was picked up, he was found to be stunned by the heavy fall he had received, and perfectly insensible.

"Fitzhugh is unable to renew the combat," cried Wingrove ; "he is fairly beaten."

"'Tis unfair," cried Agatha. Then, turning to Eldred, she whispered :— Cry out that it is unfair."

"Oh, thank you for nothing," said Eldred. "A nice topper on the head that great fellow in black armour would give me if I was to say a word. I sha'n't do any such thing."

"You say the tilt was unfair, lady?" said the knight, curvetting his steed up to Agatha.

"I do," she cried.

"Oh! how I wish you were a man," he replied, "and not the sweet gentle creature you are."

"'Tis manly of you, sir," said Agatha, bitterly, "to taunt a woman."

"And 'tis womanly of you," said the knight, "to interfere in men's quarrels. Stick to your distaff and your embroidery, madam, and don't interfere between knights. At the same time, I say, for your especial caution, beware of what you do, for there is a Heaven above which sees all and knows all. Beware, madam, beware."

Agatha looked the picture of dismay as the knight spoke, and could only falter out,—

"Tell me who you are—for Heaven's sake, tell me who you are?"

"It matters not," said the knight, as he flung himself from the steed. "I shall go as I come." He then turned to the men-at-arms, and waving his hand, cried,—

"Friends all, farewell. We shall meet again."

In a moment he had gone by the doorway through which he had entered the court-yard, leaving every one in the deepest astonishment.

"Follow him! follow him!" cried Agatha. "How come he here? Is this the watch and ward you keep that an armed man can make his way into Brandon despite of you all? Oh, you are fine soldiers! Where were you when this audacious stranger found his way hither? Follow him, I say—follow him!"

Wingrove darted through the doorway after the stranger, for he was as much surprised as any one could be at his appearance, and could not imagine who or what he was, or how he could have gained admission to the castle. His object, however, in following him was a friendly one. He meant to beg his confidence, and offer him what assistance to leave Brandon he might require, for that he was, let him be who he might, a friend to Sir Rupert, there could be no reasonable doubt.

Wingrove, however, could see no traces of the knight, although he spent considerable time in searching the castle for him, and finally he returned to the court-yard, more surprised than ever at the singular occurrences of the morning. Upon examination, it was found that Fitzhugh was so much bruised although no bones were broken, that it would be out of the question for him to think of leaving the castle, and he was accordingly carried back to his chamber in nearly as bad a condition as the unfortunate Sir Kenneth, who still lay in a deep sleep from the potent influence of the narcotic drug he had swallowed.

Agatha, in a wild tumult of feelings, retired from the scene of the conflict, closely followed by Eldred, who was so much alarmed at all that had taken place that he could not make up his mind to leave his sister a moment if he could help it.

"Agatha, Agatha," he said, "did you ever in your life see such a whack as that Fitzhugh came down with when that great fellow in black armour poked him off his horse?"

"Peace, peace," said Agatha.

"Peace, was it? Odd peace, I think. Why, it gave me a pain in my own inside to see any one have such a poke in the stomach. Oh, what a dab he did come down with to be sure."

"If you," cried Agatha, passionately, "had been other than the mean, shrinking, cowardly wretch you are, you should have been in the midst of this affray yourself ; but you have no soul for warfare."

"No, thank God, I haven't," said Eldred. "I'll be a wretch or anything else you like, rather than get such toppers on the head, and such progues in the stomach as I've seen given to-day."

"Dastard !—Coward !"

"Oh, go on ; abuse don't break bones. You may just say whatever you like, sister. I prefer being scolded to being thumped, any day. Give me a whole skin, say I. Fitzhugh must have been mad to put himself in that black fellow's way. Now, if I'd been him I should have said :—' Sir, if it's all the same to you, I don't like it. You may get somebody else to practise knocking about like a shuttlecock, but you won't have me, I can tell you. You may just proclaim me whatever you like, but don't come running up against me, knocking my head, and punching my ribs.' That's what I would have said to him."

"Eldred !" exclaimed Agatha, turning furiously towards him, and drawing a small poniard from her breast ; "if you follow me another step, I'll take your life."

"Murder ! murder !" cried Eldred, as he ran off in the opposite direction as fast as his legs would carry him.

Agatha then retired to her own room, and throwing herself into a seat, covered her face with her hands, and remained in deep thought for some moments. Then she rose, paced her apartment with unequal steps, while her passion distorted her features, and ran riot in her heart.

"What can all this mean ?" she exclaimed. "Where am I to seek for an explanation of the strange events of this morning ? Who can this stranger be ? Some knight of rank and skill he is by his noble bearing. I must seek Morgatani. He will discover all by his wondrous power and many confederates. He said 'Beware !' Beware of what ? Does he know all ? Can he have discovered ? Oh, no—no ! Impossible. That thought were madness. The secrets of this castle, and of the deeds which have taken place within its walls, can be known only to Morgatani and to myself."

A low knock on the other side of the secret entrance to her apartment now met Agatha's ears. She flew to it, and touching the spring which confined the narrow revolving door, admitted Morgatani.

The monk stood for a moment on the threshold of the secret entrance, regarding Agatha with fixed and earnest attention.

"What," he said, "has happened to cause the unusual whirlwind of passion that is depicted on your face ?"

"We are in danger," said Agatha.

"Danger !" responded the monk.

"Yes, great danger."

"Where comes it, Agatha ? Can there be danger while I am with you, which by my subtle arts I cannot convert even to safety ? No. Let what dangers may lower upon our horizon, I will still triumph over them all, and you shall still accomplish the dearly-cherished purpose of your heart. You shall have your revenge on Sir Rupert Brandon, Agatha Weare. What more do you desire ? That, on my word, I promise you."

"Nay, but, Morgatani," replied Agatha ; "you know not what has occurred since sunrise this morning." She then proceeded to relate to him the incidents connected with the two combats, and it was with an expression of some disquietude that the monk heard of the sudden and mysterious appearance of the stranger knight, and his great prowess in the lists. When Agatha had finished her recital, he remained some minutes in silence, and his

shaggy brows met, almost concealing his eyes as he contracted them in deep thought.

"Tall, and in black armour?" he said.

"Yes," replied Agatha, "of noble bearing. You are much troubled, Morgatani."

"No, Agatha, I am not troubled. 'Tis strange I do not know this stranger knight. You are aware as well as I that such an one as he could not be away from the ranks of the Crusaders, and had any one of note besides Sir Kenneth Hay arrived from Palestine, I might have heard of it."

"It bodes us harm you think?"

"No. I never think so. What mortal ear, Agatha Weare, has heard our secret counsels? What mortal eye hath seen that which only the dim spirits hovering around the dead in the vaults of Brandon Castle have witnessed? I fear no one!"

Agatha trembled as she said,

"But, Morgatani, does it not seem as if the hand of Heaven was growing perceptible in the midst of all our acts? It may be that my weaker spirit is more easily daunted than yours, but sometimes such a trembling fear will creep across my heart that I could lay me down and die, if that by so doing I could ensure extinction."

A dark, sneering smile crossed the face of the monk, as he said,

"We Jesuits are not superstitious; we wished to be the lords of our fellow-men, and we knew that it was not by reason that we could obtain the mastery, —nor was it by fear of our strength, for we could be but a small section of the great family of man; but we appealed to the imaginations—we enlisted superstition on our side, and by painting to the ignorant multitude a fearful future, over which we affected control, we succeeded in claiming as a compensation the present. You understand me, Agatha? I am not superstitious.'

"Do you mean that ——"

"That what?" sneered the monk.

"That you believe ——"

Agatha paused, and the monk filled up the sentence by saying in a hissing whisper,

"Nothing!"

A chill crept across the heart of Agatha Weare as she heard this awful avowal, and she involuntarily shrunk from the monk with a secret dread that he might be himself not of this world, but some bad spirit of the regions where no light of joy ever enters, who had clothed himself in mortal guise for the destruction of all who he could drag within the meshes of his frightful influence.

"Morgatani, Morgatani," she cried, "are you human?"

The monk laughed as he replied,

"Sweet Agatha, the time has surely passed away when such minds as yours can believe in the wild superstitions of the nursery. I am as you see me. By my acts you know me; I am mortal, but I am so far elevated above ordinary mortality as to defy all that it dreads, disbelieve all that it believes, and laugh to scorn all that it regards with fear and trembling. But this is idle talking. We must adopt some instant step with regard to this Sir Kenneth Hay. In a short time the baneful effects of the poison he has taken will subside, and although weak as one but merely recovered from a sickness which has brought him even to the grave's brink, he will be comparatively well again."

"Would not his death," said Agatha, in a low tone, "be the safest means of disposing of him?"

"No; rather let him be placed in one of the dungeons lying deep beneath the castle. I wish for some information from him regarding the proceedings of King Richard in Palestine, which he alone can render, and which I may wring from him in his weakness of body and half delirium of mind."

"How can he be conveyed there?"

"We, with the assistance of your brother Eldred, must accomplish that. I have not been so long in Brandon without possessing myself of the means of egress and ingress to every part of it. From the small court near the old Grey Turret there opens a grated door, which leads apparently to a stone staircase, terminating in the turret which flanks the southern rampart, but upon that staircase is a secret door conducting to the dungeons—not those that are known, but a range of them that I believe have never been used since the castle was built. In one of those shall this Sir Kenneth be immured until it shall by me be deemed politic to take his life, when be assured I shall not be backward in making him one of the things which have been."

"When shall this be done?"

"To-night. You must procure your brother's assistance for two reasons. In the first place, I am determined that he shall be committed as an accessory in every transaction that we may deem necessary for our purposes; and in the second, I cannot carry—which I shall have to do—Sir Kenneth Hay and open doors as well."

"This Fitzhugh—what shall be done with him?"

"Leave him to mourn his grievous fall as best he may; he will be very useful to us yet. The whole power of the church is bent upon making John King of England, instead of his brother Richard, who has ever shown a wild and untamed spirit, more than once breaking through the power of the church, and braving her anathemas. It will not be so with John, and this Fitzhugh will aid us in our views with regard to this splendid domain of Brandon, for, remember, you never have a man so much in your power as when you have aided him in the commission of some act which he dare not avow. You may consider Fitzhugh henceforward as a creature of our's. Farewell, now, till one hour before midnight, when I will meet you here to remove Sir Kenneth Hay."

"Farewell," said Agatha.

The monk, with a slow and haughty step, left the room by the same secret means he had entered it, and the plotting, scheming, but still wretched Agatha Weare was again alone.

For some few moments she stood in the exact attitude she had been in when the monk left her. Then with a deep, hollow groan she sunk into a seat, and said in a voice that sounded strange and unnatural,—

"When, oh, when will all this end? Each day involves me more and more in the intricacies of guilt. It seems as if one circumstance of iniquity became the prolific parent of a hundred others. How short a time has elapsed since Sir Rupert Brandon left his ancient home, and yet what an awful whirl of frightful circumstances have occurred to nearly sting my brain to madness. Oh, God! oh, God! although Morgatani can avow a disbelief in a world to come, and sneer at what he calls the superstition of an age he soars above in intellect, I cannot—I cannot."

The door of the secret passage was slowly opened at this juncture, and the monk, who had been listening to what Agatha was saying, appeared on the threshold. He raised his voice, and while an unholy fire seemed to flash from his eyes, he said,—

"Agatha Weare. Think of your revenge!"

Agatha, with a cry of surprise and alarm, sprung to her feet, and cried,—

"Who speaks—who speaks? Save me, Heaven!"

"Your revenge!" said the monk.

"Morgatani? It—it is you."

"Your revenge! Slighted woman—scorned of Sir Rupert Brandon. Rejected—spurned. Ha! ha! ha! Agatha Weare, have you forgotten your revenge?"

"No, no," shrieked Agatha, stung nearly to phrenzy by his words. "Morgatani, though all hell should gape at my feet I would go on."

"Right," said the monk, as he disappeared again, leaving Agatha in a state of mind which it is impossible to describe.

CHAPTER XLI.

ELDRED AND THE PAGE.—THE VISION ON THE BATTLEMENTS.

"The page, he was a gallant youth,
  He loved the battle's cry;
And yet he'd sing of maiden's love,
  And echo maiden's sigh."

THE intense excitement throughout the castle occasioned by the morning's proceedings, rather each moment increased than diminished, as all were lost in conjecture as to what the stranger knight could possibly be. The men-at-arms crowded round Wingrove when he returned from his fruitless search after the stranger knight, and all were eager in their questions and surmises upon the subject.

"Peace, peace, all of you," said Wingrove, "I just know as much about it as yourselves. You saw all that I saw, and you heard all that I heard."

"Well," said Bernard, "I am quite astonished; I hardly know if I'm on my head or my heels, and you would hardly believe, comrades and Master Wingrove, how dreadfully thirsty curiosity always makes me; it's a fact, I assure you."

"You are devoured with a perpetual thirst, I think," said Wingrove, "and, I believe never would be otherwise so long as there was a flagon of ale left in Brandon Castle. Let us now to breakfast, and I must confess a stranger morning's work than this we have just witnessed never fell to my lot to see."

"Ah, Master Wingrove," said Anstey, "do you know it's my firm belief that there's some dreadful juggling going on in the castle. That knight now lying in his bed, is no more Sir Kenneth Hay than I am."

"Not Sir Kenneth Hay!" cried Bernard. "Now you are going to perplex me still more, and I'm quite thirsty enough. What do you mean by saying he ain't Sir Kenneth Hay?"

"Why, because he couldn't fight. It's some evil spirit who has put on the form of Sir Kenneth on purpose to bring him into disrepute, and the reason he couldn't fight was, because I stood in the court-yard with one of St. Augustine's holy toe-nails in my pouch."

"You don't mean that?" cried Bernard.

"Anstey," said Wingrove, "you are a fool."

"So he is," said Bernard. "It's a great deal easier to believe Anstey is a fool than to be battered about with spirits and St. Augustine's toe-nails. However, the mention of it has made me a trifle thirstier."

"Now, be hanged to you," said Wingrove, "I see there will be no peace until you have some ale, so just go to the cellarer and get some; and hark ye, don't be lightening the flagons on the road, because, if you drink it you know you have to carry it all the same."

"Ah, that's very true," muttered Bernard, as he walked away on his errand, "but it's a mighty deal pleasanter to carry ale inside than out."

When the soldiers reached their guard-room, they found already seated there the young page of Fitzhugh, who Wingrove did not regard with any very kindly feelings as belonging to one who he held in utter contempt. The boy saw at a glance that his presence was unwelcome, and rising, he said,

"I have no wish to intrude here, but, believe me, no one more than myself can lament the sad mischance of the gallant Sir Kenneth Hay."

There was such an air of genuine sincerity and pathos in the tone in which the page uttered these words, that Wingrove felt his heart warm to the boy, and he said in his rough manner,

"Hark ye, master page, I don't like your master, and don't care who knows it; but I think you are an honest lad, and if you like to stay here with us you may, but mark me,—there must be no babbling of what passes in the guard-room."

"I understand you," said the page; "you need be under no apprehension from me on that score. I am no teller of tales."

"Then you can stay, boy, and the worst wish I have for you is, that you may have soon a better master."

The page turned away his face, and heaved a deep sigh.

The entrance of Bernard now with the ale soon occupied the exclusive attention of the guard, and the page retired to a corner, seeming wrapped up in his own meditations.

"Well," remarked Bernard, as he kept a fast hold of one of the tankards; "I never saw anything so beautiful in my life as the way that strange knight, bless him! for a whopper as he is,—unhorsed Fitzhugh. It was really lovely —it was."

Here Bernard took a deep draught of the ale, after which he allowed the flagon to pass round, remarking, however, at the same time, that he rather hoped they would pass it quick, as he felt quite as thirsty as ever.

"Here, youngster," said Wingrove to the page; "come forward, and make one among us."

"That will I gladly," said the page.

"Ar'n't you thirsty?" said Bernard.

"No."

"Then I pity you. Hilloa! Anstey, are you never going to take your head out of the flagon? I haven't had a drop these ——"

The conclusion of Bernard's words were lost in the flagon, from whence issued only a confused hollow sound for some moments.

"Since you have been kind enough," said the page, "to let me remain here, I will essay my humble powers to sing you a song."

"Ah! do," said Bernard; "I'm a sweet singer myself, only it makes me always so wonderfully thirsty, that between each verse I require something, and that spoils the interest."

"Hold your tongue, you sot," cried Wingrove, "and let us hear the lad sing."

Without further prelude the page began :—

> "A gallant lord, renowned in fight,
>   Left his castle grey and old,
> To battle do in the Holy Land,
>   With Paynim fierce and bold ;
> Yet, e'er he went, a tear he shed
>   For her who was laid low—
> The gentle lady of his heart,
>   With brow of spotless snow."

"Why, by the mass, boy," cried Wingrove, "that's just what our brave Sir Rupert Brandon did."

"Indeed," said the boy. "It is an old romance I picked up from a wandering minstrel."

"Go on, boy. Go on."

The page continued,—

> "Within the castle's ample space
>   There was an ancient tower,
> With morticed walls and loophole small,
>   A hold of strength and power.
> What hidden purpose had the monk—
>   For such an one was there—
> To hide him in the Turret Grey,
>   To think I may not dare."

Wingrove sprung to his feet, as he cried,—

"Peace, soldiers—peace. Cease your revelry. Hear you not what the boy says? By Heavens! it is the very moral of what has happened here. A monk—an old turret. Boy, explain yourself. You know more of this."

"Nay," said the page, "it would be passing strange were the old verses of the minstrel to apply to aught that has happened here. Would you like to hear more?"

"Aye, would I. Go on, boy. This is the strangest circumstance that ever I heard tell of."

The page continued,—

> "The men-at-arms, who loved the knight,
>   Who then was far away,
> Betook them to the mouldering tower,
>   So ancient and so grey.
> They were not scared by hidious sights,
>   Nor yet by frightful sounds ;
> Nor aught that could be heard or seen
>   In superstition's bounds.
> The wicked monk was in the tower,
>   Weaving many a spell,
> But what the end he wished to work
>   The minstrel cannot tell.

For all unskilled is he in craft,
He only sees there's guile,
And that a monk is plotting safe,
While fear looks on the while."

" I have forgotten more," said the page. " My memory is rather treacherous, but if you have been amused you are right welcome to my humble lay."

Bernard looked hard in the boy's face. and being perfectly astonished and nonplussed by the resemblance between the strains he sung and the events actually in progress in Brandon Castle, he took up the empty flagon and ran off to have it filled again before he could venture an opinion on the subject.

" Follow me, boy," said Wingrove, in a whisper to the page.

The words were scarcely out of his mouth when the door of the guard-room was flung open, and Eldred Weare made his appearance, looking so terrified that one and all of the guard rose to their feet, demanding what was the matter.

" Oh! oh! oh!" cried Eldred. " Oh! oh! oh!"

" What is it?" shouted Wingrove.

" A thingummy—a thingummy!"

" A what?"

" A ghost on the battlements. Dear me, I thought ghosts never came but in the night. Oh, dear! what will become of us now they have taken to coming in broad daylight? Oh! I shall never get over it."

" On what part of the battlements?"

" The eastern bastion, I think you call it. I was coming along, thinking of nothing at all, just as usual — I was, in fact, going to say, ' How do you do?' to the old cellarer, you know — when something all of a sudden peeps over the battlement. Oh, dear! oh, dear! I'm all of a shiver—I am, indeed. This Brandon Castle will be the death of me quite,—I am sure it will!"

" The eastern battlement!" said Wingrove. " Come, some of you, and let us examine the spot."

The whole of the guard rose, and followed Wingrove to the battlements, leaving Eldred in a state of great perplexity as to whether it would be safer to follow them or stay where he was. At length, espying the page, he thought he would remain in the guard-room.

" How are you this morning, Mister Page?" he said. " I dare say you are like me, now, quite a lover of peace and quietness."

" No," said the page; " I like war."

" You do, do you? Well, there's no accounting for tastes. You'll get your little body some day bruised to a jelly if you have any such foolish propensity."

" We must take our chance, Master Weare."

" Must we—I should say decidedly no, thank you, to that. Now, I'll tell you what—if I was forced to be in a battle, you know, I should like to be inside a great barrel, you understand, with only a few little holes to breathe through, and they might thump away outside of it as long as they liked; and then, when the battle was over, I should come out, you know, with a whole skin, though I might have been in the very thick of it. There's an idea for you, Mister Page."

" A brilliant idea, truly," said the page. " What can be more glorious than war?"

" Why, peace, to be sure! You are a little idiot, Mr. Page, and I prophecy that some of these days you'll be poking yourself into a quarrel, and some great fellow will hit you such a stinger as will settle your business."

" Do you doubt my courage ?"

" Oh, bother your courage !"

" I wear a sword," said the page. " Draw and defend yourself, Master Eldred Weare, or I will wash out in your blood the insult you have given me. Draw, I say."

The page, as he spoke, drew the small ornamental sword which he wore, and flashed its bright blade before Eldred's eyes, who exclaimed—

" Come, come, don't be violent ! Why you are quite a little spitfire. Murder !"

The page had made a pass with his sword purposely so near Eldred's throat, that the latter was put in the most terrible fright.

" Murder ! murder !" he cried.

" Will you fight ?" said the page.

" No, I won't," said Eldred. " Don't ask ridiculous questions. You ought to know better, you insolent little—come, come, now, don't be flashing that sword before me, you make me so dreadfully nervous. A boy of your age ought to be more mild."

" Eldred Weare, I am older than I look, and I must take your life for my honour's sake."

" My life—let me go."

" No," said the page, slipping between him and the door. " One of us must die, unless you tell me this instant what is the secret object of the monk."

" The monk !" cried Eldred. " Why—why, who told you ? Ah, I'm ruined—I'm undone—fire, fire !"

Eldred wrung his hands, and betrayed so much trepidation, that the page in vain strove to bring him back to the subject he wished to converse about, and then feeling that it was hopeless then to extract any information from Eldred, he contented himself with saying to him,

" If you report to any living soul the question I have asked you, be assured that the black knight you saw unhorse Fitzhugh this morning, will come and knock your head off."

" Dear me, will he, indeed ?"

" He will, as sure as you now have it tolerably safe on your shoulders."

Eldred felt his head, to assure himself that it was tolerably safe. Then he said, with what he thought was a very cunning expression,

" You won't get anything out of me, Mr. Fage, and I sha'n't tell my sister that you asked me, because she'd just get in a rage."

" True," said the page. " Hush—the guard come."

<hr/>

CHAPTER XLII.

" A man of holy faith was he,
Of spotless life and fame ;
To pray for that sad woman's soul,
With trembling limbs he came."

THE SICK KNIGHT.—THE ABBOT.—AGATHA'S RAGE.

WHEN Wingrove and the castle guard reached the eastern battlement, they all paused, as with one accord, for standing between them and the clear sky, was a figure, which for a moment struck them all with dismay and terror. It was the half-clad, wild Nemoni, the Wizard of the Red Cavern, that faced them. He seemed unconscious of their vicinity, but stood tossing his arms wildly in the air for some seconds, after which he cried,

"Woe, woe, woe—to the young and the beautiful—to the brave and the good—woe, woe to the innocent—woe to Brandon, Brandon!"

He then, with the speed of a hunted hare, rushed along the extreme verge of the battlements, and turning an angle, disappeared from the astonished eyes of the guard.

"How in Heaven got that man into Brandon Castle?" said Wingrove. "It is the poor maniac who calls himself the Wizard of the Red Cavern."

The guard, without waiting for orders, rushed along the ramparts in the direction Nemoni had taken, for they expected nothing more nor less than to find him dashed to pieces by a fall from the giddy height upon which they had seen him.

Well acquainted, however, as they were with the castle, and all its fortifications, it appeared that the wizard knew far more, for not a vestige of him could be found, and even the still surface of the moat presented not a ripple, to indicate that anybody had fallen into its quiet waters.

"This is most mysterious," said Wingrove. "I cannot myself imagine how any one could gain admittance into the castle, or leave it unobserved. But Brandon swarms with mysteries, and I should not be surprised some morning to find it in possession of a host of devils. I suppose it is my duty to report this circumstance to Agatha Weare."

Wingrove made a wry face as he mentioned Agatha's name; for if ever a man had a mortal aversion for a woman, he, Hugh Wingrove, certainly had for Agatha.

"Well, it can't be helped," he muttered to himself; "I must even go and tell her; but my mind strangely misgives me about that page. He must know something which I don't about the mysteries that at present make Brandon Castle a place of so much tumult; but whether he be a friend or an enemy it is hard to say. The Black Monk may inhabit the old Grey Turret, and yet not be easily dislodged, for who knows what unearthly assistants he may have there with him. These monks, I take it, if they be bad, sell themselves altogether to the devil, in which case there's no contending with Morgatani, who I have always thought to be at the bottom of all these strange proceedings. And yet I have my duty to do, and I must do it. I would that Sir Kenneth Hay were well. He and I would make yet another attempt to storm the Grey Turret. I will even seek him now before I go to Agatha, and see how he is."

Wingrove then hastily walked to the chamber of the poisoned knight, who he found still in a state of stupor, which did not seem at all alleviated.

A grim soldier of the castle guard was waiting on him, and in answer to Wingrove's questions, he said,—

"He has been saying strange things, Master Wingrove. He fancies himself with good King Richard in the Holy Land. It strikes me, do you know, that he has been bewitched by some means."

"I pray Heaven he may recover," said Wingrove.

"Hark!" said the soldier; "he speaks."

"To the rescue—to the rescue!" said Sir Kenneth Hay, as he tossed his arms wildly about him. "A lance—another lance. Charge, for King Richard and the Holy Land. Charge! charge! charge!"

His voice sunk into inarticulate murmurs, and Wingrove, with a deep sigh, said,—

"Alas! alas! he is very ill indeed. Some grievous malady has taken possession of him surely. Do you go to Peter Watkins, he is off guard, and tell him to hie to the neighbouring monastery, and beg the holy abbot to come to see Sir Kenneth Hay. He has great skill in human ailments, and may tell us what has taken possession of the knight."

"That's a good thought, Master Wingrove," said the soldier. "I will do your bidding right cheerfully."

As the soldier turned to leave the chamber, Agatha appeared at the door, and affecting an appearance of concern, she said,—

"How does Sir Kenneth Hay?"

"He sleeps," said Wingrove. "I fear he is not better."

"His sudden illness was surprising," said Agatha; "but, doubtless, he will soon recover. Have you no notion of who the audacious stranger could be who must still be hidden in Brandon Castle?"

"I don't think he is hidden," said Wingrove. "He did not appear to be exactly the kind of person to hide himself, whatever others may do."

Agatha slightly changed colour, as she said,

"I trust we shall have no more brawling in the castle. What sound is that?"

"The drawbridge being lowered to allow a man-at-arms to pass out to the abbot, in order to beg him to come and minister to Sir Kenneth Hay."

"Who dared," cried Agatha, with a scream of passion, "send for him?"

"I," said Wingrove.

"Insolent hind. You ——"

"Madam," cried Wingrove, while his cheek flushed, and he drew himself proudly up, "when you want a harsh word said to a soldier you should get some man to do it, and then it could be resented."

"So, you dare exchange words with me?"

"I dare anything, madam, but do injustice, or plot for the destruction of the innocent."

Agatha's face assumed an ashy hue, so she replied in a subdued tone.

"What mean you?"

No. 22

"My words are simple," said Wingrove; "they cannot require explanation. Such authority as I was left in here by my honoured master, Sir Rupert Brandon, I will exercise. Towards you, Mistress Agatha Weare, I have ever behaved with respect; but I am a soldier, and must resent insult, even from a woman, if she so far forgets her sex as to offer it to me."

Agatha had an angry answer on her lips, but her fear—that fear which the guilty, however powerful they may think themselves, ever feel in the presence of the innocent and pure of purpose, checked her, and muttering something to herself indistinctly, she hurriedly left the chamber of the sick knight.

"Well," said Wingrove, when Agatha had gone, "we have come to an open rupture at last. Let it be so. Perhaps I and Mistress Agatha will get on better now that we understand each other. I wonder what she will contrive next to annoy me. She is a woman who will have her revenge if she can, and I must take care of myself. Alas, alas, what a wreck of bravery is here. Poor Sir Kenneth, I would give something to see you restored once more to what you were this time yesterday, when the hues of health were mantling your cheeks, and you looked the noble, gallant knight report had ever pictured you."

"Charge—charge," murmured Sir Kenneth Hay, in his uneasy sleep. "Charge for King Richard;—for him of the lion heart. Down with the infidel!"

"He thinks himself now in the midst of the battle," said Hugh Wingrove, his eye kindling as he spoke. "Oh, would that I had, instead of remaining here, prayed harder than I did, to follow my noble master to the field."

"Another lance! another lance!" muttered Sir Kenneth Hay. "Give me another lance."

"He raves. Poor Sir Kenneth. Well, I had forgotten to tell Mistress Agatha of the vision on the battlements. It's as well as it is. She might as well take it into her head to abuse the poor wizard, who, I believe, is nothing but a lunatic, as to carp at the presence of the saintly abbot. Oh, what would I give to see Sir Rupert's face once more in his ancient halls."

The monastery was but a short distance from Brandon Castle, and the abbot readily obeyed the summons of Wingrove, although he had not been in the castle since the departure of Sir Rupert himself.

While Wingrove was still keeping watch by the bedside of Sir Kenneth Hay, he heard the clank of the drawbridge as it descended to admit the man of God, and fearful that his progress to the chamber of the knight might be stayed by Agatha, he walked hastily down to the gate of the castle, in order to receive him.

It was well for the sake of the reception which the abbot got, that Wingrove did repair to the castle gate, for Agatha was there, and with a scowl upon her brow, ready to repulse the aged man the moment he should set his foot within the gates.

The abbot glanced around him, with feelings of sad regret, as he thought of the last occasion upon which he had entered that lordly abode, which was when the Lady Alicia lay dead, and the gallant Sir Rupert was mourning her decease with that frantic grief which we are aware possessed his soul at the loss of her whom he had loved so fondly.

"Peace be to all here," said the abbot.

"Holy father," said Agatha, "we accept the benediction, but ——"

"Are very sorry," interposed Wingrove, stepping forward, "that you are not here oftener to give it."

"How now," cried Agatha.

"I am here to welcome the holy man," said Wingrove. "You must know, holy sir, that we have a knight sorely afflicted now in the castle. The hand of Providence is heavy upon him."

" I will gladly, my son, bestow upon him what aid I can in his extremity," said the abbot.

Agatha turned, and darted into the castle, without another word, resolving to consult, as early as possible, with Morgatani, as to some means of getting rid of Hugh Wingrove, to whom her feelings were now of the most rancorous description.

" He shall die," she muttered. " He has braved his fate, and he shall now die."

In the meantime Wingrove conducted the abbot directly to the chamber of Sir Kenneth, who still lay moaning, and apparently in great pain.

The aged man looked long and fixedly in the face of the knight, and then he took his fevered hand in his as he said,—

" Wingrove, this gallant soldier has been poisoned."

" I guessed so much," replied Wingrove. " Heaven help him, he has fallen a victim to the arts of him you recollect, holy father —"

" The Black Monk?"

" Yes; notwithstanding the instructions of Sir Rupert Brandon, and all the efforts which we have made to keep him from Brandon, I am convinced that Morgatani has found a means of entering the castle."

" No doubt—no doubt, my son," said the abbot. " The arts of that dreadful man are great and many. I think I can send an antidote to the poison which has been by some one administered to this warrior, and as I can see he has been sadly betrayed here, and my own presence is evidently far from welcome, I counsel you to help him on with his armour, and be ready, with some assistance from the castle guard, to convey him from here to our monastery, where he shall receive all the kind attention his situation requires, and which even were he in kind hands, he could scarcely receive here."

" I much approve of your proposition, holy sir," said Wingrove ; " and myself with Bernard shall see it executed."

" Do so; I will now hasten to my own quiet home, and after making such needful preparations for the reception of this knight as I know to be necessary, I will send the antidote to the poison which I expect will conquer its bad effect sufficiently to rouse him from the state of stupor he appears to be in, and enable him at least to walk to the monastery with a little assistance."

" At what time will you have him removed ?"

" Let it be at night, my son," said the abbot, " and in secret; I am a man of peace, and would fain avoid any contention with Agatha Weare upon the matter."

" Send your messenger when you will," said Wingrove, " all shall be ready, and I myself will assist Sir Kenneth to the monastery."

" Bless you," said the old man, as he walked with trembling steps from the room, and was conducted by Wingrove to the castle gate.

" Let one of the guard go with you," said Wingrove, " as far as the monastery gate."

" I thank thee, son," said the abbot. " I have a holy brother awaiting me some short distance off. Peace be to you all. My prayers are daily offered for the welfare of the good Sir Rupert Brandon. May he soon come again among his people, and assume the management of his own ancient home."

" Ah, holy sir," said Bernard, who stood by the gate, " we are all ready and willing to say amen to that, whether we are thirsty or not—ahem !"

" Peace," said Wingrove. "Peace, I say. How dare you talk of thirst to his reverence?"

" Well, I only ——"

" Peace—peace, you great sot you, and get out of his reverence's way."

" Who can help being thirsty?" muttered Bernard, as he walked away grumbling.

In a few moments the abbot had passed across the drawbridge, and once more turning, and stretching forth his aged hands towards the castle, as he blessed the inmates of it, without even a mental reservation as regarded those who he knew little deserved one, he slowly took his way towards his own venerable home.

Agatha in vain sought Morgatani. In vain she sought the window of the southern gallery, and made signs towards the old Grey Turret. Morgatani did not, or would not attend to her, and she dared not, in spite of his stern interdict to the contrary, attempt to seek him in the Grey Turret itself.

" I must not till night," she muttered. " I must control my passion, but then some sure and speedy means shall be concocted, of depriving this Wingrove of the power to cross me."

Agatha then sought her own chamber, for there was no one in the castle whom she could speak to but her arch tempter, the monk. A more solitary being than Agatha could not have been found. She had made, as it were, a moral desolation around her by her bad passions. She lived in a world which she herself had rendered desolate, and from which she had divided herself by her crimes, and her awful association with the monk, who was by his dreadful counsels and dark mysterious actions, hurling her to a destruction which she shuddered to think of, and which would occasionally cross her mind with a flash of horror, that would nearly drive her to despair.

CHAPTER XLIII.

" There are ancient pillars of Gothic mould
Within that dungeon dark and old,
And never a wandering ray of light
Breaks the drear stillness of the night."

THE DUNGEON.—THE PAGE AND THE PONIARD.— MORGATANI'S MALIGNANT SPIRIT.—THE APPEAL TO AGATHA.

FITZHUGH either was, or affected to be, very much hurt in his encounter with the stranger knight, for he would not rise from his bed the whole of the day succeeding the early hour at which the battle had taken place. His page had paid many visits to his chamber, and upon the last of those occasions, just as the sun was setting upon that most eventful day, he found Fitzhugh asleep, and noiselessly taking his station by the bedside, he determined to await his awakening from the uneasy sleep in which he was.

Although when the page first sat down by his iniquitous master his manner and countenance were calm and collected, yet not for long did he preserve his equanimity. The most painful and oppressive thoughts seemed to possess him, and after two or three deep sighs he drooped his head upon his hands and wept audibly, although in a suppressed tone, for fear of awakening Fitzhugh.

It would appear, though, as if his master had heard him in his sleep, for he groaned heavily, and muttered disjointed sentences expressive of great perturbation of spirit.

"Edith—Edith," he said, "torment me not—curse me not. Edith, remove your icy hand from my heart. Oh, save me, Heaven, save me—save me from the—the dead!"

"Fitzhugh," said the page, softly.

A deep groan was his only answer.

"Fitzhugh," whispered the page again. "Do you hear and do you repent? Speak—oh, speak!"

Fitzhugh, with a loud cry, awoke, and started half up from the couch on which he lay.

"Help! help!" he cried. "Save me. I—I—oh, are you here? I—have had a dream."

"A dream?" repeated the page.

"Aye, boy," said Fitzhugh, throwing himself back upon his pillow, "a dream which quite unmans me. I would not often have such visions for Brandon Castle and all its possessions."

"Indeed!"

"What is the time, boy?"

"The sun has but just set beneath the distant hills. Shall I light your lamp?"

"I—I hate darkness; it is always peopled with such frightful images, and—and—I don't like it, so light the lamp."

The page lit the lamp, and then, while his back was towards the knight, he said—

"You mentioned a name, sir, in your sleep."

"A name—what name?"

"Edith."

Fitzhugh was silent for a moment, and then he said—

"Boy, tell me truly—what said I else?"

"Nay, sir, nothing of import. You called on Edith not to curse you, and spoke of her as one numbered with the dead."

"She is dead," muttered Fitzhugh.

"But, were she living, you—you—"

"What means this emotion, boy? You seem strangely agitated."

The page shrunk back, as he replied coldly—

"I am quite calm, sir, but, perhaps, too over-fond —"

"Over-fond?"

"Aye, sir, of romance; and, from what you murmured of this Edith, I thought some pretty episode of love and chivalry was, perchance, connected with the maiden."

"Pshaw, boy, you speak of things you do not understand. Tell me, is Sir Kenneth Hay recovered from the—I mean, from his indisposition?"

"I hear not," said the page.

"I cannot leave here," muttered Fitzhugh, "before he does recover, at all events. Sing to me, boy."

"Shall I sing you a grave or merry strain, sir?"

"As you please."

"Then shall I sing you of a gentle maid who was by him she loved betrayed to sin and shame, and then —"

"No," cried Fitzhugh, his face turning paler than before, "I like not such ditties. I—I suppose the maiden in the song consoled herself with another lover?"

"No, sir; she pined away and died.'

Fitzhugh groaned.

" You will find a book," he said, " upon yon table. Read me from that some more cheering incident. I like not such reproachful strains."

The page took the book with a sigh, and, opening it at random, he said,

" Here is an old romance, by the learned Chevalier de Burno. It will interest you, sir."

" Read," said Fitzhugh. " My own thoughts pain me."

The page commenced in a low, sweet voice, as follows :—

" For some hours Guillaume Devereux had been chasing the agile chamois from rock to rock, but without success ; and, weary with his exertions, he sat down to rest upon a projecting precipice.

" The sun was going down to rest in the distant west, and cast his lingering ray upon the snow-clad summits of the mountains, while the glaciers reflected his beams with intensest brilliancy.

" Although Guillaume had often seen the sun produce more gorgeous effects than he now witnessed, yet he gazed on the scene before him until forgetfulness closed his eyelids, and he sunk into a deep slumber.

" Upon awaking, he felt refreshed ; but on looking round discovered that the light with which every object was illumed, was not that of the sun, but of the moon, which appeared now riding high in the vaulted arch of Heaven.

" He quickly rose from the spot upon which he had been reposing, and, leaning upon his staff, he bounded from rock to crag, with the agility of the goats and animals he had been in chase of for so many weary hours.

" Born and bred in the mountains of Savoy, every peak and glen was to him as well known as any beaten road to the traveller ; and, although far distant from his father's cottage, he calculated upon reaching it before midnight.

" With hurried steps he hastened, and at length reached the base of the mountain, and proceeded till he came to a deep ravine between two hills, where the moon's rays scarce penetrated one-third of the distance down, and at each step he took the darkness seemed to increase ; the part he had now reached was overshadowed with larch and other shrubs, which, joining their branches from either side, excluded every ray of light, and afforded shelter to those birds to which the solitude of such a place is congenial.

" Upon his first extrance into the glen he felt certain that his knowledge of the locality was correct, and that it was the road he had often travelled ; but now he became dubious on the subject, and was half inclined to retrace his steps ; yet, at the same time, he felt he could not be mistaken in his course, and therefore pressed forward with redoubled energy, hoping quickly to pass through the glen.

" The gloom, however, thickened, and the screechings and hootings of the nocturnal birds echoed fearfully through the place, while the hisses of some hidden reptiles caused him every now and then to arrest his steps.

" To return now was as bad as to progress, and with a kind of superstitious feeling of dread, he ran forward, hoping soon to escape the horrors of this locality.

" At length he reached a spot where the light of the moon seemed to shine with redoubled brilliancy, and at a short distance before him he perceived an aged man in deep meditation upon a large book, which he laid in his lap as he sat upon a stone.

" His robe was loose and flowing, and fastened at the waist by what appeared to be a serpent twined in folds. His beard descended to his waist, while his white locks fell abundantly upon his shoulders.

" Near him, upon the ground, lay a wand, which every now and then he waved in a mystic manner ; and, as Guillaume approached, he took his eyes from off the book, and rose to meet him.

" ' Who art thou, young man ?' said he, addressing Guillaume, ' that darest penetrate into the recesses of the wizard of the Alps ?'

" ' Father !' said our hero, 'unwittingly have I come thus far ; ere this I hoped to have reached my father's cottage to rest after the days fatigue !'

" ' Knowest thou not, young man, that all who come here are subject to the demon of the mountain, whose servant I am ?'

" ' I have once heard so, father,' replied Guillaume ; ' but deemed I was far from the glen of the Alpine Demon.'

" ' From hence thou canst not escape,' replied the magician, ' until thou hast sworn to yield up to the Demon's power the soul of her you most love on earth in exchange for your own.'

" ' Oh, my beloved Pauline !' cried Guillaume, in the intensity of his mental suffering, ' how can I thus betray your pure and holy spirit ! To what a straight have I not reduced myself and thee !'

" ' Even so it must be,' returned the magician ; ' there is no escape.'

" ' Then,' replied Guillaume, ' sooner would I suffer ten thousand tortures in this world and the next, than sacrifice the spirit of so pure a being to your infernal laws !'

" ' Be it so !' returned the magician, and waving his wand above the head of Guillaume, the latter found himself unable to recede from the spot.

" ' Follow me,' said the magician.

" Guillaume complied, and they entered a gloomy cavern, where skulls and bones were scattered around in heaps.

" ' And what is my destiny ?' asked Guillaume.

" ' That you shall henceforth know ! for the present be content to follow where I lead.'

" Resistance was in vain ; the enchantment was too potent to resist, and Guillaume, half petrified with fear, kept close at the heels of his conductor.

" At length they reached a chamber, in the centre of which appeared a kind of altar, upon which burnt in a livid flame two human hearts.

" At a distance and around the altar was a magic circle of skulls and serpents, from whose mouths breathed forth sulphureous flames, at which Guillaume stopped in terror.

" Follow !" cried the magician, waving his wand.

" Guillaume stepped within the charmed ring, and approached the altar, where for the first time he perceived the form of a female ; but of so hideous a figure he was compelled to avert his head.

Her eyes burned with a phosphorescent light, and glared with a horrid satisfaction upon him, while her hair seemed composed of braided snakes, around which was a garland of flame.

" ' Behold thy future bride !' exclaimed the magician to the frightened Guillaume.

" ' And am I destined to become the husband of a demon ?' said Guillaume in agony.

" ' Yes,' replied the magician.

" ' And wherefore ?'

" ' That the power, empire, and influence of the demon may continually increase through the medium of the sons of men.'

" ' Oh, Pauline ! Pauline !' cried the agonised Guillaume ; ' never shall I again behold you !'

" ' Never,' said a voice, which echoed through the horrid cavern with a noise like thunder.

" ' The bride tarries !' said the magician, authoritatively.

" ' Spare me ! spare me !' returned Guillaume, from the recesses of his soul, as he lay prostrate before the fiery altar.

" ' I have sworn fealty to the demon !' cried the magician, who seemed to officiate as priest, ' and dare not forego my duty !'

" ' In mercy hear me ! Oh, my beloved Pauline ! Pauline, to what has your Guillaume been reserved.'

" ' Seize him !' cried the magician, and immediately Guillaume felt himself lifted from the floor of the cavern by attendant sprites and placed beside the horrid bride, whose burning hand was placed in his.

" Who could speak the agony of his soul at the moment? his hair stood erect upon his head, while large drops of blood oozed from his brow with the intensity of his feelings.

" The magician now pronounced some cabalistic words, when again the loathsome place echoed with the sound of ' the ring! the ring !'

" The magician raised his wand, and, in an instant he received upon its end a small red ring in the form of a small serpent.

" Upon Guillaume's receiving it, he found that the red glow upon it proceeded from its intense heat, which his fingers now seemed capable to bear.

" ' On the bride's left hand !' said the magician.

" Guillaume was about to comply; but the agony of his mind was so great that he involuntarily placed his hand within his bosom, and there grasping a small cross which Pauline had given him, he exclaimed, fervently,

" ' Oh, God ! have mercy on my soul !'

" As he pronounced the sacred name, a peal of unearthly laughter resounded through the cavern ; the bride vanished with a flash of light, while magician, altar, and magic ring of sculls, scrolled up like a cloud of smoke and dissipated with a noise of the most dreadful thunder.

" The terrific explosions he had heard, caused Guillaume again to prostrate himself upon the earth with fear, and upon coming to his senses he found himself upon the ledge of rock where he had fallen asleep.

" Pale and haggard he started to his feet, and looked wildly around him ; the sun had long gone down, while around him raged the most dreadful storm ; the lightning flashed and hissed and the thunder roared, while the cataracts fell into the vallies with a deafening rush of water.

" The effect of this, combined with his horrid dream, near rendered him senseless ; but recovering his wandering mind, he hastened to a shepherd's cot, not far distant, till the storm abated.

" On the following day he departed for his home, still faint from the horrors of his evening's dream, where he arrived to bless the expectant eyes of his beloved Pauline.

" In order that he might not be separated from her by any casualty, he prevailed upon her to accompany him to the nearest priest, when they were united firmly in the bands of Hymen."

The page ceased, and the deep unbroken breathing of Fitzhugh showed that he slept.

The castle clock at that moment struck ten, and as the solemn tones died away mournfully on the night air, the page rose to his feet, and looked long and earnestly in the sleeper's face.

Then a convulsive sob of deep passion shook his frame, and drawing from his vest a dagger, he muttered :—

" Shall I kill him now, as he sleeps, and be the avenger of the wronged ? Shall I even now send him to his long account with Heaven in the full freshness of his sins ?"

The dagger glittered in the air, and what, in the wild excitement of the moment, the page might have done, was stayed by a sudden gleam of light, which, coming through the key-hole of the door, fell upon the sleeper's face, which otherwise was shaded from the rays of a lamp. The page started back and at once concealed his dagger. Then he slowly and cautiously opened the chamber-door and looked out. A tall figure was gliding along the corridor.

" The monk ! the monk !" murmured the page, and with a noiseless step, he foll wed the figure.

CHAPTER XLIV.

" Woe—woe to the just and good,
    The wicked are in power ;
And evil hearts and evil hands,
    Shall triumph for their hour."

THE KNIGHT AND THE MONK.—THE SPY.—THE PROJECTED MURDER.

IT was just about the period when the page was having the conversation we have recorded with Fitzhugh, that Agatha summoned Eldred to her own apartment, and when he came, which he did with fear and trembling, she accosted him with the words :—

" We shall want your aid to-night, in something which it is requisite you should assist in."

" Oh, dear ! couldn't you manage without me ? I'm sure, sister, you and the black—I mean Morgatani, can do just as well by yourselves. I ain't at all fond of adventures."

" Eldred," said Agatha, " you have gone too far to retreat. You must carry through all that Morgatani projects, or consent even now to die."

" To die ? What am I to be killed if I don't do just what I'm told ?"

" You are. Morgatani holds that all persons concerned in a plot are either useful or dangerous."

" Does he indeed ?"

" You will find he does. Do you know that from the court-yard at the base of the Grey Turret, there opens a communication with some dungeons ?"

" Oh, dear ! oh, dear !" sighed Eldred. " We are to go poking under-

No. 23

ground again, are we? I do hate that, upon my word I do. I like to be a great man, and I like to have lots of money, but, do you know, sister, if I'd have thought that this affair had been one half the trouble, and a quarter the danger, I wouldn't have had anything to do with it on any account."

"Hush—hush! Do not let him hear you."

"Him! Bless my heart. Oh, dear!"

The latter part of Eldred's exclamation arose from the monk having just entered the room.

"Eldred," said Agatha, with a sneer, "has, as usual, some scruples about what, for his own benefit, we wish him to do."

"Has he scruples?" said the monk, in a deep hollow voice, stepping up to within an inch of the terrified Eldred's face, who stammered :—

"Scru—scru—scruples? Oh, dear, no. It's quite a mistake of Agatha's, it is. I never had any."

"You will cheerfully do all that is required of you?"

"Yes, of course. Needs must, you know, when the —"

"What?"

"Oh, dear me, nothing. I didn't mean it. Upon my word I didn't, really."

"Eldred Weare," said the monk; "do not tempt your fate too far. As yet you know not a tithe of my power. Agatha, go you to Sir Kenneth's chamber, and see if he be alone."

"I'll go," said Eldred, who dreaded being left alone with the monk. "Let me go."

"Peace!" said Morgatani. "You remain with me, and we will consult about your brilliant future destinies."

"My brilliant destinies? Oh, I'm afraid I shall be frightened out of my life before they come."

Agatha took a small hand-lamp which was upon the table, and walked slowly from the room towards the chamber of Sir Kenneth Hay.

When she reached it, to her surprise, she found that the knight had his armour on, although he was still in the same state of stupor, to all appearance, that he had been in earlier in the day.

The same soldier was in the room who had been sent by Wingrove on the message to the neighbouring monastery, and in answer to Agatha's question of how it was that Sir Kenneth Hay was completely attired in his armour, with the exception of his helmet and gauntlets, he said,

"May it please you, lady, Hugh Wingrove and Master Bernard came and helped to place his armour on. I understand he will be removed to the monastery some time during the evening, in order that he may be tended by the monks."

"Indeed!" sneered Agatha.

Without another word she then left the chamber, and hastened to report to Morgatani the state of the knight.

A dark scowl came across the face of the monk as he heard the proposition concerning the removal of Sir Kenneth Hay to the monastery, and he remained for a few brief moments in deep thought.

"Are soldiers there?" he then said.

"But one," was Agatha's reply.

"I have bethought me of a plan," said Morgatani, "which will so wrap the fate of Sir Kenneth Hay in mystery, that let him live or die within the dungeons of Brandon, none shall suspect his presence there. Do you both wait here while I go to the armoury."

Without pausing then for a reply, the monk strode off towards the armoury.

"What's he going to do now, sister?" said Eldred.

"I know not," replied Agatha; "but be assured it is something which will further your objects."

"My objects? Ah! that's all very well. You and the black—I mean Morgatani, would like to persuade me that all you are doing is for me, but I—"

"Once for all, Eldred," said Agatha, bitterly, "I tell you I will not listen to your cowardly ravings. You must and shall proceed in the undertaking in which we are embarked."

"Bless us, what's that?" suddenly cried Eldred, as he saw a shadow of some one flit past the half-open door.

Agatha started as she exclaimed :—

"What see you?"

"I don't see anything, but I did see a shadow."

"Are we watched?" muttered Agatha, as she went to the door of the chamber and listened attentively. A slight sound met her ears, as of a retreating footstep, and she rushed forward in the direction of the sound.

"Who goes there?" she cried, but a faint echo along the ancient corridor alone replied to her, and in another moment she saw the tall form of the monk approaching from the direction of the armoury.

"Morgatani !" she said, with an expression of fear, "we are watched by some one. Even now I heard a footstep yonder."

"It were death," said the monk, "to any one who should cross my path this night. Let him beware ! But your imagination may have deceived you."

"It didn't deceive me, then," said Eldred, who, dreading, as usual, to be left alone, had followed his sister from the room into the corridor.

"Saw you anything?" said Morgatani.

"I saw a shadow, and that, you know, is good ground of belief that there was a substance."

"Hold that," said Morgatani, as he handed to Eldred a heavy breast-plate which he had brought from the armoury. "Hold that, while I search the corridor."

The monk then with a stealthy step walked to the different windows, which were let into deep recesses, leaving ample space for concealment ; but he could see no one, although, had he looked outside one of the windows, he would have found, crouched on a narrow parapet of stone, the page of Fitzhugh, who was determined to watch the night's proceedings, and discover what object the monk and Agatha had in view.

"There is no one here," said Morgatani, as he returned. "Let us proceed to our work."

"But—but," stammered Eldred ; "you forget that there is a soldier in Sir Kenneth's room."

"I do not," said Morgatani, "although he will soon be forgotten."

As the monk spoke he held up his right hand, and Eldred saw that he grasped a ponderous mace, which he recollected to have frequently looked at in the armoury, with a doubt if any mortal man could be found strong enough to wield it effectually. The monk, however, appeared to handle it as if it had been but a straw, although its weight was very great, and it was a fearful ponderous weapon. Even Agatha shrunk back a moment, as the rays from the lamp fell upon the spikes which were upon the end of the mace, and her blood ran cold as she thought of the hideous crash that would follow a blow from such a weapon, wielded by such a hand as Morgatani's.

A grim smile crossed the face of the monk as he marked the effect which he had produced upon his companions, and, turning to Eldred, who had enough to do to carry the heavy breast-plate, he said :—

"Come on to Sir Kenneth's chamber. When we reach it, do you knock at it, and leave the rest to me."

"You ain't a-going to hit anybody a nobber with that mace, surely?" said Eldred.

"Leave that to me," said the monk. "On—on—we have no time to lose."

"If there should be a row," thought Eldred, "I can hold my head behind this breast-plate, and they may hit that as many knocks as they like. Bless me, I'm quite in a perspiration; I know there will be a row. I hope that man-at-arms, who is in Sir Kenneth's chamber will be quiet and prudent, and just let Morgatani knock his brains out without making a fuss."

Agatha shrunk back as they neared the door of Sir Kenneth's room, for she dreaded the scene which might ensue, and Eldred would have run away altogether but that his fear of the monk overcame his fear of anything else.

"Knock," said Morgatani, in a low voice.

"I can't," replied Eldred; "I'm holding this great heavy thingummy with both hands."

"Put it down," said the monk in such a startling whisper that Eldred dropped it with a loud crash.

Before the monk could utter an imprecation, which rose to his lips, the door of Sir Kenneth's room was opened, and the man-at-arms put out his head, saying,

"What's that?"

The words were scarcely out of his lips, when, with a hissing sound, the mace descended upon his devoted head, and he fell with one deep hollow groan like one struck by lightning. Agatha covered her eyes with her hands, and Eldred, in his terror, sat down on the ground, trembling in every limb. Without a moment's pause then, the monk stepped across the prostrate body of the murdered man-at-arms and entered the chamber. Sir Kenneth Hay lay upon the couch in a half sleep, and, for a moment, the monk glanced at him. Then, with an effort of strength that was perfectly Herculean, he lifted him from the bed, and incased in heavy armour, as he was, he flung him across his shoulder, and making the oaken boards crack again as he went, he stepped into the corridor with his burthen.

The weight of the knight and his suit of mail was so great, that even Morgatani, notwithstanding his prodigious strength, felt it sensibly, and his voice was thick and short, as he said,

"Follow me quickly. To the dungeons—to the dungeons."

"Eldred," said Agatha, "rise—rise, I say."

A broad flash of light at this moment came from the other end of the corridor, and the monk seeing it upon the opposite wall, turned for a moment with a face expressive of such demoniacal passion, that Eldred scrambled to his feet in the greatest alarm.

Agatha clasped her hands, as she said,

"A moment's delay and all is lost."

"Follow," said the monk; "follow, or by all the powers of evil, I will leave you to your fate."

He strode along rapidly, and Agatha followed him, pushing Eldred before her, who was nearly fainting with fright.

Had they delayed another moment, they would have been seen by Bernard and Wingrove, who were approaching for the purpose of assisting Sir Kenneth to the castle gate, and thence to the monastery, but, as it was, Agatha just descended the staircase in time to avoid being seen.

The party were now in darkness, for the light which they had had was in the hurry left upon the floor by the side of the murdered guard. When they reached the bottom of the staircase, the monk paused, and in a whisper, said,

"Have you brought with you the breast-plate, Eldred?"

"Yes—yes—I—I—have," stammered Eldred.

"'Tis well. Leave it here while you go somewhere and procure a light."

"What, me?"

"Yes. Go at once, or I will scatter your brains upon these stairs."

Eldred put down the breast-plate with a groan, as he said,

"Where shall I find a light?"

"In my chamber," said Agatha; "but remain where you are, I shall be quicker myself."

She ran along a passage which was at the foot of the stairs, and which led to the principal staircase up which Wingrove and Bernard had come. To bound up that was but the work of a moment, and her room being close at hand, she procured the light, and was some steps down the staircase again, when she heard the voice of Wingrove, in loud accents, cry,

"Guard—guard—call the guard. Here has been murder done. Guard—guard."

"Curses on your brawling tongue," muttered Agatha, as she rushed down the remaining steps. "You shall meet the same fate as he you are now raising so much clamour about, before you are many days older. Hugh Wingrove, you shall die by the hands of Morgatani, or I have no power to raise his passion."

In a few moments she was by the side of Morgatani, but before she could speak the alarm bell of the castle smote their ears with a hollow sound, and struck additional terror to the heart of Eldred, who firmly believed that that night would see his death.

"Oh, dear! oh, dear, what will become of me?" he said. "Here am I, quite undone. I'm a victim. Why did I ever come here at all? It's all your fault, sister Agatha; you are a violent woman, and like rows and danger, but I don't; I'm lost quite, and shall come by my death."

"A general alarm is spreading through the castle," said Agatha. "What shall we do?"

Deep groans came from Sir Kenneth's breast, and he struggled to free himself from the grasp of the monk, who cried,—

"This way—to the southern gallery, quick; there is one window there looks into the moat.

The tramp of feet in the corridor they had so recently left now proclaimed that danger was at hand, and the monk rushed onwards with his burthen, followed by his two alarmed confederates. Loud cries now were heard in all directions, and the alarm bell continued to toll dismally; rapid steps began descending the stairs, and just as Morgatani reached the commencement of the southern gallery, the voice of Wingrove was heard exclaiming:—

"This way—this way! Let us capture the Black Monk! Forward, men, forward! To the Grey Turret! To the Grey Turret! Death to the assassins!"

Morgatani threw down Sir Kenneth Hay close to the door which led from the gallery to the court-yard, at the base of the Grey Turret, and snatching from Eldred the heavy breast-plate, he said:—

"Agatha, attend to me! Remain here, and say you followed Sir Kenneth Hay from his chamber, and that he seemed frantic. Say you tried to stop him, but that like a madman, he dashed through yon window, and found a grave in the moat which flows below."

As Morgatani spoke, he raised above his head the massive breast plate, and flung it with such tremendous force through the air towards the window, that it smashed glass, frame-work, and every obstacle, leaving a large opening, and falling in the moat with a splash that must have been heard by every one in the castle.

CHAPTER XLV.

"The dungeon, it was dark and drear,
  Foul insects crawled around;
And above, the tread of armed men
  Was heard with mournful sound."

THE FATE OF SIR KENNETH.—THE DUNGEON BENEATH THE MOAT.

So sudden and unexpected to Eldred and Agatha was the action of the monk, that the former uttered a loud cry of terror, and Agatha almost echoed it on the impulse of the moment, but excited as she was she had her feelings under better control than Eldred could pretend to, and remained silent, while Morgatani stooping over the nearly lifeless form of Sir Kenneth Hay, again lifted him in his arms, and rushed with him into the court-yard.

"Follow him with the light," said Agatha to Eldred. "If you remain here another moment I will leave you to the vengeance of the men-at-arms."

Eldred thought his safest plan would be indeed to follow Morgatani, and he accordingly did so with a precipitation that nearly rolled him into the court-yard upon his back.

As we have before had occasion to remark, the paved court was of small dimensions, and two or three steps of the stalwart monk brought him to the door leading to the turret opposite to that which possessed so fearful an interest in the eyes of the inhabitants of Brandon.

"Open the door," said Morgatani, as he threw some keys at the feet of Eldred. "Quick, quick! The largest key is the proper one."

With trembling eagerness Eldred unlocked the door of the turret staircase, and the monk passed through with his burthen, followed by his cowardly and shrinking companion. His first act was to relieve himself of Sir Kenneth Hay, by laying him on the stairs, and his next was to lock the turret door on the inner side to prevent surprise.

"Let them attack the Grey Turret," he muttered. "It will go hard, but they will be taught a lesson there which will repress their ardour."

"You—you don't mean to say there's anybody there?" said Eldred.

The monk laughed a bitter short laugh as he replied,—

"There are some spirits there, which when once raised even I could not quell."

"Spirits?"

"Yes! Subtle spirits, raised by that profound science which is known only to my order. The secrets of nature are not secrets to us. We know the hidden mysteries of the earth, and so surely as any one attempts to force the door of yon turret will they light upon their own destruction."

"Hark, hark," cried Eldred. "They are coming."

Loud shouts rent the air as he spoke, and from the noise and clatter without it became clear that the small court-yard was full of armed men.

The monk snatched then the keys from Eldred, and running his finger down the wall at a particular part, he touched a spring which immediately opened a small oval piece of metal, behind which was a key-hole. The lock was stiff and untractable, and it required all Morgatani's strength to turn the key, but when he had succeeded in so doing a small square door opened inwards, presenting a dark abyss, which could only be descended by a narrow staircase scarcely sufficient for one person.

"Are we to go down there?" asked Eldred, in terror.

"We are," said the monk. "Take the light and descend first, I will follow."

"First?—I—I'd rather not—I never like to go first except it's to go away from any danger."

"Descend," said the monk, angrily, " or I will pitch you down head foremost."

"If I must—why I suppose—oh, dear me, I suppose I really must."

"Descend !"

Eldred took the lamp and with the most abject fear depicted upon his countenance, commenced the somewhat perilous descent down the narrow staircase.

"Hold," cried the monk, when he had got down some distance, " now assist me with the knight."

He then dragged Sir Kenneth Hay, who was to all appearance, almost dead, to the door-way, and grasping him firmly by the arms he let down his feet, telling Eldred to take hold of them, after which, still holding the unfortunate knight by the arms, he himself slowly descended the narrow staircase.

"How deep is it?" groaned Eldred.

"Descend," was the only reply of the monk, and guiding the feet of Sir Kenneth with one hand, while he held the lamp with the other, Eldred went down step by step, until, to his great relief, he reached a large open space, which, but dimly lighted as it was, by the feeble rays of the lamp, seemed of great extent.

"Bless us, and save us, where are we now?" said Eldred.

"Beneath the court-yard by the Grey Turret," replied the monk. " Hark."

He pointed upwards as he spoke, and Eldred could distinctly hear the heavy tread of the men-at-arms above, as they crowded towards the old Grey Turret, where they expected to find the monk concealed.

"The poor fools," muttered Morgatani, " I could hurl them all to destruction if it so pleased me ; but their punishment will be sufficient."

A cold damp atmosphere was in the gloomy underground place, and Eldred trembled in every limb as he felt a chill at his very heart. The miserable Sir Kenneth Hay muttered some incoherent words, and moaned as if in pain, while the monk stood as if resting himself from the exertions of carrying the knight so far.

"Charge—charge," said Sir Kenneth. " Drag me from among the horses' feet. Help—help."

"'Tis horrid to hear him," said Eldred. " Where are we to take him now?"

"To the first of a range of six dungeons which commence a little further on. Move directly forward and you will see a door studded with nails."

Eldred did as he was directed, and soon perceived a low arched door, which was secured by a massive bar across it as well as by two huge bolts that seemed so firmly rusted into their sockets as to render it next to impossible to remove them.

"How did you find out this place?" said Eldred.

"We Jesuits," replied Morgatani, " have plans of all the principal castles, palaces, and public edifices in Europe. We know many secret places, and entrances, and exits, from such abodes as Brandon, which are unknown to the proprietors themselves."

"It's very odd," said Eldred ; " but I'm sure we shall never get this door open, for the bolts are quite rusted in, and so is the bar in its iron hasps."

"Give me the lamp," said Morgatani, and taking it from the hands of Eldred, he placed the flame against the sockets of the bolts until the heat expanded them sufficiently to separate the long existing contact between the two pieces of metal.

The bolts were then easily withdrawn, and as for the massive bar that went across the door, the monk with a great effort succeeded in removing it.

"Stand aside, Eldred Weare," he then said, " or the blast of foul and fœtid air from these dungeons may seize upon the springs of life and destroy you."

This caution had not to be repeated twice to Eldred, for he gave such a start as placed a considerable distance between him and the dungeon door, which Morgatani then flung wide open, himself stepping on one side to avoid the unwholesome exhalation that rushed forth as from a charnel-house.

"These dungeons," he said, "go under the moat, and its stagnant waters drop through the arched roof, forming putrid pools below."

"That must be remarkably pleasant," said Eldred.

The monk made no other remark, but, after waiting a few brief moments, he dragged Sir Kenneth into the dungeon, and propped his exhausted frame against one of the short columns that supported the roof.

"Bless me, there's a chain, too, all ready," said Eldred, as he pointed to a rusty chain that hung from an iron staple, firmly embedded in the column.

"Each of the pillars here are so provided," said Morgatani. "Here I think we have the mirror of chivalry tolerably safe."

"If he gets out of here he's a conjuror," said Eldred.

"Hush!—he speaks."

"To England—to England," muttered Sir Kenneth Hay. "Save the king."

"The king," sneered Morgatani, "will be much beholden to your services."

"On—on," moaned the knight; "another lance. For my country—and my king—down—down—down."

"I—I don't like to hear him," said Eldred. "There's something very horrid about his noise. Let's come away now we've done it."

"You can come with me to the Grey Turret. There is an underground communication with it, which I can show you."

"What!" cried Eldred, "I come to the Grey Turret? I should say decidedly not. Oh, no. Why, my hair would stand on end, it would, at the very idea."

"As you please; you can remain here if you like; but it will be unsafe for the secret of this place for you to leave it at present, by the same way we come. The court-yard is too well watched at present."

"I—I can creep out," whined Eldred, "and nobody will see me. You know nobody suspects me of anything. Oh! let me go—let me go."

"Coward!—would you run the risk of ruining us all, because you are afraid to remain in a dungeon a short time?"

"I can't stay here indeed; I don't feel very well now, I assure you. I've got a sort of pain everywhere."

It might have been the cool air of the dungeon, or the exercise he had had by being carried from his room, which in some measure revived Sir Kenneth Hay, but he languidly opened his eyes, and fixing their lack lustre orbs upon the countenance of Eldred, he said, in a faint voice,—

"Where am I?"

The monk immediately stepped before Eldred, and, confronting the still confused Sir Kenneth, said, in a deep solemn voice,—

"You are where you never can emerge! You have passed the boundary which separates the living from the dead."

Sir Kenneth shuddered, and Morgatani continued,—

"You are required to say where and when you last saw Richard Cœur De Lion."

"Charge—charge," gasped Sir Kenneth, as he relapsed again into unconsciousness.

"'Tis too soon," muttered Morgatani. "This poison still clings to the springs of life. He cannot yet answer me that which I would fain know. Go out, Eldred, and listen if you still hear the tramp of feet overhead."

Eldred went to the door of the dungeon, and listened, but all seemed still.

"I don't hear them," he said. "I think you may let me go now. They are gone. Don't you mean to let him have any victuals?"

"For my own purposes I will take care to keep life in him. In an hour I shall return here with refreshment to him."

"I shouldn't object to some refreshment myself," said Eldred; "I'm as thirsty as that great wretch Bernard always says he is, and ——"

At this moment an explosion took place in the direction of the Grey Turret, which seemed to shake the castle to its very foundation. Then followed shrieks and cries, in the midst of all which, Eldred, half dead with terror as he was, could hear a low, devilish chuckle from Morgatani, as he gloated over the mischief that he had said would happen to those who were adventurous enough to storm the turret in which he carried on his unholy machinations.

CHAPTER XLVI.

Hark! hark! to the bugle horn.
Ope, ope the castle-gate,
The good and brave shall yet be saved
From treachery and hate.

THE ABBOT'S MESSENGER.—THE PILGRIM LOVER.

In order now properly to connect the events of our narrative, we mus go back to an earlier period of the evening, where, in the guard-room of Brandon, was waiting Wingrove most anxiously for the abbot's messenger with the promised antidote to the poison which had produced so disastrous an effect upon the nerves of poor Sir Kenneth Hay.

The guard could not but see the agitation and impatience of Hugh Wingrove; and, wondering much at its special cause, they sought as much as

No. 24

possible, in their rude way, to amuse him. Minute after minute, however, flew by, and still the messenger came not, while Wingrove's fears for the safety of Sir Kenneth each moment increased.

"Why, Master Wingrove," said Joyce Evans, "you look quite melancholy. Let Anstey tell you one of his old tales of love and war."

"Let Anstey tell what tale he lists," said Wingrove, "I shall hear him as I pace up and down here."

"Did you ever hear how De Valance ran off with the Lady Blanche Gondolphe?"

"Never—never," cried all.

"Then listen to me. You must know Blanche was as fair as the day, but she was under the care of the bear Gondolphe, as he was called, from his churlishness.

"'Never shall the Lady Blanche wed other than the man I choose!' said the Baron Gondolphe, as a scowl of darkness crossed his brow.

"'She was betrothed to me in her father's lifetime,' urged the Knight Valance, a handsome youth, who now pressed his suit with fervour.

"'Maybe; but times are changed,' returned Gondolphe; 'your father at the time had a good estate, which at his death would have devolved on you; you now are little better than a beggar; his estate was seized by the Crown.'

"'In that the Lady Blanche and I are equal,' said the knight; 'but I have a sword and arm to protect her.'

"'Ha, ha! a sword is but a poor inheritance to support a lady on,' returned the baron.

"The knight bit his lip in anger at the insult he had received; he then exclaimed, 'you then refuse my right?'

"'I do,' growled Gondolphe.

"'Then hear me,' replied the knight, as he struck the oaken table with his clenched fist. 'In spite of you or yours, she shall be mine!'

"'Ha, ha! the empty vauntings of a brainless youth,' laughed Gondolphe.

"The taunt sunk deep into the heart of De Valance; hitherto he had suppressed his rage; it now burst forth; and, seizing a boar spear that stood beside him, he hurled it with fearful violence at the baron's person.

"'Hell and furies!' roared Gondolphe, as the weapon missed him; 'your miscreant soul shall pay for this. Ho, there, seize the villain, guards.'

"Before, however, any one had time to answer, the knight had leaped from the window, near which he was standing, into the court-yard below; another second he was in the saddle, and had crossed the drawbridge.

"'To horse, to horse!' roared the baron; 'a hundred marks for the villain's head.'

"No sooner were the words uttered, than a dozen steeds were led forth, and a dozen lances glittered in the mid-day sun; but their movements were not so quick as their master's wishes.

"'Quick, quick!' called the baron, 'or your worthless lives shall answer for it.'

"With all possible haste the men-at-arms were seated in their saddles, and scouring the plain before them; but De Valance had had such ample time for flight, that nothing of him could be seen except the reflection of the sunbeams as they played upon his corslet in the horizon.

"Pursuit was useless, and the guards returned.

"'How now, knaves!' cried the baron, 'has he not returned with you?'

"'He had too much grace, my lord,' replied the foremost of the party.

" ' Ye laggard hounds !' returned the baron, ' you are too well fed ; it makes you heavy in the saddle.'

" ' My lord,' expostulated the leader.

" ' Off, off, I say, or the skins shall be torn from your recreant carcases.'

" Without staying to parley, the men returned their chargers to their stalls and themselves to the buttery, to recruit their spirits after their ride and the effects of the baron's anger.

" The Lady Blanche was seated in her chamber, when her uncle, the baron, entered, and by the scowl upon his brow, she knew that something was amiss.

" ' My lord,' said she, rising from her seat, and bowing low before him, ' to what am I indebted for this early visit ?'

" ' To a beggar's impudence, Blanche, and one who has conspired against my life.'

" ' Good Heavens ! uncle, and who has dared to thus brook your anger ?'

" ' One that you know well.'

" ' Ah, say you so, dear uncle,' replied the trembling girl. ' I know of none but Hubert the Rough that would have presumed so much.'

" ' It was not he, child, but the beggarly knave, Valance.'

" The agitation of Blanche became excessive at the mention of her lover's name ; she trembled from head to foot, for full well she knew the revengeful nature of her guardian ; at length she demanded ' what provocation had he ——'

" ' Provocation ! faith, I know of none, except that I refused your hand in marriage.'

" ' He was my betrothed, dear uncle,' meekly replied the trembling Blanche.

" ' I know it ; such was the bad policy of your father.'

" ' My father !' ejaculated the fervent Blanche. ' Oh, that I could be but with him in the realms of bliss.'

" ' Yes, your father, Blanche,' hoarsely resumed the baron. ' I say such was his bad policy ; but while you are under my protection I shall expect you to think but as I wish you.'

" ' I hope, dear uncle, I have not proved remiss in aught ?'

" ' I did not say that, child ; but henceforth you must forget that you had been betrothed to Sir De Valance.'

" How can I, dear uncle ? he was the companion of my childhood, and on him was fixed my first and only love.'

" ' Childish nonsense, Blanche ; I have brighter prospects in store for you ; and him I expect you never will see again.'

" ' Never !' ejaculated Blanche. ' Never !' and she repeated the word musingly, as if she could not comprehend the whole meaning of the word.

" ' Yes, never !' vociferated the baron.

" ' Merciful Heaven !' ejaculated Blanche, clasping her lily hands, ' and thus to part without even a kind farewell.'

" ' Would you mate with a rascally varlet that has dared to raise his arm against your protector and kinsman ?'

" Blanche replied not.

" ' The cowardly knave ! he hurled the spear as I stood unarmed ; and for his head I have offered a hundred marks !'

" ' Heaven forfend !' cried Blanche, ' and did Valance do this and without provocation ?'

" ' Ask no questions, girl ; I say you must forget him, and prepare to become the bride of the Count Bretagne.'

" ' Never! never! I swear it!' cried Blanche. ' Never will I prove false to my early vow; and never will I marry the Count Bretagne!'

" ' Disobedient and ungrateful girl!' cried the baron, his eyes darting fire; ' from hence I renounce all kindred with thee!'

" ' Uncle, dear uncle! recal those dreadful words!' said the kneeling Blanche.

" ' Will you comply with my wishes?'

" ' In aught else, dear uncle—but —'

" ' Ho, there! Pietro! Ricardo!'

" At the summons, two men-at-arms appeared from the adjacent rampart.

" ' Convey this girl to the castle keep!' continued the baron, ' a little abstinence will cool her blood.'

" ' Surely, dear uncle, you cannot mean to be so harsh with your unhappy Blanche?' said the suppliant girl, as the rough warriors took her by the arm.

" ' Away! away!' cried Gondolphe, and stamped his foot with passion.

" ' Have mercy! mercy!' cried Blanche.

" ' Begone!' shouted the baron.

" ' Come, come, my lady,' said the men-at-arms, ' do not irritate him by parley; he will relent when he sees your submission.'

" ' Good Pietro—Ricardo! do not hold me; do not force me to that horrid keep!' said Blanche, in a tone of mild entreaty.

" ' We dare not but perform our duty,' replied the men; ' 'twere as much as our heads were worth.'

" ' Merciful God! protect me!' ejaculated Blanche. ' What will become of me? Oh, Valance! Valance! Oh, my blest father, look down upon your unhappy child.'

" As Blanche uttered this the door of the castle keep was opened, she was thrust in, and as they drew the heavy bolts upon her, the grating of the iron seemed to enter her very soul.

" In an agony of despair she cast herself upon the floor. ' Oh, my beloved Valance!' said she, ' what do I not suffer for your love? What rashness could tempt you thus to irritate the anger of my uncle?' For awhile she wept loud and bitterly, and when more recovered, she looked around to discover the horrors of the place.

" It was a dark and dreary dungeon : the only ray of light that entered was from a grated window near the roof; the walls were cold and bare, with the exception of the names of the various prisoners that had been confined therein, scratched in the solid masonry, and the heavy chains and bolts therein inserted to confine them.

" No hope of escape appeared, and unless her cruel uncle relented or Heaven interposed in her behalf, she feared she should die in this gloomy and horrid vault.

" The only variation to the monotony of her captivity was the tramp of the men-at-arms upon the adjacent rampart, and they seemed there more effectually to prevent assistance in case any should attempt to rescue her.

" She had now been confined some hours, when the bolts were withdrawn, and Pietro placed a small loaf and a pitcher of water on the ground beside her.

" ' Good Pietro,' said Blanche, ' for one moment I would speak with thee!'

" Pietro placed his finger on his lip, and without uttering a syllable, left he keep to the great dismay of the timid Blanche.

*   *   *   *   *   *

On the following day, at noon, an aged palmer drew near the castle ; his long white beard descended to his girdle, his hair floated in the wind, and was only confined by his hat, around which were a number of shells.

" As he approached the drawbridge, his venerable appearance and tottering step gained for him respect by the men-at-arms, who loitered near.

" ' A crust of bread and a mouthful of cold water, in the name of the Virgin ?' said the pilgrim.

" ' Walk to the buttery, good father,' said the warden ; ' there they will relieve thy necessities.'

" ' And where shall I find the Baron Gondolphe ?' asked the palmer.

" ' Most likely in the hall ; 'tis near the hour of dinner.'

" ' I pray thee show me to him.'

" ' Ho, there ! Paulo !' called the warden, ' this holy man would see the baron.'

" ' This way, follow me,' said Paulo, a domestic, who was leaning idle at the portal of the hall.

" The aged pilgrim tottered after him ; scarce could he support himself upon his staff, he seemed so weary.

" ' A pilgrim would see you, my lord,' said the servitor, ushering in the pilgrim, where the baron was seated with his guests.

" ' A pilgrim ! eh ?' returned the baron. ' Bid him enter.'

" With trembling steps the old man entered. ' Peace, peace to all !' said he.

" ' You seem weary, friend ?' resumed the baron ; ' you have travelled far.'

" ' I am faint and weary, and have journeyed far and late to bear you tidings !'

" ' From the war ?'

" ' Yes, from Palestine, where your sons were doing deeds of valour in our holy cause.'

" ' And they both still live ?'

" ' When I left they were both alive and well !'

" ' And how goes the warfare ?'

" ' The infidels are swept away like chaff before the wind !' replied the pilgrim.

" ' Know you aught of my cousin, the Count de Grouchy ?'

" ' He bid me to recommend him to you,' said the palmer, ' and also to the Lady Blanche.'

" ' Humph !—but, holy man, you need refreshment. Ho, there, knave ! pass him the wine cup !'

" ' My drink is water !' replied the friar.

" ' A stoup of wine will not do you harm ; forget your vow for once— give him the wine !'

" The palmer bent his head in token of thanks, then said—' My lord, I would crave a boon !'

" ' Say on.'

" ' It is that I have a cover for my head to-night within these castle walls, to recruit my spirits for the next day's journey.'

" ' Where go you, father, on the morrow ?'

" ' To Saint Austin's, in the Vale.'

" ' A good day's journey for a feeble man,' returned the baron ; ' to reach it, you must rise betimes.'

" ' Who ever knew a pilgrim a sluggard on his couch ?' replied the heary man.

" ' Well, well, good father, thy request is granted.'

" ' Thanks, most noble lord; but before I seek my rest, I would pray with those who need it.'

" ' I think, good father, you may save your prayers till a fitter market; here we are all sinners of the deepest shade.'

" ' 'Tis such as need my counsel,' quickly returned the pilgrim; 'is there any would confess?'

" ' None that I know of,' replied the baron; ' but old Joceline, the cook, they say, has turned religious.'

" ' Ha, ha, ha!' roared several at the table.

" ' Your mirth is unseemly,' said the pilgrim, ' and more so in the presence of a servant of the Most High.'

" ' No preaching, good father,' resumed the baron, ' but yet you may do me service.'

" ' Then let me know it, ere the sun goes down to rest.'

" ' You can perhaps give a refractory and love-sick damsel a lesson on obedience.'

" ' Children should obey their parents,' replied the pilgrim, solemnly.

" ' They should. Paulo, convey the holy man to the Lady Blanche. Pietro has the key; and don't fail, good father, to instil into her mind the danger to her soul in thus resisting my authority.'

" ' With the assistance of the Virgin, I will do what you require,' replied the pilgrim, and with tottering pace he followed the servant Paulo to the battlements.

" They arrived at the dungeon door, and Paulo sought the man-at-arms who had the key; he then returned, and admitted the palmer to the keep.

" The grating of the rusty hinges seemed to have aroused the Lady Blanche from a fevered sleep; half awake she rose from the dismal corner that she had made her couch, and with wild and earnest supplication she exclaimed,

" ' Mercy, mercy! oh, spare me yet a little longer; oh, Valance, Valance! why dost thou not come to thy sorrowing Blanche?'

" ' Peace, peace, my sister,' said the palmer, ' I came to give thee counsel.'

" ' Ah, holy man, Heaven knows how much I need it,' replied the lady, as her scattered senses became more collected.

" ' You have suffered much, my sister,' returned the friar, ' your pallid face bespeaks your sufferings.'

" ' I have, indeed, good father, and willingly would repose my thoughts within your bosom.'

" ' You would wish to confess, sister?'

" ' I would, holy father.'

" ' Do you not know, young man,' said the friar, turning to Paulo, ' that a confession is sacred and not intended for other ears than those of Heaven, through the medium of its servant? Retire!'

" At this rebuke Paulo left the dungeon, locking it after him, and then sauntered on the rampart till he judged the confession should have ceased.

" No sooner was the pilgrim alone with the Lady Blanche, than he addressed her thus, but not in a tremulous voice :—

" ' Lady, I am here to serve you; sad indeed am I to see you here.'

" ' That voice,' cried Blanche, ' surely I know it; it is—it must be ——'

" ' Your own Valance,' interrupted the assumed pilgrim, and raising up the beard that half concealed his face, he implanted a fervent kiss upon her red and fevered lip.

" ' Good Heaven, Valance! what could have tempted you to run this danger?'

" ' Love, dear Blanche ! the love of you.'

" ' Do you know the risk you have run ?'

" ' I do, my life ; a hundred marks are offered for my head.'

" ' Why then this rashness on my account ? Sooner would I die a thousand deaths alone in this gloomy keep, than the baron should find you here.'

" Gentle and generous Blanche !' exclaimed her lover, ' I live but in your presence.'

" ' Fly while your disguise is a secret !' continued Blanche, ' and leave me to my doom.'

" ' Never will I leave this castle again without you, Blanche !' replied Valance.

" ' Then you will leave it a corpse, for my uncle's revenge is deadly.'

" ' I know it, sweetest.'

" ' Then why increase my anguish by such rashness ? Valance, ere long, my uncle might have relented.'

" ' Could I endure to live without an effort to save thee, loved one, from the cruelty of so merciless a tyrant ? Am not I your own betrothed ?'

" ' You are, dear Valance ; but how can your presence aid me ?'

" ' Much.'

" ' If discovered, death must be your portion, and I, your Blanche, be left to wail your loss. The idea is indeed too terrible to dwell on.'

" As Blanche said this, she covered her face with both her hands, and De Valance perceived the warm tears gush through her taper fingers with the agony of her feelings.

" ' For Heaven's sake, dear Blanche, do not thus distress yourself—it quite unmans me !'

" ' Excuse me, love, but the idea was more than I could bear.'

" ' But let us not waste our time idly, Blanche. See,' continued he, taking off his palmer's frock, ' I have a disguise beneath.'

" ' Ah, that may be of service.'

" ' Put this in the corner of your dungeon, out of sight,' continued De Valance, taking off his under disguise, which was a monk's frock and cowl. ' And when the first faint streak of morning streams through yonder grating, ready equipped, prepare to meet me.'

" ' I will—I will. Heaven preserve us !' sighed the sorrowing Blanche.

" ' Now, father, art ready ?' called Paulo from outside the door.

" ' In another minute, friend,' replied Valance, as with the greatest haste he resumed his palmer's frock and beard. Scarcely, however, had he adjusted them, before the voice of Paulo was again heard, and the key grated in the rusty lock.

" ' A long confession, father,' said Paulo, as he entered. ' You holy fathers have a merry time of it with the ladies.'

" ' Speak not thus irreverently of God's servants,' replied the palmer, with trembling accents, which the sudden entrance of Paulo had made real.

" ' A little faster, father,' said Paulo, ' for I must find a bed for thee before I get my supper.'

" ' Adieu, sister—be comforted,' said the palmer, as he tottered from the keep. ' To-morrow I will visit thee.'

" ' Farewell,' sighed Blanche, and the heavy door once more was closed upon her ; but not without hope.

" ' I shall visit the lady at sunrise,' said the palmer to Paulo as he locked the door.

" ' You keep early hours, then ?'

" ' I do, my son—sooner than you like ?'

" ' Rather,' replied Paulo ; ' for at times the baron keeps late hours, and care little to be disturbed thus early.'

"'And how shall I gain access to the lady if you sleep till mid-day?'

"'Nay—nay, good father; now you overshoot the mark,' said Paulo.

"'I must rise with the lark; it is the baron's orders,' said the palmer. 'I have far to go, and the Lady Blanche requires my holy counsel. You had better let me have the key.'

"'Eh, what?' said Paulo.

"'Let me have the key to-night, that I may not disturb your morning slumbers.'

"'And how shall I regain it?'

"'I will give it to the warder that keeps the morning watch,' replied the palmer.

"'Well—well,' said Paulo, 'it can be so; but you friars are mighty favourites with the women. Don't you visit the Lady Blanche yourself to-night.'

"'Boy,' replied the pilgrim, gruffly, 'do not thus insult my grey hairs by such ribaldry.'

"'No offence, I hope, good father; I did but jest,' returned the merry Paulo.

" He then put the key into the palmer's hand, and having conducted him to a bed in a small room adjacent to the ramparts, left him, but soon after returned with food and ale.

"'Thanks—thanks, my son; the lord provides for his children,' said the palmer.

"'And don't forget to leave the key,' said Paulo. He then departed.

" When De Valance was alone he ate the food, for he had come far that day, and had not tasted anything. He then commended his soul to Heaven, and praying for a successful termination to his enterprise, he fell asleep.

*   *   *   *   *

" While De Valance slept, the Baron Gondolphe was keeping it up merrily in the hall. The wine flowed briskly round, and healths were drunk till all looked blue.

"'Ha! ha!' laughed the Count Bretagne—'a capital idea that, to beard you in your very hall.'

"'See,' said the baron, pointing to the wall, 'the mark where the boar spear struck.'

"'A thousand mercies it did not strike you,' replied Bretagne.

"'And now pledge me in a toast,' said the baron, filling high his cup, and passing the flagon to the count, 'Here's confusion to the knave Valance!'

"'Confusion to the knave Valance!' returned Bretagne and the others present, while the sounds of their noisy mirth and revelry reached even the ears of the drowsy palmer on the rampart, and awoke him from a horrid dream.

"'And here's to the Lady Blanche!' said Bretagne; 'again fill high your goblets.'

"'To the Lady Blanche!' cried all; and drained their wine-cups to the dregs.

"'She shall be yours to-morrow,' rejoined the drunken baron; 'I swear it by my sword!'

"'I'm hardly yet prepared,' replied Bretagne; 'and the duties of a bridegroom require attention to the toilette.'

"'For once, then, we will dispense with custom; to-morrow, count, she shall be yours.'

"'You forget, my lord, she is in the keep; it is not well calculated to improve the beauty of a bride.'

" ' It is not,' returned the baron, with a hiccup; ' but there she shall remain till I see her fairly married.'

" ' Ahem !' coughed Bretagne.

" ' And, by the morning's light, the monk that called to-day shall make you man and wife.'

" ' He made his visit seasonably, then,' returned Bretagne; ' ha! ha!'

" ' Capital, isn't it ?' rejoined the baron.

" ' Ha! ha !' laughed both; while several of the parasites at the lower end of the table echoed their loud and boisterous ' Ha! ha !'

* * * * * * *

" The tumult in the hall for some hours kept De Valance awake; at length all was hushed in silence, with the exception of the heavy tread of the armed sentinel upon the rampart,

" Who walked his weary round."

" As the night advanced, the watch approached to change, and the iron-shod heels of the warriors clanked along the battlements with a martial sound.

" ' Who goes there ?' demanded the sentinel.

" ' The rounds,' was the answer.

" ' What rounds ?—and the pass?

" ' Castle rounds, and Gondolphe for ever !' was the short reply.

A fresh man now took the other's place, who, after having promenaded till he conceived all had retired to rest, leaned against an angle of the building, and endeavoured to follow the example of the others.

" There were two, however, who could not sleep, and those were Blanche and De Valance. The former, filled with hope and fear, from time to time raised her humid eyes to the grating in the dungeon ceiling, to watch for

No. 25

the first breaking of the morn, and as oft she supplicated protection from the Virgin.

" On the other hand, De Valance anxiously regarded the glowing firmament, and, when the first star began to recede from his sight, he left his pallet, and for some moments listened attentively to the snoring of the sentry on his post.

" Before leaving the chamber, De Valance unwound a long silken ladder from around his body, and, taking it in his hand, he crept softly to an embrasure in the battlement, and, throwing one end over the wall, made the other fast with a spear that was lying near the spot.

" He then, with stealthy steps, approached the keep, and, taking the key from beneath his frock, he applied it to the lock of the donjon door, which shot back with startling noise.

" ' Who goes there ?' demanded the sleepy soldier from his post.

" De Valance made no reply, and, for the time, the challenge was not repeated.

" ' Quick, quick, my love !' said the knight, as he entered ; ' we have no time to lose.'

" In an instant Blanche was at his side, and softly replied, ' I am here, and ready.'

" ' Tread lightly, for the love of Heaven !' ejaculated the lover, in a tremulous whisper, ' or we are lost.'

" Blanche complied, and, as they hastily passed along the works, the shuffling of her foot betrayed her to the sentinel, and he again exclaimed, ' Who goes there ?'

" ' A friend,' said Valance, in breathless agitation, as he hurried on.

" ' The pass,' cried the sentinel.

" ' Gondolphe for ever !'

" ' Countersign,' demanded the man of war.

" De Valance was completely baffled—he had not heard it. He muttered something indistinctly, and, pressing Blanche forward, hurried to the spot where he had made fast his silken ladder.

" With haste he ascended the embrasure, and proceeded a few steps down the ladder, almost dragging the fearful girl after him. He preceded her, and with caution guided her trembling feet to each cord of the ladder in their descent.

At the same time they distinctly heard the approach of the sentinel above, who paced the parapet with hasty steps, and called to the men at the other posts, who answered plainly, ' No one had passed them.'

" Another difficulty now awaited the fugitives. De Valance was fearful that the length of ladder was not enough to reach the ground. He had guessed the height as near as possible, but, as the ladder oscillated with their weight, he was fearful, and trembled at the idea that his companion might be injured by a fall of many feet.

" As, however, he approached the bottom, to his joy he heard it sweep upon the grass and nettles at the base, and the next instant he and the lovely Blanche were safe on terra firma.

" ' Haste thee, my own dear love,' said the knight ; ' the horses are in yonder clump of trees : the morn advances, and we may be discovered.'

" The ground now seemed to impede their progress as they hastened towards the trees, and their legs seemed to refuse their office. Not an instant could be lost, for they now heard the trampling and neighing of steeds in the castle yard, eager for the pursuit.

" They now had reached the trees : panting as if for life, De Valance raised the Lady Blanche into her saddle, and, leaping into his own with a single bound, in another moment, with the swiftness of an eagle, they gallopped forward, and the traces of the castle were soon lost in the morning twilight.

" ' God be praised !' said De Valance, as for an instant he checked his steed ; ' we now for a time are out of danger.'

" He was mistaken, for the next moment the tramp of horses was borne upon the wind. ' Forward ! forward !' was the word. They applied both whip and spur, and soon left the sounds of their heavy pursuers far behind.

" They had now reached the shore, where a boat had been engaged, and a servant ready to take their jaded steeds. In an instant they leaped from their saddles, and entered the boat. The wind was fair, and, as the mariners braced up the flapping sail, they were soon carried to a distance upon the dancing wave ; and, upon looking towards the shore, saw the baron had just reached it, and with Bretagne stood shaking their swords in defiance at the fugitives.

*   *   *   *   *   *   *

" After a short voyage, they reached their destination. A priest was soon found, who united them in the bonds of wedlock, and they lived for several years in perfect bliss and harmony.

" The intelligence of the death of the Baron Gondolphe reached them some years after, and, as Blanche was the next of kin, she took possession of the estates, which of course became her husband's right by marriage ; but long since the remains of the once stately castle have crumbled with the dust."

" Bravo, Anstey," cried Evans. " It's a good tale."

" Hark !" said Wingrove.

As he spoke the blast of a bugle came faintly to their ears.

" It is the abbot's messenger—admit him instantly."

<div align="center">~~~~~~~~~~~~~~~~~~~~~~~~~~~~~~~~~~</div>

CHAPTER XLVII.

" Again from moat, and tree, and tower,
The sound of bugle came,
A sound it was, full well they knew,
For oft they'd heard the same."

THE BUGLE HORN.—NEMONI'S LUCID INTERVAL.—THE ABBOT'S MESSENGER.

ONE of the guards hurried to the postern gate in order to give instant admission to the messenger ; but when the drawbridge was lowered no one came across it. All was as still as the grave, and not the least sound or sight of any human being could be discovered on the opposite side of the moat.

" You heard the horn, warder ?" said the guard, with a perplexed air.

" I did," said the warder ; " and hark, there it sounds again. It seems further off than before."

The low sound of a horn quietly broke the stillness of the night as he spoke, and the soldier strained his eyes across the moat, in order to detect any lurking form that might be at the other side of it ; but all was in vain, nothing could he see but the night sky and the distant trees of the ancient forest.

" This is very strange," he remarked. " I don't like to go across without orders to do so. I'll report the matter to Master Wingrove, before I do anything in it."

He then hurried back to the guard, and informed Wingrove that the abbot's messenger, if it were indeed him, would not cross the drawbridge.

" Not cross the drawbridge ?" exclaimed Wingrove. " I cannot understand his reluctance. What says he ?"

" Nay, he has said nothing, for I can't even see him."

Again the horn sounded, and Wingrove, after a moment's thought, went himself to the postern, and called in a loud voice,

" Cross the drawbridge whoever you are. The gate of Brandon Castle is open to all friends."

There was no reply to this whatever, and after pausing for some moments, Wingrove again said,

" Cross the drawbridge, be you friend or foe, and let us at all events see you."

Another tone from the bugle now sounded still further from the moat, and Wingrove drawing his sword, turned to the warder, saying,

" Keep good watch and ward, but leave the drawbridge down till I return. I am resolved myself to endeavour to penetrate this mystery."

" Are you not fearful," said the warder, " this may be something dangerous to approach ?"

" My trade is one of danger," replied Wingrove, " you forget that I am a soldier."

He then with a rapid step crossed the drawbridge, and in a few moments was on the other side of the moat. Then he paused and glanced around him carefully, but he could see no one, and conjecturing that whoever had blown the horn, if he were mortal, had retreated to the forest, he, Wingrove, walked hastily in that direction, determined fearlessly to call upon the Wizard of the Red Cavern, and not only ascertain if possible how he himself had succeeded in entering the castle, but if he had seen any persons lurking in the forest.

" I have been told," thought Wingrove, " that at particular times and seasons, he who is called the Wizard of the Red Cavern, but who to my mind is but some poor creature driven mad by grief or oppression, is quite collected, and will converse rationally with any one ; so, indeed, he has done occasionally with Sir Rupert, before his departure."

With this feeling Wingrove approached the forest, and fearlessly plunged among the trees that skirted its edge next to the castle. Then he paused a moment, and said in a loud voice,

" Is there any one here who desires communion with the inhabitants of Brandon Castle ?"

A deep groan was the only reply that was made him, and in the darkness that reigned around, he found it impossible to decide with certainty in which direction it came from. His resolve, however, to discover if possible who it was who had blown the horn by the castle gate, was rather increased than diminished, by the seeming difficulty of so doing, and again he spoke in a loud voice, saying,

" Speak, be you friend or foe ; I, Hugh Wingrove, a faithful soldier of Sir Rupert Brandon's, call upon you to make yourself known."

" Who talks of Sir Rupert Brandon ?" said a low hollow voice, which appeared to Wingrove to come from a clump of trees close to his right hand. Without a moment's delay, Wingrove dashed on in the direction, and passing through the trees, he came to an open space, which was sufficiently light to enable him to see kneeling in the middle of it, a wild uncouth-looking figure, in which he had no difficulty in recognising the Wizard of the Red Cavern.

" Nemoni !" said Wingrove. " Nemoni !"

The poor creature looked up, but did not betray the least perception that the name was his.

The straggling clouds at this moment partially cleared away from before the sun's disc, and Wingrove could see the face of the wizard. It was ghastly pale, but there was none of the wild ferocity about it, which was its usual characteristic. His voice too, sounded very different as he said, in the weak accents of one sick at heart,—

" Oh ! God, where am I—where am I ?"

" Nemoni you are here, in the forest by Brandon," said Wingrove. " Are you ill ?"

Nemoni clasped his head with his hands a moment, and then turning to Wingrove, he said,—

" I am not mad now. This is the second lucid interval I have had since by the conduct of Morgatani ——"

He had no sooner pronounced the name of Morgatani than, like a spell, it seemed to act upon his weakened faculties, and with a loud scream he became in a moment the raving creature Wingrove had always seen him.

" Help ! help !" he said. " A knife to stab the Black Monk. Tear down the wall. They will bury her alive. Help !—oh ! help !"

He dropped again upon his knees, and as he did so, Wingrove saw something glittering at his waist, and upon eyeing it more narrowly, he saw, to his great surprise, that it was the very silver bugle which Sir Rupert Brandon had taken with him when he bade farewell to his ancient home and his gallant followers to speed to the Holy Land.

" How, in the name of Heaven, could he have come by Sir Rupert's bugle ?" said Wingrove. " Nemoni—Nemoni, I charge you, by all you hold sacred, to tell me how you came by this silver bugle ?"

Nemoni threw his arms frantically upward, as he shrieked rather than said,—

" Might is right—might is right now, but the innocent shall surely triumph. The father shall look through tears of joy upon his children, and the children shall lisp blessings on a father's love. The monk—the monk. Ha ! ha ! ha !—I have him now. Revenge—revenge ! Long has it been pent up like a raging fire, but the time has come—the time has come."

He bounded forward as he spoke, and before Wingrove could be aware of his intention, he tore to the earth a person dressed in ecclesiastical garments, who seemed but as an infant in the hands of the wild maniac.

" Down—down !—to hell—to hell !" he screamed. " I will have my revenge !"

" Help ! help !" cried a smothered voice, and Wingrove just arrived in time to save a harmless monk, who had been sent by the abbot with the antidote to the poison under the effects of which Sir Kenneth Hay was suffering, from strangulation.

" The Black Monk—the Black Monk !" shrieked Nemoni, as he struggled with Wingrove, and would not leave his hold of the terrified man. " I have him now. Heaven has granted me my prayer. The sword has not been sharpened in vain. Revenge ! revenge ! Monster, you shall now die, and the pangs you now endure shall be as nothing to those that will drive your soul to howling madness beyond the grave."

" Help—mercy—help," cried the monk.

" Nemoni," shouted Wingrove, in a voice that rang again on the night air. " You mistake. This is not Morgatani. On my soul this is not the Black Monk. Nemoni ! hear me."

" Mercy—mercy," said the half stifled monk, for it acquired all Wingrove's strength merely to keep Nemoni from killing him outright. Disengage his hands altogether from the monk's throat, he could not. What would have been the result of the struggle Heaven only knows, if Bernard and Anstey, who had been somewhat alarmed at the long absence of Hugh Wingrove, had not at that very moment, guided by the cries, arrived on the spot of the encounter.

"What's the matter?" cried Bernard.

"Help me to rescue the holy man," shouted Wingrove, "unclasp Nemoni's hands from his throat, while I hold him."

Wingrove then held Nemoni round the waist, while, with some difficulty, Anstey and Bernard succeeded in freeing the half dead monk from the terrible clutch he had taken of him.

"My revenge—my revenge," screamed the wizard, "who will baulk me of my revenge that I have wearied Heaven for so long."

"You are wrong," cried Wingrove. "Nemoni, have you sufficient intellect left to hear and understand? Surely you know Morgatani from another, or else why not attack me or anybody."

A cloud which had come over the face of the moon now cleared off, and a stream of light fell upon the face of the ecclesiastic, as, pale and trembling, he leant upon the arm of Bernard for support. The wizard's eye fell upon him, and, on the instant, with a deep groan, he left off struggling with Wingrove, and his arms dropped powerless to his sides, as with a voice of deep pathos, he said,

"I—I—am wrong. God help me, if left to my own wild passions I should have shed innocent blood. It is not Morgatani. It is not my enemy."

"Thank God he sees his mistake now," said Wingrove; "had I not been by the special mercy of Providence here you would have lost your life, holy father."

"I should, my son," gasped the monk, who could still scarcely stand.

"Was his vengeance directed against the monk," named Morgatani, we all have heard of?"

"It was, your garb made him mistake you for him. You come, I presume, from the good abbot, to see the sick Sir Kenneth Hay?"

"I do, and am charged with some medicaments of blessed power."

Nemoni, while this brief dialogue was proceeding, stood still as a statue. Then suddenly, with a loud and awful shriek he darted from the spot, and was lost to sight in a moment amid the heavy foliage of the forest.

CHAPTER XLVIII.

"Strange phantasies had filled the brain,
Strange madness filled the heart,—
The monk had triumphed o'er his mind,
And stolen the better part."

THE WIZARD'S REVENGE.—THE RESCUE.—SIR RUPERT'S BUGLE HORN.

WHILE the fearful shriek of Nemoni was yet ringing in their ears, neither Wingrove nor those who were with him moved or spoke. But when the fearful sound had died away, the monk said in a low voice,—

"I thank Heaven for this great mercy, for although with my vows I have renounced the world and all those glittering vanities that make man cling to life, yet would I fain linger still in this fair world, until by prayer I have endeavoured more to fit myself for the world which is to come."

"You had a narrow escape, holy sir," remarked Bernard. "All I can say is, that the very thoughts of it now make me quite ——"

"Thirsty of course," put in Anstey.

"What business is that of yours?" cried Bernard, in great indignation. "Who told you what I was going to say? Besides you are wrong now, for I wasn't going to say thirsty at all. Come now, booby; don't you be so ready another time, or else I shall put you in one of my boats, you understand, and then give a stamp. Where would you be then, clever Master Anstey, eh?"

"Peace, peace," said Wingrove. "Let us hasten into the castle; we have yet to administer this restorative to Sir Kenneth Hay, and assist in his removal from Brandon, where my mind much misgives me he is very far from being safe."

"He who is on guard in the chamber of Sir Kenneth," said Anstey, "is a stout and brave soldier, and I'll warrant no harm can happen while he is on duty."

"Of that I am well assured," added Wingrove, "but come on, let us lose no time."

Wingrove led the way, followed by the monk, who had now sufficiently recovered from the alarming attack that had been made upon him by Nemori, to walk without assistance, although he still trembled and looked very pale.

The rear was brought up by Anstey and Bernard, and in a few moments the little party was within the portal of the castle.

"We will proceed to the chamber of the knight at once," said Wingrove. "Pray lean on my arm, holy sir, for you seem yet but faint and weak."

"It's all very well leaning on people's arms when you are faint and weak," remarked Bernard, "but in my humble opinion, mind you, there's nothing in the whole world equal to a drop of ——"

"Ale," said Anstey.

"Now, the devil take you," cried Bernard; "I was going to say ale, what business have you to take a man's words out of his mouth."

"I am better now," said the monk, "and must decline the expedient you propose, my friend. Ale is but a false friend, and holds a man up awhile, but to slip from under him and make him fall the heavier."

"Humph," said Bernard.

The monk then took the proffered arm of Wingrove, and followed by Bernard and Anstey they proceeded towards the chamber of Sir Kenneth Hay, in which we are aware had been enacted such a scene of horror in the atrocious murder by Morgatani of the guard.

Had Wingrove and his companions been five minutes earlier, he would, as the reader will recollect, have surprised the Black Monk in the act of carrying the sick Sir Kenneth Hay across the corridor towards the southern gallery. This meeting, however, was avoided by a moment only, and Wingrove was the first to enter the chamber of Sir Kenneth.

As he did so, he trod upon something which felt soft under his foot, and, calling to Bernard, he said,—

"Come forward here with your light. God of Heaven, there is something wrong, for no guard is here."

In a moment the room was illuminated by a torch that Bernard lighted from a small lamp he carried, and then the awful truth of what had occurred was visible to them all. Lying just within the doorway, in a pool of blood, was the lifeless guard; his head was literally smashed by the blow of the mace which Morgatani had given it. Soldier as Wingrove was, and used to sights of terror on many a well-fought field of battle, a thrill of horror shot through his frame as he looked at the stiff stark form of him who but a few short hours since had been a comrade around the blazing chimney of the guard-room.

"Good God!" said Wingrove; "what a sight is this!"

Bernard and Anstey looked on in silent horror, and the monk, raising his hands, said,—

"May Heaven receive his soul, and have mercy on his murderer!"

Twice Wingrove passed his hand across his brow, for he felt quite stunned for the moment at this most unexpected event, and then he said,—

"In the name of Heaven what can have become of Sir Kenneth Hay? He was by far too sick to move. Comrades, hear me! This can have been the work of none other than Morgatani. The Black Monk's hand is visible in this affair—none but he could have committed such a crime as this. In Brandon Castle he must be; and, as faithful followers of Sir Rupert, as comrades in arms of him lying here dead at our feet, as men, as soldiers, we are bound to resent this most atrocious deed."

"Vengeance is Heaven's!" said the monk; "but still justice is human, and whoso sheddeth man's blood, by man shall his blood be shed."

"There shall be a retribution for this deed!" cried Wingrove. "Summon hither all the guard: we will storm the old Grey Turret, and satisfy ourselves whether it is man or devil that inhabits it."

At this moment each started, for a loud crash came upon their ears which sounded as if some portion of the castle had suddenly fallen into ruins.

Bernard and Anstey rushed out into the corridor, followed closely by Wingrove and the monk. Bernard held the torch high in the air, and then it became evident to them all that there was some unusual current of cold air rushing through the southern gallery, for the wind came from that direction, tossing the flame of the torch about, and momentarily threatening its extinction.

In a minute more they were in the southern gallery, and then Wingrove saw at once the window which had been smashed by the monk, with the long breast-plate, which Eldred had carried about with him so long.

"Hold, my son," said the ecclesiastic, as he placed his hand upon Wingrove's arm, "a thought has struck me. May it not be that your sick friend to whom I have brought an antidote, which well I know is only applicable to a poison which, during its operation makes strange havoc with the brain,—may it, therefore, not have been that in some paroxysm of his disease, he has himself slain the guard, and now has rushed into the presence of the Eternal by jumping through yon window into the castle moat."

"Holy father," said Wingrove, "I cannot take upon myself to gainsay your words, but even if such as you have supposed, be, indeed, the fact, the original crime of administering to him the poison which has worked such mischief remains still with the perpetrators of it, and those I am convinced are Morgatani, the Black Monk, and Agatha Weare."

"If it be that she is guilty in such ways," said the monk. "Heaven have mercy upon her."

"Amen," said Wingrove. "A more wicked woman never breathed in this world. Call the guard, Bernard, at once. We will storm the Grey Turret, despite of Mistress Agatha and all her prohibitions."

In about five minutes Bernard returned with a well-armed guard; and, when they appeared, Wingrove immediately said,—

"Follow me, soldiers; I wish to show you a sight which, if it stir not your blood to shrink from nothing to-night, I know not what would. Come on—come on."

He then led them to the chamber where lay the murdered guard; and, taking the torch from Bernard, he held it so as to throw a strong light on the ghastly remains.

"There," he said, "is your murdered comrade. Will you follow me to avenge his death?"

"We will," was the universal answer.

"Then come to the haunted Grey Turret, where, I am convinced, lies hidden Morgatani, the Black Monk, the deadly enemy of our lord and master, Sir Rupert, and, on my conscience, I believe the murderer of him who lies dead before us."

These words animated the men, who with one accord declared they would follow him, Wingrove, to death, if it should appear in their path.

"Let us have more torches," he said, "and it will go hard with us, but we this night rid Brandon Castle of the pest that has now so long inhabited it."

Half a dozen more torches were procured, and their united blaze of light gave a strong light that threw into broad relief the stalwart figures of the men-at-arms, and lighted up the gloomy corridors and gallery of the castle with a broad glare of light, such as had not visited them for many years.

The southern gallery was hastily passed through, and a few moments more sufficed to bring the party into the court-yard, which, from its confined dimensions, was nearly filled by the men-at-arms, and from which arose the two turrets, one of which had so memorable a notoriety in the Castle of Brandon.

The monk now stepped up to Wingrove, and said,—

"My son, I have left the antidote to the poison which our holy father Abbot believed had been administered to Sir Kenneth Hay in his chamber, so that in case I should be wrong in my supposition that he lies drowned in the moat, you can give it to him, should he appear."

"Thanks, holy sir," said Wingrove ; "I will spare one score men-at-arms to see you safely to your convent walls."

"Nay, I will remain here, and see the issue of your present enterprise. Should you have to contend with beings of another world, I pray you summon me, for in the name of God, and my sacred profession, I have no fear."

No. 26

"We are much beholden to you," replied Wingrove, " and will gladly have our expedition favoured by your presence."

"How now ?" cried Agatha from a casement of the gallery which she had thrown open. "What new brawl is afoot to summon from their beds those who would sleep in Brandon Castle ?"

Wingrove looked up to her, and, waving his arm for the men to be silent, he said, in a firm voice,—

"Agatha Weare, Sir Rupert Brandon, my noble master, left me in command of this castle along with you. Now I am quite willing to leave you as your share all the feminine occupations and domestic affairs within the walls ; but in all that regards the military proceedings—as the defence of the castle from internal as well as external foes, I am resolved to be master."

"You, master ?" cried Agatha.

"Yes. Men-at-arms, which will you obey, Mistress Agatha Weare, or myself ?"

"Hurrah, for Hugh Wingrove," cried the soldiers.

"Now, madam, I hope you will perceive the propriety of retiring to your chamber."

Agatha's rage seemed almost to threaten her with suffocation for some minutes, and it was evidently for that space of time quite out of her power to speak. By the time she had recovered herself sufficiently that she could have spoken, she apparently saw the uselessness of so doing, for she suddenly disappeared from the window as quickly as she had come to it. Probably she had accomplished her principal object, which was to delay time a little, so as to enable Morgatani to cope with his unexpected visiters.

"Now, comrades," cried Wingrove, "let us on. This is no secret attack, but an open assault. We will, please Heaven, enter the mysterious turret and satisfy ourselves one way or the other concerning it."

CHAPTER XLIX.

Who can contend with shapes of air,
'Gainst whom no swords avail ?
Better to be in thickest fight
With warriors cased in mail.—SCOTT.

THE SHOWER OF FIRE FROM THE TURRET.—THE DEATH VAPOUR.—A NIGHT OF TERRORS.

HUGE masses of heavy black clouds were careering across the sky, obscuring the silver radiance of the moon and rendering objects more indistinct and uncertain by the occasional bright glimpses of light that penetrated the intertices of the clouds, which only seemed to make the sudden succeeding darkness look more intense.

The old Grey Turret stood against the sky, tall and black, like some dismal apparition, while a curious effect was produced in the situation which Wingrove stood in, by two opposite loop-holes coming exactly together and admitting a glimpse of moonlight now and then through both of them.

To say that the men-at-arms did not regard the expedition they were bound upon with some degree of terror would be to give them credit for a knowledge which did not belong to the age in which they lived—an age in which superstition was rife, and in which the supernatural was as readily believed as it is now by almost all persons repudiated.

They were well armed and they were brave, but the thought crossed their minds of what avail were their arms, and their courage against things not of this world, beings of thin air against whom no sword could have power, but who themselves might possess means of offence of which mortals were not aware.

Nor was Wingrove himself entirely free from some such feelings ; but then he was one of those stern characters with whom right sanctifies all things, and although he would have been ready to admit with any one that Morgatani might be leagued with the powers of darkness, yet he would have added, that he trusted in the higher power of Heaven to aid him in the justice of his cause.

"On—on!" he cried, and stepping to the door which opened upon the staircase leading to the turret, he with one vigorous push sent it wide open.

"Give me a torch," he said. "I will lead in this affair, since it is at my request you are all engaged in it. Follow me, comrades ; follow me. The old Grey Turret shall no longer be a terror to Brandon."

The moment he stepped through the doorway his torch was extinguished by a rush of air, which was so powerful as to make him almost stagger back a pace or two.

"Another torch! another torch!" he said, and when one was on the instant handed to him, he delayed not, but stepped within the doorway again. Again came the same rush of cold air, and the second torch was as completely extinguished as the first.

The men-at-arms looked at each other, and a feeling of trepidation began to creep over them, which it gave Wingrove no little concern to see, and impressed him with a fear that he should not be effectually backed in his attack upon the turret.

Without a torch he now entered the lower part of the turret, and all seemed as calm and still as any atmosphere could possibly be. There did not seem the least breath of air, far less sufficient to extinguish a torch.

Wingrove was somewhat surprised, but he was resolved that no trifling cause should have the effect of deterring him from pursuing his enterprise, and he cried to the men-at-arms :—

"Advance. There is no enemy here, mortal or immortal. Advance, men. We shall have an easy conquest of the Grey Turret."

Emboldened by Wingrove's tone and manner, the men-at-arms advanced, but, to the surprise of all, the moment a torch was brought within the doorway, a rushing wind descended the staircase, which extinguished every one in a moment, leaving the party who had crossed the threshold in complete darkness.

"Bless us all!" ejaculated Bernard, "where can this wind come from ?"

"Why, the old one from below is surely up stairs with a legion of devils!" remarked Anstey.

Wingrove suddenly pointed to the sky, saying,—

"See, comrades, the clouds are rapidly disappearing and in a few moments we shall have a clear moonlight to help us on. Its beams will penetrate the loop-holes on the staircase, and we need not fear their being blown out—on—on."

As he spoke he rushed up the narrow staircase. For a moment he was alone. The men-at-arms evidently wavered. Then, Bernard going after him with a quicker step than he had ever been known to assume, exclaimed,—

"Let the devil and the monk, or both of them, blow away as long as they like, it sha'n't be said that Bernard left Hugh Wingrove to encounter the danger alone."

The same feeling animated every one on the moment, and with a loud cry of—

"Wingrove for ever!" they dashed forward, and the narrow staircase of the turret was full of armed men.

"Halt," cried Wingrove. "Some one hand me an axe; we will try the strength of the turret door against a piece of good steel."

Scarcely had the words passed his lips, when a groan so terrible, so loud, so wild and awful, came from the turret, that even he recoiled a step in horror. Then with a wailing shriek, a voice cried,—

"Beware! Beware! Beware!"

"Heed not such sounds as these," said Wingrove, "they are common tricks of men who make such matters their study. The axe, comrades, the axe."

A powerful battle-axe was handed from one to the other until it reached Wingrove, who was longing for some glimpse of moonlight to enable him to see where he was to strike; but the clouds, although, as he had said, they were certainly dispersing, yet did so but slowly, and as yet had not left the fair face of the moon sufficiently clear to allow it, except at intervals, to beam forth its silver light.

Wingrove, however, raised the axe and was upon the point of bringing it down upon the door, when a low hissing sound, evidently coming from within the turret, caused him to pause an instant to listen. Two or three bright sparks of fire flew from about the middle of the door, and then in an instant, before he could strike a blow, Wingrove was staggered and half blinded by such a volley of hot sparks, which kept pouring out from some small spot in the door, that he was compelled to retreat several steps backward, which brought him upon Bernard's toes, who immediately pushed the man behind him again. The sparks of fire each moment increased in quantity, and now they took a wider range and fell upon the hands and faces of the men-at-arms, making them smart with innumerable little burns, which for the moment were quite intolerable.

A general rush was made from the staircase into the court-yard, and even Wingrove found it quite impossible to resist the torrent of fire which, with a hissing sound, kept pouring from the door of the Grey Turret. When he reached the court-yard, he felt faint, weary, and in pain. His face and hands were covered with little black spots, where the fire sparks had fallen and become extinguished, and there was upon his face a look of doubt and uncertainty with respect to his next proceeding, as he glanced round him upon the alarmed and dispirited men-at-arms.

To the great joy of Bernard, Wingrove then said,—

"I am almost choking with thirst."

"Thirst?" echoed Bernard. "I declare I never was so thirsty in all my life. I'll run to the cellarer in a minute, and bring such a flagon of ale as shall astonish you—to find it half gone before you see it," he added to himself, as he hurried off on the, to him, always most welcome of all errands.

"Comrades," said Wingrove, "do not be dispirited at what has happened. We will recruit ourselves a little and then commence the attack again."

"My friends," said the monk, stepping forward; "what saw in yon place?"

"What we felt, holy father," replied Wingrove, "was of much more importance to us than what we saw. The knave has succeeded in burning us all a little with red-hot sparks; but here comes Bernard with the ale. We shall be all right again in a few minutes."

As he spoke Bernard approached with a flagon.

"Drink first," said Wingrove.

"Oh—I—no—no. After you—after you."

Wingrove glanced into the flagon, and then shaking his head, he said,—

"I think you may wait a little, Bernard, considering all things."

This remark Bernard affected not to hear, but before Wingrove could finish his draught, some one cried,—

"Look at the turret! look at the turret!"

All eyes were immediately directed to it, and through the various loop-holes streamed such intense gleams of red and yellow light that the whole of the interior seemed as if it was a furnace throwing forth fierce jets of flame.

"Who will venture in there, I should like to know?" muttered Joyce Evans. "It's all very well to have a few stand up fights for Sir Rupert, and I am as willing as any man, but when you come to getting into a fire kindled, no doubt, by the devil himself, it's quite another affair."

"Very true," echoed several, "Joyce Evans is right."

Suddenly then the glare of light within the turret changed its hue, and now it shone forth a sickly green, which, falling upon the countenances of the men-at-arms, gave them an awful ghastly appearance, making them look like so many resuscitated corpses.

"This will not do," whispered Wingrove, to the monk. "I have every reason to believe that Morgatani, the Black Monk, is concealed in that turret. Think you, holy sir, that he has art enough to produce all that we have seen to-night?"

"The order to which he belongs," said the monk, "possess many secrets of science and art; but yet it is more than probable that he has assistance direct from the great enemy of mankind."

"I would not willingly lead the men-at-arms into serious mischief, and if I thought there was much danger in this matter, I would alone undertake it."

"You would be sacrificed for no good purpose, my son. I pray you do not be so rash."

"One more attempt—one more. Men-at-arms, will you again follow me to the turret door? I ask you, not command you. Those who dislike the enterprise can remain where they are."

"Look you, Master Wingrove," said Joyce Evans, "we none of us like the enterprise, but if you are resolved to make one more attempt, we are not the men to leave you to make it alone."

"Come on then—come on."

Once again Wingrove entered the doorway leading to the turret stairs. All was still as the grave. An impenetrable darkness reigned around, and this time, although they reached half way up the staircase, not the slightest opposition was offered them by sight or sound.

"We will try a light here," said Wingrove. "Some one bring a torch."

One was lighted and brought, but not the least breath of air disturbed the steady flame. It would seem as if the monk, or the spirits who occupied the old Grey Turret, were tired of opposition, and were content to give up quiet possession.

The torch, however, which from the first had not seemed to give out so clear a flame as might have been expected, now evidently began to get dimmer and dimmer each passing moment.

In vain Bernard shook it, and held it in different directions. It was going, or at least showed a strong disposition to go out.

Then Bernard suddenly left of trying to better the light, and leaning against the wall, he said in a very unusual voice for him,

"Wingrove, I pretended to be ill once, to oblige you; but now I think I am getting ill in real earnest, for I can hardly breathe."

"Not breathe?" gasped Wingrove.

"It is—a fact."

"Why—why—I was just going to make the same remark myself. I feel nearly choked."

A confusion lower down upon the staircase now induced Wingrove to turn, he when saw that one of the men-at-arms had fainted on the stone steps.

"Anstey, are you well?" cried Wingrove.

" Far from it," said Anstey; " I—I can scarcely breathe."

" There is something in the air," gasped Bernard. " There goes the torch out, and if we stay any longer here we shall all of us die."

" To the court-yard, comrades.—Quick. To the court-yard," cried Wingrove, as loud as he could, for he felt a deadly sickness creeping over him, and was certain that he could not exist where he was many minutes longer.

Those of the men-at-arms who were highest upon the stairs evidently suffered most from the strange and sudden illness which more or less had attacked every one, and now they, as quickly as they could, for some of them were nearly in a fainting state, left the staircase, and sought relief from the cool night air of the court-yard. The relief was instantaneous, and Wingrove thought he had never breathed fresh air that was so delicious in his life, as when he stepped from the doorway, and drew a long, invigorating breath of the breeze that blew around the battlements and turrets of the castle, within whose walls such mysterious and inexplicable circumstances were occurring.

" This is beyond mortal endurance," remarked Wingrove. " If the turret is to be attacked at all by me, it must be from without, and not from that staircase which is so full of dangers and terrors. I never was so near suffocation in my life."

" Suffocation, my son ?" said the monk.

" Yes. There is even now some noxious vapour on the staircase which nearly killed us all."

" Alas, alas ! what can be done ? I will to the holy abbot, and he shall give counsel what proceeding to adopt in this emergency."

" Do so," said Wingrove. " Tell him that Brandon Castle is full of mysteries and terrors. Tell him that to all appearances it is beleaguered by a set of demons, directed by the Black Monk, Morgatani ; and likewise inform him most particularly of the disappearance of Sir Kenneth Hay, who, from my heart, I do not believe has come by the melancholy end you have surmised. Nor had he a weapon which would have enabled him in any paroxysm of madness to slaughter the guard in the manner we have seen he has come by his death."

" It may be so, my son."

" But we will have the moat searched to-morrow, holy father. Sir Kenneth Hay was in his armour, and if it be that madness has driven him to death in the castle moat, he must lie exactly under the broken window, for the weight of his armour would be more than sufficient to prevent the body from floating."

" The blessing of Heaven be with you all," said the monk, as crossing his arms upon his breast, he slowly walked towards the postern gate.

Wingrove looked round him upon the men-at-arms, and he saw upon every countenance an expression of suffering and alarm. His heart told him it would be madness to press them further upon the enterprise, and, although with a feeling of deep disappointment in his breast, he said,—

" To your quarters, soldiers ; Heaven may direct us to some better means yet of discovering the secret of the old Grey Turret. Oh! would that Sir Rupert were once more in his ancient home."

CHAPTER L.

THE APPEAL OF THE PAGE.—AGATHA'S REMORSE.—THE ANTIDOTE TO
THE POISON.

" One act of gentle charity,
A world of sin will cover ;
Some angel bright above the stars,
Will that one act discover."

FOR the remainder of that night nothing occurred to disturb the repose of Brandon Castle, although there was not one heart within that ancient pile but had its own peculiar sources of grief, anxiety, or remorse.

Agatha as usual passed the restless night consequent on

" ——— A mind diseased,
Whose rooted malady no earthly skill
Can compass."

While Wingrove felt all the deep anxiety arising from an uncertainty of the fate of Sir Kenneth Hay, and the gloomy anticipation of what other iniquities might yet be perpetrated in Brandon before the much longed for return of Sir Rupert.

The morning dawned, at length, and then most of the weary watchers in the castle sunk into dreamless slumber. There was one, however, who had not retired to rest at all, but who had wandered about the castle the live-long night, with deep melancholy, and such occasional bursts of frantic grief, as would have surprised any one to witness. That was the page of Fitzhugh. He had seen the monk, as we are aware, carry Sir Kenneth Hay's nearly insensible form to the dungeons, but how to succour the unhappy knight—how to render him any kind of assistance, was a proposition which he, the page, could not answer, for deep in the recesses of his heart there were secret feelings, which, sooner or later, will come to light in the course of this history, which prevented him from communicating openly to Wingrove what he really knew of the iniquitous proceedings of Agatha and the monk.

At morning's dawn the page was seated in one of the deep window seats in the southern gallery. His head was resting on his hands, and now and then he murmured disjointed sentences, indicative of a mind ill at ease.

" When is all this to end ?" he murmured. " When am I to be enabled to strike the blow which I have gone through so much to be enabled to strike—which I have sighed for an opportunity of doing, and yet ever deferred with a foolish irresolution whenever such opportunity has presented itself."

He was then silent for some time, and when he spoke again he said, in different accents,—

" Be still, my heart ! Close for a brief space over your own wrongs, and let me think of the sacred claim to my best exertions which Sir Kenneth Hay, in his present sad state, has. How can he be succoured ?—how can he be rescued from his present state of suffering ? I have overheard Agatha speak such words of remorse, that surely there must be some spark of human feeling still lingering at the bottom of her heart. That spark might possibly be fanned into a flame. Shall I, or shall I not, try an appeal to her better feelings."

The xperiment seemed a very desperate one, and yet what other course was open to adopt? for he, the page, although he knew in which direction the dungeon of Sir Kenneth lay, yet felt that it was more than probable he should not be able to reach it were he to make an attempt so to do. In the absence of keys how could he unlock doors, and how would his feeble strength suffice to overcome obstacles purposely constructed to resist strong and stalwart men?

"I must make the appeal," he said. "I will make it, though it cost me my life; and what is life to me?—a cheerless waste, without one sunny spot. Agatha may be moved to pity. I have heard of guilty wretches who the world would say were destitute of all feeling, awakened by a few well-timed words to do some act of justice at variance with the glaring iniquities of their whole previous existence."

The page had scarcely come to the conclusion that he would, despite the danger of so doing, make an earnest appeal to Agatha to spare the life of Sir Kenneth Hay, than, as if Heaven had so specially willed it, a door opened at the other end of the gallery and no other than Agatha herself appeared.

Her steps were uncertain and slow; her face was very pale, and every now and then seemed convulsed with some passing passion or great agony of the soul. Her eyes were fixed upon the ground, and she did not observe the page, who allowed her to pass on without interruption, contenting himself by following her footsteps, with the determination of addressing her at the first more fitting opportunity, for the gallery was too general a thoroughfare to and from different parts of the castle to make it a proper spot for urging Agatha to the purpose he, the page, had in view.

The wretched woman—for wretched indeed she was as mental disquietude and agony could make her—walked on until she came to a door which opened into a small sitting-room, whither she was accustomed to repair in the morning, and leaving the door but half shut, she threw herself into an arm-chair, and covering her face with her hands, she groaned aloud.

"Am I never—never again," she said, "to know the common luxury of quiet sleep—such sleep as the poorest, the meanest, the most abject creatures enjoy upon stony pallets and beds of straw, while I in vain court the blessing of one brief hour's repose, unvisited by visions that nearly drive me mad!"

The page thought that a more fitting opportunity could scarcely present itself for preferring his suit concerning Sir Kenneth Hay than the present, when Agatha was evidently suffering from the pangs of remorse, and might eagerly snatch at the chance of performing one good act upon which her mind might fall for comfort in its hour of bitterness.

He accordingly quietly approached the door which had been left partially open, and pushing it sufficiently wide to allow himself to enter the room, he presented himself to the alarmed Agatha, who, starting from her seat, exclaimed,—

"How now—what means this intrusion, boy?"

"Lady," said the page, "will you allow me to speak to you about a matter upon which I feel deeply, and hope that you, too, will feel?"

"To me?"

"Aye, lady, to you, on behalf of one who never did you harm—one whose death would lie heavy on your soul at that last hour when the account we have to render to Heaven can no longer be delayed."

"What—what mean you, boy?" faltered Agatha.

"I plead for Sir Kenneth Hay."

"Ah!"

"Yes, lady. Let him live. Do not—oh, do not allow him to fall a sacrifice to one who knows no pity—feels no pangs of remorse : one mingling with humanity, and yet surely not human."

Agatha shuddered as she said faintly,

"Tell me who—who you mean by so appalling a description? Tell me, boy?"

"I mean the Black Monk."

"The Black Monk?"

"Aye, lady, Morgatani,—the much dreaded Black Monk. For your own soul's sake, as well as for the sake of heavenly reason and God-like justice, I intreat you to save from him the gallant knight, Sir Kenneth Hay!"

Agatha sunk into her seat, and trembled violently, while her countenance betrayed the agitated and tumultuous feelings of her mind.

"On my knees, lady," said the page, "I pray you to be merciful, and save him."

It seemed as if Agatha spoke with great difficulty as she said,

"Tell me how you became acquainted with the fact, you presume upon, that Morgatani is in any way connected with the fate of Sir Kenneth Hay. Tell me that ; tell me that !"

"I saw him."

"Where—where ?"

"I saw him in the gallery leading to the old Grey Turret."

Agatha was silent for awhile. Then she said,

"Are you not page to the knight Fitzhugh ?"

"I am."

"Then know you not that Sir Kenneth Hay is an enemy of him and his master ?"

No. 27

"I know nor care whose enemy he may be," said the page; "but I do not like to see great wickedness done. To you I appeal as a woman—one who surely must possess tender sympathies and gentle feelings, and I implore you to save the knight from the monk."

"What, if I cannot?"

"Will you try?"

"You say you saw him," said Agatha, evading the question; "know you not that it is sometimes dangerous to overlook the secret actions of others?"

"I do know so much; but, lady, I throw myself upon your confidence and your mercy."

"You are very bold. There is not a man in this castle would venture to say so much to me as you have done this day."

"I am one," said the page, "who never will, who never can believe that there can be a human heart without some ray of generous feeling, which if properly appealed to may be awakened into action. You will save the knight!"

"Know you where he is?"

"Not wholly."

"Hear me, sir page: I do not dislike or feel angry at your audacity; but know that there are events now in course of progress which such hands as yours or mine.—"

She paused, and for a moment a hysterical gush of feeling impeded her utterance.

"I pray you speak on," said the page.

Agatha lifted up her hands and cried,

"I am powerless!"

"Heaven then help the innocent," said the page, rising. "But when you think of Heaven, lady, tell yourself that you would have done a noble act had you possessed the means."

Agatha shook her head as she strove to repeat to herself the awful words of the monk—there is no Heaven; and then with a burst of frantic weeping she hung her head upon her hands, and alarmed the page by the wild vehemence of her grief.

When he saw that she was recovering from her gust of passionate remorse, he said,

"Lady, bethink you well of the future: that earthly future, I mean, which in its more important aspects it is in the power of all persons to shape as they please."

"Too late—too late," said Agatha.

"Nay, not so," said the page, with a deep drawn sigh. "If I thought so I would wish to sleep the sleep of death in your castle moat."

"You, boy?"

"Aye, even I. I am young, and yet old enough to have known sorrow."

"Can it be that you, on the very threshold of existence, as you are, can have felt the heart's deep anguish—that goes by such a name."

"I have, and at some more fitting time and place I would gladly recount to you a passage in my young life, which has robbed me of my peace; and were it not that I look to those days to come, which for your own sake I implore you to make days of happiness and repentance to yourself, I tell you I would wish that I were dead."

"Dead," repeated Agatha, "I would that I were dead. Boy, I cannot grant your prayer. Sir Kenneth Hay is a doomed man."

"Doomed by Morgatani, the Black Monk?"

"Hush! Let not that name pass your lips. There is much danger to you in the very sound."

"Ah, Mistress Agatha Weare," urged the page, "shake off the fearful trammels of that bad man, and exert your native strength of mind in virtue's cause, rather than in aiding him in carrying out dark designs, in which he will make you an abject tool, to be thrown aside when he no longer requires your aid."

"Peace! peace!"

"Nay, lady, know you not the creed of these Jesuits? It is that all persons who have been once useful in any of their intrigues, become dangerous and troublesome if not still useful."

Agatha shuddered, for she had several times heard a similar sentiment from the lips of Morgatani, and the page continued,—

"Be warned, then, while yet 'tis time; and, when Sir Rupert Brandon ——"

No sooner had the page mentioned the name of the knight, when every dark and malignant passion of Agatha's breast seemed to rise with increased strength, and, with a half scream, she cried—

"Sir Rupert Brandon! I thank you, boy, for mentioning that name, for it has recalled me to myself. Heavens! have I been so weak as to weep when my revenge is still ——"

She paused, for her fears told her she was confiding by far too much to the page, especially after his avowed feelings in favour of Sir Rupert Brandon and Sir Kenneth Hay.

"You pause," said the page. "What can Sir Rupert Brandon have done to thee?"

"Sir Page," said Agatha, "you are in danger."

"In danger?"

"Yes—much danger. Think you such as I am can risk the pert tongue of a page, who might repeat throughout the whole of Brandon that he found Agatha Weare in a moment of weakness, when she wept, and made use of strange expressions which might be tortured to mean far other things than they really were intended to convey to the ear."

"Surely," said the page, "you will not take my life because I have pleaded to you for the innocent?"

"You know not on what a precipice you stand. One word of mine, boy, would ensure your destruction. You have attributed a sentiment to the Jesuits which may recoil upon your own head."

"You mean that Morgatani will kill me."

"He would."

"And you will denounce me to him? Agatha Weare, I do think that some latent feeling of horror at such a deed will spring up in your heart. You cannot—will not do it."

"There are circumstances," faltered Agatha, "which, in their awful consequences, submerge all feeling. Yet on one condition I will spare you."

"Name it, lady."

"It is that you solemnly promise me not to communicate to any one in this castle the secret you are possessed of as regards the fate of Sir Kenneth Hay, or one word of our present conversation. And I—I promise in return that if I can I will save his life."

"On your soul you promise that?"

"I—do."

"Then I promise what you require of me; and let this be the commencement of an understanding which may in its results work good for you Agatha Weare, and, perchance, save you from the steep descent down which Morgatani would fain plunge you."

The page abruptly left the room as he spoke, and Agatha remained for some moments in silence, while her working countenance betrayed the feelings that agitated her mind.

"The steep descent!" she muttered. "Save me—oh, God, no!—'tis too late. I have already made the frightful plunge which has separated me from even a hope. My hands are red with blood — a hell is raging at my heart! Help! help! Morgatani—Mor ——"

The violence of her feelings overcame her, and she fell heavily on the floor in a swoon.

~~~~~~~~~~~~~~~~~~~~~~~~~

CHAPTER LI.

" This will restore the tide of life,
Make the warm blood to flow,
And lend the cheek of pale disease
A healthful, radiant glow."

THE ANTIDOTE TO THE POISON.—THE PAGE'S ATTEMPT TO FIND THE DUNGEON.—THE MEETING WITH THE MONK.

ALTHOUGH he had failed in extorting from Agatha's fears or remorse a positive and unconditional promise to save the life of Sir Kenneth Hay, still the page considered that he had effected something on behalf of the knight in her promise not to be an active agent in his destruction. Moreever, he thought that Agatha would not interfere now with any perambulations he might make about the ancient castle, or any attempt which he should feel himself enabled to pursue for supplying Sir Kenneth with comforts in his dungeon.

Anything, in fact, short of aiding the knight in escaping, the page considered he might do undisturbed by Agatha, because she was equally in his power as he was in her's, and she must well know that he could disclose to Wingrove and the men-at-arms the secret of the imprisonment of the knight, although he could not lead them to his dungeon. There was likewise a view of the knight's position which, to the page's mind, appeared an important one, and that was, were he to make known that somewhere beneath the castle Sir Kenneth was kept in durance, the alarm which would be of necesssity given to the monk by the instant efforts that would of necessity have to be made for his liberation would, in all probability, ensure his immediate destruction, and the disposal of his body somewhere where it could never be found again.

Then in his attempts to better the condition, or save by aiding in the escape of Sir Kenneth, the page was forced to proceed with the greatest caution, and after his interview with Agatha he took long counsel with himself as to what course he should first pursue in his self-imposed enterprize of humanity.

His promise to Agatha prevented him from engaging any one to assist him in his task, and even were he to forget his word, and communicate to Wingrove freely what he knew, how could he control him again from giving publicity to the whole affair, and so involving a general confusion, in which Sir Kenneth Hay might suffer death at the hands of the monk, while Fitzhugh would scarcely escape the vengeance of the men-at-arms.

He then determined to make an attempt to visit Sir Kenneth Hay in his dungeon, in which, should he succeed, there could be no difficulty in the knight escaping by the same route.

A sudden thought then struck him that could he secure by any means the antidote to the poison, he would, in the event of reaching Sir Kenneth Hay, be enabled to do him the most essential service, provided he was still suffering from the effects of the baneful drug which had been administered to him.

With great anxiety the page then hastened to the chamber from whence the knight had been removed by the monk, but when he reached the doorway he shuddered as he asked himself if the murdered man-at-arms had been removed or not from the scene of his awful death with the mace.

For a few moments only he paused, and then said,

" Why should I be deterred from a purpose surely holy in the sight of Heaven by the terror of the sad remains of one who may be laying in this room. I will shake off these idle fears which cling to me from hearsay, and place my trust in a higher power than belongs to superstition and its wayward fancies."

He cautiously opened the door; but a dim light from a lattice window illumined the room, which appeared empty; but when the page cast his eyes towards the bed a slight tremor shook his frame, for there he could see by the folds which it assumed that a sheet only concealed the ghastly body of the man-at-arms from his view.

For some moments the page could not take his eyes from the sad spectacle, which was as clearly defined beneath the sheet as if it had been completely removed, for the drapery had sunk to the still proportions of the dead soldier, and, if possible, presented a more awful appearance, because more was left to the imagination than had the corpse been uncovered.

" Alas," said the page, " what fearful crimes are committed within these ancient walls, and what a sad position is mine that I am following one who knows not virtue himself, and yet who I dare not—cannot sacrifice, by at once proclaiming the fearful knowledge I have of the deeds of blood committed by Morgatani. Heaven help me! Heaven help me!"

With a trembling step the page hastened across the room, and eagerly looked over the miscellaneous contents of an open drawer which was in the room. Among the various articles was a small phial with a scrap of paper tied to its neck on which was written the word " Benedicite," in large letters.

" This must be the antidote," said the page; " it is the fashion of the monks thus to label their medicinal preparations. Thank Heaven, however, I have found it."

In the drawer, likewise, was a small poniard in a sheath, which the page also took, for he thought that in the event of his reaching Sir Kenneth Hay, it might be most useful.

He had no desire to prolong his stay in an apartment which was occupied by so terrible an object as the mangled corpse of the man-at-arms, and with an instinctive dread which he could not master, of turning his back upon the body, he moved backwards from the room; and with a feeling of intense relief, closed the door upon the gloomy spectacle within.

Scarcely had he done this, when he heard a heavy footfall coming along the gallery, and shrinking back until he saw who it was, he observed Bernard plodding along rather out of breath, from ascending the winding staircase leading from the rooms below.

" It's all very well," muttered the thirsty soldier, " but I'm sure there is no occasion to lock up a dead man. Here's Master Wingrove bothering me to lock the door on our poor dead comrade, and bring him the key. How uncommonly thirsty I am, to be sure. Upon my word, I'm generally, that is, I may say in a manner of speaking, always a little thirsty, and sometimes a great deal."

The page breathed a mental thanksgiving that he had already secured the antidote to the poison, and cautiously slipping on one side, he allowed the bulky soldier to pass him, and then, his light footstep quite unheard by Bernard, whose senses were not very acute, he hastened along the corridor towards the southern gallery.

So far, and indeed a little farther had he been able to trace the monk, but a dread of being observed, had prevented him from discovering the secret entrance to the vaults under the moat, through which Morgatani had conducted the unhappy Sir Kenneth Hay.

That there must be some other and more accessible entrance to the dungeons, the page could not but believe, for he knew it was usual in these ancient edifices to have secret modes of egress and ingress to their prisons, as well as those which depended alone for security upon the multitude and strength of the locks and bars that closed their doors.

After some consideration then, and carefully concealing the antidote about him, he resolved to repair to the guard room, and endeavour to extract in the course of casual conversation with the men-at-arms, if there was any easily accessible passage to the dungeons.

He with a noiseless step now glided towards the ancient guard-room, where he found assembled all the men-at-arms who were off duty, and the conversation was full of remarks and conjectures concerning the frightful and appalling mysteries that beset the Grey Turret.

The entrance of the page by no means disturbed the conversation, for Wingrove's good opinion of the lad had impressed the men-at-arms in his favour, as much as his own quiet and unobtrusive manners had done.

" Brandon gets worse and worse," remarked Anstey. " In days long gone by, there was generally something or another happening within its walls, of a mysterious or a violent character."

" That's true enough, Anstey," said Wingrove, " but I never could have supposed that Sir Rupert's absence would have produced all the troubles we now labour under. I would to Heaven he would return, for I cannot help thinking that with his presence, would cease all the horrors that infest us."

" It may," said Anstey, " and I hope it will. I, and all my family have lived in the service of the Lords of Brandon for these last hundred years and more, and yet I never heard ——"

" What!" cried Bernard, who had just returned, " do you mean to say you have lived here a hundred years? Upon my word, it makes a man thirsty to hear you."

" No, stupid, I don't mean that," said Anstey, " but I mean that from father to son, we, the Ansteys, have been for so long in the service of the Lords of Brandon. How long is it since you've sharpened up your wits, Bernard, to be so critical?"

" Since I couldn't get any ale," said Bernard.

" Well, well," responded Anstey, " you may laugh as you like, but I tell you that I know more about Brandon Castle, and the many strange scenes that have occurred in it, than any of you. My father, who had eleven children ——"

" One fool makes many," said Bernard.

A loud laugh from the men-at-arms, testified their relish for the wit of the not often witty soldier, and Anstey in great dudgeon, cried,

" Give him some ale to stop his mouth. I was going to tell you that my father had from the lips of his grandfather, who was, of course, my great grandfather, an accident that I'll strive to tell you in his own words —that is my great grandfather's own words—you know ; and this is how he begun :—

" The bell of the Castle of Brandon had just tolled the hour of midnight when the blast of a horn was heard from without. The warder opened his drowsy eyes, and at the same time demanded from his station on the out-works the business of the stranger at that hour.

" ' I bear despatches from the Lord of Wintoun to his noble relative the owner of this castle.'

" ' The baron's pass-word ?' demanded the warder.

" ' Right, not might,' returned the visiter.

" ' 'Tis well,' said the warder, and immediately lowered the drawbridge, when the sound of his horse's iron hoofs reverberated among the ramparts from the wooden floor.

" ' Stay here,' said the warder, ' till a message is sent to his lordship, who has retired to his chamber, to inform him of your arrival. Did he expect a messenger ?'

" ' He did.'

" The warder then retired to the interior, and informed the Baron of Brandon that a messenger had arrived from the Lord of Wintoun. The latter ordered him to be admitted, and soon after the trooper was admitted to the court-yard, his despatches given up, and himself ordered to the guard-room to await the baron's reply to his kinsman.

" The soldier's first care was to see his horse attended to ; he then, with a tired air, his spurs and sword clanking as he walked, sought the guard-room, where a cheerful fire cast its ruddy light on a score of thickly musta-chioed visages that were seated round it.

" The room was nearly square ; rough oaken benches and tables were placed for the convenience of the men, while around the walls were pikes, shields, arquebuses, and other weapons of feudal warfare.

" ' Make way there for a stranger,' said a halberdier to the group round the fire, as the new comer entered.

" At this the guard, who were mostly young men, ceased their jests, and turned their eyes upon the stranger at the same time making room for him to approach the fire. In a few minutes after, a domestic of the castle brought him refreshment from the buttery.

" For some time the weather-beaten trooper sat in silence, content to discuss the viands that were placed before him ; and when sufficiently re-vived by a long and hearty draught of ale, he seemed to be inclined to be more communicable.

" ' You seem tired, friend,' ventured one of the baron's men, uncertain whether he should get an answer.

" ' I am,' replied the trooper ; ' but the cheerful fire and a drop of the baron's ale has considerably refreshed me.'

" ' You, no doubt, have travelled far, and the night is bleak and cold.'

" ' It is ; and I have come from Wintoun. The sight of this old guard-room puts me in mind of former times.'

" ' You, then, have been here before ?' asked another of the halberdiers, as he attempted to rub a spot of rust from the point of his pike with the sleeve of his jerkin.

" ' Aye, have I, before you were born,' returned the trooper. ' You are not above twenty-six, and I have numbered fifty summers. I was in the service of the old lord for many years.'

" ' And why did you leave the service of the family ?'

" ' You shall hear. You no doubt have all heard of the Lady Isabel, the sister of the present owner of this castle ?'

" ' Never,' replied several ; ' we never heard the baron had a sister.'

" ' Well—well ; but he had as beautiful a lady as the sun ever shone on, and the old lord, her father, made sure he should marry her to some duke or earl, and thereby strengthen his interest at court ; but the Lady Isabel had a mighty fancy for her cousin Wintoun, my present master, whom her father deemed too poor to become her husband.'

" ' And did he have her ?'

" ' All in good time, lads,' said the trooper, taking another draught from the cup of beer. ' It happened while I was on duty in the hall young Wintoun arrived at the castle, and demanded admittance to the baron. He was ushered in.

" ' Good morrow, uncle,' said he. ' I have come once more to ask your leave to marry my cousin 'Bel, for you know she will never like another.'

" ' I have already twice before told you, Wintoun, that it is to the interest of the family to marry into other families, and thereby strengthen our connexions. The day may arrive when we shall want help.'

" ' You then refuse me, uncle ?'

" ' I do, and moreover forbid any intercourse between you, as I well know it only tends to increase a passion I shall never sanction."

" ' Dear father !' said the Lady Isabel, who was present, ' it is impossible for me ever to love another than my cousin Wintoun, and no other will I have—I vow it before the God of Heaven !'

" ' Hence to your chamber, malapert !' cried her father, in a towering rage ; ' and you, Dennis,' said he, turning to me, ' take your station in the corridor, and see that none gains admittance to her.'

" ' Father ! dear father !' sobbed the lovely Isabel, ' hear me but one moment.'

" ' Begone, I say !' cried the baron, ' and the sooner you leave my presence, Wintoun, the better.'

" ' With tears streaming from her eyes, Isabel left the hall, while Wintoun regarded her with a sorrowful aspect ; he then, with a deep muttering, followed her example, while I took my station in the corridor and allowed none to have access to the chamber but her maid.

" ' On the second evening of my watch, which I took alternately with another, I fancied I heard voices in the room of Lady Isabel. I listened attentively and heard a conversation kept up in a low, deep, murmuring tone, and distinctly heard the Lady Isabel say, ' Hush ! hush ! or the guard will hear you.'

" ' Feeling confident no one had entered by the legal passage, I knocked at the chamber-door. A scuffling took place within and immediately after the lady unbolted the door and in a drowsy tone, as if just awakened from her rest, demanded what I wanted ?

" ' My lady,' said I, ' I have been placed here purposely by the baron to prevent any one coming to your chamber—I hear voices within and I must therefore ascertain the cause.'

" ' The Lady Isabel offered no opposition to her father's commands ; I therefore entered, and, after a diligent search, found no one concealed.

" In the morning I reported this circumstance to my lord. ' Dennis,' said he, ' are you not mistaken ; do you not think the Lady Isabel was at prayer ?'

" ' My lord,' I replied, ' she would hardly tell our lady, the Virgin, to hold her tongue, lest the guard outside the door should hear her !'

" ' True, true ! there is some mystery here which must be unravelled.'

" ' It would appear so, my lord.'

" ' Are you sure you have not slept on your post, and allowed young Wintoun to pass you unseen ?'

" ' I am positive, my lord.'

" ' Then this shall be unravelled ; to-night I will watch with you in the corridor.'

" ' Good, my lord, you then can ascertain the truth of what I state.'

" ' At ... ppointed time, his lordship arrived in the corridor, while I walked up and down as usual ; the domestics had long retired to rest, and not a sound was heard, except the ticking of the old clock in the western tower.

" ' If I catch that Wintoun in her chamber,' whispered her father to me, ' I will tan his features on the drawbridge for a month, let the consequences be what they may.'

" ' Hour after hour passed away, but not the slightest sound arrested our attention, and at the first beaming of the morning, the baron went to his chamber muttering something about the trouble I had given him.

" ' On the third evening I took my watch as usual in the corridor, and not thinking it was likely I should be disturbed, I folded my arms and leaned against the door of Isabel's chamber to take a dozen winks of sleep, making sure that if any one attempted either to go in or out, they could not do so without disturbing me.

" ' At length the clock tolled one, and my attention was awakenedby the whispering in the room ; I listened attentively and could plainly distinguish the voices of Isabel and another person.   There seemed to be much moving about within, and lastly a heavy sound, like the shutting of a door, then all was quiet.   I knocked several times, but received no answer, and finally sought the chamber of the baron to communicate what I had heard to him.

" ' Nonsense,' replied he. ' I wager you have been sleeping and dreamed.'

" ' Indeed, my lord, the voices are the same as on the first evening.'

" ' Well then, we shall know all about it in the morning.'

" ' Seeing the baron half doubted the truth of my assertion, I left him to his repose and returned to my station on the corridor, but not the slightest sound was heard till the sound of the trumpet at sunrise.

" ' It's very strange,' said the listeners, in chorus.

No. 28

" ' And did you discover the cause in the morning ?' asked the halberdier.

" ' In the morning,' continued the trooper, ' the Lady Isabel's maid came to awaken her; she entered the room, but immediately after returned declaring she was not there.'

" ' At the same time I heard the footstep of the baron approaching along the farther end of the corridor and stood ready to receive him.

" ' Now Dennis,' said he, ' we will see our daughter and ascertain the meaning of this nocturnal conversation.'

" ' Oh, my lord! my lord!' cried Agatha, ' my Lady Isabel is nowhere to be found.'

" ' Eh, what ?'

" ' She is gone, my lord, and not the slightest trace of her escape, is left.'

" ' Gone!' cried the baron. ' Hell and furies! who durst assert as much ?'

" ' It is true, my lord,' timidly returned Agatha, falling on her knees.

" ' The baron then entered the chamber followed by myself; but no traces of the Lady Isabel could be seen; her bed had not been lain upon; we examined the floor and wainscot, but not the slightest aperture could be found that could lead us to suppose she had escaped by any secret passage.

" The next supposition was that she must have cast herself from the window into the moat beneath, and this suspicion was favoured by the circumstance of a light scarf being seen floating on the surface.

" The water was then drained from the castle moat; but not a vestige of the body could be seen, and this, in conjunction with the conversation in the chamber, favoured the idea she had been spirited away; but sure it is from that hour to the present nothing has been heard of the Lady Isabel, and her chamber has ever since been closed.'

" At this part of the narrative the superstitious soldiers regarded each other with looks of deep amazement, while Dennis continued,

" The loss of the Lady Isabel, worked deeply on the mind of the baron, and for some time he was confined to his bed; but upon his recovery he did not fail to censure me for neglect of duty, and believed I was cognizant of her escape, of which I was as innocent as the child unborn; fearing some catastrophe, at the first opportunity I made my escape, and upon application was received into the service of my present master De Wintoun, where I have remained ever since.'

" ' But do you not imagine he was acquainted with the flight of the lady ?'

" ' I have often thought he must have been,' replied the trooper, ' and that he must have found access to her chamber by some secret passage with which he alone, and the Lady Isabel were acquainted, and which there was discovered by chance, and had some outlet in the forest beyond the moat; and I further imagine he must have concealed her somewhere till all inquiries were at an end, and then have carried her to some distant land, where perhaps he married her—he is now often abroad. The old baron, however, made application to him and vowed a deep revenge; but as he could not prove he had been concerned in her disappearance, he was forced to submit; inquiries were instituted all over the country, but the Lady Isabel was never found.'

" ' Your despatches are ready,' said a domestic, who now entered the guard room. ' The baron now waits to deliver them into your own hands.'

" The trooper then rose and followed to the baron's chamber, where he received an answer to his message; he then returned to the stable, where he found his charger equally refreshed, and leading him forth, leaped into the saddle; he then looked to the priming of his pistols, and after a few moments the horse's hoofs were again heard in the court-yard, then across the draw-bridge, and finally lost in the distance.

" The men-at-arms in the guard-room were now summoned to their midnight watch upon the ramparts where they had leisure to ponder upon the fate of the Lady Isabel as they walked their dreary round."

Anstey ceased, and the page, in a low soft tone, said,

"I dare say your father was well acquainted with the various vaults and dungeons of Brandon?"

"I should say he was," replied Anstey. "He knew every turn and passage about Brandon, as well as if he had built it himself."

CHAPTER LII.

"Gloom was around, above, and below,
The flickering light burnt dim;
And the shadows of grim warriors old,
Seemed all to frown on him."

THE MARBLE MONUMENT.—THE SECRET ENTRANCE TO THE VAULTS.—THE INTREPIDITY OF THE PAGE.—A WILD ADVENTURE.

"But—but, the vaults under the moat?" said the page.

"Well, the vaults under the moat. My father knew all about them as well—aye, better than the owners of Brandon themselves."

"Indeed! I always heard they were blocked up, and quite inaccessible," said the page.

"So they are, but that's no reason why there should not at one time have been an entrance."

"Not now, surely."

"Of course not, and that entrance, as I've often heard my father say, was at the back of the monument of old Sir Hugh Brandon, the fourth baron of the name, who was six feet five without his shoes, and lies buried in a copper coffin in the east aisle."

"I have seen the monument you speak of," said the page. "It is of black marble."

"It is, and blacker than ever it gets year by year."

The page now gradually backed, as it were, out of the conversation, which in a few minutes more ran upon the wonders of the Grey Turret, when he took an opportunity of quietly and noiselessly leaving the guard-room.

"To the chapel!—to the chapel!" he muttered, as he walked rapidly in the direction of that part of the castle. On his route he did not encounter any one, and after traversing a great portion of the vast pile of building, he came to a stone staircase, at the foot of which he knew there was a door opening into the chapel, for in his lonely wanderings throughout the castle he had discovered many modes of egress and ingress to different parts of it, which were scarcely known even to those who had dwelt within its ancient walls for years. Since Sir Rupert's departure the chapel had not been used, and the dust lay thickly upon some parts of it, softening the sound of the page's footsteps as he entered the precincts of the holy building.

But a dim religious light found its way through the stained glass windows, and, in fact, it ever required a very strong sunlight to illumine with anything like brilliancy that gloomy monastic-looking spot.

The page paused for a few moments in order thoroughly to assure himself that he was alone, and then casting his eyes towards the gloomy black monument of Sir Hugh Brandon, he walked towards it with a solemn step, for the place was one in which to feel the deep solemnity of silence, and to awe even the boldest to gravity and circumspection.

"If I can," he said, "but find an entrance to the dungeons from here, surely, by perseverance and much patient search, I shall discover the one in which the persecuted Sir Kenneth Hay is placed, and rescue him from the the fate, which, if no friendly hand find him, will surely be his. For some purposes of his own only, would Morgatani yet let him live, if, indeed, he be not already numbered with the dead."

With these and such like reflections, the page went towards the monument, and walking round it several times, he carefully examined it to note if he could see any opening, or the signs of one about it. This monument consisted of a huge square pedestal of black marble, on the top of which was a sculptured urn, which was represented as broken, and some flowers falling from it, the whole being, for the period at which it was executed, a very meritorious work of art.

With all his care, however, he could see no opening. The monument stood some paces from the wall, and the page thought that possibly the entrance might be there ; but it seemed to be composed of such massive blocks of granite as to defy the possibility of any doorway ever having existed there.

"After all," he thought, with a sigh, "the information I supposed myself to have gained from the man-at-arms may be but mere hearsay, and have no sort of foundation in fact."

This reflection was to the adventurous page a sad one, as it threw him completely again upon his own conjectures as to where to search for an entrance to the dungeons.

A sudden thought, however, struck him, and he took from his vest a small poniard which he had found in Sir Kenneth's bed-chamber. With the hilt of it he sounded the wall, but there was no answering hollow echo ; all seemed hard, dense, and firm as solid rock. He then did the same by the black monument of Sir Hugh, and, to his surprise, he found that one side of it returned a far different sound than the others. He struck that side again and again, and became convinced that it was for the most part composed of a plate of metal, which returned a ringing echo to his blows, while the other three sides only presented to him the dull sound of stone.

There was hope from this discovery that something of more importance might result, and the page knelt down by that side of the monument which was so evidently composed of a metal plate, carefully to examine it.

In vain he ran his fingers over its surface. He could find no sort of mark or indication which could lead to a means of opening it. Whatever the metal was, it had evidently been painted so as exactly to resemble the colour of the marble, for as the page touched it, the paint, which had rotted, came off in thin flakes, falling then to the ground, and breaking up almost instantaneously into dust.

After a time he became convinced that there was no means of moving the plate to be found upon its surface, and then he endeavoured with the aid of the thin point of his dagger to loosen it from where it was let into the stonework, which seemed under-cut to receive it. In this, however, he was not successful, and he felt certain that if he exerted more force he should but break off the blade of the poniard.

Disappointed, and somewhat wearied, he rose and leaned upon the tomb, remaining for some minutes in deep and painful thought.

"Am I, or am I not," he said, "to be the instrument employed by Heaven to rescue the innocent Sir Kenneth Hay from his most unjust imprisonment ?"

His words found a faint echo in the gloomy building, and came back to him in a strange and unearthly whisper.

The page guessed the cause of the sounds, but he could not forbear a slight start as they came faintly to his ears in that lonely place.

As he thus started he found that he had caught the sleeve of his habit in something, and upon releasing it he found that it had been detained by a slight projection in one of the sculptured wreaths of flowers which hung from the broken urn.

The projection seemed to be loose, and curiosity, rather than any hope that he should discover anything by it, induced him to lay his finger on it with a slight pressure.

In an instant a strange rushing noise, terminating in a loud clank, met his ears, and he stood for some moments immoveable from astonishment, mingled with fear.

All then remained as still as the grave. The last echoes of the strange sound died away, and then the page found voice to say :—

"Protect me, Heaven! What strange and awful sound was that?"

For a few moments longer then he listened, but there was no repetition of it, and he slowly and cautiously walked round the tomb.

What was his surprise when he reached the back of it to find the metallic plate completely gone, and a yawning chasm in its place.

The truth, however, flashed across his mind in a moment. The little projection in the flower was a spring, which, when pressed upon, released the plate of metal, which, sliding in grooves, had then by its own weight rapidly descended, causing the strange rushing sound, and then the clank when it reached the bottom of the groove in which it slid.

"Success! success!" cried the page.

He immediately knelt down, and endeavoured to pierce the gloom of the chasm with his eyes, but the rush of noxious vapour that came from it almost deprived him for a moment of his senses, and he was compelled to remove some distance, in order to breathe a purer air.

It was clear that that metal doorway had not been opened for many years.

After waiting for the space of about five minutes, the page ventured once more to approach the chasm, when he found much of the noxious air had escaped, although there was still a noisome fetid smell arising from that gloomy place which had so long been closed from the eyes of mortal man.

In vain he strove to pierce the obscurity of the place. He could see nothing but a black, dreary-looking void, that might be deep or shallow for all he could pronounce upon it then.

"I must procure a torch," he muttered, "and then, with Heaven's help, I will brave whatever dangers may present themselves in this adventure."

With this resolve he was about to turn from the opening, when he bethought him of the necessity of finding how to fasten it up again in case any one should accidentally pass through the chapel and discover it. To do this, however, appeared to be no easy task, for the metallic plate went so low down that he could not get a sufficient hold of it to move it, and he began to think there must be some mechanical contrivance for raising it to its former position, which, by an attentive examination, he should discover and be able to use.

All his efforts were in vain. Without a light he could find no such means ; and, resolving for the brief period of his absence to risk a discovery of the secret spring, he hurried from the chapel towards the domestic offices of the castle in order to procure a link or lamp which should enable him to make a more careful scrutiny.

As good fortune would have it, there was no one in the servants' hall, and, taking from a shelf a small hand-lamp, he lighted it by the embers that gleamed upon the hearth, and then, as fleetly as his footsteps would carry him, hastened back to the chapel.

He met no one either going or coming, or he might have been questioned as to what he wanted with a light at that hour of the day, and to his great relief he found himself once more by the marble monument without having experienced any interruption.

With great eagerness he then examined the metallic slab, and he in a moment perceived that at each side were two very small pieces like buttons, which, when he pressed on them, evidently moved springs that, had the plate and the groove in which it moved, not been exceedingly rusty, would have enabled him to move the former up into its place again.

As it was he could not move it, but he bethought of the oil which was in the lamp, and pouring some of it down the groove, he waited a few moments for it thoroughly to descend, and then he found he could slide the plate up with ease and perfect silence. When it reached the top it fitted in with a clicking sound, and remained fast as it had originally been.

The slightest pressure, however, upon the small projection in the wreath of flowers again released it, and this time the page, by placing his hand upon the plate, guided its descent softly, so that there was but very little noise made by it.

For a moment then he paused. It was to address a brief prayer to Heaven for success in the enterprise he was about to go on. Then he examined the lamp and felt satisfied there was enough oil in it, to last some hours.

"Yes," he said, "I will dare all to save him. With Heaven's aid he may yet be restored to life and liberty."

He held the lamp at arm's length into the gloomy opening, and then he saw there was a ladder of some kind which, through being blackened by age, he had not before observed. Upon placing his hand upon it he found it was composed of metal, and appeared to be of considerable strength. How deep it went he could not see, but he thought by its firmness that it could not be very long.

In a moment he placed his foot upon the first round, and commenced slowly a descent into the unknown regions he was determined to explore. A sickening sensation for a few moments came across his heart, and the blood rushed tumultuously through his veins as he paused after descending a few steps. The air was very bad, and that combined with the excitement he was in, produced the alarming symptoms which, however, in a few brief moments subsided.

He felt the necessity of closing the entrance to the vaults after him, as well as of thoroughly ascertaining the mode of opening it from the inner side. This he found very easy, for there was no concealment there attempted of the apparatus by which it was slid up and down in its grove.

In another moment the adventurous page was shut out from the light of day, and cautiously desending the narrow iron ladder into the vaults of Brandon Castle.

He counted thirty steps ere he touched a flooring, which by the feel he found was damp earth. Then he raised as high as he could his lamp, and looked around him with intense interest and curiosity.

The place in which he was seemed of considerable extent, and the dim rays of the lamp, which burnt but very badly in that damp noxious atmosphere, showed him but a small distance around.

He could have no choice to go either to the right or to the left, and guided by chance he turned to his right hand, when about twelve paces brought him to a wall of flints and hammered earth. Here and there likewise were wooden supporters, which were very rotten and in some cases quite crumbled beneath the touch. The page then adopted one precaution, which in the intricacies of these gloomy under-ground places might be of the greatest importance—he with his poinard cut from one of the firmest of the wooden supporters several slips, which he further made into small pegs, one of which he resolved to place in the ground or the wall at every ten or twelve paces he went, in order that they might guide him safely back again to the foot of the ladder.

This accomplished, he with a slow but steady step, walked onwards with his lamp in one hand and the wooden pegs in the other.

The wall seemed to extend a long way, for the page had used six of his pegs before he came to an ancient mouldy-looking door-way which was arched, and from one side of which there hung by one of its hinges, only what had once been a massive door of great strength, but which appeared to have been burst open, for it was splintered and broken.

Scarcely had the page tried to examine the broken door, when a strange rushing sound came from the other side of it, and he drew back instantaneously with a beating heart, and placed his hand to shield his lamp.

CHAPTER LIII.

"No carpet knight in sooth was he,
A warrior tall and bold;
His feats the theme of minstrelsey
By many a bard were told."

THE ASSASSINS IN THE FOREST.—THE SPY IN THE TREE.—THE PILGRIM'S ARRIVAL.

THE noon-day sun was gleaming in beauty on the ancient trees of the forest in the immediate vicinity of Brandon, and secretly peeping downwards through the clustering leaves speckling the walks and ancient glades with rare beauty. The buzy hum of many insect things was making vocal the still air, an l the free denizens of the old forest—the birds, were singing from bough to bough, and winging their airy way throughout that wild spot of natural beauty where the foot of man so seldom trod, and where they were so rarely alarmed except by some larger creature of their own species.

Lying, however, concealed in a brake which was shielded from the direct rays of the sun, lay three stout men of ferocious aspect. They were well armed with short double-edged swords, and one of them had lying by him one of the immense long-handled axes of the period which required the two hands of a strong man to wield, but when so wielded it was indeed a frightful and dangerous weapon.

These three men were conversing in low tones, and ever and anon shifting their positions as if tired of waiting in such anxiety and quiet.

"How much longer, by the mass," said one, "are we to wait here ? It's dull work and dry work. Nothing but the water from yonder spring to drink is enough to drive a man well nigh mad."

"We must make up for it when we have done our job," said another. "We have our instructions, and I suppose we must carry them out."

"A plague on our instructions," said the other.

"Ah, that's all very well for you to say so now," replied the other speaker, "but we are promised a capital reward, a reward that will enable us to live on the best at any tavern in London, and get drunk every day for three months' at least if we do but succeed in our enterprise."

"Well," growled he who had the axe by him, "as far as that goes I don't see how we are to fail. Here are we three men waiting to stop one only."

"Aye, but that one may be rather a difficult customer, as perhaps our employer knows."

"So he may, but I consider myself a difficult customer, and with my axe we are two difficult customers. I tell you, comrades, I would have taken the job myself, not that I object to your good company on the occasion."

"Well, the sooner it's done the better; we are to stop and massacre a tall man, who will in [all probability pass through the forest dressed in the garb of a pilgrim from Palestine, but likewise in all probability well armed and a tough customer in a fight."

"Ah, that's it, and all I have to say is, I hope he'll come soon. Do not let us forget the evidence we are to produce, that we have done what we engaged. We are to carry his right hand severed at the wrist to London, and lodge it with Cardinal Ambrosini, the chief of the Jesuits."

"Yes, that is a gage with a vengeance; but what do you say, comrades, to taking somebody else's hand if we don't happen to fall in with this pilgrim?"

"That I fear wouldn't answer," said the other; "for, no doubt, the hand would never have been asked for if it did not possess some mark by which it could be at once identified."

"You are right. Hang me, I didn't think of that. Where's Vin?"

"Why, he's on the tree top on the look out, still, if he has not gone to sleep as he did yesterday."

"By the mass, that must be seen to," said he of the axe, "for we might stay here long enough if the pilgrim, or whoever he may be, should pass through the forest while Vin was asleep, and we not know it."

One of the desparadoes then rose, and walked some distance from the brake, in which his companions were hid, till he came to the foot of a gigantic tree. He then said, in a voice more clear than loud,—

"Hilloa—Vin—Vin."

"Here," said a voice, from among the topmost branches of a tree.

"Keep a good look out."

"I am."

"You have seen no one?"

"Not a soul has come near the forest for some hours. I have a capital view of Brandon Castle from here, I can see the men-at-arms on the battlements."

"Can you?"

"Yes, quite plainly. I never saw such a castle in my life."

"Mind you don't let your stupid head run too much upon the castle, or you will keep but a poor look out for him whose approach you are placed where you are to give us warning of."

"Never fear, never fear," cried he who was in the tree. "I can see for miles around. No one can enter the forest without my being aware of it."

"Very good."

"I shall be able to come down and let you know in plenty of time."

The ruffian walked away, muttering to himself,—

"I wonder how the boy relishes staying in the tree so many hours, but he seems amused rather than wearied with his watch."

He then went back to his companions, and throwing himself down upon the mass of dried leaves, which they had collected and made a rude couch of, he said,—

"All's right, Vin is on the look out, and will warn us in time."

"It's just possible, comrades," said he of the axe, "that this pilgrim may be somebody of consequence, and if he be so, he will doubtless have about him money or jewels of value."

"A good thought."

"A capital thought," cried both the others.

"If it should be so, comrades, mind we share and share alike, and who knows but we may make double what we have been promised of this adventure."

"Agreed, agreed."

At this moment a footstep alarmed the assassins, and they sprung to their feet—it was the boy Vin who had been watching in the tree.

"He's coming, he's coming," he said, as well as his want of breath would let him, for he had descended the tree with great swiftness.

"Who? The pilgrim?"

"Yes, a tall man."

"Which way?"

"From the side opposite to that where the castle stands. He is making his way swiftly across the meadows towards the forest."

"Then we must be stirring," cried the man who had the axe, as he shouldered the ponderous weapon.

"What shall be our plan of attack?" said one of the others.

"Why this: do you two suddenly start out from behind a tree and stop him, then I will come behind, and with a sweep of my axe cut him down."

"Ah, that will do; he must fall if you hit him."

The ruffian laughed, as he said,—

"I will not leave his head on his shoulders, or if I do it shall be in two pieces. Now, Vin, do you get through the wood, and meet this pilgrim as quickly as you can. Tell him you know the forest well, and offer to guide him through it in which direction he pleases; then do you bring him to this spot where we will remain concealed, and the job can be executed finely."

"I will," said the boy, "but mind you I'm to have fifty marks for my own share."

"You shall, Vin—you shall; we will keep faith with you on the honour of gentlemen."

The boy started off through the mazes of the forest in the direction where he thought he should at once meet with the pilgrim he had seen from his exalted station in the tree.

The information given by the boy to the three assassins was quite correct, for advancing from the open country in a direction, which, if he became not

No. 29

lost amid the mazes of the forest, would conduct him directly to the gate of Brandon Castle, came a man in the garb of a pilgrim from the Holy Land. He was of tall and commanding stature, and his firm step as he strode forward betrayed great strength and activity. In his hand he carried a pilgrim's or falconer's staff, which was of unusual thickness and length, and far from being any support to him, would, had he not been the strong athletic man he was, soon became a very troublesome burthen to carry. Masses of auburn hair hung to his neck, and a short thick moustache of the same colour was on his lip. His eyes were particularly fine and expressive—they were of a deep blue, and had not his face been bronzed by long exposure to the sun and air, he would have had a complexion which many a court beauty might have envied.

There was altogether about his manner and bearing a fearless, reckless daring, and confidence in his own courage and strength, which looked as if it belonged far more to a soldier than a pilgrim.

Beneath the pilgrim's long frock, his feet seemed to be encased in buff leather, such as it was the custom of knights to wear under their armour, and a projection at his left side looked uncommonly like the hilt of a sword which hung there.

Such was the man who the three desparadoes in the forest had been hired to assassinate, and well might three be employed, for a glance would have told any one that it would be no child's play to stop such a man as he in forest or on plain where he choose to go on.

He paused a moment as he reached the outskirts of the wood, and glanced up at the sun as if to guide him on his way through the wilderness into which he was plunging. Then he said, in a clear manly voice,—

"By the holy rood, if I don't lose my way I should reach Brandon shortly, for here is the very wood which I have had described so well. The sun is in the south; let me see, I am to keep my face eastward. Well, that cannot be difficult, except I get into some deep places of the wood where all is darkness. Well, well, I can but push on, and sooner or later I shall surely reach Brandon. The cool shadow of these trees is welcome indeed after the heat of the meadows."

Pushing aside with his staff the low hanging branches of the trees which impeded his progress, and occasionally glancing upwards at the position of the sun, he plunged into the forest, little dreaming of the danger that awaited him within its recesses.

He had not proceeded far when he heard some one approaching and whistling a lively air. He paused, and called out loudly,—

"Hilloa, friend; whoever you are, make your appearance. You may shew me my way better than I can find it if you be a native of the soil here."

The boy Vin on the instant made his appearance, and saluting the pilgrim courteously said,—

"Was it you who spoke just now, holy sir?"

"It was, boy. Are you well acquainted with this wood?"

"I have lived on its outskirts all my life; I know every tree, every bush, every glade in it."

"Indeed?"

"It is true, holy sir."

"Then you are just the person who will be of use to me for the next half hour or so."

"I shall be very proud," said the boy.

"Aye, will you, but better pleased, I'll warrant, with a few silver groats," said the pilgrim, "which shall be yours when you bring me to Brandon Castle."

"You wish to go direct to the castle, holy sir?"

"In faith, boy, I do. So e'en take the nearest road across these brakes, and trees, and bushes, with which you say you are so well acquainted."

"I will. Shall I carry your staff for you?"

"No, I prefer carrying my staff myself."

The pilgrim as he spoke fixed his eyes scrutinizingly upon the boy's face, which he had scarcely glanced at before, and he could not help being struck with the expression of ferocious villany therein depicted.

"Boy," he said, "I may wrong you, but your countenance is no recommendation."

A slight flush of colour came to Vin's face as he answered in some confusion,

"I will guide you fairly and safely."

"Be sure you do," said the pilgrim. "I have taken a good look at you—now, do you take one at me."

The boy looked steadfastly in his face.

"Enough," said the pilgrim. "If you are any judge of countenances, my young friend, you will see that mine belongs to one who will not be trifled with. You quite understand me?"

The lad trembled as he thought to himself, "I don't half like the job—I'm afraid he'll find me out, and as sure as he does he'll lay that staff across my shoulders most amazingly."

"I will guide you fairly," he then said aloud, and the pilgrim with a brief "Do so," followed close upon his steps.

Vin was half a mind really to conduct the pilgrim to the castle, for he was dreadfully afraid he should not be able to get out of the way quick enough to escape his vengeance when he found himself betrayed; but then, what should he, Vin, be able to say to his rough companions, who, if disappointed, might revenge themselves upon him to his very great personal detriment. Altogether, the boy found himself in far from a pleasant position, as the tall stalwart pilgrim kept close upon his heels.

CHAPTER LIV.

Oh, for a tongue to curse the slave,
  Whose treason, like a deadly blight,
Comes o'er the counsels of the brave
  And blasts them in their hour of might.—MOORE.

THE FIGHT IN THE FOREST.—THE COMBAT.—THE RESCUE.

THEY proceeded onwards now for some time in silence, the boy being busy with his own thoughts, which were so rapidly changing to fears, and the pilgrim, with a shade of care upon his brow, as if his mind was travelling to other persons and other scenes of a painful character.

The boy took him by a round about path to where the three hired bravos were waiting, for, although he could not bring his mind to let him escape altogether, yet his fears and the state of indecision he was in prevented him from taking the most direct route to the shady brake where he was expected with the man he was betraying.

"Did you know Sir Rupert Brandon?" said the pilgrim, with a suddenness that made the boy start.

"Yes—yes," he replied. "I have seen him. But I was very young—very young indeed."

"He has been long away from his castle?"

"So I have heard, holy sir."

"You are quite certain you know your way?"

"Quite; the forest is familiar to me."

"Well, perhaps you are right, but I made the remark, because, it appeared to me by the occasional glimpses I can catch of the sun, that you had nearly doubled on your course."

This was, indeed, the fact, for the boy had gone a little past the brake, and then had made a slight detour to return to it. He replied, however,

"The forest is intricate, and there are pools of water here and there, hidden among the trees where you could least expect them, which enforce a devious track."

"That is a good reason enough," said the pilgrim. "Lead on, boy, I will follow you."

The lad now trembled as he came near the trees, behind which he knew his atrocious companions were hiding, and he quickened his pace to try and increase his distance from the pilgrim; but in this he was defeated, for two or three longer strides than usual brought the latter again close to him with the remark,

"You seem in a hurry, young friend, suddenly."

"Hurry? ah, sure I am in no hurry, I was only anxious to get on as quickly as possible lest you should think your way long."

"Oh, you are very kind," said the pilgrim, in a sarcastic voice, "but it looked mightily as if you were attempting to run away."

"Run away; oh, no—I—I—don't—want ——"

At this juncture the boy knew that he was some paces past the one of his comrades who was armed with the long axe, and close upon the hiding-place of the other two, so without waiting to finish his sentence he fairly took to his heels, and would have secured his own safety by flight had he not caught his toe in a long bramble and fallen flat on his face.

"So, so," cried the pilgrim, "trying to escape again."

The words were scarcely out of his mouth, when, in immediate advance of him, there started forth the two ruffians with their swords drawn, crying,

"Yield—yield—or die."

Their object was to get him, as most persons would naturally have done, to fall back a few paces, when their hidden comrade would make the treacherous assault with the axe. In this, though, they were grievously mistaken, for it appeared the pilgrim was not one to be easily daunted at danger. Instead of stepping back he made two strides forward, and brought the end of his staff with such effect upon the head of one of the assassins that it made the very staff ring again, and felled the ruffian to the earth with a dab as if he had been struck by lightning.

"Help—help!" cried the other, as he moved backwards, in momentary expectation of the one with the axe finishing the affair, nor was he disappointed as far as the inclination of that one went, for he ran from behind the tree and taking the ponderous axe in both hands, he gave it a preparatory swing round his head, and was in the act of then bringing it down with a crash upon the pilgrim's head, when he was clutched round the waist from behind with such an iron grip, and such a wild horrible unearthly scream sounded within a hair's breadth of his ear, that he became perfectly stunned and paralysed with fright.

"The devil!—the devil!" cried the assassin, who was in front of the pilgrim, and throwing down his sword, he attempted to run off, but he was in a moment brought flat upon his face by such a lusty whack across the shoulders with the pilgrim's staff, that escape or resistance was out of the question, and he could only lie writhing like an eel, and groaning on the dried leaves that plentifully strewed the ground.

"Mercy!" shrieked he of the axe.

" Murder !—I'm a dead man !" shouted the last felled ruffian.

" Oh, spare my life, holy sir," mumbled the boy, who sat on the ground rubbing his head and looking around him with a rueful countenance.

Another shriek, more terrible than the former, now nearly drove him with the axe crazy.

The pilgrim glanced in that direction, and he saw a strange, wild, uncouth figure, attired in skins, and altogether presenting a terrible aspect, holding the ruffian in his arms, and every moment or two screaming so frantically in his ear.

It was Nemoni, the wizard, who had come so very opportunely and saved the life of the palmer.

" Ha ! ha ! ha !" he laughed. " Caught—caught. You are not Morgatani, the Black Monk of Brandon, and yet you are as wicked as he. Caught —caught—ha ! ha ! ha ! Caught !"

" In Heaven's name, who are you ?" said the pilgrim, in amazement.

" My name is Nemoni. Men call me the Wizard of the Red Cavern. God help me, I am but a persecuted piece of clay. Ha ! ha ! ha ! Yet have I caught the spiller of blood—the despoiler !"

" You have done me good service, whoever you are," said the pilgrim, " for this ruffian with his axe would surely have killed me but for you."

" Oh, save me from him," said the discomfitted ruffian, dropping the axe from his trembling hands and shaking all over like an aspen leaf.

" You don't deserve my interference," said the pilgrim.

With a wild shout the wizard lifted him off his feet, and carrying him to a tree, would, but for the instant stepping forward of the pilgrim, have in all probability, dashed his brains out against it.

" Hold !" cried the pilgrim. " Leave him alone now. He shall not escape, but do not kill him, for I want to ask him a question or two."

" Blood for blood !" cried the wizard.

" Not now—not now. I pray you let go your hold of him, for my sake."

" Mercy—mercy !" cried the man, sliding to his knees, and clutching at the hem of the pilgrim's garment.

Nemoni left go of him, and crossing his arms upon his breast, he leant against the tree, as if listening with great curiosity to what was taking place.

" Now, hark ye, scoundrel," cried the pilgrim ; " if you don't answer me at once what I shall ask of you, I'll brain you on this spot, or, at all events, give you up to this mad but honest creature, who has saved my life from you."

" I will—I will," groaned the fellow. " I will tell all—I will tell all."

" Be careful you do."

" I will—I will."

" He will lie," said the wizard.

" On my soul, no ; I will tell the truth."

During this short colloquy the boy tried to creep away, but the wizard caught sight of him, and darting forward with a yell that awakened echoes far and near in the forest, he seized hold of him and threw him headlong into a hedge of brambles, into which he fell with a scream and crash that testified his terror and pain.

The pilgrim laughed as he said :—

" Think yourself well off, traitorous guide, that you are not more severely punished than you are."

" Oh, take me out ! take me out !"

" Indeed I shall not. You may get out the best way you can, and may you get well scratched in the process."

The boy kicked and floundered about till he had scarcely a particle of clothes left on him, and he was terribly scratched. Then he broke through the hedge, and fell into a pool of stagnant water that had collected from the rain in a hollow, where for a moment he was drenched over head and ears, and came out like a half-drowned rat.

"Now," said the pilgrim to the kneeling assassin, "who employed you to waylay me?"

"The cardinal, chief of the Jesuits in London."

"Ambrosini?"

"Yes, holy pilgrim."

"Humph!" said the pilgrim, "I suppose he is now a great man at court, and much in John's confidence?"

"Yes, he is."

"So he employed you?"

"He did indeed. I throw all the blame upon him. He tempted, me poor man as I am, and I'm very sorry—very sorry, indeed I am."

"Peace—peace. Do you know me?"

"No—no."

"If you did I would intrust you with an important mission to London. Are you sure you do not know me?"

The man looked hard at him, and then said, with a groan,—

"I wish I did."

"He knows me not," said the pilgrim in a low voice. "I am glad of that. How came you to know that I was the person Ambrosini wished to waylay?"

"You were described to us, and said to be in a pilgrim's habit—and——and——"

"And what?"

"He told us a mistake or two would be no great matter."

"The blood-thirsty villain!"

"Yes, he is."

"You are a fine one to echo such a sentiment. What were you to do if you had succeeded in murdering me?"

"We were to cut off your right hand and take it to Ambrosini in London."

"Ah!" cried the pilgrim, "indeed. That would have identified me by a scar the villain knew was on it. Thank Heaven I have escaped his toils. Tell me in what state you left London?"

"King John was holding royal feasts."

"Indeed?"

"Yes, he was everywhere prayed for by the clergy, and made much of by some of the nobles."

"'Tis well. We shall see! Now my friend I shall just trouble you to follow me."

"Whither go ye?" said the wizard, stepping close up to the pilgrim, and laying his hand upon his arm.

"To Brandon."

"Come to my cavern—I have there the clearest waters, from springs none but I, and the old forest trees—from among whose gnarled roots they come— know of. I have fruits too, brought by the one kind hand that still—sti" trembles as it touches mine—the same kind heart that still feels for poor, poor, Nemoni!"

"The heat is oppressive, and my contest with these ruffians has made me somewhat thirsty," said the pilgrim. "If your cavern be not far out of my way I will avail myself of your hospitality. If it be I will thank you the same, and proceed to Brandon Castle."

"Come, come," said the wizard. "'Tis close at hand, this way, come."

"I will follow you, but first let me see if these rascals be dead."

He stepped up to the two assassins he had felled with his staff, and found that the one he had struck on the head was quite dead, while the other, although he affected to be very bad, had evidently not much the matter with him, the staff having lain pretty severely across his back.

To the great surprise then of the two living assassins the pilgrim slipt off his frock, showing under it a complete suit of the most exquisite chain armour that could be imagined. A sword was by his side, and he looked noble and magnificent in the extreme. Leather russet leggings were drawn over that part of the armour, and with this one exception his costume was costly and resplendent indeed, for there were links of gold and of silver introduced among the steel rings of his mail which glistened and shone so brilliantly that the knight, for such he evidently was, looked more like the impersonation of some gorgeous dream than a living warrior of flesh and blood.

Without heeding the bewildered stare that the men regarded him with, or the undisguised admiration of the wizard, he tore up his pilgrim's garb into strong strips, which he then twisted up into a very tolerable imitation of a rope, after which turning to the men he said,—

"Safe bind, safe find, is a good maxim; so I shall take the liberty, my friends, of tying each of you to a tree, in order that I may send for you when I get to Brandon Castle."

In spite of the supplications and protestations of the men he bound them firmly to two trees, and then turning to the bewildered wizard, whose eyes were fixed as if fascinated upon his armour, he said,—

"Lead on, I will follow you."

CHAPTER LV.

" Of wild revenge was still his talk,
His eyes were flashing bright,
Deep injury had moved his soul,
His heart was dark as night."

THE WIZARD'S CAVE. — THE CHILDREN OF THE UNKNOWN. — THE KNIGHT'S PROMISE.

THE wizard led the way with a peculiar bounding step, and the knight followed him closely through thicket and briars, until the former paused by the huge trunk of a majestic oak, that seemed, by some freak of Nature, to be inclined so far forward and off the perpendicular, as to bring its topmost boughs within a few feet of the ground. A nearer inspection told the knight that this strange appearance of the tree was in consequence of its growing on the side of a declivity, whence from its own weight, as it increased in growth from year to year, it had gradually dropped forwards in the manner described.

The wizard, when he reached this spot, turned and took the hand of the knight, saying,

" Welcome, welcome."

" The poor creature's wits are quite distracted," thought the knight, " for there is nothing to be welcome to more than is to be found in any other part of the forest—namely, dry leaves and grass."

As these reflections were passing through his mind, Nemoni led him round the trunk of the tree, and tossing aside some intervening boughs, he showed the entrance of a cavern which had been either by art or nature hollowed out of the same steep bank or hill-side on which grew the gigantic oak.

" Enter, enter," he said.

"I follow you," replied the knight, as he strove to pierce with his eyes the darkness in which the wizard's cave seemed to be completely shrouded.

In a few moments every obstruction was removed to their entrance, and the knight found himself in a spacious apartment, the flooring of which was beautifully even and soft to the tread.

"It is very dark here," he remarked.

"Your eyes," said Nemoni, "will soon get used to the dim, soft light of this my quiet home,—the happiest I have ever known. I would not leave it now for a palace."

"How long have you lived here?"

The wizard answered mournfully, and it was evident his mind was not equal to a calculation of time.

"I sometimes," he said, "think how long; but I cannot tell exactly if this be only a dream or a new state of existence. I think it is a dream."

"Poor fellow," thought the knight, "some great grief surely must have cast this mental blight over him."

Every moment now, as if the dawn of morn was lengthening, the cavern seemed to get lighter and lighter to the knight, for his eyes were becoming accustomed to the dim radiance which had succeeded a profound darkness, to him, as he first came out of the broad daylight.

A delicious coolness spread itself over his limbs as he gazed around him, and he felt much invigorated and refreshed by the cool air of the cavern after the long walk he had had since sunrise, for he had travelled far that day to reach Brandon Castle early.

The wizard now brought him a rough seat, which was composed merely of some boughs of trees tied together, and upon the top of them spread the skin of some wild animal of the forest which the recluse had slain to provide himself with animal food.

"You were right," said the stranger knight, as he removed the pilgrim's cap from his head, and enjoyed the cool refreshing air of the cave. "You were right when you told me I should soon become accustomed to this light. I can now see plainly around me."

"Drink," said the wizard, as he brought the knight a small earthen vessel in which was some deliciously cool spring water, which was inexpressibly refreshing.

The stranger partook of it with evident pleasure, and then as he made a tolerable meal off some fruit which his strange entertainer handed to him, he said,

"I hope some day you will dine with me, and if you come with as good an appetite as I have to you, you will do justice to such cheer as I may be able to place before you."

The wizard shook his head as he replied,

"I belong not now to the great family of man. I have been preserved by Heaven for one purpose."

"And what is that?"

"Revenge!" shouted the maniac, as he sprung from the floor on which he had seated himself, and his whole frame seemed to dilate with the violence of his passion. "Revenge — revenge — Morgatani—The Black Monk of Brandon will surely some day be given up to me by Heaven. Oh! that it may make me the minister of its just vengeance against him. Death—torture—despair to Morgatani, the Black Monk. Let vultures feed on his heart; and I must have my revenge on him. My sword—aye, my sword."

He rushed to a corner of the cavern and returned in a moment with a naked sword in his hand, the blade of which was so highly polished that it shone like glass.

He would have rushed out of the cavern with the weapon in his hand had not the knight forcibly stayed his furious progress, and cried,—

"Morgatani is not here. Where would you seek him just now? Be calm. You surely would not leave me your guest here alone?"

"Where—where is he?" said the wizard.

"Nay, I know not; but place your sword aside again, and tell me what deep cause of enmity you have at that man, whom I confess I have myself heard of as a deep, dangerous, and intriguing Jesuit?"

"What—cause—of enmity?" said the wizard, as he dropped the point of the sword.

"Aye, what cause?"

"Look at me—look at me. The wild creatures of the forest are better than I, for they rove in the wilderness and hide themselves in rocks and caverns, because it is their nature, and God has said so shall they do; but such is not man's nature. Think of some heavy cause—some heart-smiting agony which could take a human creature from his kind and make him what I am, and then say Morgatani, the Jesuit—Morgatani, the murderer —the fiend did that!"

The sword fell from the grasp of Nemoni with a clank upon the floor, and his breast heaved for a moment or two with deep emotion.

"Why do men call you the wizard?" said the knight, for he wished to give a turn to a conversation which was so evidently distressing to the poor maniac.

"People ever seek for some extraordinary explanation of that which they do not understand. They will have it I am something supernatural, because I do not do as they do, live as they live, and bear oppression's chain as easily as they wear it."

No. 30

" Then you make no pretensions yourself to supernatural power ?" asked the knight.

" Sometimes," replied the wizard, " strange voices will whisper things to me that are hidden from mortal knowledge."

" Indeed ?"

" Yes—yes—yes.

" Even in Brandon strong and old,
    Where evil natures dwell,
The power of right shall hold its way,
    Sweet as a marriage bell.
The father shall behold his own—
    Shall kiss away the tears
That flow adown his children's cheeks,
    And smile away their fears.
From out the grave the gentle dead
    Shall see the light of day;
Two wicked hearts may then despair,
    Their hope shall pass away,
And agony of soul and brain
    Shall call them all her own.
They dare not pray to Heaven, but sink
    With many a shriek and moan."

The wizard ceased, and then with a shudder, that shook his whole frame like a convulsion, he sunk down at the feet of the knight, and was silent for many minutes. When he spoke again it was in a low voice, he said,—

" I have made the sword bright—very bright, that it may be dimmed in the blood of the betrayer. Then I can look at it and remember what it was, and why, like the joy of my heart, its radiance and beauty is for ever quenched."

The knight then rose, saying,—

" I thank you for your hospitality, and must now take my way to Brandon Castle."

" Ere you go," said the wizard, " tell me who you are, for you are brave and noble ?"

" I am a crusader," said the knight ; " and when I say that I am one of the poorest, I believe I am not far wrong, for my present possessions consist of my armour, my sword, and a few silver pieces."

" But your name ?"

" I will tell it you when next we meet," said the knight, " till then adieu ; but keep you this in remembrance of me."

He gave the wizard a rough, but massive gold ring that he had on his finger, and then stepped from the cavern once more into the wood.

" I will show you on your way," said the wizard, as he bounded after him.

Scarcely had the knight got twenty steps from the cavern of Nemoni, than he was astonished at suddenly hearing the musical voices of children, and glancing in the direction from whence the sound proceeded, he saw playing beneath the shadow of a tree, the same two young children which have before been mentioned to the reader.

A few paces from them was the female who took so deep an interest in the fate of the poor maniac, and who was in the habit of visiting him in the wood.

The knight gazed for some moments at the group in undisguised astonishment, and then hastily walking up to the female, he said,

" What children are these ?"

Struck by his noble appearance and gorgeous armour, the female made her respectful obeisance, as she said,

"I know not, sir."

"You know not? That is passing strange. Come hither, little ones."

The children shrunk back slyly for a moment, but then assured by the smiling countenance of the knight, they walked towards him, and laid their small hands with great admiration upon his armour.

"Now tell me who you are?" said the knight.

The children both replied without the least hesitation,

"We don't know."

"I have taught them," said the female, "to make that reply to any one asking such a question, with a hope that it may lead some day to such inquiry concerning them, as I am not in a position to make, and perhaps their restoration to the arms of those who may possibly be mourning their decease."

"You are right, so far," said the knight. "Do they reside with you?"

"They do."

"And how come you by them?"

"Nemoni brought them to me; but, alas! there is a blight upon his mind, and he cannot tell me whose they are. They seem twins."

"Right lovely children are they," said the knight, "whosoever they are. I presume you reside hard by?"

"Yes, in a hut given me by Sir Rupert Brandon, on the outskirts of the forest."

"Nemoni," said the knight, turning to the wizard, who having followed him, was leaning against a tree, listening to the preceding conversation, "what do you say of these young children?"

"They are fair and beautiful as sunlight," replied Nemoni.

"True—but their history?"

"They came from Heaven to bless him, who will in time be blessed."

"Who?"

The wizard shook his head.

"I have often questioned him," said the female, "but he cannot, or he will not tell."

"Ask him once again, and tell him that I will protect both him and them, if he will relate truly who they belong to."

"Nemoni," said the female, while the tears gathered in her eyes, "Nemoni, brother, dear brother, tell this noble gentleman what you have denied to me."

The wizard seemed moved for a moment, and then he advanced a step towards the knight, but a second thought held him back, and throwing his arms wildly about his head, he cried,

"Not yet—not yet.

"Twice in its strength and its wondrous power,
Will bring forth the day, will bring forth the hour;
The father shall clasp his children fair,
And joy shall sing in the sunny air.

Not yet—not yet. There is a power above which says, 'Not yet.' Who shall dispute the judgment?"

"It is in vain," said the female.

"I fear you are right," remarked the knight. "Just now I am myself so harassed by some matters upon which hang more lives and fortunes than I can number, that I am quite powerless as regards aught else; but soon, by God's help, I hope to be in a condition to seek you out, when right shall be done to these lovely children. I swear it."

"May Heaven bless and reward you, sir," said the female, as she clasped her hands in gratitude.

"Heaven will reward you," remarked the knight, "for your pious care of these young ones. I have given Nemoni a token from me, for he this day saved my life from ruffians in the forest, who would have assassinated me. Take this gold chain, and sell it to whoever will give you its value. Use the proceeds for the children, and perchance ere all be gone, you may see me again."

The gold chain which the knight took from his own neck, was a very massive one, and composed of beautifully engraved links, of the most rare and exquisite pattern and workmanship.

"Alas, sir," said the female, "where can I dispose of such a costly article as this?"

"Take it to some of the monks in the neighbouring monastery," said the knight. "I dare say they will manage to exchange it for gold."

"I will show you to the gate of Brandon," muttered Nemoni, as he walked hastily onwards, apparently as if he wished the knight away.

The latter then kissed the children, and bidding their kind-hearted nurse adieu, he walked after his guide.

CHAPTER LVI.

"So beautiful was she in death,
　Though silent, sad, and lone,
One scarce could think her dead, and that
　Her spirit it had flown."

THE VAULT OF THE DEAD.—THE PAGE'S ADVENTURES IN THE
SUBTERRANEOUS PASSAGES.

WE left the page, who was making such strenuous and gallant exertions to reach the dungeon of the persecuted Sir Kenneth Hay, at the entrance of the narrow passage, from whence there suddenly arose sounds of such strange import, and so unearthly a character, as made him recoil from the spot and stand in suspense and fear for some minutes.

When he stepped back and shaded his lamp with his hand, the sounds after a few moments gradually died away, as if they had been produced by something which was momentarily increasing its distance from him, rather than decreasing.

"What, in the name of Heaven, can that be?" murmured the page, as after waiting for some time he began gradually to recover from his first fright.

His own voice found a faint echo in that gloomy spot, and then all was as still again as the grave.

For a few moments more he now waited, and strained his ear to catch the least sound, but there was not a vestige of the singular rushing noise now to be heard. Commending himself, therefore, once more to Heaven, the adventurous page removed his hand from before his lamp, and with a slow steady step passed the broken door.

A sudden dimness now of his light, even if his own difficulty of breathing had not told him so much, proclaimed the badness of the air in the narrow passage he had now entered. He walked very slowly, for he thought the light might consume the bad air, and then that necessarily purer would find its way from the vaulted place he had just left, which, bad as it was, was certainly far preferable to the one he was in, in which heavy, dense, noxious vapours seemed actually to hang like clouds, threatening suffocation to any living thing which should venture to pass through them.

As he advanced he either got more used to the inhaled atmosphere, or it became really, as he imagined, purer, and he breathed with far less difficulty than he had done at the first entrance to the wretched place.

He found, likewise, that his lamp burnt tolerably clear if he held it low instead of high, and he accordingly did, while he followed several windings in the passage which seemed to be perfectly interminable.

" I will keep bearing to the right hand," he thought, " whenever I can, and at all events if that leads me wrong, I shall have less difficulty in avoiding the same track upon a second attempt."

As he went, even along the narrow passage he was in, he occasionally stuck one of his wooden pegs in the walls as a guide to his return; but from the length of the passage, he began to fear he should exhaust his stock where there might be no means of making more. For the last fifty paces he therefore abstained from using any, and then he came to another turning which was quite open, not having the least remnant of a door at it.

Without hesitation, as it was upon his right hand, he entered it, but scarcely had he done so, when the same strange rushing noise that before had so much startled him, came upon his ears.

He paused in terror, and this time he did not shade his lamp. The noise momentarily increased, and before he could move from the spot on which he stood, a monstrous bat flew headlong towards the lamp, and would certainly have extinguished it, or knocked it out of the page's hand had he not suddenly, more from impulse than reflection, stooped when the creature continuing its headlong career, being dazzled by the light, struck itself with such force against the opposite wall, that it fell stunned to the ground, only giving signs of life by an occasional slight movement of its large leather-looking wings.

" Thank Heaven!" said the page, with a feeling of great relief, " I now know what that is."

He stepped up to the creature as it lay on the floor, and was perfectly astonished at its monstrous size. It had in all probability, been an inhabitant of those gloomy, dark passages for years, and had grown to its unnatural dimensions by feeding on the many insect things that came into existence in that pestiferous region.

" I cannot bring my mind to kill thee," said the page, as he looked at the bat; " but still you might have been my destruction, for how could I with any hope of safety emerge from these wretched subterranean passages without a light to guide my steps."

The bat now lay quite motionless, to all appearance dead, and the page turned again towards the passage, which he entered with a much lighter heart, now that he was aware of what had occasioned the strange sounds that had shaken his nerves.

The passage he was now in was but short, having at its further extremity a door which, to his great chagrin and disappointment, the page found was fastened.

He placed his lamp on the floor and carefully examined the door; it seemed massive, but to be composed of wood only, and that appeared from the touch so old and so rotten, that he thought there could be but little difficulty indeed in making a way through it.

Taking then his dagger by a firm hold he struck it against one of the panels, when the weapon went through it with the greatest ease, a quantity of dust falling from the crumbling wood.

To break the panel off now by long spongy-looking pieces was the work but of a few moments, when the page made an opening large enough for his slight form to pass easily through, and which availing himself of directly, he passed, and was at the other side of the obstacle which, at first sight, he had thought would be an effectual bar to his further progress in that direction.

The passage on the other side of the door presented to the extent of a few paces no difference from its first part; but the page was very nearly falling down a short flight of stone steps, which, from the shadows cast by his lamp, he did not perceive till he was quite close upon them.

These steps were composed but of large loose blocks of stone laid one below the other in corresponding indentations in the earth. They were but eight in number, and when he reached the base of them the page found that there was a solid wall before him, and circuitous passages right and left, neither of which were secured by doors, but having merely arched entrances formed by square blocks of stones embedded in earth and clay.

He stuck one of the pegs into the wall at the foot of the steps, and then without the least hesitation followed the right hand passage according to his previous determination. This passage appeared to curve round in a complete semi-circle, and as far as he, the page, could judge, was conducting him in the direction of the chapel again, but he nevertheless pursued it with the hope that it would take him to the dungeons.

Suddenly the circuitous pathway terminated in a small octagonal vaulted apartment, on the floor of which were strewn rushes in abundance. From the ceiling hung an iron lamp, and in a niche in the wall was a crucifix.

"This," said the page, "has surely at one time been an oratory."

He walked round and round the room, and on one of the eight walls he found the following inscription in a tolerable state of preservation :

"Here ye piouse Sir Monktone Brandone
Made muche prayere and holie supplicatione
For ye soule of Maude, his ladye."

The next thing that attracted the attention of the page was a small and very neat gothic door; it yielded to his touch, and immediately on the other side were two wide stone steps, which, when he had descended, the page found himself in a spacious vault.

There were niches all round the walls, which in many cases were filled up by coffins, while on trussels and stone beds, or supports, lay several others, some of which were still covered by rich mouldering palls.

The page placed his lamp on a vacant slab of white marble, and gazed around him with astonishment, not unmingled with awe.

"This, then," he said, "is the burial place of the Brandons that I have reached, instead of the dungeons. In seeking for him whom I still hope is among the living, I have discovered the gloomy resting place of the dead."

He shuddered, and sat down upon the slab upon which he had placed his lamp.

"How still and solemn," he murmured, "is this place. What ideas does it not give birth to. There is an awful interest about these trappings of the dead, which, while we men approach with curiosity, we feel inclined to shrink from with dismay."

Suddenly a sound came upon his ears—so slight a sound, that in any other place it would scarce have been heard, but in that solemn, silent vault it made itself conspicuous.

A pang of terror shot across the page's heart as he turned his eyes in the direction from whence the sound proceeded, when, to his great relief, he was able to make an immediate guess as to its cause. A heavy bullion tassel had just, by its own weight, and the decay of the material that had fastened it to the corner of one of the palls, fallen to the stone flooring.

That was a sad and mournful lesson to human vanity, and the page could not help saying—

"So shall the glitter of wealth fall away before the cold corruption of the grave!"

He shuddered as he made the remark, for life to the young is full of joy and hope. The portals of the grave present to them ever a gloomy and horrifying aspect.

With a feeling of anxiety which he could not resist, he approached the bier, from the pall covering of which the tassel had fallen. The face of the corpse was uncovered, and the start of surprise which the page first gave when he ascertained such to be the case, was in a moment exchanged for a feeling of great curiosity.

The pall was mouldering away. The upper of the clothing of the body which was visible presented evident signs of crumbling into dust; but the body itself which lay there, and would have been supposed the most corruptible substance on that bier, appeared as fresh — as uncontaminated by decay—as untouched by decomposition, as if life had not an hour passed from it, and it still lay but a sleeping picture of vitality.

The form was that of a female, and even in death how lovely was that form! How exquisitely chiselled were those features, that, by some means, had escaped the contamination of the tomb! What a soft languor seemed to sit upon the fair cheeks! The page was stricken with amazement, and exclaimed,—

"God of Heaven! how is this that, surrounded by all the signs of having lain long here in this gloomy vault, this body presents no repulsive tokens, but would seem almost to be sleeping in beauty rather than a ghastly tenant of the tomb?"

He went for his light, which he had left on the slab at some little distance, and threw its rays upon the calm, cold face. Not a muscle had fallen—not a trace of decay was there. The long, silken eyelashes fell upon the cheek as they were wont to do in life. He could not believe he looked on death. The grave seemed robbed of its victory, and, by some high and holy power, to be kept from harming so fair a thing.

His eye now caught a few words which were cut upon the side of the marble bier, and, stooping, he cast the light of his lamp upon them, and read,—

"Alicia Brandon."

"This, then," said the page, "is the young wife of the absent Sir Rupert, who, I have been told, he loved so fondly when living, and mourned so deeply when dead. How could her body have been thus wonderfully preserved?"

He cast his eyes on the pall. It was evidently in the last stage of decay. He saw something glittering there just by the breast of the corpse, and, stooping down closer to see what it could possibly be, he exclaimed, with unfeigned surprise—

"A dagger!"

Yes—there was the dagger, which it will be recollected by our readers Morgatani forced the trembling Eldred Weare to plunge into the heart of his own dead sister.

The page was quite lost in astonishment at what he saw. Once he thought he would remove the weapon; but, even as he approached his hand to its glittering hilt to do so, he shrunk from the task, saying—

"Heaven knows by what means it came there! I will not disturb it. Alas, poor lady, I much fear you came by your death most foully! May justice light upon those who have in any way injured you!"

He then left the side of the bier, and slowly walked round the vault to ee if there were any other bodies in such a state of preservation as the Lady Alicia's ; but such was not the case, and he could draw no general conclusion that it was customary to preserve the dead in the Brandon family thus, and they had some secret means of doing it ; but he was compelled to the belief that heaven itself in this case, for some special purpose of its own, had stayed the hand of decay.

Outlet from the vault he could find none, save the narrow door at which he had entered.

" Once more," he said, " I must, by taking the left hand of the two passages, the right of which has brought me here, essay to reach the dungeon of Sir Kenneth Hay."

CHAPTER LVII.

"Blow, warder, blow thy sounding horn;
Thy banner raise on high :
A warrior bold is at your gate—
He comes from the east country."

THE CRUSADER.—THE WELCOME.—THE MEETING WITH AGATHA.—THE MYSTERIOUS FEAR OF FITZHUGH.

' The man-at-arms who kept watch and ward in what was called the gate turret at Brandon was lounging lazily upon his partisan, and ever and anon glancing through the narrow loophole which commanded a view of the moat and the country on its other side to the verge of the wood, when he suddenly started at the unexpected sight of a knight in such complete war panoply as he to whom we have already introduced the reader, and who at that moment emerged from among the trees, and stood gazing upon the frowning battlements of Brandon.

He then turned, and waved his hand, as if bidding some one a courteous adieu. It was the Wizard of the Red Cavern, who had accompanied him so far as a guide.

The guard then, recovering from his first surprise, placed to his lips the bugle that hung by the side of the loophole, and blew two short blasts upon it, which in a moment reached the ears of the men-at-arms in the guardroom, letting them know that some one of quality was at the gate of Brandon.

The knight then placed a very small silver horn to his lips, and blew a low, winding note, which, although it was scarcely louder than that of a flute, still, by its exquisite clearness, made itself heard quite as far, if not much further, than could a louder and a rougher strain.

In a few moments Hugh Wingrove reached the portal, and, giving one glance at the knight, he said,—

" All are friends to us who come in such a guise. Lower the drawbridge, and admit him. God knows but he may bring us news of Sir Rupert."

The order was obeyed with an alacrity that shewed the soldiers' hearts were in the work, and the chains ran rapidly over the pulleys till the drawbridge fell with a heavy clank upon the stonework fitted to receive it on the opposite side of the moat. The knight, with a few rapid strides, crossed over, and the ponderous gate, creaking upon its hinges, admitted him within the precincts of the castle.

" Welcome, sir knight," said Wingrove. " You come from Palestine ?"

" I do," said the stranger. " Peace be to all here !"

"' May we ask your name and title?'"

The men-at-arms. who had followed Wingrove, pressed eagerly forward to hear who it was that presented so gallant a bearing, and wore armour of such a costly nature.

"My friend," said the knight, "rather than impose upon you with a false name and title, I tell you candidly, that I have urgent reasons for concealing my real one. If you will trust me as I am, and receive me not knowing who I am, further than I tell you I am a crusader and have fought by the side of King Richard, I shall thank you?"

"We live, I know, in evil times," remarked Wingrove, "and far be it from me to question the wisdom of your incognito, Sir Knight. Your word is a sufficient guarantee for your honour. Your are right welcome to Brandon."

"I shall not forget your courtesy," said the knight, "and the time may come when I may requite it fully. Till then I must remain your debtor; I pray you step aside with me."

Wingrove walked a few paces with the knight, who then turning to him and looking him fully in the face said,—

"Is your name Wingrove?"

"It is, Sir Knight."

"By the wars, I thought so, for there is honesty in your face. Sir Rupert has spoken of you to me."

"My honoured master? Oh, tell me, sir—is he well?"

"As I hope for Heaven, I hope he is. But there was one who came here on a message from Sir Rupert, the purport of which I am aware of. What has become of him?"

"Sir Kenneth Hay?"

"Aye, Sir Kenneth Hay. Tell me he is dead and I will give a tear to his memory; but what else could have befallen him to make him fail in his mission know not."

No. 31

"Nor I," said Wingrove. "Let me crave your patience for a brief space while I relate you incidents that may well make you hold up to Heaven your hands in wonder."

Wingrove then related to the crusader the circumstances connected with the combat in the court-yard, and the mysterious disappearance of Sir Kenneth Hay, concluding by saying,—

"Morgatani, a Jesuit, is, I believe firmly, in conjunction with Mistress Agatha Weare, the sister of the deceased Lady Alicia, at the bottom of all these mysteries; and I really believe too, that they must have the devil himself to aid them, for I know not how otherwise they could contrive as they do."

"So," said the knight, when Wingrove had finished his narration, "this is news indeed. One of the bravest of the crusaders spirited away by the artifices of a woman and a monk. I have heard of this Morgatani as a wily agent of Rome, and a Jesuit of great art and skill. Let him beware. Let him beware, I say. The time may come ——"

The knight paused, and while a slightly heightened colour testified to the excitement of his feelings, he strode to and fro for some seconds with haughty strides.

"You feel this matter deeply, Sir Knight," remarked Wingrove.

"In truth I do, and will by the assistance of Heaven find out the truth. What now—who are you?"

These words were addressed to Eldred, who had been sent by his sister to see who it was that had been admitted to the castle, and who was so struck by the noble bearing of the knight and the glitter of his costly chain-armour, that for some moments he had stood staring as if moon-stricken, without saying a word.

The manner of the knight, however, was so imperious, that Eldred immediately stammered out,—

"I—I—ah—I only—bless me, come to see how you was."

"How I was?"

"No—I—mean who you was."

"Leave off that shaking and tell me who you are?"

"My name is Eldred Weare; I'm very glad to see you, sir—oh, very. What a walloper!"

"A what?"

"Nothing, nothing."

"Who is this man?" said the knight, turning with a gesture of impatience to Wingrove.

"He is the brother of Agatha Weare," said Wingrove.

"Indeed, and she by all accounts a bold, bad woman, while this man is such a slinking hound."

"Well, I never," muttered Eldred. "This fellow don't mind much what he says, at all events."

"Tell your sister, Master Eldred Weare," said the knight, "that a crusader desires an audience of her. What are you muttering—eh? Speak out."

"I—I wasn't muttering—really I wasn't. Don't be in a rage. I'll tell her."

Eldred then made a precipitate retreat, and when he had got fairly out of ear-shot of the knight, he stopped for breath, and said :—

"Ah! it's all very fine; I will tell Agatha. Of all the impudent fellows that ever I come near, this one beats 'em. A bold bad woman, he says she is. Won't she be pleased. Oh, lor'! I daren't have said so much for my life. I wish I was a great walloping fellow, and didn't mind fights and rows, and knocks and cracks on the noddle. How I would bully everybody, to be sure. This chap who has just come is worse than Sir Kenneth Hay, and he was bad enough; but this fellow, independent of being quite as big, is enough to alarm anybody dreadfully.   Well, I'm sure if I was to try to come it in such a way, I should get such a stomacher as would double me up.   I wonder, now, what Agatha would say if I was to try and look a little heroic, and say :—

"'Woman, female woman! how dare you speak to me ? How dare you —'"

"Fool!" said Agatha, as she clutched Eldred's wrist suddenly, and confronted him.   "Have you lost the small quantity of brains that you did possess ?"

"Oh—oh—oh—lor'! what a turn you did give me, Agatha, to be sure.   I was only a joking.   Really, I was ; you know I never thought ——"

"Peace—peace !   Answer my questions."

"Ye—ye—yes."

"Who is the stranger ?"

"I really don't know."

"What does he want here ?"

"I really don't know.   He—he is a whopper, rather, and he says, says he, 'Tell Mistress Agatha she's no better than she should be, and not quite so good.'"

"He dared say so ?"

"Yes, he did ; and then he says, 'Tell her I desire an audience of her immediately at once.'   Then, after nearly having my very nose snapped off, I came away."

"Go back, then, and tell him that Agatha Weare will not condescend to reply to so impertinent a message as he has sent."

"I think I see me," thought Eldred.

"Do you hear ?" cried Agatha.

"Yes, I do ; but—but ——"

"What?   What does your fear suggest now, that you pause when I command you to act ?"

"Why, you see, sister, I'm rather in what some folks would call a quandary. If I don't take your message, you get in a rage, and then there's the devil to pay ; if I do, why, I'm more than likely to get what may be called a stunner from this knight, who has come home fresh from fighting the Turks, and who, I dare say, is just as likely to fall foul of him who brings a disagreeable message, as the sender of it."

Before Agatha could reply, Bernard, with a slow steady step, and a twinkle in his eyes, which showed he was very far from displeased with the message he was on, made his appearance.

"Well," cried Agatha, "what now?   Are you the bearer of some second impertinent message from this stranger ?"

"A stranger he is," said Bernard, "but as to the impertinence, I shall give no opinion ; not that I am too thirsty to think, although I haven't had anything to drink for three quarters of an hour nearly, but ——"

"Cease this silly prating," said Agatha.   "If you come with any message to me, speak it at once."

"Why, the crusader says he will be here in a few moments."

"Here ?"

"Yes ; and by the mass, he is not much worse than his word, for here he comes."

The knight advanced with a haughty stride and a knit brow to where Agatha was standing, and just when she was prepared to resent some insolence on his part, he stopped, and made her so courteous a bow, that she was compelled, on the impulse of the moment, to acknowledge his presence with equal civility, while she whispered to herself,—

"This can be no common man.   Who in the name of Heaven can he be ?"

"I believe," said the knight, "I have the honour of addressing Mistress Agatha Weare?"

"That is my name, sir," said Agatha, abashed, in spite of herself, at the calm glance of conscious power and dignity which was bent on her by the crusader.

"As a friend, then, of Sir Rupert Brandon's," he added, "I claim the hospitality of this castle, which I am quite sure will be accorded as freely as it is required."

Agatha was puzzled to know what to say for a moment, and then replied :—

"For how long, Sir Knight, do you purpose honouring us with your anonymous presence?"

There was a tone of insult and irony in these words which the knight received with a slight smile, as he said,—

"So long, lady, as it shall suit my convenience, and your kind heart to welcome me."

"We are ill provided with accommodation," said Agatha.

"Ah, I am far from particular," replied the knight. "If you have no other chamber for me, I will put up with even the old Grey Turret, which has so very ominous a reputation."

"The old Grey Turret!—What—what know you of that place or its reputation?"

"Much, lady. Sir Rupert Brandon has often mentioned it to me during his campaigns."

"Is Sir Rupert well? and will he soon return?"

"I do not know, lady; but my hopes say yes to both your questions."

Agatha was silent for some moments, during which she considered how exceedingly inconvenient to the proceedings of Morgatani it might be to have such a visiter remaining for an unlimited period at Brandon, the more especially too as he concealed who he was, and there could be no means of ascertaining how far he was to be dreaded or trusted. Full of these thoughts, she said,—

"Surely, Sir Knight, you would not wish to accept of our hospitality, at the same time that you mistrust us so far as not even to tell us who you are?"

"There," said the knight, with a slight smile, "is my misfortune; I have made a vow not to tell my name until—in fact until it is quite convenient to do so."

"Then," said Agatha, making a great effort to overcome the fear which was at her heart, "I decline receiving you as a guest here."

"Indeed?"

"Yes, sir. I will not receive a nameless adventurer as a honoured guest in, Brandon."

"Lady, I have lived the better part of my life in camps, and the smallest courtesies of life will suffice for me. I am, as you see, here, and if you can get any one to turn me out, I will go, but not otherwise, until it suits my good convenience. Nay, lady, you may spare a reply, for I have an enterprise on foot which may even induce me to invite some score or more other persons here, for whom I expect some sort of accommodation to be provided."

Agatha was perfectly bewildered at the cool impertinence, as she considered it, of the knight, and she gazed in his face, which wore a smile partly of contempt, and partly of amusement, as if she would study from his physiognomy if he were really serious.

"Sir," she said, "are you such a desperado that you will take forcible possession of people's homes however unwelcome you may be?"

"Why," replied the knight, carelessly, "my fortunes just now, lady, are not very bright, although I have considerable expectancies; but in the meanwhile Brandon Castle will suit me as a residence very well, and if you and I are to be at war while I remain here, all I can say is, that you will find me an honourable opponent, and that if your brother there will throw down his glove in your cause, I am as willing to break as many lances with him as he may think necessary for his honour."

"I?" cried Eldred; "I break long thingimys with sharp points at the end? I think I see me. Do I look like a fool?"

"Rather," said the knight.

"You shall repent, sir," said Agatha, biting her lips.

"Truly, I hope so," interrupted the knight. "I have often promised my confessor I would, and some day I really shall begin. Come, Bernard, show me to the chamber of Fitzhugh; I have something to say to him now that Mistress Agatha and I have settled matters so lovingly."

He then followed Bernard with rapid strides, who was so much delighted with the scene that had ensued between Agatha and the knight, that he was fain to stop every now and then to laugh so loud and long, that the castle echoed again with the sound.

CHAPTER LVIII.

" 'Twas frightful in that holy spot
To hear the din of arms;
Instead of prayer and gentle sounds,
Uprose dread war's alarms."

THE STRANGE COMBAT IN THE CHAPEL.—THE PAGE'S TERROR.—MORGATANI'S DANGER.—THE ESCAPE.

THE page felt very weary from his long sojourn in the underground passages of Brandon, but his spirit was undaunted. His only fear was that even should he now succeed in finding the right track to the dungeon of Sir Kenneth Hay, he might himself be too much exhausted to render him the assistance of which in all probability he stood in need.

He felt sick and faint, for the air of the gloomy subterranean habitations he had passed through had begun sensibly to affect his strength. He trembled excesssively, and a conviction began to creep over him that unless he recruited himself by breathing a purer air, he should perhaps fall a victim to the pestiferous vapours he had been breathing for so long, and thus sacrifice his own life without even the consolation of saving that of another.

"I must ascend," he thought, "to daylight, and strengthen myself for another attempt to discover the dungeons, in which I am now far more likely to be successful than before, for I know what passages to avoid, while hitherto my progress has been directed by chance alone." Having come to this resolution, the page rapidly retraversed the various passages through which he had come, until he arrived at the tomb of Sir Moncktone Brandon, and in a few moments he emerged into the chapel much exhausted; there he seated himself upon a neighbouring tomb, and the air he now breathed, in comparison with that which for some hours visited his lungs, seemed to him perfectly delicious and full of life.

"I will rest here awhile," he thought; "and then again adventure the deliverance of Sir Kenneth Hay, for I should not sleep to-night unless that I had done all that in me lay to rescue him from the direful fate evidently intended for him."

Then it occurred to the page that he might be many hours in the gloomy underground passages, in which case his lamp would scarcely last him, and what then would be his fate if left in the darkness of those damp regions?

Acting upon this supposition, which was one of no small moment, he hastened from the chapel, and betook himself to the domestic offices of the castle, where he procured more oil for his lamp, as well as a small case bottle of wine, which he thought he might require during his wearisome and anxious search.

Much reassured then by the preparations he had made, and his acquired knowledge of some, at least, of the localities of the vaults beneath Brandon, he returned to the chapel, and opening the tomb, was upon the point of descending, when he heard a strange sound, as of the creaking of a window close by him.

Casting his eyes in the direction from whence the sound proceeded, he saw to his surprise one of the gothic windows gently opened, and a strange, unearthly looking head presented itself at the aperture.

The page drew back right within the tomb, and kept his eyes fixed upon the singular appearance. In the course of a moment the window was opened wider, and with wonderful agility Nemoni, the wizard, drew himself up from without and effected a safe entrance into the chapel.

Wondering what object he could have in making so very mysterious an appearance, the page forbore making any alarm, but kept a continued gaze upon the actions of the wizard.

The strange creature, after gazing about him for some few seconds, took from a rough leathern belt at his side a long and brightly polished sword, the same he had spent so many hours at his rocky retreat in sharpening. He held it up above his head, and after gazing at it in silence for some seconds, he said,—

"Avenger! avenger! you are bright and beautiful, but you shall be dimmed in the blood of him, the wicked and accursed."

Then he sunk his head upon his breast, and repeated some name several times in tones of deep feeling and emotion, which, however, was too low for the page to catch the exact sound of.

"Surely he comes here on some wild errand," thought the page, "which may be productive of much mischief and bloodshed. Can I prevent him by giving an alarm to the castle guard?"

"Has Heaven heard my prayers," suddenly said the wizard; "and shall I this day have vengeance on the destroyer? Yes, yes; a something seems even now to whisper to my seething brain that he will come this way, and I shall have revenge."

"Who speaks he of?" thought the page.

"Morgatani, Morgatani," cried the wizard, with a suddenness that made the page start, for it sounded almost like an answer to his mental question. "Death! death!" continued the wizard. "Death to the Black Monk!"

"Let Heaven," murmured the page, "use what instruments it may in its judgments, I will not interfere to save such an one as Morgatani from the retribution which may be awaiting him."

He then descended one step downwards towards the vaults, and in another moment would have been below the chapel floor, but his attention was suddenly arrested by the sound of a heavy footstep, and advancing from the gloom at the further end of the chapel he saw a tall figure, which from its gait, he pronounced at once to be Morgatani.

Curiosity then to see the issue of a meeting between two such strange beings, each equally desperate in his way, chained the page to the spot, and he scarcely breathed as he watched the slow and steady approach of the Black Monk to where the wizard was nearly hidden from his observation by a statue that adorned one of the ancient monuments of the place.

Morgatani was muttering to himself, as he was in the habit of doing when quite alone, although in too low a tone and too disjointed and indistinct a manner to enable any one to catch the purport of his thoughts.

Suddenly then the wizard, when Morgatani had passed on without observing him, stepped out from his place of partial concealment, and in a voice of triumph shouted rather then said,—

"Morgatani! Morgatani!"

The monk uttered an imprecation, and then suddenly turned to face the speaker.

"Morgatani!" again cried the wizard.

The monk stepped back, and thrusting his hand among the folds of his dress, he drew a sword, which was otherwise quite concealed by his monkish costume, and, standing upon the defensive, he said,

"Man or devil, you shall rue questioning me, when I would pass unknown."

"Morgatani!" repeated the wizard, evidently only repressing the wild rage which was struggling, like a caged tiger, in his breast—"Morgatani, do you know me?"

"Madman! How should I know thee?"

"No, no. Ha! ha! ha! How should you know me, indeed, Morgatani. It was not to be expected that you should retain a memory of all your victims."

"My victims!"

"Aye, your victims!—that is the word—your victims! I did not expect you to know me."

"You are some wretched maniac."

"I am; yes, I am a wretched maniac; but God has left me one memory, that of my wrongs—one feeling, that of revenge."

"Against whom?"

"Thee! thee! thee!"

"What have I to do with you or your wrongs?"

"Listen. There was once a nun—a young, fair girl, beautiful as the dawn, and innocent as an angel at the throne of Heaven—"

"A nun?"

"Aye, Morgatani, a nun. Then there was a monk, and he looked upon her beauty with unholy eyes; he cursed with bitter oaths the very innocence which placed between him and her a barrier he never could surmount."

Morgatani was silent; but, by the gigantic shadow that it cast on the chapel wall, the page saw the sword shake in his grasp.

"When the monk," continued the wizard, "found that the fair and innocent young novice scorned alike him and his unholy suit, revenge took possession of his heart, and he vowed to destroy her—to take her life, if he could not prove the destruction of her pure soul."

"Peace!" said the monk, "what want I to hear of such wild tales?"

"Ask your own heart."

"Madman!"

"Villain!—worse than villain—hell itself should coin some word more terrible than human ears have yet heard, to describe such fiends in human shape as thou art."

The wizard made a step forward as he spoke, and his eyes flashed with an unearthly brilliance, as he raised his sword towards the monk's breast, threateningly.

"Beware! beware!" said Morgatani, stepping back several paces, as if he dreaded the encounter with the wild, haggard being, who thus defied him.

"Had you two lives, I would take them," cried Nemoni. "Know, villain, that she who, by your barbarity, was doomed to a horrible death because she would not listen to your unholy solicitations, was my sister—the one most loved—she who had most twined herself round my heart."

"Your sister!" gasped the monk.

"Yes. Die!—die!"

The wizard commenced on the moment a furious attack upon Morgatani, so sudden and furious that he, the monk, received a wound before he could place himself thoroughly upon his guard against his reckless opponent. The greatness of his danger, however, as well as the smart of his wound, aroused him from the partial state of tremour into which he had fallen, and the combat in a moment became fast and furious.

The great stature and immense strength of Morgatani, aided, as both were, by a consummate knowledge of the weapon he used, would quickly have terminated the contest in his favour, had he had any other than a madman to contend with; but, as it was, the insanity of the wizard lent him a strength and recklessness which placed him upon an equality even with the Black Monk, who, for several minutes, acted upon the defensive merely, for the purpose of tiring his antagonist, if possible, who was fighting with such wild fury.

But as well might Morgatani have waited to tire some machine, which, as long as iron could hold together, would maintain its action. The wild blood which ran riot in the brain of the wizard prevented him from feeling the fatigue which any sane man would have sunk under.

"Die!—die!" he shouted, and he pressed on the monk more and more furiously, while sparks flew from the clashing swords, and the din of the conflict, considering that but two persons were engaged in it, was absolutely terrific and astounding.

The page, with suppressed breath, and a beating heart, watched the issue of the fight. So wrapt in alarm and wonder was he, that, had he wished, he could scarcely have found words in which to give any alarm.

The monk did not speak during the conflict. His whole attention seemed taken up in defending his life against the wild and desperate attack which was made upon it. The wizard, however, was far from silent, for he filled the chapel with such demoniac cries as would have appalled any one but Morgatani.

"Die! die!" he shrieked. "The avenger has come. The day of triumph and revenge. Die! die!"

Then with bursts of frantic laughter, although blood was pouring from several wounds he had received, he pressed more and more closely upon Morgatani, who fought with the greatest desperation, and was compelled to put forth all his strength and all his knowledge of fence to save himself from being slaughtered on the spot.

So great was the noise, and so loud the clashing of the swords, that a result ensued which filled Morgatani with dismay, and unnerved him so much that he could scarcely defend himself.—That was the sudden rushing into the chapel of several of the men-at-arms, who had distinctly heard the sounds of the combat, and traced them to proceed from the chapel.

Morgatani had been gradually retreating before this towards a particular corner of the building, and when he saw the men-at-arms he fairly turned and fled.

That his destruction was now certain the page believed to be beyond a doubt; but the monk had a chance of escape of which all were ignorant but himself. The fact was, that when he entered the chapel it was but to use it as a thoroughfare to another part of the castle, by means of a secret door leading from the aisles, and known only to himself and Agatha.

To gain this door, then, without receiving any mortal wound, was his ob-

ject, and no easy one was it, for the door had to be opened by pressure upon a small spring, when he reached it.

By making, however, a slight deviation from the direct track, he puzzled Nemoni, who, in his haste, darted too much to one side, and thus gave Morgatani the space of about a moment to himself.

The monk did get the door open, but as he passed through it, Nemoni made a slash at him, which, from the deep execrations that followed it, had evidently been effective.

Another instant, and Morgatani was gone, fastening the door securely on the other side.

A wild shriek burst from the wizard, as he saw that his prey had escaped him, and so awful was that shriek that the men-at-arms, who were on the point of rushing forward to secure him, shrunk back in dismay and terror.

Then Nemoni's eye fell upon them, and in a moment he banished everything but what he conceived to be the necessity of escaping from them. With the agility of some wild animal, he rushed to the window at which he had entered the chapel, and before any of the soldiers could recover from their first amazement, he had climbed up by the assistance of the old carved stone work to the sill, and then he appeared literally to throw himself out, so suddenly did he disappear from their distended eyes.

"Well," exclaimed Anstey, "if he is the devil himself, he has broken his neck now."

"I'll run round and see," said another of the guard and he forthwith departed on the errand.

"Who, in the name of Heaven, were they?" added Anstey. "One looked like the devil and the other a monk."

"What, in the name of Heaven, is all this?" said Wingrove, who now arrived from another part of the castle, whence he had been fetched by one of the men-at-arms who had first heard the clashing of swords.

No. 32

"That, Master Wingrove," said Anstey, "is just what we are all puzzling our heads about."

"But I was told there was a combat."

"And so there was. As we were quietly walking in the guard-room, we suddenly heard such a clashing of swords and shouting as if a dozen armourers were at work, and when we came out, the sound directed us here."

"And you saw nothing?"

"Oh, yes, we saw two things, but they have both gone off in some extraordinary manner. Between you and I, Hugh Wingrove, I have a shrewd guess."

"Indeed?"

"Yes. Incline your ear."

"Well."

"One of these combatants was the Black Monk."

"The villain!"

"Yes, you may well call him that."

"But the other, Anstey, the other?"

"Why, in my opinion, he has had a quarrel with his master. You understand?"

"His master?"

"Aye. Him down below. The old one. That's my idea, and they came here to fight it out."

"I fear, Anstey, that Morgatani was attempting the destruction of some human creature."

"You wouldn't have said so if you had seen the creature jump out at yon window; and what's more, I can take upon myself to say, that he who was fighting with the Black Monk was the same strange-looking being we all of us saw lately by moonlight on the battlements."

"He's quite gone," said the soldier who had run round to the outer side of the chapel window.

"Dead?" said Anstey.

"No, vanished. There were two or three drops of blood to be seen on the flag-stones of the old court."

Wingrove held up his hands, as he said,—

"Brandon Castle is as full of mysteries as—as—"

"As its cellar is full of empty ale barrels," put in Bernard; "and the sooner they are filled and the mysteries sent to the right about the better."

"What, you here," said Wingrove. "Where is the crusader?"

"Oh, he's gone for a walk round the battlements; but I'll just tell you what has happened."

"What! what! what!" cried the men-at-arms, crowding round. Bernard, who continued,—

"This crusader gets the better of me altogether. First he went to Mistress Agatha Weare, and made no more ado but told her he meant to stay as long as he liked, and do what he liked, and then he walked off to Fitzhugh's chamber, and when we got near the door, he said,—

"'Bernard, wait a minute for me.'

"'Very well,' says I, 'I'm rather thirsty, and it always makes me thirstier still to wait, but I will.'

"Well, he said nothing to that, but he walks in. Then in a minute I heard Fitzhugh give a great cry, as if an arrow had gone into his inside. What's amiss now, thought I, and then I got uncommonly thirsty."

"Commonly, you mean," said Anstey.

"Don't interrupt me, if you please, confound you. Where was I now?"

"Thirsty, as usual."

" Now, if you say another word—"

" Peace, peace," said Wingrove. " Go on with your statement, Bernard."

" Well, as I was saying, then I heard Fitzhugh say,—

" ' Mercy ! Mercy ! Mercy !' Three times, just so. Then the crusader I heard him say,

" ' Beware ! You have not another chance for your head. Play me false, and, by the holy sepulchre, I will make you a head shorter within the hour afterwards. Rise, and mind that you obey me to the very letter, in all that I shall think proper to command you."

" ' Yes, most gracious,' says Fitzhugh, and what he was going to say besides I don't know, for the crusader said in a voice that made even me jump—and Heaven knows I don't often jump,

" ' Peace. Is this your caution ?'

" Then Fitzhugh mumbled something in a very humble way, after which the crusader came out, looking quite cool as if nothing had happened.

" ' Are you thirsty ?' says I.

" ' No,' says he, ' thank you, I am only going for a walk on the battlements.' "

" Who can this crusader be ?" thought the page, who heard all. " Well, well, my present business is to attempt the rescue of Sir Kenneth Hay. Heaven aid me—Heaven aid me."

CHAPTER LIX.

" The 'wildered bats flew shrieking by
With many a frantic dash,
And drops of moisture fell around,
With a deep and sullen splash.—Anon.

THE DUNGEON.—THE MONK'S PROPOSAL TO SIR KENNETH.—THE REJECTION.—THE PROMISED VISIT.—THE ANTIDOTE.

WITH much more confident steps, the page—for he knew now part of his route, and there was not the same uncertainty about every footstep which before had oppressed him—made his way down the narrow staircase, conducting from the tomb above to the underground portion of Brandon Castle.

Making as much speed as was consistent for the safety of his lamp, he hurried along the passage he had before traversed, until he came to where it branched off in different directions. His object, of course, was to take a different path from that which had been productive of nothing but disappointment, and he accordingly entered, without hesitation, the left hand passage.

" Now," he whispered to himself, " I am again upon unknown ground, and I must be cautious as before."

Slackening then his speed, and holding his lamp as high as he could, so as to have the greatest benefit from its rays, he proceeded forwards at a slow pace, which was rendered the more necessary, as the ground he was walking on was very damp and slippery.

The passage wound about in various eccentric turns, but the page was well aware that many such passages beneath ancient buildings, were, of necessity, very tortuous, in consequence of the foundation of different parts of the structure frequently barring their progress in some particular direction. With hope, therefore, still holding a warm place at his heart, the chivalrous young page pressed onwards on his errand of charity and humanity.

Gradually now he found the passage narrowing, until it became so close

that the small portion of humid air which it contained, was scarcely sufficient for the support of human existence, and the lamp flickered ominously
and appeared upon the point of expiring.

The page paused one brief moment in irresolution, but then he blushed
for his momentary cowardice, and holding the lamp low down, where he
found was a purer air than that which ascended, he proceeded slowly and
noiselessly.

Suddenly then his heart beat tumultuously, and he stopped and shaded
his lamp, for he thought, nay, he was certain, he had heard a noise resembling the closing of some door not far from where he was. He listened
for several minutes in the most painful state of suspense, but as the sound
was not repeated, he began to think his excited imagination must have
deceived him.

"It may be," thought he, "that the dull echo of sounds in the castle above
may reach these gloomy passages—I will not be deterred from my enterprise;
my trust is in Heaven, which will surely protect me in rescuing the innocent from the oppression and violence of the wicked."

To his great joy, for the air had become frightfully oppressive, he found
the passage suddenly widen; but how great then was his disappointment
after walking forward another twenty yards, to find his further progress
stopped by a stone wall, in which there appeared no door whatever.

"Surely," said the page, "I must have passed some opening or door in
my progress hither, for this long passage would never have been excavated
merely to terminate on the face of one of the foundation walls of the upper
building."

Even as he spoke, a dull heavy sound met his ears, and he could suppose
it to be nothing but the heavy tread of some one in the immediate vicinity.

Nearer and nearer it came each moment, until the page felt perfectly clear
that it was approaching from the other side of one of the walls of the passage. He immediately concealed his lamp completely, by covering it with
a portion of his clothing, and crouching down at some distance, he waited
the issue of the adventure.

Scarcely had he thus concealed himself from observation, than the sound
of the footsteps suddenly ceased—a portion of the wall of the passage
opened—a broad glare of light came through the aperture, and the Black
Monk, bearing in his hand a lamp, appeared.

It was well for the page that he had concealed himself where the shadow
of the door at which the monk had entered, fell strongly so as to assist in
his concealment, or that minute might have been his last, for Morgatani
scrupled not at sacrificing the young or the old, the weak or the strong, so
long as they interfered in any manner with his vile machinations.

The monk paused when he had passed through the doorway, and uttered
a deep groan. The page could, by stretching out his hand, have touched
the hem of his garment, and not a murmered word that fell from Morgatani's lips escaped his hearing.

"I am faint," groaned the monk. "May the fellest curses of the foul fiend
light on him who has made me lose so much blood! I never yet met my
equal in fight, save this one; never yet did I receive such wounds—flesh
wounds truly, but weakening me sadly, when it may be I shall too soon
require my utmost strength of mind and body to carry me through the
scenes I have resolved shall be enacted at Brandon."

He was evidently then in pain, for he groaned heavily several times, and
then there was a dead silence of some few minutes duration, after which he
again spoke in a voice of much bitterness, saying,

"The mad, wild being, who attacked me in the chapel, was surely set
upon me by those in the castle, who would fain destroy me, but have not

the courage themselves to essay the dangerous work. Oh, I would glory in the agony of them all. The day may come when my vengeance shall reach from the highest to the lowest, and blood shall flow in Brandon like a torrent. I will not, because I carry some wounds with me, forsake my enterprize. I have staunched the bleeding, and cannot be weaker than I am; and surely I am strong enough to subdue a chained and half-dead prisoner."

"He means the knight—he means the knight," thought the page. "Now Heaven give me power to follow in his footsteps!"

Morgatani now, with one stride, crossed the passage, and the page heard the rattle of a key in a lock, immediately after which a door creaked on its hinges. Crawling forward, so far as was at all consistent with safety, he watched the monk pass through the opening, leaving the door half-open, and the key in the lock.

"I will follow him," whispered the page. "If it cost me my life, I will follow him."

Placing then his own lamp in a corner, and recommending himself to the care of Heaven, he slowly crept after the monk, who had descended a flight of stairs, the top one of which the door opened upon.

The gleam of the lamp which Morgatani carried was an ample guide to the page, and he pursued him with the lightness of an antelope. The steps were quickly descended, and still at some distance he saw the gleam of light. On, on, he went, and his excitement and hope grew greater each moment, as he firmly believed himself nearing the dungeon of Sir Kenneth Hay.

It is doubtful, even if Morgatani had looked behind him, if he would have seen the shrinking small figure of the page, in the gloom of those dreary passages; but never suspecting that any one was following him, he turned not, and for all the danger there was of being seen the page might have been almost treading upon his heels.

At the bottom of the flight of steps there was a wide vaulted passage, from which numerous doors opened on each side, conducting, as the page presumed, to dungeons, where unfortunates might be confined at the will and pleasure of whomsoever, for the time being, might have power in Brandon Castle.

The monk rapidly passed many of these doors, and then pausing at one, he took a key from his vest, and with apparent difficulty turned it in the rusty lock. He then removed a ponderous bar, which was across the door, as an additional security, and in another moment the page was in profound darkness, for Morgatani had passed into one of the dungeons with his light, and the door had, with a loud creaking noise, swung nearly close shut.

"Found, found," whispered the page; "without a doubt that door opens to the dungeon of Sir Kenneth Hay."

Without a moment's hesitation he then advanced and placed his ear to the door, when he heard the voice of the monk in deep hollow accents, saying,—

"Rise, rise—Sir Kenneth Hay, rise."

A low moan was the only answer that the page could hear made to this demand, although it would appear that some words had been spoken, for in a moment Morgatani added,—

"Your life and liberty are in your own hands."

"Is it not all a dream?" said the voice of Sir Kenneth Hay, in weak, trembling accents.

"No, no," cried the monk, "you will find it, Sir Knight, a stern and painful reality."

"Who and what are you?" said the prisoner.

"Your conqueror."

"Never, never. Disease and treachery may conquer me, but mortal man, never."

The monk laughed discordantly, as he said,—

"Think you death would conquer you?"

"Even so, but ——"

"Hear me out. I mean would the fear of death, such a death full of torments, as I could inflict, would conquer the mind, and bend it to purposes, which in the hey-day of its health and strength, it would scorn?"

"I understand you not."

"Then open your ears and listen. You came here on a secret mission for King Richard, whose throne and title are seized upon by his brother John, now reigning in London. It behoves me much to know the true condition of Richard—his strength—his resources, and what friends by name, he counts upon at the court of London, should he escape the great dangers that environ him, and reach these shores."

"King Richard," said Sir Kenneth Hay. "God bless good King Richard! there is strength and renewed health in his very name."

"Where is he?"

"Under Heaven's protection."

"What was your secret object in coming to England from Palestine? Tell me that, and name me Richard's staunchest friends at the court of London, and you are free."

"I am weak," replied Sir Kenneth Hay, "so weak, that I cannot raise myself from the damp floor of this dungeon, which in all probability will be my tomb. There is still strange disorder in my brain, but thank Heaven I have strength yet sufficient both of mind and body, to defy you, and tell you to your teeth, you are a cowardly and despicable villain."

"Harsh words," muttered the monk. "Know you not that you are entirely in my power?"

"I am not," cried Sir Kenneth Hay, with greater energy than he had yet shown. "You may take my life, as such dastards as you only dare to take life when your victims are under circumstances of bodily depression, but there is one possession you cannot rob me of, were you aided by a thousand such as yourself."

"Indeed?"

"Aye, indeed, sneering devil. You may kill me, but my honour and my name will live yet."

"Your honour."

"Yes, my honour."

"Pshaw—an empty sound. What is honour to you, when you are mouldering in the grave? Call a skeleton a king, and will it smell less loathsome than the festering bones of a beggar?"

"You reason in vain," said Sir Kenneth, "because you reason on what you cannot comprehend. An honourable man alone knows how to appreciate that feeling which feels a stain like a wound."

"So you would sacrifice your life for this shadowy phantom you call honour?"

"You have sacrificed a dearer possession for a more worthless, hideous shadow."

"A dearer possession than life?"

"Yes—your immortal part, which when your bodily form is lapsed in the corruption of the grave, must live for ever in joy or in despair. That you have sacrificed for the feverish ambition of power over creatures as frail and short-lived as yourself. Tremble—tremble. I know you well. You are he who is named the Black Monk. You are the curse of Brandon, and all that is good and great connected with it."

"So you know me, do you? Then know, along with the knowledge of who I am, that I despise the superstition which you call your faith—that I dread nothing—hope nothing—believe in nothing."

"Impious man!"

Morgatani laughed scornfully, as he added,—

"Fool! I cannot believe you are so mad as to prefer rotting in this dungeon, in compliance with the dictates of what your fancy has nicknamed honour, to breathing the pure air that blows over the face of nature, and preserving yourself for years to come to indulge in such enjoyments as our nature is capable of."

From the tone in which Sir Kenneth Hay replied to Morgatani, it was evident that the momentary strength which had enabled him to raise his voice had passed away, leaving him again in a state of great weakness and half delirious.

"Hence—hence, evil spirit!" he cried,—"phantom, hence. God save King Richard. Drag me from among the horses' feet. There, there—unclasp my visor, I shall breathe then. How goes the fight? St. George for merry England. On—on, for Richard and England!"

"The poison still works," muttered Morgatani. "'Tis useless to press my inquiries further now. To-morrow—to-morrow. He shall then surely die; for if he tell me all I wish to know, why, then he lives for no purpose but to be a trouble to me, and if he tell me not, he shall die for his great contumacy. In either case, to-morrow shall be his last day of life. He raves—he raves."

"Victory—victory!" said Sir Kenneth. "Ho, there! Give me another lance. Hurrah for Bethlehem! Where—where is the king?"

"The dose was to the full," muttered Morgatani; "much less would have sufficed."

During this dialogue between the monk and his prisoner, the page had pushed the door gently a little way open, so that he could command a view of the dungeon and its occupants. Sir Kenneth Hay had a chain round him which confined him to a stunted-looking column that supported the roof, and the monk stood at some few paces from him, with his cowl drawn very much over his face.

When the page now found that Morgatani was upon the point of leaving the dungeon, he, with a sudden movement, took the key from the lock of the door, and secreting it in his vest, he darted some distance down the passage.

In another moment the monk was outside the dungeon door, and the page heard him mutter,—

"The key—surely I left the key here."

Then followed a few moments of great anxiety and suspense to the page, while Morgatani was searching on the damp ground for the key which he thought must have dropped from the lock.

After some minutes' search his patience appeared to be exhausted, and, with a bitter oath, he put up the massive iron bar, muttering,—

"This will be security sufficient; but what in the name of hell can have come of the key?"

Another glance he then cast about him before he walked hastily away. As the light from his lamp became weaker and weaker by his increasing distance, the page felt more and more rejoiced, and finally, when he stood in a darkness such as he had never before experienced, he clasped his hands and cried,—

"Thank Heaven he still lives, and may yet be saved!"

CHAPTER LX.

When the air feels warm and healing,
    O'er the green encircled plain—
When sweet-odour'd, soft, on-stealing
    Twilight, sinks to earth again,
Then whisper him soul cheeriness.—FAUST.

THE GRATING BY THE MOAT.—THE PAGE'S DANGER.—THE CRUSADER'S
    COURAGE.—THE MEETING IN THE DUNGEON.

THE only fear of the page now was, that the monk might discover the
lamp he had left by the narrow passage—a discovery which would at once
assure him he had been watched by some one, and in all probability induce
a search, which would be his death.

With this thought in his mind, the next five minutes passed in great
anxiety and dread; but when about that period of time had elapsed, and he
heard no sounds of returning footsteps, he began to feel more assured, and
to think, as was highly probable, that the greater light which came from
the large lamp carried by Morgatani himself had so much obscured the dim
radiance of the one which he, the page, had left behind him as to prevent it
attracting attention.

Still he paused a little longer ere he adventured to grope along the passage towards where he had left the lamp. No sound came upon his attentive ears—not a gleam of light met his eyes.

"The monk must be gone," he said, "and I am safe."

With considerable difficulty he found his way to the staircase, and ascending carefully till he came to the door, he never, such had been the flurry and
agitation of his mind, till that moment thought that, as a matter of course,
the monk had locked it after him, and that he was equally with the unfortunate Sir Kenneth Hay, a prisoner in the dreary vaults and subterraneous
passages beneath Brandon Castle.

This supposition was a terrible one, and it no sooner darted across the
page's mind than he flung himself with a cry of terror against the door,
and found his worst fears at once verified, for it was quite fast.

This unthought of misfortune for a few moments entirely overcame
him, and he sat down on the dark staircase paralysed with dread at the
fate which seemed to be staring him in the face.

"God of Heaven!" he cried, "am I doomed to a lingering death of
starvation in this gloomy place, or to be murdered by the ruthless Morgatani?"

As he then crossed his hands upon his breast in his despair, he felt the
key of Sir Kenneth Hay's dungeon. A faint hope that he scarcely dared
dwell upon, for a moment crossed his mind that it might fit the door
which shut him out from life, light, liberty, and hope.

In a moment he rose, and feeling about nervously for the key-hole, he
made the trial. Alas! with a pang of disappointment he found the key
was much too large for the lock, and there was not the faintest hope of
release by its agency.

"Lost! lost!" cried the page. "Heaven aid me now. What but a
miracle can save me? I will even go to Sir Kenneth Hay's dungeon, and
speak to him. Companionship may rob even death of some of its gloom
and horror."

With this resolve he crept again down the staircase, and feeling his
way by the walls and doors he strove to reach the dungeon, but of all the
numerous doors that presented themselves to his touch, how was he to
decide upon which belonged to the place of confinement of Sir Kenneth Hay?

Tears nearly burst from the eyes of the page as difficulties thus each moment seemed to rise before his eyes, and the whole aspect of his adventure was so suddenly changed from the most cheering hopes of success to the greatest chances of failure and destruction.

By a great effort of mind he saved himself from sinking on the damp earth in a state of hopeless despondency, and he whispered to himself,—

"Courage—courage. Accident has produced all this great difficulty, and some unexpected accident may even yet end them."

He then thought of the small flask of wine he had with him, and taking a draught from it he felt much strengthened both in mind and body as the generous liquor warmed his blood and sent it flowing in a quicker current through his veins.

"I will not despair—I will not despair," he said. "Let the evil-intentioned abandon hope. My trust is in my cause and Heaven."

He commenced then one after another lifting off the bars that secured the dungeon-doors, feeling that such was the only means of at length finding the one which contained the unhappy knight.

After much fatigue he at length came to a door, which yielded to his touch after the bar was removed, and, with something like fresh hope springing up in his heart, he called loudly,—

"Sir Kenneth Hay—Sir Kenneth Hay!"

"Who calls?" was the low, mournful reply.

"A friend—a friend."

"Alas!—alas!—my friends are far away."

"No; not all. One is here who will be faithful to you as you can wish."

The page entered the dungeon, which, to his joy, he found was not quite dark, for a small portion of light struggled in through a grating, near the roof, on the opposite wall, which, while the monk was there with his lamp, was not discernible.

No. 33.

Coming, too, as the page did from the intense darkness of the passage, the dim light which found its way into Sir Kenneth Hay's dungeon seemed to him much more than it would have done had he emerged from daylight into it.

"Thank Heaven!" he cried, " there is not darkness everywhere."

"Who thanks Heaven here?" said Sir Kenneth. "Surely some kinder soul than I have yet seen lately is now near to me in my captivity."

"A friend is near you," said the page, as he knelt down by the side of the knight ; " one who abhors the Black Monk and his infamous designs, has, with some danger and trouble sought you out, and brings you comfort and assistance."

"The blessing of Heaven be upon you !" said Sir Kenneth.

"Rouse yourself: you have been poisoned."

"So I think—so I think."

"I know it, but by Heaven's help you shall yet recover, and defeat your enemies."

"Who are you that breathes such words of hope into my ears? Your voice is soft and musical."

"I am a young page ; but we will talk of that anon. Here, in this phial, is an antidote to the poison you have had administered to you."

"Art sure, boy ?"

"On my life. This mixture was prepared by the holy abbot of the neighbouring monastry. He brought it to Brandon himself, but ere then you had been removed by the villain, Morgatani, to this sad gloomy dungeon. Drink—drink, and you may yet be saved. Oh! drink quickly."

With what strength he was master of, the page assisted the knight to raise his head, while he placed in his trembling hand the phial containing the antidote.

"I will trust you," said Sir Kenneth, faintly. " If there be falsehood in your heart, Heaven forgive you."

"As I live, and hope for mercy hereafter," cried the page, " I come here as your friend, and wish you well."

"Enough, boy ; if you can restore me to myself by this potion, it shall be my care to show you such gratitude as shall convince you there are yet warm hearts in a world of sin, sorrow, and crime."

"There are—I know there are," said the page. " Drink—oh ! drink ; upon your strength I believe that my own fate depends."

Sir Kenneth Hay took the phial, and emptied it of its contents at a draught. He then dropped the fragile vessel on the floor of the dungeon, and a dead silence ensued, for the page was too anxious concerning the result of the antidote to speak, and the knight himself was lost in wonder at the effect that was stealing over him.

Each moment the distressing symptoms that had tormented him decreased. The deathly sickness, that made speech and movement painful to him, vanished; a sensation of renewed strength diffused itself over his frame, and, when he did speak, it was in a tone of voice so different from the weak, plaintive accents he had used before, that the page started to his feet, scarcely believing it was the same person who spoke.

"Now, Heaven be thanked !" he said, " and you, Sir Page, accept my grateful thanks, for I am myself again."

With a cry of joy the page knelt down by his side, saying,—

"Thank Heaven indeed. Blessings on the antidote which has done its work so well. Ah ! Sir Knight, speak again, that I may hear your voice in the strong accents of renewed life. Speak again."

"I am much better, although weak, and my heart throbs. It seems to me now that a few hours' sleep would quite recover me from my illness."

"Have you food here ?"

"Bread and water I see within my reach. I am very sleepy now : I think I will lie down."

To the dismay of the page a drowsiness, which he could not resist, was evidently stealing over the senses of the knight : he knew it not, but such was the intended effect of the antidote which, during the sleep which was sure to succeed it, would thoroughly recover the frame from the baneful effects of the poison which had been administered. This state of things, however, brought despair to the breast of the page, for how was he to escape from those vaults, and how long was he to wait Sir Kenneth Hay's awakening again, even should he awaken with fresh strength and renewed energies.

"Sir Kenneth Hay," he cried, "for the love of Heaven sleep not now ; Sir Kenneth Hay, awake ! awake !"

The knight heard him not. His senses were steeped in oblivion. A sound, refreshing slumber had thoroughly seized hold of every perception ; he breathed calmly and easily, but nothing that the page could do sufficed to rouse him from that deep repose.

"What will become of me now ?" cried the page, as he stood in the middle of the dungeon, with his hands clasped, and looked around him with a feeling of despair.

He had been long enough in that gloomy place to become accustomed to the dim light that came in from the high grating, and he could discern with tolerable clearness every object that was there. These consisted but of chains, some fragments of broken pitchers, and in one corner a huge mass of rusty iron, machinery which, with a shudder, the page guessed had been used in a more barbarous age for the inhuman purpose of torturing prisoners.

"Oh, that he would awaken !—oh, that he would awaken !" sighed the adventurous and generous boy ; "I shall be starved to death in these dungeons, or the monk, on his next visit, will discover me, and assuredly take my life as a punishment for my interference with his diabolical projects."

These were indeed gloomy misgivings to the boy, and for some minutes his imagination could suggest to him no possible means of escape. Then he directed his eyes to the grating which was so high above his head ; and, from the observation of it he was enabled to take, it struck him that, could he reach it, and remove it, he should be able to pass through the aperture. But how was he even to make the experiment? How could he reach it ?—and even then, could he, with the assistance only of his small poniard, remove it from its place?

Wistfully he looked at the grating, and then he felt the wall, which he found composed of stone, presenting no sort of foothold for any one to climb by. A thought, however, struck him, that could he find any pieces of iron strong enough to support his weight, and, at the same time, thin enough to be introduced between the stones, he might construct a rude flight of steps up the wall to the grating. This idea had no sooner found a place in his brain, than with fresh hope he commenced looking about him for the means of carrying it into execution. It is astonishing with what elasticity the human mind will recover from the very depths of despair, when it finds that there is something yet to try which may present even the faintest hope of a rescue from the calamitous circumstances which have reduced it to such an abyss of abandonment and sorrow. No sooner did the page feel assured of the probability of his scheme, could he find the means of carrying it into effect, than his eyes sparkled with fresh lustre, and he walked with a firm step towards the mass of machinery in the corner, which before had excited so painful notion in his heart, but which now he looked upon with eyes of hope, because he thought that from it he might succeed in wrenching some materials that would answer his purpose.

The machine was composed partly of wood and partly of iron, but the wood work was so decayed that it crumbled beneath the page's touch. With great joy he found there were abundance of long iron bolts about it which would answer his purpose well, provided they were small enough to insert between the stones.

With a palpitating heart he approached the wall to try one, and the joy he experienced when he found that the cement by which the stones had been held together readily gave way before the slightest pressure, admitting the bolt freely, can be better conceived than described.

In less than ten minutes, he had inserted several, and soon succeeded in bringing his face on a level with the grating. Holding on to one of his temporary steps with one hand, he pushed the grating with the other, when it fell with a loud splash into some water. The aperture was now free, and the page, looking through it, saw that it was nearly on a level with the waters of the moat, and looked out upon the uninhabited side of the castle.

This discovery brought a pang to his heart, for he could not swim, consequently, escape by that means would be vain.

"Lost! lost!" he cried. "Oh, what will now become of me?"

"Who speaks?" said a manly voice from the dungeon, and the page, glancing round, saw Sir Kenneth Hay gazing up at him, and wide awake.

In a moment the boy descended, and rushing to the side of the knight, said :—

"Oh, tell me you are well. Sir Kenneth Hay, bless me with the news of your recovery."

"My kind young deliverer," said the knight, "I never was better, with the exception of feeling as weak as if I had been laid up with some grievous wound."

"Rise—rise."

"I would," replied the knight, "but some scoundrel has taken the liberty of fastening a chain round my ancle, you see, and I doubt my strength to remove it."

"The villain Morgatani," cried the page, "has used you thus, after in your wine causing you to swallow some poison which completely unnerved you, taking all your faculties prisoner."

"So it seems; and now, Sir Page, if you can get into the armoury and bring me a sword, I will soon release myself."

"Alas! alas!" cried the page, "what can I do? Yet, wait, I will look again."

He then climbed up to the grating, and leaning far out, he saw a narrow shelving place, formed by the jutting out of some of the stones, which was only partially covered by water.

"Hope! hope!" he cried, and to the knight's surprise, he scrambled through the opening, and disappeared from his eyes.

CHAPTER LXI.

"——— Who is this stranger?
With a look he awes the boldest,
And directs around him like a king.
What gives him such a wond'rous power?"

AGATHA'S CONSULTATION WITH THE MONK.—FITZHUGH'S STRANGE CONDUCT AND APPREHENSIONS.—MORGATANI'S ANGER.

WHILE the young page of Fitzhugh was thus laudably endeavouring to rescue from his dungeon Sir Kenneth Hay, Agatha Weare was a prey to the most uncomfortable and alarming feelings. There was a tone and manner about the crusader who had just arrived that filled her with a dread she could not explain to herself. It seemed to her excited imagination, that in some strange manner he was doomed to be the instrument of much woe to her and Morgatani, and if ever a coming evil cast its shadow before it, it did so in this instance to Agatha Weare.

When the crusader, after defying her so haughtily, and yet, withal, so courteously, that she could not lay hold of one word which, when repeated, could be construed into a ground of complaint against him, left with the avowed intention of visiting Fitzhugh, she was in an agony of suspense to discover what could be the subject matter of his discourse to the craven knight. Before, however, she took any further measures in the business, she determined to consult with Morgatani, and rely upon his firmer mind to adopt some mode of action which should, if possible, rid Brandon Castle altogether of its most unwelcome guest.

Her immediate search for Morgatani was quite unsuccessful, for even then he was engaged in the manner we have related, and it was not until his return from the vaults of Brandon, and his interview with Sir Kenneth Hay, that Agatha found a means of communicating with him and asking his advice.

The urgency of her wish to see him, induced a ready compliance on his part, although he was weak and exhausted, in consequence of the wounds he had received in his terrible conflict with the wizard Nemoni. These wounds he hastily bound up, and saying nothing to Agatha of them, he met her as usual stern, cold, and implacable, although she was not slow to notice the unusual paleness of his countenance, nor some signs of exhausted strength which he could not help betraying.

"Can it be, Morgatani," she said, "that illness has power to assail you?"

"No, Agatha," he replied, "no—I am well and able to listen to advice, and if needs be to act."

"Hear me, then, Morgatani. There is now in Brandon one who, I fear, will give us much more trouble than Sir Kenneth Hay did."

"Indeed, Agatha! I have heard of an arrival, but have not yet seen the man."

"He defies all things and all persons," added Agatha. "He is rude of speech and stern of purpose. He declares his intention of using Brandon Castle at his pleasure, and upon my sacred word, I believe there is some secret understanding between him and our foe, Hugh Wingrove."

"Is he a soldier?"

"Ay, and if he belie not his bearing, a gallant one."

"Of rank?"

"By his arms, yes."

"And none here name him?"

"None. He preserves an impenetrable incognito. That he is some one of distinction returned from the holy wars, I can well and truly believe."

The monk mused a moment, and then said,

"Since the dismemberment of the crusaders' force, in consequence of the many dissensions between Richard Cœur de Lion, and the other chiefs, many an adventurous knight of gallant bearing, but great poverty, will in one guise or another seek again the shores of Britain."

"But the richness of his armour?"

"That may be a gift from some one of more ample resources than himself as a reward for services rendered in a battle-field. Such things are common. Nevertheless, there are few of the great crusaders unknown to me, and could I once catch a glimpse of this stranger, I think it is more than probable I can name him if he be much above the common herd of knight adventurers."

"He attempts no concealment of his face, and you can have little difficulty in seeing him. I will, however, hear from Eldred, whom I desired to watch his movements, where he now is."

Going then to the next apartment to that in which she always held her secret meetings with Morgatani, Agatha summoned an attendant, who she sent in quest of Eldred, with directions to tell him to hasten to her as quickly as possible—an order she knew the timid Eldred dared not attempt to disobey.

In a very few moments a tap upon the door announced his presence, and Agatha at once admitted him to the apartment.

When he saw the monk he gave a slight groan which he tried to carry off by an affected cough. He always dreaded some disagreeable mandate from Morgatani, and now, when the monk bent from under his shaggy brows his piercing eyes upon him, he trembled with dread.

"Where," said Morgatani, "is the stranger now but lately arrived in the castle?"

"He—he is making himself uncommonly at home. He's walking about looking at the fortifications, and ordering one thing to be altered, another to be added, a third to be taken away. Oh, he orders about like I don't know what."

"And is he obeyed?"

"Why, yes. They don't know who he is, but Hugh Wingrove pays him a deal of attention, and whatever he orders Hugh cries out for them to do it in Sir Rupert's name."

"'Tis strange."

"Well, that's my opinion, says I to myself ——"

"Peace, fool," cried Morgatani, and Eldred shrunk back, thinking to himself, "That's mighty civil, at all events. Perhaps he'll ask me to take this crusader by the collar and bring him here. I think I see me. I ain't quite an idiot."

Morgatani paced the room with long strides for some minutes, then suddenly halting opposite to Eldred, he said,

"Where is he now?"

"I don't know, upon my word, I don't know. When I saw him last he was sauntering along the eastern battlements."

"Is he armed?"

"I believe you. First of all, there's his long sword, which, in its way, is a slasher; then ——"

"Enough—enough. Would that I was not weakened as I am. Curses on that madman, or devil, be he which he may, who has made me part with so much blood. I am stiff too in my wounded arm, and unequal to a fight."

These latter words he muttered to himself, so that they were too indistinct for Agatha or Eldred to catch the full meaning of. The latter, indeed, thought that Morgatani was shrinking from encountering the stranger knight, after his description of him, and he added,

"I should say that was enough. Such a whopper as this fellow is, I never saw in all my life. Why he'd think nothing of in a moment ——"

"Another word till you are asked a question," interrupted the monk, "and I will silence your loquacity for ever as you stand before me. By the mass I would as leave hear the incessant clatter of a scarecrow."

Eldred was silent, and after a moment's pause, Morgatani added,

"Go now, at once, and tell me exactly where he is."

As Eldred reached the door and was rushing out in great haste, for he was quite willing to leave Morgatani, on any pretence or message, he ran against some one, who, with a hearty curse, nearly flung him down. A glance shewed him Fitzhugh, fully attired, but looking pale and spiritless.

"I'm sure I beg your pardon," said Eldred, "how was I to know you were coming in at the same moment that I was going out? Did I tread on your toe?"

"No matter—no matter," said Fitzhugh, as he tapped at the door.

"Who knocks?" said Agatha.

"Fitzhugh," was the reply. She then turned to Morgatani, saying,

"Will you see him? I believe he has had a visit from this new comer, and may, perchance, have come to tell us who he is."

"Admit him instantly," said the monk.

Fitzhugh was admitted, and the monk as well as Agatha could not fail of being struck by the terror that was depicted in his face. It was deathly pale, his very lips being destitute of colour, and he was trembling in every limb.

"Fitzhugh," said Morgatani, "whence arises this sad state of physical and mental weakness?"

"I was more hurt by my heavy fall," he said, in a hollow voice, "than any of you imagined. It is with difficulty I have now risen from my bed."

"I scarcely thought your fall so very heavy," said the monk, with a perceptible sneer; "but if it were, how comes it that you have left your couch?"

"I was tired of bed."

"Have you not had a visitor to-day?" asked Agatha.

"Yes," replied Fitzhugh, with visible embarrassment. "I certainly have had a visitor."

"Do you know him?"

"No—no. Do you? I was in hopes you would, by some means, have found out his name and condition."

"We know him not," said Morgatani; "I have not seen him—but it seems strange to me that you, Fitzhugh, do not recognise in him some well-known crusader. Residing as you have done so much at court, the faces of all of note must be familiar to you."

"I know him not," said Fitzhugh, "and much marvel who he can be. Do—do you communicate much with the chief of the Jesuits in London?"

"Wherefore that question?"

"Oh, nothing—nothing—it was a passing thought, believe me."

"So far as you are useful to me, and no further," muttered the monk to himself. "You will inform us what this stranger said to you on his visit to your chamber."

"Certainly. He asked me how long Sir Rupert had been gone, and threatened a visit to the Grey Turret."

"Indeed?"

"Yes; he said he loved mystery and would take it by storm, and—and—if you can assure me of his death when he does so—if you can show me his body that I may be quite certain—I can promise you honour—wealth ——"

"Honour and reward for the death of one you know not even the name of, Fitzhugh?—Pho! pho! You are not serious."

"I am—I am."

"Then you do know that this person is one, in whose destruction you, or more probably those much higher than you, have a great interest."

"Indeed no—I—I only ——"

"Peace! The lie shows itself upon your face. You do know the name of this bold stranger."

Fitzhugh trembled, as over and over again he denied his knowledge of who the crusader was, but he could plainly perceive his denial availed him nothing with the Black Monk, who wound up the matter by saying,—

"I am, myself, no stranger to the faces of the most famous of the crusaders, and when I catch a glimpse of his, I doubt not I shall be able to give him a name."

"Here is Eldred," said Agatha.

" Well, where is he?" cried Morgatani.

" In the southern gallery."

" Alone?"

" No. That great brute Bernard is with him, but ——"

The monk was gone from the room by the secret door-way, at which he always made his egress and ingress, before Eldred could add what he was going to say, which was to the effect that his, Morgatani's, seeing the crusader would be of little avai   as he had wrapped himself up in an immense cloak, which he had borrowed of Wingrove, and wore on his face a velvet mask, which effectually hid the greater portion of his features from observation.

All this, however, Eldred duly explained to Agatha and Fitzhugh, while the latter's fear seemed each moment to be on the increase.

At this instant, too, the drawbridge was heard to be hastily lowered, and Agatha flew to a window which commanded a partial view of it, when to her surprise, she saw two of the men-at-arms coming home with a prisoner of whom they kept a very tight hold.

" What can this mean," she cried ; " go, Eldred—yet no, I will go myself. This is beyond all comprehension."

She hastened to the gate and arrived just as the prisoner was admitted within the portal. He was a robust, but ruffianly-looking man, and there were blood and dust upon his face and hands.

" Hold," cried Agatha, imperiously. " What means this?"

" This," replied Wingrove, calmly, " is a prisoner, madam."

" What has he done?"

" I don't know ; but the crusader who is here desired he might be brought in as he had left him tied to a tree in the forest, and half forgotten him."

" How dare any crusader command here?"

" Mistress Agatha Weare," replied Wingrove, firmly, " nothing is more difficult to do than force people to obey what they don't like ; but nothing is easier than to command when there are willing servants."

" What mean you?"

" I mean, that for the love I bear my master, whose good friend I am convinced this crusader is, I will obey him, and cause him, as far as in my power, to be obeyed here."

" And yet you cannot name him?"

" I cannot."

" Ah! fair lady, are you here?" said the voice of the crusader, as he strode up to the gate.

Agatha turned and looked at him in surprise. He was enveloped in a large cloak, and his face was hidden by the mask Eldred had mentioned.

" I am here," she replied, " and I would that all here had an equal right."

" Ah, so do I," said the crusader ; " but some folks have impudence enough to stand in lieu of everything else."

" In truth they have, sir."

" I am delighted we agree. So, Wingrove, you have the prisoner?"

" Yes, Sir Knight. What is it your pleasure that we do with him?"

" His pleasure?" screamed Agatha.

" Yes, my pleasure," said the crusader ; " am I not a pleasant person, and is not the little mystery connected with me quite interesting in its way?"

" Insolence!"

" Well, Wingrove, just clap this knave into some secure lodging. Let him be fed. Sooner or later he must be hung, but in the meantime we will not starve him."

" Your orders shall be obeyed," said Wingrove, and to Agatha's chagrin the prisoner was forthwith dragged away.

" What has yon man done," she said, " that he should be thus treated, and Brandon Castle made his prison?"

"Brandon Castle," replied the crusader, "I fear, is made the prison of worthier subjects, and as for what he has done, why, he offended me."

"Offended you?"

"Yes, as I came through the forest; so I take the liberty, in an old friend's house you see, of locking him up."

"This insolence, from a stranger too, is quite unparalleled."

"No doubt. Madam, shall I have the pleasure of conducting you to your apartments?"

"Oh, that I were a man," said Agatha.

"By the mass, I wish you were," laughed the crusader, "for then—but no matter, I will not be uncourteous."

Agatha gave him a look of anger and hatred, and then hastily left the gate where she found she had no more real authority than if she had been a hundred miles from it.

Rage, humiliation, and mortification beset her heart, and when she reached her own chamber, she shut herself in, and gave way to a perfect storm of passion.

"Am I ever to be thus foiled," she said, "treated as a thing of no account, where I expected to rule with despotic sway? and he, too, the one being to whom I have surrendered my very soul, he seems of late more full of his own political ambition than thoughts of me! He has sworn that when he has once gratified his revenge and mine against Sir Rupert, that he will with me repair to some country where he is unknown, and, throwing off his monastic garb, make me his wife! Will he keep his word, or will he leave me here to ruin, degradation, and shame? Oh! will he keep his word?"

"Yes," said the deep tones of the monk.

Agatha started as Morgatani advanced towards her.

"Yes," he repeated. "He will keep his word, but first let his own honour

No. 34

have its vengeance, and let her, the scorned, slighted one, see him who laughed at her love laid low in the dust—then he will keep his word!"

"On your soul?"

The monk laughed bitterly as he replied,—

"Rather let me swear by my revenge, for that I know of!"

CHAPTER LXII.

"Much courage dwelt within the breast
Of that adventurous page;
A youth he was of feelings high,
An honour to his age."

THE DESCENT FROM THE BATTLEMENTS.—THE DUNGEON.—SIR KENNETH'S RESTORATION.—THE PAGE'S EXULTATION.

It was indeed a most hazardous attempt to leave the dungeon of Sir Kenneth Hay, which was made by the page, as he passed through the small aperture from which he had unmoved the grating that looked into the moat. All that he had to save him from destruction in the dark waters of the turgid stream, was the small foothold he could procure on the ledge of projecting stone-work, which was scarcely six inches in width, and sloped fearfully towards the moat.

The object, however, which that young page had in view, and his pleasure at the success that had attended the exhibition of the antidote, nerved him to the task of creeping along the narrow ledge, which he accomplished with safety, until he came to a part of the battlements which presented a flight of rugged steps, cut into the face of the wall, for the purpose of bringing water from the moat, which, in the case of Brandon Castle, was not an artificial, stagnant pool of water, but a running stream, taking its rise among the Welsh mountains, and winding through many a fertile valley, till it reached the domains of Brandon, where an artificial channel had been dug for it to induce it to surround the castle in its progress, after which it travelled on for many miles.

The sight of these steps was delightful to the page, and with renewed strength and hope he clambered up them, nor halted till he found himself on the battlements.

The part of the castle at which he found himself was as still as the grave, for it was one which had been allowed to go almost to decay, and long suits of rooms there situated had not been inhabited for many years.

The successive lords of Brandon, however, had been careful to prevent any of the external defences from suffering much from the ravages of time, and the battlements there, although overgrown with moss and creeping plants, were as capable of being defended by an adequate force as those of the front of the huge building.

"Success, success," cried the page, as he clasped his hands and glanced around him upon the sweet sylvan scene that the surrounding country presented to his enraptured gaze. "I will now proceed to the armoury, and select a weapon for Sir Kenneth Hay, which will assist him to regain the liberty of which he has been so unjustly deprived."

He then hurried along the battlements until he came to the other part of the castle, and entering a doorway, which he knew was in the direction of the armoury, he with impatient steps, and a flush of pleasure upon his face, rushed rather than ran onwards.

He soon reached the corridor, at the end of which he knew was the armoury, and he would at once have entered it had he not been accosted in his progress by the sound of voices from within it. Pausing a moment he listened attentively, and felt convinced that one of the voices belonged to El‑dred Weare, and the other to the monk.

"Will you," said Morgatani, with bitterness, "obey my commands or not?"

"I—I can't," stammered Eldred, "indeed I can't. What, I take a a sword in my hand?"

"Coward—the task I would set you on could be performed by an infant. This sword is smeared from hilt to point with a deadly poison. You have but to secrete yourself somewhere until the stranger crusader passes you, and in‑flict upon him the least wound, it will prove mortal."

"But—he—he might smash me before it had any effect upon him."

"Wretch, dare you refuse me?"

"I can't fight, and never would. Why don't you do it yourself if it's so uncommonly easy?"

"My hands are full of other matters. Moreover, why should I be the councillor of your acts, and the executor of them likewise? Take the sword."

"I daren't. Indeed I can't."

The page heard then a scuffle and a stifled cry of murder. He drew back into the recess of a window, and it was well he did so, for the next moment the door of the armoury was flung violently open, and Morgatani appeared, with the sword to which he had alluded in his hand. A bitter execration came from his lips as he strode along the corridor, and dashing open a door with his foot, he disappeared from the eyes of the page.

The youth no longer now hesitated to enter the armoury, where he found the trembling Eldred sitting on the floor with a ridiculous expression of fear depicted upon his countenance, and glaring around him like one newly awakened from a dream.

"Why, what's the matter, Master Eldred!" said the page.

"The—the matter?"

"Yes; you look scared, and your vest is torn as if you had had a fight with some one."

"I a fight! I think I see me. Certainly some one has set me down here with never such a thundering whop on the floor, but as for fighting, oh dear?"

"Who has used you thus?"

"Who? Oh, why—I don't know."

Eldred was beginning to recover from his confusion, and to see how dan‑gerous it would be to answer the questions of the page, so scrambling to his feet he said—

"I don't know anything about it. What do you want here?"

"I like to look at arms and armour, and fancy what noble deeds have been done by their assistance."

Eldred held up his hands as he left the room muttering,—

"Well, there's no accounting for tastes. I shall go and have a talk with the old cellarer; he's the only sensible and peaceable person in Brandon."

"That man," said the page, as Eldred left the room, "suffers much more from his cowardice than ever he could do by the greatest and most reckless courage. But, to my task—to my task; a sword for Sir Kenneth Hay."

He glanced round him upon the various weapons of all ages that thronged that spacious chamber, and selecting a sword which was in a plain black sheath, the hilt of which, however, was so curiously wrought as to lead him to believe such pains would not have been taken upon a worthless blade, he determined upon taking it to the knight.

He likewise selected two poniards, which he concealed about him, and con‑sidering that he had ample arms then for the knight, he hastened from the armoury, lest some one should come and question him about his appropriation of the arms.

When he reached the battlements on the side of the castle where the dungeon of Sir Kenneth Hay was situated, which he did without meeting any one, it struck him that he should never be able to descend to the grating encumbered by the sword, which was of great length and considerable weight.

The thought then crossed his mind that perhaps he had better at once speak to the crusader who had newly arrived, and leave him to complete the liberation of Sir Kenneth ; but then the pride of doing it all himself came across his mind, and, moreover, he thought that the violent measures which might be at once adopted by the crusader, would possibly defeat their object, and cause the destruction of the prisoner by the alarmed monk, before he could be rescued from his dungeon.

" No," cried the page, " I will ask no help yet. Alone I will endeavour to rescue Sir Kenneth, and should I fail I can but call other assistance."

He bethought him then that in one corner of the armoury he had seen several coils of rope lying, and at once the idea struck him that they would be eminently useful in his attempt to reach again the dungeon of the knight.

Hurrying then back to the armoury, he seized one of the coils, and once more without interruption reached the battlements. He then walked on until he came above the grating looking into the dungeon. Uncoiling the rope he fastened one end of it securely to some iron stanchions which held the topmost of the massive blocks of stone which formed the parapet of the fortifications together. Then he tied to the other extremity the sword and carefully let it down the face of the wall. He found that the rope was long enough to reach the moat, into which the sword plunged.

" This," he thought, as he swung himself down the rope, "will be an easier as well as a safer descent than by the crumbling steps which I ascended."

A few moments sufficed him to reach the grating, and he stood firmly on the narrow ledge close to the moat.

The voice of Sir Kenneth Hay immediately met his ears, crying,—
" Ho, Sir Page, is it you?"

" Yes, yes. Can you climb up and assist me into your dungeon, for I find it easier to get out than in."

" You forget I am held by the leg," said the knight. " If you can give me a weapon I can release myself."

" That can I," replied the page, and holding by the edge of the opening, he dragged up the rope till he reached the sword, which he untied from where it was fastened, and cast into the dungeon within reach of the knight.

With a feeling of joy which showed itself in his countenance, he seized the weapon, and drawing it from its sheath, he with one blow broke the chain which bound him to one of the columns that supported the roof of the dungeon, and was, comparatively, a free man.

To climb up to the opening and assist the page to enter was the work of a moment, and when they were both on the floor of the dungeon, Sir Kenneth said,—

" Thanks to you, I am well again, although not very strong. The very feel, however, of a sword seems to give me new vigour."

" Here is some wine," said the page, " I pray you drink it; it will recruit your energies."

The knight took the wine flask and drunk some of its contents, then, as he returned it to the page, he said,—

" Tell me who you are, that I may know to whom I am so much indebted?"

" I am the page of Fitzhugh."

" Ha! of that cowardly traitor ?"

" Name him not ; be satisfied with what good I have been able to do you, and—and—if your gratitude will suffice to grant me one boon, I shall be amply repaid."

" After the services you have rendered me, I surely can refuse you nothing consistent with my honour. Speak freely, boy, I am much bound to you."

" All I ask is that you will spare the life of Fitzhugh—that you will not endeavour to be avenged on him in any way for what he has done or contrived against you."

Sir Kenneth Hay was silent some moments, then he said,—

" I know not how to reconcile your own noble and courageous conduct with the interest you take in a man who possesses neither of those high qualities."

" Seek not for my reasons. All I ask of you is to forego your just revenge. As you are powerful be merciful, and for my sake do not harm him."

" It is a hard thing," said Sir Kenneth, " for a soldier like myself to make such a promise, but I cannot forget how much I owe to you, and I will here promise that if Fitzhugh gives me no new ground of offence, I will not interfere with him. My object now will be, of course, to leave Brandon Castle as early as possible, for I am charged with missions from King Richard, upon which may hang his throne and life. Shew me, Sir Page, the way from these dungeons, and rely upon my knightly word for what I have promised."

" I do, I do," said the page; " but the way from here has still to be found."

" Show me in which direction to direct the energies of my arm and sword."

" This way, then—we can now both leave this underground and dismal place much easier than I have now entered it."

" Why, truly," said the knight, " I doubt much if I could force myself through yon narrow opening."

" This way," said the page. " We will find a better passage."

He then led the knight from the dungeon, and advising him, as the darkness was most intense in the outer passage, to place his hand upon his shoulder and follow him closely, he conducted Sir Kenneth to the staircase which led to the door that shut them within those gloomy precincts.

" Ascend carefully," said the page. " At the summit of these stairs is a door which you will have to force. I believe it is the only one which stands between us and liberty, but it has been locked by the Black Monk."

" It seems of wood merely," said Sir Kenneth Hay. " I pray you stand some steps lower, Master Page, or I may give you, to my great regret, an unintentional blow with my sword, which I shall use against this door."

The page quickly retreated to the foot of the stairs, and then Sir Kenneth Hay dealt the door such a blow with the sword, that it at once dashed through the thick panelling. Another and another followed in quick succession, until a large piece of the woodwork fell out, leaving space enough for the page, but not the knight, to get through.

All was darkness, for the light had long since expired which the page had left on the other side of the door.

" Wait yet a moment," said Sir Kenneth, and seizing the door, he at length tore it from its hinges. The way was free, and the page sprung up the staircase, saying,—

" Follow me now, and I will lead you to life and liberty."

Carefully then feeling his way, he led the knight along the passage until they reached the iron steps which terminated at the tomb of Sir Montague Brandon, in the chapel. Without a light, to touch the proper spring that would cause the iron plate to open, was a task of some difficulty, and it took several minutes ere the page could do so. At length the plate descended. A flood of light burst upon the gaze of Sir Kenneth Hay, and springing on to the chapel's marble floor, he said, in a voice of exultation,—

"Thank Heaven, I am free again! and the cause of King Richard is not lost."

"Use your freedom cautiously," said the page, "and remember your promise to me."

"Be assured I will not forget it; and now, Sir **Page**, do me one favour more. Go to Hugh Wingrove, and bid him come here to me at once, for I must leave Brandon as quickly as may be on business of the highest import."

"It shall be done," said the page, and he, with a quick light step, glided from the chapel.

CHAPTER XLIII.

THE CRUSADER.—THE MYSTERY.—SIR KENNETH'S JOY.—THE DISAPPOINTMENT OF THE MONK.—THE MISSION TO LONDON.

> "What joy it was again to feel
> The balmy, sunny air—
> What joy to look on Nature's face,
> So beautiful and fair."

THE page thought the shortest way to find the crusader would be to proceed at once to the guard-room, and ask Wingrove where he was to be found. He accordingly made what speed he could to that part of the castle, and his light step and sparkling eye—for he was indeed delighted at saving Sir Kenneth Hay from the fate which otherwise, in all human probability, would have befallen him—at once gave token that he was more than usually delighted.

"Well, Sir Page," said Wingrove, "you seem much pleased; may we ask what has given your spirits such a hoist to-day?"

"Oh," said Bernard, "the kitchen-maid has smiled on him, or the cook has offered him a greasy sop whenever he may think proper to come to the kitchen."

"No, good Bernard," said the page, "you have not guessed rightly; and I can only attribute your lack of wit to the want of faith the cellarer has had in you to-day. You are like an ale barrel, potent and strong when full, but when empty as hollow and worthless as can possibly be. Good Bernard, rub up your wit again, unless, as I much suspect, it be past scouring."

"Oh, bother you," said Wingrove, "I ain't a magpie, and therefore would never attempt a war of words with a page. I am thirsty, though."

"Ah, so I thought. A word with you, good Master Wingrove."

"What would you say to me, boy?"

The page drew him aside, and said,

"Follow me, Wingrove; you will not repent your pains. Quickly follow me."

"But where?"

"To the chapel—to the chapel. There is one there you will be as glad to see as though he had risen from the dead. Follow—follow."

' So saying, and without waiting for further questioning, the page hurried away. Hugh Wingrove was not one who considered long about anything, and wondering to himself what the page could mean, he went after him, with quick strides, towards the chapel. If the old soldier had for one moment surmised the agreeable surprise that awaited him when he reached there, he would have gone at a much quicker pace than he did, but the idea of any such pleasure as meeting with Sir Kenneth Hay there never for one moment crossed his mind.

When he reached the chapel he was met by the page, who had advanced some paces towards the door.

"Hugh Wingrove," he said, "I wish to introduce to you a friend of mine."

"A friend of yours? Who mean you? I tell you, boy, it is unseemly of you to jest with one so much your senior as I am."

"Nay, I do not jest—I am perfectly serious. Come this way, good Wingrove, and you shall be convinced that I have conjured up a welcome spirit."

"A spirit?"

"Yes—from the vaults of Brandon Castle."

"Whence he is right glad to escape," said Sir Kenneth Hay, suddenly advancing towards the astonished Wingrove. "How dost thou, my honest friend?"

Wingrove gazed for a moment on the knight with much astonishment; he could scarcely believe the evidence of his own eyes.

"Are—are you really Sir Kenneth Hay?" he gasped.

"As real as ever I was."

"God bless you, Sir Knight. Where have you been?—who spirited you away?—how did you get back?—where ——"

"One question at a time, good Wingrove. I have been in a dungeon beneath this abominable castle—I was spirited away by Morgatani, the Black Monk—I have come back through the gallantry and unaided courage of this young page, to whom I owe my life."

Wingrove turned to the page, and grasping both his hands, gave him such a shake as nearly dislocated his shoulders.

"You shall be a soldier, boy," he cried, "and a gallant one you will become. By Heavens, I long to see a beard upon your smooth chin."

"Thank you," said the page; "I am not ambitious, and yet ——"

"Yet what?" said Sir Kenneth, noticing the sudden dejection of the page's face, tone, and manner.

"No matter, sir—no matter; we all have our griefs; some only are more hidden than others; some admit of kindly sympathy, while some must needs remain in the heart's inmost core until it breaks."

"You have a grief," added the knight, "of no common order. I am at present on service connected vitally with the life of King Richard, and the future welfare of this great country. When I have discharged faithfully the missions with which I am entrusted, you shall command me, and woe be to them who have done you wrong."

The page answered by a deep sigh, and then he said, with an effort at self-composure—

"May fame and fortune attend you, and the cause you espouse. Heed not me and my private griefs."

"What will be your first step now?"

"I must proceed to London."

"To London?" said Wingrove.

"Yes—on service of the king. His liberation from a foreign prison may depend upon my exertions."

Hugh Wingrove looked at the page for a moment with an air of confusion, and twice he opened his lips to speak, but said nothing, while Sir Kenneth Hay looked surprised at his strange emotion. In a moment more he said,—

"Sir Page, pardon me, that I dare not say before you what I now wish to say to Sir Kenneth Hay, but it is no secret of my own; if it were, I would trust it to your keeping with all my heart and soul."

"I will retire," said the page.

"Nay, if Sir Kenneth will step aside with me a moment."

The knight did so, and said,—

"What mystery is this, Wingrove?"

"Incline your ear."

Wingrove whispered something to the knight, which made him give such an extraordinary jump, that the page thought him stricken with some sudden frenzy.

"You—you cannot mean what you say?" he cried.

"'Tis true," said Wingrove. "On my soul, 'tis true."

"Thank Heaven, then. My young friend, excuse me now—I will seek you again soon, but—but—I don't know just now if I am on my head or my heels. Hurrah! hurrah!"

So saying, the knight who seemed suddenly transformed from a tolerably discreet individual to a maniac, rushed from the chapel, closely followed by Wingrove, who seemed as much pleased as Sir Kenneth.

"Well," said the page, "this is extraordinary. What can be the meaning of it all? he will seek me me again soon. So be it, but I need not wait in this cold chapel for him."

The page had scarcely made this determination, than he heard the creaking of a door, and instinctively hiding himself, he saw Morgatani enter the sacred building.

In his hand was a lamp, while slung upon his arm he carried a basket of provisions. That he was going again to the dungeon where he believed Sir Kenneth Hay to be confined, the page had no doubt, and if he had had any, they would have been dispelled by the mutterings of the monk himself.

"He shall live another day," he said. "Yes, another day, during which I will terrify him by what he shall consider as supernatural sights and sounds. By so doing, I may so far weaken his mind, for terror plays strange havoc with the brain, as to wring from him the information I require, and which is of so much importance to King John, and the cause of my order."

The page could not refrain from a smile, as he thought of the deep disappointment Morgatani would experience, and the impotent rage he would be in, when he discovered that his prisoner had escaped him.

He waited until the monk had fairly left the chapel, and then he commenced an examination of the secret door, through which he had now twice seen him pass; but so very artfully concealed were the means of opening it, that the page could by no means discover them, and after noting the spot well, he left the chapel.

As he did so, he heard the sound of many voices towards the postern gate, and hurrying thither, he heard that on the opposite side of the moat was a minstrel, who craved admission into the castle, and the hospitality of its owners. Ever and anon he struck a few wild but sweetly melodious chords upon the small harp he carried. The men-at-arms were nothing loth to admit him, but they dared not lower the drawbridge without orders, so one of them went in search of Wingrove, while another called loudly across the moat,—

"Tarry awhile, minstrel, and you shall be admitted. We but wait regular orders."

When Wingrove came, he was accompanied by the crusader, who still wore the mysterious mask upon his face, and kept himself enveloped in the capacious mantle lent him by Wingrove.

The moment he heard a few tones from the minstrel's harp, he cried,

"Thank Heaven, 'tis he. Admit him instantly."

The drawbridge was lowered, and in a few moments the wanderer made his appearance. He was strikingly handsome, but much bronzed by foreign travel. The moment his eyes fell upon the crusader, a cry of joy escaped him, but what he would have said or done was stopped by the nameless knight saying,—

"I am nameless."

The minstrel bowed, and then struck a lively measure from his harp, while his eyes sparkled with joy.

"I leave him," whispered the crusader, to Wingrove, "in your care; treat him with special kindness."

"It shall be done."

"I will be with you in the guard-room anon, but I have still something further to say to Sir Kenneth Hay."

The crusader then strode away, while the minstrel, who appeared in the highest spirits, said, as he entered the guard-room,—

"Well, soldiers, shall I sing you a merry lay, or tell you a tale of chivalry?"

"Are you thirsty?" said Bernard.

"Methinks I could help to drink a flagon of good old English ale."

"Then hang me if you ain't a good fellow, and I'll go and get it. Eh, Wingrove?"

No. 35

" Well, well, go and get a couple of flagons."

Bernard soon executed his message, and returned with the two flagons, and a message from the old cellarer, to the effect that he would draw no more that night for any one whatever.

The minstrel laughed as he swept his hand over the strings of his harp and said,—

" I can tell you something of this very castle that will amuse you, if you are inclined to listen to it. It has the two merits of interest and brevity."

" By all means," said the guard with one voice, and the minstrel commenced thus :—

" This castle of Brandon, as you all know, stands on a rock, the base of which is washed by the stream which gives the castle its name, and at that time served as a barrier to the Welsh, who often made inroads into the fertile vales of Shropshire and Salop. These fierce borderers, for such they were, seldom remained long at peace, even with a powerful neighbour— for a short peace was sufficient either to give them disgust at inaction, or their restless habits made them bad cultivators of the earth, and want often drove them to deeds of daring.

" The Welsh had, not long before the return of the noble castellan, Sir Huge de Bracy, from Palestine, made a hot and fierce excursion into the country, and laid waste with fire and sword all that were too weak to defy their hordes ; and this comprised all those who had not time to shut themselves up in stone walls, and trust to the chance of repelling violent assault, for there was little else to be feared, as they had no means of assailing save with such weapons as naked men bear. They usually rushed on with resistless impetuosity as well as in countless numbers.

" Did they besiege a place, it turned to a mere blockade ; and could they not take it by sudden escalade and assault, they were in their turn usually surprised by the cavalry of the Lords Marches, and fell by thousands—the chief duty of the defenders of the castle being therefore to guard against a surprise, as their incursions were very sudden and often in the night.

" The castle of Brandon was one of importance, as its garrison had often checked the advances of the Welsh ; because, if the Welshman penetrated far, he would, on his retreat, have to encounter the castellan, loaded and encumbered with spoil, and, as it often happened, with diminished forces ; while his enemy would have collected more force, and sally out and cut them off.

" For this reason the castle was constantly well guarded, and the walls manned with a sufficient body of men. But now it was a scene of festive enjoyment—the wine-cup was replenished, and the toast went round with more frequency than was usually permitted in a place so situated, where men where liable to be called on for instant service.

" Sir Hugo de Bracy had not many days returned to his castle, and rejoicings were continued among the soldiery as long as there was the shade of an excuse, or indeed as long as they could obtain liquor. With Sir Hugo had returned a number of the vassals who had followed him to the holy wars, and it was between these returned warriors and those who had been left behind, that these repeated carousals took place.

" The guard were about to be turned out, when one of the crusaders said to one of his companions,—

" ' It will be a dreary night for watch and ward. I am glad I have not to be walking the battlements such a night as this is.'

" ' Your turn will come soon,' replied his comrade. ' Sir Hugo will not long grant you a holiday from duty. In fairness you ought to have relieved us from a duty we have been doing for many years ; it would be a novelty for you.'

" ' Ha ! ha ! ha !' shouted the crusader—' you talk finely. Pray who should be exempt but he who had been made so by his valour, he who has helped to recover the Holy Sepulchre—who else, indeed ?'

" ' A fine thing you have done, old comrade, when you have it ; but you have not even done so, for it remains in the same hands. What say you to that ?'

" ' Why, friend, my answer is, that it is no fault of ours that a peace was agreed upon between the parties just as we should have taken it, had we won another battle.'

" ' Had you won another battle !—but listen to a traveller, and you shall hear strange tales,' replied the third soldier, as he left the guard-room in company of those who had to relieve the guard upon the walls.

" These soon entered the guard-room, and sat down to their meal in company. After that they all drew round a blazing fire, when they began to converse over all that had occurred since the departure of their master, Sir Hugo, and his return, while the crusaders, as those were termed who had been to the holy war, in distinction from such as remained at home, related their adventures, both by flood and field, until the time came for their retirement to their quarters.

" Morning frequently surprised these veterans who had spent the time allotted to rest in revelry.

" The wind whistled round the embattlements and towers as the evening set in, while the rain could be heard driving against the windows, rendering the warm room more comfortable by the contrast afforded without.

" A few anecdotes were related by the men one to another, and there was a jocund laugh against one of the returned soldiers for something for which the remainder could not account.

" ' What was that you were talking about just now ?' said a crusader, as he quaffed his flagon.

" ' Roul says that his family is increased since his absence,' was the reply.

" ' What !—that is nothing new in the life of a crusader,' returned one of the relieved guard, who felt jealous of the importance his traveller comrades assumed.

" ' How so ?' inquired the man. ' Are all women turned false, then, as well as men who stay at home to play the traitor ?'

" ' Well, you shall judge ; there's Roul, he leaves his wife and two children, and follows my lord to the holy wars ; well, his dame becomes disconsolate, and is, in fact, a widow and her children fatherless. I will say nothing of what the soldiers of the cross do on the road—all sins then being forgiven ; but when Roul returns, he finds that instead of two children she has four.'

" ' A miracle ! a miracle !' exclaimed the soldiers, with a burst of laughter.

" ' And that is what you must teach old Roul, but he is not patient, for he is swearing at his spouse all day long, and she trying her utmost to persuade him that his memory has failed him and he cannot recollect how many he had before he left.'

" ' Ha—ha—ha !' shouted a chorus of voices.

" ' What can a man do ?' inquired a burly fellow who had followed the cross. ' He cannot please God and a woman too ; it's a plain impossibility.'

" ' True, comrade, all women are not so many Edith Mortimers.'

" ' No, you may say that truly, comrade, she was a jewel of price, which none but a crusader should wear, and such as we shall never see again.'

" ' Who was Edith Mortimer ?' exclaimed a dozen tongues in the same breath.

" 'A heroine,' replied the crusader ; 'but it is a long tale, and the wine pot is low, I pray you fill it. I could never abide a good tale and an empty flagon in all my life.'

" ' I readily believe that, for thou couldst always drink thy share, but now thou art not content with less than a week's consumption at once ;' so saying, the man arose and proceeded with a large vessel to obtain a fresh supply of the required liquor, with which he presently returned, saying, as he set it down,

" ' You had best draw it slowly, for the cellarman says there will be no more after this.'

" ' He must broach another cask when this is gone ; but go on with thy tale, crusader, about Edith Mortimer.'

" 'Oh, ay,' said the crusader, as he drew near the fire, which some had heaped up with fresh fuel, and all had seated themselves in a semi-circle and disposed themselves to listen. 'Well, then, this Edith Mortimer came of the celebrated family of that name, which you all know well.'

" 'Yes, yes,' replied his auditors.

" Well then, Edith Mortimer was as beautiful as she was illustrious, and one day while enjoying the freshness of spring, around her father's castle, she left the bounds and entered the forest in search of wild flowers, which were then scarce, and in the ardour of her pursuit she became bewildered and unable to return. For some time she endeavoured to find the path, but these endeavours only seemed to involve her the more in uncertainty and doubt ; but amongst her wanderings she came to an old fort or tower, which had fallen to decay for many ages, for trees grew upon the spot where the defences once stood, and plants throve upon its walls, as climbing plants overrun the whole spot.

"Thinking there might be some means of telling where she was if she could mount the roof and look towards the castle she had left, she tried to push aside an old door, but she was startled to hear voices within. She would have remained concealed, but her attempt to open the door had been noticed, and one of the robbers, for such they were, rushed to the door and opened it, and on seeing nobody but Edith, uttered horrid imprecations ; he called his comrades, saying to them,

" 'Here's a prize for us ! but she must not be allowed to escape.'

" Poor Edith stayed not to hear this, it was borne after her on the gale, for she instantly took to flight ; where she went she knew not, but onward she flew and could hear the heavy tread of her pursuers as they followed her light and rapid footsteps, with which she strove in vain to distance the robbers, who were, however, too swift and better able to endure the fatigue of the chase than she was.

" She was overtaken and roughly seized. She begged for mercy, to which the fellows replied, that they would not hurt such a pretty chick as she was, but as she had once seen their hiding-place, she must for security's sake become an inmate, and besides she would grace their festive board, and be a handsome mistress for the captain ; such being the case, she need not fear anything, as she would have mercies enough shewn her presently.

" Terrified at this picture of misery and dishonour, she screamed out, upon which they laughed, and were cramming a kerchief into her throat to prevent her from making a noise, for they were now in the open road. While they did this they were assailed by a single knight, who rode along and came upon them unawares ; perceiving they had but one man to deal with, they turned round and attacked him with great vigour, but the knight being on horseback and encased in massive armour, their blows for the most part fell harmless, while the knight's heavy falchion cut through steel-cap, breast-plate, and armlets, as if they had been so much pasteboard, and no less than four of their fellows lay dead on the green sward. Terrified at such unequal strength and skill, those who remained, though eight or nine in number, fled for their lives and escaped.

" The knight, without speaking or dismounting, offered his foot for the lady to mount by; she immediately stepped lightly on it, and was in front on the saddle. She was scarcely there ere the outlaws returned, and reinforced by numbers meditated an attack, but the knight spurred his good horse and was speedily beyond their reach.

" ' Whether would you go, damsel ?' inquired the knight, after a quarter of an hour's gallop, but in a faint voice.

" ' To yonder castle,' she answered, pointing to the stately edifice which now rose to their view. ' I am a Mortimer, and well shall this deed be repaid by those who love me.'

" ' The deed is its own reward; to have served you, lady, is happiness enough.'

" ' I fear you are hurt, Sir Knight,' said Edith, but before he could reply, they were met by her father, the earl, who, alarmed at the unusual absence of his daughter, caused his followers to mount and ride in search of her. When Edith alighted and flew into her father's arms, she saw her dress was covered with blood, and that the knight could scarcely sit in his saddle from faintness. He was immediately borne to the castle and his wounds attended to.

" They were found to be not dangerous, but he was weak from loss of blood, and after a time he recovered from his wounds, and expressed his intention of serving in the holy wars; before he left, Edith sought him out, presented him with a ring and chain of gold of great value as a remembrancer, which were received by the knight with great reverence, and he swore to keep it for the donor's sake. The Lady Edith saw there was much dejection in the knight's manner, he sighed often, and she often caught him gazing upon her. Edith sighed too, but thought the knight was poor, and inquired how it was he had no 'squire and page. He was too poor to offer any advantage to induce any one to offer themselves, and he was too proud to solicit.

" Edith promised that, three days after his departure, she would send him a youth, well nurtured, whom he was to use well for her sake. Before the knight left the castle, he could not refrain from divulging his love for Edith : the interview was a long one, and the moment which made them happy in each other's love, saw them separate for years—perhaps for ever.

" On the third day, at the appointed place, the knight was met by his page, whom he saw possessed the token; he led a sumpter horse with a beautiful suit of mail, of the best Milan steel. The page was beautiful and expert, and in the course of his travels more than once saved the knight's life by his watchfulness and care, which seemed never to tire, though the knight gave him but little trouble, and behaved to him with more than the ordinary kindness of a master. They would often converse together, and the subject of their conversation was usually the Lady Edith. The knight had fought hard for three years in Palestine, when a peace was concluded between the powers, and the knight prepared to return to England.

" On their road home they were wrecked on the coast of Sicily. The knight escaped with little hurt, but not so his 'squire, who was nearly killed—and when he recovered from the effects of his wounds fell into a fever, when it was discovered that the page, or 'squire, was a woman—a lovely, blooming woman. Greatly astonished at the discovery, when she was well enough to rise the knight was introduced to her, and he at once recognized Edith Mortimer.

"Yes, it was Edith—when she heard that her knight was poor and would encounter the perils of a long and toilsome journey, she determined to share it with him. For that purpose she disguised herself, and used the stratagem related. When she related all the motives which induced her to act so, she threw herself at the knight's feet, and asked if she had forfeited his good opinion.

"'No, fair Edith; but are you willing to wed a nameless stranger, and a poor one to boot, and anger your family?'

"'I would not have done all I have if I would not do so.'

"'Your love and devotion deserve its own reward. I am not what you see me, but a belted baron. I made this pilgrimage under a vow, and left my father's hall unattended—and, if I hear rightly, death has deprived me of a parent, but it has made me the Baron of Faversham and lord of many acres.'

"The joy of Edith was great, for well she knew that he was an ally of her father; they were wedded immediately, and the favour of the good knight, and the beauty and virtue of his lady, were well known in their day.

"The speaker ceased, and casting his eye on the almost empty flagon, poured out the remainder, and having drank it, he said in a lugubrious tone—

"'Since the flagon holds out no longer, and we can get no more, unless we assault the cellar, I shall turn in till the sun again thaws the heart of the cellarer.'

"This speech was commended by all, and the guard-room fire was deserted by all except such as who were by duty bound to stay there, till the watch was relieved on the following morning at sunrise."

"All cellarars are alike," remarked Bernard, "and a more flinty-hearted wretch than ours don't exist."

CHAPTER XLIV.

—— This mystery is terrible.
Let him declare himself in any shape,
He will relieve my fainting heart, for now
'Tis full of dread.   OLD PLAY.

THE MEETING WITH FITZHUGH.—SIR KENNETH'S AMAZEMENT.—THE SUDDEN DEPARTURE FROM BRANDON.

BERNARD had hardly done speaking, when the crusader himself entered the guard-room, with the free, joyous, careless manner which was so strikingly manifest in all his actions.

"Good wishes to you all, brother soldiers," he said; "don't let me disturb you, I merely wish to say a word to Wingrove."

Wingrove, who had risen when the crusader entered the guard-room, now advanced towards him, and with a marked deference that quite astonished the men-at-arms, for they were more accustomed to see Hugh Wingrove behave rather roughly than otherwise, he advanced to the knight, saying—

"I am ready, sir, to obey you."

"Why, all I want, good Wingrove, is a flagon of ale, and ——"

"Ale!" shouted Bernard. "Ale—good God, how very odd, I want some ale myself."

A roar of laughter, in which the crusader heartily joined, followed this speech of Bernard's, and Anstey cried—

"How very odd that Bernard should want some ale. Did any of you ever hear of such a thing before?"

"Oh, no, never—never," cried the merry soldiers, while Bernard stood rather discomfited, not knowing what to say or do to ward off the laughter that had arisen at his expense.

In vain Wingrove tried for some time to make his voice heard, and at length succeeding, he said—

"Go one of you instantly to the cellarer, and bring some of the best. Yet stay a moment; get Sir Rupert's large silver tankard that is in the oaken parlour."

"What," said Bernard, "the—the tankard King Richard—bless him for a hard fighter—gave Sir Rupert? Why, I've heard him say a hundred times, that nobody but himself or the king should ever drink out of it, and besides ——"

"Go along," said Wingrove, giving him a not very gentle push. "Do as you are bid, you great calf."

"Hold," said the crusader, "I am but a soldier, and a very poor one now. Let me have my ale from one of these earthen vessels."

"No, no," said Wingrove, and as Bernard still lingered, he seized one of the jugs the crusader had alluded to, and holding it in a threatening attitude, added—

"Will you go?"

"I'm going, but wonders will never cease," said Bernard; "however, so long as ale is going, it's all one to me."

"I want you likewise, Wingrove," said the crusader, "to bring refreshments to the room I occupy here."

"Certainly," said Wingrove; "all that the castle affords is at your service. Here, Anstey, go to the monastery, and ask them if they have any rare confections, or a good fat haunch, they can send us. Quick—quick."

The crusader smiled, as he said—

"For myself I would not give so much trouble, but I have a friend whose health wants recruiting, and his appetite a little pampering, perhaps."

"Well, I'm sure," thought Anstey, "here's a bustle. However, this crusader, be he who he may, is a gallant-looking fellow, and as civil as needs be withall, so I'll go willingly."

"Here's the ale," cried Bernard, appearing suddenly, "but Mistress Agatha says she'll see us all d——d, no, I don't mean that, but she won't let me have the tankard."

"She shall," cried Wingrove.

"Since it has been asked for," said the knight, "I likewise say she shall. Tell me where it is?"

"In the oaken parlour."

"I'm as wise as before. Where is that?"

"This way," said Joyce Evans, drawing his long legs from under the table; "I'll show you—I like a row—I don't like Agatha Weare."

"Special reasons, truly," laughed the crusader; "but while I am here I have a special objection to Mistress Agatha Weare having her own way in anything, so the tankard I mean to have, whether she be agreeable or not."

"Where are you going, Anstey?" said Bernard.

"To the monastery, to borrow a haunch of venison."

"Bless me, you don't like going out in the evening. Let me go, will you?"

"Why?"

"Why—why the monks have some famous ale, and they always offer a fellow as much as he likes to drink."

"I know it," said Anstey, "so I mean to go myself."

Bernard looked very much annoyed, but he said no more, for he comforted himself, that as Anstey was gone, he should, in all probability, come in for an extra draught of the flagon of ale ordered for the crusader.

While this little dialogue was proceeding, the crusader, accompanied by Joyce Evans, who had volunteered to show him the way, proceeded to the oaken parlour, where was the silver cup in dispute.

"Knock," he said briefly, when he reached it, and the bluff soldier gave a kick against the lower panel, that nearly split it into a hundred pieces.

Agatha was startled at so clamorous a summons for admission, and she had scarcely courage to say, "Come in." The moment she had done so, the crusader entered, and casting his eyes round the room, he said—

"I have come for a silver cup."

"Insolent braggart," cried Agatha. "You shall not have it. How dare you ——"

"Madam," interrupted the crusader, "in one word, I dare anything and everything. I am here, and I mean to make myself quite at home."

"Hurrah," cried the man-at-arms, who was in an extacy of delight.

"Ruffian! robber!" cried Agatha.

"The cup—the cup," said the crusader.

"You shall not have it—as I live you shall not have it. Dare to force it from my keeping, and I will summon aid to force you from Brandon as a lawless plunderer, such as I believe you are."

"You may summon who you please," growled Joyce Evans, "but they won't come. Ho! ho! ho!"

"Peace—peace!" said the crusader. "Where is the cup?"

He watched the direction of Agatha's eyes, and saw them turn to a cupboard which occupied one corner of the apartment. Guessing, then, immediately that the silver tankard was there, he, with one kick, knocked the door in, seized the object he sought, which was just within, and left the room before Agatha could recover from her rage and surprise.

As for Joyce Evans, he kept stopping every half dozen paces, as he went back to the guard-room, to laugh, until the crusader gave him a tap on the skull with the edge of the tankard, at the same time saying,—

"Be quiet. You are big enough to know better;" when Joyce Evans admitted that he was, and strove to smother his laughter, which made him look as if he were blowing a trumpet, and could not leave off on any account.

The guard-room was soon gained, and the crusader, having drunk a health to all, beckoned to Wingrove to follow him, which the honest soldier did with a celerity which showed how cheerfully he obeyed the command.

When they were some distance from the guard-room, the crusader turned and said,—

"This night, at twelve, procure a good horse."

"Sir Kenneth's steed is in the stable," said Wingrove.

"'Tis well. Let it be ready at twelve to-night, for then Sir Kenneth will leave here for London on business of the first importance, I hope, to all of us."

"I am sure of it," said Wingrove.

"Be secret and faithful. Now, fetch Fitzhugh to me here—I would speak with him."

Wingrove at once went in search of the cowardly Fitzhugh, who quickly made his appearance, betraying by his trembling the great dread in which he held the stalwart and mysterious crusader.

"Approach," said the latter, in a very different tone to that in which he usually spoke.

Fitzhugh came close to him with a cringing gait and manner. He seemed scarcely able to lift his eyes to the face of his questioner, and a more strik-

ing contrast could not have been found than was presented by the different bearing of those two men.

"Have you done as I desired?" said the crusader, with much coldness and hauteur.

"I have endeavoured," murmured Fitzhugh; "but the monk is a man of much craft, and I cannot procure information from him."

"Now, by the mass!" cried the crusader, "I much suspect you of double dealing."

"No—no—on my word."

"Your word?"

"On my hopes hereafter, I swear I have done my utmost. Indeed, you may believe me. You have spared my life, gracious sir, and how can I be too grateful? The answer Morgatani made to my questions was to load me with invective, and told me broadly that he suspected my faith towards him and his cause."

"These crafty Jesuits," muttered the crusader, as he paced to and fro for some moments, "are at the bottom of all evil. Could I but once convict them of a political act of importance; but no matter—no matter. This poor, cringing fool Fitzhugh has, I believe, done his best. Sir Kenneth Hay must to London to-night, and be active in the cause."

"Can I do anything more?" murmured Fitzhugh, in a subdued tone.

"No," said the crusader; "but you will remain here, and be cautious, or your life shall pay the forfeit. Wingrove, send a cloth-yard shaft through him if he attempts to leave the castle."

"It shall be done," said Wingrove.

"Mercy—mercy! spare me!" said Fitzhugh, dropping on his knees, and looking the picture of terror.

"Coward!" said the crusader, "your life is in your own hands. You

No. 36

may preserve it, or you may forfeit it.   Oh! Fitzhugh, does not even your heart cry shame upon you for your conduct towards me?   Had I such reflections as you must have, by the Heaven above me I would not live another hour so abject in my own esteem."

Fitzhugh groaned, and either really was, or affected to be, very much distressed, for he leaned his head upon his hands, and would not look up till Wingrove and the knight had walked away.   Then he slowly rose, and with faltering steps sought his own chamber, when he threw himself on the bed, quite ill from intense terror and excitement.

The crusader and Wingrove proceeded to the chamber in which Sir Kenneth Hay was reposing, for although the antidote had removed all the real effects of the narcotic poison from his system, it could not suddenly replace him in the same state of health he had been in previously, and the long toilsome journey he had to take at night made it most desirable that he should recruit his strength as much as possible.

He was sleeping when they reached the room, but the sound of their steps awakened him.

"Now beshrew me," said the crusader, "but I ought to have known better than to have awakened you, Hay.   Sleep will do you as much good as food."

"I think the pleasure of seeing you safe and well," replied Sir Kenneth Hay, "does me more good than either.   I feel quite a new man again."

"Think you you can undertake the journey to London to-night?"

"Assuredly."

"Then all will be ready for you at twelve; but you know, even in all circumstances, I am fond of a little bit of malicious sport with those who have behaved badly.   Now, what I want you to do, Hay, is to attire yourself just as you were when Mistress Agatha Weare and her friend the monk put you in that uncomfortable apartment under the moat, and walk to her room.   Just look in, and assume as ghastly an appearance as you can.   By Heavens! she deserves a fright."

"I will do so," said Sir Kenneth; "and I should be glad if Morgatani were there."

"That should not I," remarked the crusader, "for I cannot spare either you or him just now.   You will be useful to me as a friend on whom I can rely.   He, though an enemy, I will make useful, for, sooner or later, I expect he will do something to compromise the heads of the Jesuits in London."

"But I only want to alarm him."

The crusader shook his head as he said,—

"Don't deceive yourself, Hay.   These monks are not easily alarmed by supernatural matters.   They use such weapons to terrify the vulgar, but they have no faith in them themselves.   Do you rest until I come to you again, and as soon as may be you will have a good meal brought to you."

"Our messenger to the monastery will soon return," said Wingrove.

"One thing I would say," remarked Sir Kenneth to the crusader, "before you now leave me.   It is concerning the page of Fitzhugh, to whose courage and noble perseverance I owe my life.   Will you protect him for my sake?"

"I will.   He shall have no cause to repent of his residence in Brandon Castle, or to regret making the acquaintances he has made while here. He's a noble little fellow; but he looks weakly and delicate.   I'm afraid he will never be strong enough for a knight; but should he, you may depend upon my care of him and his future fortunes."

"I thank you from my heart."

."Now, Wingrove," added the crusader, turning to the old soldier, who stood at a respectful distance, "I have some letters and other matters of importance to write before Sir Kenneth goes from here. Can you place me in some room where I shall be free from interruption?"

"Most certainly. You shall have Sir Rupert's own room, and I will place a sentinel at the door."

"Aye, do so; that will be a good arrangement. Farewell, Hay, till a little before midnight."

"Farewell, and Heaven bless and prosper you," said Sir Kenneth, with fervour and animation.

In the course of a quarter of an hour the crusader was snugly ensconced in Sir Rupert's room, with the huge, bulky form of Bernard fully armed at the door, he having orders to allow no one to enter the room on any pretence.

"Well," thought Bernard, "this must be somebody, or old Wingrove would never have put me on duty here. I don't care, however, who he is, so long as I know what he is, and that he is a brave, big, strong fellow, who don't object to a glass of ale. I should like to know who he is, though. Bless us, here's some one coming. Now what a pleasant relief it would be if some one would come and try to force my post. I'd stand a gallon of ale to any one who would make a row with me."

To Bernard's great disappointment, the approaching figure turned out to be the pacific Eldred.

<hr>

CHAPTER XLV.

Such superstitious terrors haunt the guilty soul,
That trifles bring despair, and what to purer hearts
Resolves itself to simple wonder, is to them
Brim full of terrors!—FARQUHAR.

THE DEPARTURE.—AGATHA'S FRIGHT.—MEETING WITH THE WIZARD.

BERNARD drew himself up exactly in the doorway as Eldred Weare approached his post, and more with a view of frightening him, than because he thought it part of his duty, he cried suddenly,—

"Who goes there?"

"Lor, bless me," said Eldred, giving a start of terror. "It's me. What makes you call out in that way?"

"Stand."

"Well, I am—what's the matter?"

"My orders here are, to take charge of all persons who try to force my post. Now Master Eldred Weare, do you like ale?"

"Yes, moderately."

"Then if you will make a disturbance I will treat you to a gallon."

"I make a disturbance? I wouldn't make a disturbance for a whole cask of ale, not I."

"You wouldn't?"

"No, to be sure."

"Then you may pass on, for I don't want to have anything more to say to a man who has no taste."

"But, good Bernard, I want to go into that room on a message from my sister Agatha."

"You do? hurrah—that's right—do push me."

"Push you?"

"Yes, give me a blow. Do now. You see, I'm in your way. Why don't you drive me on one side, and insist upon going in?"

"Do you think I'm a fool? No, indeed, I know better. A nice topper on the head you'd give me. Come now, do just be so good as to let me in."

"No, listen to me, Master Eldred. I'm here as a sentinel to prevent the crusader from being interrupted by impertinent visitors. Neither you nor Mistress Agatha shall enter this room, you may depend, while I hold watch here."

" Well, I never heard of such a thing. I say, Bernard."

" Well, what ?"

" I—I—am quite sure I can promise you ——"

" What ?"

" A whole barrel of ale to yourself."

" The deuce you can."

" Yes. If you will be so good, Bernard, as just to whisper in my ear, you know, who this crusader is. You understand me, Bernard, a whole barrel of ale all to yourself. You can sit down upon it, you know, and drink away. Eh, Bernard ?"

The indignation of the honest man-at-arms was to the full as great as if he had known who the crusader was himself, instead of being as profoundly ignorant as Eldred himself. He made no answer for a moment, but when he did recover himself sufficiently to make a reply, he made a practical one, which consisted in placing his foot against Eldred, and giving him so sudden a projection forward, that after making two desperate plunges to recover his centre of gravity, he fell down roaring with all the strength of his lungs,—

" Murder! murder !"

" Ah, you may make what noise you like," said Bernard. "You'd better be off."

Eldred was wise enough to act upon this advice, for he scrambled to his feet, and made a precipitate retreat, holding his nose, which had suffered some danger from his fall. He paused not until he reached his sister's room, into which, without any ceremony, he rushed, exclaiming,—

" Murder, murder! I'm killed! assaulted—I'm murdered by Bernard, and my nose bleeds !"

" Peace !" cried Agatha, " what means this uproar ?"

" Just this. There's that great long fellow, Bernard, won't let me go into the wainscot parlour, and when I wanted, he knocked me down never so flat. I shall never be the man I was again."

" Pshaw !"

" Look at my nose."

" Idiot !"

" Oh, it's all very fine of you to call me an idiot, but Solomon himself would have come on his nose with just such a whack, if he had had just such a kick behind, in the small of his back, as I've had to-day."

" Do you mean to assert that one of the men-at-arms have dared to kick you ?"

" Rather."

" Unpardonable insolence !"

" So I say, but it's a very disagreeable fact, notwithstanding."

" He is keeping guard, do you say, at the door of the wainscot parlour ?"

" Yes. There he is, and he says the crusader is inside, and he is not to be interrupted by any one."

The rage of Agatha for some moments prevented her from speaking. That the whole authority in the castle should be usurped by the audacious stranger, exceeded belief, and yet how utterly helpless was she under the circumstances—what could she do or say to put an end to a state of things which galled her to the very heart ? To Eldred it was useless to speak. The monk was not a powerful auxiliary, because he dared not show himself, without at once risking his life from the enraged men-at-arms, who would make no scruple of cutting him down at the very first opportunity.

Terror, anger, agitation and despair, alternately ruled in her breast, until, actuated by an impulse which prompted her to bring things to a crisis, she rushed from her room towards the wainscot parlour, where stood Bernard, fully expecting her, and mightily amused with the prospect of the scene of violence which in all likelihood would ensue.

When she reached his post, she stood facing him for some few moments without speaking, while he drew himself up to his full height, and returned her gaze with one of such fixed stolidity, as greatly added to her previous angry feelings.

"Well, sir," she screamed, rather than said, for her voice was harsh and shrill with passion.

"Pretty well, thank you," said Bernard, calmly. "Only a little thirsty or so."

Agatha bit her lips, and then summoning all her command of temper to her aid, she said in a voice of assumed calmness,—

"Who placed you here?"

"Hugh Wingrove," was the prompt answer.

"What are your orders?"

"To allow no one to pass into this room while the crusader is in it."

"Then I command you to leave your post, and go to the guard-room this moment."

"Can't think of such a thing."

"What hinders you?"

"'Cos I won't. I'm placed here, and here I shall stay till my watch is over, which will be when the relief comes, and not before."

"You—you refuse me admission into that room?"

"I do."

Agatha rushed to the guard-room, and making her sudden appearance among the men-at-arms, she cried,—

"Soldiers, you know well I was left by Sir Rupert Brandon in authority here during his absence. Will you support me in that authority, or will you desert me, because I am weak, and unable to chastise those who are insolent to me, and slight the commands of Sir Rupert?"

"If," said Wingrove, "you will explain yourself more fully, Mistress Agatha Weare, I will answer you."

"Why, then, is a sentinel placed at one of the rooms of this castle, and refused admission?"

"Simply for this reason, lady. The crusader who is here has told me that he has full authority from Sir Rupert Brandon, our honoured master, to do just what he pleases here. We believe him, and award to him accordingly the full and entire command of the castle."

"Indeed?" sneered Agatha, "and pray who may this authoritative crusader be?"

"That I know, but am at present forbidden to tell."

"Then I am to be treated with absolute contempt?"

"No one will treat you with contempt, if you will not bring contempt upon yourself, by resisting that which you cannot help."

"'Tis well," said Agatha, bitterly, "I now understand my position, and I know my remedy."

She then left the guard-room with great precipitation, and seeking her own apartment, she opened the secret door, and made the signal agreed upon between her and Morgatani, when she should require his counsel.

A few moments sufficed to bring the monk to her, and bending his shaggy brows upon her, he said,—

"Whence this unusual agitation, Agatha? your looks are disturbed, and you tremble with passion."

" Well I may, Morgatani.—Hear me."

She then informed him of what was taking place in the castle, and as she spoke his countenance each moment grew darker, while he compressed his lips till they became bloodless. In his own mind he was considering, along with other things, if he should inform Agatha of the escape of Sir Kenneth Hay, which he had discovered, or not. The information he knew would alarm her excessively, without one whit forwarding his views, so that rather than make it a subject of idle discussion with her, he determined to say nothing about it. When she had done speaking, he said,—

" Agatha, the presence of this mysterious crusader, I own, troubles me much, and I cannot think of a means of arriving at a knowledge of who he is. Twice have I lain in wait for him, when, had he passed my post alone, I could have rushed upon him and stabbed him to the heart: but each time he was in company with another, and I dared not make the attempt, for too many high and important interests depend upon my life for me to be justified in merely exchanging it for an enemy's."

" True, true," said Agatha. " Without you what would become of me ?"

" Aye, what ?"

" I have a proposal to make."

" Name it."

" It is this, that you send some trusty messenger to London at once, with letters praying King John to send a force to take possession of the castle."

" Who could I send ?"

" Could not Fitzhugh go on such an errand ?"

" Doubtless, he would, although he is scarcely a trusty messenger; yet does his interest square with the message. I will bethink me further of it, Agatha, and should I resolve upon the step, he shall start this night."

" Let him go on the errand by all means."

A low knock at the door, at this moment, arrested their attention, and Agatha, upon demanding who was there, received an answer in the voice of Eldred, who added through the keyhole,—

" I've got something uncommonly particular to say, sister."

" Shall I admit him ?" she said to Morgatani.

" Do," replied the monk. " He may bring some useful intelligence. He is fit for nothing but a spy."

Agatha opened the door, and Eldred, with an appearance of great mystery, entered the chamber.

" Speak your errand quickly," said Agatha.

" Well, I'm going. In the first place, my nose is a little better, but not much, you must know."

" Be brief," said the monk, who had not been noticed by Eldred, who gave a start of alarm.

" I—I—will.—Well, you must know, as I was coming along by the corridor near the great kitchen, who should I see but Wingrove himself, sneaking along, with a tray in his hands, covered with such nice things as made my mouth water again. Where's all that going ? thought I ; so I got into a corner, and let him go by, and then I followed him."

" Quick," said the monk. " Where went he ?"

" To the small chamber by the oratory. I saw him go in, and then out he came without the tray ; so, thinks I to myself, there's some one there, but who can it be ?"

" 'Tis Sir Kenneth Hay," thought the monk, " and I may yet triumph over him. He must not get to London with the messages he brings from Palestine, or he may raise a party in favour of the absent Richard, which may hurl John from his throne in a day."

Agatha looked in the face of the monk, who merely said,—

"Leave this affair to me."

"Then it is important?" said Eldred, quite delighted with what he believed his own cleverness.

"No!" said Morgatani, in a voice that nearly made him fall down.

"You may leave the room," said Agatha.

"Oh, thank you—I ——"

"Begone!" added the monk, advancing a step, and Eldred rushed from the room in great alarm.

"Well, I never," he muttered to himself when he was some distance off. "I never get credit for anything. Well, well, I'll go and have a chat with the old cellarer. He is a reasonable man—a very reasonable man. He's rather deaf, and he never disputes what one says. Moreover, I've promised him, if ever I'm master here to make him a great man, and so I will. I won't have any fighting and soldiers here. There shall be nothing but good eating and drinking going on. Really my nose feels very odd and uncomfortable."

Thus muttering to himself, Eldred repaired to the cellarer, with whom he sat in congenial conversation for some hours afterwards.

Agatha expected that the monk would at once have imparted to her who he thought the person was that Wingrove so mysteriously supplied with food, but as he had kept the escape of Sir Kenneth Hay a secret from her he could not well tell her that he thought it was no other than that knight who was kept so secretly. To her chagrin, therefore, he merely said,—

"This matter is a political one of which you will care not to know. Leave it to me, it concerns not your affairs and fortunes."

He then, without another word left the room, repairing to his lonely home in the turret, from whence he wove the various dark contrivances which were eventually to recoil upon himself and involve him in their own destruction.

The evening was rapidly progressing, and the castle clock had already given notice of ten o'clock having arrived, when the crusader emerged from the room in which he had been engaged in writing. Addressing the man-at-arms who had relieved Bernard some hour or more previously, he said,—

"You may leave your post a few minutes, my friend, to fetch to me Hugh Wingrove, who I wish to see immediately."

The man-at-arms, as he had been ordered to do, obeyed him with alacrity. While he was gone, the crusader walked in musing forgetfulness to and fro in the corridor from which the apartment he had so many hours occupied opened.

The small velvet mask he had made a practise of wearing, he had in his hand. A gleam of light from a lamp which was in the room shone out through the open doorway, and occasionally fell upon his tall handsome figure as it came within the sphere of its influence.

"These letters," he said, in a low tone, "will be most efficacious in my cause. What a mercy it is to me that Sir Kenneth Hay has escaped from the clutches of that rascally monk. Let me consider. Ride as he may, he must be two days and a night reaching London. Then a day performing his errand in London. A day, too, may be consumed in unavoidable delays By the most it will be near a week ere anything can be really expected."

He strode to and fro now with impatient gestures for some minutes, and then said,—

"Well, well, there is no help. After all I have much to be truly thankful for, or I should not be here among the living."

He suddenly started as a light touch upon his arm warned him that some one was close to him. Turning quickly he saw the page, who placed in his hand a small scrap of paper, and then glided away without speaking a word to him.

" What can this mean ?" he said, as he strode into his room, and by the light from the lamp read the following words on the paper :—

" ' Put on your mask if you wish to be concealed, and beware of an ambuscade for your assassination. Be perpetually on your guard in Brandon.' "

" Humph !" said the crusader. " No doubt a friendly caution."

As he spoke he placed the mask on his face, and turning towards the door, he saw a dark tall figure move from it with great precipitation.

To rush into the corridor was the work of a moment, but all was still, and not the least vestige of a human being could be seen.

<hr/>

CHAPTER XLVI.

What form is that which speeds along,
　At midnight's lonely hour,
Nor heeds he if the sky be fair,
　Or if dun tempests lour?—SCOTT.

THE HORSEMAN.—THE GRATEFUL STEED.—AGATHA'S AMAZEMENT.— MORGATANI'S WILD PASSION AND RAGE.

HALF-PAST eleven sounded solemnly from the castle clock, when three persons stood in the chamber occupied by the gallant Sir Kenneth Hay; one was that knight himself, the others were the mysterious crusader and Hugh Wingrove.

Sir Kenneth was fully armed and equipped, presenting the same appearance he had done as when first he appeared before Brandon Castle. A flush of pleasure was upon his face, and in his hand he held a small packet of letters which the crusader had just given to him.

" Help me, Hugh Wingrove," he said, " to unclasp this gorget. I will place these letters next my heart, and whoever would possess himself of them must take it as well."

The letters with the assistance of Wingrove were soon safely stowed away, and then the crusader said,—

" Now, Hay, for a flying visit to the Mistress Agatha Weare, during which time your horse shall be caparisoned and brought to the postern gate."

" By our lady," laughed Sir Kenneth, " she deserves a fright, for she did succeed in giving me one ; I shall not be many moments."

He then strode from the room, and having before traversed the same route, he found no difficulty in reaching the door of Agatha's room. There he paused a moment and listened attentively. He fancied he could hear an uneasy footstep pacing to and fro, and he was not deceived, for it was Agatha Weare herself who had risen from her dream-haunted couch to endeavour by exercise to fatigue herself sufficiently to snatch some few hours of healthful repose. A more favourable opportunity for the experiment upon her nerves, meditated by Sir Kenneth Hay, could not have been desired, and when he knocked at her door the sound went to her very heart.

She paused instantly in her uneasy walk, and grasping the corner of a bureau for support, she gasped in a low and nearly inarticulate tone,—

" Who is—there ?"

The only reply to this was another knock as before.

"Who—who knocks?" said Agatha. "Is it you, Eldred?"

Another knock excited all her fears, and she sunk into a chair in an agony of apprehension.

The mysterious knocks continued, and she after some moments made a desperate attempt to overcome her fears and open the door. Once more, however, she thought she would ask who was there, and accordingly grasping the handle, she said,—

"Speak, speak, be you who you may?"

There was no answer, and she opened the door, when she saw upon the landing, standing perfectly motionless, the figure of Sir Kenneth Hay.

The notion that he was dead and that was his spirit, came across her in a moment, and with a loud cry she fainted on the threshold of the door.

CHAPTER XLVII.

THE DEPARTURE.—THE MINSTREL AND ELDRED WEARE.—THE SECRET.

THE castle clock was pealing forth the hour of twelve when the crusader and Sir Kenneth Hay stood by the portal, while the drawbridge was being lowered, in order to allow the latter to pass from the gloomy fortress in which he had experienced so much misfortune, and from some of the inmates of which he had so narrowly escaped a death that, to him, as a soldier, did indeed present, as he looked back upon it, a most terrible aspect.

No. 37

Most of the men-at-arms who were not on duty at different parts of the battlements were grouped about near to the gate, in order that they might see the departure of the gallant Sir Kenneth, under whom some of them had fought, and who was so well known to them all by the voice of fame.

They betted among themselves, and hazarded many a conjecture as to the mysterious disappearance of the knight for some time, when they felt assured he had not left by any of the ordinary means of exit the castle of Brandon, and his as mysterious reappearance among them from they knew not where.

There was not one among that picked few brave soldiers, who had been so carefully selected by Sir Rupert Brandon, who might not have been fully and completely trusted, but the crusader had decided not to take more persons into his confidence than were absolutely necessary; and hence Hugh Wingrove's mouth was sealed, and he replied to all questions by saying,

"You will know all soon, I hope; but I am forbidden at present to communicate anything."

For the space of about a quarter of an hour, the crusader and Sir Kenneth Hay conversed in earnest whispers, during the course of which some familiar names of knights and nobles of high birth and repute struck upon the ears of the men-at-arms.

Then the crusader suddenly clasped Sir Kenneth's hand in his, saying,

"To you and to Heaven I commit my cause. Farewell, and God speed you."

In a voice of deep emotion, Sir Kenneth replied,

"What can be done by all the devotion, all the zeal which mortal man can feel in a just and holy cause, shall be done by me."

"Farewell—farewell."

"The charger waits," said Hugh Wingrove. "The good wishes of an old soldier attend you, Sir Kenneth Hay."

It was with a voice slightly tremulous with emotion that the knight turned to Hugh Wingrove, saying,

"From my heart I thank you; I am, as you well know, bound on no common enterprise. The good wishes of all honest and brave men must surely be of assistance to a Christian warrior. Farewell—farewell."

"Heaven speed you!" said the crusader. "I shall not stir from Brandon Castle until I see or hear from you again."

Sir Kenneth Hay waved his hand to the men-at-arms, who crowded the ancient gateway, and then, with a slow and stately step, he crossed the drawbridge, on the other side of which his charger stood in readiness to receive him.

One torch, which was carried by the guard on duty, shot its rays across the moat, glancing brightly from the armour of the knight, and lending a strange beauty to that rough and uncouth scene.

"Farewell," cried Sir Kenneth Hay, as he waved his arm. "Hurra! for England and King Richard."

The charger's head was turned away from the castle, and in a few moments the dull sounds of his hoofs upon the bright green sward was entirely lost.

"Heaven help him!" said the crusader, in a low voice, as he turned away from the gate, at the same time replacing the velvet mask upon his face, which he had withdrawn during his brief converse with Sir Kenneth Hay.

Scarcely had he proceeded many paces towards the guard-room, when he encountered the wandering minstrel who had so recently arrived at the castle. No word was spoken on either side, but the minstrel's face glowed with pleasure as he gently bowed his head, while the crusader, holding out his hand, said, with a pleasant smile,

"My well-tried and most excellent friend, a cordial welcome to thee. Be cautious yet, for although we once more tread the soil of merry England, all are not friendly eyes that are even now bent upon us."

"Not friendly?" said the minstrel. "What caitiff dares ——"

"Hush, hush!" said the crusader; "trouble not thyself, good friend, with such matters; make merry with your happy minstrelsy, and be assured that Heaven will not desert a righteous cause."

"It is my fervent hope—my ever fervent, holiest hope," said the minstrel.

"Let us part now," said the crusader; "we are observed."

The minstrel glanced in the direction which the crusader's eyes indicated, and saw Eldred Weare gazing with ill-suppressed curiosity upon himself and the crusader.

"May I presume to ask," he said, "who is that that dares make himself so obnoxious as to listen to your conversation?"

"I will advise you to have nothing to do with him," said the crusader; "for, although as you see, he scarcely looks it, he is a most doughty and dangerous foe."

"Were he ten times what he is," said the minstrel, as he placed his hand upon the hilt of his light rapier, "I would tell him he is insolent to watch the conversation and actions of ——"

"Hush!" said the crusader—"hush! be cautious—be more than cautious; utter no name until I bid you within this castle's walls."

"I am mute—I am mute," said the minstrel, "and yet I would fain seek permission to say a word to yonder prying knave."

"You have it freely," said the crusader, with a smile, as he turned towards Hugh Wingrove, who was standing a few paces distant in a respectful attitude.

The minstrel really believed that Eldred Weare might be what the knight in his overweening love of a joke represented him, and walking up to him with a stern air, he said,—

"May I be so bold, sir, as to ask your name?"

The manner of the minstrel was sufficiently belligerent to awaken Eldred's fears, and he immediately replied,—

"Keep off—keep off, Mr. Minstrel. What's the matter with you? If you want to pick a quarrel, or knock up a row with anybody, there are plenty in this castle, I can tell you, who like it. I don't, so no nonsense now."

"Are you a coward?" said the minstrel.

"Anything you like, my dear sir, so that I keep a whole skin and an uncracked crown. Come, now, don't come after me. I shall tell my sister if you do, and she's the one."

"An idiot!" said the minstrel, as, with a look of ineffable scorn, he walked away in the opposite direction.

"Now, if I dared," muttered Eldred, "how I should like to run after that fellow and give him a horrid kick, only he looks such a determined wretch. He'd be sure to give me another kick, and then where should I be? Oh, dear, I think I see. Ah, it's all very well of Morgatani to tell me about honour, and riches, and power, and all that sort of thing. If I had known half the trouble, and botheration, and rioting, and thumping, and hauling I should have to go through before I came to it, I'd never have tried it, not I; but if I happen to presume to say so much now, my sister says, with a great scream, 'You have gone too far.' And then the Black Monk, he bends his great shaggy brows upon me and says, in a voice like thunder coming from the bottom of a well,—' Tremble, you have gone too far.' Well, I do tremble—that's easy enough ; but the best of the joke is, I don't know how far I have gone, or how far I have got to go, and sometimes I don't know whether I am on my head or my heels. Then sister Agatha tells me that I ought to think that an agreeable excitement. Every one to their taste say I. Agreeable excitement certainly ain't mine. I like ale when it ain't too strong, for then I am afraid it would get into my head and make me valorous, and I might get into a row, when who knows how I should ever get out of it again. I like sops in the pan and nice deep cuts in venison pasty. I like to be snug and nice, and I rather like the cook ; but I don't like armour, and swords, and battle-axes, and maces, and fights, and honour, and all that sort of thing, that makes a fellow so dreadfully nervous. Oh, here's Bernard. Who it is that's gone out of the castle at such an hour?—I am quite sure sister Agatha would be glad to know, and she'll think it vastly clever of me to find it out without being asked."

The huge, bulky form of Bernard was passing Eldred, when the latter touched him slightly on the arm, saying,—

" Bernard, my good friend, Bernard."

The man-at-arms was either too indolent, or too much occupied in his own thoughts, to reply; but, when Eldred added,—" Don't you feel thirsty ?" he at once aroused himself, crying,—

" Thirsty—I am always—that is, sometimes thirsty, and when I ain't, I have no objection to a glass of ale, for fear I should be. Prevention is better than cure, you know, Master Eldred."

" Ah," said Eldred, " that's what I think, when I move my pate out of a row to prevent its being cracked. But, my good Bernard, I'll take care that you have a flagon of ale, if you tell me two things."

" Do you mean drink it up in two draughts ?" said Bernard.

" No. First of all, I want to know who the crusader is."

" I'll tell you a secret," said Bernard, " if you promise to stand the ale."

" I will—I will," said Eldred, inclining forward his ear, into which the bulky soldier whispered,—

" So do I."

" Then you don't really know ?"

" I'll think again after the ale."

" Who went out of the castle, then, just now ?" said Eldred.

Bernard again beckoned him to place his ear in convenient proximity, into which he whispered,—

" A man in armour."

" I know that," said Eldred, with an air of vexation.

Bernard nodded three times mysteriously, and then walked away.

" Well, now," said Eldred, " if I was a whopper, I mean, about eight feet high and four feet wide, I'd run after that fellow, and give him such a topper as never was seen. Everybody's insolent to me. Hugh Wingrove is insolent; the men-at-arms are insolent, and even that little upstart of a page of Fitzhugh's actually pretended he'd shake me. Times have come to a pretty pass indeed. I'll go to bed, and sister Agatha may find out herself who leaves the castle, and who comes to it."

¡CHAPTER XLVIII.

" The knight has left the castle walls—
Well known was he to fame.
'Twas night, and through the silent air
A sound of sadness came."

THE FIGURE.—THE PURSUIT.—THE SECRET ASSASSIN.—A TALE OF DEEP VILLANY.

WHEN the postern gate was closed, and no further sight or sound of Sir Kenneth Hay could be obtained, the crusader turned to Hugh Wingrove, and said,—

" I shall, in all likelihood, my good friend, be a sojourner in this castle for some weary days, during which time I cannot employ myself better than in discovering some of the mysteries that seem to beset and make it such a place of terror."

" If," said Hugh Wingrove, " those mysteries are ever to be unravelled, such a result will be achieved by you, or by Sir Rupert himself, for I believe no others will have sufficient power over the daring and iniquitous spirits that haunt Brandon, and make it so fearful an abode."

" I will try, however," said the knight ; " but ere I attempt a solution of the old Grey Turret, if you can spare time to accompany me, I will make a tour through the gloomy vaults of Brandon, and become master of whatever strange sights they may present to mortal eyes."

" My duty," said Wingrove, " as well as my inclination, prompt me to such a course, and much honoured shall I feel by the permission to accompany you, sir. It will be a tale of pride and pleasure for an old soldier to tell, such as few can boast of."

" The hour is propitious," said the crusader, " let us go at once ; and if you know of any ready means of admission to the vaults of Brandon, be my guide, and I shall be much your debtor."

" From the western corridor," said Wingrove, " there is a door leading to the vaults, which was pointed out to me by Sir Rupert himself as he said, jestingly,—' Here, good Wingrove, is a resource for us, and a means of escape, should we be thoroughly beleaguered by a foe. This door leads to the numerous vaults and secret passages beneath Brandon, in the intricaces of which we might defy the most active search.' "

" That would be the very thing," said the crusader. " Conduct me to that door, Hugh Wingrove, and through it let us pass, daring the adventures the fates may have in store for us when past its portal."

" That will I," said Wingrove, " and should we be attacked by mortal foes, I have a heart and arm ever ready to do you service."

At that moment they both turned their faces in a direction away from the guard-room, when the crusader observed a dusky figure rapidly rushing up the narrow passage which led to the domestic offices of the castle. To Wingrove, likewise, the figure was apparent, and his hasty exclamation of " The monk ! the monk !" by no means tended to stop the lightning speed with which the crusader dashed after the retreating figure. In vain, however, was his pursuit, for Morgatani, if indeed it were he, was too well acquainted with the intricacies of Brandon Castle to allow himself to be caught if he had anything like a fair start of his pursuers.

The crusader was not one of those persons who too easily gave up a pursuit, and, heedless of the fact that he no longer saw the fugitive, he darted onwards, in the hope of coming up to him in some unexpected corner or doorway. Heedless of what new danger he might be plunging into, he rushed down every passage he saw, and entered every apartment he found open, in some cases letting his impatience get so much the better of him as to place his foot against one that offered any particular obstruction, and forced the lock from its hold. Nowhere, however, could he see him he was pursuing, nor the least indication of his presence.

Meanwhile, Hugh Wingrove began to be really uneasy at the continued absence of the crusader, who, with the expectation that he would return immediately, he had allowed to proceed without him, until he had proceeded so far that any chance of coming up with him became as doubtful as that of the crusader's himself was of reaching the Black Monk.

"Merciful Heavens!" cried Wingrove, "he will lose himself in Brandon, and be assassinated at some corner or turning where he least suspects treachery."

With these apprehensions full on his mind, the trusty old veteran drew his sword, and, breathing a short prayer to Heaven for him whose life he held so dear, he hastened forward in the direction the crusader had taken.

But the wild impetuosity which had hitherto dared the crusader onwards began to give way to the suggestions of a better and calmer reason, and he paused in one of an extensive suite of apartments, in which he had been rapidly hurrying, and which bore all the marks and indications of the rude magnificence of an age gone by. He had, by accidentally bursting open a door, reached the wing of the castle which had so long been uninhabited, and which looking to the bleak and cold east, opened upon those battlements, which, from their extreme height, were considered impregnable, and upon which only in times of strife and danger were any sentinels posted.

The room in which the knight paused was one of considerable extent, although its low roof took much from its nobility and appearance. The window sills and huge chimney-piece were richly carved, and here and there depended from the walls, faded pieces of damask, which had once been the pride of the ancient residents of that feudal building.

"This castle," said the crusader, "is indeed of vast extent. Much as I had heard of Brandon, and of the great additions which had in succession been made to it, I little dreamed to find a very town in miniature enclosed within its massive walls. What materials for sad contemplation might here be found, and how strange and mysterious do all objects appear by the silvery light of yon moon, which shines through these party-coloured windows."

The crusader stood in a broad streak of moonlight, which came in many strange coloured masses, through a gothic window of stained glass; and scarcely had the last low murmur fallen from his lips, when he was conscious of the sudden obscuration of the light, which a glance up at the deep azure sky, showed him could not have been caused by any passing cloud over the moon's disc.

Again then a shadow flashed across the streak of moonlight, and he felt certain some one must have passed the window through which it proceeded.

To act upon the suggestion of his mind was the work of a moment, and rushing forward, he would have reached the window, had he not slightly stumbled over a piece of fallen arras.

That stumble saved his life, for at that instant an arrow, shot by no weak hand, whistled over his head, and buried itself to the feathers in the opposite wainscoting.

The crusader, during the many scenes of active warfare he had been engaged in, had become too familiar with such sounds, to doubt for a moment from whence they proceeded. Regaining his feet in a moment, he dashed forward, and with one blow of his sword brought the greater part of the window down in a crashing mass. A rush of cold air immediately came through the aperture, and the moonlight falling with its own sweet silvery whiteness into the room, gave him ample opportunity to see that, whoever his enemy was, he had escaped, leaving behind him on the window sill, a heavy cross-bow, which it would require a person of no ordinary strength to use.

"Now, by our lady," cried the crusader, "the bowman who drew this twanging piece of gut must have been most intent upon my destruction, and stout and strong withal. I would give him better fair play for his life than he seemed inclined to give me for mine. Now, however, I believe that I am safe, for a discomfitted assassin seldom musters up sufficient courage in one night, to again attempt the life of him he would make his victim. I must find my way back to Hugh Wingrove as best I may, for this, after all, is but a foolish chase, seeing that I am unacquainted with this castle, and without a guide may double repeatedly on my course."

He then turned round several times before even he could find the door at which he had entered the apartment, and when at length he thought he had done so, he became convinced, after proceeding a few paces in the dark, that it was not the same, and that in all probability he was further mystifying himself, amid the intricacies of those gloomy chambers.

Moreover, it was only in those, the windows of which faced the east or the south, which received the benefit of the moon's rays, so that when by chance he passed into a chamber having neither of those aspects, he found it dark as a dungeon, and was but too glad to grope his way out again, without stumbling over any obstacle. At length, after feeling anxiously for some time around the walls of an apartment, for some other door than that by which he had entered, he found one that readily yielded to his touch, and passing through which, he, to his astonishment, observed on the other side a broad streak of light, which seemed to proceed from a partially opened doorway, at some short distance down a passage close at hand. At the same time a faint murmur of voices met his ears, and pausing involuntarily, he heard a voice say,—

"Listen, listen, and you shall know all. Oh, how I have panted for a moment such as this, to find in my deep wretchedness some kindred soul who will listen to the story of my wrongs."

"That will I," said a soft tender voice, "and most patiently too. I have known suffering and misery myself; Heaven forbid that I should refuse that kind sympathy to another, which would be so dear to me, but which, alas, I fear I can never know."

"That," said the crusader, "must surely be the voice of the young page, who has been so strongly recommended to my kind offices by Sir Kenneth Hay. What can he mean by holding secret colloquy here with so mysterious a person? By the mass, Brandon Castle is indeed full of mysteries, and they by no means seem to diminish in amount or intensity, upon better acquaintance."

The crusader paused for some moments, as if considering whether he should break in abruptly upon the conference, or remain a passive listener to what was taking place.

"Such as I," he muttered to himself in a low tone, " hear more to the purpose frequently when we are not supposed to be listening, than were the words spoken or addressed especially to our ears. For once, master page, I will play the eaves-dropper with the hope of more readily and easily as well as effectually performing my promise to Sir Kenneth Hay, to be of service to you."

The crusader, however, was disappointed if he supposed that he was to hear much of the page's history or the secret cause of his grief, for in a moment the other voice spoke, and that was one which the knight could identify with no particular person.

Its tones were wild and full of grief, and there was a deep impassioned earnestness in every accent which was convincing of the truth of what was uttered.

"You shall hear," he said, "a tale of such woe, such deep humiliation and abject sorrow as may well make you wonder not that I am what I am, but that I am not still further removed from the appearance and the habits of humanity than you now see me."

"And do you say," remarked the page, "that Morgatani, the Black Monk, worked you all this woe?"

"I do, I do; let me hail his name with curses. I tell you, boy, he is a fiend. No mortal man could war with such deep devilry against his species."

"I will hear you," said the page, "and such kind sympathy as I can afford you, shall be yours. Moreover, I will not be sparing in my exertions to see justice done you. I will speak to those who have the will, and I believe, have the power to right the oppressed, and they will do you justice."

"Can they restore the dead?" shrieked he who complained so loudly of his wrongs. "Can they bid the warm blood flow which has congealed for ever in the veins of the young and beautiful? Can they make me what I was? Can they restore her to me who was made the victim of a living tomb?"

"Alas! no," said the page.

"Then talk not to me of justice—of sympathy—of commiseration! What I want is revenge, a deep and damning revenge. A revenge which shall in some measure reach the height of my most frightful injury. What is sympathy to me? What to me is that weak mockery called human justice? Revenge, revenge! I must have revenge, and then I am content to die."

"This Black Monk," thought the crusader, "seems to have the unenviable felicity of being abused by everybody. 'Tis well that I know much of him, for I shall then be the better prepared to confound his villanies when I have the opportunity."

"I will be brief," continued the strange voice. "It is now some years ago since I and my sister resided at Florence."

The page felt in considerable doubt, as he marked the feeling of excitement which shone in the eyes of his companion, whether he should not at once rise and call for assistance, or remain and please the imagination of him who might be a maniac, by listening to the recital of his real or supposed wrongs.

The singular looking man commenced his narrative as follows:—

"Some years gone by, from circumstances which are unconnected with this narrative, I went to reside at Florence. I lived in the same house with my sister. For some time after I took up my residence at this city, I spent my time in looking at and seeking out the various beauties with which that place abounds. I spent many weeks and months in happiness, until at last I met with the fell monster, Morgatani.

"He I met at a house where I was received as a visitor and a stranger to the country; he was officious and civil—knew and had possessed powers of observation and remark that gained him my attention, though I could not esteem him, for there was that reserve and forbidding appearance in feature that would invariably dissolve the newly formed sentiment of friendship, and cold civility took its place.

" 'Twas he who took me to the Convent of Franciscan Nuns, who re-sided in the environs of the city.

" I had expressed a desire to witness the induction of a new devotee to the order, of which circumstance I had been informed.

" ' And would you like to see the ceremonies ?' he inquired of me, ear-nestly.

" ' I would,' I replied. ' I never saw such—indeed I never had the desire ; but being in a place where I am known to none, I have much time upon my hands, and my curiosity is excited in proportion to my idleness.'

" ' Strangers are rarely admitted,' he answered, ' but I think that I have influence sufficient with the abbess to induce her to permit your being pre-sent ; but you must be very circumspect, and place yourself implicitly under my direction.'

" ' I will do that gladly,' I replied ; ' I have heard much of this order of nuns, and especially those of the Convent of St. Francis.'

" ' And they deserve it,' replied Morgatani, and while he said this, a singular expression of features crossed his countenance. He proceeded— ' for they are of the highest born, and of the best families which Florence and her territories can boast of. The young, beautiful, and the pious are all within the walls of yon sacred edifice.'

" The young, the beautiful, and the pious,' I repeated ; ' are they all within the walls of St. Francis ?'

" ' And the high-born,' he added.

" ' It were a sight well worth seeing, and yet is it not sad to think that such beings should be shut out from the joys of life—they who have all that is needful for its enjoyment ?'

" ' Stranger,' said Morgatani, ' beware how you give utterance to such thoughts. Our holy church tells you that these maidens are happy —hap-
No. 38

pier than mortals torn by more than mortal passions—they escape all the evils that the intercourse with the world is sure, sooner or later, to bring upon the head of its followers. They do but sacrifice the evanescent joys of life, chequered as they are, for the more lasting happiness of eternity.'

" He spoke so solemnly and impressively that I had no desire to reply, but looked upon him with a higher opinion than I had yet formed of him.

" ' He is devoted and sincere in his calling,' I thought, ' and deserves esteem despite of those nameless things which would cause distrust.'

" Morgatani left me with the promise that he would seek the abbess and endeavour to obtain her consent to my presence at the ceremony about to take place, and which, as he had prophesied, he had interest enough to obtain.

" In the meantime I learned something of the maiden who was about to become one of the sisterhood.

" Report said she was the daughter of a noble house, whose vast wealth and possessions were to be lavished upon a son, while, that this overgrown mass of worldly goods should come to him unimpared, the daughter was induced to become a nun in the convent of St. Francis.

" Morgatani returned to me the next day, and said,—

" ' Be ready to accompany me to the convent of St. Francis in a few hours, as then this ceremonial will probably take place, but you must not gaze too hardly at the sisters, else it might be misconstrued.'

" The latter portion of this was said in a sneering tone that I could not well account for, but I have since found out, boy, that this fearless and belief-less man contemned all that men hold in respect and veneration,—that strong in mind, he places himself above humanity, and affects a superiority over all mankind."

" Alas! this description does but terrify me," replied the page. " Alas! it is too like the man—he is feared and hated by all."

" But not feared by me, boy; and mark me, I will baffle his machinations and beard him in his utmost power and wrath. But to proceed :—

" We arrived at the convent and were admitted by the portress within its walls. I will not describe all I saw to you, but this I will tell you, that no human form could be half so lovely as the maiden who was about to immolate herself—to quit the world, its cares and joys, its miseries and blessings, its light and shade. Yes, the sunny side of existence might have been her's had she not sought this refuge; all that could be desired, or wealth procure, might have been her's, but the unseen spring of her actions —a father who commanded, nay goaded her to this act of immolation—prevented any other course being adopted.

" I knew this—I saw that lovely girl led between two rows of sisters of the order, while the pealing organ gave forth solemn and majestic sounds that added interest to a scene almost indescribable. Then the chant began, and they reached the altar, and after a few moments spent in prayer, a solemn silence ensued.

" Her beautiful brown tresses, the most beautiful I had ever beheld, were gathered together by a sister and severed from her head. I could feel the severance in body by sympathy—a wound inflicted on my own body would have been less painful. But—but, boy, I tell thee what thou canst not understand.

" By this right hand, I loved, madly loved; a burning liquid fire rushed through my veins as I gazed upon this scene. The form and features of that dear girl were indelibly imprinted upon my heart; my very soul knew nought else but the beautiful being before me. I at one moment turned to my companion.

" He gazed intently upon the scene; his piercing eyes were fixed upon the trembling noviciate, who was being inducted to the order. I could not read his thoughts; but his expression was singular—something betwixt admiration for the lovely being before us and utter contempt for all else.

"I turned to the ceremonies, and beheld the pale, trembling creature, standing shorn of those locks, the pride and glory of woman; but even now she was beautiful—exceedingly beautiful. The ceremonies were concluded.

"'Let us be gone,' I whispered to Morgatani—'let us be gone, my heart sickens. I would quit these walls where the very air is too thick to breathe—laden, as it is, by the solemn sights and sounds we have just heard and witnessed.'

"He turned his bulky form, and with a grim smile, which the expression of his eyes belied, he motioned me to follow him.

"For many days I know not what I did. The form and features of the beautiful nun haunted my mind, and I could not think of aught save the beautiful being I had seen so sacrificed. I wandered about by day, but I was always found by the convent. I strove to obtain permission to enter, but that was denied me. I wandered round it repeatedly, and at length I discovered a spot where I could scale the wall.

"Some alder trees grew near a part of the wall which surrounded part of the garden, or orchard, in which were many fruit trees. The wall was a high one; but at this spot it had fallen down, so that by climbing these trees, and some exertion, I found myself on the top of it. Fortunately there was a large tree growing close by the wall, and assisted me in my descent on the other side; but I remained on the tree concealed among its leafy branches, waiting anxiously until I should see the object that had raised such a tumult in my soul.

"I left the spot after dark, and returned by daylight. This I did for several days, until one evening, when the sisters had nearly all retired, she whom I sought came there by herself. Sad and melancholy came this beautiful girl; her breast throbbed and heaved in a manner that convinced me she was unhappy. I gazed for some time fascinated with the beauty of the newly-made nun, and then slowly descended the tree, with as little noise as possible, that I should not alarm her.

"'Heaven preserve me!' she exclaimed on seeing me, and crossing herself. 'Stranger, what do you here? This is no place for such as you. I pray you begone, for if I call the sisters, you will pay sorely for this intrusion.'

"'Do as you will,' I replied, 'I am a slave to your beauty, and I would sooner expire in your sight than live without you.'

"'Do you know that such as I are shut out from the world, and such converse is ill-fitting for our ears? You might at least spare the unhappy an unnecessary pang.'

"'Say not unnecessary. But hear me—I love you above all mortals.'

"'Hush! conceal yourself, stranger, for here comes the portress; and should you be seen, I fear your fate and mine would be a very melancholy one.'

"'I will be here to-morrow. For Heaven's sake grant me an interview.'

"I then sprung up into the tree, and was over the wall before the portress came in sight.

"The next night I was there, and saw her. We conversed for a long time, and on many subsequent occasions; and I at length persuaded her to listen to the tale of love I poured out to her willing ear.

"It was eventually agreed that she should escape from the convent, and under an assumed disguise travel to some part of the world, and live in quietude and happiness. I had arranged all. I had horses in waiting, which I had placed with my own hands, not choosing that another person should be cognizant of the circumstance, as there would be so much the less chance of treachery.

" I was at the spot at the appointed hour, but my adored one was not come. I concealed myself carefully in the old tree, and watched the rising moon gradually shed its silver radiance over the face of nature, and the Convent of Saint Francis. The old building was thrown in strong relief, and presented a scene of architectural beauty seldom seen. But I had no eye for such a sight, but sat on the tree tormented by a thousand fears and a sadforeboding of evil.

" The bat flapped his monstrous wings, and took his unsteady flight around me, as if scared that a mortal had taken his post there.

" ' It is an ill omen,' I thought; ' may Heaven preserve my soul's dearest treasure, and guide her safe to my arms, and then I care not for all the ills that flesh is heir to.'

" At that moment the solemn bell tolled a funeral knell. I started as if bitten by an adder. The bell tolled solemnly and continually. I knew not what I did or how I acted, but I found myself in the convent, which I entered by an open door, at which no one stood to guard. The dismal bell kept tolling, which indicated the death or burial of some person.

" A dreadful feeling of awe and terror crept to my heart. I feared I knew not what, but still crept onward, and, after passing through many passages, I heard a low, solemn chant below. I descended to the vaults, and came to a spot where there was a small grating, through which I could see all that passed before me.

" There was a newly built niche, or rather a place built more like a well than a cell, into which they lowered a small pitcher of water, and a loaf of convent bread. The chanting ceased, and a pause ensued ; I looked around and standing near the pillar, stood Morgatani, the Black Monk. My soul trembled with horror, as I gazed upon him, but I had not time to look upon him or meditate upon the cause of his presence, for a movement took place, and some one was brought forward, over whom was thrown a white veil.

" The individual's back was towards me, but my fears suggested the worst, the veil was lifted off the unfortunate being, who started as her eyes met Morgatani's gigantic form, but recovering herself, she said, in solemn accents, that struck like an electric shock to my soul,

" ' Monster ! inhuman monster ! had I consented to your vile will I had not now been in this strait ; but I tell you, and let all hear the words of a dying daughter of man—that a day of terrible retribution will overtake you.'

" The truth flashed upon my soul, Morgatani had watched us, and overheard all, and finding his own base passion scorned, he had betrayed her he would have debauched, to the abbess, and she was caught, condemned, and this was her slow execution.

" A slight, almost imperceptible sneer, passed across the features of the monk, but he replied not, nor seemed to move a muscle, or change the direction of his eyes, which were full upon the unfortunate woman, who was now thrust forward into this living tomb.

" She turned her last gaze upon the faces of those who stood around, and the glare of the torches fell full upon the features of her I adored above all human things.

" As she was about to utter some words to the abbess, a thundering chant was sung, while the loud tones of the organ drowned all that the unhappy nun spoke, if speak she did. I saw the spot built up, the tomb closed over, the living buried ; and yet, boy—I—I—live—but 'tis for revenge, a deep, terrible, and complete revenge, upon her destroyer.

" I flew from the spot. I was unarmed, and had I not been so, any attempt however mad, was useless. I quitted the orchard by the means I had got in, and flew to my residence.

" What happened after this I know not ; a fever seized upon my brain, and I became delirious, and for months my life was despaired of.

" I, however, recovered ; but only partially. At times, when the thoughts of the past cross my imagination, I am mad—ay, wildly mad ; but yet I have lucid moments, which are dedicated to revenge, and which purpose I have always in view,—no earthly or heavenly consideration can ever drive it from my thoughts, and he who is so great and strong in his own iniquity, shall tremble and gnash the dust before my arm."

" And how came you to know that he was here ?" inquired the page, tremblingly.

" I'll tell you, boy. When I recovered from my fever fit and delirium, I inquired for the monk, intending to sacrifice him to my just resentment, but he had left Florence. When I was fit to travel I followed his footsteps, and dogged him from city to city, town to town, one place of concealment to another, till I crossed the seas in search of him, in this country, where for a time I lost him.

" However, after a time, I obtained a clue to his haunts, and heard that he had come to Brandon Castle, where he would remain—and—and—I know his purpose. I will baffle every scheme he lays, and he shall be my prize."

" But how came you into the castle ?" inquired the page, his fears mounting higher and higher.

" It matters not. I came to yon wood, where I determined to lay in ambuscade, till opportunity should serve, when I found the cavern I inhabit, and from that I am called the Wizard of the Red Cavern, by which name I am known to the common people, and which well suits my present purpose, and gives me more facilities for my intents than I could otherwise expect.

" I often wandered round about Brandon, and I found the means of ingress and egress unseen and unsuspected by any soul breathing, and Morgatani— the fell betrayer, Morgatani, must be more than mortal if he escapes my power."

As he related this tale of woe and passion he gradually became wild and even frantic in his manners, tossing his arms to and fro in the air, and the wild fire of insanity gleamed from his frenzied eyes, till the page shook with mortal fear, and the Wizard of the Red Cavern gave a wild laugh, saying,—

" I live for revenge ; if death comes accompanied by revenge, I have an elysium in store for me. Ha! ha! ha! Life is the race, and the dark red stream that flows through the veins of Morgatani is the prize. All men live but for an object, and mine is the revenge of the wrongs of that dear soul who perished a long and lingering death, not more terrible to the imagination than its dreadful reality."

Then, with another wild laugh, he sprang from the room, by what way the page's fear was so great that he could not discover, but he fled the spot in terror and dismay at the thoughts that crowded on his own brain.

CHAPTER XLIX.

Now, who is he, who, with such mild discourse
And winning cadences, awakens memory's ear ?
SHENSTONE.

THE PAGE AND THE CRUSADER.—THE MYSTERIOUS HORN.

THE alarm and consternation of the page was by no means diminished by his falling directly into the arms of the crusader in the corridor.

" Help! help!" he cried; " the monk! the monk!" for he fancied, indeed, that he had fallen into the hands of the terrible Morgatani.

"Hold, my young friend," said the crusader ; "not so fast. Do you not know me ?"

The page started at the voice, which once heard, no one could mistake, and in a voice of thrilling pleasure, he cried :—

"This is a relief, indeed. I did think, Sir Knight, that my last hour was come, and that, after listening to a recapitulation of some of the villanies of Morgatani, I was doomed to become myself another of his victims."

"I have overheard all," said the crusader, "and so soon as I have settled some important affairs which shall give me power and liberty of action, I will see that that rascally monk is made shorter by a head. But, tell me, master page, can you act as my guide from here to the guard-room ?"

"I can," said the page ; "for since I have been here I have used myself to ramble over this old castle, and there is scarcely a part that is not familiar to me. I will but get my lamp, Sir Knight, and then I am at your service."

"By the holy cross," said the knight, while the page was gone for the lamp, "'twas well I met with the boy, for else I might have wandered for some hours through this place, and been exposed over and over again to the evil acts of that rascally monk, whom I have no doubt sent that winged messenger of death with such resistless force."

The page quickly returned, bearing the lamp in his hand, and saying,— "Sir Knight, if you will follow me, I can take you by a quick route to the guard-room," he preceded the crusader, who followed with rapid strides the light agile steps of the youth.

When they had proceeded some distance down the corridor the page moved aside a piece of arras that hung from the wall, and opening a small gothic door, he turned to the knight, and said—

"Here is a staircase that will lead us directly to the chapel, and from thence, as you are aware, it is but a short distance to the guard-room."

"Truly," said the crusader, "there is a great difference between knowing the way and being a total stranger to it, for it seems to me that I must have wandered half over Brandon had I not so opportunely found you."

"Not knowing this secret means of getting to the eastern wing of the castle," said the page, "you must of necessity take a long round, but here we are, Sir Knight, at the door of the guard-room, and I must bid you adieu."

"Yet, tell me," said the crusader, "before we part, who told you the tale of Morgatani's deep iniquity, which I heard related so circumstantially ?"

"He came upon me unawares," said the page, "as I was wandering through those deserted chambers, and although his appearance was sufficient to alarm me greatly, yet, his voice was so gentle as he begged me to banish my fears, and not to be under any apprehension from him, since he was one who had suffered far more than ever he had inflicted, that compassion and curiosity had chained me to the spot. Then he told me the wild tale of mortal suffering which you heard, and which from my heart I believe to be true."

"Then you know him not ?"

"I believe him to be one who is known to the inhabitants of Brandon, and its vicinity, by the name of the Wizard of the Red Cavern."

"Alas! poor fellow," said the knight, "if he has suffered but one half of what he relates, he is truly an object of the greatest compassion."

A hasty "thank Heaven!" from some one beside him now called the attention of the crusader, and turning, he beheld Hugh Wingrove looking pale and exhausted from the long and fruitless search he had had throughout the castle for him, whom he now was so rejoiced to see alive and well.

"I have been very foolish, Wingrove," said the knight, "and I have been nearly punished for my temerity. He is an indiscreet soldier who chases a foe too hotly over an unknown country."

"You are safe," said Wingrove, "and I am myself again."

"Thanks to this page, yes," said the crusader; "and now, Wingrove, for our enterprize."

"Will you still pursue it on this night?"

"Most certainly; my spirits are well attuned for such adventures, and it shall go hard but before the morning's dawn I have a peep at the old Grey Turret which has caused so much alarm in Brandon."

"This way, then," whispered Wingrove, and turning to the page, he said, "pleasant slumbers to you, young sir; you are a gallant youth, and if you were but a little taller, and a good deal stouter, you would make a good soldier."

The door of the guard-room was this moment flung open, and Bernard, with an ale flagon in his hand, made his hasty appearance; in his hurry he nearly ran over the page, and when he saw Wingrove, he, with great difficulty, prevented himself from dropping the flagon, so annoyed was he at being intercepted by him.

"What now," cried Wingrove; "who told you to get some ale?"

"Don't stop me—don't stop me," cried Bernard; "the minstrel don't feel very well, and he asked me to get him a glass of water."

"And you mend the order," said Wingrove, "into a flagon of ale."

"Why you see I thought it would do him more good, and being just a little thirsty myself——"

"As usual," interposed Wingrove, "you seized the excuse to coax the old cellarer to filling your flagon."

"Oh, you are as good as a witch, Wingrove," said Bernard; "so now for Heaven's sake let me go at once."

"Nonsense," cried Wingrove, "I cannot permit it."

"At my request," said the crusader.

"At your command," said Wingrove, "most certainly. You can get the ale, Bernard."

"Well, now only think of that," said Bernard, as he hurried to the cellar; "that crusader is somebody, and a remarkable civil-spoken, good-looking, big, strong fellow he is. I hope he'll stay here and keep on with such commands all day long."

"Now, Wingrove," said the crusader, "after so many interruptions, let us proceed to solve some of the mysteries of Brandon."

Wingrove took a lamp from a niche over the guard-room door, and leading the way, was followed by the knight up a stone flight of stairs, to the upper story of the castle. He then said,—

"Our armoury is close at hand, and should you feel inclined to select any other weapons than the one you have, to take with you on your expedition, we have ample store."

"If you have a sturdy battle-axe," said the crusader, "I should certainly prefer it."

"Sir Rupert has some of the finest specimens of the weapons of warfare that the age can boast of," said Wingrove, as he led the way to the room in which was a choice collection of offensive and defensive arms and armour of all descriptions. The crusader cast his practised eye around him, and at once selected a ponderous axe, the handle and blade of which were composed of one solid piece of highly wrought metal.

"This will do," he cried, as he flung it up singing in the air, and caught it in its descent, as if it had been a toy. "Think you it has a fine temper, Wingrove?" Then whirling the axe round his head once, he dealt so ponderous a blow with it upon the breast-plate of a piece of armour which hung close by, that he cut through the iron as if it had been lead, and from the violence of the shock the whole suit of mail fell to the floor with a tremendous crash.

Far and near throughout Brandon Castle was the fall of that heavy suit o mail heard; the soldiers started from their seats in the guard-room, with inquiring glances—the domestic retainers huddled more closely round the huge hall fire, and Eldred Weare, who was slowly ascending the steps of the southern gallery to his chamber, fell down with affright, and his light becoming extinguished, he rolled down the staircase again into the great hall, where his sudden re-appearance caused no little panic among the domestics, and immediately produced hysterics on the part of the fat cook, to whom he professed the ghost of an attachment.

Even Hugh Wingrove, although he knew the cause, started at the enormous clatter, and remarked to the crusader,—

"There will be scarcely any one in Brandon, but who will be full of surmises as to the cause of this noise at such an hour of the night."

"It will add another," said the knight, smiling, "to the many mysteries with which this place is peopled. Lead on, Hugh Wingrove; lead on."

It would seem, however, as if the very fates conspired to prevent the crusader from carrying into effect his resolution, for at that moment the long winding sound of a horn, sounded at the castle gate, awakening many echoes in the stillness of the night, was heard.

"Sir Rupert's horn! Sir Rupert's horn! as I am a living man, that is Sir Rupert's horn," cried Wingrove.

"Sir Rupert's!" echoed the crusader.

Then before Wingrove could reply another long blast from the horn filled the air with its long wailing sound. Then at the interval of a minute, came a third, after which all was as still again as the grave.

"I have my doubts," gasped Wingrove, "it may not be my lord and master after all, for such sounds as that at the gate of Brandon have more than once warmed every heart that loved Sir Rupert with joy at the expectation of his return, but to plunge them into deeper disappointment at the nonfulfilment of their hopes; and yet, I could swear it is his horn. Of all the mysteries which are in and about Brandon, this is the one which clings most sorrowfully to my heart."

"Can you be sure," said the crusader, "in your identification of the sound of a horn?"

"Quite, in this case," said Wingrove. "It is a small silver horn, which Sir Rupert had himself slightly bent, so as to produce a particular sound which I never hear from any other instrument. By it we always knew when he returned from the chase, and flew with joy to admit him to his ancient home."

"To the postern, to the postern," cried the crusader, "this is surely a mystery, if mystery at all, which can be easily solved."

CHAPTER L.

"What wonders will not love achieve?
Seas, deserts, continents oppose not its
Triumphant march."   ANON.

THE SUSPICION.—THE GUARD BY THE CRUSADER'S CHAMBER.

WINGROVE needed no urging to hurry to the postern-gate, which he and the crusader reached in the course of a few moments. As on the former occasions, when the supposed sound of Sir Rupert's horn had struck upon the ears of the men-at-arms, they had rushed from the guard-room and assembled in an anxious throng by the small wicket, through which the moat could be

seen, and any stranger on its opposite side duly observed and commented upon ere they were permitted to enter the fortress.

Anxiety sat on every face, and the moment Hugh Wingrove made his appearance half-a-dozen voices at once exclaimed :—

"Sir Rupert's horn—Sir Rupert's horn again, Wingrove."

"And that puts me in mind of my ear," said Bernard ; "don't you recollect the twinge I got by some infernal fool shooting an arrow through the open panelling ?"

"Yes," said Wingrove, "and I remember the wild message that was appended to the shaft of the arrow."

"What message ?" said the crusader.

"It was to the effect that so long as we heard that horn occasionally blow before the castle-gate, we might be assured that Sir Rupert Brandon was still among the living."

"That is strange," said the crusader. "Lower the drawbridge, and endeavour to discover who this mysterious horn-blower can be."

"For Heaven's sake do not risk your precious life on such an occasion," said Wingrove. "Remember how many thousand lives ——"

"Hush," said the crusader ; "you forget, Wingrove,—I pray you to be cautious. I have ever found. that from the greatest danger I have ultimately plucked the greatest safety."

At this moment another and still louder blast from the horn came from some spot on the other side of the moat, evidently very near the castle. Wingrove instantly dashed forward, and drew the bolt of the wicket-gate, when a general scuffle to get out of the way ensued among the men-at-arms, for, brave soldiers as they were, when they saw and understood the danger they had to encounter, they shrunk with a superstitious terror from the consequences that might ensue after the blowing of that mysterious horn. Hugh

No. 39

Wingrove alone stood exactly in the opening of the wicket-gate, and thrown into strong relief as his figure was by the glare of lights behind him, for several of the soldiers had brought torches from the guard-room, he presented as fair a mark as could be desired by any one who chose to level a deadly missile at him.

"Out of the way, you Wingrove, out of the way," cried Bernard. "What's the use of having a cloth-yard shaft through you when there's actually nine barrels of old ale in the cellar, for I counted them to-day?"

"Ale comes between you and your wits," said Wingrove; "there is no danger here, or I should have met it ere now; give me a torch some one of you."

A soldier handed him a torch, and holding it as high as he could, he shielded his eyes with his other hand, and strove to pierce the dim obscurity which lay between him and the opposite side of the moat.

The moon lay behind the castle, throwing a broad shadow across the moat, and for some distance beyond it, and Wingrove strained his eyes to pierce the darkness, and discover, if possible, what was on the other side. After a few moments he fancied he could discover, but indistinctly, something that bore a resemblance to a human form.

"By Heavens," he cried, "there is some one there this time," and raising his voice to a loud key, he shouted,—

"Who claims admission to Brandon at such an hour as this? If you are a friend, speak fearlessly; if an enemy, declare your name and calling."

The only reply was a low mournful blast of the horn, and the figure appeared to be walking to and fro on the bank of the moat. A cold feeling of fear crept over the heart of Hugh Wingrove as he thought, that after all the strange flitting looking form which he saw so faintly by the dim rays of the torch, might be something more than human, and that this time the blowing of Sir Rupert's horn might be rather an intimation of his death, than one of the strange proclamations of his continued existence.

"What see you, Wingrove," said the crusader, "that you fix your eyes so intently across the moat?"

"On my faith I scarce can tell," said Wingrove; "but there is certainly some one on the opposite side restlessly pacing to and fro, and I have thought once or twice, as the wind rose and fell, that I could hear a voice in such low plaintive accents, that the words were not distinguishable."

"Lower the drawbridge," cried the crusader, with a loud voice. "I am but a visiter here, comrades; but you have shown me so much courtesy that I trust you will let me do a little duty for my bed and board. I will cross to the other side of the moat, and I give you my sacred word, that if yon flitting figure run not away, in which case I am not good at a chase, be it man or devil, I will bring it into Brandon."

"For the love of Heaven go not," said Wingrove. "I entreat, I implore you."

"Nay," cried the crusader, "there can be little danger, and if there were much, I am sure you would not have me shrink from it."

"No," said Wingrove; "but when I consider ——"

"Hush—hush," said the crusader, "say no more; hark! the chains are rattling over the pullies—the drawbridge is down. Let go my arm, I beg of you."

"I am old and worthless," said Wingrove. "Let me go. What is such a life as mine compared to yours. I pray you let me go. I ask it as a most gracious boon."

"Nay—nay," said the crusader, laughing, "if you be so urgent we can both go; follow me if you please, but let the adventure be mine; it will go far to relieve the monotony of my stay at Brandon."

So saying, and wielding the heavy battle-axe in his hand as if it had been a straw, the crusader strode out of the castle through the wicket gate, and his heavy tread, as he crossed the drawbridge, was echoed back by the walls in endless cadences.

Wingrove rushed after him, bearing the torch in one hand, and his drawn sword in another.

Then Bernard, after turning to his comrades, and exclaiming,—" For God's sake any of you don't drink my ale," strode after Wingrove, determined that should there be any hard fighting he would be in the midst of it. Before then the crusader could reach the opposite side of the moat, a short abrupt note was again blown upon the horn, and he could plainly see a small slim figure, with its arms outstretched towards the Castle of Brandon, standing on the verge of the precipitous bank that led down to the rushing waters of the stream that encircled the fortress.

"Speak—speak," he cried ; " let us know ere we exchange courtesies or blows who and what you are?"

"Help—help," cried a soft feminine voice. " Oh, tell me if this is Brandon Castle? 'Tis like what they described it to me. Bless me with one word, and let that be yes, for I am faint and weary."

"Here's danger, Wingrove," said the crusader, with a laugh. " Why this is but some poor benighted wayfarer who claims our hospitality." |

"But the horn—the horn," said Wingrove ; " beware of an ambuscade ! Who knows what danger may lurk under those soft tones."

"Faint and weary," ejaculated Bernard ; " there's been no ale down that throat for a week, I dare say ; I always feel faint and weary between breakfast and dinner, and then between dinner and supper ; and the very sight of an empty ale flagon makes me drop down flat."

"I am on my guard," whispered the crusader ; " but I never anticipate danger ; then raising his voice, he cried,—

"This is Brandon Castle ; whom seek you here?"

" Joy—joy—joy," said the same low, gentle voice, which had in it some sweetly musical accents ; " my pilgrimage is over—my weary journey done ! Oh, what joy is this ! Did I ever hope to see this happy hour !"

The crusader in another moment stood by the side of the small fragile form from which came such extraordinary manifestations of pleasure, on the mere assurance that the edifice before it was Brandon Castle. Wingrove stood by the side of the knight, and the rays of the torch fell clearly and distinctly upon the face and form of what appeared to be a young lad, clothed in such garments as belonged to a sailor-boy of the period. The face was exquisitely beautiful ; the dark lustrous eyes shone with uncommon brilliancy ; and the glowing coral of the lips, together with the complexion slightly bronzed by the exposure to the weather, set off to the greatest perfection teeth white as alabaster.

"Who are you, boy?" said the stranger ; " and wherefore do you show such signs of extravagant joy at reaching Brandon Castle?"

"Because he is here ! because he is here !" said the stranger, clasping his hands, and speaking with fervour.

"Who?" cried Wingrove.

"Sir Rupert Brandon, the bravest, the noblest, the best : he is here, my heart tells me he is here ! This is his ancient home—the home of him and his high and noble race ! He has told me so himself a hundred times, and now, God be thanked, after much peril by land and sea, I stand in the shadow of his walls ! I press delightedly the verdant sod that he has trodden ! I am near him ! I am near him ! and my weary pilgrimage is done !"

To describe the tone of high enthusiasm, intense feeling, and exquisite pathos with which these words were uttered, would be impossible. The crusader and Wingrove looked at each other in astonishment, and Bernard stood with open mouth, and eyes rivetted upon the countenance of the youthful speaker, forgetting for full five minutes the very existence of ale as an article of human consumption.

The silence was broken by Hugh Wingrove, who said in a voice of deep emotion,—

"If from your heart you speak in such terms of dear love towards Sir Rupert Brandon, you are welcome here to the best we can give you, and to the services of every honest heart within this castle."

"Sincerity in every word," cried the crusader. "Come into the castle, and we will have some further conversation."

"He is there? tell me he is there?" said the young stranger.

"Sir Rupert has been away from his home for a long and weary time."

"Yes—yes—that I know full well; but he has returned—he has returned?"

"Heaven send he had; the sight of Sir Rupert again would bless my eyes and warm my heart to youthful vigour."

The boy clasped his hands despairingly, and looking in the face of the crusader, he said,—

"Do you too tell me that he is not here?"

"Sir Rupert has not returned from the crusades," was the reply, when the young stranger uttered a loud cry of anguish, and would have fallen to the earth had not the friendly arm of the crusader supported the fragile form, which to him was a matter of the greatest ease, as to his great strength it was no more than the weight of an infant.

"By the mass," he said, "this is most singular! the boy has fainted! Walk on with the torch, Wingrove, and I will carry him into the castle; there is some deep mystery in this transaction, which neither you nor I can at present understand."

"There is indeed," said Wingrove, as he hastily preceded the crusader, in his mind rapidly revolving every possible circumstance that could account for the sudden and strange appearance of the unknown boy before the Castle of Brandon. In a few minutes the crusader reached the guard-room with his burden, whom setting down by the fire-side by the rough soldiers, he called for some wine, an order which Bernard for once did not endeavour to translate into ale, and some being quickly procured, he poured a small portion into the mouth of the boy, who opened his singularly beautiful eyes, and fixed them with a look of intense disappointment on the face of the knight, as he murmured faintly,—

"You are not he! you are not he!"

"True I am not Sir Rupert Brandon," said the crusader; "but still I can even be as he is, a friend to the unfortunate."

"Still you are not he," was the earnest reply; "and yet, deem me not ungrateful; your air is noble, and your mannner compassionate. I am deeply thankful to you, although you are not he I have come so far to seek!"

"Boy," said the crusader, "you speak in riddles. Who are you? and whence come you?"

"I come," said the boy, "from the far east; what I was matters little; what I am now is a poor, lonely thing—a weed without the sunshine to give it life or beauty; for what am I without him?"

"Without Sir Rupert Brandon, mean you?"

"Aye, without Sir Rupert Brandon. There is music and beauty in his very name."

"But you will tell us who you are," said Hugh Wingrove. "We like not nameless persons here."

The honest soldier forgot at the moment that the crusader not only concealed his name, but his features likewise, on many occasions, and it was not until he said with a smile,—

" You know, Hugh Wingrove, people may have many reasons for concealing who and what they are, and for my own part I do not feel exactly justified
just now in pressing this young lad for an answer."

"Oh," said Bernard, "odd things are coming over Brandon. Why one
half of us in a little while won't know who the other half is."

" Never mind, Bernard," said the crusader, " you and an ale flagon will,
I make no doubt, be always on most intimate terms, and make no difficulty in
recognizing each other." Then he whispered to Wingrove,—

" Let this boy have food and refreshment, and then we can question him
apart."

" Will you consign him to my care ?" said the page of Fitzhugh, suddenly
stepping forward, and gazing earnestly in the face of the young stranger.

An odd expression of countenance came over the crusader's face, as he
said,—

" Thank you, no, I will see that this lad is safely bestowed for the night."
Then placing his mouth close to Wingrove's ear, he whispered,—

" Good Wingrove, are there women in the castle ?"

" There are several female domestics, besides Mistress Agatha," replied
Wingrove, surprised at the question.

" Ah," said the knight, " I had forgotten her, sweet amiable creature.
Take this young stranger to some kind female domestic, for between you and
I, Wingrove, I much suspect it is a girl."

" Lord bless me," said Wingrove, " but if you should be mistaken ?"

" Well, then," said the knight, " they can but turn him out into one of the
corridors, and we shall soon hear of it."

" Wonders will never cease," ejaculated Wingrove. " Oh, that Sir Rupert
Brandon would himself come home, and put an end to all these troubles and
mysteries."

" But you know, Wingrove," said the crusader, with a laugh, " people will
be mysterious and troublesome, and I doubt even if Sir Rupert Brandon could
prevent them ; so take the boy at once, and I shall now endeavour to snatch a
few hours' repose, as the night is so far advanced."

CHAPTER LI.

Fear is a medium through which trifles become gigantic. Like jealousy, it makes its own
food.—BACON.

ELDRED'S ALARM.—THE FALL.—THE MYSTERIOUS DISAPPEARANCE.

WHEN Eldred Weare recovered from his terror at the sudden clattering fall
of mail in the armoury, he once more bade good night to the domestic servants, in whose company he certainly passed the happiest hours of his existence, and again adventured to ascend the staircase leading to the gallery,
from which his bed-room opened.

With trembling steps he slowly proceeded, but when he reached the top,
without anything very terrifying crossing his path, he began to be a little reassured, and fancied after all the alarm was nothing, and had been occasioned
by some accidental circumstance, which would explain itself in the morning.

" I shall be glad when I am snug in bed, though," he muttered ; " not that
I am ever very snug in Brandon Castle ; but it is something to be in bed at
all—anywhere—for there one does feel safe, for if one sees anything extraordinary, one can put one's head under the clothes, and see it no more ; or if
one hears anything one don't like, one can pull one's night-cap about one's

ears, and then at all events one don't hear it quite so plain, and can almost fancy it is nothing at all. Well, I declare it's two o'clock, and what with one scrimmage and another there's hardly a soul asleep in the castle ; as for the men-at-arms, they sit up drinking ale, pretending they are forced to watch everybody else while they are asleep, and everybody else can't go to sleep for noises and riots, and great things coming down with a whack, and trumpets blowing, and all sorts of uncomfortables. Then there's the servants, they are as bad as anybody ; there they sit round the hall fire, and keep putting on logs. I wonder they are not ashamed to look an old tree in the face. And then one begins and tells something about a ghost that he had heard of some-body who knew somebody else—who was told of a man who had a friend, whose mother had a married sister, who had read about it somewhere ; then they all draw in a little nearer to the fire, and on goes another log, and so on they go till it's two o'clock in the morning, and I am nearly frightened out of my wits."

Eldred now proceeded for some paces half asleep, indulging in such dreamy reflections as those he had just given utterance to, when he came within a few paces of his sister's apartment ; there his eyes suddenly fell upon the form of Agatha Weare as she had been left after her fright from the visit of Sir Kenneth Hay.

Not knowing then at the first glance what it was, or who it was, who lay there half in and half out of the chamber, so still and so motionless, Eldred gave a great spring back and shrieked,—

"Murder—murder! fire—fire! what's that—what's that? help—help! —thieves—take my money and clothes, but spare my life!"

Retreating backwards until he again arrived at the top of the stairs, El-dred made a precipitate plunge head foremost down the whole flight, and arrived again in the great hall just as one of the domestics had concluded a ghost story in the following words,—

"And then as they were sitting as we are sitting now, and very quiet, as we are now, there came a rumbling sort of noise."

"Gracious Heavens!" said the cook, "there is a rumbling noise, and it sounds just as if some one was coming with a bump—bump—bump down the stairs."

"You—you—you don't say so," said the narrator of the tale.

Hardly had the words escaped his lips, when the latch of the door was burst off by the violence with which Eldred came against it, and for a second time on that eventful evening he rolled into the servants' hall, where he lay on his back, kicking out like a man attempting to swim on an emergency, and not exactly knowing how to do it.

A simultaneous scream arose on the part of the female domestics, and one of the males made a frantic attempt to climb up the chimney, which ended, after a few fruitless struggles, in his utter discomfiture, and coming down again with a face as black as a negro's, which so effectually dis-guised him, that no sooner did he show himself to his fellow-servants than, with one accord, they made a wild rush from the fire-place, upsetting El-dred, who had just regained his feet, and rolling over him, with such shrieks, oaths, cries, groans, and prayers as never were before heard in that ancient hall.

The best of the fun then was, that he who clambered up the chimney, feeling conscious that he had added greatly to the dismay of his fellow-servants, trampled about them, shouting, with his mouth full of soot,—

"It's only me—it's only me."

This confirmed them more in opinion that the old gentleman, who is not to be mentioned to ears polite, had actually made them a flying visit down the chimney. Confusion became worse confounded ; and when the men-at-arms in the guard room, who had heard an unusual tumult, rushed to the scene of the commotion, they found the household of Brandon Castle kicking about in all directions ; while of Eldred Weare there could be seen nothing but two thin legs incased in red stockings kicking convulsively, while the fat cook lay in hysterics exactly on his face.

It took a quarter of an hour or more to raise the affrighted domestics from the ground and convince them they were not surrounded by a legion of ghosts and devils.

As for Eldred Weare, he gave so confused an account of seeing somebody or something lying somewhere, that he was abused by all parties as having by his absurdity been the cause of all the uproar and confusion.

"Why, you coward," said Bernard, "you are always making some fuss or another with your fears."

"Ah," said Eldred, "go on—abuse me all of you ; but if you doubt what I say, come up to the southern gallery and look for yourselves, when you will see what alarmed me so much, and you'll all fall down yourselves, as I did."

The men-at-arms laughed at the idea of falling down ; but the proposition to go up and see if anything of an alarming character was really there they thought but reasonable, and, headed by Bernard, they ascended the staircase, leaving the terrified servants in expectation that something terrible would happen in a few moments.

Eldred gathered courage sufficient, now that he was surrounded by others, to approach the exact spot where he had seen the figure lying to all appearance dead ; but when he reached it, to his dismay, he saw nothing, for Agatha had in the interim risen and staggered into her own chamber, where she lay in an agony of terror, thinking that henceforward she should be the slave of supernatural appearances.

Such a conviction to a mind formed in the mould of Agatha Weare's was terror indeed, and the moment that it found a place in her bewildered imagination, every trifling sound became an object of terror, and the silence of her chamber became to her pregnant with horrors.

In the fitful blast, as it moaned past the ancient battlements of Brandon, she fancied she could hear the wild shrieks of departed spirits, and the merest incidental noise was converted by her teaming brain into the voice of Sir Kenneth Hay, reproaching her for being the cause of his untimely and terrible death ; for that he was dead she fully believed, as it had not entered into the plans of Morgatani to inform her that, by some means he knew not of, the imprisoned knight had escaped from his dungeon and was either still in Brandon Castle, or making what speed he might from its time-worn walls, for the purpose of taking measures to avenge himself for the injuries he had there received.

Deep groans burst from the labouring breast of Agatha ; one moment she would clasp her hands with agony, and the next she would twine her long fingers in her raven hair, and utter such deep sobs in her mental disquietude as would have moved the most obdurate breast to pity.

"Why—oh, why," she cried, in despairing accents, "did I suffer the wild passions of my slighted heart so far to triumph over reason, justice, and right as to plunge me into the frightful chaos of despair I feel around me ? Why did I league myself with that fiend in human shape, Morgatani, the Black Monk, the much-dreaded, wily Jesuit, of whose deep selfishness, want of faith, and frightful cruelty I had ere then heard so much ? Oh, it was madness—madness—madness !"

She buried her face in her hands, and throwing herself heavily upon her couch, she remained for nearly half an hour as still and motionless as if her erring spirit had indeed fled to its last account.

But how fearful—how intense—how agonising were the thoughts that during that period of time ran riot in the hapless brain of Agatha Weare.

She thought of her first wild, boundless passion for Sir Rupert Brandon—of the deep anguish with which she had marked the growing symptoms of his increasing admiration of her sister Alicia. Then she run over in her own mind how she had watched the progress of that dear love until it reached the full meridian of its glory; and with fearful, terrible minuteness came to her memory each word and action of the scene which she then wondered at the time had not driven her mad, but which had indeed virtually done so by depriving her of the command of her better reason.

A half stifled shriek burst from her lips as these recollections forced themselves with such painful minuteness on her mind.

" I," she cried, " even I, proud and haughty as I always was, I stooped from my maidenly dignity and station to tell him, Sir Rupert Brandon, that I loved him. In the violence of my emotions, in the deep debasement of my maddening passion, and in the utter abandonment of all thought and feeling, which should have saved me, I even knelt at the feet of that man, as he should have knelt at mine, to implore him to pity the heart he had so easily captured."

She sprang to her feet, and wildly paced to and fro in the apartment, then raising her hands wildly above her head, she cried,—

" Heaven save me from these thoughts! they rush like liquid fire through my brain. Oh, what a reply did I receive to that wild, passionate declaration of attachment, which flowed with all the wild, fervid adoration from a heart which like mine only fosters such feelings once, and when blighted, becomes choked up with the noxious weeds of demoniac passion.

" He said that he would pity me.—His pity! It was that one word that raised the unholy flame of revenge in my heart. With wild laughter, and shrieking accents, I then told him that the time would come when even I, hating him and abhorring his very name, as from that time forthwith I should, would pity him : and great indeed should be his sufferings and mortal agony, before such a feeling found place in my anguish-stricken heart. I saw him smile, and by that smile I vowed a deep and terrible revenge.

" This monk then found me apt. He had but to apply the kindling torch of his fiery eloquence to my half smouldering passions, when they burst into a blaze which knew no control. I have had my revenge, and, God of Heaven! what am I now ?"

" Mine," said the deep voice of the monk, as he glided into the chamber. " Mine, Agatha Weare, soul and body, mine. You have sold yourself to the gratification of your passions, and if the price be paid—as it shall—as it shall—you cannot, you dare not shrink from the compact."

These words were spoken to Agatha Weare with a hissing vehemence that made her tremble with terror.

" Morgatani, Morgatani," she cried, " spare me, spare me! make me no longer the poor tool of your unholy designs. Spare me, spare me, as you have one lingering ray of mercy left, spare me."

The monk laughed loud and long, like a very fiend, as, grasping Agatha's wrists, he said,

" You shall have your revenge. You shall have your revenge That was the condition, and it shall be fulfilled to the very letter."

Agatha flung herself upon her knees, and clutching the hem of his robe, hrieked,—

" Mercy! mercy! Morgatani, you are yet human."

" No," cried the monk, "I am mortal—curses on the fate that made me

so!—but I am not human. The passions—the feelings of humanity move me not—the belief of mankind is not my belief. What they reverence I scorn—what they shrink from I approach undismayed—what they worship I taunt and defy. Call me not human, Agatha Weare, for I am as far apart from humanity as are the poles asunder."

"Horrible! horrible!" said Agatha.

"Not so," said the monk. "Why should it be horrible to you to be associated with one who you know will keep his word to the very letter, although all hell should stand between him and his purposes."

"It is horrible—it is horrible," said Agatha.

"This paroxysm of mortal weakness will pass away," sneered the monk, "and those delightful feelings which a benign and amiable Providence has implanted in your breast, will arise again in all their gory beauty, pointing you the way to your revenge, through clinging pools of blood."

"No, no," gasped Agatha.

"I say yes," added the monk, with a bitter laugh. "So you loved Sir Rupert Brandon, you adored him—and—ha, ha, you told him so. But with man, the rose that falls is never worth the plucking, and he promised you, kind gentle heart, his tender pity. He was not angry—oh, no, he could only pity the fond tender fool who threw herself into his arms to be repulsed. Poor slighted, rejected, scorned, pitied Agatha Weare."

"Peace, tempter, peace," cried Agatha, dashing aside her disordered hair from her eyes. "What would you tempt me to?"

"Nothing, nothing," said the monk.

"Yet your words are such as to stir up the latent fires or passions of my heart."

"Are they, indeed," said the monk. "I thought all Agatha Weare's fiery
No. 40

passions were quenched in the floods of tears with which she lamented that Sir Rupert Brandon pitied, instead of loving her."

"What would you tempt me to? what would you tempt me to, Morgatani?" said Agatha.

"To conclude," replied the monk, "what is already so well begun. The commencement was a bridal, which left you in despair; the end shall be an execution, which shall leave you in triumph."

Agatha was silent for a few moments, and then in a low voice she said,—

"Morgatani, I feel that I cannot now retreat; from your employer in the wild purpose of my revenge, I have changed, to become your slave."

"Not my slave," said the monk, "but the only human heart for which I would feel deep sympathy. This shrinking remorse which occasionally oppresses you, is but the fleeting remains of those early imbibed feelings and prejudices which such a mind as yours is never very late in shaking off. Trust me, you shall have your revenge, and with it power and wealth. King John has promised under his own hand and seal, that Brandon Castle shall be placed in your hands and mine solely, if we but succeed in ridding him of so dangerous a personal follower and friend of Richard's, as Sir Rupert Brandon."

"Then Eldred," said Agatha, "is not taken into account in such an arrangement."

"He is not," said the monk, with a sneer, "but he will be a useful tool to us as evidence, regarding those matters in which we wish to implicate Sir Rupert Brandon."

"Direct me as you will," said Agatha, "I must obey you. But know, Morgatani, we have more then mortal foes to contend with."

"Indeed?" said the monk, with an incredulous air.

"Yes," continued Agatha, "Sir Kenneth Hay is doubtless dead, for this night his spirit has appeared to me, and caused me such shivering pangs of terror, as I trust I may never know again."

"His spirit?" said the monk.

"Ay, his spirit, fully armed, even as he appeared when he first came to Brandon."

"Banish your fears, Agatha Weare," said the monk. "Sir Kenneth Hay has escaped, by the damnable agency of some one whom I cannot as yet even suspect. It was his mortal form, if any had greeted your vision."

"Escaped?" cried Agatha.

"Ay," said the monk, "but you seem rejoiced."

"I am—I am," cried Agatha. "Thank Heaven at least for so much. Ah, I am free from a terror which would have preyed upon my very soul."

"Weakness," said the monk, "weakness engendered by early superstition."

"And yet I thank Heaven," added Agatha.

CHAPTER LII.

What strange unearthly light is that,
Which with an awful lustre chases night away?—ANON.

THE GLEAM OF LIGHT FROM THE OLD GREY TURRET.—THE CRUSADER'S
DETERMINATION.

THE strange and exciting dialogue we have attempted to record between Agatha Weare and the Black Monk, was taking place during some period of the time that Eldred Weare was making himself so ridiculous to the assembled servants in the great hall of Brandon, by an exhibition of his many fears, and the abundant cowardice of his heart. The feelings, too, of Morgatani, were unusually bitter, for he had just failed in his attempts to assassinate the crusader, being likewise unsuccessful in obtaining a view of his face, in order that he might come to some conclusion as to who he was, for the monk said no more than the truth, when he said that the principal crusaders were well known to him. Hence, perhaps, arose some of the more than common bitterness of his tone, and from the accumulation of those aggravated feelings most unquestionably came many of the deep oaths and frightful curses he muttered, after he left Agatha Weare's chamber.

"Richard Cœur de Lion is a prisoner in a foreign land," he muttered, "but it is astonishing the efforts made by his adherents to rescue him. This last emissary, who affects a mystery, by keeping a mask upon his face, is no doubt one of his most intimate associates, and one high in his confidence. There seems to be a charm about his life, for twice have I attempted it, but to fail twice most signally. Yet will I not be discouraged. He shall die, for no human soul shall live to thwart my hopes, and destroy my highest and dearest expectations. If I could but now discover where they have lodged him for the night, my exceeding intimacy of all the intricate windings of Brandon Castle, would surely enable me to take him at some disadvantage, and destroy his life."

The monk then remained some moments in thought, after which, he said—

"Surely Eldred Weare, who is intimate with the domestics of the castle, must know where this much thought of stranger has been lodged. I will seek the information, even if I procure it not."

Without another moment's hesitation, the Black Monk with rapid strides sought the chamber of Eldred Weare, who trembling and frightened at his own shadow, just then contrived to get into bed.

It never occurred to Morgatani that his visit at such an hour to Eldred would go near to be sufficient to kill that far from courageous individual from fright. He was only intent upon his own purpose, and when he knocked at the chamber door, he as little thought of Eldred Weare's feelings as he did of the oaken panelling against which he struck his knuckles.

The moment Eldred Weare heard the summons at his door, he made but one dive under the clothes to the very middle of the bed, where he remained shivering and shaking to such a degree that the bedstead creaked amazingly, and the old hangings threw out volumes of dust.

Again the monk, who was not over-gifted with patience, knocked, and Eldred, with a deep groan, attempted to fish up from the depths of his memory the fragments of some prayers he had been taught by the family confessor, when a child.

A third and louder knock at the door now made Eldred Weare wish that a trap-door would open, and let him and the bed right down, to any depth, so that it could set him free from what he believed to be an unearthly visitor.

"Eldred Weare—Eldred Weare," said the monk, in a low, deep tone; for he was far from wishing his voice to be carried further than to Eldred's own ear.

"Go away," said Eldred, whose terror was far too great to allow him to recognize the monk's voice. "Do go away, if you please, good Mr. Ghost, and come again some other time. I have tumbled down stairs twice already to-night, and I am sure if I see you, I shall have to get out of the window, and tumble into the moat with never such a splash."

"What does the fool mutter?" said the monk. "Open the door, Eldred

Weare, or you will compel me to force it.   I must and will speak with you this night."

"The Lord have mercy upon us !" said Eldred.   "Amen—give us our daily bread—and for what we receive the Lord make us thankful."

"Open—open," said the monk, again knocking at the door.   "Do you not know me ?"

"Good gracious !" said Eldred, popping his head out of the bed-clothes, "it's the voice of the Black Monk, I mean Morgatani.   He'd just twist my neck in a minute, if he heard me call him the Black Monk." Then, raising his voice, he said in a broken tone,—" What do you want, eh?   I'm fast asleep, and have been for ever so long."

"I would speak with you, Eldred Weare," said the monk, solemnly.

Eldred groaned, as he muttered,—

"Needs must, I suppose, when the thingamy drives.   Well, I do wish, with all my heart, I was out of Brandon Castle.   There's no peace all day to one, and when one does get to bed, somebody comes to frighten one out of one's wits.   How cold too.   I never will go to bed another time without a light.   No, never—for I——"

"Open," cried the monk, as he dealt the door a furious kick, and Eldred, with renewed alarm, hastened to obey the imperious mandate.

The stupendous figure of the monk filled up the entire doorway, and a more striking contrast than he presented in his dark ecclesiastical garments, and look of bold, fearless determination, to the diminutive, shivering, half clad Eldred Weare, could not well be imagined.

"May I presume to ask you what you want ?" said Eldred Weare, shivering and trembling, as he stood before the monk.

"You may," said Morgatini ; "but wherefore do you tremble thus, Eldred Weare ?"

"It's the co—co—co—cold," stammered Eldred.   "I ain't afraid a bit, it's only the cold."

"Tell me," said the monk, with a sneer, which he did not attempt to conceal, "where the crusader lodges this night in Brandon ?"

"The—the—crusader ?" stammered Edgar.

"Answer me, you idiot, for your life's sake, and repeat not my words."

"No—oh, dear !—certainly not.   They have put him into the chamber with the green arras, where they said King Henry once lodged."

"The chamber with the green arras," muttered the monk, as he walked slowly away.   "I know it well ; 'tis most fitting and convenient for my purpose ; for now I do bethink me, I can see its exquisitely worked window from the old Grey Turret.   Beware, bold and haughty crusader, beware ! for be you whom you may, it shall go hard with Morgatani, the Jesuit, this night, if he leave you light enough to break your morning fast."

"Well," said Eldred, as he closed his door, "I would not be in the chamber with the green hangings for a trifle.   There will be a row there to-night, as sure as eggs _is_ eggs ; and it strikes me that that crusader is very nearly as much of a whopper as the monk, in which case, the row won't be very soon over.   They'll cut each other up like the two strange foxes I once heard of, for one of them had nothing but his tail left after the fight, and the other nothing but his left whisker.   Well, they ain't above me, so they can't come through the floor ; and they ain't below me, so they can't poke anything through the ceiling ; so I'll just go to bed again, and hope nobody will disturb me till breakfast time, when I shall hear the sweet voice of that amiable creature the cook saying,—' An' it please you, Master Eldred, I warmed up the venison pasty for your breakfast, and here's a glass of spiced Canary—Canary'—the cook—rather fat—the Black Monk—Heaven keep us with a whole —skin—skin—skin—"

Eldred was fast asleep.

Meanwhile the crusader had been conducted by Hugh Wingrove to the chamber that Eldred had mentioned. It was a spacious and elegant room, which had been fitted up specially for the accommodation of King Henry upon his making one of the frequent royal tours through his kingdom, in which he took so much delight. Everything of elegance or cost which the rude magnificence of the age in which he lived could produce, was collected to grace the chamber of the king. When, however, the visit was over, the smaller portable articles of rarity or magnificence were removed to different rooms of the spacious edifice, leaving little more than the massive bedstead, with its carved cherubims at the corners, and its lofty dais of cloth of gold.

The hangings likewise remained untouched, and, being of a dark green colour, they had greatly resisted the changes of time.

The window, to which the monk alluded as seen from the Grey Turret, was one of rare and costly beauty, and had been let into the room for the king's admiration. Its many curiously shaped points of singularly coloured glass, when the sun was shining, gave the chamber a most dazzling and beautiful appearance, and dappled the oaken flooring with so many beautiful colours, that the rarest carpet of the present day could scarcely have vied with it in splendour.

Even the cold, pale moon-beams, as they passed through the gorgeous medium of coloured glass, borrowed a beauty beyond their own sweet simplicity, casting long streams of coloured light upon the rich damask hangings.

Hugh Wingrove had been careful that every comfort should be added to the chamber that could in any way add to the satisfaction or the repose of the crusader; although he might have well spared himself so much trouble, for that gallant warrior was more accustomed to sleep in the tented field than upon downy beds of state, and cared little for those arts of life which pamper the body, and, in too many cases, succeed in enervating the mind.

" Beshrew me, Wingrove," he said, as he glanced around, on reaching the chamber; " but you have lodged me right well. This room might well befit the royal Henry, who, you say, one night slept within its walls."

" It is my humble and pleasant duty," said Wingrove, " to lodge you as well as Brandon Castle can afford. I will place a sentinel at your door, who shall be regularly relieved on his watch, until you issue from your chamber in the morning."

" Thanks for your attention, good Wingrove," said the knight, " although I hardly think it necessary. It is true, that I sleep heavily, because I have been accustomed to repose amid the din of war's alarms; but surely no one could break through this massive oaken door without awakening me ?"

" My fears are scarcely for your safety in this chamber," said Hugh Wingrove; " for that I believe your own arm would always insure, but I should be unhappy if I thought your rest was disturbed, therefore, I pray you, allow me to place the sentinels."

" As you please, Wingrove," said the crusader. " I will consent, rather to please you, than because I think there is any necessity for such a measure."

As the crusader happened to pass between the lamp and the window, his eyes were attracted by a light on the outside, at a considerable distance off.

" Wingrove," he said, " what light is that, which streams so far on the night air ?"

Wingrove stepped to the window, and, shading his eyes with his han he said,—

" By Heavens! it is in the Grey Turret.   The devil, or Morgatani, is at his work to-night."

" Then think you, really, that Morgatani inhabits that ancient turret?" said the knight.

" I do, on my soul," said Wingrove; " but so subtle and dangerous a man is he, that even if he be not leagued with evil spirits, he seems to possess all their power of mischief, and to hold possession of the old Grey Turret as an impregnable fortress."

" He must carry on his game boldly," said the crusader, " to permit so strong a light to glance through those ancient loopholes. One would think there could now be little trouble in bearding him in his den."

Wingrove shaded his eyes with his hands, and looked long and earnestly at the light, after which he said,—

" I pray you, sir, not to adventure your precious life by approaching that Grey Turret. When I come to think of how much less importance it is that Morgatani, or the devil, or both, should hold their highest revelry within that ancient place, than that you should come to any injury, I am induced to pray of you not to tempt the dangerous subtlety of that dark, mysterious man, who, for all we even know, may be throwing out yon light as a lure for your destruction."

" It is likely enough," said the crusader, " that a Jesuit might adopt such means. I will, however, disappoint him to-night, Hugh Wingrove, for I feel most specially wearied and long to retire to rest."

" May the saints guard you," said Wingrove, as, after lighting and trimming a lamp which was in the room, he left the crusader to his repose.

The latter, however, was too much interested by the phenomena of that mysterious light from the old Grey Turret to retire instantly to bed ; and more from curiosity than any intention of pursuing the adventure further, he placed himself behind one of the high-backed chairs, which effectually shaded its rays from the window.

As he then approached the gaudily stained glass, the effect of the mysterious stream of light from the loop-hole of the old Grey Turret was beautiful in the extreme, for it changed its hue as it passed into the crusader's chamber through one or the other of its various tinted panes on his window.

After some efforts in vain, he succeeded in opening one-half of the lower part of the window, and then upon the clear night air he saw that brilliant scintillation of light streaming without a break from the loop-hole. The night air was cold as it came off the moat and swept occasionally in gusts howling around the ancient battlements, but the crusader would have been as little aware of the state of the weather had it been pouring with rain instead of being, as it was, dry and cold, for his attention was altogether absorbed by the light in the turret, which he puzzled himself in vain to account for.

" No common source of light," he said, " could produce so strong and brilliant a ray as that which now presents itself to my eyes. What can that infernal Jesuit be doing? It would seem as if the flame from which that strong beam of light proceeds, must be immense."

Even as he spoke the light totally disappeared, and then to his surprise a shower of bright sparks shot up apparently from the roof of the turret, streaming high in the air, and some of them exploding with a loud report.

Then again a light green, but of a strange and sickly hue, proceeded from the loop-hole. The source from whence it proceeded seemed to be moving from left to right in such a manner as to make the long ray fall each moment upon a different part of the castle. Then a slight confusion in his eyes convinced the crusader that it was directed full against his window, and by an involuntary movement he stepped on one side and allowed it unmolested to stream into the room, which it did for some seconds steadily.

Then as suddenly as before it disappeared, and so strong had been the glare of light that it threw into the apartment, that its sudden departure was followed by a comparative darkness, which the lamp in the room appeared to have no effect upon.

" This is indeed very strange," said the crusader ; " I have heard wild tales and legends of this kind, and when encamped on the battle plain, many a tale containing such incidents as this, has wiled away the weary hours of night until the morning watch. Do these appearances belong to the natural or the supernatural ? I am far more inclined to believe the former than the latter, and yet why do I pause upon the question when I can satisfy myself so easily? It can be but a short distance from this wing of the castle to yon old Grey Turret. Sleep seems to have deserted me, my weariness is fled in the surprise at the curious sight I have seen. I am not used to delays, and such an opportunity of solving one of the greatest mysteries that clings to Brandon Castle, may not occur again. Come of the adventure what it may, I will attempt the dangers of the old Grey Turret.

CHAPTER LIII.

A sound so horrible and full of terror,
That the vexed soul suspends its functions
As at the bidding of a God.—BARRY.

THE ADVENTURE IN THE TURRET.—THE SOUND OF TERROR

TAKING then his lamp in his hand, the crusader opened his chamber door, at which he found the soldier, whose name was Anstey, keeping watch and ward as he had been ordered to do by Wingrove.

" I shall return anon, my good friend," said the crusader, as he passed on after receiving a respectable salute from the guard.

After he had proceeded a few paces, he bethought him that the soldier would, in all probability, be well acquainted with a near route from the chamber to the small court-yard, immediately adjoining to the mysterious turret ; he, therefore, returned, and addressing him in the familiar frank tone of voice which so much pleased the men-at-arms, and came so gracefully from the lips of the crusader, he said,—

" My friend, didst ever see a light beaming from the loop-hole of the old Grey Turret ?"

" Often, Sir Knight, very often," replied Anstey ; " there is not a soul in the castle but has seen it, and I may add not a soul without fear and trembling."

" Indeed !" said the crusader.

" Yes," added Anstey, " there cannot be a doubt but that some evil spirits have leagued themselves with Morgatani, the Black Monk, and made the old Grey Turret their home."

" There are more evil spirits of mortal flesh and blood," said the knight, " than any which inhabit the airy regions of space. I have to-night seen that light, and intend, if it be possible, to enter the turret and discover from whence it proceeds."

" Heaven preserve me !" said the soldier, " the whole of the men-at-arms, headed by Hugh Wingrove, who shrinks not at a trifle, attempted in vain to storm the old Grey Turret."

" What deterred you ?"

" Such frightful sights and sounds, and such real danger in the shape of showers of fire, that mortal man could not stand against it."

" I am inclined to think," said the crusader, " that the adventure is one of those which are much more likely to be brought to a successful termination by one person than by a hundred. What I require of you is that you should direct me which is the shortest way to the small paved court which I have so frequently seen from the battlements, and from which springs the turret."

" That I can do," said Anstey, " but you must recollect, Sir Knight, that I have my duty to do besides."

" I will not detain you five minutes," said the crusader ; " all I require is to be put into my proper road, in order that I may not waste any time."

" You misunderstand me," said the soldier, as he settled his iron head-piece on his head. " I conceive it to be my duty to accompany you, since I was placed here as your guard, and if you are indeed bent upon this adventure—from which, sir, I would fain persuade you—at least let me share its dangers with you."

" Come on," said the knight, without a moment's hesitation, " we will endeavour to be back by the time your comrades come to relieve your watch."

The crusader then handed the lamp to the soldier, and swinging the heavy battle-axe in his hand, which was his favourite weapon, and which he had been careful to bring from his chamber, he followed the soldier, much amused in his own mind at the tale he should have to tell Hugh Wingrove in the morning of his success in storming the turret, for that he should be successful he never entertained the shadow of a doubt.

So daring and bold, and so generally happy in their issues had been most of the actions and adventures of that fearless man, that when he started upon any new enterprise, whether it were great or small, he never allowed himself to dream of failure.

Descending a flight of stone stairs, the soldier pushed open a door and then six steps which immediately presented themselves brought him and the crusader into the long gallery, the windows of which looked into the paved yard, from which sprung the old Grey Turret.

" Here we are at once," said the soldier, as they merged into the open air ; " the turret looks solemn and black as usual. When the moon rises it stands out in the clear sky quite like a great blot upon it. By the mass, if I were Sir Rupert, when I returned from the holy wars, I would not leave one stone of it standing upon another."

" It was light enough but a short time since," said the knight. " Think you the door from the court-yard is open ?"

" Most likely, Sir Knight," said the soldier ; " I never knew it otherwise—not that I have paid many visits to the place."

The crusader followed the soldier closely to the door, and then he said,—

" My good friend, if it was your duty to follow me in this adventure, it is surely mine to lead you in it. Therefore, allow me if you please, to precede you up these stairs."

Anstey made no particular objection to this arrangement, but looking rather grim and setting his teeth firmly, he grasped his sword tightly in his hand, resolved that come what might he would be in an active and ready condition to strike a few blows for his life.

" Upon my word," said the knight, as they ascended a few steps of the staircase, " these ghosts, if such they are, are singularly unmindful of the advantages of their situation ; two or three of them at the head of these

narrow stairs might keep a strong force actively employed, and at bay below."

"Never mind, never mind," said Anstey; "I pray you not to make such remarks, for they hear every word that is uttered."

"If they do, then," said the knight, "they will receive a lesson in generalship, to which I will add for their special edification, that if the staircase were so defended, I would not trouble myself to lose men by storming it, but I would pile up lighted faggots outside until it became too hot to hold them. When for fear of being baked, they would either make a ghostly exit through the loop-holes, or creep down the stairs and surrender at discretion like mere mortals."

Scarcely had these words passed the lips of the knight when Anstey said,

"I have just trodden upon something."

"D—n it, so have I," said the crusader, and he half stumbled on the stairs, when there immediately ensued so stunning and terrible a report that they thought that the drums of their ears were split, and that they never should be able to hear again. The lamp which the soldier carried was as completely extinguished by the concussion of the air as if it had been suddenly dipped into the castle moat, and the darkness that remained around was so dense and profound that the crusader could not see his own hand when he held it up within an inch of his own eyes.

Whether or not the soldier made any remark he could not tell, for his sense of hearing was completely stunned, and when he attempted to cry, "Courage, courage, my good friend; do not be scared by a noise," he quite started at the sound of his own voice, which, after the tremendous explosion that had taken place, sounded to him as thin and weak as an infant's.

No. 41

To hear each other was out of the question, and they continued for some moments shouting out mutual remarks, without in the slightest degree answering each other, or carrying on any rational conversation.

"For Heaven's sake, come away," said Anstey.

"Why don't you speak ?" said the crusader.

"Sir knight! sir knight!" cried Anstey, "let me hear your voice, that I may be assured of your safety."

"They have killed that poor fellow," remarked the crusader.

"Alas!" said Anstey, "that gallant man is no more; I will get a light and bring the men-at-arms to search for his body."

"I won't leave the poor fellow lying dead here," said the crusader; "I will call Hugh Wingrove to my assistance."

They then rapidly descended the staircase together, when the crusader overtaking the soldier, ran up against him, and immediately seizing him with an iron grasp, cried,

"So, villains, I have one of you, and you shall not so easily escape me."

"Murder !—help !" cried Anstey—"the Black Monk !—the Black Monk ! —I am a dead man !"

The crusader dragged him through the low doorway into the court-yard, and then, by the dim light of the rising moon, that was attempting to struggle through the clouds that opposed its brilliancy, he saw who it was that he held in his grasp.

By this time the violence of the effect upon their sense of hearing was beginning to abate, and the crusader could hear Anstey say,

"Heaven be thanked, you are safe, sir knight; in my own mind I had numbered you with the dead."

"And so had I you," replied the crusader; "but tell me, do I speak in a little thin whisper, as if I were afraid to trust my voice ?"

"You do, indeed," said Anstey, "for I can scarcely hear you."

"Then," said the knight, "I quite understand the effect produced upon us—that noise has half deafened both of us; by the mass, two or three such sounds would destroy one's sense of hearing altogether. Let us, at all events, procure some lights before we think of proceeding further."

As the knight spoke, a broad glare of light came from one of the windows of the gallery, and several of them being thrown open, he saw a crowd of the men-at-arms and the domestic servants of the castle, many of whom had torches, looking with eager eyes in the direction of the Grey Turret.

"Heaven preserve us !" said one, "I thought the castle was coming down about our ears."

"It must be shaken to its foundation," said another.

"I don't know whether I am on my head or my heels," screamed a third.

"And it tumbled me bang out of bed," said Eldred, rushing into the room. "I am sure I shall never get another night's sleep in the castle. Oh, dear, oh, dear, what was it ? Is the castle all of a shake, or is it me only ? Is everything going joggle-joggle, or am I only ?"

"Where is the crusader ?" cried Hugh Wingrove, in a voice of anxiety and alarm, for he conjectured that the tremendous noise which had awakened every inhabitant of Brandon, and really startled Eldred Weare quite out of his bed on to the floor, might be, in some manner, connected with an attempt on his life.

The crusader heard the voice of Hugh Wingrove, for he was now nearly recovered from the shock his sense of hearing had experienced, and the voices of those who spoke were gradually to him assuming their usual character.

"I am here—I am here," he cried; "and here, too, is Anstey, in a whole skin, and only a little bewildered by the crash, which seems to have had such an universal effect in Brandon."

"A crash!" cried a dozen voices in chorus.

"Why," cried Wingrove, "it was more like a hundred claps of thunder rolled into one."

"Where was it?—where did it come from?" cried everybody in a breath.

"From the old Grey Turret," cried Anstey; "and if ever I go near it' again, I'll give you all leave to call me a fool."

"And so you are," said Bernard, looking from one of the windows; "what business had you going to the old Grey Turret making such a noise? Upon my word, it's dreadful; you don't know the harm you may have done."

"Yes, I do, stupid," said Anstey, "I have given all your ears a tingle, and my own the most."

"No, you don't, stupid," said Bernard, "curse you. It strikes me very forcibly, you know—that is, I think ——"

"What?—what?" cried everybody.

"That that awful noise—that frightful, horrid noise we all heard ——"

"Yes, yes, yes," said a dozen voices.

"Was enough to turn all the ale in the castle sour."

A general expression of discontent at this climax to Bernard's mysterious opinion pervaded the men-at-arms and domestics, and just as the crusader and Anstey reached the gallery, Agatha Weare rushed, with wild, disordered looks, into the midst of the throng.

"God of Heaven!" she cried, "what has happened?—what awful sounds were those which burst upon the ear of sleep?—what is it that now makes the night so terrible at Brandon Castle? Is it real, or did I dream that I heard the castle was rent to its deep centre, and a yawning chasm opened to receive those guilty of human slaughter? Speak, speak some of you—was it real, or but the hideous phantasma of a dream? My brain throbs—my heart beats wildly in my bosom—that dreadful sound is still ringing in my ears. Speak, I charge you, for the love of Heaven—speak!"

CHAPTER LIV.

"What pangs the guilty heart must feel when terrors of the supernatural assail it. The wonder of the innocent is to it an agony."—ANON.

AGATHA'S TERRORS.—THE SAILOR BOY.—THE NIGHT OF ANXIETY.

THE appearance and manner of Agatha were such as to create alarm in every breast. She was loosely attired in a flowing morning dress, which made her look taller than she really was, and the long, snake-like, black hair, that hung in wild disorder about her face, joined to the anxious and terrified expression of every feature, gave her an appearance scarcely human.

It was some moments before any one could reply to her, so intent were all in gazing at her, and endeavouring, each according to his or her judgment, to found some conjectures concerning the strange words she had uttered.

"Speak, speak!" she shrieked; "are you all dumb? Do I look so terrible that you do nothing but bend your eyes upon me in stupid wonder? Was it a dream, or was it real? Speak, I charge you; and yet it must be true, or why, at such an hour as this, are ye all assembled, looking at each other with such ghastly faces?"

She glanced rapidly around the group, and then suddenly exclaimed,

"Hark! hark! How tardily the time passes when the heart is full of woe. Help—oh, help me, Heaven!"

The castle clock at this moment struck solemnly the hour of four, and when its melancholy reverberations had ceased, the crusader broke the silence in which the curious throng were wrapped by saying,

"Agatha Weare, it was no dream; there was certainly a sound sufficiently loud to have awakened the far-famed sleepers. By the mass, it still rings in my ears as if a dozen bells were jingling in my brain."

"True, true!" said Agatha.

"I can vouch for that," said Anstey, shaking his head and rubbing his ears.

"And I—and I," said several.

"And I," cried Eldred, in a squeaking voice of alarm; "I can vouch that I fell out of bed with a bang that nearly broke every bone in my skin, and look at me now."

Eldred had a piece of faded tapestry rolled round him in the form of a cloak, and now by his words that he challenged general attention to his appearance, those who had rushed so hastily from their beds began to look curiously at each other, and so strange a group of persons so oddly attired could scarcely have been found. Many would have immediately rushed back to their chambers, but that curiosity to know the cause of the tremendous uproar detained them, and upon others fear had taken so strong a hold that they had determined not to retire to rest again that night.

Among those latter was Fitzhugh, who stood by one of the windows, looking pale and ghastly, surmising much in his own mind that a violent attempt had been made upon the life of the crusader by the Black Monk, and that he, Fitzhugh, might rationally enough be suspected of being a participator in the intended crime.

"Retire to your couches," said the crusader; "there is no harm, that I am aware of, done, nor can I at present perceive any danger. The tremendous sound which seems to have disturbed the repose of Brandon Castle did certainly come from the old Grey Turret, but by whom, or in what manner produced, remains a mystery."

"A mystery!" muttered Agatha Weare—"yes, a terrible mystery to me, for it has shaken my very soul."

She folded her arms across her breast as she spoke, and after a convulsive shudder, she slowly walked away to her chamber.

At that moment there stepped up to the side of the crusader the strange lad who at midnight had been admitted into the castle, and looking up appealingly in the face of the knight, said,

"Does that sound, think you, bode evil to the great and good Sir Rupert Brandon?"

"I hope and believe not, boy," replied the knight, "and I regret that your first night's repose in Brandon has been so roughly broken in upon."

"Heed me not—heed me not; if he be safe I care for nothing else. Oh, when will he return to bless those who love him in his ancient home?"

"I will speak to you more of Sir Rupert Brandon in the morning," he replied, in a low tone. "Till then retire to rest, for I am quite sure from your appearance you have need of repose."

Then turning to the men-at-arms, he cried,

"Comrades, let us hope that the perils and disturbances of this night are over. At broad day-light another, and I hope a more successful, effort shall be made to relieve Brandon Castle of those mysteries which make it a residence so much to be feared."

The boy placed his small hand in that of the crusader's, and whispered a gentle good night; he then glided away in the gloom of the gallery.

"Who'll sit up with me?" cried Eldred.

A general laugh was the response to this question, and then he cried, frantically,

"What are you laughing at? I can't go by myself, and you know I can't. I ain't afraid, of course, only I don't like it. If you won't sit up with me any of you, for goodness sake come some of you and see me safe in bed. Hilloa, hilloa—stop, stop, stop. Where are you all going? Goodness gracious, don't leave me alone, I can't bear it."

So saying, he ran frantically after the servants, who were rapidly retreating to the domestic offices of the castle.

Before they reached the great hall through which they had to pass, in order to reach their own chambers, Eldred came up with them, and represented so vividly the great dangers they would undergo in retiring to rest, after so strange a noise had disturbed the serenity of the castle, that he prevailed upon two or three to assist him in throwing some fresh logs upon the hall fire, and to sit up for the remainder of the night, rather than encounter the terrors of such another disturbance.

"It is no use going to bed after four o'clock," said Eldred, "you couldn't get much sleep; and besides, if there should be such another noise and disturbance as we have experienced, only think how dreadful it would be to find oneself undressed and in bed, and fancy the devil pulling one's great toe, when as long as we sit here and talk, we surely must be tolerably safe."

This reasoning had its effect upon those to whom it was addressed, and Eldred Weare, with a feeling of great rejoicing, drew the largest and most comfortable arm-chair he could find to the fire-side, placed his feet with great gratification on each side of the grate, and assuring himself that the morning would soon come, he gave himself up to a feeling of security, which he would have been far from feeling in his own chamber.

In the meanwhile, the crusader, accompanied by Wingrove and the men-at-arms, whose duty it was to relieve the guard of Anstey, proceeded to the chamber with the green hangings, on their way to which, the crusader related how he had been induced to leave his room, and attempt a solution of the mystery of the old Grey Turret, and concluded by saying,—

"So perfectly terrible and awful a noise I never before heard, or supposed it was possible for human ears to listen to."

"That Black Monk," said Hugh Wingrove, "must surely be leagued with things unearthly, for he could never command the very elements of nature so to do his bidding."

"Rather," said the crusader, "let us wonder at the exceeding lore of the Jesuits, and the skill and art with which they confine to their own body a knowledge of many wonderful secrets of nature, which to those entirely ignorant of them, have the appearance of being perfectly super-natural."

"Think you so?" said Wingrove.

"On my soul I do," said the crusader, "and I have heard so much of the study that the monks have given to that strange and wonderful science called alchemy, that I am inclined to believe the very sound which so alarmed every inhabitant of Brandon, terrible and superhuman as it appeared, was produced by some means extremely simple and easy, could we but know the secret springs that brought it into existence."

" I bow with deference to your better judgment," said Wingrove. " I am but a soldier, and know little more than some of the ancient arts of war, except that I have been so much honoured lately, and am so much honoured now, that I scarcely know how sufficiently I can express my own deep thankfulness to one who ——"

" Hush, Wingrove, hush, no more of that," said the knight; " the time may come when we shall talk with more pleasure, and under more fitting circumstances on such subjects. This, I presume, is my chamber door, and I will wish you a good repose for the very short time which will elapse, ere the sun's light will warn us again to be up and stirring."

" I will leave you another light," said Wingrove, " which I will humbly advise you to keep burning—how damp and cold the wind comes in at your window."

" I opened it," said the crusader, " in order to obtain a better view of the strange light I saw gleaming from the Grey Turret."

" Is this your glove ?" said Wingrove, as he picked one from the floor.

" I have none but mailed gauntlets here," said the knight, " that is none of mine. Good heavens, what a size it is. My hands are by no means small, and yet I could very nearly put them both within its capacious dimensions."

" It is gigantic," said Wingrove; " I never saw but one hand that there was the slightest chance of its fitting."

" And that ——"

" Was the Black Monk's."

The knight took the glove, and examined it curiously.

" I will keep this," he said, " and he whom it fits shall one day render an account to me of how it came to the floor of my bed-chamber."

" Gracious powers !" suddenly exclaimed Wingrove.

" What alarms you ?" said the crusader.

Wingrove held the lamp above his head, so that it shed a strong reflection upon the crusader's couch, and pointing towards it, he exclaimed,—

" There is a sight which affects me more strongly, and excites more bitter feelings in my soul, than any battle-field I ever witnessed."

The crusader advanced and looked with surprise upon the bed, when he saw two poniards struck up to the hilt at some few inches distance from each other, as near as possible in the centre of the couch, and where, in all likelihood, he would have lain, had he been sleeping.

" Some assassin has been in my room," he said.

" The villain—the monster !" cried Wingrove. " Oh, what an escape have you had."

The crusader drew one of the daggers from the couch, and holding it up to the lamp, he saw that it had a long double-edged blade, of apparently exquisite workmanship.

" We never know, Hugh Wingrove," he said, " when Heaven is most kind to us. I have been complaining to myself that my head was confused by the tremendous explosion that took place in the Grey Turret, when in all probability by leaving my chamber as I did, I have escaped having these daggers in my heart."

" True," said Wingrove, " the hand of especial Providence is in this night's proceedings. You are evidently preserved by Heaven for better and nobler objects; but how could your secret foe have gained admission to your chamber?"

" By this window," said the knight, as he pointed to some damp footmarks upon the heavy window-sill. " Had I not by a sudden impulse which I could not resist, gone forth to explore the turret, when the deep sense of drowsiness so suddenly left me, I should ere this have been numbered with the dead."

"Even so," said Wingrove, "I shrink from a contemplation of what you have escaped. These daggers, I make no doubt, were planted here by Morgatani, the Black Monk, and by some oversight, he has left you a glove as an indication of his presence."

"Do you keep the daggers and glove," said the crusader, "the time may come when I shall ask you for them, as an evidence against him who would in so dastardly a manner have assassinated me."

"They shall be preserved with religious care," said Wingrove; and then approaching the window, he took what measures he could, carefully and effectually to fasten it, saying,—

"Allow me to sit in your chamber this night as your guard, to-morrow I will see that a more commodious and not so easily accessible an apartment is prepared for your reception."

"Nay, Wingrove," said the crusader, "I can't permit you to deprive yourself of rest upon my account. Retire to your own couch, you have had fatigue enough. I myself will keep a watchful eye, now that I am assured of danger."

Wingrove would not dispute the commands of the crusader, and bidding him a courteous and respectful good night, he retired from the chamber. When, however, he reached the outside, he said to the guard,—

"Be vigilant and careful on your watch. Should any one disturb you on your post, give me instant notice, for when the crusader sleeps, I intend myself, in my great anxiety for his safety, to steal into his chamber and there keep watch and ward over his most precious life."

CHAPTER LV.

"The morrow's morn was beautiful,
  A fairer could not be,
The winds were hushed, the bright sun shone
  In cloudless beauty free."

THE MORNING.—THE CONVERSATION WITH THE SAILOR BOY.—THE VISIT TO THE VAULTS.

THE morning broke in radiant beauty upon Brandon Castle, the loud gusty wind which the previous evening moaned and howled around the battlements was hushed, retreating before the glorious and gently coming light of day, like some wild creature who had chosen the dusky obscurity of night, in which to prowl about the habitation of men, seeking whom it might destroy as its prey.

In a streaming flood of glorious hues, the sun-light fell broadly through the painted windows of the crusader's chamber, producing an effect beautiful in the extreme ; the dazzling brilliancy of which, when he first awoke, was almost painful to his eyes, and it was some moments before he could accustom them to the brightness and vivid colouring with which his chamber was filled.

"The morning must be far advanced," he cried, as he sprung from his couch, "or the sun would not possess such dazzling power."

An exclamation of surprise then burst from his lips, for lying upon two chairs exactly under the window, lay the recumbent figure of a man fully armed, and apparently sleeping, although his hand grasped a sword which lay across him.

The crusader seized his axe in a moment, and in two or three strides reaching the recumbent figure, he cried aloud,—

"Awake, awake, whoever you are. By the mass, this is the strangest circumstance that ever I heard of."

The sleeper immediately sprung to his feet and placed himself in an attitude of defence, crying,—

" Over my prostrate body alone shall you reach him. Awake, awake—there is danger, there is danger !"

" Hugh Wingrove !" exclaimed the crusader; " why, what on earth brought you here? but that it is contrary to the rules of honourable warfare, and my own feeling, I might inadvertently have slain you as you slept."

Wingrove, for it was indeed he, lowered the point of his sword, as he replied,—

" Forgive me, sir knight, for my hasty exclamation, and still more must I crave forgiveness for this intrusion into your chamber."

" Freely," said the knight, with a laugh; " you hinted a desire to watch me during the night, and I presume you waited until I slept, and then had your own way."

" I could not have rested anywhere but here," said Wingrove; " believing that you were in danger from the vile machinations of Morgatani the Black Monk. The door I knew was well and sufficiently guarded, but I was fearfully apprehensive of the window, and could not even feel satisfied after I had placed a sentinel below it. The power and strength of the Black Monk I knew to be prodigious, and by some secret and subtle means he might take the life of the man-at-arms, and then, entering your chamber by the window while you slept, attack you at a serious disadvantage."

" And for that reason," said the knight, " you placed yourself in the way of danger?"

" Why, truly," said Wingrove, " I thought that by lying down under the window exactly, should he attempt to enter the room by that means, he would inevitably tread upon me, which would enable me to give you a sufficient alarm to arouse you from your sleep."

" You deserve and have my sincerest thanks," said the knight, " for I would not willingly perish by treachery; a soldier's death in the open field in gallant conflict with a worthy foe, I covet as the end of my career. I have as great a horror of assassination as I have of a sick-bed."

" May you live long," said Wingrove, " for the good of the many who have so great an interest in your existence."

" Thanks, thanks, good Wingrove," said the crusader, as he placed the velvet mask on his face previous to leaving the room. " My first proceeding this day—always with the reservation of a good breakfast—shall be to have some converse with the singular being who arrived last night at the castle in boy's apparel, but who, as I strongly suspect, will turn out to be some low-born maiden smitten with a wild passion for Sir Rubert Brandon, and in some way aware of his present proceedings."

" It is evident," said Wingrove, " that he or she, whichever the new arrival may be, expected to find Sir Rupert in the castle, from that I gather a hope that to me is very dear indeed—namely, that Sir Rupert cannot be far off, and will shortly arrive to bless us again with his presence."

" 'Tis more than probable, and I have no small anxiety to learn from this new guest at Brandon, what chances there may be of so fortunate a circumstance, for such it would be both to me and every one here."

" It would give life and animation to us all," said Wingrove, " and there is not an inhabitant in Brandon, excepting Agatha and Eldred Weare, who would not rejoice heart and soul at the event."

" By your leave, good Wingrove, I will occupy the same apartment in which I spent most of my leisure yesterday, and when I am satisfied I have obtained all the information I can from our new guest, it is my purpose to occupy my further leisure by another and searching examination of the castle, for which I have several reasons. In the first place there must

be some mode of ingress and egress to Brandon, of which even Sir Rupert himself is ignorant, otherwise how could this Black Monk, this crafty and dangerous Jesuit, carry on the intrigues which we may be sure he is immersed in ; and likewise, how could that strange creature who did me such good service in the forest by saving me from the assassins who were employed to take my life, by one whom I am ashamed to name, find such ready access here ?"

"I perfectly agree with you," said Wingrove, "that there must be such an entrance into Brandon Castle. If we can discover it, we can either shut out or shut in the Black Monk, and so hold him at bay without, or cut off his supplies from within ; for that he is the inhabitant of the Grey Turret I cannot for a moment doubt ; but whether he be aided by supernatural power, or has at his command some rare secrets of nature, he does certainly appear to possess powers sufficient to defy all exertions to dislodge him."

"We must starve him out," said the crusader ; "for it is not worth while losing a single life in an attack upon the citadel, which I give him the credit for holding so well."

It was about an hour after this time, that the crusader was sitting in the parlour which Wingrove had prepared for his reception. He was attired in a magnificent brocade morning gown, which Wingrove had unhesitatingly broken open Sir Rupert's wardrobe to supply him with, upon Agatha's refusal of the necessary keys.

Various other articles, likewise, of costly apparel, which from time to time had graced Sir Rupert's commanding form, on his occasional visits to the court, were piled upon chairs, and placed half around the blazing fire of logs which roared and crackled upon the ample hearth.

Every article, too, of luxury or convenience, which Hugh Wingrove could lay his hands on throughout the castle, he had collected in that one apartment.

He had quite a tussle with Eldred Weare in carrying from his room

No. 42

some decorative articles, and, to the indignation of Agatha, he had taken from her own private apartment a richly covered arm-chair, the seat and back of which was composed of the richest Genoa velvet, and on which the crusader was now sitting.

The slight which had been put upon her by the abstraction of the costly chair, nearly drove Agatha Weare frantic; and, but that her reason told her how very futile such an attempt would be, she would have resisted its abstraction by force of arms.

Who, however, had she in all that castle upon whom she could rely for the slightest assistance in such a matter? As for Eldred Weare, so terrified was he of the crusader and his martial appearance, as well as the ponderous battle-axe which he carried about with him, that, had he been required so to do, he would almost have attempted of himself, for fear of the consequences of a refusal, to put the chair on his own head, and carry it to the required room.

Morgatani, too, in such a matter, was entirely useless; for when Agatha sought him, and mentioned the circumstance, he answered her rather testily, intimating that such matters were far beneath his notice.

Thus Agatha Weare felt herself a mere tool in the hands of the monk for his own ambitious purposes, and she began to suspect—what she might well before have guessed—that she might in vain seek for assistance and countenance from him in any matter which did not exactly square with his own views and objects.

An ample and as luxuriant a breakfast as the castle could afford was spread before the crusader, and altogether the ancient apartment, with its richly carved mouldings, its painted ceiling, and the beautiful drapery that hung from its walls, presented an appearance of considerable comfort as well as elegance.

Hugh Wingrove was himself respectfully waiting upon him, and as the knight concluded his repast and leaned back in Agatha's chair, he said,

"Now, Hugh Wingrove, will you seek out the stripling, with whom I wish to hold converse, and let us ascertain as much information as we can concerning Sir Rupert Brandon."

Hugh Wingrove at once departed on his errand, but on the road he met with Eldred Weare, who, saluting him with an aspect of fear and deference, said,

"I tell you what, Master Wingrove, I have had a dream last night, and do you know my dreams always come true. I thought Sir Rupert Brandon was really dead, as was likewise Richard Cœur de Lion, and that King John, on account of great services and abilities, had ceded to me Brandon Castle."

"Indeed!" said Wingrove.

"Yes, upon my life," said Eldred, "I would not say such a thing if it wasn't true upon any account."

"Well, but what is it to me?" said Wingrove.

"Why, only this, my good Hugh, that I have been thinking if such were to turn out to be really the case, I should require a man of your singular judgment and great experience to conduct most of the affairs of the castle, and there is nobody to whom I would sooner commit so important a trust than yourself. You understand me, good Wingrove?"

"I understand you are a fool!" said Wingrove; "and if you so much as again hint at the death of Sir Rupert Brandon, by virtue of my authority here, I will have you shut up in one of the vaults until he himself returns to contradict your presumptuous dream, which, I assure you, is far from pleasing to any one in Brandon."

"Eh!" said Eldred, in great alarm, "shut me up in a vault! Good gracious! What made you think of such a thing? I should expire in a moment. By-the-bye, who is the crusader after all, good Wingrove? As you and I are such excellent friends, you may as well tell me at once. Rely upon my prudence. Oh, dear, I am as close as an oyster when you want to open him."

"I rather rely upon my own, idiot," said Wingrove ; "and as for Brandon Castle ever being your's, I'll see that it's made a bonfire of first, and you shall then be welcome to the ruins, but in no other shape or manner need you hope to become possessed of it ; and as for King John, there is no such person, and any traitor who maintains there is had better look sharp, or he'll run a shrewd chance of being hanged, while he himself may have his head chopped off for his impertinence on Tower-hill."

"Hanged !" cried Eldred.

"Yes, hanged! You don't seem to like the notion, so get out of my way, and be specially careful of what you say in future."

"Good gracious ! I will," said Eldred. "I never thought of being hanged until just now. Here's a nice thing I've let myself in for. Sister Agatha will be the death of me, and then she'll pretend to be sorry ; but that won't be any consolation to me—oh, dear, no—not a bit."

So saying, Eldred Weare turned from Wingrove, with the firm resolution in his own mind that, for the preservation of his neck, he would never name King John again until the whole world should agree that King Richard was really dead.

Wingrove easily found the object of his search, and whispering in the ear of the boy who had arrived so strangely, and used language of passion and interest apparently so far beyond his years, he said,—

"The crusader, with whom you had some slight conversation last evening, is desirous of further converse with you in his own apartment ; I would advise you, in a friendly spirit, to trust him wholly and entirely with your history."

"Is he a true friend to Sir Rupert Brandon ?" said the boy.

"As true as ever lived, and the best of all."

"Then I will trust him, he shall know all. Oh, how I longed for the hour when I should see the ancient towers of Brandon rising high into the sky ; oh, how I longed to set my foot within its walls, so dear to me as they were from the very name by which they were known. He is not here—he is not here though to meet me, and my heart is very desolate indeed. One smile, one cheering smile from him were worth kingdoms—one welcome word a rich jewel that I would wear for ever in my heart. Oh, when will he come—when will he come to bless these eyes with his presence that have wearied for him so long ?"

"You cannot weary for his presence," said Hugh Wingrove, "more than do many warm hearts in Brandon ;—but come to him I spoke to you of and you will receive sympathy as well as much kindly feeling."

<hr />

CHAPTER LVI.

" It was a tale of war and love—
Of sighs to memory dear ;
A tale of girlish constancy,
Devoid of guile or fear."

THE CONFERENCE WITH THE CRUSADER.—SIR RUPERT'S DANGER.—THE POWER OF AFFECTION.—THE PROMISE.

THE sailor boy followed Hugh Wingrove in silence till they reached the crusader's chamber ; then, as the old soldier was about to lay his hand on the lock, his young companion said,—

"I pray you pause a moment, that I may recover breath, and still have time for a moment's thought ere I make so great a confidence as that which is asked of me."

"Still fearful," said Hugh Wingrove. "Now beshrew me, boy, but when you grow up you'll make a bad soldier; a good one seldom hesitates. But once again let me assure you, you may thoroughly and safely trust the greatest secret you have with him you are about to visit."

"I am assured," said the boy, "my confidence shall be complete."

As he spoke he passed into the chamber of the crusader, into which Wingrove did not enter.

"Come hither," said the knight, in a gentle voice, when the door was closed—"come hither, young stranger. If you are indeed, as I suppose, some hapless maiden in disguise, I would fain spare your blushes and confusion in letting me by myself thus intimate my suspicions. Ah! I have guessed aright; that downcast look, and that vivid accession of colour, are ample confirmations of what I have stated."

"You have guessed rightly," said the supposed boy, covering her face with her hands; "I am not what I seem."

"Nay," said the crusader, laughing, "say rather you seem not what you would fain try to be—a boy; that timorous, yet beautiful glance, that gentle speech of your's, and the style of your language, are so many evidences against your affected appearance; but do not fancy I think harshly of you because you have thought proper to change the habiliments of your sex."

"I will tell you all—I will tell you all," said the disguised maiden.

"Unreserved confidences," said the knight, "are ever the safest. I shall listen attentively."

She sat down on one of the brocade chairs, and, with a timid voice, recounted the motives of her strange appearance.

"It is now some time since the crusaders began to return to their native lands, as you, sir knight, must well know, and, no sooner had Richard Cœur de Lion turned his horse's head towards Europe, than men of all nations sought to return to their long deserted homes.

"My father fought under the banner of the house of Austria, and, no sooner was the time of his pilgrimage expired, than his banner pointed towards Lower Germany, anxious to arrive with the first who reached their castles; for it has often happened, that those who turned their backs upon the Holy Sepulchre, and were united in the bonds of amity, and animated by the same chivalric desire of rescuing the holy ground from the infidel, no sooner did so, than all their former jealousies and heartburnings returned, and he who reached his abode first, did so that he might thus be better able to make some inroad upon his neighbour's property that he would be unable to resist; and when he arrived, probably fall into the hands of his late comrade, but present foe, and be cast into a dungeon, to linger out the remainder of his existence in hopeless captivity, or a speedy but cruel death.

"The dissentions among the leading crusaders are well known to you, sir knight, and you cannot but be aware that the treacherous ally of Richard, Philip of France, is at this moment intriguing to place the imbecile and cruel John upon the throne of the lordly Richard; but he is not the only enemy of Richard, the Archduke of Austria is a bitter and sullen enemy. He has seized upon the person of Richard, and he is confined in some strong castle, but where no one can tell, since it is kept a close secret.

"My father owes fealty to the house of Austria, and, of course, looks upon the policy of the duke and his neighbours as that by which he should be guided.

" During the crusades, Sir Rupert Brandon had given ample offence by his daring contempt of many of the German barons who followed the Duke of Austria, and would not hold them his equals; and to none did he offer greater offence than to Reinwold, Baron of Stettin, whose enmity was by no means allayed when Sir Rupert offered to meet him in the lists, which Reinwold would assuredly have done, had he not been suffering from a recent hurt."

" By the mass," said the crusader, " it is well for the Baron of Stettin that he did not do so, for Sir Rupert is as good a knight as ever wore harness; but proceed."

" It was with no feelings of displeasure that, on his arrival at Stettin, he received a special messenger from the Archduke, who intimated that his highness's pleasure would be best consulted by staying all English and Norman knights who might pass through his territories, and to refuse all ransom.

" He was further informed, that it had been discovered that, as soon as Richard's captivity became known, Sir Rupert had parted from his followers, appointing a place of meeting near home, and travelling himself alone, and in disguise, and it was presumed that he would thus pass through Reinwold's territories.

" The prospect of securing an old foe, who had given him such cause for deadly hatred, was pleasing to a degree to Reinwold, who immediately had spies in all parts where it was probable, or even possible, that he could pass.

" The baron had scarcely been in his castle a week, before he had certain news that Sir Rupert Brandon was travelling, unattended, through Reinwold's territories.

" He was not molested for some time, as every day's journey brought him nearer to the castle, and one evening late, I heard a great commotion among the men-at-arms. The drawbridge was lowered, and my father, the baron's lieutenant, at the head of a strong party of men, rode out.

" I inquired what was the cause of so unusual an occurrence, for we were at peace, but I could obtain no reply, but that night I heard the drawbridge lowered, and the noise of armed men entering the castle, and passing through it to a lonely tower, called the Spring Tower, as in it arose a supply of water from a spring.

" The upper part of the Spring Tower was wholly disused, the vaults below being the only part that was ever visited, and that only for water.

" The next day I endeavoured to learn something of what was going on, but all was enveloped in mystery; but this I could learn, that several of the men-at-arms were sorely wounded, and there was a prisoner confined in the Spring Tower. I was much dissatisfied with only this information, and was desirous of learning something more; I questioned the baron, my father, with much perseverance, but he evaded all my inquiries, and at length bade me ask no more questions of him, on pain of his high displeasure.

" I was actuated by an irresistible impulse, I was urged forward by an unseen and unknown hand—fate drove me to do that which at any other time I should have shrunk from.

" Between the tower and ramparts, which here were very high, and for that reason seldom guarded, was a broad platform, upon which were in times of war raised large engines for throwing missiles at the besiegers. This was empty now. I determined to traverse it, and endeavour to discover who the prisoner was, as I knew that some of the iron gratings which gave light to the prisons, were accessible from that place.

" I succeeded in my attempt, and found that there was neither a sentinel near the spot, nor one so placed, that he could observe me. I looked in at the gratings, till I found by one of them I could see a knight dressed in a plain leathern suit, such as a warrior wears under his armour.

" He stood looking towards one of the windows through which the sun was shining. His noble form showed to much advantage as he stood, and his captivity had not robbed his eye of its fire, or his brow of its gentleness.

" As he stood thus, gazing earnestly, I was unseen, and stood admiring, and unable to withdraw my gaze from him.

" ' And has my father doomed such a form, so noble, so commanding, and so frank and generous, to suffer and waste in the wretchedness of a dungeon? no, no, no, it cannot be—he would not, could not do it.'

" These last words were uttered half aloud, as I gazed upon him, nearly unconscious of where I was. The knight started, and looking round, at once perceived me, and advancing towards the window, said, oh, with such accents that I can never forget,—

" ' Kind maiden, canst thou tell me in what place I am imprisoned? Tell me, I beseech of you, the name of this castle?'

" ' It is the Castle of Stettin, sir knight.'

" ' And its owner is ——'

" He paused for a moment, and I answered,

" ' The owner's name is Reinwold, baron of ——'

" ' Reinwold,' he replied. ' Ay, I know how it is then, my old enemy has sought and found me at a disadvantage; and so I am to be cooped up here, and die the death of a dog—poisoned, starved, or stabbed in the dark by assassins' hands.'

" ' Starve you shall not, sir knight,' I said, prompted by the moment to speak before I well knew what I would say.

" ' A kind maiden,' said the knight; ' could I but escape from this hole by thy aid, you would lay Sir Rupert Brandon under so heavy a debt of gratitude that life itself would be an inadequate repayment.'

" ' Talk not so, sir knight, I cannot do it; but tell me, have you received provisions?'

" ' None.'

" ' I will be here after sunset,' I replied, ' and will bring you some.'

" I need not relate the thanks of Sir Rupert; they were short, but sincere and frank, such as became a knight and soldier, but they were uttered in accents that I never before heard, and struck a chord in my heart that vibrated with pleasure and joy.

I went to him after sunset. A few coarse provisions had been left him by his guards, but who spoke not a word in answer to his many inquiries; and the food they brought was in such a small quantity that, should it be persevered in, it was plain Sir Rupert must have wasted away, and thus gradually fall into the arms af death.

" ' The churlish hounds,' exclaimed the crusader, ' are not fit to attend a herd of swine.'

" I took him the best that I could obtain, without being noticed, and thus I saw him daily, and carried to him all that he required.

" I need not say that I was much interested in the fate of Sir Rupert Brandon. I often tried to obtain some information respecting the object of my father's keeping him in custody, and what he intended eventually to do with him; but I could obtain no kind of satisfaction, and whenever the subject was broached, my father became stern and repulsive to a degree that alarmed me for Sir Rupert's fate, and I determined to watch every movement of my father, or any of the men whom he might converse with privately.

" From Sir Rupert I learned my father's motives for thus imprisoning him, and after he had thus been confined for a few weeks, I heard, by accident, a conversation between my father and his lieutenant, which told me that, if Sir Rupert remained another night in his dungeon after that, he would be slain.

" I flew to Sir Rupert, and informed him of what I had heard. A flush of anger at first crossed his martial countenance, but it was succeeded by a shade of sorrow as he looked round the walls and said,—

" ' And is it thus I am to quit the world, not one word of adieu from gallant companions? Well, they shall not find me unprepared, but these bare hands shall work them evil, while I have life to use them ; but say, maiden, are there no means of escape? Cannot you aid me—give me but a weapon?'

" ' Hold, sir knight, here is a dagger, and should you be molested before night defend yourself ; but when the castle is enveloped in darkness I will return, and, if possible, assist you to escape.'

" I heard voices in the distance, and, quitting the spot, I entered my own apartment, and when it was too dark to discern anything with certainty, I sought Sir Rupert's cell, and letting down an iron bar, bade him attempt to wrench the iron gratings off the windows, which, after much labour, he succeeded in doing, and a moment after he stood by my side on the platform.

" ' Thanks, maiden, thanks—I owe my life to you, and be sure that Sir Rupert Brandon cannot be ungrateful ; wouldst thou but accompany me, Brandon Castle and its fair domains are thine, and I thy slave.'

" ' Rather my lord,' I replied—' but what would Sir Rupert say when he looked upon the daughter of his enemy?'

" ' Art thou ——'

" ' Yes, I am the daughter of Reinwold.'

" ' Thou deservest a better parent,' he said, gently embracing me.— ' Wilt thou come?'

" I shook my head and gave him a sword, while a coil of rope which lay at our feet informed Sir Rupert how he was to leave the castle.

" ' I cannot—dare not leave my father,' I replied.

" ' It would be ungenerous to urge you,' he replied, ' but I go straight to Brandon, and should this act call down your father's anger, Brandon Castle will ever be a shelter for you, and you will there find a grateful heart ready to protect and shield you from all danger.'

" He made fast the rope to the iron grating, and taking a tender leave of me, he descended to the ground on the outside of the castle, and when he stood firm on the earth, I could hear him say distinctly, ' Farewell, dear maiden—remember, Sir Rupert is a debtor.'

" I drew up the rope mechanically and replaced it, and returned to my own apartment to wait the issue of the adventure.

" It was not till the next day that the flight of Sir Rupert was discovered, but no sooner had night set in, than those who were to assassinate him entered the cell for that purpose and found it empty. A terrible commotion ensued among the inhabitants of the castle, and every hole and corner was searched in vain, for though the grating was seen to have been broken through, yet it was deemed impossible for him to have got quite off ; but the prisoner could not be found, and Reinwold became dreadfully enraged, and threatened death to all who should keep the slightest occurrence from him that in any way might tend to explain this affair.

" It was eventually said that I had been in that part of the castle. On the platform a large coil of rope had been displaced. Reinwold caused all the sentinels to be brought before him, who could even see the platform where the window was situated, and also those whom I had passed ; these he interrogated until he had accumulated such a mass of evidence that, though unwilling to believe me guilty of the offence, yet he was constrained to do so.

"His anger was extreme—he called me to him—I came with fear and trembling, and had scarcely courage to look upon him. His face was swollen with passion, and his eyes distended and bloodshot. Oh! it was a fearful picture to look upon."

Here the stranger paused much affected, but after a while her emotion subsided, and she proceeded as before :—

"My father, the baron, stood some moments unable to articulate a word, but at length in a strong harsh voice, he said,—

"'Dost know aught of the escape of the prisoner from yonder tower, girl? Speak, speak the truth as you value my favour.'

"'I—I do.'

"'It was you who assisted him to get out of the tower, eh?' he said, in a tone of suppressed fury, and stamping.

"'I did.'

"'You did!' he roared, in a voice of thunder.

"'Yes, I did. Oh, for the love of Heaven and its bright hereafter, do not—do not kill me!' I said, throwing myself on my knees, for I really feared he would kill me.

"'Hold,' he cried—'tell me—he—he cannot have got out of the castle—tell me where he is, and I will forgive all.'

"'He is gone— he is escaped.'

"'How?—where?—which way?' shouted Reinwold.

"'The rope,' was all I had time to answer, for, no sooner had the words escaped my lips, than I was felled to the earth by a dreadful blow, which deprived me of my senses.

"The blow that laid me bereft of sense and motion was a kind one, since I escaped the horrors that followed ; and, perhaps, it was the only thing that saved my life; for his fury arose to such a pitch, that he spurned me as I lay bleeding, till some of the attendants took me to my apartment, where I recovered, and heard of the storm that followed. This was too violent to last long. It was not in nature to sustain anger and passion at such an extreme, and Reinwold was fain to seek his wine cup as a restorer of his exhausted frame, and thus I escaped from any further persecution that night.

"The next day, however, made matters worse, for my father came to me in my room, and, after having interrogated me respecting the escape, poured forth such a stream of bitter invectives, and called down from Heaven all the curses a parent could find words to utter for the deep and lasting destruction of his child, that I could not articulate a word for weeping and the depth of my soul's anguish.

"He left me ; but before he did so, he told me I was no longer his daughter, but a criminal, whose punishment was certain, and when I was capable of enduring I should suffer.

"I was dreadfully agitated, and knew not what course to pursue ; but my attendant, who had been informed by the baron that she must quit the castle by sundown on the following day, as he had no longer a daughter, came to me, and advised me to make my escape, as she was sure I was in danger of imprisonment in the vaults, at least. This had the effect of arousing me from a death-like stupor, and I determined to trust all to her ; and I then quitted Stettin Castle, determined to seek Brandon Castle and Sir Rupert.

"We escaped to her cottage, where she lent me the disguise I now wear,

and procured me the guidance and protection of a peasant, who was ignorant of who I was, for a part of the way to the shores of Normandy, where lay many vessels daily returning to England, laden with the toil-worn knights returning homeward from the crusades.

"I was fortunate enough to get a passage; for the bustle did not allow the captains of the vessels to look at me very attentively, else I had been refused, deeming me too weak to pay my passage by the performance of my work. I reached the English shores; but I had no money, nor provisions. Trusting to the chance succour of the way-side and peasants' hovels, I last night found myself exhausted, and all but incapable of speech, at the portals of Brandon Castle, the dwelling of the good Sir Rupert. But tell me, Sir Knight, for you are good and gentle, tell me where I shall see Sir Rupert?"

"I would," said the crusader, "that our means were as powerful as our wishes, he should soon be here; but at present all is doubt and uncertainty, but in all your relation you have not told me your own name."

"My name is Bertha," said the maiden, timidly.

CHAPTER LVII.

Ths monk was crafty, bold, and strong,
A Jesuit was he,
More full of villany and guile
None other could there be.—*Old Romance.*

THE crusader continued musing for some moments after Bertha's eventful narrative, then he said in a tone of gaiety,—

"Be cheerful, Bertha; that you should admire Sir Rupert Brandon, and particularly in the hour of affliction, for then a great man is ever greater,

No. 43

I do not at all wonder. You are aware, I presume, that he has been already married to one whom he valued so much, that her sudden and unexpected death cast a fearful gloom over his mind—a gloom, which I believe only the excitement and bustle of the crusades could at all have dissipated. Your love, therefore, strange and full of romance as it appears, in my opinion, does you honour, and if I could possibly feel more earnest then I was before, in a wish for the return of Sir Rupert Brandon, it is on your account. In all likelihood, I shall remain some time, welcome or not, a guest in Brandon. Look upon yourself, therefore, as most especially under my protection. I will take care that you are properly lodged and tended upon. Retain your disguise, and hope for happier days, as I do myself, for I am as much under a cloud of an evil destiny at present as you can be, and although once my possessions were sufficiently ample, I am scarcely the owner now of what clothing is upon me, for most of that is borrowed."

The crusader spoke these words with a gaiety of demeanour, that showed he either set no great store by the goods of fortune, or looked forward to ample means of renewing his exhausted resources.

" How can I sufficiently thank you for such generous sympathy," said Bertha; "my heart is a thousand times lighter than it was, now that I feel I have a friend who knows my history."

" Be tranquil," said the knight, " and depend upon me for arranging everything for your comfortable sojourn here. Without means at my own disposal, I yet have some power in Brandon Castle; it shall be exerted, believe me, to render your stay agreeable."

" Then you think," said Bertha, " that he will come?"

" I do," said the knight; "but there is one thing, Bertha, that you have not told me, and that is, how you produced so good an imitation of Sir Rupert's silver horn when you first came to Brandon. The men-at-arms all declared it to be his, and rushed with exhilarated spirits, and happy countenances to the postern gate, expecting to see their much revered master himself."

" They might well fancy so," said Bertha, " for it was Sir Rupert's horn— his first, last, and only gift to me; when he gave it me he said, ' Bertha, should you ever reach Brandon Castle, be it in the dead hour of the night watch, or when the midday sun is shining on its time-worn battlements, the faintest sound from this horn will procure you instant admission; keep it for my sake, Bertha, 'tis the only gift Sir Rupert has to present you with.' "

As Bertha spoke she produced from her breast the curiously-fashioned small bugle of silver, the low plaintive note of which was so familiar to his followers.

" Keep it then, Bertha," said the crusader, " until you see Sir Rupert himself, which may yet be sooner than any of us expect."

It was some half hour or more after that interview that the crusader with Hugh Wingrove and Bernard stood in the ancient chapel of Brandon; the knight was speaking with earnestness, and his concluding words were,—

" Most completely am I convinced not only that Brandon Castle is made a grand point, or species of head-quarters, by the Jesuits to carry on their machinations in favour of John, as king of this realm; but there seems to me to be some under plot of dark and deep malignity, the object of which is to do some serious injury, if not utterly destroy Sir Rupert Brandon; something seems to tell me that the bursting forth of this plot, and the showing itself in all its malignant fury, waits but his return; therefore is it that before that event takes place, which I hope from my soul may be soon, I wish to possess myself of the knowledge of everything both above and below ground in Brandon Castle, for I wish if necessary to be fully prepared to stand forward in his defence. Now let us seek the vaults, for I would fain ascertain if any objects are there concealed which may prove detrimental to his safety."

"Our united strength," said Wingrove, "would suffice to move the marble slab that covers the entrance to the vaults, but Fitzhugh's page is aware of another mode of entrance to the vast subterranean passages of Brandon, and he was to have been here by this time to have pointed it out to us."

"I am here," said the page, stepping from behind the monument of Sir Sir Montague Brandon, "I am here, and what poor service I can render, I pray you to command."

"Boy," said the crusader, "do you know what ticklish ground you stand on?"

"Ticklish ground?" echoed the page.

"Yes," continued the crusader, "the slightest breach of faith with us would precipitate you into an abyss from which there would be no return."

"Let me answer for his faith," said Wingrove. "Show us the way, boy and the time may come when you shall be amply rewarded."

The page replied nothing, but touching the requisite spring permitted the iron plate which formed one side of Sir Montague Brandon's monument to slide down, revealing the narrow staircase down which he had himself gone on his mission to the dungeon of Sir Kenneth Hay.

"Will you not guide us, boy?" said the crusader.

"I will," said the page, "I have but one prayer in Brandon Castle, and that is Heaven preserve the right." As he spoke he passed down the staircase, followed by the crusader, after which came Wingrove and Bernard, the latter of whom muttered,—

"Well, now if we were to come across in our researches, some old cellar full of hogsheads of ale, that had been kept secret so long by somebody that at last he died and said nothing about it—that would be an adventure, and one worth having."

Scarcely, then, had the last sound of the retreating footsteps of Bernard died away upon the staircase, when there glided from a gloomy recess in the chapel, Morgatani, the Black Monk himself.

For some moments he stood gazing down the aperture which had been left open by the little party that had just descended from the light of day; then he spoke in those low deep tones which he always used when some bitter feeling was crossing his mind, or when he meditated some act of more than usual wickedness.

"So!" he said, "the subterranean portion of Brandon Castle is to be explored in order to discover, if possible, what plot the Jesuits are contriving against Sir Rupert Brandon. Well, be it so. The Jesuits can lay snares as well as contrive plots; but no snare ever answers its purpose half so well as that which men fall into of their own accord; and I rather think that this party of four, each individual of which is an enemy of mine, have fallen into a snare for their own destruction."

He crossed his arms over his ample chest, and a sneering laugh burst from him; then he added,—

"This tomb, then, opens by a secret spring—the plate of iron seems heavy —if I can destroy the spring, and fix it in its place, it may defy their efforts to remove it, for the staircase is so narrow as to cramp all exertion, and the strongest man, with the heaviest weapon, in such a confined place, could not strike a blow."

He then drew from his side a short two-edged sword, with which he was always armed, under his ecclesiastical garment, and with one blow of the weapon he broke the spring, and lifting up the plate of iron, in the grooves through which it moved, he held it in one hand, which no ordinary man could have done, while, with the handle of his sword, he hammered the lower part of the tomb until he bent the iron casing, and fixed the sliding piece so firmly that it would move in no direction.

"I would fain yet," he said, "find some other security against their outlet from this place."

He glanced round him as he spoke, and saw a large marble slab let into the wall, on which was an inscription commemorative of the virtues of one of the Brandon family, long since dead.

With his sword he hewed down the cement by which it was fastened in its place, and with one stupendous effort, then, he tore the marble slab from where it had been so long, and carrying it in his arms, he placed it over the once moveable piece of iron in the tomb of Sir Montague Brandon.

Then he muttered, "I will defy the strength of any one human being to remove now the obstruction I have placed to an exit from the vaults by this sepulchre, and but the strength of one can they bring to bear against it. Curses on the caution of that crusader in keeping his face so closely masked by that velvet vizard. I must have known him could I have seen his face. The voice sounds strangely familiar to me in some of its tones, and yet I could not, for my life, charge my memory with the when and where I have heard it."

He remained, then, some minutes longer in deep thought, after which he muttered,—

"To the battlements—to the battlements; ay, to the battlements. There must be some means taken to prevent their escaping through the opening near to Sir Kenneth Hay's dungeon ceiling, for that is well known to Fitzhugh's page, and would, of course, be made immediate use of. Let me consider—let me consider."

As he spoke he glided to one of the windows of the chapel, and silently un-bolting it, he cleared the ledge at a spring, then gliding along by the exterior of the wall, he ascended the broad moss-grown steps, leading from what was called the lower keep, to the eastern battlement, and which lay on the unin-habited side of the castle ; taking then one of the largest of the huge square blocks of granite which lay there, in case of occasional repairs being required, he placed it on the extreme verge of the battlement, exactly above the narrow opening through which the page had squeezed himself during his operations for the rescue of Sir Kenneth Hay.

"This is the spot," said Morgatani ; "they will be some hours before they will seek to return from their explorations, and long before that time I will place Eldred Weare here on the watch, with strict instructions to topple the stone over upon receiving a given signal from me, at the Grey Turret, of which, from here, he can see sufficient for such a purpose. Such a measure must prove the destruction of the page, and no other individual of the party is small enough to get through the narrow opening."

Morgatani then glided from the spot as he had come to it, and casting a grim look of satisfaction as he passed again through the chapel at the marble slab which lay against the tomb of Sir Montague Brandon, he muttered,

"I shall have revenge if I cannot obtain information, and those who would have crossed my path shall meet death for their temerity, so perish the enemies of Morgatani."

CHAPTER LVIII.

"Grim death seemed waiting for his prey,—
A ghastly form was he—
But Heaven shall save the good and brave,
And they shall yet be free."

THE PASSAGE THROUGH THE VAULTS.—THE STORM.—THE RETURN.—THE CLOSED ENTRANCE.—THE PAGE'S EXPEDIENT.

WINGROVE had taken care that the party on its mission to explore the vaults of Brandon Castle should be well provided with lights, and at the suggestion of

Bernard, who never forgot the essentials of existence, Wingrove took with him a flask of wine, which, as circumstances turned out, became of great value to the adventurers.

At the foot of the staircase a torch was lighted, and Fitzhugh's page taking it in his hand walked forward with cautious steps, noting carefully, as he went, the various tokens by which he knew the passages through which they had to pass.

"I cannot pretend," he said, as he paused and half turned to those who followed him, "that I have intimate knowledge of the intricacies of this underground portion of Brandon Castle. I can certainly lead you to the vault in one of which lies the body of the Lady Alicia, Sir Rupert's ill-fated wife, and I can take you to the range of dungeons in one of which was confined Sir Kenneth Hay ; for anything further, I should be but a wanderer and an useless guide."

"Do your best, boy," said the crusader, "and we will trust to ourselves and our weapons to force a passage in every direction."

"I cannot say," remarked Hugh Wingrove, "that I am thoroughly acquainted with the vaults of Brandon, for I never had any strong motive to explore them, but in the various conversations I have had with Sir Rupert I have acquired sufficient information to assist somewhat in threading these mazes."

"Then among us all," said the crusader, "I think it will go hard but we shall thoroughly explore them."

As he spoke, a low rumbling sound reached their ears, and he added, instantly,

"Ah ! a storm is rising—that sound is distant thunder. I have frequently heard such lately when confined in a dungeon far deeper below the earth's surface than we at present are."

They paused for a moment, and listening attentively they could plainly distinguish the distant sound of roaring elements, which sounded distinct and strangely upon the ears of Wingrove and Bernard, who looked to the crusader expecting to hear from him their directions.

"It will not reach us here, nor be in the neighbourhood of the castle for some time," remarked the crusader ; "it will not retard our progress." Then turning to the page, he added, "Go forward, boy, with the torch, and fear nothing."

The page who had stood still listening to the mutterings of the storm, now turned and walked forward followed closely by the crusader, and Wingrove and Bernard bringing up the rear of the party.

They proceeded through a long but winding passage for some distance, until they came to a spot, which enlarged itself almost to the extent of a hall, and from which branched various passages in different directions. There was a large stone pillar rose in the middle of the space which appeared to assist in supporting the roof. The crusader paused, looked around, and after a moment or two's consideration, he said,

"By my faith this would form a convenient spot to meet and harangue traitors."

"It would be a secure place for such a purpose, or to rally men who sought to escape from a foe. But, hark, how loud the storm rages."

It did rage, and seem as if the numerous passages all contributed to increase the din without, by each conducting the sound of a single storm, and when it reached the ears of the little party, seemed multiplied in sound by the number of conductors.

They proceeded to examine these passages, and at the suggestion of Wingrove took that on the right, which they pursued for some distance, and which terminated in a door which, being only bolted, they, after a little difficulty in drawing the bolt, entered a subterranean corridor in which were several doors.

"These are dungeons," said Wingrove, as he gazed on the lock of one of them.

"Then we will examine them," replied the crusader; "there may be some hapless prisoner who owes his fate to the Jesuit."

The dungeons were examined one by one, but nothing remarkable was found, and they left them to return, as there was no further outlet in that direction. Retracing their steps in silence, they listened to the deep roll of the thunder which now broke over the spot on which the castle stood, with fearful violence. Crash on crash succeeded each other with great rapidity, while the many echoes, the trembling of the earth, which seemed to rock the substantial walls around them, rendered the spot gloomy and fearful.

The page appeared to faulter and looked pale, but yet proceeded, holding the torch with a steady hand, while Bernard still bringing up the rear, muttered to himself.

"A flagon of right sparkling October, and a good rousing fire, were worth all these damp and dark passages—faugh—my tongue clings to my mouth with drought."

They had now returned to the spot where all the passages met, and they could listen to the storm without, which was heard here more plainly than elsewhere, and the din which the elements caused was so great that the crusader turning to Wingrove, said,

"Dost know, good Wingrove, a spot which we have not yet seen, but which would serve as a place secure to wait in till this storm is over?—it is too violent to last very long, and I am loth to return over ground we have already explored."

"I think that passage," replied Wingrove, "will lead us to some such place as you desire, sir knight, though I fear I shall be but a poor guide, since I only know it by description."

"Lead on," said the crusader to Wingrove, and the whole party were soon lost to view in the passage; but they had not proceeded far when they found their course impeded by a strong door, which they were compelled, with much labour, to force, and then they again proceeded, until at length Wingrove stumbled against a stone step, and on examining the spot, said,

"This must be the place I spoke of. See, here is the door; but how to open it is beyond my skill to tell."

Fitzhugh's page now stepped forward, and, touching a spring, the door slowly opened with a grating sound upon its iron hinges, and disclosed to them a small room, enclosed with high walls. At one corner was a rude altar, with a crucifix, and on one side a stone bench.

"Beyond this," said the page, "we shall find the vault in which lies the Lady Alicia. I know this room from my former visit, although I came not the same road to it."

"The storm seems abating," said the crusader; "do you not hear the peals of thunder get more and more distant each moment? We may now proceed as rapidly as possible on our task."

The page led the way, and the vaults in which were buried the dead of the ancient Brandon family were entered; the tomb of the Lady Alicia, which has already been described to the reader, attracted greatly the attention of the crusader, and his surprise was strongly manifested at discovering the fresh state of the body.

"How can this be accounted for?" he said. "All around here is decay and unwholesome moisture, while this body alone seems to have suffered nothing from the withering hand of Time."

"I know not," said Wingrove; "the fact is glaring and manifest; but what object Heaven has in permitting so extraordinary a violation of the general order of nature, it is impossible to guess."

" It is indeed most strange," mused the crusader ; " and here, too, Sir Page, as you have stated to me, is the dagger plunged into the breast of the corpse. There is some frightful meaning in all this—a meaning that will show itself, I believe, when Sir Rupert returns. Let us leave everything as we find it, and it may be a great object for us to know the real condition of the body in these vaults."

" It is strange, indeed," said Wingrove, in a saddened voice ; " I could almost fancy I saw before me the poor Lady Alicia, as she was in life—so like reality do her poor remains still look. But several hours have now elapsed, and, from the space we have traversed, I feel quite sure that we have left but little of the vaults of Brandon unexplored."

" We have not yet," said the page, " visited the dungeons, in one of which was confined Sir Kenneth Hay."

" True," said Wingrove ; " but there, at least, we shall find nothing to repay our toil ; there is but a long range of dungeons, in none of which has any one been confined, excepting the knight, for many years."

" Then let us be content," said the crusader, " and let us return once more to the light of day ; for, to tell the truth, I am sufficiently tired of being cooped up in this dreary, underground place."

The party then made a retrograde movement, and, with far greater facility than they advanced, took their course towards the narrow passage, which was terminated by the narrow staircase leading to the chapel.

Little suspected they the trick which had been played them by Morgatani, the Black Monk—little deemed they that any difficulties would arise in emerging from the gloomy subterranean passages which they had wearied themselves in exploring.

Wingrove was now preceding the party with a torch in his hand ; and, when he reached the top of the narrow staircase, which, in truth, obliged a man of ordinary stature to stoop, as he ascended or descended, he turned to the page, who was following him, and said,—

" Now, master page, if you know how, I will trouble you to undo this intricate entrance."

" Undo it ?" cried the page ; " why we left it open."

" By the mass, so we did," said Wingrove ; " but it's fast enough now, and it's only to be hoped that you know the way to open it, master page, or else we are like so many mice in a trap."

" Thank Heaven, I do," said the page ; " but this staircase is so narrow, that we must all descend it again, to allow me to go first."

This was a measure so self-evident, that it was immediately adopted, and the page then, taking the flambeau in his hand, tripped lightly up the narrow staircase, wondering much who had fastened the iron door, but with the full expectation of being able to open it with a touch. A cry of terror escaped him when he saw the devastation which the sword of the monk had committed and he said,—

" The springs are destroyed—the springs are destroyed ! Morgatani must have been here, for none but he would feel an interest in confining us within this dreary abode."

" Confine us, master page ?" said the crusader ; " that, give me leave to hope, a hundred monks would find difficult, and it would go hard with me, indeed, if I cannot find strength to make our way out of this gloomy place."

" Heaven send you may," said the page.

" Confound the narrow staircases," added the crusader, " we are forced to dodge each other up and down them, in order to find any room for action."

The crusader, however, when he found himself at the summit of the narrow staircase, began rapidly to alter his opinion with regard to the easiness of forcing an exit from the vaults of Brandon. When he calculated upon his strength, he quite forgot for the moment that he required space in which to exercise it ; and when he reached the iron plate, which he rightly calculated his strength would have easily enabled him to force, he found that, by the cramped position in which he was compelled to stand, he had no opportunity of calling into action the extraordinary strength with which he was gifted.

In the first place, he could not stand upright in the small space ; and, so restricted was the movement of his hands, that, instead of striking a vigorous blow with the battle-axe, he could only give a succession of very inefficient taps to the iron plate.

"Now, by the mass, this is provoking," he cried ; "it seems, Wingrove, that we are indeed fixed here, unless you know of some other mode of exit from this place."

"I do know of one," said Wingrove, "the existence of which I have before intimated to you, and which was once pointed out to me by Sir Rupert himself, but it is as awkwardly situated as this from the inside, and being firmly fastened on the out, I am sure we shall have no chance of forcing it."

"Upon my word," said the crusader, "that is remarkably pleasant—time becomes valuable, for our strength will not increase in this place. Let us proceed at once to some part of the vaults where at least there will be freedom of action, and then commence a continued attack in some particular direction, until we work our way into safety."

"In that we must be extremely cautious," said Wingrove, "for we are below the level of the moat, and if we open a communication with it, our immediate destruction will be the consequence."

"My good Wingrove," said the crusader, "you are an excellent Job's comforter. You have quite a talent that way ; but do something we must, for I have not the remotest disposition in the world to terminate my career under ground ; it is quite a sufficiently disagreeable idea to be there deposited when one is of no further use above."

"Hold," said the page ; "why should we despair ; what is to hinder me from getting through the same aperture near the roof of Sir Kenneth Hay's dungeon that I before found so serviceable in assisting him to escape ? I can then go round, Wingrove, and open the secret door you have mentioned as having been shewn to you by Sir Rupert."

"That will do," said the crusader. "I wonder that none of us thought of that before."

"By'r lady," said Wingrove, "the suggestion is a great relief."

"A monstrous relief !" said Bernard ; "you can't think how dreadfully thirsty I'm getting. Oh, if I had but thought of it, to have brought over a quart, or a couple of quarts of ale in anything, it would have helped to sustain nature till I got back."

"I have a small portion of wine with me," said Wingrove to the crusader, "which I brought with a hope you would condescend to partake of it."

"Such condescension," said the crusader, as he took the flask, "brings with it its own reward ; and now, sir page, hasten on, and let us thank our fates that we brought you with us, and that you are small enough to creep through a little space, otherwise these gloomy vaults of Brandon might acquire an historical celebrity I have no wish to bestow upon them."

The page led the way as before, and without pausing to note any of the objects they passed, the party proceeded rapidly to the line of dungeons, in one of which Sir Kenneth Hay had been confined.

"You may have some difficulty, master page," said Wingrove, "in finding

the keys of the door I mentioned, for it has two massive locks ; but I will give you as accurate directions as I can where to search for them in my bedchamber.''

" Oh, a page will find out anything," said the crusader.

"Wingrove," said Bernard, " you must be tired—let me carry that wineflask for you."

" You are very considerate," was the reply ; " but I am afraid you would find it fatiguing likewise, and find out a means of distributing the weight by carrying part of it inside ; so I'll even carry it myself, if you please."

CHAPTER LIX.

Revenge is a passion, which may be made to grow in the human heart, like a rank weed choking the fair luxuriance of the sweetest flowers.—BOSWELL.

ELDRED'S AMBITION.—THE MESSAGE FROM THE MONK.—THE STORM ON THE BATTLEMENTS.

IT was with a grim and ghastly smile of demoniac triumph that Morgatani glided from the battlements to seek further means for the completion of his murderous intentions as regarded the page of Fitzhugh, and the party that were exploring the vaults.

" 'Tis well," he muttered, " they have laid a most admirable trap for themselves ; without provisions, in bad air, and probably within a few short hours without light, they must surely perish—their strength must be decreasing—terror will seize upon them, and their efforts to escape will become more irra-

No. 44

tional each moment. I shall triumph! I shall triumph! By what other fortunate chance could I have got rid of so many enemies at once? This crusader, whose face I have not been able to see, but who is none the less a bitter enemy of mine, that I do not know his name or rank—Hugh Wingrove, likewise, and the page of Fitzhugh, who I more than suspect to be playing a double part, all will fall together; and that lump of mortality, Bernard, from a stroke of whose sword I once narrowly escaped, is a good riddance, for he is much looked to by the men-at-arms, on account of his physical power and brute force."

With a lighter and freer step than that with which he was wont to traverse Brandon Castle, Morgatani walked towards the chamber of Agatha Weare, for there was scarcely a person in that building whom he dreaded to meet.

To have encountered any of the domestics, he knew would produce in them but a feeling of terror, while to come across one of the men-at-arms would have been to him rare sport, for he would unhesitatingly have murdered him; and all which would by no means have detracted from his already ominous reputation, since the deed, as a matter of course, would be attributed to him.

As it happened, however, he pursued his way unmolested, and consequently unmolesting, until he reached Agatha's room, which he entered with so unusual a smile upon his features as convinced her at once that something of an unusually satisfactory character must have occurred.

" You are pleased, Morgatani," she said, " what has happened?"

" I am pleased, Agatha Weare," he replied, " more pleased than I have been for many a day."

" Indeed?"

" Yes. Pious people, I believe, when they have achieved any extraordinary villany, usually thank Heaven for its kind assistance; let us therefore do so, and not be behind hand with the age."

" That something has happened," said Agatha, " that is favourable to our interests I am certain; but keep me no longer in suspense."

" I will not," said the monk, " the features of the dead do not alter much in a few days."

" The dead," echoed Agatha, " wherefore that remark?"

" Because before the expiration of that time I shall be able to discover who the dead crusader is, although he has failed me while living."

" You have murdered him?" shuddered Agatha.

" No," said the monk, calmly, " most heartily I tried to do the deed, but failed; he has himself chosen, together with Hugh Wingrove, Bernard, the man-at-arms, and Fitzhugh's page, to step out of the air into the grave; they're in the vaults of Brandon, which their curiosity has tempted them to explore. There I have blocked them up, and to the best of my belief they cannot escape. So that when any future adventurous persons wander in those gloomy passages or dungeons there will be really something to speculate upon, in the mouldering skeletons of our enemies."

" It is very dreadful," said Agatha; " was it necessary to destroy them all?"

" Ay," said the monk, " both necessary and pleasant. Providence is good to us, and at some idle moment when time hangs heavy on me I will compose a special prayer of thanksgiving."

" Oh, Morgatani! Morgatani!" said Agatha. " Do you not tremble at such bold impiety? Can you indeed look upon the boundless wealth and beauties of nature and dream that there is not a Heaven above us?"

" I never indulge in any dreams," said the monk; " but let us quit such a subject upon which of late you have become alarmingly sensitive. Where is Eldred Weare? I have something for him to do which will about suit his great capacity of mind."

" I will seek him," said Agatha, " his cowardice provokes me past endurance."

"What I wish him to do," said the monk, "requires no courage. It is just such a nice little act of sneaking villany, which comes fully up to the capacity of Eldred Weare ; seek him, Agatha, for I will lose no further time."

Much as Agatha felt the truth of Morgatani's not very flattering description of her brother, she thought in her own mind that it was bad taste in him to utter it so broadly to her ; but she obeyed his requisition to seek Eldred, without making any remark, for she was too far committed with that dreadful man, and too much in his power to quarrel about any little incidental circumstance that might be a mere matter of private opinion.

The monk was alone for some time before Agatha returned with her brother, a circumstance which arose from Eldred, in great terror, positively refusing at first to meet Morgatani, for well he knew he was never sent for by the wily Jesuit except to be instrumental in the performance of some act of a disagreeable nature, which he, the monk, either shrunk from himself, or could not conveniently perform.

"I tell you, sister," said Eldred, "I can't—I won't—that is to say, I'd rather not. Tell him I have got a cold in my head, and can't see, or that I have sprained my ancle, and am unable to walk. I have just hit the funny bone of my arm never such a knock, and you may tell him that too—and anything else you like, for I positively will not come. I know that it is always something uncommonly disagreeable that he wants me for."

"These are idle excuses," said Agatha, "you must come. Where is your ambition ?"

"I don't know," said Eldred ; "you and Morgatani persuaded me to be ambitious some time ago, and I have done nothing but repent of it since. I'm afraid it will be of very little consequence to me whether John or Richard is king. The idea of you and Morgatani persuading me, that if Sir Rupert had his head chopped off I should drop in for the castle and all the estates, and be able to tyrannize over everybody, just as I liked. I begin to think it is a horrid delusion, and that if I did drop in for anything it would be something in the shape of a malletting from Morgatani some day for trying to say my head was my own."

"But your revenge, Eldred—your revenge," said Agatha.

"Ah ! my revenge be bothered," said Eldred ; "you and your revenge are enough to drive any one out of their wits. Suppose Sir Rupert Brandon, who was courting poor Alicia, what's dead and defunct, did kick me dreadfully for peeping behind a screen when he was a kissing her. What, then, d'ye think I'm a fool ? He was a wholloper, and I wasn't, and I never thought of being so ridiculous as to make any fuss about it, for if I had the end of it would have been, I'd have got my head punched as well."

"Pshaw !" said Agatha, "that I should have to speak to such a dastard."

"Ah ! it's all very well, sister," continued Eldred ; "but if I hadn't been as wise as I am, you wouldn't have had me to speak to at all. After Sir Rupert had kicked me he was kind enough to offer to break a lance with me, as he called it, to make things a little square."

"And you refused," said Agatha, in a sneering tone.

"Do I look like an ass ?" said Eldred ; "of course I did. No, said I—I thank you. You may break your lances by yourself, don't add insult to injury ; perhaps, while you were breaking your lance, you might include breaking one of my bones, and that might be the one that joins my head to my neck. None of your nonsense, said I, if you ain't satisfied, kick me again."

"Cowardly dastard," said Agatha, "can you not resent an injury?"

"Of course I can, when there's a good opportunity of doing it quite safely ; but when you and Morgatani gammoned me so about my revenge, I never thought of being dragged through the mire as I have been. Revenge, indeed, why it's been all against me. I have had nothing but trouble and hard knocks ever since I began in that line."

" You have gone too far to retract," said Agatha.

" Ah! of course, that's the cry," said Eldred. " A good while ago it was —' ha! you have not gone far enough, Eldred, to taste the fruits of your revenge,' and so I was pushed on a little further, till it was, ' you've gone too far, Eldred, to retract ;' and then, I suppose, I have had all the fruits, and all I can say is, they've been uncommonly sour."

" You must come," said Agatha, " your weak arguments are utterly useless ; if you don't come to him, you may depend that Morgatani will come to you, and that not in the best of tempers."

" Ah!" groaned Eldred, " there it is ; I suppose I'm booked. I feel for all the world as if I had sold myself to the old thingamy, and been uncommonly bilked in the agreement. I suppose I must. Needs must when the old gentleman drives. I shouldn't wonder if there's somebody's old corpse to pull about."

" No," said Agatha, " I am sure such is not the case. Morgatani tells me that the task he wishes to assign you is easy, and well suited to your talents."

" Ah! he's uncommonly polite," groaned Eldred. " I don't aspire to-day to a greater effort of genius than will include the demolition of my meals, and having a little innocent flirtation with the cook, who is certainly a fine woman—an uncommonly fine woman, and it strikes me, if she wasn't always in the state of perspiration she's in, she would be the finest woman I ever saw, and go near to break down the drawbridge if she were to go across it. There's a female for you, and no nonsense."

" Come on," said Agatha. " Come on."

" Well, I'm a coming ; I suppose I must rub up my revenge a bit now."

The monk was, as Agatha had anticipated, not in the best of tempers at the delay in Eldred's appearance, and when he saw him, he said, " Eldred Weare, you must surely forget both your revenge and your ambition ; wherefore do you so long delay attending my summons?"

" Ah!" said Eldred, " my revenge had very nearly got the better of me, and I was half asleep ; but is there anything disagreeable I can do for you?"

" No," said the monk ; " but follow me, and I will set you a task that will delight you, and materially faciliate your magnificent projects."

" My magnificent projects," thought Eldred, as he followed the monk ; " that's a good un ; I'm dreadful taken in, that's quite clear, and I suppose I must be resigned to my fate. No sop in the pan to-day, that's evident."

The monk strode along so rapidly in his fear of losing his victims, that Eldred, to keep up to him, was forced to break quite into a little run, until they reached the battlement, where the huge stone stood tottering upon the brink.

" Crouch yourself down there," said the monk, " but keep an eye on yon small loophole of the Grey Turret, which you can just command a sight of from here. When you see from thence a small black flag projected, topple the stone over—that is all you have to do."

" Oh," said Eldred, " I suppose it is to be a nobber for somebody who is to be down below."

" It will further," said the monk, " your deep-laid schemes and high-reaching ambition."

" Oh, indeed!" said Eldred ; " the schemes are so deep, and the ambition so high, that I don't very well comprehend either one or the other of them ; and now it's beginning to rain—the deuce, that's a clap of lightning, and a flash of thunder. It's beginning to rain dogs and cats."

" Remain by the stone," said the monk, " or remove from it at your peril."

Eldred crouched down by the stone, and in another moment Morgatani had left the spot.

The rain now came down in resistless torrents on the battlements of Brandon Castle, and all around, washing the grey stones of which they were made, and running in little channels over the moss-grown sides.

Far around but one dreary scene met the shrinking gaze of Eldred Weare, who stood trembling under the united effects of cold, wet, and fear; creeping as close to the large stone as he could, he endeavoured thus to shelter himself from the pitiless pelting that deluged the spot.

He now and then cast his eyes towards the moat, but little could he see there save the plashing of the rain, and the streams of water that rushed into it from several parts of the battlements, and descending into it from projecting points in torrents, and mingling itself with the dark and muddy waters of the moat beneath.

All around, as far as the eye could reach, presented but a dreary prospect of one wide watery vapour, which hid from the sight the distant prospect which at other times cheered the vision of the beholder; and, did he turn his eyes to the Heavens, a still more uncomfortable scene presented itself, in the shape of heavy leaden coloured clouds, overcharged with watery particles, and which promised no speedy cessation—but a mere collection of humid clouds could be seen as far as the eye could reach.

Eldred instinctively shut his eyes to such a scene of discomfort, with a fear almost amounting to horror, but he opened them again as he recollected the necessity for his obeying the behest of the Black Monk.

While he was thus placed, the roll of the distant thunder raised up dreadful images in his mind, and his fears amounted almost to an agony as he beheld the vivid lightning dart along the dreary sky, and was then followed by peal on peal of the thunder, as it neared the castle, until the crashing reports which were so distinctly heard by the party in the vaults, caused him to shrink into the smallest possible space, burying his head in his hands, firmly believing his last moment at hand, and that the next sound would be that of the falling structure of Brandon Castle.

But such was not the fate either of this noble pile or of Eldred Weare, for the thunder passed over, and he could hear each vibration as it proceeded further and further from the castle, till the lightning was no longer seen, and the thunder was only heard in indistinct mutterings, and then it ceased altogether, or was lost in the distance.

Though the thunder thus passed off, yet the rain still continued to fall in deluging drops; upon this spot it appeared as if the floodgates of Heaven were opened, and its waters let down to wash the structure from its base; but yet its ancient and timeworn walls showed but the trace of the flood as it chased its way down the many indentations on its stone surface, and had worn for itself a channel which strongly contrasted with the darker hue of the adjacent stone.

The huge stone which Morgatani had placed upon the battlement, ready to be launched upon the unsuspecting page, stood in bright contrast with the battlement itself, for the latter was old and timeworn, while the stone, though it had lain a long time, was now so cleansed by the shower, that the granite looked new, and many bright spots were visible upon its surface.

As the storm decreased Eldred began to recover a little the equanimity of his mind, and for the first time since its commencement he remembered what the monk had said about watching the loophole of the Grey Turret, and with a cry of alarm he raised his eyes in the direction Morgatani had indicated.

"Here 'll be a row," he said, " if he's been waving away all this while with his little black flag, and I've not seen it. I suppose all my deep schemes will be spoiled, and my revenge go to the dogs."

CHAPTER LX.

" Now Heaven speed thee, gentle page,
    And guide thy footsteps right,
Or never will the brave and good
    Again see morning's light."

THE DUNGEON.—THE ALARM.—ELDRED'S DESPERATE CONDITION.—MORGATANI
    AT THE LOOP-HOLE.—THE WIZARD'S REVENGE.

IT was with some feeling of anxiety that the page himself hurried onwards to Sir Kenneth Hay's dungeon, for he felt that on himself depended the rescue of so many persons from a terrible death, which else would be surely inevitable. Moreover, the undertaking itself was attended with no little difficulty, and it would require but a trifling degree of nervousness, or vertigo, to precipitate him from his narrow foothold, after his leaving the aperture in the dungeon, into the gloomy moat below.

To think of such a catastrophe was to go a long way on towards producing it, and the nervousness of the page was such, that it became noticed by the crusader, who said,—

" Boy, you tremble ; why should you do so, you have essayed before the feat you are now about to accomplish ?"

" True, sir knight, I have," said the page, " and yet now I tremble, for a mightier stake depends upon my exertions. Here are four lives at risk, and I did tremble with apprehension at the possibility of failure."

" Banish your fears," said the crusader, " nothing was ever done well with apprehension. A firm resolution to succeed is the greatest element of success. Waste not a thought upon us as you attempt the dangerous passage."

" If I fail," said the page, " I will, at least, prove the sincerity of my wish to succeed, for I will perish in the attempt."

" And if you do succeed," said the crusader, " I have fought so often by side of King Richard that I have good interest with him, and can promise you any boon you may ask when he shall dispossess the usurper who at present fills his throne, and resumes his birthright."

" Any boon ?" said the page, earnestly.

" Yes, any one," said the crusader, " within the bounds of possibility."

" Think you," said the page, " King Richard could force a great act of justice from one who has done a great wrong ?"

" I think he could," said the crusader ; " because, if the person so acting refuse to perform the justice that was required of him, King Richard would make him shorter by the head if he were a knight, and hang him on the nearest tree if he were of meaner quality."

" I'm satisfied," said the page, " and some day, sir, will put you in mind of your promise."

" As soon as you like," was the reply, " so soon as the performance shall be practicable."

They were now in the dungeon which had been so very near proving the tomb of Sir Kenneth Hay. A gleam of light came in through the enlarged orifice through which the page made his escape, mingling strangely with the torch-light that was brought into that gloomy place by its present visitors.

" Ay," said the crusader, " there, sure enough, is the opening. Now, Wingrove, tell this youngster where to get the keys of that same door which you speak of, and, in the name of Heaven, let us emerge from this place as quickly as may be."

" I will," said Wingrove. " Sir page, you may know the apartment that

I occupy, and if not you can have no difficulty in getting a ready direction to it. Take this key, it opens a small box which you will find in the corner of the room, and at the bottom of which you will see two massive and old-fashioned keys; they are linked together with a piece of twine, and are those which we require for the secret door. Go now at once, boy, and Heaven speed you."

"Allow me," said the crusader, "to lend you my assistance to reach the aperture."

"I need not trouble you," said the page; "there are the same means existing in the wall for my easy ascent that there were before."

"Call it not a trouble, boy," said the crusader, as he caught the page up from the ground, and with one arm lifted him up quite level with the aperture. "Now, off with you, and may this day's work make you the luckiest page that ever lived."

At this instant so tremendous a splash took place in the moat below that the page was covered with water, and had he not been caught in the arms of the crusader, in the surprise of the moment he would, in all probability, have fallen from the ticklish ledge on which he was, and met his death in the troubled waters.

"Good Heavens! what is that?" cried Wingrove.

"Some heavy body," said the crusader, "has fallen into the moat."

"I should say a heavy body," muttered Bernard; "somebody about my size, I reckon. Now, what a great lump of luck it would be if that was the Black Monk!"

"I never heard such a splash in my life," said Wingrove. "Do you go up again, master page," said the crusader, "and reconnoitre."

The page trembled, but made no opposition, allowing himself to be again lifted to the narrow opening.

"I see nothing," he said, "but the troubled waters of the moat; but did you hear that cry?"

"I did," said the knight; "it was some one crying murder, and appears to come from the battlements above."

A voice could now be distinctly heard crying,

"Murder!—help!" in loud accents.

"That is the voice of Eldred Weare," said Wingrove. "By the mass, I am puzzled to know what has happened above to cause so great a disturbance."

"The sooner we get above, then, and ascertain the facts ourselves the better. Come, sir page, why do you hesitate?"

The page offered up a brief prayer to Heaven, and then clambered through the aperture, soon disappearing from the eyes of those who watched his movements with so much interest from the dungeon.

In order now to explain the cause of the premature falling of the stone from the battlements, we must go back to Eldred Weare in his uncomfortable position, by the huge block of granite, which, by the diabolical cunning of the monk, was destined to work the destruction of Fitzhugh's page, and in all human likelihood to embarrass the little party in the vaults, until famine should incapacitate them from making exertions for their own deliverance.

The rain had been too violent to last long, and although Eldred Weare, in consequence of being soaked to the skin, derived but little benefit from its cessation—cease it did, and a cold wind succeeded it, which was anything but agreeable to a person situated as he then was; but he dared not move from the position he occupied, for he imagined that the eye of the Black Monk was upon him, and that he would take ample vengeance for any neglect of his imperious behests.

Eldred Weare, however, was mistaken in supposing himself so closely watched by Morgatani, it was only occasionally that he glanced from his narrow turret window towards the huge block of granite which nearly hid the shrinking form of his weak companion in guilt from his sight. His attention was too much engrossed by watching the opening from the roof of the dungeon, while he held in his hand the small black flag that was to be thrust out at a moment's notice when the page should appear on the narrow shelving.

All through the continuance of the storm he remained in that watchful attitude, and now, when Eldred Weare, recovering his terror at the rude strife of the elements, in reality fixed his eyes on the loophole, he fancied he could see a portion of the monk's face, and one of his eyes glaring with unholy fire from that small opening.

"Oh," said Eldred, "here's a pretty situation I'm in, soaked through and no exercise, and then being dried up by as comfortable a cold wind as one could wish to have. I was talking about a cold in the head a little while ago to Agatha, and now I shall have one. I shall be as hoarse as a raven, that's a settled point, and the rheumatism for a month is as good as bespoke. Flannel next the skin is a pleasant thing when it happens to be dry, but I believe I must be wet through skin and all. Now, whoever's to have this little pebble on his head might just as well come and have it at once, it couldn't make much difference to him surely, and may to me make a good deal. I suppose this is more revenge—hang it, everybody seems to get revenged upon me, and as for ambition, I have been so knocked about lately, that I mount no higher than an ardent wish to be left alone, and be allowed to sleep quietly in bed at nights."

Just as Eldred had got thus far in his solitary ruminations, he gave such a start of terror, that he nearly fell over the battlements, stone and all, for as he crouched down behind it, something gave him a terrible tug at the legs, which precipitated him upon the flat of his face, and a great weight came with a thump upon his body, that made him gasp again.

He was perfectly paralysed and nearly distilled to a jelly with fear; then he felt two hands or paws rummaging about his head, when his ears, which appeared to be the objects of search, were taken hold of, while some frightful long nails or claws were made to meet through them, while at the same moment a voice growled—

"Dare to make the least noise and I'll drag your tongue out by its roots —dare to look round and your eyes shall be twisted from their sockets before you can close them."

Eldred Weare lay to all appearance dead—think, he could not; he was, as it were, in a kind of trance—the operations of life went on mechanically, but terror had almost upset the small portion of brains he possessed.

"Answer me what I shall ask of you," growled the voice in his ear, "and answer me truly; if you don't, I'll smash your head as you lie here against the battlements."

With a faint tone Eldred could just manage to say "Yes," to which he added, "your majesty," for who could it be but the devil himself who had pounced upon him.

"What were you doing here?" said the voice.

"N—n—n—nothing, only throwing stones into the moat."

"Where is the Black Monk?"

"In the G—G—Grey Turret. Your majesty may see him through the loophole."

"Oh," cried Eldred's mysterious interrogator, and he gave such a jump upon him that he thought his back-bone was broken; "I do see him—revenge! revenge!"

"There it is," groaned Eldred to himself; "more revenge and I'm the victim."

The reader will surmise that Eldred's strange assailant could be no other than Nemoni, the Wizard of the Red Cavern. It was indeed he, who, having found his way at that juncture into Brandon by the mysterious mode of ingress and egress known only to himself, had suspected Eldred Weare to be stationed where he was for no good purpose, and being likewise aware of his cowardly nature,—for he had been a hidden witness to many of the strange scenes that had occurred at Brandon, he had pounced upon him as described—with a determination of wringing from his fears an account of his errand on that spot.

The name of Morgatani, however, always acted as a spell for calling into existence the darkest feelings of the unfortunate Nemoni's mind, and, although he knelt upon Eldred Weare's prostrate form, he forgot his very existence as he strained his eyes in the direction of the Grey Turret.

He shrouded himself at the same time from observation behind the huge block of grey granite, and his sight, rendered more acute by his long residence in the forest, and the necessity there existed for carrying on a warfare with its feathered and four-footed inhabitants, enabled him far more readily than Eldred had done to discover the face of the monk just within the loop-hole of the old Grey Turret.

The wizard crouched down still lower, and while Eldred Weare only gave an occasional groan to intimate that the superincumbent weight upon him was far from pleasant, the wizard unstrung from his side an exquisitely tempered small cross-bow, made entirely of steel, and which he had possessed himself of from the castle armoury in one of his singular visits.

He fitted an arrow into it with great nicety, and then resting the weapon by the side of the block of granite, while all but his eye was completely shrouded from view, he took a long and steady aim at the face of Morgatani.

No. 45

An uneasy movement of Eldred's, however, disturbed his aim, and then taking the arrow from its groove, he gave him, Eldred, several rather disagreeable pricks in the back with it, saying, in a low voice,—

" Another such movement, I'll cut off your head and throw it into the moat."

Eldred Weare's terror must have been great to induce him, suffering, as he was, more downright physical pain than he ever suffered in his life, to remain silent; but silent he did remain, while the wizard again placed the arrow in the cross-bow.

Then a thought suddenly struck him that Morgatani might possibly glance in the direction of the battlements, and not seeing Eldred, become alarmed.

With the quickness of thought, he snatched from Eldred's head his cap, and placing it upon himself, he hesitated not, in order to take a surer aim, to raise himself a little higher and peer over the edge of the granite stone.

CHAPTER LXI.

What hideous shape was that,
Which, with such direful meaning,
Stepped between me and my soul's revenge?
Let it come again—I'll speak to it.—OLD PLAY.

THE SUCCESSFUL SHOT.—ELDRED'S INJURIES.—THE WOUNDED MONK.—
THE DANGER AND COURAGE OF THE PAGE.

FOR a few moments the wizard knelt as motionless as the cold granite stone upon which he rested the deadly cross-bow that was levelled full at the loop-hole where was the dark and demoniac face of Morgatani, little dreaming of the danger that awaited him, or that his deadliest foe had him at such great vantage.

Once, during the time the wizard took in perfecting his aim against the life of the monk, Morgatani did look in the direction of the battlements, and then he was satisfied, for he saw the top of the velvet cap which Eldred Weare usually wore, and with a grim smile he said to himself,—

" He knows my eye is upon him, and he dared not flinch; weary and uncomfortable work he has had indeed during the storm,—but what care I? such as he are the poor tools with which subtle spirits, like myself, work out our schemes of deep ambition."

The wily monk then turned his eyes again in the direction of the aperture of the dungeon, which showed itself like a dark speck just over the moat in the castle wall, and from thence he determined he would not again remove his gaze until he should see the page emerge; and little dreamed he of the sudden interruption of his lonely watch that was in preparation.

The small black flag which was to be the signal for Eldred Weare to throw over the block of granite lay upon the side of the loophole, with one of the brawny hands of the monk upon it, ready at an instant's notice to thrust it forward into the open air, where it must catch, as he proposed, the fixed gaze of Eldred.

Was ever diabolical scheme so wilily planned to be so completely marred, as was that of the wily Jesuit's?

The wizard was at length satisfied with the aim he had taken; the small arrow flew from the cross-bow with a whistling sound; quick as a flash of light it entered the loophole,—Morgatani's face immediately disappeared, —and by design, or by accident, the little black flag was pushed outwards, and remained fluttering in the light breeze, as it lay partially upon the cell of that narrow casement.

The wizard saw in a moment that his aim had been true; and rising to his feet, with a cry of exultation, he stamped wildly upon Eldred Weare, who, in the despair of the moment, kicked wildly with his feet, like a strong swimmer attempting to stem an advancing tide.

The wizard paid no attention to him, and seemed to have forgot his very existence; for, after crying out—

"My revenge—my revenge—I've had my revenge!—the thought by day and the dream by night, is fulfilled,—Heaven! I thank thee—I have had my revenge!" he walked across the prostrate body of Eldred, and disappeared from the spot.

For full five minutes after the wizard was gone, Eldred Weare lay as flat as possible upon the battlements, in a state of mental confusion and bodily pain, that completely chained up his faculties. It had so happened, that the last step of the wizard had been upon the back of his, Eldred's, head, and the consequence was, that his nose was brought into such frightful and sudden collision with the worn stone-work of the parapet on which he lay, as to cause a serious injury to that organ; and, in fact, to widen and compress it in a manner that it never recovered fully. So violent was the concussion, that Eldred was under the impression that he had no nose at all, until returning circulation assured him of the fact, by visiting him with such an infernal aching in that once prominent organ, that he forgot all his other pains and bruises, and rolling over on his back, kicked wildly in the air, exclaiming—

"My nose—my nose—my precious nose! I think I have had enough of revenge and ambition now. Ah, my nose!—ah, my nose!—I wish I was dead and buried!"

From his back, in another few moments, he struggled to a sitting posture; and, wiping the mud and tears from his eyes, he looked in the direction of the Grey Turret.

There, sure enough, was the black flag; and all Eldred's evil passions rising in a moment in his breast, he felt a gratification in the prospect of at least being able to do injury to somebody, so with a "'Cuss you, take that," he toppled the mass of granite over the battlements.

The loud splash it made alarmed him as much it did any one else, and he turned to fly from the spot, when he suddenly confronted Morgatini, who seized him by the throat with the grasp of a demon, and with eyes that seemed to shoot fire from their glances, glanced into his terrified countenance.

The appearance of Morgatani was sufficiently frightful: his face and hands were covered with blood, and his apparel was torn in several places.

Then it was that Eldred, fancying that the next movement of the monk would be to pitch him over the battlements, raised the cry of "Murder," which had reached the ears of the crusader and his party in the dungeon.

"Peace!" cried Morgatani; "villain—wretch—tell me, what—what—damnation—tell me, what fiend has been here?"

"Murder," said Eldred, "look at my nose?"

The monk shook him to and fro with tremendous force, and then suddenly leaving go of him, down went Eldred again, rolling over in the rainwater which had collected in the hollows of the battlement.

This was too much for human nature, and Eldred Weare made a sudden resolution to remain there lying on his back, and as he said, "Let them all have it out," for that his murder by degrees was fully resolved upon he no longer entertained a shadow of a doubt.

The cause of Morgatani's precipitate retreat was, that he suspected Eldred Weare's cries might have been sufficiently loud to reach the ears of some of the men-at-arms on the battlements; flight then became his most prudent course under his then uncomfortable circumstances, for the arrow from the wizard's cross-bow had struck him on the cheek near the corner of his mouth, but taking an oblique direction, had done him no further injury than inflicting a ghastly flesh wound, which, in addition to being very painful, had covered him with blood in the manner we have described.

He was right in his conjecture that the men-at-arms would take an alarm from the cries of Eldred Weare, for such turned out indeed to be the case. An alarm was given by the nearest sentinel on duty, and so communicated to the guard-room, from whence issued four or five of the soldiers, to take the round of the battlements, and ascertain the cause of the cries.

When they reached Eldred Weare, their first impression strengthened too, as it was, by his cries of murder, was that he must certainly be dead.

" It's no joke," said Anstey, " here he lies. Now I could have sworn that fellow would never have died out of his bed. Somebody has met him, and settled him at last."

" Then whoever it was," said Joice Evans, " jumped into the moat just about the same time for I never heard such a devil of a splash in my life."

" Nor we, nor we," said the other men-at-arms.

" Gentlemen," groaned Eldred, who heard the sound of voices near him, but would not open his eyes,—" gentlemen, you had better put me out of my miseries at once. I have been persecuted quite enough—amen. Salve, domini, for I've lost my nose."

" He ain't dead, after all," said Anstey.

" Not quite," said Eldred; " but by the time I've been danced upon, I shall be."

" Come, get up," said Evans, giving him a poke with his partisan.

" I've tried that before," said Eldred, with a groan, " and only came down again with a more horrid whop. My nose is crunched, and I've no wish to live. Let me be peaceably buried—amen. Tell sister Agatha I have had quite enough revenge. Revenge has settled me. I'm a dead man. I've been a great donkey, and it's been all through ambition—amen."

" Somebody's pulled his nose," said Anstey.

" No," said Eldred, " somebody pushed it; if anybody pulled it with half such vengeance, they would have carried it away with them."

" He's been rolled in the mud, and soundly beaten by somebody," remarked Joice Evans. " Let's lift him up and carry him into the guard-room."

" I'm resigned to my fate," said Eldred, as they raised him to his feet, " quite resigned; take warning by me all of you, and if any of you get well kicked, never try after revenge—pocket it, just pocket it. Take warning and look at my nose, and, as I said before, I'm resigned to my fate."

" Who has ill-used you so ?" said Anstey.

" With reverence be it spoken, the devil," said Eldred.

" The devil !"

" Yes, he danced a sort of hell-jig upon my body—he had it all his own way; I never interfered."

" Did you see him ?"

" No, but I felt him, and if seeing is believing, I am sure feeling is ; and after he had danced on me a little while, it rather damped curiosity. Amen, let me be quietly buried."

The men-at-arms could preserve their gravity no longer, but burst into a simultaneous roar of laughter, which echoed again round the ancient battlements. They then lifted up Eldred Weare, and carried him bodily to the guard-room, where propping him up on a bench before the fire, they gave him something to drink, which partly seemed to restore him.

" You'd better go to bed," said Anstey, " at once, and I dare say you'll wake to-morrow quite well."

" I'll go to bed," said Eldred, " but noses don't grow in a night—this comes of revenge. I don't know whether I've got any inside or not, it has been so trampled upon."

" Assist him to bed, some of you," said Anstey, " for he does indeed seem to be sadly knocked about."

Two of the men-at-arms conveyed the unfortunate Eldred to his chamber, where they pitched him on to the bed, and walked away with all the unconcern imaginable, for in their earlier lives they had been so accustomed to fights and skirmishes, and the consequences arising therefrom, that they thought very little of Eldred Weare's injuries, nor indeed did they trouble themselves much about wondering who inflicted them, for so accustomed had they been lately in Brandon to mysterious circumstances, and likewise so accustomed to attribute everything of that character to the infernal agency of the Black Monk, that they at once placed upon his shoulders the burden of the present proceedings, only deeply lamenting, as usual, to each other, that Sir Rupert Brandon himself was not in his ancient home, to expel the daring intruder.

As all remained tolerably quiet after the heavy splash in the castle moat, and the cries of murder which had reached the ears of the crusader and his party ceased, the page gathered courage to pop through the aperture, and make his way, which he did in safety, to the battlements of the castle.

By that time, however, Eldred Weare had been removed by the men-at-arms, and no trace remained of the singular events that occurred so recently.

Heeding, little, however, of anything but the important mission he was on, the page hurried forward, and darting through the long corridors of Brandon Castle, he reached the chamber of Hugh Wingrove.

To unlock the box which had been mentioned, and to find the large antique keys, was the work of a few moments. Securing them, then, safely about him, the adventurous boy hurried back without a moment's delay to the battlements, and with eager haste he commenced descending the crumbling wall towards the opening from the dungeon.

Scarcely had he reached half the troublesome descent, when he began to find that indeed his danger was great, for an arrow, sent on its errand with no weak arm, so nearly touched him, that it pinned a portion of his garments between two massive stones, of which the wall was composed.

The page trembled for a moment, but he felt that to pause was death, and the only way to distract the aim of the marksman, was to continue descending as rapidly as possible.

In another moment a second arrow splintered to fragments against the wall just above his head.

" Help, help," he cried, and his footsteps were visible to those in the dungeon.

With one tremendous spring the crusader caught the edge of the opening, then drawing himself up, he supported the whole weight of his body upon one arm, and seizing the page round the waist with the other, he dragged him in safety into the aperture.

CHAPTER LXII.

" That gallant page, through deadliest hate,
A joyful day shall see,
When Richard of the Lion Heart
From treacherous toils is free."

THE ANCIENT DOOR.—FREEDOM.—THE UNHOLY CONSULTATION.

IT was when he was in safety that the courage and fortitude of the page seemed most to give way ; and when the crusader had sprung down the narrow opening, the page hung heavily upon his arm, and for a moment or two it seemed as if he would have lapsed into insensibility, so overcome was he by fatigue, excitement, and the narrow escape he had just had from a painful death.

Beyond his cry for help, the crusader and his party were not aware that any danger had menaced him, but they were soon made conscious of what it was that had made the descent from the battlements so extremely perilous, for, just as the crusader had said with rough kindness,

" Come, master page, cheer up your drooping spirits, and give a fairer promise of the man you one day may be," a cloth-yard shaft came in at the opening, and whistling over the heads of the party, buried itself in the further corner of the dungeon.

" Ah, indeed," said the crusader, calmly, " we have some enemy without who is getting angry, and wasting his arrows. By the mass, sir page, were you treated with a few of these messengers as you descended the wall to us, even now ?"

" I was," said the page, faintly. " Pardon my timidity, but I am not yet well used to war's alarms."

" Your timidity," said the crusader. " Why, boy. I don't wonder at your fright ; the oldest, bravest soldier might well have shrunk. A fair fight in an open country, with plenty of daylight, is a pleasant enough pastime, but to be made a living target of for some one's archery practice, while descending the face of a crumbling wall, is rather a serious proceeding. Let me but come across the knave who went so dastardly to work, and I'll let in daylight to his brains."

" It could be none other but the Black Monk," said Wingrove, " and now I bethink me, there are loopholes in the Grey Turret, which command the outer walls of these dungeons."

" Now the devil Black Monk him," said the crusader. " I desire nothing better than to meet that ruffianly priest face to face. By the mass, I would let him see that the church cannot stand well against—but no matter, the trial may come."

" I shall be sufficiently rewarded," said the page, " for all dangers and all fatigues, if the time should come, if you would ask of King Richard, for me, the boon I so much desire."

" Be assured that time will come," said the crusader ; " and now, Wingrove, take the keys, if the boy has brought them, which I doubt not he has, and let us leave this place as quickly as may be."

" They are here," said the page, as he handed the antique keys to Wingrove. " They are here, and, thank Heaven, I have reached you safe with them."

" Follow me," said Wingrove. " The door, which would have defied our utmost efforts to force, would readily yield to these ancient keys."

With rapid steps—for one and all were deeply interested in gaining the upper air, after so long and tiresome a sojourn in those subterranean passages, where the atmosphere was loaded with noxious vapours—the little party followed Wingrove, who, after a time, stopped at a deep recess in the wall, saying,—

" Here is a narrow staircase, which I remarked before, as we passed this way, and as it is the only one I have observed, I have no doubt but it is terminated by the door I have mentioned."

These stairs were so exceedingly narrow and steep, and the roof came down so close to them, that it was only in a crouching posture that any of the party could ascend. Even short of stature as was the page, he could not stand upright in that small space.

The stairs ascended to a considerable height, and then terminated in a massive door, which Wingrove immediately proclaimed to be of the same shape and size as that which had been pointed out to him on the other side by Sir Rupert Brandon.

" We are safe," he said. " We are safe ; there are two massive locks on the door, which my noble master assured me these keys would open."

The keys passed readily enough into the locks, but to turn them seemed to be a task beyond mortal strength, for, from long disuse, and the damp vapours arising from the vaults, the locks had become perfectly set with rust.

" I cannot turn the keys," said Wingrove, after making several ineffectual efforts, " and what to do I know not."

" If you can let me squeeze by you," said the crusader, " I will try my strength upon them."

" But, there is the danger of their breaking," said Wingrove.

" Nay," said the crusader, " were we to abstain from action, lest such an accident should occur, we might remain here and court death. The keys must be forced come of it what may."

He took a small poniard from his vest, and passing it through the handle of the key, he acquired a leverage which enabled him to exert so much power, that the lock must inevitably turn, or the key break.

To the great joy of the whole party, the key stood the test, and the door, which was of enormous weight and thickness, slowly revolved upon its rusted hinges.

All seemed darkness beyond, and, in answer to the crusader's glance of surprise and inquiry, Wingrove said,—

" This door opens behind some heavy tapestry, which effectually precludes the light of day,"

" Indeed," said the knight. " I thought we were scarcely free of the vaults ; but lead you the way still, Wingrove, and let us see daylight as quickly as may be."

Wingrove felt carefully along the tapestry, until he came to a part where two pieces met, hanging over each other in massive folds ; these Wingrove opened, and a flood of daylight immediately fell upon the little party.

The crusader drew a long breath, as if with the feeling of great relief, and then he said,—

" It certainly was of no use mentioning it before, but I am tremendously hungry."

" And I am thirsty," cried Bernard. " I have been thirsty for an hour and a half ; there's suffering for you. It's positively dreadful, and I don't know what will become of me. In another quarter of an hour, I think I should have wished myself a gallon of ale, and drank myself up, and there would have been a catastrophe."

" Well, Wingrove," added the crusader, " do you look after our young friend, the page, for he seems the most tired of us all, and I will myself seek some refreshment."

Bernard was by no means unwilling to be at liberty at once to proceed to the cellarer; but, knowing the obstinacy of that ancient servitor, he was careful to procure an unconditional order from Wingrove for ale, before he proceeded to quench his terrible thirst.

The crusader repaired to his own chamber, whither Wingrove was, of course, careful to send him ample refreshment, and in the course of another half-hour the little party were thoroughly recruited, and the dangers they had encountered in the vaults of Brandon only remembered as such men are in the habit of remembering hair-breadth escapes, and narrow chances of death by flood or field.

It was some short time after the escape of the crusader and his friends from the subterranean passages of Brandon, that, in the small chamber where Agatha Weare usually held her conferences with the Black Monk, on account of the facility of escaping from thence to his own gloomy habitation in the Grey Turret, were assembled a small party, in deep conference as to what could be done for furthering the dark schemes in which all were so much committed, and which, by a singular train of events, appeared to be continually frustrated in their progress.

That party consisted of Agatha Weare; Morgatani himself, with his face bandaged up, and a frightful paleness on those parts of it which were visible; the dastardly knight, Fitzhugh, scarcely less pale than he, although in his case it arose more from mental terror than from bodily injury; and lastly, the exhausted and trembling Eldred, who, by the stern mandate of the monk, had been compelled to rise from his bed, and with many bitter groans attend the conference, which—by a species of hypocrisy which nearly drove him mad when it was urged, but which he dared not resent—was affected to be solely for his benefit and advantage.

Agatha was seated, and her face was of an ashy paleness; the recent events seemed nearly to have convinced her that the wild scheme she had entered into for the accomplishment of as frantic and unholy a revenge as ever found a home in a human breast, were, by the interposition of Providence, doomed to be abortive, and to recoil upon her own head.

This was the same idea which possessed Eldred, only that it took a different complexion, according to the very different genius or disposition of the parties, for the same passions and feelings, which in Eldred Weare partook largely of the ludicrous, were in Agatha dark and gloomy as the night, and full of fearful import. She was listening attentively to the monk, who, with a voice of extreme bitterness, was talking rapidly.

"We have been foiled," he said—"foiled, I know not how; some cursed agency has been at work to destroy my schemes, and those plans, upon the success of which I could have staked my very life, have been those that have most signally failed. How, or wherefore, I scarcely know, but it seems as if the malignant fates took a pleasure in thwarting us; but this morning I could have calculated upon a success to our hopes and wishes beyond our utmost expectations, but now all is confusion again, and we seemed tossed at the mercy of the winds of destiny, like a ship upon the wide ocean, without a rudder; but yet we will not despair; some scheme yet more desperate —yet more subtle, yet more full of likelihood, must be thought of which shall ensure us success; we must yet triumph, and these puny puppets who oppose us must yield before the energies of higher spirits."

"What can be done?—what can be done?" said Agatha, wringing her hands. "Oh, that we could undo the past!—oh, that I could be as once I was—so pure and innocent in comparison to what I am, that my soul shrinks, and ——"

"Peace!" cried the monk, in a voice that filled the apartment with its awful reverberations. "Peace, I say, this is a consultation and not a la-

mentation; we have not met to groan over the past, but to consult for the future. Agatha Weare, let us hear no more of this idle talk; when I had stated the difficulties we had encountered, I did not consult despair—it was but a necessary preliminary to what was yet to be accomplished. That mysterious man, the crusader, whose face I have not been able to see, voluntarily appeared to throw himself into my power; he assembled together those who I believe are most inimical to our interests in Brandon Castle, and descended to the vaults as if he had sworn to place himself in my power, and was fulfilling his vow.

"The narrow entrance by which they reached those gloomy underground abodes I closed behind them—closed so strongly, too, that, situated as they were, they could not hope to force their way to light and liberty; then did I calculate upon the progress of starvation—upon famine slowly decreasing their strength, until at last what could there be left but to lay them down and die with despair at their souls, and not a hope of rescue.

"In this I have been foiled, and that they have escaped by some means unknown to me, I do fully believe.

"You, Eldred Weare, I stationed above the only orifice from one of the gloomy dungeons beneath Brandon through which there was a chance they would attempt to pass, or as a consequence of which they could hope to receive succour."

"Yes, you did," groaned Eldred. "It rained dreadfully, and somebody had their revenge if I didn't; look at my nose, and discard ambition."

"At a given signal from me," continued the monk, unheedful of Eldred's admission, "he was to topple over from the battlements a huge stone, which, in its descent, would have assuredly crushed and drowned in the moat any one who had attempted to pass through that orifice.

"While waiting at the turret loop-hole to give Eldred Weare the agreed

No. 46

upon signal, an arrow struck me in the face, inflicting this wound, which you all perceive. Unwittingly, then, I suppose, I gave the signal, and Eldred Weare cast over the stone, without injuring those whom it was intended to destroy."

"Yes," said Eldred; " I saw the black flag, and over it went. After that, you know, you shook me so dreadfully, and after that I gave up the ghost, but it came back again ; and I beg to add I have had enough revenge to last me all my life, and such a dose of ambition as never was known."

"These," added the monk, " are the circumstances under which I have failed, wherefore I can scarcely tell, and now it appears to me that but one good course of action remains."

" What is that ?" said Agatha.

"Avoiding the coarser methods of attempting to take life, we must adopt the more subtle, unless you, Fitzhugh, in your greater experience, have something to suggest."

"No," said Fitzhugh. "I have nothing to suggest; my wishes are well known to you ; I am a partizan of King John's, to whom I owe my knighthood; I would fain see him undisputed King of England, and I am an enemy of Sir Rupert Brandon's, because he is a friend of Richard's. So far, then, my inclinations all go with you, but what course of action to adopt I know not."

" Then," said the monk, " I have but to recommend one scheme, and that is, that, perfectly heedless of how far it may extend itself, so that we ourselves are careful to escape its malign influence, we use liberally ———"

" What ?—oh, what ?" said Agatha.

" Poison !" said the monk.

CHAPTER LXIII.

Oh, can there be a mind can ere conceive
A crime so dark, so deep, so dangerous,
As that which in the festal bowl will place
A lurking poison ?   FLETCHER.

THE MONK'S SUGGESTION.—THE CONSULTATION.—THE VISIT TO THE WIZARD.

FOR some moments after these words had been spoken by the monk, a death-like silence reigned in that small apartment, and those to whom this sweeping proposition had been made looked in each other's faces in doubt and uncertainty.

The monk saw the effect he had produced, and, in a hollow voice, he repeated the word,

" Poison !"

" Can it be accomplished," said Agatha, "with safety ?"

" It is a weapon," replied the monk, " in the hands of those who are skilful in its use, of far greater power than the sword—a weapon which the bravest cannot fight against, which truly defies the boldest warriors, the most skilful generals. We have tried other means, and failed; let us now try that only one which still remains—a means which surely will succeed, and which can be attempted with the smallest possible risk, if indeed risk there can be any."

" We had need be particularly careful," said Fitzhugh, " not to compromise ourselves too far—it's dangerous poisoning food wholesale."

"It is," said the monk ; "and, besides, liable to detection ; so we will not poison food ; but wine is drunk in Brandon—into that we can place a deadly drug, and by abstaining wholly ourselves from drinking any, we shall be sure to escape any evil consequences. What say you to the plan?"

"I consent to it," said Fitzhugh ; "it seems to me safe and practicable."

"Do what you like," said Agatha—"do what you like ; I am powerless, but my soul does indeed shrink from such frightful slaughter."

"You will think less of the deed when it is done," sneered the monk. "The path to the revenge you have so long panted for will then be wonderfully cleared."

Agatha made no reply, but Fitzhugh remarked,—

"When this matter is accomplished, I must leave Brandon, and proceed at once to the metropolis, to make my report to King John of that which has occurred. You will recollect that I came here but as an agent from him to secure to him the interests of those occupying this important fortress."

"You may," said the monk ; "but you will not carry with you, Fitzhugh, the young page you brought from London."

"Indeed."

"No : the boy has leagued himself with our enemies—of that I have been for some time well assured—and he shall stand or fall by his party ; but that he will, of course, be included in the general destruction that must ensue from my plan, he should not live another day in Brandon."

"The youth forced himself upon my service in London, and with such great pertinacity and offers of rare fidelity did he assail me, that I could not shake him off."

"His conduct can be no fault of yours," replied Morgatani. "I have known a youth like that, apparently of little power, prove a serious stumbling-block in the way of the greatest designs. But enough of him, he shall perish!"

"So be it," said Fitzhugh. "I have been at times suspicious of the boy myself, for his language has been ambiguous and strange, and I have little desire to interpose in his favour. Let him die!"

"He shall," said the monk, with sudden vehemence, "for to him principally is to be attributed the failure of my plan this morning. Already have I once essayed to take his life, but he seemed to wear a charmed existence, and the arrows I directed against him touched him not, else he must have perished."

"I give him up—I give him up," said Fitzhugh, hurriedly. "No more of him, I pray you. I have no need of him, and, as I tell you, he may die!"

"Can you not spare him?" said Agatha ; "he is but a boy, and his death or life can surely be of little consequence to the designs of men."

"You mistake," said the monk. "It is a most mistaken policy to neglect a foe on account of his seeming insignificance. But there is one with whose destruction I must charge myself, and that is he who is called Nemoni, the Wizard of the Red Cavern. He has some means of secret entrance to Brandon, and his insanity has taken the peculiar phase of deep enmity against me. He must be destroyed, and for that purpose I will this day proceed to the forest, soliciting, Fitzhugh, your good company in the adventure."

"I am unacquainted," said Fitzhugh, hurriedly, and in some degree of alarm, "with the person of him you seek, and I should think could be of but little assistance to you."

"I will shew him to you," said the monk, sarcastically ; "but as I happen to know by experience, this wizard is not a pleasant opponent to attack single-handed, nevertheless will I engage him in combat while you steal behind him, Fitzhugh, and inflict upon him some dangerous wound : so shall we overcome him. By the foul fiend, I have a shrewd suspicion that it was from his hand came the wound from which I now suffer."

"I trust it is by daylight you purpose going?" said Fitzhugh.

"Yes," said the monk; "I have a means of getting into the forest without troubling the drawbridge of Brandon."

"Then, I suppose it's all settled," said Eldred, "and I may go to bed once more?"

"You may," said Morgatani; "we do not require your valuable counsel any more just now; you will, nevertheless, perceive, and be grateful, for the great pains we are taking to ensure you your revenge, and to place you at the summit of your lofty ambition."

"Oh, thank you," said Eldred. "Of course, I'm grateful; I'm only sorry to see you give yourself so much trouble on my account; and, on the whole, I rather think I should be as well pleased if you were to give it up now, for I really have had ample revenge. Look at my nose."

"But you shall have more," said the monk, sarcastically; "you shall have much more. Look upon this as but the beginning."

"The devil!" said Eldred; "it was very near proving the finish to me; but I suppose it's no use arguing—all I've got to say is, if there is any more revenge to be had, I hope you'll be so good as to divide it among you. I make it a free gift, for I have had quite enough. Good day to you all; I'm going to bed, and have an idea of not getting up till to-morrow, by which time I hope you'll have settled all this poisoning business, and there'll be a quiet house."

So saying, Eldred slunk away from the room, cursing his own folly as he went, for ever engaging in those undertakings which had proved to him so calamitous, and which, he firmly believed, unless he speedily escaped from, would terminate in his destruction, an opinion which was not so ill founded, when we consider the rough spirits with which Eldred had to deal, both as regarded friends and foes.

*   *   *   *   *   *

The circumstance of the arrows being shot with such savage ferocity, betokened an energy and determination to destroy, on the part of the Black Monk, if it were indeed he who shot them, that called for the serious attention of those who were making Brandon their temporary home, as well as of those who permanently inhabited the ancient structure.

When the crusader had thoroughly refreshed himself, and felt no longer the fatigue incidental to his adventures within the vaults of Brandon, he desired the man-at-arms, who was placed as sentinel before his door, to tell Hugh Wingrove he would be glad to speak to him, and in a few minutes that ancient servitor appeared.

"Wingrove," said the crusader, "although I know not a day nor an hour when Sir Rupert Brandon may return to his castle, yet adverse circumstances may possibly detain him much longer than any of his friends wish or expect. In the meantime, Heaven only knows what may occur as regards this monk, who seems to have effected so complete a lodgment in Brandon Castle; that he will continue laying plots for our destruction, and that we shall be kept in a continual state of apprehension of the possible success of those plots, there can be no doubt, therefore is it that I think we must adopt some plan for making him a prisoner."

"There is, indeed," said Wingrove, "a strong necessity for such a measure. But your mention of the word prisoner puts me in mind of the one we already have, who you brought in from the forest. Have you any further instructions as regards him?"

"None," said the crusader, "and let him be kept in safe durance until the return of Sir Rupert Brandon; but, there is one circumstance connected with his capture, which I would fain look to. As the only reward which I had about me, I gave the wizard, Nemoni, a gold chain, in gratitude of the services he rendered to me; or, rather, I gave it to a female, who I thought required money ; now, that chain I valued much, and would fain redeem it of her, if in Brandon Castle there is sufficient to enable me so to do."

"By the mass," said Wingrove, "there must be ample store of money in Brandon Castle ; but Mrs. Agatha takes care that none but herself has the fingering of it."

"That is awkward," said the knight, "for I want at least fifty broad pieces."

"I will do my best to discover the place where she keeps the money, and by main force procure the sum you require. It would be hard indeed if, in Brandon Castle, we could not lay hold of fifty pieces for service."

"Do so," said the knight, "and I shall be thankful to you."

"I will about it instantly," said Wingrove ; "and, now I bethink me, it is more than probable that the coin is in an old oaken cabinet that stands in the private parlour of Sir Rupert, a room which Mrs. Agatha Weare, at his departure, selected for her own private use."

"If you succeed," said the knight, "I will repair at once to the forest, and, in the hut of Nemoni, endeavour to reclaim my chain."

"In that expedition, may I hope you will allow me to accompany you ?" said Wingrove. "I shall be unhappy, and filled with alarms, until your return."

"There is no danger," said the knight ; "but, if you wish it, Wingrove, I will not refuse your company."

Wingrove bowed, and, with a gratified air, hastened from the crusader's chamber.

In his anxiety to perform the behests of the knight it was evident he knew no scruples, for repairing at once to the apartment he had mentioned, and not finding the key in the open cabinet, he deliberately wrenched it open with his sword, and, rummaging over its contents, he at length found a small bag of gold, with which he hastened to the crusader, who, strange to say, accepted it without the least hesitation.

"Now, Wingrove," he said, "as soon as you please we will proceed on our expedition, for, in addition, I wish to have some conversation with that singular creature, as it strikes me he knows something more of the mysteries of Brandon than he might tell to every chance visitor."

"'Tis a strange creature," said Wingrove, "and has a love amounting to veneration for Sir Rupert, and, as you say, I believe he does know something which it would much import us to be acquainted with. I am entirely at your service whenever you please to proceed on your expedition."

"Then we depart at once," said the crusader, rising at once, and grasping his battle-axe. "I will take this good companion with me, in case of accidents."

The day, though advanced, had lost none of its beauty, for though the morning had been sullied by a tremendous storm, yet it had passed over, leaving behind it only the recollection of its power, while the sun shone out in his meridian splendour.

The pleasing and refreshing sensation borne upon the air after a storm is known by all, for few there are, even of the inhabitants of crowded cities, but remark that the air is clearer, purer, and more pleasing, than previous to its occurrence.

This the crusader and Wingrove experienced, and found it grateful to their senses, which had been so oppressed by the damp and unwholesome vapours they had encountered in the vaults of Brandon, as they passed over the drawbridge, which had been lowered to permit them to pass over the moat, and set out towards the forest.

The sward was damp to the foot, but the freshness of the verdure, the clearness of the sky, and the warm rays of the sun, cast an air of gladness around that was cheering to the mind which had suffered from anxiety as they must have suffered in the morning.

They neared the wood; every bough was charged with moisture, which sparkled in the sun like pendant diamonds, darting back his rays with various colours. The birds, too, as if grateful for the cessation of the storm, fluttered gaily from bough to bough and tree to tree, pouring forth their wildest harmony, and making the woods re-echo to their notes.

" This is a lovely scene," said the crusader, " and one amply worth visiting, were it but to exchange the gloom and dreariness of Brandon Castle for something heart-cheering and full of life."

" It is indeed lovely," said Wingrove, " and one could almost cease to pity the recluse who inhabits this wilderness of nature."

" Pity him !" cried the crusader. " He is happier than a king, for what can he have, comparatively speaking, to torment him? The wild fruits of the forest deck his table, and he earns an appetite by chasing the wild creatures who must afford him sustenance. But we are now near the spot; I recollect this winding brook, it leads directly to the hill side in which Nemoni has his singular abode. By-the-bye, saw ye ever the interesting female, with the two children, Wingrove, who seemed to be on such intimate terms with the recluse ?"

" No," replied Wingrove, " but I have heard of them from the men-at-arms, who have occasionally gone out to hunt in the forest. Some mystery appears to be wrapped around them, which probably the wizard himself could explain, if advantage were taken of one of his lucid intervals, which I am told are frequent, to ask him."

" I will try it," said the crusader; " but see, we are already within the gloom of the hill side."

Even as he spoke, a crashing among the underwood announced that some hasty footstep was approaching, and in the next moment Nemoni himself stood before them.

" Who seeks the wizard? Who seeks the wizard?" he cried. " Who has faith in the wizard, who thought he had killed his enemy, and afterwards saw him alive, with but so slight a wound, as if Heaven had turned aside the shaft and wished to save the guilty? If it were so, it were surely that greater vengeance might fall upon him. Approach me not, for the dangerous spirit is upon me, and the society of man is hateful to me. Away—away—be warned—approach me not !"

" Do you not know me ?" said the crusader.

The sound of his voice seemed to awaken recollection in the breast of the poor maniac, who said—

" Your tone is friendly—your tone is friendly; I would not that all hearts should be driven from the hut of poor Nemoni, I would fain that some should be welcome."

" Then let me be one of those,". said the knight, " for, believe me, I come as a sincere friend. Do you not recollect saving me from the assassins in the forest ?"

" Yes—yes," said the wizard. " You are welcome—you are welcome—I wished for you."

" And you know me, Nemoni ?" said Wingrove.

" Your voice is a friendly one to Sir Rupert Brandon," was the reply; " I know you well, and you are right welcome."

" We may enter his hut now," said Wingrove, " for he is most hospitable when so inclined, and never breaks his word."

" We will follow you," said the crusader. " Lead the way, Nemoni; thanks for your welcome—we will follow you."

" This way—this way," cried the wizard; " through tangled bush and briar. This way to the wizard's hut. Men hold me as a thing cursed and full of guile, but who will not say I am gentle to my friends. 'Tis true honesty to be a lamb to friends and a lion to foes. Of a truth you are right welcome. Come on—come on."

"I thought he would make us welcome," said the crusader; "he regaled me with his utmost means while I was in this forest, and I sincerely hope to be able to return the compliment some day, when I shall take pains to endeavour to restore him to a better frame of mind; for it is sad to see him thus, evidently possessing, as he does, too, an intellect of a high order. What can he mean by saying he thought he had killed his enemy?"

"I know not," said Wingrove; "it is likely some mere conceit of his over-burthened brain. He is full of strange fancies, and it will not do to be too critical at what he says or does."

"Poor fellow," said the crusader; "injuries make some people angry and others mad; but it seems to me, from the many lucid intervals he has, that his insanity cannot be of an incurable order."

Thus conversing, in low tones, the crusader and Hugh Wingrove reached the hut of Nemoni, whither the wizard preceded them with a quick bounding step.

CHAPTER LXIV.

> Oh, what so vile as treachery!
> What blight on earth, or air, or heaven,
> Can equal the deceit
> That with a glozing tongue would lure to death ?
>
> SHENSTONE.

THE FOREST.—THE WIZARD'S CAVERN.—THE ATTACK AND THE RESCUE.

It was somewhat singular, and may be looked upon as one of those accidental circumstances which occur sometimes in real life to puzzle the acutest calculators, that Hugh Wingrove and the crusader should have been nearly at the same hour traversing the open glades of the forest in search of the hut of Nemoni that Morgatani, the Black Monk, and the cowardly Fitzhugh were seeking the same place of destination, by a subterranean passage, known well to the monk, and which, as we have before hinted, had been constructed by a former possessor of Brandon Castle as a rapid and easy means of communication with the monastery which was in its immediate vicinity.

The underground communications of the strongholds of the feudal nobility and any religious house that might be in the neighbourhood, were common during the thirteenth and fourteenth centuries, for there was such continued warfare between these petty lords of the soil, that no one could know a day on which his circumstances might prove so disastrous, and to induce him with what portable valuables he might possess to seek safety wherever he could find it—and where could it be found so well in that superstitious age as in the walls of a superstitious house, for at the anathemas of the church the boldest then trembled, instead of as now most irreverently laughing.

So it was, then, that scarcely had the crusader and Hugh Wingrove reached the wizard's hut, when Morgatani and Fitzhugh emerged into open air in the hollow of a gigantic elm, where terminated the secret passage from Brandon Castle.

We shall leave them for a time to their hellish machinations, while we occupy ourselves more agreeably in the cavern of the poor heart-stricken

Nemoni, who had suffered such fearful injuries at the hands of that atrocious monk, who cared not, so that he achieved his own ambitious projects, if he waded through the blood of a hundred victims to do so.

" Do you remember," said the crusader, " a chain of gold which I gave to a female who I saw here a short time after you rescued me from the hands of assassins ?"

" I do, I do," said the wizard.

" Has she parted with it ? Not that I blame her for so doing, for I gave it her for such a purpose."

" She has not," said the wizard.

" Then I myself will become its purchaser. It is fairly hers, but I will take back the chain, and give her in its stead fifty gold pieces, which would be of greater service to her."

" You are generous," said the wizard; " and something tells me you are one of the great ones of the earth."

" Indeed !"

" Yes. It is a simple lore which enables me to pronounce from tones and manners what a man is, although I may err largely in saying who he is."

" Well," added the crusader, " I will not say if you have guessed wrongly or rightly. But, tell me, why did she to whom I gave the chain not dispose of it ?"

" She set a higher value upon the chain than its intrinsic worth."

" Wherefore ?"

" Because you accompanied the gift of it with words that made her hope the day would not be far distant when you would exert what power you might possess in doing something for those children, for whose sakes alone she seems to live and have her being."

" Now, tell me," said the crusader, " for you are as rational at this moment as mortal man can wish to be—tell me, to whom do those children belong, and how is it, that of gentle blood as they appear to be, they are so utterly neglected by those who should be most watchful of them, and left to the chance kindness of a stranger."

As the crusader spoke, the wizard rose and stood in an attitude of listening. He then threw himself down, and laying his ear close to the ground, he remained motionless for some seconds, after which he sprung to his feet, saying,

" There are footsteps in the forest—there are footsteps in the forest; belong they to friends or foes, there are footsteps in the forest. Hark, they come this way. Do you not hear—do you not hear? there are two men approaching."

" I hear nothing," said the crusader.

" My sword, my sword," cried the wizard, his eyes flashing with a wild fire. " The sword that I have sharpened to drink the blood of the Black Monk. Where is my sword—there is ample room for dead men's bones in the wood of Brandon. There they may lie and bleach, till time shall be no more. My sword, my sword."

He suddenly disappeared in a recess of the cavern which led to the right of the principal apartment, if it might be so named, and in a moment returned with the naked sword in his hand, that he was in the habit of whiling away so many hours with, by sharpening and polishing up to a most brilliant lustre.

He then assumed an attitude of defence near the mouth of the cavern, and it was evident that all the wild frenzy of his disposition, which had slept for a time, was roused into activity by the approaching footsteps, which now the crusader and Wingrove began faintly to hear.

" Some one, indeed, is approaching," said the former, " Some chance wayfarer in the forest, in all probability."

" 'Tis likely," said Wingrove; " it may be accidental, of course, but the

steps appear to be approaching here with great precision. I do advise that we step aside into this inner portion of the cavern, from whence we can hear if those who are here be friends or enemies."

"Be it so," said the crusader; I am glad I have my mask with me, for I would not be seen at present by friend or foe."

So saying, he placed upon his face the small velvet mask which had so perplexed Morgatani, and prevented him from arriving at a knowledge of who the crusader was.

"Nemoni," he said, "fear not: if those are foes now approaching, they shall work you no mischief. One good turn deserves another. You saved me from death in this very forest, and I shall not be backward in rendering you assistance."

The wizard evidently heard him not, but continuing in the same attitude of defence, he kept muttering,—

"He lives still—he lives still—he, whom I thought was dead—he lives still, and yet I must have my revenge. Why has Heaven prolonged my life but that I may have my revenge of Morgatani, the Black Monk? The arrow sped well on its errand, but it failed to execute its mission. The sword will be more successful—the sword, the sword—ay, the sword."

"He hears nothing but those footsteps and his own dark mutterings," said Wingrove. "Let us retire, we shall hear all that passes, and can advance to his rescue in a moment."

The crusader accompanied Wingrove to the inner portion of the cavern, and there waited anxiously what was to ensue.

It was Morgatani and Fitzhugh who were approaching so rapidly the wizard's humble abode, little dreaming of the efficient assistance he had at hand to repel the meditated attack upon him, and but which, without such assistance, combined as was the projected attack with great treachery, he would most probably have fallen.

No. 47

"My person," said Morgatani, "is, I am well assured, perfectly known to this madman we are about to visit; I, therefore, wish you to enter his cavern."

"I enter his cavern!" said Fitzhugh, shrinking back; "nay, Morgatani, you must be jesting. I expose myself to the rage of a maniac! you cannot surely suppose me so foolish?"

"You need not provoke his rage," said the monk; "approach him with a friendly aspect and say you have lost your way in the forest, that you are a friend of Sir Rupert Brandon's on your route to his castle, in the right track to which you require to be directed; then, when he answers you with courtesy, which, doubtless, he will, you can crave leave to rest awhile in his cavern, being faint and weary from your journey."

"What then?" said Fitzhugh.

"Then, in a short time, I will appear with a drawn sword at the entrance of his cave; he will instantly rush out to combat with me, for his enmity to me is his fiercest passion. I can well maintain a fight with him for some minutes, but ere that time has expired, you can steal behind him and plunge your dagger up to the hilt in his back. He must then fall our victim, for what can save him?"

"You think that may be done safely?" said Fitzhugh.

"Not quite," said the monk; "but you are a knight, and have surely no objection to a little danger."

"If it's very little indeed," muttered the dastard, "I certainly have no objection, but otherwise, the greatest."

"It is little," said Morgatani. "Surely you can run but small risk in such an assault. You have but to use your dagger firmly, and he must fall."

"I will do it as you suggest," said Fitzhugh, "but should he turn upon me, remember I must depend upon your greater strength to assail him. The violence of a madman is to be dreaded."

"Hush, we are here. We must succeed, for be assured this madman has been hitherto a serious hindrance to the prosecution of our schemes."

Fitzhugh evidently disliked the business he was upon, but in addition to his dread of obeying the behests of the monk, he had as deep a hatred of Sir Rupert Brandon, and who in any way befriended him, as it was possible to have; for the lamentable exhibition of cowardice he had made, as regarded his encounter with Sir Kenneth Hay, had, while he could not avoid it, galled him to the quick, annoying him past endurance, and begetting in him a desire to do anything he could, in order to have vengeance upon those who had caused him so much uneasiness.

It was an easy exercise of thought to such an unjust and vindictive nature as Fitzhugh's, to class together those who had really offended him and their friends; he was one of those men who liked to be revenged upon a whole party, because an individual might have given him offence—hence, he had no objection to the destruction of the wizard, although he did tremble at the danger there might be, in taking part of the transaction.

It was now too late, however, to retreat, and he proceeded in advance of the monk to poor Nemoni's hut, without the slightest compunctions as to taking part of the dastardly act by which his destruction was meditated.

Fitzhugh was unknown to the wizard, and at his wildest moments Nemoni had been never known to inflict unprovoked injury upon any traveller in the forest. There was, therefore, the greatest possible chance of his being deceived by the false statement of Fitzhugh, and falling a victim to the rage of the Black Monk.

"Hold, hold," cried the wizard, as Fitzhugh appeared in sight from among the overhanging branches of the trees. "Hold, stranger, at your peril. What is your errand here? proclaim yourself a friend or foe, which it matters little to Nemoni."

"I am a friend," said Fitzhugh, in a hesitating voice, that showed his alarm.

"A friend," said the wizard. "My friends are among the bold and adventurous. Your tone and bearing bespeak you a dastard. Away, away, I hold no such communion with such as thee."

"You mistake me greatly," said Fitzhugh. "I am a knight, and an old friend of Sir Rupert Brandon. I have come from Palestine, and wish to know the way to his castle?"

"An old friend of Sir Rupert Brandon," said the wizard, "methinks should know the way to his abode."

"But surely one may lose one's way in a forest," said Fitzhugh; "you are strangely suspicious."

"My intercourse with human nature," said the wizard, "has certainly not made me trustful and confiding; but will you swear you are a friend to Sir Rupert Brandon?"

"I swear it," said Fitzhugh.

"By Heaven?"

"Yes, by Heaven!"

"Then Heaven pity you, if you have sworn a false oath. You may enter, and such food and shelter as I can give you, you are welcome to. When you have rested awhile, I will show you the route to the castle."

By Fitzhugh's reluctance, it would seem that the invitation was rather more unwelcome than the rejection of his suit, but nevertheless, whatever were his fears, he did walk forward, and fairly enter the wizard's cavern. Mindful then of the plot which he had concocted with the monk, he retreated as far within the cave as he could get, saying,—

"Do you lead a solitary life in this forest?"

"I do," was the reply. "I have not an evil conscience, and therefore a solitary life for me has no terrors."

"Ah," said Fitzhugh, "I suppose you are not wholly unprovided with provisions, I am somewhat weary?"

"I have fruit of the forest, goat's flesh, and some sparkling water from a stream that flows like a thread of molten silver among the tangled brushwood. For Sir Rupert Brandon's sake you are welcome."

"He has got rid of his suspicions," thought Fitzhugh, as he carefully freed the hilt of his poniard, so that it could be taken hold of at a moment's notice. "He has got rid of his suspicions, and will surely die. What can save him? what can save him? The Black Monk is strong, and I—"

The word that rose to Fitzhugh's lips was treacherous, but he scarcely liked to confess that even to himself, and turning to Nemoni, he said aloud,

"I have no doubt your sylvan retreat possesses to you many charms."

"It does," said the wizard. "Human nature and I have sadly quarrelled, and I am happier in this solitude, awaiting the one event, for the consummation of which alone I live, than I should be mingling again among the busy haunts of men."

"Ah," said Fitzhugh, "virtue is its own reward. After my own exemplary and pious life, I should just like to turn my thoughts to Heaven, and think of all the good I have done, in such a quiet spot as this, far away from the jarring discord, and with nothing to disturb the peaceful tenor of my existence."

"There's an infernal scoundrel," muttered the crusader.

"A scoundrel indeed," was Wingrove's reply. "Some treachery is surely intended against the poor maniac, or Fitzhugh would never have made his appearance here."

"There is no doubt," said the crusader. "I am only glad we are so opportunely on the spot to thwart his villany."

Fitzhugh felt himself in anything but a comfortable state of mind, and most anxious was he for the appearance of Morgatani, to relieve him from his embarrassment.

The monk, however, appeared to think the moment had not yet arrived, and Fitzhugh was most uncomfortably left to his own resources to amuse the mind of Nemoni, and keep him from suspecting the treachery that was really intended.

The wizard placed before his despicable guest the homely viands he had mentioned, but Fitzhugh had but little appetite for their consumption ; he was too full of apprehension that at some unexpected moment the wizard might have his suspicions awakened, and suddenly rush upon him to his great personal detriment, and before the monk could interfere, even if he were so inclined, to save him from his destruction. The reader therefore may imagine how very uncomfortable were the feelings of such a man as Fitzhugh, while thus waiting the conclusion of an adventure which was none of his seeking, and the result of which might possibly be anything but pleasurable.

"For Heaven's sake," said Wingrove, "let us keep most strictly upon our guard, for we know not a moment when some diabolical treachery may be perpetrated."

"The wizard is safe enough," whispered the crusader, "as far as regards Fitzhugh. You may depend that he has not the courage, of himself, to attempt anything."

At this moment such a wild shout of rage and defiance arose from the maniac, that the wood rung again, and both Wingrove and the crusader involuntarily uttered the exclamation of—

"Good Heavens! what is that?"

CHAPTER LXV.

"Foul treachery had done its work
But for a noble hand,
Which interpos'd to save the right
From a revengeful brand."

THE COMBAT.—THE PROJECTED TREACHERY.—THE WIZARD SAVED.—
FITZHUGH'S TERROR AND THE MONK'S ESCAPE.

The voice of the wizard then rose loud and shrill, as he cried,—

"You have come—you have come, and vengeance shall be mine. Who shall now step between me and my wrath? Morgatani—devil—Jesuit— were you fleet as a hound, you should not escape me. Had you the strength, in your single arm, of a host, I would cut you down. Vengeance shall be mine."

"By Heavens! the Black Monk," said Wingrove.

"Hush," said the crusader. "Keep back a moment ; let us hear more. This may indeed be a most auspicious day."

"Nemoni, or wizard, as you call yourself," said the deep tones of the monk, "you have sought my life—wherefore I know not—but I am no shrinking coward, and when I hear of one who wishes to do battle with me, I care not if it cost me some trouble to gratify his wish."

"That's an uncommonly sensible speech," said the crusader, "for a scoundrel like that. If it comes to a fair single combat, Wingrove, we must not interfere, except in the way of seeing that the monk has no undue advantage in the way of weapons."

"Keep an eye on Fitzhugh," was the reply. "I could take an oath some treachery was intended."

"So, Morgatani," said the wizard, with exultation, "you've come to meet me. For that gracious act I do, indeed, owe you thanks; but has time, indeed, so altered me, that you know me not?"

"I have no knowledge of you," said the monk, "further than as an inhabitant of this forest, and one who, for some inexplicable reason, seeks my life."

"Look at me well—for I will have you know from what hand you receive death."

The wizard parted the long elf-like locks that hung round his brow, and looked fixedly at the monk; but the latter shook his head, saying,—

"I know you not; but, if you wish to fight with me, come on, I am ready, or do you shrink from the contest?"

"I shrink!" said the wizard. "I shrink!—no, Morgatani; but know me you must, or the contest will avail little. Do you remember Claudio Pinto?"

"Claudio!" said the monk.

"Ay. And do you remember a novice, named Beatrice, whom you pursued with your unholy love, even to the gates of Heaven? Do you remember, priest, the cries of that victim? Do you remember that dreadful process which entombed the living, and ——"

"Peace," said the monk, in a loud tone. "By Heaven and hell! I know you, and yet, a suspicion of who you were, never, till this moment, crossed my brain. Without this, I was resolved upon your death, but now no power on earth shall save you. Come on—come on."

With a wild yell, the maniac sprung forward, and the ringing of the swords testified the nature of the conflict that ensued.

The crusader and Wingrove, to obtain a view of the fight, emerged completely from their concealment; but they were nearly enveloped in gloom at the back of the cavern, and were not perceived by Morgatani, whose whole energies were directed to saving himself from the murderous attack of the wizard.

They were, consequently, behind Fitzhugh, who began then, in pursuance of the atrocious scheme for the destruction of Nemoni, to slink up carefully behind him, having in his hand the dagger with which he was to terminate the conflict.

'Twas some moments before the crusader and Wingrove could see what he was about, for their attention was much engrossed by the combat; but, as he turned partially aside, they saw the gleam of the poniard he held in his hand.

With two strides, then, the crusader reached him, and, to his sudden terror and dismay, seized him by the back of his head, and, without uttering a word, dragged him into the inner part of the cavern, where, with one tremendous kick, he sent him nearly insensible to the further end.

At this moment, the voice of the monk was heard, calling,—

"Fitzhugh—Fitzhugh—where are you? D——n! Fitzhugh—the dagger—the dagger!"

The moment the crusader had thus become fully aware of the treacherous nature of the attack upon Nemoni, he resolved to interfere, and, grasping his battle axe, he strode to the side of the wizard, where he was at once seen by the monk, who, with a shout of surprise and anger, turned immediately and fled.

The wizard rushed after him with the fleetness of the wind, crushing down all obstacles in his way, and ever and anon raising loud shouts of demoniac fury. The very violence and preternatural strength of the maniac defeated its own object, for it was no match for the wily cunning of the monk, who, in a few seconds, allowed Nemoni to pass him.

If ever Morgatani felt real terror, it was then, for, single-handed, he felt that even he, with all his extraordinary power, was no match for the madman who sought his destruction.

Nemoni soon found that he had outstripped his opponent, and, throwing himself upon the ground, he applied his ear to it in the manner the crusader and Wingrove had seen him.

The monk, from behind the trunk of a gigantic tree, saw this movement, and, with a diabolical cunning, he made the very acuteness of the wizard's hearing serviceable to himself. Taking some loose coins from his pocket, he threw them a considerable distance over the tops of the trees; they then fell dropping from branch to branch, producing a faint sound, but, the moment this reached the ears of Nemoni, he arose, with a loud yell of defiance, and rushed in the direction it proceeded.

The monk then cautiously left his place of concealment, and making the best of his way towards the ancient elm, in the hollowed trunk of which was the aperture conducting to the subterranean passage which lay between Brandon Castle and the forest, he quickly descended, leaving Fitzhugh to his fate, for little Morgatani cared what became of his associates in crime when they were no longer serviceable to him.

"Thwarted in every way," he muttered, "by that infernal crusader; turn which way I will, I am crossed eternally by him. There is a ban, surely, upon these proceedings; I never so much failed before in my undertakings. These enemies who now surround me, appear to work together, merely from the result of accident, with all the d—ble excellence of well organized proceedings; but surely the day will come, and that quickly, when fortune will change in my favour. One triumph over them shall be enough, for it shall be the triumph of death, and as for Fitzhugh, why, I suppose they will kill him if he resists, and if they take him prisoner, they may, perhaps, hang him upon the next forest tree they may come to.

"Well, what matters, let them do it. I begin to think he will not be of much service; and, consequently, he may as well be hanged as not. It is a good maxim of us Jesuits, that all people who are not useful are likely to become obnoxious, and the sooner they are got rid of the better."

So saying, and without wasting another thought upon the unhappy comrade in his guilt, the monk hurried to the castle, disappointed and vexed, certainly, with the result of his day's work, but still inwardly congratulating himself that he had escaped as well as he had, for he felt that he might have received, but for his own adroitness in escaping, great personal injury in the transaction.

And then, the more his failures came strongly to his mind, with great assurance, he over and over again told himself that poison must ultimately be his weapon, and that it would be one more likely to succeed than any other, for no bravery, no power, no skill, could guard against its insidious attacks.

"I will yet rule in Brandon," he muttered. "I will yet be master here, and King John shall find that the Jesuits can efficiently aid him, more especially when their own private interests—their own private passions—and their own private feelings of vengeance against individuals, square well with the public cause they choose to advocate. Poison—poison; ay, poison."

Turn we now to the hut of Nemoni, where were the crusader, Hugh Wingrove, and what might be called their prisoner, the craven knight, Fitzhugh.

To attempt to follow the wizard through the winding paths of the forest, at the tremendous pace with which he started from the mouth of his cavern, would have been a task of no small difficulty, and neither the crusader nor

Wingrove chose to attempt it, so that their attention was not withdrawn from him whom they had so happily frustrated in his infernal design.

As for Fitzhugh himself, who still lay where the crusader had kicked him, he was at first so stunned and perplexed, that his faculties were useless; but he lay on the same spot, only sensible to an extreme of fear and horror, induced by undefined danger, and he dared not move a limb, lest he should fall a victim to the blow, that he believed only momentarily withheld, which would be his destruction.

" What on earth, good Wingrove," said the crusader, " shall we do with this ruffian ?"

" I really know not," said Wingrove, " he deserves the worst fate that can await him. Treachery such as his is the most indefensible of crimes."

" But," said the crusader, " there is no doing anything with the scoundrel. We cannot ourselves become the executioners, and he is not one who will come out into the open glade of the forest and have a fair fight. If he would do so, I could knock him on the head with some degree of satisfaction and comfort to my own feelings ; but as it is, there is no knowing what to do with such disagreeable people."

" What would Nemoni do with him," said Wingrove, " if we were to leave him to his mercy ?"

" In all likelihood crack his crown," said the crusader. " Now, at present, he don't know who has assaulted him. It would be an awkward thing to take him a prisoner to Brandon ; and, perhaps, the best way of proceeding, after all, will be to tell him to make what haste he can to the castle, and then we can take some convenient opportunity of visiting upon him his transgressions when other and more important affairs are settled."

" It would be the best way," said Wingrove. " Shall I tell him ?"

" Yes," said the crusader ; " but tell him in a feigned voice, and leave him still in ignorance of who has frustrated his treachery."

Wingrove proceeded to the entrance of the inner part of the cavern, and said, in a loud voice, which he made differ as much as possible from his usual tones,—

" Fitzhugh, wrongfully made a knight by him who wrongfully calls himself a king, you are free to rise and fly for your life to Brandon Castle, or to wait, if it so please you, the wild vengeance of the wizard when he shall return."

" I will fly—I will fly," cried Fitzhugh, scrambling to his feet ; " Heaven help me, I will fly. Let me go with life—let me go with life—do not kill me as I pass out."

" The treacherous always suspect treachery," said Hugh Wingrove. " You may pass free."

The crusader and Wingrove then shrunk back into the inner part of the cavern, and Fitzhugh rushed out of it with the speed of a hunted hare, making the best of his way through the forest to the castle, which he reached long before the crusader and Hugh Wingrove could arrive, at the moderate pace they walked.

They did not wait for the return of Nemoni, for they were satisfied they had done all that was requisite for his safety, in freeing him from Fitzhugh, whose treachery was much to be dreaded.

The drawbridge was quietly lowered, at a private signal from Wingrove, to admit him and the crusader, and they entered the castle, without being observed by any one except those who were friendly to them.

" We have not succeeded," said the crusader, " in our object of questioning Nemoni, nor have I recovered my gold chain, upon which I set such store ; but we have certainly accomplished something more important still, for we have assuredly saved the life of that poor creature, who would have been sacrificed to the evil passions of that ruffianly priest."

" Of that there cannot be a doubt," said Wingrove ; " his mortification must be extreme, indeed, to find himself so utterly defeated in his most vindictive schemes."

" I live in hopes that his defeat will be still greater," remarked the crusader ; " if that scoundrel is not hung on the battlements of Brandon, I shall be grievously disappointed, and a great act of justice will remain unfulfilled. But I presume we must wait with patience until circumstances further develope themselves, before we take any active steps against him. A regular siege must be laid against the turret ; by some means it must be demolished, and when forced from that, his stronghold, he will, in all likelihood, fall into our hands."

" Amen," said Wingrove, " I desire nothing better."

CHAPTER LXVI.

" Strangers came to the castle gate,
Of gallant mien were they ;
The day was gone, the moon was high,
And beautiful its ray."

THE MIDNIGHT HOUR.—THE TRUMPET.—THE ARRIVAL OF THE THREE STRANGE KNIGHTS AT BRANDON.—THE HERALD.

THE moon that evening rose in its proudest lustre over the ancient battlements of Brandon Castle, showering upon the moss-grown walls its sweet silvery light with a prodigality that lent them a rare and exquisite beauty, and made the ancient and venerable structure look like the palace of some fabled enchanter of old, a palace reared by no mortal hands, and surrounded by a beauty not of the earth.

Then, too, the quiet beams fell sweetly upon the moat, making it more resemble a broad thread of silver tissue than the narrowing stream of water it really was.

The midnight hour had sounded solemnly from the castle clock, and the wild passions, and the redundant fears, the many warring interests of the inhabitants of that gloomy pile seemed for a time to be lost in the oblivion of gentle sleep. An unusual repose reigned throughout the edifice, for both the parties who dwelt beneath its roof, and who seemed even coming into such active collision with each other, paused as if with common consent, as if each were awaiting the movements of the other, or that the one was satisfied that it had resisted all the apparent machinations of its enemies, and the other was brooding in silent and gloomy discontent over the failure of those plans and projects which had surely been thwarted by the hand of Providence itself.

The very sentinels on the battlements appeared to feel the sombre loneliness of the hour, and paced to and fro in quiet and subdued steps as if they feared to disturb that rapt repose.

The " all's well " with which they greeted each other occasionally was spoken in a subdued tone ; and holy sweet, and solemn was the dim repose of nature.

The very sentinel who watched by the door of the crusader leaned heavily on his partisan, and longing for the sound of footsteps of his comrades when they should come to relieve his guard, so that the oppression on his spirits of the stillness around, might be broken.

A fourth of that hour immediately succeeding midnight had just passed away, that hour which is clothed by superstition with so many terrors, and which, hovering between the night and the succeeding day, seems scarcely to belong to either, has been by common consent given up to the supernatural

and unholy. A fourth of that hour then had but slowly winged its leaden flight, when a trumpet blast so loud, so long, and so startling, sounded before the gates of Brandon that not a sleeper in the ancient pile preserved his or her attitude of repose, but springing up in alarm, wondered whence such a volume of sound could come.

Not long, however, had they to await in doubt and uncertainty, for ere the echoes of the first trumpet blast had died away among the distant hills there came another, if possible, more loud and sonorous than the former. After which there was not a person in Brandon, with the exception of Eldred Weare, who had not risen, and dressed with rapidity, in order to descend to the postern-gate, and ascertain who could have arrived with so regal a flourish.

So astonished was the warder, that for some moments he answered not the loud challenge. Then, however, he blew his horn, which sounded weak indeed, when contrasted with the trumpet flourish that had preceded it.

A dead silence then prevailed for the space of about a moment. After which a loud voice from the other side of the moat cried,—

"Open the gates of Brandon,—knights from Palestine crave admittance on hospitality."

Suddenly, then, the crusader dashed in among the guard that were assembled around the postern-gate, and in a loud exulting voice he cried,—

"Admit them instantly—down drawbridge, and open gates; can you hesitate a moment—knights from Palestine, by the mass, and right noble ones—heard you not the trumpet sound?"

The gates were thrown open and the drawbridge was lowered so suddenly that it met its supports on the other side with a crashing sound. Then bareheaded as he was, and but lightly clad, the crusader, after exclaiming,—"Let no one follow me," rushed hastily through the postern-gate, and across the drawbridge, disappearing in a moment, in the darkness of the night, from the astonished men-at-arms.

No. 48

There was a dead silence of a moment or two, and then a loud laugh from the other side of the moat, after which several voices mingled together in hearty tones, but the crusader's was heard above all as he said,—

"Follow me—you are right welcome; I will sleep no more to-night. By the mass, I scarcely expected you so soon; but follow—follow, we will awaken the old cellarer of Brandon, and see what he can do for us."

As quickly then, as he had bounded across the drawbridge, the crusader returned, and addressing the men-at-arms, he said, in merry accents,—

"More guests—more guests for Brandon. We shall make the old pile ring with glee. Knights from Palestine, my men—knights who have fought with King Richard."

"May we make so bold," said Bernard, "as to ask their names?"

"No, man-mountain," said the crusader; "like me, they must depend upon their own merits, and be nameless."

"Ah, well," said Bernard, "it's all one to me. I dare say there'll be more ale going, and I am sure that's needed. Let me see, the last drop I had was at a quarter to twelve, and now, by our lady, it's getting on to one. Ah, how thirsty I am."

"Your thirst is perpetual," said Anstey; "if the castle moat was ale, I expect Brandon Castle would want one of its defences, for you would swallow it up."

"The Lord preserve us," cried Bernard, quite struck with the idea. "The moat all ale! goodness gracious, the moat! There would be a nice lot indeed. I'd forgive anybody for throwing me in any morning, directly I woke."

The trampling of horses' feet upon the drawbridge announced the rapid approach of the new comers, and in another minute three knights, armed *cap-a-pie*, with their vizors closed, and mounted on the most superb chargers, dashed into the court-yard of Brandon.

So unusual a sight, and so gratifying a one to the men-at-arms, had not occurred for many a day, and they burst into a simultaneous cheer, as the torches they carried glanced upon the superb armour of the warriors, and showed the completeness and richness of their equipments. But the wonder of the men-at-arms, and Hugh Wingrove, was not yet at its height, for the clatter of another horse's hoofs sounded upon the drawbridge, and in a moment there arrived after the knights a herald in his full tabard and coat, on which was emblazoned the royal arms of England. In his hand he bore a silver trumpet, from which depended a square silken banner, richly embroidered. The magnificent animal he rode, as likewise were those belonging to the knights, was covered with foam, and it was evident from the general appearance of the whole party that they had travelled far and hastily.

"How now," cried Wingrove; "a royal herald!"

"Yes, good friend," said the herald, as he descended from his horse. "Did you expect a Griffin? I came from London; I suppose you'll ask me why? and, as I like to stop people's mouth's at once, particularly the mouths of magpies, I ——"

"Peace," said the crusader, in an imperious tone; "there are friends as well as foes here, Montjoy, though your addle head may not know it."

The herald immediately took off his cap, and shrunk back evidently abashed:

"Sir Herald," said Wingrove, with a smile, "you may expend your wit as much as you like upon an old soldier, the only risk is in carrying it a little too far, and then a practical joke in the shape of a crack on the head might follow."

"I crave your pardon," said the herald, "I knew not to whom I spoke."

"Granted, friend," said Wingrove; "instead of cracking heads or jokes we will crack a flagon or two of choice ale to the health of King Richard."

To the surprise of the men-at-arms the three strange knights took no notice of any one around them, but dismounting from their horses without unclasping their visors, they stood whispering together, but with their faces turned towards the crusader as if they expected some directions from him.

"Hugh Wingrove," he cried ; "we will make merry, and it shall be in my own chamber ; we have all fought side by side, frequently, and it is long since we have met even under such pleasant circumstances as the present. Let us have some of your choicest wine."

"From the butt marked seventy-three," said one of the knights, in a deep hollow tone from beneath his vizor.

The three knights then turned hastily, and mingled together in such a manner that it was impossible to tell which it came from.

Wingrove looked amazed, and the men-at-arms stared at each other in astonishment.

The crusader laughed aloud, and giving Wingrove a smart blow on the shoulder, he said,--

"Why, Hugh Wingrove, you tapped this same seventy-three cask for me, I believe, some few days since, and truly it comes of a choice vintage."

"I did," said the bewildered Wingrove ; "but how comes it that one of these knights knows so well where the best wine is kept in Brandon Castle ?"

"Never mind," added the crusader, "we learn strange things in the east ; I dare say Sir Rupert Brandon, in one of the gossips in the camp, told him."

"Nothing more likely," said Wingrove. "Well, it's a good thing seventy-three is tapped, for it saves trouble. I will have brought up to your chamber the best the castle affords."

"Do so, and as quickly as may be."

"The silvery Epernay," said one of the knights, "and the dried fruit in the east closet."

Wingrove gave such a jump, that he trod upon Bernard's toes, and looking from one to the other of the knights, he said,—

"Which—which of you spoke ?"

They all three shook their heads with great gravity, and turning one and all the same moment as if they had been mere machines, they strode after the crusader, their armed heels sounding heavily on the stone staircase as they ascended to the corridor, at the further extremity of which a door opened into the magnificent chamber, whither they had been invited.

Wingrove glared after them until they were out of sight, and then he said,—

"Am I awake ? For the love of Heaven, shake me, some of you ; this is surely a dream ! Butt seventy-three, and the preserved fruits in the east closet. How did they know a supply of preserved fruits was always kept in the east closet ? Am I awake ?"

"D—n you," said Bernard, "you trod on my toes hard enough, that was no dream."

"Shake yourself a little," said the herald, as placing the bell-shaped mouth of his silver trumpet close against Wingrove's ear, he blew a shrill sharp blast that made the old soldier jump again.

"Are you awake now ?"

"Quite," said Wingrove, taking hold of the herald's nose, and giving it a hearty pull, that it looked fiery for an hour.

The men-at-arms laughed uproariously, and the herald himself, truth to say, took the jest amazingly well, and slinging his trumpet behind him, cried,—

"The ale, the ale—there's nothing like ale."

"You are an uncommonly sensible man," said Bernard ; "but if that's your opinion, don't sit next to me, or else they'll be sure to say we two drink it all."

"Come, come," said Wingrove, "let us, among ourselves, wait upon these knights, the domestics are all asleep; come, bustle comrades, seize upon whatever you can find in the larder of a choice character, and one of you waken up the old cellarer—scream seventy-three butt in his ears, and don't leave him till he's dressed. I will myself see to the preserved fruits in the east closet."

Thus urged, the men-at-arms did what they were desired, and in a few minutes such a clatter of platters and such a scuffling up and down the stair-case ensued, as filled Agatha with a thousand fears, and alarmed Eldred to such a degree that he slipped down under the bed-clothes in the shape of a large ball, and would not stir till the morning.

The domestics crept down one by one to the great hall, where they found numberless articles broken by the clumsy efforts of the men-at-arms to render themselves generally useful; such a scene of clamour and confusion at such an hour in Brandon Castle was unprecedented.

Fitzhugh arose, and stood listening outside his chamber-door, but nothing could he hear save the running up and down of the men-at-arms. He, too, was lost in wonder as to what could be the cause of the unusual tumult. Two o'clock boomed forth from the castle time-piece. The moon still continued to shed its flood of beautiful light upon Brandon Castle, but how animated and full of life was the scene it now illumined in comparison with the rapt repose it had shone upon two hours previously.

CHAPTER LXVII.

"Flow the regal purple stream,
Tinctured by the solar beam;
In the goblets sparkling rise,
Cheer their hearts, glad their eyes."

THE SINGULAR DEMEANOUR OF THE THREE STRANGE KNIGHTS.—WINGROVE'S SURPRISE.—THE POISON MAKING IN THE GREY TURRET.

DURING the whole time that an ample repast was being spread in the crusader's chamber, the three strange knights sat on chairs as still and motionless as if they had been three effigies cased in armour, leaning grimly upon their swords, and looking neither to the right nor to the left. As for the crusader, he, with his arms folded across his ample chest, paced up and down in the magnificent room, neither speaking to the knights, or they to him.

It was not until the table was completely covered, that Wingrove said, in a respectful voice,—

"We have but poor cheer with which to entertain distinguished guests at Brandon. If my honoured master was here we could do better; but such as we have it's placed before you right heartily along with our respectful service."

The three knights gravely nodded their heads, and the crusader said,—

"We shall do well enough, good Wingrove; be assured these are friends of mine, and if they at present remain concealed, it is from prudential reasons, and not from any doubt of your trustworthiness."

The three knights again gravely nodded their heads, and Wingrove said,—

"I am much honoured, and I will place two sentinels outside the door, the duty of one of whom it shall be to bring me any orders you may have."

He then left the room, and he had scarcely got half-a-dozen paces from it, when he heard the door locked on the inside.   He involuntarily paused, and in another moment he heard such a tremendous clatter in the room, that he was perfectly astonished to know from what cause it could proceed. Then a thought suddenly struck him, and he said,—

"By the mass, they are getting rid of some of the troublesome portions of their armour and throwing them down.   I much wonder who they can be.   Knights of high renown I make no doubt; but it is not my business to conjecture, and that I do right cheerfully."

He posted, as he had said he would, two sentinels at the door, which was by far too massive a structure to permit the sound of ordinary conversation to be heard through it.   These sentinels were Joyce Evans and Bernard, who, fully armed, took up their posts in the corridor, while Wingrove himself waited anxiously in the guard-room for any orders which might be issued by his distinguished guests.

He had not to wait very long, for in about a quarter of an hour Bernard, with his usual deliberate step, made his appearance.

"What is it?" said Wingrove.   "Anything wanted?"

"Yes," said Bernard.   "What do you think they want now?"

"Come, be quick.   Tell me—they will get impatient."

"Why, they say you are to go to the oaken cabinet in Sir Rupert's par- lour, and bring them some of the golden liquor which was brought by Sir Rupert Brandon from the Netherlands, and which you will find in the left hand corner cupboard."

"The devil!" said Wingrove.

"God bless me, where?" said Bernard, looking anxiously around him.

"Who told you this?"

"I don't know exactly.   I was standing very near the door, grinning at Joyce Evans, when suddenly there comes a thundering whack on my head with a silver flagon, to make me attentive, I suppose, and then one of them says what I have told you; after that, bang went the door again, and they all laughed."

Wingrove held up his hands in amazement, and then seizing the light, he hurried off to execute the orders of his mysterious guests, who seemed to know far better than he did himself the resources as regarded good cheer of Brandon Castle.

Exactly as he had been directed he found the liquor, and was about to leave the room with it, when Agatha Weare, pale and disordered, entered by an opposite door.

"Hold! Wingrove," she cried; "for the love of Heaven tell me what is the meaning of all this uproar and rioting in Brandon Castle at such an hour?"

"I don't know," said Wingrove.   "There are some more friends of Sir Rupert come, and I'm not going to quarrel with them because they do not tread so softly as they might."

"Insolence!" said Agatha.

"Call it what you please," said Wingrove, "these friends of Sir Rupert s shall do just what they like.   I and the men-at-arms will back them in everything, and we defy you and the Black Monk, and all the devils you can muster.   Now you know my mind, Miss Agatha Weare, and I hope you'll never speak to me again."

Agatha was so surprised at this decided speech of Wingrove's, that he had left the room before she could recover the faculty of speech.   He pro- ceeded directly to the chamber of the crusader, and himself tapped at the door with the liquor.

"Come in," cried the crusader, and Wingrove, with some little curiosity, opened the door of the apartment.

There sat the three strange knights with the small caps on their heads usually worn by warriors of rank, even when in complete armour, when they do not wish to be encumbered with the helmet, and likewise on each of their faces a velvet mask, similar to that worn by the crusader, who said, in a jocular tone,—

"So, Wingrove, you've found the golden liquor?"

"Yes," was the reply, "it is here. Is there anything else I can procure?"

"We will take a thought," said the crusader; then turning to the knights, he said,—

"By-the-bye, didn't one of you say there was a curious drinking-horn in a cabinet somewhere about Sir Rupert's bed-chamber?"

The three knights nodded their heads, and one of them, in a sepulchral voice, said,—

"In the bottom draw, standing on a stag's foot."

Wingrove actually staggered, and then he said,—

"Noble sirs, I know not how you came by this rare and accurate information; but Brandon Castle is evidently better known to you than it is to me. I grieve that you will not trust me."

"Hush—hush!" said the crusader.

"Hush—hush!" said the three knights, mysteriously; and then one of them rising opened the door for Wingrove, while the other two significantly pointed to the corridor, so that he had no resource but to walk out as wise as he walked in.

Wingrove felt hurt and annoyed more than he chose to acknowledge to himself, at the want of confidence that was shown in him by those who he knew might safely trust him. These emotions, however, he strove, as much as in him lay, to stifle.

"Why did I be curious," he said, "in what concerns me not? I am sure of one thing, and that ought to be sufficient for me, and shall be, namely, that these warriors, be they who they may, are friends of Sir Rupert."

With a praiseworthy determination then he resolved that he would simply do his duty, and make no further inquiries, but blaming himself at the same time for the one he had made so unsuccessfully.

Every soul was now up in the castle, and the revelry of the knights continued without the slightest intermission, while the two sentinels kept steady watch and ward by the chamber-door.

Agatha Weare was both angry and alarmed; she knew not what to think or how to act; circumstances seemed thickening around her in the most uncomfortable manner, and it was evident to her she was a complete cipher in Brandon Castle, and that all her efforts to assume a far higher authority than had been delegated to her by Sir Rupert Brandon had ended in the entire loss of that which she might fairly have claimed.

Even then had she listened to the voice of conscience and of reason, she might have been happier, far happier, than she permitted herself to be; for not so far had she gone in the career of vice and dissimulation which had been opened to her by the Black Monk as to make retreat and repentance utterly hopeless. What had been yet done bore more the character to her mind of the preparatory steps to something of more direful import still, which was yet to be accomplished, and yet to reflect upon the acts that had already been committed.

But hers was a nature which was constantly struggling with its own darker passions; from earliest childhood she had detested to be foiled in anything. Defeat upon the most trivial occasion would rouse her to the most ungovernable fury, and then had arisen the one grand passion of her existence—an admiration and wild love of Sir Rupert Brandon—which knew no bounds, but he preferred the gentler virtues and more feminine graces of Alicia—Alicia, whom she, Agatha, had ever despised and treated with contempt. Then indeed had arisen a storm of passion which transcended everything that succeeded it, overpowering in its wild career her better judgment, and making her the tool and slave eventually of that artful priest, who made the worst passions of humanity the stepping stones of his own ambition, and the accomplishment of his private revenges.

Feeling that he had disappointed her hitherto, and that everything which had been attempted to be accomplished had failed, notwithstanding all the diabolical means which he had to ensure success—feeling that his words were, in many instances, mere idle boastings, and that his vaunted power was liable to be defeated by the merest accidental circumstances—still, where could she turn for succour, where for even a doubtful assurance of success, but to him, the Black Monk—for what other congenial soul was there in Brandon?

She accordingly hastened to the chamber in which they held their secret meetings, and opening the concealed door which led from it on to the staircase of the old Grey Turret, she, with a throbbing heart and an aching brain, repaired thither, and making the accustomed signal which had been agreed upon between her and Morgatani when she required to see him, in order to communicate something of importance, she hastened back again to her chamber; for never even had she ventured to cross the threshold of that turret apartment from whence the monk spread such terrors, and issued such singular sights; and in which he concocted these schemes which were intended to bring destruction upon the brave and the innocent.

Minute after minute passed away and the monk made not his appearance; with anxious steps Agatha paced to and fro in her chamber, and as each passing minute brought with it an assurance that Morgatani was not in the turret, and, consequently, that her signal could not reach him, she felt more acutely the utter desolation of her situation.

The Black Monk was otherwise engaged in his turret abode, he had heard those trumpet calls that had produced so great an effect on Brandon, and despite the danger of his prowling about the castle, his was not the nature to remain idle when anything of moment was proceeding.

Hence he glided from place to place about the ancient pile, concealing himself here and there, in order to listen to any conversation that might give him a hint as to whom the new comers were, but no benefit did he reap from his cunning, for all that he heard was conjecture, so that he became convinced in a short time that the new-comers preserved their incognito to all alike.

This was a circumstance that gave him additional vexation, inasmuch as it gave him additional reason to believe that the preservation of such incognito was of vast importance, and not the mere whim of a moment.

"It will be strange indeed," he muttered, as he was hidden behind the arras in the southern gallery—"it will be strange if some of the partisans of King Richard have decided upon making this castle a place of rendezvous for themselves, and yet such may be the case, for that these new arrivals are from London instead of from Palestine, I can well believe. If such be the case, it is indeed most essential that I should discover who and what they are, and after all the mysterious circumstances which have centered two plots in one edifice may be beneficial to the cause which I advocate. These four persons who are now in Brandon are, without doubt, parties of importance. When they have fallen victims to the poison which I mean to administer, I shall have an opportunity of carefully examining their features and of ascertaining how far they were calculated to become obnoxious to me."

Finding then that he could discover nothing, and feeling that in his attempt he was incurring great danger, he quietly and silently slunk back to the Grey Turret, from whence, in a short time, shot a singular and lurid glare of light.

The monk was preparing the deadly poison—a few drops of which, mingled with the wine in Brandon, would ensure excruciating pain and ultimate death to those who partook of the beverage.

That strange and preternatural-looking light was seen by many within the Castle of Brandon. The sentinels on the battlements paused and crossed themselves as the lurid glare fell upon their arms and accoutrements.

" The Black Monk," they whispered to each other. " The Black Monk is at his work to-night."

'Twas seen too by the crusader and his friends through the painted window which was in his chamber, and they with one accord, paused in their revelry to gaze upon the singular phenomenon.

Any active interference, however, with Morgatani at that time, seemed not to be contemplated by them, and they turned again to their wine as if with perfect heedlessness of what the dark designs of that wily priest might bring forth.

Welcome and comprehensible to but one person in Brandon was that mysterious light, and that person was Agatha Weare, who hailed it as an intimation that the companion of her crimes and her tempter to iniquity had returned; without delay she, therefore, once again made her way to the turret staircase, and giving the signal which before she had given in vain, she retired to her own chamber, with the expectation of the speedy arrival of Morgatani; nor was she disappointed, for in a short time the monk made his appearance.

CHAPTER LXVIII.

" From the twelfth to the fifteenth century there were many persons who, affecting to study alchemy, made a trade of compounding poisons, which were freely vended in the Italian cities."
—ROCHEFOUCAULT.

THE CONSULTATION.—THE POISONED WINE.—THE VENETIAN GLASSES.

The monk had obeyed the summons of Agatha the more promptly because he thought it possible she might have made some discovery of an interesting character with regard to the strange knights, although he did not think it likely that such was the case.

He met her with an inquiring look, but by her trembling aspect and generally disturbed demeanour, he guessed that she had nothing to communicate beyond her fears, or if she had, that it was not of a pleasant character.

" Well, Agatha," he said, " you have heard of the mysterious arrival?"

" I have," she said. " Oh, Morgatani! who can these be, who so strangely, and in such deep disguise, have come to Brandon? What evils are in store for us? Whither shall we turn for succour?"

" Hush! Agatha Weare," said the monk; " wherefore do you give yourself up to such strange excitement? What is there now in our situations and prospects that should fill you so full of fears?"

" Are we not surrounded by enemies?" said Agatha. " What am I now in Brandon?—what are you?"

" What am I!" said the monk, with a bitter laugh; " I am the evil genius of Brandon Castle—my spells are only working; when they are ac-

complished, you shall discover in their effects how great has been design." that

"Morgatani," said Agatha, "you cannot tell me that as yet I have met with anything but promises from you?"

"Ah!" said the monk, in a tone of passion. "Do you begin to upbraid me now because I am not omnipotent, and cannot command every small circumstance that steps between you and the accomplishment of your wishes?"

"No," said Agatha, "I do not upbraid; but what have we yet reaped from our exertions but bitterness and woe?"

"You think so?" said the monk.

"Do the facts not speak glaring for themselves, Morgatani?"

"Woman!" said the monk, "when first I leagued myself with you, it was for the accomplishment of a higher object than the gratification of your womanly spite against the man who rejected your addresses."

"My addresses!" cried Agatha.

"Yes, your addresses. Did you not yourself tell me that you confessed your tender passion to Sir Rupert Brandon, and that he kindly proffered you his pity?"

"His pity!" screamed Agatha. "I will have his life—his life, I say. I must see his heart's blood flowing ere I shall be satisfied; he shall die, and if I could have my way, he should die a thousand deaths. His pity!— curses on the word. He shall die—he shall die!"

"Ay," said the monk, sarcastically, "that is right—that is right; now you are yourself again. Truly, I had as lief be hanged as pitied—ay, much rather, after you had condescended to tell him of your love. By-the-bye, I have forgotten—my memory is treacherous on some matters—did you kneel to him?"

No. 49

"Morgatani," said Agatha, in a suppressed tone, while she trembled with passion, "devil! you have said enough. I am yours; give me but my revenge, and lead me on what frightful downward path you will—I ask but my revenge."

"And you shall have it," said the monk, in a tone that rung through the apartment. "Ah! who knocks?"

Agatha walked to the door, while the monk concealed himself in the gloom at the further end of the apartment. She opened it carefully a short distance, when Fitzhugh presented himself.

"I would fain speak to Morgatani," he said, "if he be here."

"He is here," said the monk, in some surprise; for he thought that Fitzhugh had surely been killed, either by the wizard or by those who had stepped in to his rescue. "Come in, Fitzhugh—I would fain have a word or two with you."

Fitzhugh entered the apartment, and the monk, fixing his eyes upon him, said,

"So you escaped safely from your little adventure in the forest."

"Little adventure," exclaimed Fitzhugh. "Another such little adventure, I believe, would be my death. Never again will I venture into the cavern of that infernal maniac, for he has surely some devils at his command that step between him and danger. I was flung into an inner recess of his abominable abode with a vehemence that nearly deprived me of my senses, and then, I suppose, you ran away?"

"Yes," said the monk, calmly; "it would not have been absolute wisdom to remain. I thought your natural wit would enable you to escape, and that I might be more an hindrance than an assistance to you—so I left you to your own great resources—the issue proving how correct was my judgment, for here you are."

"D—n your judgment," muttered Fitzhugh. "I certainly am here, but how I can scarcely tell myself; nevertheless, that was not what brought me to this chamber. I dread these new arrivals, who, from what I can hear, are knights, and no doubt favourable to King Richard."

"You dread them," said the monk. "Why you ought to fight them; you come here on an errand from King John, who has made you a knight, and you suspect there are parties in Brandon who deny your master's title. Your duty is plain and straightforward; you must fight, then."

"I decline the honour," said Fitzhugh, coldly. "If I were four men instead of one, I might feel inclined; but as it is, I most emphatically and decidedly decline."

"But, Fitzhugh," said the monk, "have you any objection to a little bit of treachery, which, in order to give it a more palatable sound, we will, if you please, call policy, leaving the world in after ages to call it by what name it will, since it cannot matter to us?"

"I have no objection," muttered Fitzhugh, "to anything which will advance our cause, and in which there is no danger."

"Candidly spoken," sneered Morgatani; "in this there is certainly no danger; all that is required of you is to assist me in poisoning certain wine casks."

"Poison!" said Fitzhugh.

"Ay, poison," said the monk. "It is prepared. These gallants who have arrived will not live without choice wine, and plenty of it—they shall have their fill, and in so having it they shall discover that death is in the winecup, and be able to moralise more scripturally upon the delightful uncertainty of human life."

"I am willing to lend such assistance as I can," said Fitzhugh.

"Be it so," said the monk; "Brandon Castle is now in a state of commotion—but in the course of a few short hours its inmates will be sleeping again, and then we can proceed to the cellar and execute our purpose. All that we have to be particular in, is to take care among ourselves that we drink no wine."

"Of that I shall be sufficiently careful," said Fitzhugh, with a shudder.

*   *   *   *   *   *

The morning broke serenely beautiful on the moss-grown towers and battlements of Brandon Castle. The grey light in the east gradually brightened and expanded over the sky, giving life and beauty to the earth. The sun soon emerged from the obscurity and gloom of night, dispensing gladness and joy in the hearts of the sentinels, who watched his progress on their solitary posts on the walls.

Another day was begun, and the grey pile of Brandon seemed once more to emerge from darkness into life and glorious day—while the rising sun, whose rays became stronger and more vivid, began to illumine and warm the chill atmosphere, at the same time drawing up the damp vapours engendered in the night.

No tongue can tell the feelings with which the wearied and benumbed soldier watches the progress of dawn—it spreads a gladness over his heart and a warmth over his body—he again traverses the allotted spaces with lighter feelings and invigorated energies, and thus the sentinels on duty on the ramparts, gave the watchword with a gladdened tone, which of itself said "day was come."

The scene was one which would have been viewed with pleasure by a less interested observer, who could watch how nature grew as it were into life, as each spot became more and more lightened by the sun's rays, which now assumed a bright golden tinge through the clouds and vapours which were fast dispersing under the influence of his warmth.

It was at this solemn and beautiful hour, that Agatha having ascertained that no one was moving in the castle, save the guard, the sentinels by the crusader's door, and those who held their accustomed watch upon the battlements, informed Morgatani that such was the case, and then he, with Fitzhugh, departed on their unholy errand of poisoning the wine.

"You must affect, Fitzhugh," said the monk, as if he were making a very indifferent proposition, " you must affect great kindness towards your young page, and offer him a cup of course ; the boy deserves all the advantages of having made himself friends among our enemies."

" I have some dislike to poisoning the lad," said Fitzhugh.

"Ah ! that is a pity," replied the monk ; " but it only shows how public necessities war against the beautiful and kind feelings of human nature. You must even let him be poisoned, Fitzhugh. Who knows what evils of after life we may be sparing him. Perhaps Providence may take us into consideration for the act."

" I cannot there go with you," said Fitzhugh, with a shudder, " in your daring scepticism, but if the boy must perish I cannot save him, and in a great measure it is his own act. He is my page, and entertained by me, therefore he should not league himself with my enemies."

" Most admirably spoken," said the monk ; " most logically spoken ; such reasoning ought to convince the very page himself of the propriety of poisoning him."

" Should the cellarer encounter us, Morgatani," said Fitzhugh, " what shall we do ?"

" To avoid suspicion," said the monk, " it would not be a bad plan to knock in the head of one of the wine vats, and put him in."

" That would be a plan, indeed," said Fitzhugh. "But what a wonder—

ful knowledge you have of the localities of Brandon—here we are in the cellars."

"Truly," was the reply, "but here is the poison. In every cask that has been tapped I will place a few drops of this harmless looking fluid, but in those few drops are contained the deaths of hundreds of men."

As he spoke the monk performed his diabolical errand, and in a few minutes the casks of wine were poisoned, and he looked with a grim satisfaction upon the frightful work he had committed.

"Let us hasten now from here," he said. "All is as it should be. Let us cheerfully await the event, feeling that the watchful eye of Providence, which never sleeps, is upon us, and what we are doing must surely be the will of Heaven, and consequently pious, which you must be aware, Fitzhugh, is a reach even above virtue."

"But," said Fitzhugh, as they reached the southern gallery, "there is some wine drawn, and how shall we distinguish it from that which may be in the barrels?"

"In the oaken cabinet," said the monk, "which stands in Sir Rupert Brandon's own room, there are several Venetian goblets, do you secure one and leave me to do so likewise; if there be poison in the wine that is poured into them, as you may have heard, they will fly into a thousand pieces—if they show no effects you may drink in safety."

"Truly," said Fitzhugh, "I am glad there are Venetian glasses here; I do not like, if I can help it, going without a tankard of wine occasionally."

"You need not, since you have a test," said the monk. "I shall now wait patiently in my turret the effect of the offensive operations I have adopted."

In a few minutes Fitzhugh and Morgatani separated, but the former was careful not to retire to his own apartment until he had really possessed himself of one of the glasses the monk had mentioned; with that he had no fear, for he had heard from too many undoubted sources, tales of the efficacy of those glasses, to entertain any doubt concerning them.

To say that he felt no regret at the destruction of the page, would be almost to libel Fitzhugh, but still whatever he might feel, it was not sufficient to induce him to adopt any active steps in order to save the young boy from the dreadful effects of Morgatani's villany, and he satisfied his own mind with the mere regret, instead of adopting any measure that might have the effect of saving the victim.

Thus the poor page seemed doomed to suffer a terrible death, a death which he little deserved, but still from which there seemed no possibility of escape, as he, Morgatani, appeared willing to sacrifice any one who might stand in the way of his infamous projects.

Scarcely, however, had the infamous and cold-blooded associates left the gallery, than there stepped from the deep recess of a large window, the young maiden who had confessed her sex, and the reasons why she had wandered so far from home, to the crusader. She looked for a few moments in the direction of the retreating forms of Morgatani and of the recreant knight, Fitzhugh.

"Venetian glasses," she muttered; "what want they with Venetian glasses? Is there any villany afloat that requires such extraordinary aids to detect it? Venetian glasses—Venetian glasses, surely that speaks of poison. I have heard of such most frequently. Can there be any frightful tragedy about to occur at Brandon, which Heaven in its goodness has given me the power of averting? There must be a warning given. I must charge myself with the preservation of those who may be in danger. Oh, how I shall rejoice if I should become the happy means of rescuing from so terrible a death as that of poisoning, that noble knight, who with such kindly words has made my stay so full of pleasant expectation.

Morgatani was right in supposing that after the disturbance and revelry of the night, the inhabitants of Brandon, who had not some particular motive for remaining up and active, would be seeking repose from their fatigues, and lie unusually late in the day.

By the assistance of Wingrove the three stranger knights had been well accommodated in the crusader's chamber; but nothing could induce them to consent to his again taking up his nightly watch beneath the window. He, however, such was his great anxiety for the crusader's safety, himself visited, every half hour during the darkness, the parapet beneath the huge pointed casement, for he could not be satisfied, without the repeated inspections, that the Black Monk was not making some desperate effort to do mischief.

Little did he think how much mischief that he, Morgatani, had done; but the faithful soldier would not leave his self-imposed task until he heard the knights stirring in their chamber, and was perfectly sure there was no further cause for fear; then he sought that repose of which he was so much in need, and of which, perhaps, his deep anxiety, he had less than any other man throughout Brandon.

CHAPTER LXIX.

There is a tide in the affairs of man,
Which, taken at the flood, leads on to fortune.—SHAKSPERE.

THE BANQUET.—BERTHA'S COMMUNICATION.—THE ALARM.—THE TERRORS OF
AN EVIL CONSCIENCE.

SUCH was the situation of parties in Brandon on the morning after the arrival of the three strange knights, who, in all human probability, would have fallen victims to the machinations of Morgatani but for the little accidental circumstance of Bertha overhearing a portion of their discourse; and, having her suspicions sufficiently awakened, to present, at all events, some chance of escapé to the crusader and his associates.

The morning meal had scarcely been despatched, when she sought Wingrove, and besought him to inform the crusader that she had something of importance to communicate concerning his and his comrades' safety.

This was a theme upon which Wingrove himself felt too deeply for him to neglect paying immediate attention to, and he instantly replied,—

" If such is the fact, I pray you come with me instantly, and communicate your intelligence. It may be of more importance than you may imagine; but to whom does it particularly refer ?"

" The persons," said Bertha, " whom I suspect of evil intentions, is a tall man, attired in ecclesiastical garb, and answering well to the description of him whom I have heard talked of since I have been in Brandon as the Black Monk."

" Then you could not suspect a better person," said Wingrove; " for, if there is any villany going on, or projected in Brandon, he is assuredly at the bottom of it."

" But there was another," said Bertha, " who was conversing with him."

" Who was that ?" said Wingrove.

" I do not know, but I can give you his description. It was a tallish man, attired in half armour."

" The cowardly Fitzhugh, I'll be bound," said Wingrove; " you have indeed hit upon two notable subjects for suspicion—two greater scoundrels than Morgatani, the monk, and the tall man in half armour, cannot exist. What is the nature of your suspicions?"

"You'll excuse me," said Bertha, "but I wish to communicate them only to the crusader."

"Certainly," was the reply, "I should be sorry to lose another moment in leading you to him."

Wingrove preceded Bertha until they came to the crusader's chamber, at which he knocked.

"Come in," was the reply; and, when he entered with Bertha, there sat the three strange knights, with their velvet masks upon their faces, looking as solemn as ever.

"I have something to communicate," said Bertha; and, glancing at the crusader as she spoke; "I believe it concerns all here present."

The three strange knights nodded their heads with the gravity used on such occasions; but Wingrove did not wait for them to point to the door as a signal for her departure, he having left the room hastily the moment he had introduced Bertha to the crusader's attention.

Bertha distinctly related all that she had heard between Fitzhugh and the monk, to which the crusader listened with the greatest attention, and the three knights with the greatest gravity.

"This is most important," said the crusader, when Bertha had finished: "we shall all of us, I hope, live to thank you truly for this information. We intended ordering a slight repast, in the shape of a mimic banquet, to-day; and, but for the caution you have given us, we might indeed have lost our lives."

The three knights nodded in acquiescence to this sentiment; and Bertha, seeing that her presence must, of necessity, be a restraint, left the apartment as speedily as possible, a measure which the knights did not oppose, inasmuch as they no doubt really did wish to be by themselves, to consult concerning the important information which had been given to them. What was the result of their consultation will appear as we proceed; but, at all events, it seemed to make no difference in their preparations, which the crusader thought proper to make for the entertainment of his friends.

He sent for Wingrove very shortly after the interview with Bertha, and, without the slightest allusion to it, or the subject matter of it, he desired to know if there were sufficient resources in the castle to prepare a repast of more assumption and appearance than usually graced the board.

"We have plenty of game," replied Wingrove, "and it can be washed down by as choice wines as can be found in the country side."

"Ay," said the crusader, "we will have choice wine—there is nothing like choice wine. I shall rely entirely upon your management, Wingrove, to provide us everything in as pleasant a manner as possible."

"I will do my best," was the reply; "the wine is abundant; and, if we lack delicacies, we must make good the deficiency by a greater welcome to our guests."

"Of that we are assured," said the crusader; "and, as we should never harbour malice against a fair lady, pray carry the joint regards of four unnamed, but not unknown, knights of the cross, and tell her we shall be glad of her company, and that of her brother, Eldred Weare, as well as any other guest she may have in Brandon, whom she wishes to honour."

"It shall be done," said Wingrove, although he much marvelled in his own mind at the message, and would rather have not been the messenger; but, if that crusader had asked him to go to the devil with a message, he would have endeavoured to have accomplished the task; therefore he departed at once to obey the command.

If Wingrove was surprised at having such a message to deliver, Agatha was still more surprised at its reception, and after a few moments' consideration, she returned an answer to Wingrove, to the effect that she would consider of the invitation, and that, as she considered herself a prisoner in Brandon Castle, at the mercy of lawless intruders, she knew not if she should accept it or not.

To this answer Wingrove made no remark, secretly hoping in his own mind that she would be by far too indignant at the numerous slights which had been put upon her to attend to the crusader's invitation; in fact, as he told himself, he did not see very well how she could go, after the angry scenes that had taken place between her and the individual who had assumed to invite her. But in this Hugh Wingrove was mistaken, for upon Agatha seeking the advice of the monk, he said, after musing for some moments :—

" The invitation must be accepted, for good and substantial reasons : firstly, it would be pleasanter for you to appear innocent of any knowledge of the poisoning transaction than not ; and secondly, you will have the pleasure of seeing how the scheme works, and of marking the gradual progress of those whom we wish to destroy from health to sickness, and from sickness to death, and in their pangs you will read a confirmation of my policy. Take with you, if you please, Eldred Weare, as well as that craven hound Fitzhugh ; all they have to do is to be cautious respecting the wine, and if they should not, why the fault will rest with themselves ; and, after all, when one comes to think of it, perhaps if they were to make a little blunder and get poisoned, it might be better for our plans, as, on my life, I do not see what use either of them are, and as far as I am concerned myself, it so happens, that, as a churchman, I would rather not be suspected, for, of late, by some mischance, priestcraft does not seem to be thought so much of as formerly."

" I cannot consent," said Agatha, with a shudder, " to such wholesale destruction."

" Well, well," said the monk, " I give up the point ; but be sure you let me know immediately that the poison has taken effect."

" How shall I let you know ?" said Agatha. " What message can I send to you ?"

" Dash a wine-cup through a window," said the monk. " I shall be sufficiently near to hear the crash, and will immediately make my presence, for I am all impatience to see the faces of those men, who have hitherto so artfully eluded my observation."

" It shall be done," said Agatha. " I would that it were over."

" We cannot fail," said the monk, emphatically ; " success now amounts to a certainty. Can you fancy that these men would sit at the festive board and not drink wine, and that deeply, too ? Agatha, this day will put us in undisturbed possession of Brandon, by the death of those men, who else by their residence here might render all our schemes fruitless. Likewise, if these men should turn out to be, as I fully believe they will, men of note, and personal friends of Richard, we shall be doing so acceptable a service to King John, that the condemnation of Sir Rupert Brandon for the crimes we shall lay to his charge, would follow as a piece of gratitude to us, even were he to succumb to the new order of things, and acknowledge peaceably the new monarch."

" Well," said Agatha, " I will attend this feast ; Eldred and Fitzhugh shall accompany me, but they shall be amply warned, each of them, for I wish not to shed unnecessary blood."

" As you please, as you please ; remember the signal you are to give me of the success of the stratagem."

* * * * * * *

Neither Fitzhugh nor Eldred very much relished the rather unpleasant invitation to dine with men against whose lives they were plotting barbarously, and who might, before the consummation of the scheme which was to prove their destruction, become very obstinate and uncomfortable table companions.

Fitzhugh shuffled and turned in every possible way to escape the job, but Agatha assured him that not only would he incur the vengeance of the monk, who, she took occasion to remind him, was not over scrupulous in his behaviour towards those who seriously offended him, but, likewise, and she found this argument had great weight, she assured him that the crusader had insisted on his appearance, and likewise promised his vengeance if he came not; between the two, therefore, the unfortunate Fitzhugh had not the shadow of an escape, and with a groan he consented to be one of the party.

In consenting so to do, however, he insisted that Eldred should not escape, and, to the latter's great dismay, he was informed that he must positively go to the banquet, whether he liked it or not, for that, if he did not go, it would give rise to a well-grounded suspicion that he had poisoned the whole party, and so draw down upon himself the vengeance of the laws.

"Certainly," said Fitzhugh; "I shall pretend to be very ill, and only to recover from the effects of the poison by a miracle and the strength of my constitution."

"Gracious goodness," said Eldred, "I don't see what you can want with me. Why should I be dragged into it?"

"You must go," said Agatha. "It is no use disputing the point; Morgatani says it, and you must go. After this your ambition will rise triumphant."

"Now, don't," said Eldred, "don't say any more about my ambition. You know perfectly well, sister, it's all gammon. You'll begin telling me about my revenge next, and I know what that means well enough, a skinfull of sore bones, and lots of vexation. No, no, I have had enough revenge and ambition too, to last me all my life, and now I mean to pluck up a spirit. You may say what you like, all of you, and do what you like—with awful solemnity I say I won't ——"

"Won't what?" said the monk, putting his head into the apartment.

"Oh, dear!" said Eldred, giving a great jump. "I—I—I—was going to say that I won't refuse anything, from a hit in the eye to an invitation to dinner; from a kick to a coffin."

"'Tis well," said the monk, and bang went the door.

"If that," said Eldred, in a mysterious whisper, and jerking his words out at intervals; "if—that—is—not—the—thingamy—that—lives—below—I—ain't—a—sinner."

"The devil?" said Fitzhugh.

"Exactly," said Eldred; "and all I mean to say is that ——"

"Enough," said the monk, as he strode into the apartment. "Be satisfied with the skill you have already shown in guessing. The banquet is being laid; be quick and join the guests. There is an old English proverb of 'the devil take the hindmost.' Beware!"

"By my ears, so there is," said Eldred, as he rushed from the room. "A pretty figure I am for a banquet, with, I am sure, not above half a nose, and that plastered over with little white strips of sticking-plaister, till it looks as if I carried a picture of the sun in my face, with the rays all around it. Why was I born? Why wasn't I smothered? Why didn't my nurse get beastly drunk and drop me in the fire? Why am I here? Why am I anywhere? Why am I at all? Why is anything? Why is nothing? Why ——"

"Why don't you get out of the way?" said Bernard, as he ran against Eldred with a shock that sent him sprawling.

"There's philosophy for you," cried Eldred, continuing his speed. "Murder, thieves, fire, and water! What the devil did you do that for, you elephant on its hind legs?"

"How could I see you?" said Bernard. "There's rare doings in the castle,

I've been to get two flagons of ale. One of 'em I was carrying in my hand and the other I was looking into to see whether the bottom of it was cleaned out well."

" Do you mean to say you've drunk all that ?" said Eldred.

" Not quite," said Bernard, as he finished the remainder, and giving his lips a great smack, "I was forced to leave off, running against you, 'cus you."

" There's a sot," said Eldred, as he looked after Bernard. " That's knock down the first for me to-day. Lots of revenge; oh, dear, yes, of course. Here's a lump on my head. Well, I suppose I must go; but I'll get near the door, and the moment I see anything queer, or one of 'em looking odd, I can shoot out in a moment."

The hour for the banquet was fast approaching, and Eldred Weare, fearful of offending those who had invited him, made some hasty changes in his dress by way of compliment to them, and then seeking Fitzhugh in his chamber, he said to him,—

" I say, let's go together. There may be a scheme in it, you know; if they give you a nob on the head, just you give a cough, and that will be a signal for me to be off. They are not over particular, those kind of men, you know, and would give you a crack on the skull as soon as look at you, and think it fine sport, and laugh at it, and ask you how you liked your entertainment, or some such insult."

" That's very kind of you to ask me to go first; but I'll tell you what I'll do, Eldred, I'll hold you fast behind, while you put your head in first, and then the moment I hear them give you a nob, I'll pull you out again."

" You are a great deal too kind," said Eldred. " If you won't go in first, I shall open the doorway wide, and say, ' how de do ?' outside, before I venture in, just to see what sort of humour they are in. They won't, surely, be such dreadful hypocrites as to say, ' pretty well, I thank you,' if they meant to do harm to me."

No. 50

" Where are they ?" said Fitzhugh.

" Why, they have taken possession of the little painted hall, where the banners hang, and around the walls of which is hung that sweet tapestry that they tell me Sir Rupert brought from Flanders."

" Well," said Fitzhugh, with a sigh, " I am ready, and we may as well go at once. I don't think there can be much danger, Eldred."

" Danger, good gracious! I hope not ; but I suppose we must go. I'm in a dreadful perspiration, and my hose are sticking to my feet, and I am all over a revenge and ambition sort of feeling."

CHAPTER LXX.

The feast was spread in the ancient hall,
The festive cup was there;
But what began in revelry
Was ended in despair.—ANON.

THE BANQUET.—THE POISONED WINE.—RETRIBUTIVE JUSTICE.—THE
DECLARATION.

THE room which Eldred Weare had correctly enough described to Fitzhugh, was, although by no means the largest, the most magnificent one that Brandon could boast. The roof was elaborately and beautifully carved, being supported by groined arches, beautifully adorned with fret-work, upon which there remained still sufficient of the dazzling brightness of former gilding to catch the rays of the wax candles that burned profusely in the apartment, and reflect them in dancing beauty ; in every direction stained glass, of the rarest colour, and the most exquisite designs, filled the casements. The walls were hung with the most gorgeous tapestry, which, by the directions of Hugh Wingrove, had been well shaken, and freed from the accumulated dust which had collected in the massive folds during the course of the few years that Sir Rupert had been absent from his home. Upon the ample hearth there burned a blazing fire of logs, and the floor was strewn with the finest rushes, which were used at that period, and long after, instead of the more modern luxury of carpets.

Massive and richly carved chairs, the seats, and a portion of the backs of which were covered with the richest Genoa velvet, were ranged around the festive board, which groaned beneath the weight of the ample cheer that had been provided for the repast.

The glancing of the many lights upon the massive silver tankards and huge candelabra that stood upon the table, combined with the rich and ruddy glow lent to everything by the fire-light, gave an air of massive splendour to the scene, which daylight could scarcely have imparted. A warm and agreeable atmosphere filled the apartment, and before any of the invited guests made their appearance, the crusader and his three mysterious companions descended the staircase, preceded by Hugh Wingrove bearing the lights, and entered the hall.

They were none of them without some defensive armour, and it was remarked by the men-at-arms, who saw them proceed to the banquet, that two of them carried in their hands the long straight swords, which were such powerful weapons when grasped by a man of strength and skill, while the third brought with him a heavy mace, the end of which was furnished with a frightful array of spikes, and the crusader, to the great admiration of the men-at-arms, brought up the rear with his mighty battle-axe, which he whirled round his head, and ever and anon tossed in the air, catching it again dexterously by the handle, to their unbounded delight.

THE SECRET OF THE GREY TURRET.

Thus did these four mysterious men proceed to the festive board, placing their arms beside them in such a manner, that they could be laid hold of in a moment.

They took possession of chairs next each other, and still wearing their masks, which came down just to the upper lip, while their heads continued covered with their velvet caps we have before alluded to, they awaited the arrival of their timorous visitors.

Not long had they to wait, for a knock at the door announced some one, and the crusader cried out in such a stentorian voice, "Come in," that Eldred Weare, for it was he, was near running back to his chamber and locking himself in ; but he, in some measure, conquered his fears, and whispering to Fitzhugh to stick by him, he entered the hall.

"Welcome," said the crusader, laying his battle-axe on the table with such a clash, that everything shook again.

"Thank yer," stammered Eldred. "I am very much obliged to you—how are you ? I hope all your family is quite well ? don't you think you'll find that chopper inconvenient ?"

"No," said the knight. "I like to carry it about with me. After a feast sometimes comes a fray, and it's useful to be prepared."

The three stranger knights nodded their heads, and those who had swords, rattled them ominously in their sheaths, while he who brought in the ponderous mace, placed it upon the table beside him, not so quietly, however, but two of the iron spikes sunk deeply into the solid oak.

"Allow me to remark, gentlemen," said Eldred, in a hesitating voice, "that we are uncommonly peaceably inclined here. You may do just whatever you like, and we sha'n't think of resisting. We arn't quite idiots, gentlemen, and I am sure, rather than have that iron what d'ye call em, with the genteel-looking spikes, near my head, I consent to be kicked twice round Brandon, and back again. I am an individual, gentlemen, who would make any sacrifice for peace. Look at my nose."

"Sit down," said the crusader, dealing the seat next him a bang with his fist.

"Ah, ah !" said Eldred, with an hysterical laugh, "it's a funny fancy of mine, but I want to sit on this chair next the door. Ah, ah ! it's quite funny."

The crusader made no reply to this by words, but rising from his seat, he at one stride reached Eldred Weare, and seizing him by the collar, he dragged him to the seat he had indicated, on which he seated him with such a thump, that Eldred was some moments in recovering his breath.

His misfortunes, however, were not quite at an end, for the crusader glancing towards Fitzhugh, said,—

"I believe, sir, you are a knight ?"

"I am," said Fitzhugh, looking very pale, and trying to screw up his courage.

"Then you ought to have been seated first," said the crusader, and upon the word, he gave Eldred's chair so tremendous a kick, leaving him no other resource than to fall with a bang to the floor, which he did with a candlestick in his hand, which he had seized hold of, to prevent his falling.

"Knock down the second to-day," he groaned ; "revenge in heaps."

"Sit down, sir," said the crusader to Fitzhugh, dealing the chair on the other side of him just such a blow as he had that of Eldred's.

After what had befallen his companion, Fitzhugh was afraid to say he preferred the door, and with trembling steps, and great fear at his heart, he sat himself down in the chair indicated, which was between the crusader and the dangerous-looking character with the mace.

" Now you can sit," said the crusader to Eldred, " there's nothing like etiquette."

Eldred with many groans rose to his feet, and drawing the chair back to its place, sat down; upon which, another of the knights strode round the table, and seating himself on the other side of him, drew his sword, and throwing the sheath with a great clatter to the further end of the apartment, he laid the long double-edged weapon on the table before him, with a sort of growl, which was interpreted by Eldred Weare into an earnest wish that there might be occasion to use it.

The door opened then, and Agatha Weare made her appearance, upon which the third knight advancing towards her, led her on the instant to her seat, which he so hemmed in with his own, that it would be a matter of impossibility for her to leave the apartment, without scrambling over some of them.

" You are very welcome, lady," said the crusader. " You do us great honour."

" My respect for Sir Rupert," said Agatha, " brings me here. You say you are friends of Sir Rupert's, and as your tale seems to be believed by the men-at-arms in the castle, I am not myself willing to raise objections."

" That's very kind," said the crusader, appealing to the other knights, who gravely nodded their heads; " but let us to the banquet. What-ho! Who waits without ?"

The door was flung open, and several of the domestics of the castle appeared, together with Hugh Wingrove and a couple of the men-at-arms, who entered the room and busied themselves in attending upon the guests.

Eldred did nothing but wipe the perspiration off his face, and could eat of none of the dishes that were presented to him; while Fitzhugh, in great tribulation of spirit, forced with difficulty a few morsels down his throat.

As for Agatha, she looked around her with dismay, for she saw that Eldred and Fitzhugh were so completely hemmed in that they could not possibly escape, and she dreaded what might be her own fate if a discovery was made of the infamous plot to poison the knights.

As yet no wine had been drunk, and none called for, but each passing minute brought circumstances nearer to that climax at which they must soon arrive. Conversation there was none, except now and then a few sarcastic remarks addressed by the crusader to Eldred, and his timid replies.

About half an hour might have been thus passed—half an hour of seeming great amusement to the crusader, and of actual agony to those who had come to witness his and his companions' deaths.

" Ah! ha!" cried Eldred, " it has just struck me, how funny, I have left my handkerchief up stairs. I must go and get it—indeed I must—how very odd."

He tried to rise as he spoke, but the crusader gave him a knock on the top of the head that seated him in a moment, saying,—

" Send one of the serving knaves for it, if you really want it. Here you moon-faced fellow, by the door, go to Master Eldred's bed-room, and hunt through his wardrobe for a handkerchief."

" Oh, how funny," said Eldred faintly, and taking it from his pocket, " I've just found it."

" Uncommonly droll," said the crusader. " What-ho, Hugh Wingrove."

" I am here to do your humble service," said Wingrove, approaching.

" Wine !" said the crusader, with an awful blow on the table.

" Directly," said Wingrove.

" Butt seventy-three," said the knight with the mace, in a deep, hollow voice.

" The Venetian glasses, with gilt rims," said another of the knights.

" In the oaken cabinet below," said the third.

Then they all nodded their heads with great gravity, while Wingrove stood aghast, gazing from one to the other.

" Venetian goblet !" cried Agatha.

" Venetian goblet !" echoed Fitzhugh, very faintly, and the colour fled from his lips.

" Oh ! oh !" said Eldred. " I don't feel well at all ; there's something wrong in my inside. It's funny, but true. Oh ! oh ! I must go ; I never was so bad in my life."

" Pooh, pooh," said the crusader ; " a bumper of seventy-three will do you good."

Eldred sunk down low in his chair, and despairingly gave himself up to his fate, for he saw they would not let him live.

" Gentlemen," faltered Fitzhugh, " I came here out of courtesy to you, but have been recently wounded. Pray allow me to retire. I am subject to a dizziness."

" How odd," said the crusader ; " so are all of us."

The three knights nodded their heads, and the crusader added,—" a flagon of seventy-three will likewise set you to rights. The wine—d—n it—the wine."

As he spoke he took up his battle-axe, and gave it a flourish just before Eldred Weare's eyes, who sunk down a little lower in his chair, with another deep groan, murmuring,—

" I'm in for it now. The meat's got in his head already ; what will it be when the wine comes ?"

Agatha did not speak, but she clasped her hands before her, and the state of agitation she was in, was painfully observable in her countenance.

Hugh Wingrove brought in two flagons of wine, a larger and a smaller.

" Fill," cried the crusader, in the same stentorian voice he had taken to talking in ; every sound of which materially increased Fitzhugh's and Eldred's terror. " Fill, I say ; we will drink a bumper to the fair."

Hugh Wingrove filled five silver tankards with the wine, and then the crusader, as if suddenly bethinking himself, cried,—

" By the mass, we have not a Venetian glass. One will suffice, for the wine comes from the same butt."

Eldred by this time had nearly disappeared under the table, and it was with a faint voice he said,—

" You—you—surely don't suspect anything ?"

" Suspect !" cried the crusader, making a dive for his collar, and bringing him up to his seat again. " Suspect ! I scorn the idea. It's only a whim of mine to test my wine. Ain't it funny ?"

" Ah ! ah !" said Eldred, " very ; but talking of my inside, it's rather worse."

" Never mind your inside," said the crusader, giving him a blow at the pit of the stomach that, if he had eaten any dinner, would have inevitably brought it up again. " Never mind, man, we will have a good carouse, and then a little fight all to ourselves."

" The Venetian glass," said Wingrove, handing one to the crusader.

" Oh !" he cried, " the very thing ; fair play, gentles, and you, lady fair. I will test for my own glass."

Agatha rose to her feet and made an attempt to pass the knight who was at her side, but he gently though forcibly detained her, saying,—

" Nay, madam, abide the test."

Fitzhugh gave himself over for lost. The crusader poured a portion of his wine into the Venetian goblet—a hissing noise immediately succeeded it, and the wine bubbled over in a state of effervescence and the goblet fell to pieces with a loud sound, while Eldred slipped quite out of his chair and crept under the table.

"Why, Hugh Wingrove," said the crusader, calmly, "your butt seventy three, is likely to last a long while."

"God of Heaven!" he cried, clasping his hands, "on my soul's salvation I swear ——"

"Hugh!" said the crusader, raising his arm, "you are unsuspected—guard the door. We have an act of retributive justice to perform."

He and the three knights rose he spoke. He continued,—

"It is my firm belief that you, Agatha Weare, you, Fitzhugh, and you, Eldred Weare, conspired this night to poison me and my friends. We have escaped, but not so you. Your goblets shall be drunk to the dregs, although ours remain untouched."

Eldred made a rush and nearly succeeded in getting out of the door between Wingrove's legs, but he was caught, and by the orders of the crusader, brought back to his seat.

"Have mercy upon me," he cried. "I didn't do it—there's nothing in the wine, there isn't indeed, only a little cooling physic."

Fitzhugh was paralyzed with terror and unable to utter a word, while Agatha hid her face in her hands and trembled convulsively.

"I shall begin with you," said the crusader, turning to Eldred and taking up a goblet of the wine—"please to drink this."

"Murder! murder!" shouted Eldred. "Murder! murder!"

"Please to drink this," said the knight, calmly, and as Eldred continued to refuse he took up the battle-axe, and holding it poised above his head, said,—

"Which will you have, this axe in your brains, or the cup of wine?"

"Oh! neither, neither," said Eldred; "murder—murder!"

"We shall see," said the knight, and suddenly placing the corner of the battle-axe between his teeth, he poised it open and instantly dashed the whole goblet of wine down his throat to the risk of choking him, and when he let go of him, away went Eldred backwards, chair and all; then, turning with amazing quickness, he seized Fitzhugh by the throat, and taking up another goblet with his disengaged hand, he cried,—

"Now, dastard, you shall meet your doom," and at the moment he dashed the goblet with such violence against his teeth that Fitzhugh gasped with pain, and to save himself from choking, he swallowed a considerable portion of the wine.

The guilty wretch then fell in a huddled up heap on the floor, giving himself up for dead.

"Lady," said the crusader, addressing Agatha, "you are a woman, although a vile and wicked one. I will leave you to God and your own conscience."

Agatha rose from her seat like one in a dream, and staggered from the room, but ere she could reach the door, she dropped insensible to the ground.

"Wingrove," said the crusader, "the wine is poisoned, let no one, as he values his life, drink from these goblets; the tankard itself must be vitiated—let it go."

As he spoke he dashed the silver tankard through one of the windows, there was a moment's pause and then a door was flung open at the other end of the hall, and Morgatani himself strode half-a-dozen paces in before he discovered the state of affairs. One bitter oath escaped his lips and he turned to fly, but the crusader with a shout of vengeance rushed after him; that shout aroused Agatha Weare, and she clung to the knees of the knight who was nearest her, shrieking "mercy! mercy!"

"Ask it of Heaven, woman," was the reply, as the knight tore off his mask. "I am Sir Kenneth Hay!"

He then hastened in the direction the crusader had taken.

Agatha rose to her feet, and pointing with trembling fingers to the next knight, she cried deliriously.

"And you—and you ——"

"Sir Rupert Brandon!" cried the knight, a voice that rang through the hall.

A scream burst from Agatha, and she dropped dead upon the floor.

CHAPTER LXXI.

"Oh! who shall say when Heaven's mysterious laws
Shall bring to mid-day light the darkest crimes,
And in their hour of greatest joyance
Strike the iniquitous with fearful dread?"

THE ARRIVAL OF THE COMMISSIONERS FROM KING JOHN.—THE DEFIANCE.—PRUDENCE THE BETTER PART OF VALOUR.

SCARCELY had Sir Rupert Brandon time to utter an exclamation of horror at the sudden and frightful decease of Agatha Weare, in the full flush of all her iniquities, and with no opportunity of repenting of her deep wickedness, when a challenge of trumpets outside the gate of Brandon Castle, so long, and so loud, that it awakened every echo about the ancient walls, proclaimed the arrival of some parties, who, in their own estimation, were of no small consequence.

Thrice the loud brazen call for admission was wafted over the surface of the moat with scarcely a moment's intermission between each ringing blast of the trumpets; the men-at-arms, who were in the guard-room, and who little suspected what was ensuing in the banquet-hall, sprang to their feet as the warlike sounds came to their ears, and it was not until the echo had almost subsided into silence, that with one accord they cried out,—

"A visitor—a visitor to Brandon, of no mean rank. Call Hugh Wingrove. Where in the name Heaven is he?"

By this time the warder's voice was heard challenging those who in so startling a manner had placed themselves before the castle gates. Well might he and the two or three men-at-arms, who rushed up to his tower which commanded a view of some distance on the further side of the moat, be surprised at the cortege which appeared before the ancient fortress.

The party consisted of ten persons, differing largely in dress and appointments, but making upon the whole a very complete little band.

First and foremost, there were two heralds, attired in their emblazoned coats, and with all the appointments and insignia of their profession and condition. They carried in their hands massive silver trumpets, from each of which depended a square silken banner, richly wrought with the royal arms of England.

These heralds were mounted on superb horses, and the whole of their appointments being entirely new, gave them a strikingly splendid, and gorgeous appearance. Immediately following these were four persons attired in garbs half civilians, and half military; they wore each a shirt of chain mail, but from the rest of their general appointments and appearance, they rather resembled ecclesiastical or legal personages, who being on some important mission, during which some danger might be apprehended, had taken some precautions for their personal safety.

The other four making up the entire party, were stout, stalwart men, in every respect completely armed and caparisoned for the field. They looked like selected warriors, men who had been well tried in many a battle field, and who could be thoroughly depended on to act together with great effect on any sudden emergency.

Their armour and caparisons shewed they were not knights, although they were what were called esquire's at the period, all of whom were eligible to become knights on any occasion, as after a victory, for example, which justified a new creation of those hard fighting gentry.

The whole party were admirably mounted, and it was evident that a matter of no ordinary importance indeed could have brought together so well appointed and imposing a little throng.

"What ho!" cried the warder, as he blew a short shrill blast upon his horn, "who seeks admission to Brandon?"

One of the heralds spurred his horse forward six or eight yards, till its fore feet rested among the rank herbage that grew at the edge of the moat, waving his arm, then he said with a loud voice,—

"In the name of King——"

"Hold, hold, Master Norreys," cried one of the four official-looking personages. "Hold, hold; do not be so precipitate. It is far better till we get comfortably housed and have ascertained what kind of reception we are likely to get, to say in the name of *the King*, instead of naming him; by so doing we shall escape giving needless aggravation, and they may translate it to King Richard, while we owe allegiance to John."

The other three official-looking personages highly approved of this politic suggestion, one of them remarking,—

"Ay, by the mass! Master Herald, have a care. I still recollect the arrow that whistled within an inch of my eye when, but the day before yesterday, we claimed admission into Fearnshaw Castle in the name of King John,"

The herald nodded assent, and in a loud voice then said,—

"In the name of the King, we demand admittance to Brandon Castle. We bring important intelligence from court. Open your gates in the name of the King."

"Perhaps, good Master Herald," said Anstey who was on the warder's tower, "you'll be so good as to tell us which king you mean, for we've had a little squabbling at Brandon already upon that very subject."

"Irreverent knave," said one of the official personages, "we mean, of course, his most gracious Majesty."

"Exactly," said Anstey, "but——"

"Pshaw, pshaw, how dare a knave like you carp at such niceties? We come from the King of England, let that suffice; and we bear his Majesty's royal sign manual, empowering us, as his commissioners, to visit every strong hold and baronial hall in England, for the purpose of notifying some great changes that have occurred at the court. Once more, then, we demand admission in the name of the King. Sound your trumpets, heralds, and let them refuse us upon their peril."

Again the heralds blew a sonorous blast from the silver trumpets, and, scarcely had it died away, when it was answered by another within the court-yard, which was blown by the herald that had arrived at Brandon some time before, in a plight very far from the neat and trim one which his brethren outside the castle presented.

"Nay, now, what's that?" said one of the commissioners.

"It's Mountjoy, I'll wager my head," said the herald, falling back. "I know his breath on a trumpet as well as I know my own voice."

At this moment, in obedience to a command that was hastily brought to him, the warder, assisted by the men-at-arms, lowered the draw bridge, which fell with a clanking sound upon the stone supports on the opposite side of the moat.

There was a little hesitation on the part of those who had so strenuously demanded admission before they availed themselves of the tacit leave which had been given them to enter the castle. But that was only momentary, and the commissioners, whispering to each other as they went, crossed the drawbridge closely after the heralds, being followed by the four armed men, who evidently looked upon Brandon Castle with no small degree of interest.

In fact, at that period, it was the most renowned fortress of that part of the country in which it stood, and having been always in the possession of a family famous for its warlike exploits, it had seldom been so badly garrisoned, or so neglected in its exterior defences, as it had been since the departure of Sir Rupert Brandon to the holy wars.

In fact, we may date almost the decline of many of the stately baronial residences of England from the period of the crusades, when their owners, infatuated with a religious frenzy, used up all their resources in outfits to Palestine, leaving their castles in a state, in many instances, of very inefficient management during their absence.

Scarcely had the commissioners reached the court-yard, where it was customary for the visitors to alight, than there appeared before them Mountjoy, the herald, who, with his trumpet in his hand, looked with an inquiring air at the party, and evidently was resolved to wait until they chose to proclaim themselves the nature of their errand.

"We come," said the boldest of the commissioners—and he was not very bold—"we come to proclaim John King of England; and, in order that there may be no mistake hereafter upon the subject among any of the barons, we shall deliver here a circular letter, signed by the king's own hand, and addressed in most loving terms to his excellent subject, Sir Rupert Brandon."

No. 51

"Oh, indeed!" said Mountjoy. "It's remarkable polite; but as there is such a person as King Richard, we couldn't altogether appreciate it."

"King Richard," said one of the commissioners, casting up his eyes with a sanctified look, "is in Heaven's holy keeping."

"That's a lie," said Mountjoy.

"Oh!" cried the commissioner, "to speak thus to me. Retract the offensive expression, or my escort shall cut you down as you stand."

"Poh—poh!" said Mountjoy. "Civility becomes prisoners, and more especially traitors, whom we should be justified in hanging from the castle walls, without further ceremony."

"Traitors and prisoners!" cried all the four commissioners. "By the mass! you are a bad jester, Master Mountjoy."

"If he is, I am not," said Bernard, suddenly appearing, with a heavy mace in his hand, and his steel cap on, which was not commonly worn, except when active warlike operations were expected.

"Nor I," said Anstey, and he in a moment emerged from a door leading into the guard-room followed by twelve of his companions in arms, who, by a dexterous movement, separated the commissioners from their guard, and seized the bridles of their horses.

"Help! help!" cried they, and a demonstration was made by their four esquires, who immediately drew their long, straight two-edged swords, that were dangling at their saddle-bows, and prepared to charge in compact order upon the men-at-arms of Brandon Castle.

A melee would then, undoubtedly, have occurred, of a dangerous and fatal character, had it not been that there walked into the court-yard, on the instant, and placed himself between the contending parties, Sir Rupert Brandon himself.

He was bare-headed, having entirely thrown aside his helmet, and in an instant, with a shout of joy and surprise, he was recognised by the general body of the men-at-arms.

"Sir Rupert! Sir Rupert!" was the cry, and everything was forgotten in the moment of heartfelt greeting and sincere congratulation upon the appearance of their long lost and much loved lord and master. They crowded round him with the most boisterous acclamations, and it was not until he observed a hostile movement on the part of the commissioners' guard, and cried "To arms, to arms," that his own soldiers faced their opponents with a determined front.

"Now, sirs," said Sir Rupert Brandon, "you find me, perhaps unexpectedly, once again in my ancient home, from which I have so long been a stranger. Proclaim your errand, then, to me; but beware, I am not only a subject, but a personal friend of Richard of the Lion Heart, and I am apt to be choleric if anything is said disparaging to him; so speak, I pray you, as your discretion may point out to you as desirable."

The commissioners looked at each other in rather a nervous sort of way, and one of them suggested that it would perhaps be better, after all, to go away and say no more about it.

"Fetch me the ten-slayer," said Sir Rupert Brandon to Anstey.

"The what?" cried one of the commissioners.

"Why, it's a sword, if you must know," said Anstey. "There's room enough in the hilt for two good-sized hands; the blade is nine feet two inches and a tenth. It is called the ten-slayer because the first Sir Montague Brandon, who was six feet nine and a quarter without his armour, cut down ten men with it at one sweep. Now there's ten of you, so put that and that together."

" It makes one dry to think of it," said Bernard. " Come, you had better be off, all of you; you'll get no ale here, I can tell you. Take warning in time."

The faces of the commissioners lengthened considerably, and there was a whispered consultation among them, after which, one who had been appointed spokesman to the rest, said,—

" Sir Rupert Brandon, we are very glad to see you home again, and quite congratulate you on not being knocked on the head in the holy wars. Our general impression is, that we'll go now, and not give you any further trouble, as you must be remarkably busy after so long an absence from your castle."

" Not at all, not at all," said Sir Rupert; " but at all events I shall trouble the whole of you to remain here, until I have taken advice as to the future disposal of you, for, by the mass, I look upon you as arch traitors every one of you."

" Here's the ten-slayer," said Anstey, appearing with the sword Sir Rupert had sent for.

CHAPTER LXXII.

" Sad was the end of that bad man,
And awful was his doom;
May he find mercy for his sins
In realms beyond the tomb."

THE CHASE FOR THE MONK.—THE BURNING OF THE OLD GREY TURRET, AND THE TERRIBLE DEATH.

HEEDLESS of whither he was going, or into what dangers his wild chase of the Black Monk would lead him, the crusader dashed onwards, followed by the knight who is yet unknown to our readers, but who, although he has not yet figured in our history, was as valiant a knight of the cross as any we have had the pleasure of presenting in our narrative.

Brandon Castle was an admirable place for a chase to those who knew its various intricacies, and the Black Monk showed himself by no means deficient in such information; it was only the terrific speed of the crusader, and the impetuous manner in which he dashed open every door that impeded his progress, that enabled him at all to catch an occasional glimpse of the monk, who, although he closed the doors behind him in his frantic career, found such a measure no protection whatever, for they were dashed open quite as quickly as the locks themselves could have been turned.

Perhaps the most exciting part of the chase was across the southern gallery, for there the monk could be plainly seen a little in advance, and the crusader, poising his ponderous battle-axe in his hand for a moment, hurled it after him with a precision and power that must have destroyed him had not Morgatani just slipped through a door at the critical moment, leaving the axe to bury itself, which it did, deep into the oaken panel.

" We have him, we have him," shouted the crusader, as he saw that a considerable portion of the monk's habit was caught in the door; " come on, come on, we will see what this vile churchman is made of ere we part with him."

The door was forced open, but monk there was none, although his ecclesiastical habit lay upon the floor, and by its side the sheath of a ponderous sword.

" By Heavens !" cried the crusader, " the villain has escaped ; but I know his haunt, and we will not even give him breathing time. He and he only is the inhabitant of the far-famed Grey Turret of Brandon Castle. I swear by our lady, that that turret shall be stormed before I am an hour older. This day shall be a memorable one for Brandon, for on it shall be settled some affairs which have harassed the inhabitants of this stronghold, and by the mass, I go to the task with none the less pleasure because it is a Jesuit who shall pay with his life for some of the mischief he has done. To the court-yard ! to the court-yard! and let us summon Sir Rupert and his men-at-arms to the fray."

So saying, the crusader, having by no trifling effort, released his battle-axe from the oaken panel of the door, hastily retraced his steps followed by the knight who had accompanied him, and in a few minutes reached the court-yard where Sir Rupert himself had given so uncomfortable a reception to the commissioners from King John, whose grand tour to the various strongholds of England seemed destined to be brought to a stand-still in Brandon Castle.

The official personages were evidently impressed with the conviction that discretion was the better part of valour, and one of them politely intimated to Sir Rupert, that if he was bent upon being so uncivil as to make them prisoners, they would rather decline going through the previous operation of getting a cracked skull, and they forthwith ordered their escort to lay down their arms, which certainly it could be no disgrace for four men to do when opposed, shut up in a fortress, to more than ten times their number.

These pacific resolutions had just been arrived at when the crusader returned from his fruitless chase of the Black Monk, and after having ascertained how matters stood, he said in a loud voice to Sir Rupert,—

" We have a fox to unkennel and an arch traitor to boot. Collect the men-at-arms, and let us at once storm the old Grey Turret, which has frowned so ominously on Brandon Castle for ages. How now, my men," addressing the escort of the commissioners ; " you are big enough, and ugly enough, all of you to take part in a fray. What say you to joining us ? We are going to unearth a Jesuit, and an enemy to King Richard."

" Who still lives," cried Sir Rupert Brandon, vehemently, " and is on English soil."

A visible sensation pervaded the commissioners at this intimation, and a brief consultation took place among the escort, after which one of their number said,—

" If King Richard is alive we are his soldiers, and quite at your service, more particularly as there seems likely to be some fighting."

" Well spoken," cried the crusader ; " to arms ! to arms !"

A blast from the herald's trumpet collected the men-at-arms, and in a few minutes a goodly force was in action in order to dispossess Morgatani of his stronghold.

" May we presume to ask what is to become of us ?" asked one of the commissioners.

" Oh ! certainly," replied Sir Rupert. " You may walk about this court-yard and amuse yourselves. I shall leave a guard with orders to cut either of you down who attempts to leave it."

" One word, my gracious lord," cried Hugh Wingrove, " ere you go upon this expedition. It would indeed be a sad price to pay for the death or capture of Morgatani, if you or any one of these noble knights were to be killed in the affray; he is subtle and dangerous, and I am convinced possesses means of doing injury which we do not. He is far from a fair foe, and, therefore, we should meet art by art; let us pile up faggots round the old tower, and either force him to come out or leave him to perish amid its ruins."

" By my faith," said the crusader, " no bad plan; we may have fine sport in smoking the monk."

" The tower is much isolated from the castle," said Sir Rupert Brandon, " and I have long wished for its destruction; let it perish."

" To the work, to the work," cried the crusader, and with great glee the men-at-arms dived into various cellars and out-houses where were faggots piled up for the use of the castle, and commenced conveying them into the little court-yard from whence sprung up the Grey Turret.

By the directions of the crusader, the staircase was in about ten minutes completely blocked up by well-dried wood, and then many more faggots were piled up round the base of the tower, so that it became next to an impossibility for the Black Monk, will all his arts, to escape through the raging element that would soon be roaring round him.

At this moment then, and before a torch could be applied to the wood which was supplied in such abundance, a cry of surprise from some dozen or two of the men-at-arms turned every eye in the direction where they pointed, and standing upon the parapet of the overhanging battlements, considerably above the heads of the large party assembled in the court-yard, appeared Nemoni the Wizard.

Shouts of maniac laughter came from him, and he tossed his arms wildly about his head.

" Caught—caught at last," he said. " Trapped in the old Grey Turret, and by my hands—ay, and by my hands—see, they are bleeding from the work. You know not that a subterranean passage leads from the base of yon turret to the forest; through that would Morgatani have escaped, leaving you, if you pleased, to heat the solid masonry to redness, and yet harm him not. Ah, ah, ah! But I have trapped him. The subterranean passage is beaten in for many feet. I have done the work, and there is no escape for the Black Monk of Brandon."

An arrow from the loop-hole of the Grey Turret, at this moment, flew with a whistling sound over the heads of those in the court-yard, and lodged deep in the shoulder of the wizard.

" 'Tis he! 'tis he!" cried the maniac, as he slightly staggered from the shock of the wound; " burn, burn; let him feel the taste of fire, and as the forked flames lick up his blood, I will give him loud laughter in answer to his groans."

" Fire the faggots," cried the crusader, in a voice of thunder.

Long thin streaks of blue smoke began to creep through the faggots which were piled up in such abundance on the staircase and around the base of the old Grey Turret. Thicker and thicker it came, taking fantastic forms and rolling up the sides of the old grey stones, now and then completely hiding them by its dense volume; but a light wind was stirring, and even that was partially shielded from the turret by the rest of the gigantic edifice. Not a word was spoken, and the most intense interest seemed to pervade all hearts as to the issue of the enterprise.

Then came a sullen roaring sound, immediately followed by the crackling of the wood, as it yielded to the influence of the destroying element, and began to blaze fiercely; the faggots, which were piled upon the staircase, were most favourably situated for ignition, and in a few minutes such a roaring body of flame ascended to the door of the turret chamber, that the men-at-arms drew back to escape the glowing heat that was thrown into the court yard.

Then the flames from the faggots round the base of the tower ascended to a fearful height, apparently making their way through the loop-holes, and enveloping the whole of the detached building in such a blaze that its interior must have been awfully suffocating. Still all remained silent within the tower, and the Black Monk made no indications of his presence or his sufferings. Such a silence, however, was not to continue long, nor such a state of calm indifference on the part of Morgatani, for in a few moments a scene of confusion ensued among the men-at-arms, by the falling among them of little projectiles from the loop-holes in the turret, which, after they had fallen upon the ground, burst, and inflicted serious wounds upon many of them.

"Confound these knaves of Jesuits," said the crusader to Sir Rupert, "they possess secrets of warfare, which I verily believe will one day put an end to gallant knighthood."

At this moment a tremendous explosion took place within the turret; the heat from the outside had ignited some of the monk's chemical preparations, and such was the force of the explosion, that several large stones were forced out from beneath one of the large loop-holes, leaving a tremendous gap in the walls of the turret—a gap so large, that part of the figure of the monk could be seen through it, as the flames now and then cleared from before it.

" Ha, ha, ha!" shrieked Nemoni, from the battlements; " death for the Black Monk of Brandon—death to the betrayer of innocence. Morgatani, your hour is come—I triumph—I triumph!"

A cry came from the turret. It was one of pain forced even from Morgatani in his agonies. It was the first and the last they heard from him, for at that moment Sir Rupert observed the Grey Turret to rock perceptibly, and he cried with a loud voice—

"Retreat—retreat all! the turret is coming down."

The men-at-arms, and the knights who were assembled, were bold enough warriors, but they had no fancy for being buried in the ruins of the Grey Turret of Brandon. It was really somewhat indecorous to see the rush that was made to get out of the court-yard, and how, without distinction to rank, they tumbled over each other in their effort to escape. The rocking of the turret, however, appeared not to be the immediate precursor of its fall; for the crusader, Sir Rupert Brandon, and the other knights, reached a window of the long gallery which commanded a view of the turret, while it still remained apparently without further injury.

The explosion within it appeared to have done it more harm than the fire from without, for every moment there kept falling pieces of the stone work, with a loud crash into the court-yard below.

"It is a fearful death," said Rupert Brandon, "and yet probably not equal to the sufferings he would have inflicted upon us, had we not been warned in time of the intention to poison us with the wine."

"By the mass," said the crusader, "it has been his own seeking. I should have brained him with my battle-axe, but he would not stop to undergo the process—there—there, behold!"

The Grey Tower shook to and fro like the mast of a ship—now it seemed inclined to fall in one direction and then in another, then doubling over towards the court-yard, most probaby in consequence of the great displacement of the masonry in that direction, it fell with a stunning crush. Immense columns of smoke and dust fell from the ruins, and it was many minutes before anything could be seen, or any voice heard after that tremendous uproar of sound.

Then, as the smoke and dust gradually cleared away, the ruins of the ancient turret became visible. The faggots on the staircase had burned to white ash, and those that had remained unconsumed in the court-yard were covered up and extinguished.

"Thus ends the career," said Sir Rupert Brandon, "of the guilty Morgatani. Heaven only knows what may be the extent of his crimes. His attempt, however, at our destruction by poison, is amply sufficient to guarantee us in the course we have adopted."

"I feel," said the crusader, "for that poor maniac's situation. I owe to him my life in the forest; let us hasten to the battlements and see what can be done for him."

Nemoni was found lying insensible on the extreme verge of the parapet; he was bleeding profusely from the arrow wound which he had received, and at first sight they thought he was dead; upon raising him such was not found to be the case, and Sir Rupert had him conveyed to a chamber in the castle, where, after some warm wine had been poured down his throat, he rallied amazingly, and opening his eyes, fixed them with a mild and melancholy expression upon those around him. All the wild maniacal ferocity of his nature seemed to have vanished, and when he opened his lips his tone of voice was so different from that in which he usually spoke, that no one believed it could have come from the same person.

"I am dying," he said; "my last hour has come, but Heaven has vouchsafed to give me for that brief space my long lost reason. Is Sir Rupert Brandon here?"

"He is," said Sir Rupert, stepping forward; "what would you say to me, Nemoni?"

"May the great God bless and prosper you; I have that to say, which, in the period of my mental alienation it was providential I did not utter, for Heaven only knows the danger that might have occurred from the revelation of the secret I am about to disclose, while you were far away and unable to protect those near and dear to you."

"Alas," said Sir Rupert; "I have none such. My hopes lie in the silent tomb with my long lost Alicia."

"Not so," said the wizard, raising himself upon his arm; "not so, thank Heaven. On that severe night which consigned your young and loving wife to the grave, there came into the forest a woman with two new-born infants. She laid them at the foot of an aged tree, saying, with a shudder, for Heaven overheard her words,—

"'Twin children of Sir Rupert Brandon, I cannot kill you, although I have sworn to do it. Cold and want must perform the work I have not nerve to do.' She then, with bitter groans, departed from the spot, and raising the children, I took them to my sister, whom you have seen, ere now, with me in the forest, and to whom a noble knight, some short time since, gave a gold chain as an earnest of his favour."

"Children!" cried Sir Rupert Brandon; "gracious Heavens, is this a dream! Nemoni—wizard, on your soul's hope, swear to me that this is true."

"I swear," said the wizard. "Help,—help,—Morgatani! the Black——"
He sunk back with a deep sigh, and when they again raised him, they found that his spirit had flown to his Maker.

"To the forest—to the forest," cried Sir Rupert Brandon. "My children—my children."

"Hold!" cried the crusader; "be assured they are safe; I have seen them,

It appears to me we are upon the eve of the discovery of a most diabolical plot, and if a full confession is to be extracted from any one, it is from Eldred Weare, who by this time has found out, probably, that he is not poisoned; for I changed the goblets, giving him and Fitzhugh some pure wine instead of that which was drugged. A more public and ignominious death is fitter for such villains."

"In the meantime, I will to the forest," said Sir Kenneth Hay, "in search of the children; give me some one to guide my steps."

"Take me with you," said Hugh Wingrove, "and Heaven help us on our mission."

"Come on," said the crusader, taking Sir Rupert by the arm; "let us seek Eldred, and extort from him a full confession of the villanies that have been practised against you in Brandon."

<hr>

CHAPTER LXXIII.

"The bell shall be rung
The mass shall be sung,
And we'll feast right merrily."

ELDRED WEARE'S CONFESSION.—THE RESTORATION OF SIR RUPERT'S CHILDREN.—THE CONCLUSION.

WHEN Sir Rupert Brandon, the crusader, and the knights reached the small banquetting-hall, in which their lives had been so atrociously attempted, they found that no perceptible change had taken place in the state of affairs. Agatha Weare was quite dead. Fitzhugh was lying on his back, with his eyes fixed on the ceiling; and Eldred Weare was keeping up a chorus of groans, as he imagined that he felt the direful effects of the poison coming on.

"Eldred Weare," said the crusader, as he took him by the throat, and lifted him upon his feet, "we require from you a full and particular confession of the practices against Sir Rupert Brandon, in which you and others have been engaged."

"I am dead," said Eldred. "You poisoned me yourself."

"But, in the event of receiving this confession, I have an antidote which may yet save you from that species of death, although you certainly will be hung afterwards."

"What an offer!" said Eldred, with a groan. "Take warning by me, everybody, and never try to have your revenge."

"I perceive," said the crusader, "that I shall be compelled to end this wretch's miseries at once; bring here a stout cord, and we will hang him to one of the iron stanchions of the window."

"No, don't," said Eldred; "no, don't; I'm poisoned already; what's the use of hanging me? Don't be revengeful; see what I've come to; that and ambition has done me up altogether. It's beginning; there's a pain in my inside already. Oh, men, fetch me a confessor. The Lord have mercy upon me. I know I'm a sinner; but I got cuffed and kicked into it. I was harmless once, but they wouldn't let me be. Oh, dear—oh, dear; there's another twinge; this is a sort of poison that acts with a belly-ache."

Bernard handed to the crusader a stout cord, made into a noose, which being put round Eldred's neck, and drawn tolerably tight, so horrified him, that he dropped on his knees, exclaiming,

"Oh, don't! oh, don't! oh, don't!—hanging's equal to choking any day. I'd rather go out of the world with a pain in my inside. Murder! murder! I'll tell anything and everything."

"Proceed, then; we must have a full and entire confession."

Eldred, after some groans, spoke as follows:—

"It was sister Agatha who first put it into my mind to be ambitious— how I came to be revengeful I don't know exactly; but it appears Sir Rupert had offended my sister Agatha by marrying my other sister Alicia, and he had offended Morgatani, the Black Monk, too, because he wouldn't make him abbot of the neighbouring convent; and, besides, he kicked him out of Brandon for something that I never heard the rights of; and then they both got hold of me, and told me if I would join them I should in time become the lord of Brandon Castle and all its possessions, for they wanted nothing but vengeance themselves, and would give me all the profits. The Black Monk had a secret means of getting into Brandon, and he took up his abode in the old Grey Turret, where he and Agatha used to make up all their schemes. Well, it so happened that Alicia was near her confinement, and it was Agatha told me she had died, as well as two children she had given birth to. I didn't say anything, but I thought in my own mind that something very awkward had occurred, and that perhaps, although she had died, it wasn't altogether by fair play."

"Dastardly villain!" cried Sir Rupert Brandon, "did not one spark of feeling rise up in your cowardly heart to prevent such atrocious crimes?— Ah, my Alicia—my Alicia—you were murdered!"

"Will you want me to confess everything?" said Eldred.

"Yes, everything," said the crusader; "omit nothing—tell us all, or ——"

No. 52

A pull at the rope round his neck significantly suggested to Eldred the alternative, and he continued his narration.

"After that they told me that the way to get the better of Sir Rupert was to get up a charge against him that he had murdered his wife Alicia, to substantiate which a dagger belonging to Sir Rupert was plunged into her heart after she was dead, and the monk sprinkled something upon the body, which he said would preserve it for many years, making it look like quite an interposition of Providence that decomposition had not taken place in order to convict the murderer.

"Then we were all of us for King John, who, out of gratitude for our declaring for him, was to do wonders for us, and not to scruple at all at cutting off Sir Rupert's head; but, you see, gentlemen, that the cleverest things will fail, and instead of being lord of Brandon Castle, here am I, with a pain in my inside and a rope round my neck."

"Gracious Heavens!" cried Sir Rupert Brandon, "what a vile plot was this—to accuse me of crime in a quarter where my tenderest sensibilities and holiest sympathies were awakened."

"And after all that," said the crusader, "you assisted in the atrocious attempt to poison us?"

"Don't say I assisted in anything, or did anything," said Eldred; "I was partly thumped and partly frightened into it all. Of course, I'm a dead man, and I know it. Don't bother me."

"One question more," said Sir Rupert Brandon. "Was this dastardly knight, Fitzhugh, aware of the projected poisoning?"

"I believe you, rather," said Eldred.

"Then take him to the court-yard, hack off his spurs, and then hang him."

"One word," cried Fitzhugh's page, springing forward; "one word for that bad man. Fitzhugh, do you know me now?"

She removed the cap she wore, and allowed her hair to fall down in its natural ringlets upon her shoulders.

"Beatrice!" he gasped—"Beatrice!"

"Yes, I am she who yielded to your false vows, and fell from purity to shame. Now, sir," turning to the crusader, "you promised me a boon—force this man to amend the evil he has done, by making me his wife."

"By Heavens! he shall," cried the crusader. "But who comes here? Ah! is it you? Sir Rupert Brandon, I have a dear friend to introduce to you—one without whose help we should all have even now been in the cold embraces of death. Do you know this heroic girl?"

"Bertha!" cried Sir Rupert; "she who rescued me from a dungeon abroad, and to whom, as the only token I could give her, I presented a silver horn, similar to the one I had lost in the forest."

Bertha burst into tears, and hung, weeping, on the arm of the knight.

"That horn," interrupted Bernard, "we found upon the person of Nemoni, the wizard; and, by-the-bye, that accounts for all the alarm we have had when it was blown occasionally outside of the castle."

Fitzhugh slowly rose to his feet, and, in a hollow voice, he said,

"I confess my guilt, and will yet perform one act of grace in the eyes of Heaven, by wedding her I have wronged, ere I die. Send for a priest, for my hours are numbered."

Before then any one could prevent him, he seized one of the poisoned goblets, and quaffed down the wine at a draught.

"Wretched man," said Sir Rupert Brandon, "you have but anticipated your fate. As for you, Eldred Weare, I give you five minutes' time to get clear of Brandon Castle. Follow him, Bernard, and if he is not across the moat within that period of time, dispatch him instantly."

"Murder!—fire!—clear the way!" cried Eldred. "Don't stop me, anybody. Gracious Powers! five minutes!—I can't do it. Help!—help!—murder!"

With these words he made a wild rush from the apartment, and did just succeed in getting clear of Brandon Castle within the time specified.

What became of him afterwards was never accurately learned, but he is believed to be the same person who, some years afterwards, in the service as shopman of the worshipful Master Smallpin, man's mercer, of Ludgate, was whipped at the cart's-tail for robbing his master.

* * * * * *

Scarcely had Eldred left Brandon when there arrived Sir Kenneth Hay with the two children from the forest, and their kind nurse, accompanied too by the aged abbot of the monastery, whose joy was great indeed to hear of the safe arrival of Sir Rupert.

"My children! my children!" cried the knight, as he folded them in his arms, "my long lost, dear treasures, that will invest life with new charms to the disconsolate Sir Rupert Brandon; and now, Bertha, if you'll accept a widowed hand and become a mother to these darlings, it is offered to you along with a heart that will love you tenderly."

"Joy—joy!" said Bertha, as she sunk into Sir Rupert's arms.

Within a brief hour two marriages were celebrated in the chapel of the castle by the aged abbot, that of Bertha with Sir Rupert Brandon, and that of Beatrice with Fitzhugh, the latter leaving his bride a widow before sunset.

The chapel was crowded with the men-at-arms, and when the crusader had acted the part of father to the bride, as he did in the case of Bertha, he stood upon the steps of the altar, and the abbot said,—

"May we crave your name, gentle sir, who have acted no unimportant part in this ceremony?"

"My name is Richard," said the crusader, with a laugh; "some call me Cœur de Lion, and if my friends have, as I am advised, marched promptly on London, I am again King of England, and let my first devout prayer, now that I have declared myself, be for the welfare of Sir Rupert Brandon and his bride."

The shout of surprise and exultation of the men-at-arms echoed tremendously through Brandon Castle, and that night was one of feasting and revelry which the old walls had not witnessed for many a year.

It was a sad and mournful task for Sir Rupert Brandon to visit the vault in which lay the strangely preserved remains of his much-loved Alicia; he took with him his children, and they gazed with awe and wonder upon those still features, beautiful even in death, which, with deep emotion, Sir Rupert Brandon pointed to as those of their mother. He took himself from the breast of the corpse the dagger, which, by the diabolical ingenuity of Morgatani, had been there placed, in order to convict him, Sir Rupert, of a crime which the vile Jesuit did not live to have an opportunity of accusing him of. He caused a small altar and a crucifix to be placed in the vault, and kept a lamp constantly burning within it; nor did he love Bertha, his new bride, the less that he paid such attention to the cold remains of her who had been so dear to him while living.

It was not until long after Sir Rupert Brandon was gathered to his fathers, that Brandon Castle suffered from an extensive conflagration, which nearly destroyed it. And its then proprietor, in digging its extensive foundations for an enlarged plan of the building which he proposed re-erecting, came upon the secret passage, which had led from the base of the old Grey Turret to the neighbouring forest, through which the villain Morgatani had evidently attempted to make his escape, for at one point where the roof of the narrow passage was broken in, so as completely to stop it up, there was found a gigantic skeleton and a rusty sword, both of which no doubt proclaimed that there the Black Monk had ended his vicious and frightful career.

He had been entombed alive, for the passage was blocked up in the other direction by the fall of the turret.

At the intercession of King Richard, Beatrice was received back by her friends, from whom she had been induced to stray by Fitzhugh, it being considered that by her marriage with him, her wounded honour was considerably repaired.

Wingrove died some years after Sir Rupert Brandon's return, aged, but full of honour, and Bernard having solemnly promised not to take more than four quarts per diem, was permitted to succeed him as captain of the castle guard.

Sir Rupert's children grew in strength and beauty, and some years after the events we have recorded, the boy gained universal applause and admiration, on the occasion of a great fete at court, when he acted as page to King Richard, who seemed never weary of heaping favours on the Brandon family.

The sister of Nemoni was handsomely provided for by Sir Rupert, who considered her as truly the preserver of his children, and, in fact, she took as much pride in their welfare as it was possible to do, becoming their kind and affectionate nurse for many years, during which time Sir Rupert Brandon recovered the elasticity of his spirits, and in the society of Bertha, learned to look with a better and calmer spirit on the decrees of Providence.

END.